Upon a
Wheel of Fire

Paul Grieve lives in Paris.

Upon a
Wheel of Fire

PAUL GRIEVE

INDIGO

An Indigo paperback
First published in Great Britain by Victor Gollancz in 1999
This paperback edition published in 2000 by Indigo,
an imprint of Orion Books Ltd,
Orion House, 5 Upper St Martin's Lane, London WC2H 9EA

A CIP catalogue record for this book is available
from the British Library.

0 575 40256 3

Printed and bound in Great Britain by
Clays Ltd, St Ives plc

…à cette CG qui aurait pu être…
mais qui jamais n'était…et pour sa fille Emma…

PART I

1

The first time I met Lloyd George was in Paris. The early spring of 'nineteen.

Paris 1919. That was a place and a time. A year of hope. A place to start the future.

The year just to be alive, just to have survived.

I am sure that if I tried, I could remember every day and every moment of every day of that year. The year I turned nineteen.

From soft cool dawns, pinks and blues over the magic city, quiet but expectant. Each the start of yet another day to revel in the newness of my existence: to breathe and drink, to eat, to touch and smell. Just to be alive.

I walked everywhere and I watched. Street sweepers beginning the day, birch brooms flicking down gutters. A horse and cart taking away piled rubbish. Hoofs, steel banded wheels hollow and impatient on stone pavé.

Ohlà, Reina, oh. Recule-toi! Or, *Tat-tat-tat, à droite, Reina!*

Calls more of *camaraderie* than of command, Reina knew it well. Her blinkered way across the Île Saint Louis to every box and bin. Without the calls, without even a tug on the rein, content in her work, content in her Paris.

Then waiters removing shutters, straightening, wiping. Making inviting white tables from dirty furniture stacked on littered pavements.

From early morning and often round and back to dawn again I watched the day-long task, the full-time job, *la vie parisienne.*

But mostly I watched the women. Through crowded streets and boulevards in my foreground, in front of the pantomime, the spectacle of Paris

1

life. Tall, prepared, unassailable, they walked purposefully through the bustle or sat in pairs conspiratorial against me. Smoking and drinking coffee at tiny round tables in street cafés.

The tight corsetry and petticoats from before the War, all that was gone. Now it was *la silhouette garçon*, dropped waistlines on a boyish figure, sheer shiny hose over visible legs and ankles, make-up, varnished fingernails and cropped hair.

Tailored suits were popular, long straight jackets of Poiret twill, yoke skirts to the calf. Fine shoes, buckled and strapped. Veiled hats and turbans: mystery was the fashion of '19.

All day I walked if I could, smart in my new tunic. A flash of white and purple on my chest. Saluting and taking salutes, inventing reasons to be out on the street or through the parks. Anywhere and everywhere was wonderful.

Even the dead left me alone on those days.

Unclaimed, lying out in beet fields. Or the newly dead by our support trenches, blood-soaked uniforms and caked-on boots, all ranks together. Waiting for their burial patiently in the rain. A wooden cross on each chest and long down the body, as if making love, love of a deathly kind.

And later, near the end, bodies in blankets tied up with string. Post Office parcels sliding down into cleaned-out craters. Sitting, lying, some rolling over on to others like teddy bears in a nursery. As the padre says his words, as the living stand and stare. They faded for that moment, there on the bridge looking down at the twinkling Seine, sun bobbing on a hundred ripplets.

In that upside-down year of 1919 the European Section of the Foreign Office had moved itself to Paris. They said that only the dullards and the clerks were left in London.

My duties were light: I was being rewarded, Captain Vernon had told me, just for surviving. Just for being on my feet at the end. My men from Montreuil the same. We had saved our lives and we had escaped the return back to freezing barracks overflowing into tents, out in the wet again. Back to England for the eternal wait for demob papers that never came. Small wonder there were mutinies that year. Even German prisoners were treated better.

All of us in Paris had been for our leave and we were happy to be away. We had seen England again for ourselves: strikes, rationing, lighting restrictions, the terrible influenza.

So we lived it up, of course, every hour of every day. Every moment an unexpected bliss, every duty a pleasure and every pleasure a dream. Paris, Victory, the end of the War. The Great War, as I heard people call it.

At least once a week Serjeant Jones would ask me, 'The lads, sir, they'd like to know how long this 'ere picnic can go on for.' I could not tell them, but yes, I understood why they asked.

I took a shift as a driver myself. Thursday nights and over into Friday mornings. I wore a driver's suit, shamming as one of my men. Every Sunday evening when Serjeant Jones chalked up the duty detail for the week to come, *Lt.B.* was unchanged, untouched in my slot on the blackboard. Overnight, the graveyard shift, 23000 to 0700 every Thursday. There was never anything to do and I was really only there for the gramophone.

We were still in the army but my drivers all wore suits fitted out by the RASC. No badges, no insignia, nondescript like our black cars. Ready to carry any of the toffs, French, American or Italian. All intended to look as if those exalted persons were in one of their own vehicles, not in one of ours.

Descretion, anonymity and smartness. Doing our bit to make the Conference go, that was how I put it to the men.

I had my men well trained. I would stand in front of them at the garage under the glass-panelled roof. Ironed and crisp with my Sam Browne gleaming, my gloves and cane. The men in fatigues, holding rags, spanners and oil cans, a half-circle in front of the big shining motors.

'At all times, men, for every trip, you must know exactly who is in your car, full name, correct rank or title. Memorize completely. Do not forget. If you are asked, you say, *this is the car of Monsieur le Ministre Briand*, or *this is Signor Albiro's car*, or, *this is Sheik Hassani's car*. What you do not say is, *this 'ere is an FO motor, mate. An' that there in the back is an old Frog called Bree-something*. While Briand is in the car, it is his car, *Monsieur le Ministre Briand's car*.'

Laughter. Understood? Understood. There were no risks to measure then, no chance that one of us would not come back.

On that Thursday night when I first met him I was sitting in the drivers' day room playing at duty driver. Down in our dusty cellar waiting to run a message, to drive any upstairs type who needed a car after a late meeting: to his hotel, to a bar, the station.

The jacket of my driver's suit was over the back of a chair and I was lounging on our worn settee in my shirtsleeves. The car was standing outside ready by my sentry. Timing set, compression up. I could run out and crank her in a flash. I had nothing to do but to wait and play my music.

For that year the European Section occupied the offices of the ministère de l'Agriculture on the Île de la Cité, a storehouse of a building wedged between the Préfecture and the Seine. Behind the standard front, the Haussmann front, the building was split into four large open floors. Here the FO had set up shop for the Peace Conference, until the Treaty was signed.

In the foyer on the main floor, porters heavy in FO livery stood behind a long trestle table, covered with green baize. Their job was to log visitors in and out, to fetch and carry, touch their hats at senior frocks and foreign diplomats. All incongruous and British over in Frog Country.

Gu'mornin, mista Squires. Or, *Luverley day again, Sir 'oobert.*

All that rubbish. Grovelling with them almost, with the frocks in their long swallow coats. But presumptuous, uppity with my men.

My drivers and my sentries in from guard duty lurked behind a wall of FO boxes. Like war, like all government service, waiting was the main occupation. Hidden away in their bivouac with a paraffin stove, a coal fireplace and an assortment of discarded furniture from upstairs. Glass blocks in the pavement above let in some light.

On a small table stood the gramophone, our camp littered with my drivers' phonograms large and small. Their dance recordings, their hot jazz scratched and marked, torn brown paper jackets slovenly everywhere.

This marvellous contraption played a record five or six minutes long. Quite satisfactory for the men learning their steps for their *mademoiselles.* But for my longer pieces, the music I had learned before the War, as many as six records in a set, my music could be hard to follow through scratches and changes. So every Thursday night I listened alone and slowly that little box had begun to revive my heart.

It was after one o'clock in the morning when Mr Lloyd George came down the stairs. The time when the Welsh Wizard came alive, as I had sometimes heard from my men. Any other politician, any other of those frocks, would just have stood at the top of the stairs and yelled.

Dri-vah.

Or they had a porter do the yelling which upset my men no end. We were still heroes.

Mr Lloyd George looked even shaggier than in the newspaper pictures and much shorter. But I recognized him immediately. Grey and silver hair flowing down his neck, long and bushy, folding around his ears at the back like horns. A fleecy moustache shaved in from the sides to leave a small blob of white straw under his nose, curving down over his lip. A large head and strong deep jaw. An impish, puckish face, but kindly, understanding.

The face, we believed, that had ended the massacres. The face, we said,

4

that questioned everything and accepted nothing. Asking, no, demanding a straight and a human answer. LG was a deity to the men.

And into that dark and squalid room the man threw out an immediate draw, an energy that could never have been gathered from photographs. Even tired and dishevelled as he was.

Surprised in my squalor I jumped up, then smartly to attention. But without the foot stamping that would have accompanied the move in the army. Exhibitionist parade-ground drill was not encouraged by the Gentlemen of the Foreign Office. Nor was the yelling and swearing that went with it. But exhibitionist was their word. We called it smart.

I had no time to turn off the gramophone. Standing frozen to attention in my braces, next to one of the pigsty tables in the middle of the room, as the music played on.

That night it was Mendelssohn, the opening movement of the octet. My music, young and alive, even through the distractions of changing records and winding the handle.

LG stood on the bottom step, taking in the scene as the phonogram ended. The arm stuck on the inside groove repeating the crackle, over and over. He may not have known the piece but he seemed interested. He walked to the machine and he stood nodding in time with the arm trying to read the revolving words.

'Carry on,' he said. Flooding me with his smile, waving at me to deal with the gramophone.

I removed the brown paper cover from the next record and I cranked the handle.

LG sat on one of the crippled armchairs and he listened, leaning forward, his large head cradled in his hands. While I stood by the gramophone changing records, stiff and nervous.

To the end of the *Andante*, the astral call of the theme. Then the melody reprised, soaring over the inner voices again. Did LG know this music? Did he feel the call? But how could he resist?

LG stood up. 'I heard that at the Albert Hall in 'fourteen,' he said. 'Played by two string quartets together, I remember. Something from Goethe. *A breeze among the leaves, a wind among the reeds and all is scattered.*'

A high-pitched voice but friendly, a voice that asked for warmth, for openness in return. Yes, LG knew the music. But how could I have asked him then, on the night I first met him. About Events and about Unintended Consequences, about music beyond words when there are no explanations left.

'So, shall we go?' LG said. He put on his grey top hat with an affectionate little tap to the lid.

I walked close to him up the stairs and out to the car in the courtyard. He stumbled on the cobbles and I had his arm. I realized that he had been drinking, but that was certainly no sin, we all drank all the time.

I held the back door open, standing smartly now, fully dressed in my jacket, cap and driver's gloves.

The duty car that night, Number 28, was one of our 20 horsepower Daimlers from Château Beaurepaire, dark green, not black like the others. As a staff car, Number 28 had been fitted with two collapsible map tables. With the tables down the passenger compartment was cavernous like a small upholstered drawing room. The wide quilted seat looked a long way back.

LG peered in.

'I'll be up front with you,' he said, standing back for me to open the other door.

Then LG mounted the high driver's bench where he sat small and hunched, top hat well down over his eyes, grey frock coat crumpled and baggy from a long day at the conference table. The bench was protected by a roof though the sides were open like a landau, exposed to the elements. But it was not a cold night and LG was enjoying his perch.

The big four started with half a turn of the handle over the top of compression then I climbed up next to him.

'Where to, sir?' I knew we were going on a jaunt. I took my cap off and placed it on the seat between us.

'Somewhere up by the Odeon, there's a spot there.'

I steered the dark bulk of the limousine out through the narrow gate and onto quai du Marché Neuf. My sentry jerked a salute on to his rifle as we emerged.

Then across the deserted street and over pont Saint Michel.

2

From the quays and the bridges of the Île de la Cité the river was a slice through a cheese, revealing the city's inside complexion like a moist *bleu*.

The cathedral of Notre Dame was as dark as the water below, a Gothic mass, forbidding against the luminous cowl of the night sky. And on the south side of the Seine, the jumbled façades of the Left Bank faced the imperial frown across the river, the Louvre, then further down, the careful order of spare spring trees in the Jardins des Tuileries. While between the two, on the island, the Palais de Justice brooded like the Wicked Fairy's castle, gaunt, moated by the Seine.

In place Saint Michel, under the grotesque romantic fountain at the far end, lit by the last of the flaring gas streetlights from up rue Danton, milk churns were being unloaded from two hefty wagons drawn by enormous draught-horses. Their heavy pulling done, they munched quietly now from nose bags, hairy socks down to the cobbles. The square still showed some life, people on the street, muted singing from a cellar *bistrot*, bodies sleeping on benches, in doorways.

As I turned off boulevard Saint Michel, LG looked up to the Théâtre de l'Odéon at the end of the road. A Greek temple, a shadowed row of tightly packed columns framed by the cheap hotels of rue Racine.

LG could play on his Welsh accent, rolling his *rrr*-s up and down like a continuous undulating question, frothy and guttural.

'We would like to ha-ave every class of British sub-ject visit Paa-ris,' he began, 'that they may emulate its ex-cellencies and shun its vices and er-rors which distract from the glor-ry of the French capital.'

LG paused.

'Thomas Cook, boy, Thomas the great Welsh travel agent, that's what he said many years ago. And I agree with him wholeheartedly. Bring them over by the boat load, I say, do them all some good.'

LG looked up and down the quiet shuttered street.

'But do you see any vices or errors here, boy?' smiling me his impish smile.

Did I answer? Did I comment? Was Thomas Cook really a Welshman? I mumbled yes sir or no sir, I was unsure. What would one of my drivers do in such a circumstance?

Then LG was going to start on something else but we came into place de l'Odéon and he peered around for his spot.

Place de l'Odéon is small, crescent shaped, dominated by the classical façade of the theatre which also has the uphill advantage over the buildings fronting from below. André my taxi driver and architect *manqué* was passionate about the Odéon, passionate about his Paris.

When Haussmann's clearing was undertaken in the 1850s, André told me, to expose the public buildings and open the vistas and wide streets that have created modern Paris, the Odéon was not much changed. Haussmann the

Slum-Clearer, the Baron with his cavalry and his cannon, had yet to arrive in the quartier Luxembourg when the Prussian War had started in 1870, bringing public works to a halt. For André the Odéon was the real Paris, old untouched Paris, Paris that had grown as she would. Walls sloping and bulging as if ready to fall, tight streets of varying character leading up to the green open space of the Jardins de Luxembourg. Not like the artificial parts, the tricks he said, that the tourists saw. The new boulevards and avenues built on murder, on absolute power and absolute corruption, making masons into millionaires, millionaires into magnates.

'The Café Soufflot,' LG said, pointing across the square. 'That's the spot.'

There were a few motors parked. A calèche stood outside the front door. Bright lights and diners could be seen through laced windows. It was more than a café, it was lustrous and beckoning.

I pulled up next to the carriage to speak to the driver, stumbling in my army French.

'*Pouvez-vous vous avancer pour que je puisse stationner derrière?*' In my flat English monotones.

The driver pulled forward with a word to his horse and I circled the Daimler back to the pavement in front of a red and gold awning. Then I skipped around the radiator to open LG's door, leaving my cap and gloves on the front seat. I was anonymous in my suit, trying to anticipate the spirit of the occasion, whatever that might be.

LG climbed down the running board. I held his arm but he was steadier in the cool night air.

'Come in, Mr Mendelssohn-lover,' he said. He took off his top hat. 'I could do with someone who speaks the language.'

Inside the Café Soufflot LG was recognized, but whether as the Prime Minister of Great Britain, The Man Who Won The War, or merely as a late-night regular, I could not tell. But if his identity was known they were certainly very discreet.

On the short drive over I had had a momentary premonition: arriving at some dingy *brasserie* on the quai de Montebello. Or worse: I saw us, me and LG, walking in the street, LG being jostled by Bolsheviks or insulted by a Turk. Me springing to the defence. *Don't you realize who this is*, I would yell, throwing myself between LG and our antagonists. But none of that had been necessary.

While the manager engaged LG in the requisite French preliminaries, making himself understood in English, I returned to secure the car.

Outside, a uniformed doorman had materialized.

'*Voiture du gouvernement anglais. Visiteur très important,*' I started. But my naïveté was evident and the doorman was unimpressed. Our duty cars did not fly the Union Jack. I handed him five Francs from the petrol fund which we kept in a canvas bag under the driver's seat. The doorman remained unimpressed though he appeared reliable. A former *poilu* maybe.

By the time I returned to the restaurant LG was installed at the back in a deep, comfortable booth, a horseshoe banquette in plush red velvet around a crisp linen-spread table. Four sparkling *couverts* were set off by a huge silver bowl of three or four dozen white roses. Beautifully arranged, casual yet balanced, long straight stems green and leafy. The roses at the end of the table obscured LG completely.

The whole restaurant, still busy after one o'clock in the morning, animated even, gave an impression of plush mirrored excellence, exquisite attention to detail, all of the very best French quality. Yet not upright and established like the Hôtel de Crillon. Rather it was rakish, *grand luxe*, a place without restraint, a place where anything goes. For those who can.

LG motioned for me to sit. I took a place on the end of the banquette next to the flowers.

'We're having a bit of company.' LG waved to the empty spaces on each side, pulling at a cigar which had appeared while I was away. Another impish smile. 'You'll enjoy them.'

Champagne was served, wordlessly like morning tea by a smart waiter in tails.

'What a day,' LG sighed to himself. 'We've almost no idea of where we're going.'

He stared down into his glass, head forward and morose suddenly, white and silver locks at the back of his neck lifting off the collar of his coat.

The company appeared. Two extraordinarily pretty young girls in short tasselled dresses up as far as the knee, one pearly grey, one black. And even shorter hair, the very height of fashion.

LG brightened up. But I wondered immediately: was it one for him and one for me? I rose to my feet for the girl in grey. She moved into the vacant area of the banquette between me and LG. A whiff of something unbearably desirable as she passed. The other one, the girl in the black dress, sat in opposite.

As soon as they were seated LG put an elbow around each girl's neck, drawing them toward him, both his arms out like a wrestler. It was to be two for him, one on each side.

LG made the introductions.

9

'Nicole and Colette,' beaming from one to the other then over to me.

Had LG really met the girls before? And were these their real names or names just for the evening invented on the spot? I had no idea. But now he really did look like the Wizard, seated between his two apprentices.

More champagne was served by the waiter, tall, severe, unmoved by this scene, or, it appeared, by any other scene that could possibly be imagined.

The call on my services as translator was very limited. LG wanted not so much to amuse or to be amused by our visitors as to fondle them, their hands, their shoulders, caress their heads, but talking past them, rambling. Or silent for a while, dejected even, as the girls prattled to each other behind his slumped back.

Sometimes there was an attempt. *'Dis lui qu'il a la tête d'un vrai lion,'* Colette in the pearly dress instructed me. Stroking at LG's flowing mane as I stammered out the English, her fingertips a startling red on a small white hand. LG was diverted for a moment and pecked her on the cheek.

'And you tell her that the back of her neck with the scissored hair is the prettiest thing I've ever seen.' LG ran a finger up her nape and Colette giggled charmingly. Conversation was not her function.

There were moments that night when I had to look away. Impelled by a sudden explosive pressure in my chest and down under the table, by a singing in my head. As if a sniper's bullet had cracked across my quiet trench, leaving me breathless, my heart pattering.

Moments when I had to stand and leave precipitously for the night air. To secure the car again, I said. Anything, just to be away from the starched white table that separated us.

The girl in black: the even white skin of her shoulders running under narrow straps, waiting for my finger to follow her firm scented lines. Her pencilled green eyes flashing across the room when they should have been focused on me alone. Her exquisite hands on delicate fluted glass that should be releasing me through my heavy buttons. Crimson nails flashing as she lifts her slippery tasselled hem while I smother her against the etched partition behind the booth. Or over against the scrubbed tile wall outside the lavatory, on the padded back seat of the car, now, anywhere.

But despite my state, my state of months, during the next hour or more as LG rattled on in his frustration, through the champagne, through a dozen oysters, through a *terrine d'anguilles* with English toast, I learned more then, more about the Conference, more than all the newspapers or all the idle talk at the Majestic bar could have ever told me, more than all the gossip my drivers could have brought back in an entire year.

First it was the Americans. Wilson. What sort of a name was Woodrow? And did I know that he was the president, if that's the right word, the president of a university before he became President of America? An academic. That's where he'd dug up all those wonderful ideas of his, no doubt. How would this three-ringed circus *ever* come to an end? And today Woodrow had said he was going to go back to the United States. He'd called for his boat in a huff. Is that how they ran their institutions over there?

And did I know what our Woodrow thought? Our Woodrow thought that we'd been fighting some kind of a civil war in Europe, back here in the *old country*. Like three naughty boys with little to choose between us, English, German and French. A civil war like the Americans had fought in the 1860s, was that it? And which he, Wilson, President Woodrow Wilson thinks he can come over and settle like some self-righteous magnanimous uncle.

And, boy, if he doesn't get his way? Did I know what our Woodrow said he was going to do? He was *going over our heads*, he said, *straight to the people*, he said. Can you imagine? Wilson campaigning in Italy? Or in the new Poland? What was he going to do? Speechify in five languages? In Brest Litovsk? Off the back of a train like some devil of a Teddy Roosevelt?

And in any case, boy, leaning toward me, insistent, frowning now, as if LG thought that I might have an answer for what was coming, but he, LG, was going to squelch my arguments before I could even make them. In any case, what about Congress? Run by the other side it was, by the Republicans, since the election of '18.

So here was a question. A real question. Did the man really have the *power* to impose all these ideals of his?

Power. LG liked that word, *Pow-wh-rr*.

Shouldn't some of those others be over here nodding their little shorn heads? How about Senator Smoot? Oh no, this was no joke, boy, no laughing matter. There really was a Senator Smoot. There had to be someone, here in Paris, who spoke for the opposition. Other than old White, that doddering retired ambassador.

LG turned his cigar between his lips with each pause in his tirade, which seemed to emphasize the intimacy between us and the truth of what he said.

Then to General Pershing. Were us and the French really expected to quit the field in favour of the doughboys? Give over to the Americans, with less than 100,000 casualties, when we had millions? Let them press on and occupy Berlin and then tell us how to end the War? And then, expostulation, expostulation, then tell us what to do with Europe?

The Armistice had come just in time, boy. We can thank the Almighty for that.

LG rapped the table with his middle finger.

'But we've ended a war through mutual exhaustion not through superior tactics. Whatever the generals and the dukes may like to tell each other in their clubs.'

Maybe it was his working girls. That's what LG liked to think. The ones he had mobilized, their skin turning yellow in the armaments factories, maybe it was his girls who had really done it. Producing all the shells.

Did I know for example that the Americans had no arms? No ammunition? That Saint Mihiel had been fought with our rifles, our machine guns and our bullets? And yet the Professor now thinks he can dictate to us about his *ideal state of affairs*.

Then on to his friend Georges. *Le Lion des Ardennes.*

'Now there's a real lion for you,' LG said. 'But they call him *le Tigre*.'

Suddenly LG started to sing.

Oh my darling,

Oh my dah-ling,

Oh my da-ha-ling Cle-men-ceau.

LG's voice rang out from behind the roses, up and quavering. But the singing was over before we had time to be embarrassed. The girls looked at me. Was *Monsieur OK*? The new American *chic*. I reassured them, *Monsieur* was indeed *OK*. They tittered but they were still not sure.

'We've all got what we want,' LG started again earnestly. 'Clemenceau has Alsace and Lorraine, infinite quantities of German coal, Belgium has been liberated and they're getting priority in Reparations. We've got the German colonies. And we'll get the Turkish. We're getting all the Bosche merchantmen and their fleet is in Scapa Flow, headed under the waves.' LG made a little fishy motion with his hand. 'And,' shaking his finger now, 'most important of all, we've proven our point to the Germans. War of Aggression does not pay.'

LG seemed to sink. Back to his brooding, despairing almost. About Foch, who, he said, wanted to go on and on with his vengeance. Now he was trying to make five million Germans west of the Rhine into Frenchmen. The Rhenish State, if you please, a buffer zone against the Bosche, he says. And the old Tiger trying to set a price on Reparations so high that the Germans would never be able to pay. Slaves for ever.

Would I not think that taking a bullet in the neck would have softened the old boy up? But not a bit of it. He was worse now than before.

I knew about the attempted assassination of the French Prime Minister, but as to the rest, all I could do was try to remember what LG had said. Just remember the words and work out the meaning later. The references, the jumps, the presumptions of knowledge in his mutterings, it was all too much for me to absorb.

Then on again.

'We've already managed to get seven million Germans on the wrong side of the line as it is. Germans not in Germany any more. And isn't it better for us all that their economy gets going again rather than creating a nation of unproductive paupers? Vengeance, boy, that's all it is. That's why the big palace at Versailles. So that the French can get back at the Prussians for 1871.'

There was a pause. The girls, bored now, were making faces at each other, their chins down near the tablecloth.

'I'm the cucumber in the sandwich. Between the two of them. The cucumber. That's what I am.'

LG sighed and sat back sipping his champagne.

A third bottle was brought by the waiter. A Russian aristocrat, I had decided, who was used to being on the receiving end. Until he had escaped in '17 with only his life.

'But it's not the German people we've been fighting, you know, boy. It's their leaders who are the guilty ones. We don't want to punish the wrong party. I'd hang the Kaiser if I could get at him. But the German people, they need help to pull themselves together. And the sooner the better.'

LG talked on. About the Italians, Fiume, the Brenner Pass. The Roumanians. Rats, he said, changing sides twice and doing so well out of it. Poland. Such brave people, but difficult? I had no conception. They've been given their country back after all those years. But the word *corridor*. Isn't it obvious even to the simplest soul what that little word means?

And how he was sure that all the parts not settled right now would be looked after later. By reasonable offers, fair counter offers, by well-intentioned men reaching the right conclusions. In a year or two, when the passions had all worn down a mite.

'We're remaking the world here, boy. Can't get it all right the first time, I don't expect.'

LG sat back against the banquette. He blew a stream of smoke up into the air.

'Vengeance is mine,' he said quietly, almost to himself again. 'I will repay, saith the Lord.' The dark cloud hung over us, obscuring the plaster vines and baskets of fruit entwined along the ceiling cornices.

Then suddenly it was over.

'Well, that's enough of that,' LG declared, pretending to rap on the table. Then his elbows were gathering the girls' necks again. 'How about some dancing over on the other side of the town?' He looked round the table at us. The girls understood only that we were leaving. I quickly made for the car, to prepare.

With the three of them installed in the passenger compartment I headed back over pont Neuf, past the Opéra and towards Montmartre. The *premier arrondissement*, the formal part of the city, was deserted. German heavy artillery pieces lined the boulevards like Carthaginian booty, spaced between the trees, their metal wheels sunk into tar pavements as if spent, fixed, secured for ever.

But as I crawled along rue Pigalle looking for LG's next spot, we had reached that other life. *Le monde des noctambules* was all around. Le Rat Mort, LG had said, up at the end, on the corner with rue Frochot, as if I knew it well.

Le Rat Mort was a sombre and a forbidding-looking place. A large converted house, a dark wedge fronting on to two streets. No awning, nothing inviting from the pavement, only a small illuminated sign on the side street, rue Frochot. I pulled up in front of a tall double door studded and heavy like the entry to a stable.

I looked back into the compartment through the partition. I could see LG, his lion's mane drooped, asleep between the two girls. I climbed into the back and tried to wake him.

'Sir? Sir, we're here, sir.' I tugged gently at his sleeve. LG twitched and lolled back against Colette. She looked annoyed, this was not *le good time*. I tried once more, shaking his shoulder as hard as I dared. LG was completely unresponsive.

Suddenly I was panicked.

That flash of an instant, that eternal moment. I saw the counter-attack again in a split second of premonition. *Stoßtruppen* looming out of the ruined town without warning, up from craters, through doorways, out of blasted houses, rising like an army of we-thought-you-were-dead. Huge men in their *feldgrau* overcoats, bayonets reflecting the moon, faces set and determined, blurred in the shadow of their helmets.

What if LG were sick? What if he had collapsed? How much had he had to drink even before we started from the day room?

I turned urgently to the unshaven doorman, hovering and anxious by the car. This one was a real *poilu*, a former soldier of the French Army, still in his blue overcoat and definitely impressed by the standard five francs. But at that moment I would have preferred the calm, even the *hauteur* of the Café Soufflot. I closed the door to the compartment behind me.

'*Vous restez ici*,' I said to the *poilu*. 'Nobody is to leave or enter the car. *Compris?*' The imperative battlefield order with no room for error. He understood.

I hurried into Le Rat Mort only to become blockaded by a dense crowd of *les soupeurs de Paris*. A collection drawn from almost every social diversity the city could bring together: dandies in white tie; women in glistening gowns, their hair parted severely like a man; workmen in caps and leather tuckers; sickly-looking youths in dark jackets, smoking and talking earnestly. They sat at little wooden tables by candlelight under a high black ceiling, they leaned against the ornate brass bar or they stood in crushed groups on the sawdust-strewn floor.

A party of Americans, distinguishable by their bright clothes, was making a show at the back. Bow ties and straw hats, more appropriate for playing golf on the other side of the clock than slumming in the *9ème*.

A violinist and a tenor were struggling through the high point of some obscure opera, almost lost to the roar of the *soupeurs* and the clatter of waiters in long white aprons shouting to the barman.

Deux coupes, trois crèmes, trois noirs! Or, *La vingt se tirent!*

I forced my way to the back and raced up the staircase. LG had said the first floor and there I thought I might find someone reliable such as the manager of the Café Soufflot.

Here the scene was altogether different. An accordion trio was playing the tango to a packed, smoke-filled room. Couples in evening clothes danced languidly or sat vapidly at their tables. Unwilling to admit that they were about to drop from exhaustion.

A maître d'hôtel stepped from his desk at the top of the stair as I arrived. I started my breathless explanation.

'*Je suis un officier anglais. J'ai un visiteur très important dans la voiture…*'

But it was all of no importance. Once the maître d'hôtel determined that what I wanted was merely to place a telephone call he interrupted me with a stiff little bow from the waist, head up, arrogant. He opened the palm of his hand toward the lectern. On the wall behind was a telephone.

'*Un franc*,' he said. Outrageous.

I wound the handle. An ear piercing click followed by an *allô! allô!*

'*Cité trente neuf, s'il vous plait. Et vite si possible.*' Shouting over the accordion. Frantic now: the car, LG, the girls, the street at three o'clock in the morning and near place Pigalle.

Oui, oui, oui and what's your hurry at this time of night?

Bonjour. Arnaud? Yes, there was a taxi waiting. No, André was not there. But just a minute, his son Jean was outside.

Attendez. Jean came on, a voice I knew. Relief.

Certainement, he knew Le Rat Mort, he would be there immediately.

Outside, the Daimler was large and conspicuous in the narrow street, but all was well. LG was slumped into the corner on the far side, snoring heavily. The girls had somehow moved him over. They were sitting back on the seat beside him, smoking and pouting. The compartment reeked of their perfumed cigarettes.

Suddenly in my panic they looked like the last two warm and sticky glasses from a bottle of flat champagne. Post-orgasmic and overpainted. I spoke to them more roughly than I had meant. You must go. A taxi is coming to take you back to the Café Soufflot.

They were offended.

'The taxi will be paid for,' I added. But that was not the trouble.

'*Et qui va nous payer, nous?*' the girl in the pearly dress asked, suddenly showing a hard edge. I had no idea at all about the arrangements. The restaurant, the Café Soufflot, I thought.

'But they were closing,' the other one said, Nicole, the one who used to be my girl in black. I dug into the petrol fund again and gave them eight francs each. It was clearly insufficient but the fund was dry until we could sell more petrol.

I was saved by the arrival of Jean. I could have hugged him.

'*C'est notre premier ministre,*' I said in an urgent low voice as Jean stepped down. 'He's out cold. And there are two girls. I have to be rid of them. I've given them eight Francs each but there's going to be a scene.'

Jean opened the back door of the Daimler.

'*Et alors mes coquottes,*' Jean started, climbing in. He turned to look at me before he closed the door.

'Nobody's touched them,' I said apologetically. My ancient friend André would have made one of his comments. *Quel maquereau!*

I could hear heated conversation, which did nothing to waken LG, then the door opened again. Nicole and Colette followed Jean out of the Daimler and he escorted them to his Renault. They looked like two sulky schoolgirls in fancy dress, caught by their father creeping back in through the kitchen door.

'Whatever it comes to,' I said. 'We'll settle later.'

Jean held the door of his taxi for the girls then he climbed on to the driver's bench.

The Renault gearbox whined off up rue Frochot, little red tallow lamp at the back flickering away.

At the Hôtel de Crillon, before I could complete my explanation, the *concierge* referred me to his manservant, Varley, in LG's suite on the sixth floor. Varley answered the door in his shirtsleeves and I began again. Again I was cut off.

'Ah Mr Lloyd George. Right. Bring the car to the side door on Boissy d'Anglais.' I was just the driver again and that was complete relief.

In the street, Varley was waiting by a low side door and between us we manhandled LG out of the Daimler and into the building.

The service entrance was the dark side to the impeccable marble lobby. The business end I had never seen. Yellow-green walls were lined with a tangle of dusty, lagged pipes running across dark vents and gratings. Trolleys, barrels, boxes and laundry bags lay on both sides of cramped corridors leaving only a narrow space to pass. We struggled and shuffled to a lift with LG held up between us. The lift was made for rapid loading and unloading and unnervingly, had no doors. A hoisting rope passed through the ceiling and floor of the car, an apprentice pulled us up hand over hand, assisted by a counter-balance.

The lift arrived at the sixth floor, expertly matched at the threshold. Varley and I manoeuvred LG through trays and trolleys being prepared for breakfast in a cluttered maid's scullery. Then out into the familiar corridor, a world apart.

Into the drawing room of an elaborately decorated suite of gilded furniture.

With our load slumped in a large armchair Varley knelt on the floor and started to undo LG's shoes. LG opened his eyes and looked at me carefully as if for the first time that night.

'So, Mr Mendelssohn-lover, tell me. What's your name?' Slurring slightly. 'And how do you fit into all this madness?'

It was high time to say.

'My name is Beauchamp, sir,' standing at ease, holding his top hat behind my back, square to his chair in the middle of the huge ornate room. Varley had LG's shoes off, paying no attention. He started to undo LG's tie.

'I'm a lieutenant, sir, the Oxfordshire and Buckinghamshire Light Infantry, on secondment to the General Staff, in charge of the motor pool at the Foreign Office Temporary Headquarters in Paris, sir.' The full description of my position.

'So where's your uniform, Lieutenant Beauchamp?' LG inquired, bantering, but the most obvious question to follow.

'I drive one night a week, to keep my hand in, sir. To see what my men are up to.' LG liked that.

'No toffee-nose, you, eh? Lieutenant?' The Chicken-Gutter's expression. He was alive. I smiled at him. I loved him, suddenly and intensely. Our Crumpled Wizard.

Varley was standing behind the chair now, taking off LG's jacket. While LG sat forward, struggling to release the tails from under his backside.

'Well, Lieutenant Beauchamp, Mr Mendelssohn-lover, you've been good company tonight.' I had hardly said a word. LG seemed fully awake for a moment. 'Oh no,' he said loudly, 'they won't be rid of me that easily. Not over yet.' He had read my mind. Then LG was quoting again, down in the chair, eyes tight like a mole.

> '... but I am bound
> Upon a wheel of fire, that mine own tears
> Do scald like molten lead.'

He fell asleep again. I left him to Varley. I put the topper on a table by the door and let myself quietly out of the room.

~

It was the same thing week after week. Morley drove up Walnut, turned right on Birch and parked the Landcruiser, with the same anxiety rising, now into a fourth month.

Reluctantly he admired the small development on every visit. Professional offices in a townhouse format: massing and finish entirely appropriate for the transition context and cleverly articulated back from the street. Straight out of the City Planner's textbook.

But urban infill was work that Morley had left behind in his thirties, years ago. And each week the little building forced him into the same admission. That his partnership, like his life, was out of control. Forty architects and over one hundred staff run by three partners, an overhead of more than a million dollars every month. A practice that had become a furnace of design competition politics against a grind of slow receivables and meeting a huge payroll.

He should never have left being a one-man-band, working out of the house with a couple of draftsmen, minor projects as easy bread and butter.

What if he'd come home one evening and just made the announcement? Things with Jane couldn't have worked out any worse than they had.

Hi honey. I'm home. Guess what? I've canned the cash cow.

Morely pressed the entryphone button.

'Robert?'

'Come on in, Morley, be with you in a minute.' Morley's nerves tightened further at the dismembered voice and its familiar hollow cheer.

In the waiting room Robert's five o'clock patient walked out through the consulting room door right on five to six, dark glasses, head down. A shameful place, a shrink's office.

Robert was just as jovial and shallow in the flesh. With his smooth routines, recently polished up at a weekend enhancement workshop for upscale practitioners.

' 'Well, how's things this week?' Then, 'Juice?' Robert asked, before his first question could be answered. They settled down under antiqued beams and Tiffany lamps, facing Robert's triptych of posterized lily pads in matched frames.

Robert's question didn't need an answer. Heaped on the Deco sofa, Morley looked the picture of clinical psychosis. Morley could put up an appearance, but behind the red-eyed front he hardly functioned. During the early visits Robert had checked symptoms: frequent mood swings, diminished interests, fatigue, through to thoughts of death and suicide. Eight out of a list of nine that defined depression, only weight loss was missing. A tangle of rage and desperation, breathless anxiety like a bone-crushing disease.

Sometimes by the end of a session Morely could remember vaguely what *whole* used to feel like. But only until he was back in the elevator, only until he realized that there was an entire evening ahead of him, then a complete night.

And Morley's time was always filled. This wasn't a distress that could be fixed from the outside. It was a personalized acid running through his veins, eating away at his stomach no matter who he was with or what he was doing. An overwound spring that had forgotten why it was so taut, driven crazy with pent-up adrenaline but unable to connect with its intended clockwork.

Unrelieved by Robert's cool vocabulary of therapeutic suggestions. *Nurturance:* the patient treating himself well. Which Morley had somehow interpreted as a week in Los Angeles of all places, no reservations, no plans, just US $10,000 of anonymous cash in his pocket to last him the seven days. Driving around in a rented Maserati and doing whatever he wanted to do regardless of cost, time of day or moral constraints.

Then there were the emasculating visits from the decorative young girl with the *nom de profession*. Whom Morley was sure he was meant to pay in hard cash, not even concealed by an envelope. Implementing Robert's advice, he thought, to try and understand what Jane had meant by the word *object*.

Followed by *diversion therapy*, another mystery. But precipitating Morley's guilty visit to his mother in Saskatchewan during the coldest spring of the century.

And now the terminally ill. Putting in one evening a week in the kitchen of a hospice where Robert's partner was a *de bono* consultant.

'So, how's the volunteering going?'

'You just get to know them and they die.' Morley smiled weakly.

'But that's the point of the hospice, isn't it?'

'No, Robert, it's nuts. I'm play-acting.'

'I bet they don't think so.'

'One of the doctors wants me to sit on their board and help them lobby the Province for more money. They want to build a new one, for dying mothers to have their children with them. He wants to know why I'm doing the dishes.'

Robert nodded gravely.

'Just exactly how am I supposed to be *useful* over there?' Morley insisted. 'At the moment all I'm doing is listening to an old man who says that he's the same age as the century. Started late yesterday, very remote, means nothing to me at all. About being in Paris after the First World War. Articulate though, not what you'd expect in the East End.' Morley attempted another smile. 'Oh it'll actualize, I suppose, as Jane likes to say these days.'

Morley usually left Robert with even more agony than he had brought. Just being in the room where he used to sit facing her. The empty chair, wondering what she was doing at seven o'clock on a lovely sunny evening.

There had been sessions together after the split, angry resentful hours in which Morley had churned with more frustration than he knew was possible. Watching her as she sat, trying to persuade himself that she was just another of those dark-suited career women. Pushing forty or more, using their leggy tricks around the office to sell software add-ons or cheaper long-distance calls.

Or he had tried to remember the bad times. Picked thumb cuticles as a barometer of her cash flow, rings of stale make-up over a wrinkled neck. Rotting breath from too much instant coffee. Cigarette smoke in her hair from the staff room at the back of her shop. Or their drenched visit to the Cliffs of Moher in search of her mythical Irish roots. Where boredom had almost metastasized into a suicidal leap.

And he had followed Jane one evening as she drove away from Robert's office in the Jetta. He knew perfectly well where she went as soon as the hour was over. He saw right through her hokum. *Back to the shop, I suppose,* or, *really must get an early night tonight.*

'Her counsel's told her to sit through whatever,' Tim, his lawyer, had warned with a cynical smirk after the first joint counselling session had been set up through Jane's lawyer. 'So don't be getting your hopes up, amigo. Their divorce affidavits will carry a higher price tag at the end if she can say she's been co-operating with all the shrinky stuff you've asked for.'

Worse still, Jane had seemed to go out of her way to look as attractive as possible for each appointment. Always Georges Rech, the designer they had stumbled on together in Avignon and for which Jane's shop had then obtained the exclusive Vancouver rights. Morley had put up the credit guarantee.

'Jane is all I think of when I'm down there,' Morley started again. 'I watch the clock, and I picture Donald getting home at seven. I think of him coming through the door, Jane kissing him.'

Morley's real picture was of himself.

Following Jane from the front door into her little study, close behind her as she puts her purse on the desk. Then quickly moving her back against the wall and he's covering her mouth with his, across her face, her hair, her neck, a starving man. Her skirt up around her waist, her smells flaring his nostrils. Stepping on each other, pushing and fiddling through their clothes, panting, grunting.

There was something about Jane, something chemical, magnetic, a power beyond himself. Going back to the sunny day he had fallen in love at a glance across the tables of the crowded terrace at La Piazza. Something that turned Morley into a Satyr.

Robert was watching him carefully. Then he smiled, as if to soften the words of hard advice that were buried in the middle of every session.

'Try and do the hospice thing for itself, Morley. Empathize with the people you're looking after. Get involved and all the other clichés. Check the high-flying persona at the front door.' Robert's smile turned into his self-conscious laugh.

'They don't know what I do or who I am.'

'Don't be naive, Morley, you might as well wear a lapel tag. PROSPEROUS

VANCOUVER ARCHITECT, even if they don't associate the name with any of your buildings. Even if he's off his rocker, stalks his wife and sees a shrink.' Robert attempted another laugh.

The hour drifted on: Morley's missed exercise and his broken sleep, his refusal to take a drug. He wasn't going to give Jane the satisfaction. Until his fifty minutes were up, vague, without conclusions. Until he was back in the 4×4 by five to seven.

Morley thought about the old man as he started the Landcruiser. He had been delivered by ambulance from hospital the evening before. The first night was always the hardest. These were the four walls, this the last place.

It was late when Morley had made his final rounds, the eleven o'clock news was starting with the sound muted. There was some crisis on in France or Italy.

That was when the old man had started to talk about Paris. Morley had been torn. Tired after a morning of arguing with suburban tin-pots at Chilliwack Town Hall. Then back to the office after lunch to face a full day's problems.

But another of Jane's new expressions from her psycho-course had come back to him: *follow the moment*. Morley had stayed to listen.

He drove away from Robert's office down West 4th. No matter how often the view was admired, no matter how many postcards were sold, Vancouver with the coast mountains behind was always spectacular in the screened light of a summer evening. Before Jane he used to love his adopted city. A small town grown big, still manageable, no decay. A place that was everything: Pacific, European, North American all at once.

Morley could make West 4th be on the way from anywhere to anywhere and at all times of the day or night. This time the lights were out behind the window display in Jane's shop. He crept the Landcruiser around the back and into the lane. Her Jetta, his Jetta, wasn't there. But he knew exactly where it was to be found.

At the next light there was a choice. Over the bridge and find the Jetta, have his heart try to beat its way out of his chest, all his senses taken over by that running acid, or he could turn right and be home in five minutes.

Where no-name-brand would be waiting. Susan already in bed, pretending to be asleep, pretending not to care. Not the right picture of herself.

But at the house it would be the same, his house, their house, still Jane and Morley's house. Even with the furniture rearranged and the bedroom redecorated, even with Susan's things in Jane's closet.

Marriage: build yourself a house you love, give it to a woman you hate.

No, he would never move, she and lover-boy would never have the place. Nor the money. God, it was everywhere, it was now his life. Jane, anger. Anything could set him off, any familiar street corner throughout the entire cocksucking city.

Morley drove straight on, towards the hospice.

When the old man was dozing it seemed as if he had died quietly in the half hour since Morley was last in the room. Then the shape in the bed would stir or eyes would open and Morley would jump. He was a long way from being easy with the dying. .

The old man looked uncomfortable and Morley tried to straighten him up as he slept. But he came awake immediately with a loud gurgle, gripping Morley's hand. Staring into Morley's eyes, scanning back and forth across a distant horizon. As if he had the most urgent thing in the world to say and no reason left to hold anything back.

The gurgling turned into a violent cough. Morley ran for Elaine. He was just a volunteer who helped run the kitchen. He quickly felt out of his depth if the patients did anything except lie in their beds or sit quietly at the dining-room table.

Elaine the night nurse was matter-of-fact about death. She strode confidently up and down the corridors, compact in a silky purple tracksuit with her short black hair. Holding an overflowing kidney bowl or a stacked pill tray, taking everything just as it came.

'So what's your problem then?' Elaine teased as she marched into the room. 'Causing our volunteers trouble again?' The coughing came to a gagging end. Elaine wiped the old man's mouth and held the glass up to his lips, a hand slipped through pillows to the back of his head.

'This one should be on the stage,' he spluttered, 'she's a laugh a minute.'

The coughing started again. Elaine turned from the bed.

'Could you get him an Ensure? And another soda water. And straws.'

When Morley returned Elaine explained.

'He can't come up any further because of his back. He's in a cast, so he needs help with his drinks.'

A molded plastic brace held the old man at the neck then spread behind his shoulders, disappearing under his gown and down into the bed.

'What's the poor guy got?' Morley asked Elaine outside the room.

'Cancer.' She shrugged. 'Last stages. Could be a month or could be a week. They found it in emergency after his blackout and his fall. And a broken back, of course, that cast is from top to bottom. The can with the old boy is a lot of fun. But at least he's catheterized, that deals with some of it. He says that if they hadn't cut him open it would never have spread.' Elaine cracked her weary smile. 'But with cancer everyone has their pet theories.'

'Do you know anything about him?'

Elaine consulted a notebook from a top pocket.

'Lives a few blocks away, here on the East Side.'

'Seems so unlikely, doesn't seem to fit.'

Elaine shrugged again. Maisey in Room 6 was going down, she had no time.

'Would you stay with him until he's had his drinks? He could choke again.'

Morley returned to the room and sat by the bed. He held the straw in the Ensure can up to the old man's mouth, then some soda water. Cold fingers crept across on to Morley's arm.

'Events began with an accident,' the soft voice started after some deep panting breaths, 'in Cumberland, England.'

Jane's accusing babble came back to Morley once again: *follow the moment*. He took up a skeletal grey hand with his own. He tried to settle himself down.

3

The first fatal motor car accident ever recorded in the county: 5 July 1899, in a country lane near Carlisle. A year to the day before my birth.

'*Bon père rén*, you are,' Ethel the Chicken-Gutter would say of me, 'just like '*im*.' Good-for-nothing she meant, like my grandfather, the driver.

For Ethel, my grandmother, it was a rule of life, that weaknesses of characters are repeated in alternate generations. So as she would have it, I came to imagine myself as my absent grandfather and like him I became a drinker.

As a schoolboy, fourteen, fifteen, I would often sit sodden and impervious to her. Then seeing my condition, Ethel would take a small bundle of papers out of her tin and wave them in the air over my head.

'Just like '*im*,' she would scream. 'That's 'ow you'll end, like '*im*.' Not that she ever knew how my grandfather had ended.

Before the papers, Ethel's tin had contained an assortment of Carr&Co's Best Biscuits. The large round lid was covered with a kaleidoscope of scenes from 1901, for the Coronation of Edward VII, partly worn off from years of handling.

I had been drinking, there was no denying it, back for the school holidays and still under age. Writing out letters for Mr Jowett the illiterate publican to pay my way. There was no money from Ethel.

And over the years, little by little, the story of my grandfather came out. Until one day I read for myself the papers with which I had been threatened so often. A set of ragged documents, folded and refolded until they were ready to crumble, kept under Ethel's money at the bottom of the biscuit tin.

The sheets were headed *Original For The Accused, Carlisle Assizes*, beautifully copied out by a steady hand with a quill. Then between the pages I found a brittle yellow cutting from *The Cumberland News*.

My grandfather, Alfred Arbuthnot Stoat, had been playing golf at a club outside Carlisle. This was part of Ethel's plan to come up in the world and live down the rest, the slums of Botchergate in a one-up-one-down. Trying to rise from the lost generations of the Industrial Revolution. Her plan to join the new middle classes in their houses with servants up Stanwix Bank. The gentry, she called them, a word I used to think she had invented, made up from *gentlemen* and *aristocracy*.

The drinker's moment came for my grandfather after he had told his group of golfing friends that he could drive. The drunken moment when exhilaration turns to tragedy, the moment that can never be had back. After the game and all the drinking, trying to impress, trying to be one of them, the gentry who owned the insurance office where he worked.

The sheets were not in order. I started in the middle of the policeman's evidence.

'Tell the court, constable,' I could hear the Crown Prosecutor say in his best Oxford accent, 'in your own wa-ards, exactly what you *saw-ah* on that day.'

'Took top of 'er 'ead off,' the constable starts, notebook in hand, helmet under arm. ''Air and brains to be seen by the side of the roadway, milud, skull opened up like an 'ard boiled egg.'

A young girl from the golf course kitchen, crushed under thin metal wheels. A ragged heap of bloody clothing lying in a narrow lane.

'And I then observed the accused, milud, the driver of the 'orseless carriage. Unsteady on his feet when answering questions. Smelling to 'igh 'eavens. Ten or twelve pints I would say, milud.'

My grandfather admitted to his guilt. He was lectured by the judge before sentence was passed and the newspaper had printed every word. Six months in gaol as well as a fine of more than the family's entire savings. And the men from the insurance company had dismissed him, his drinking friends from the golf course. The day after the accident and long before the trial, with nothing but his last week's pay.

When my grandfather came out of gaol Ethel had moved them as far away as she could, to St Ives in Cornwall. The place, she said, where her family had first landed.

Without the hedgerow in front and Mr Dalgetty's chicken sheds behind, the ugly brick house on Riley Lane was nothing more than a Victorian working-class tenement of four small rectangular rooms. In the first years we all lived there together with my grandparents' few possessions: Ethel and Alfred, my mother Phyllis, my father Graham and me. But the men were soon refugees: out, drunk, dead, it made no difference.

The centre of the house was the kitchen and the focus of the kitchen was the Aga, hungry for coal, for beaks and feathers. The rest of the room was filled by a trestle table covered with a patterned oilcloth and benches to sit on. Yellow walls crawled with moisture from vats bubbling steadily on the stove. Draughts came in all directions at once and the nauseating smell of scalding skin and scorched chicken-down pushed right through the house.

At the kitchen table sat the Chicken-Gutter-in-Chief herself, plucking and scraping without respite. Dressed in what had once been butcher's whites, now thick with tripe.

Out at the back Ethel had her chopping block and her bucket for heads, feet and blood, which my mother boiled up with swedes for the pigs. On the clothes line, chickens hung spaced between sheets and smalls, twitching and headless, pouring from their necks. Bleeding the white meat white, the sign of a well-prepared bird.

There was blood everywhere: on the door panels, the washing line and staining the ground beneath. Inside there was more: on the floor, the table, on the door jambs, smeared on the benches.

'*Vaqui!*' my grandmother would say when she was finished for the night, her cigarette waggling, addressing my mother's back, stooped over the Aga. 'That's ten shillings thre'pence ha'penny I've earned today.'

Then as if to convey the true value of ten shillings thre'pence ha'penny she would pick up her batch of prepared birds and wallop them down on to the table together. A lumpen wad of carcasses, beheaded, disembowelled and trussed. Necks, giblets and livers neatly stacked into the scooped out void of each blanched cadaver. While my mother kept stirring and skimming, boiling up the scalding pans, always at the stove.

Later, when the postman, Mr Jowett the publican and all Ethel's other backdoor customers had been and gone, paid their cash for her clandestine birds, pilfered live from Dalgetty's sheds where Ethel worked, the money would be added to the rest of the Chicken-Gutter's treasure in the Coronation biscuit tin.

My grandfather's accident had released in my grandmother a demonic energy. The fury of a woman whose plans for herself and her daughter had been scorned by the world. From then on it was the event that drove her life. So that every feathered neck that flowed as she drew her knife, every pair of popping eyes waiting for dispatch, every condemned claw scrambling wildly in mid-air was her answer to the tattles behind her back, the crossings of the street to avoid her.

Ethel killed them all, the Carlisle gentry, gutted and bled them every one. And every penny into her tin for her stolen birds was a vengeance, a tiny tinkling triumph.

My father Graham had been drawn into the event as the boy who went with the daughter. They had walked together up to Rickerby Park, back in Carlisle, when my grandfather was still in gaol. I like to think that it was still warm that day in the park, a soft autumn in the low Cumberland hills, but my mother told me nothing except the name of the place. And there on the grassy banks of the River Eden, her life in ruins, Phyllis my mother let him in, Graham my father. So that by the next summer, when I could no longer be hidden, they too had to run to Cornwall.

My grandfather lasted two years at Riley Lane, until 1903 when Ethel put him out. A broken man, a cider drunk, sent to wander the country as a tramp and to die a lonely death in the poorhouse.

Then the next year my father left, to work in Canada, Phyllis told me later. To earn money for a house, she explained, so that the three of us could be together, on our own.

My grandmother used a small vocabulary of foreign words mixed into her speech and she had snippets of stories. She said that her family was originally from France but from where or how was never explained. The core of the fragments was missing and by the time I might have understood, there was the Chicken-Gutting Empire to run with no time for storytelling.

I knew the words, or rather I knew what the words were intended to mean, but their origin was lost. I only presumed the language to be French, garbled, I thought, after years of unredressed use.

But Ethel hung on to her scraps and snatches, right or wrong. She was implacable and unself-conscious. The attachment to her distant past was strongly felt as something distinguishing, for all the gaps and enigmas. She maintained that her family, the Beauchamps, had come from France to live in St Ives because of *Nanto*. But whether *Nanto* was a person, a place or a plague, I could never determine.

'*Que lou bon Dièu lis apare,*' Ethel would say when mentioning the names of her forefathers, something like, *God bless them*. Ethel called her family *Uganand*, which she knew to be Huguenot, Protestant, although Ethel herself had no religion left.

There was Ethel's great-great-grandfather who had lived in St Ives long before the move to Carlisle, the Yves Beauchamp for whom I was named. He was not born in France and he may well have taken the name, Yves, from the town. So allowing twenty-five years between generations, I calculated that this original Yves Beauchamp of St Ives was born in 1779 or before. And his family had emigrated much earlier, from the old France, maybe as long as a century before the Revolution.

Then Ethel would talk of wealth, of houses and farms, of wealth wasted, of what it would all be worth today. But that is probably the same in many families.

4

My schooling was more of the Chicken-Gutter's vengeance on Carlisle. If it was not my grandfather it was to be *me* the gentleman, even though I was sure to be the inheritor of all my grandfather's faults.

My boarding school career began with a hired car in the summer of 1911, an undertaker's car used for country funerals. A De Dietrich, black and formidable, that took us to a shop in Exeter to buy my new school uniform.

With Miss Trelawney at the village school in St Erth I had developed a broad Cornish accent. I led a simple healthy existence, pulling girls' hair, catching frogs, torturing snapdragons and hunting with a catapult.

Most days my mother walked me up the lane to school and would be waiting for me at the gate at lunchtime. I was not ashamed of her then, that only came later as Ethel's programme took hold.

By the Aga, at the kitchen table, the day of the shopping expedition, with Ethel at her accounts and the daily batch of pimpled cadavers on the table ready for scalding, my mother settled down to sewing names on to my new clothes. BEAUCHAMP Y.G.

'And don't go letting 'em call you Beecham, neither,' Ethel started. 'Like the pills.' One of her favourite subjects, '*É Beau-champ alor*, with the *p* silent. Means beautiful field, the good land the family once owned. And will own again one day.' Nodding vigorously.

Then the display. I wore the complete uniform, shirt and tie, blazer and cap, heavy corduroy shorts, long prickly stockings turned down over little blue garters to reveal the school colours.

By then we had moved to Plymouth Road and Ethel had tenants of her own.

'Well,' Ethel asked around, while I stood there stupid and self-conscious, still with no clear idea of what was to happen to me, 'how's about that? Proper little gent, don't yer think? *Espetadous!*'

So what did the tenant's son think? My chum from the village school who had been asked over for the spectacle, to drive home the new distinctions.

'T'wern't no good for zbread'n' dung,' he replied, not knowing how well he had made the Chicken-Gutter's point for her.

Deanswood, my preparatory school, was a converted country house in Devon. And Mr Spaggot the headmaster seemed to live the illusion that a country house it remained. Acting the squire, treating his one hundred and fifty pupils as an unfathomable inconvenience, as if we had been invited to tea to look at the armour and had overstayed our welcome.

The establishment was really run by Johnny, Mr Johnstone, a fat, red-faced failure of a man. He prowled the corridors in his flowing gown and stained frock coat sneakily catching little boys talking in class, flicking peas at meals, or best of all, throwing water and splashing in the baths. The culprit naked, white and slippery.

Johnny's wrath was the same in all cases, though punishment in the baths took him longer. He would clutch at hair, at an ear, a nose. He would squeeze and jerk the captured protuberance until the victim was a helpless creature, a calf led by a ring following Johnny's hand. Unable to breathe or think, flinching away in anticipation of the parting slap. To a stream of abuse and spittle through swollen lips and brown teeth.

But in my case there were other offences.

'There are few *zeds* in the English language, Beauchamp,' he would say, interrupting me in full stream, 'despite the opinions of your local peasantry. It's *that*, not *zarrt*, and *over there*, not *owerzear*. You may decide to be from London one day, Beauchamp, or from Brighton. It may not always suit you to be from Cornwall.'

It was Johnny who told me about my father. He called me into his class-room while the other boys were lining up for lunch. He had a letter in his hand. I recognized my mother's writing.

'It's my lot to inform you of this, Beauchamp,' he said, lighting a cigar-ette and puffing smoke into my face. 'Your father's been killed.' Johnny consulted my mother's letter. 'Somewhere in Canada, on a dam site.'

I started to cry.

'Well, you know what they say,' Johnny added, ignoring my tears and making for the door, 'you can never feel a proper man until your father's out of the way.'

The rhythm of the boarding school continued, harsh, lonely and barren. But I received an education. From the leisurely pace of Miss Trelawney's classes I found myself struggling to keep up as everything I had learned before was passed over in the first two weeks of the year.

I began Latin, French, algebra and scripture and I attended daily Anglican service. I learned to play rugby, field hockey, cricket and croquet, all the games of a gentleman. I learned the rules for conduct between boys and boys. And between boys and masters.

With Mr Melhuish it was always the lavatory. Waiting in his heavy embroidered dressing gown as I came padding along the lino. He carried a candle in a holder.

'Everything all right?' he would ask in his best mock-friendly manner, lodging himself so that I could not close the door behind me.

Then somehow the candle would go out and he would put his hand on me in the dark, perching me up on his lap as he sat on the lid. Talking still, quietly from behind, rubbing at me through the slit in my pyjamas. Working me without a pause until I cried out in pain. Then he would let me down and send me back to bed.

It was a grotesque dream that I did not understand, but inexplicably bad and for ever connected to the smell of Harpic, to the loud clank of the over-head flusher cranked by a chain. Assuring any listener who chanced to be awake of the innocence of my visit.

Soon my new furrow diverged from the lives of all my former friends. I found that I had no interest in village dances, in furtive grapples with Mary Baker in the churchyard, in lamping rabbits or stealing cider and cigarettes.

But there were corresponding discoveries at Deanswood. That in this other world boys had fathers and grandfathers with the same last name. That boys lived in houses with servants, that boys had mothers who visited the school accompanied by these fathers. Women dressed in high Edwardian fashion, inverse tulips, dresses flowing to the ground like softly melting dolls.

That boys did not have homes where, in place of musical evenings in the drawing room, chicken livers, giblets and skinned necks were cleaned, sorted, covered with cigarette ash then re-inserted into bowels while we all sat in the kitchen watching.

Slowly it built in me, resentment at the Chicken-Gutter's continuous operation, at her enslavement of my mother over steaming basins of foul-smelling offal. And at my grandmother's constant admonitions.

'È alor,' she would start during the holidays, "ow's our little pupil today?'

Ethel seemed to have a daily theme prepared with which to taunt and nag. Subjects about which I could do little to satisfy her, then, on that very day.

I could hardly improve my cricket sitting in the kitchen on Plymouth Road, watching my mother move her rendering pots around on the stove to còok me my breakfast. Or recite my French, Latin and Greek, the languages, Ethel assured me, that were spoken between gentlemen.

On my first day at Deanswood, Ethel in her Carlisle finery had been a sight to behold. Hair back in a tight bun like the old Queen herself. Swathed and layered like a nineteenth-century statue. Victorian black, appropriate for a widow. Or an unapprehended murderess.

Her gnarled hands were another prominent feature: rough and warped, joints at all angles like a pile of kindling. Unscrubbable dirt and blood caked under nails and around cuticles, skin stained black by nicotine. Twisted fingers living a life of their own, fussing and fiddling continuously: with Ethel's papers, with her skirt, smoothing, straightening. Puffing at their cigarettes.

But my mother was still the scullery maid, even out in the De Dietrich, unsure of what to do with her hands on her day off. A simple frock, no hat and heavy laced shoes.

On that first day at Deanswood Ethel's fingers were indulged in their favourite pursuit, the counting of money. New five pound notes out of her bag. Valuable, large and white, something rarely seen. Mr Spaggot was horrified. And on many later occasions I came under a distinctly uneasy gaze, as if I might at any minute try to dole him out a few more embarrassing fivers.

Ethel missed completely Mr Spaggot's attempts at patrician offence. Clearing his throat, saying he had no idea of the amount, that Ethel really should see the Bursar, by which Spaggot meant his wife. Anything, anything, to make her *stop*. But the feel of money dimmed all Ethel's other senses during the sacrament of counting, her hearing especially.

'*Vaqui!*' Ethel yelled at Spaggot, the tips of the fingers coming up to meet her tongue for a quick lick before they started to flick notes and coin onto his desk like so many trimmed chicken livers. 'That'll be thirty-six pound, fifteen shillings for the boy for a full year.'

Ethel had also missed that payment was intended to be made as thirty-five guineas, written out by cheque, posted before term began. Or at the very worst, brought in an envelope on the first day. But certainly never to be mentioned.

5

The Coronation biscuit tin may have bought me entrance to Deanswood but the next advance in my grandmother's progress was up to me. And I cannot deny that I took that step voluntarily, by humbling myself to ask Johnny for a reference, by listening to his lecturing and his accurate forecast of the examination questions for entrance to The Martyr's School, Oxford. I could have refused. But the result would have been damnation to the life of a labourer within the Empire.

With the journey to Oxford on my own, by train from St Ives, I managed to avoid the large black car and Ethel's dead fox around her shoulders, the most wilfully repulsive female fashion I have ever seen. And I was spared her inevitable attempt to flick chicken livers at the headmaster, now called the Warden.

But I missed the appointed school train, arriving late into Waterloo from Exeter and never through London before. I was an hour late at Paddington and I reached Pond House later still, by taxi up to the front steps. As the driver and I struggled through the door with my trunk and my box, a man appeared. Dark suit, high-cut jacket, striped tie denoting membership of some club, I thought, fancy paisley waistcoat, sparkling brogues.

'Sir,' I began immediately, before he could speak, taking him for a master, my accent back toward Cornish after the summer holidays. 'Could you tell me where to go, sir?'

I quickly learned that my entrance, the boys' door, was round the corner and that this man was not a master, but Elliot, Head of House. Starting his last year at that school, coming up to eighteen years old maybe.

Elliot looked down at me in my Deanswood uniform, shorts and blazer, knitted tie.

'So what's *your* name?' he asked.

'Beauchamp, sir.'

'*Bowchumpzhurr.*' Elliot sneered. 'And how do you spell that?'

Just as he had thought.

'It's pronounced Beecham,' Elliot informed me.

But I had been readied by my grandmother for this very eventuality and I was quick to the defence.

'No, sir, it's not. It's Huguenot, sir. From France.'

Elliot's face masked over with sudden anger as if I had trodden on his shiny shoes.

He repeated my words after me once again, '*Vrom Vrance*, eh?' But this time with a heavy menace. 'Well, I'm going to show you how we deal with cheeky little Frogs up here in Oxford.'

Another boy was passing at the far end of the hall.

'You, come here,' Elliot snapped. 'This specimen is Beecham, he's to go to Dorm One.'

In the dormitory I waited blithely among the beds until Elliot entered with two other senior boys in more coloured ties. The official witnesses to the punishment for my many crimes.

The first few he could have overlooked, on that, my first night. Being a Frog, not to mention my absurd accent, this ridiculous prep school outfit, coming in through the front door, not knowing who he, Elliot, was. But answering back, that was quite intolerable. Shells would be made to understand: Elliot was jolly well going to make Pond House the best house in school that year, whatever it took.

'Bend over,' he said, 'touch the bottom bar of the bed.' The cane came out from behind his trouser leg.

My public school career had begun.

Then I was taken to Mr Mather, the Housemaster. A large awkward man, a wall in front of me in a complete tweed golfing outfit. Big boned, going to fat after an athletic career.

'Ah, Beecham,' he said. 'Rather bad start, I hear. You really must...'

Mather examined me, finding me to be unworthy of the completion of his admonition.

'And doesn't the boy have any *clothes*?' Mather asked of Elliot as if I was not present. Mindful of the extraordinary spectacle that I was going to make for Pond House among six hundred other boys in their suits at the first Evensong of term.

Mather made a show of consulting a list. 'Wherever is it the boy has come from?'

But just as Elliot opened his mouth to reply, Mather found his place on the paper.

'He's from *Corn*-wall,' they both chimed together and I was scrutinized once again in the light of this fresh information.

I tried to explain, addressing Elliot, while Mather rattled the stem of his empty pipe against his teeth, apparently impatient for me to go.

No, sir, I had no school uniform and no long trousers. Because my grandmother had said, sir, that I could buy my new uniform at the school shop.

I placed what Ethel had given me on to the desk for their joint inspection, pressed and curled from the long journey in my pocket.

Mather looked up at Elliot. 'Good Lord,' he said. 'Isn't that money?' They both stared down at the tight wad once again, as if shocked.

So, Mather supposed, there was simply nothing for it, all the boy had was five pound notes. He would have to excuse the boy chapel that evening. But didn't the boy have a father? I started to explain again but Elliot motioned me to be quiet and Mather turned disdainfully away toward the window.

Once outfitted, my job as a shell was to learn by rote the names, nicknames and rules for every conceivable aspect of the life of the school and the house. And to accept without question that ours was the best school and that within that school, ours, Pond House, was best house. Beliefs to be adopted fervently, yelled out at interminable inter-house and inter-school team events. To be taken on as an instant, lesser religion.

And once initiated I became a fag in the endless year-over-year supply of juniors as the labour for pressing and cleaning uniforms, for cooking and running errands for any prefect who selected me. All in addition to my own well-being, games and school work.

And slowly, as the first term progressed, I was also initiated into the school underworld. Who took after who, who the school lush was and who was going to do what to him. An initiation I had already had. But unlike at Deanswood where it had been between masters and boys, here, like the beatings, it was between boys and boys. The reason why school bogs had no doors.

The sole objective of that school was to produce what Mather referred to as a *certain type of boy*. And although as Bow-Chump, who always had to be *different*, I knew that I was definitely not in this category, I never understood what was meant and Mather never defined his ideal any further. A games player, at which the school excelled? A *good sport*? A boy who showed a lot of *gum*-ption?

There were many new subjects at Martyr's: Roman literature, French literature, Greek grammar, ancient and modern history. And out of the classroom, survival against the rules, the sudden harsh penalties, political almost. Why did not one of them just come out and say it?

'Beecham, I'm now going to beat the living daylights out of you, merely because I detest you and your kind. Bend over.'

It was not until my first visit to France in July of 1914, with that school, that I came to pay any attention to the map of France and to the unanswered questions from Ethel's stories.

Fairy, my history master, asked me the first night of the journey, in Lille.

'So, Beauchamp,' he said with a big energetic smile, Fairy was always happy. 'Have you any idea where your French name comes from? Where were those *beaux champs*?'

On the train and on the Channel steamer Fairy had listened to my descriptions of Ethel's stories and to her language. Over the week of our visit he produced his hypothesis.

Fairy loved France, the language, culture, food, the history and the countryside. And Fairy could make history come alive, explain the present and even predict the future.

'The true inheritor of Greece and Rome,' he said to me. 'Clearly the dominant influence in Europe. Compared with France, even with our Empire, England is a backwater. *La France* is the true centre of the world.'

Such heresies. And on our way to Waterloo.

Fairy suggested that the Beauchamps might have come from the south, matching some of Ethel's descriptions of the country. Ethel's language sounded Italian as well as Spanish to him. From one of the Huguenot towns which had enjoyed autonomy under Henry IV and the Edict of Nantes.

Then we imagined the terror following the revocation of the Edict in 1685, the *Nanto* of Ethel's fragments, after one hundred years of religious peace. King Louis's Intendants start razing Huguenot towns and villages, raping, murdering whole families. The Beauchamps abandon their farm. Food for a few days is put into mule panniers including a few possessions: gold and silver, jewellery.

Which way lies safety? Fairy and I studied the map. The family may have headed north, up the valley of the River Orb, away from the larger towns and the dangers of the Mediterranean coast. They could have posed as pilgrims to the tomb of Saint Jude.

Finally over the bogs to the coast till they meet the screech of seagulls through Atlantic fog. An open boat for the crossing, dangerous and raw, maybe a fisherman from the Île de Ré, sympathetic but well paid.

From La Rochelle, the first landfall could only be Cornwall.

'QED,' Fairy said, as if he had solved a problem in geometry.

Fairy had constructed a story which I took to be the true explanation. Arrival in Cornwall to an England of toleration after the Glorious Revolution of 1688. Hard work and industry starting the Huguenots all over again, still confident in their faith.

Back at the house on Plymouth Road, during the last weeks of my first summer holiday from that school, I tried to explain Fairy's story to my grandmother. I had brought her a map of France, a thing, I realized, she had not seen before. But we never did look at the map. Within days of my return the first seven-day-olds of the season were coming ready in the hatchery, then the new sow threw a litter of thirteen and war was declared against Germany.

So I never did tell Ethel the story, Fairy's clever reconstruction, and she seemed happier with her snatches.

But in their different ways, Ethel and Fairy set up in me a longing for times past that I had never lived, for places and people that I had never known.

'It was a place,' Ethel used to say about the Beauchamp farm, '*ges de soucit.*'

Without cares, I imagined, without worries, where the *mas* produced everything the family could need. Where fruit fell into your pockets as you walked under the trees. Where beauty, comfort and contentment were the natural gifts of a benign southern god.

I began an inconsolable ache for this long-ago place that may never even have existed. And in the present it became a steady interest, a low-voiced attraction to France and to all things *françaises.*

During our return journey from Waterloo, I walked with Fairy through the narrow streets of Louvain to the library. The building was timbered like an Elizabethan house, but this structure was taller, larger, infinitely more sophisticated. The Tudor buildings I knew looked like farm cottages in comparison. Built in the fifteenth century, when, Fairy said, Berlin was just a tribal clearing in the forest. Inside the library there were manuscripts and incunabula, hundreds of volumes stretching back a thousand years. The most brilliant display of illumination and gold leaf in the world.

'One of the umbilical cords of our culture, tying us to the birth of civilization,' Fairy told me, standing among glass cases. 'Without these connections we would just be a dark, meaningless, industrial society. Without origins and without a future.'

But in August 1914, before school had started again, the old town of Louvain had been razed during the German invasion of Belgium. The fire was started by Belgian snipers, the Germans said in the American newspapers. No, the Belgians replied, by some accidental shots, some panic among the Germans themselves caused by a runaway horse. Nothing to do with their civilians. But even though no one knew how, the magnificent library, the Gothic town hall and the church, wonderfully decorated by Flemish masters in the fifteenth and sixteenth centuries, all were gone.

Fairy did not come back to school in September of that year, for the Michaelmas Term. And one morning during that winter, a dark, cold, wet December morning when the names were read out in chapel for the previous month, for November 1914, Fairy's name was the first.

'Alister John Farrington, a Master of this School.'

6

From my first term at that school I tried so hard to play the piano. But by the start of my second year, Mr Whitehouse, my music master, was ready to take me off his list.

'You're like Pinocchio, Beauchamp. Wooden.' Resting his arms on the lid of the upright with a look of desperation. 'There's no connection between your head and your ten thumbs.' I was defective in any form of mathematical instinct, the secret ingredient to a successful musician.

I looked dejected, my useless hands in my lap. Whitehouse tried to console me.

'But you can admire Christchurch quad, can't you, without knowing anything about geometry or perspective? Can't you enjoy the countryside without being Gainsborough?'

Whitehouse was right, but my removal from his list was going to leave a hole in my stomach that I could not explain. I was to be excluded from music, the new discovery to which I was so mysteriously drawn.

Whitehouse was constantly pushing back his flopping forelock with his right hand, little finger out rigid as if held in an invisible splint.

'Look, Ten Thumbs,' trying to be cheery now, letting me down gently, over a week or two maybe, 'do you think your parents would object if we spent some of these music lessons on history, music appreciation, voice coaching, that sort of thing?' I had been in the school choir for a year.

Whitehouse had no idea how irrelevant his question was. My grandmother, beyond my ability to describe to someone who did not know her, would have had one response and one response only.

'I' tha-at what gentlemen does?' Delivered as a controlled scream.

And from that day, without further introduction, on a whim, Whitehouse pushing at his forelock, with just a sudden thought, I began my endless journey. Music, a prism through which I found that I could see, understand even. A light to save me from the darkness of meaninglessness and despair.

We started with history, two one-hour sets per week, Whitehouse playing excerpts on the piano and on the organ in chapel. Teaching me with his examples through four hundred years of music. Starting with the minstrels and *Greensleeves*, ending with Bruckner and with Mahler, who had died only two years before. Until I knew that I had found my subject and I had in my head, embedded in my consciousness, a list, no, more than that. Shining images of many composers, their styles and their forms, who they were and how they fitted with my European history from the classroom.

Then we turned to the consideration of specific works. But at first, during my second year at that school, all other music was obscured by Bach and *St Matthew Passion*.

Lost in a sublime labyrinth: the recitatives of the Evangelist weaving the story around the voices from the Gospel. Words which I came to know by heart in English, the original German being almost illegal and the work itself suspect. When the programmes were printed for Easter 1915, Bach's name was left off the front cover.

Then the chorales, hymns of contemplation sung by the worshippers, originally by Bach's congregation, now by our choir. Solo arias interspersed throughout the work, heightening the tension, underscoring the emotions of the unfolding Passion.

I began to learn my parts. Whitehouse as rough and demanding as with the failed piano lessons. Forcing me, standing me on the steps to the huge empty chapel facing the vacant pews, whimpering my way in at first, thin, without conviction. Whitehouse holding me up, violently almost, pushing at my back, prodding my diaphragm. Learning to let go, to bring out my voice, beyond the self-consciousness and into the singing, large and open.

And suddenly one day it came to me. Here was an instrument I could play. The joy at entering, at projecting each and every note. Holding the score out in front of me with both hands. Breathing for the sustained notes and learning to count. Up from the chest, out through the top of the head.

After months the choir was able to take the *Passion* right through in practice, a coherent whole but missing the soloists and their arias for now. Manning, head of music for the school, an intimidating Austrian, singing the Evangelist for our rehearsals, in and out as he conducted.

Whitehouse had taught me a bass aria, weeks and weeks during our lessons, trying, stopping, starting. Up an octave for my alto voice.

One night at choir practice, without any notice, Whitehouse said, 'You're going to try your aria for Manning.'

In Part II, without any announcement we began, the others wondering, me nervous but caught up in the moment and wanting to show what I had been doing. Manning smiling his forced smile, leaning toward me, urging me, encouraging me as I came in after the soft opening.

> *Mache dich, mein Herze, rein,*
> *Ich will Jesum selbst begraben*
> *Denn er soll nunmehr in mir*
> *Für und für*
> *Seine süße Ruhe haben.*
> *Welt, geh aus, laß Jesum ein!*

The most beautiful aria in the entire work. Lilting, a waltz, taking me along with its beauty and serenity, opening me right up. At the end of the aria there was no stopping and no comments before we moved on to the next recitative.

Whitehouse spoke to me afterwards.

'Manning wants you to sing on the night. The bass will sit it out.'

There was nothing that school could have done to match my joy and my pride. They could have taken me into their establishment, made me whatever rank they chose, given me a tasselled cap for this or a striped sweater for that, let me wear some coloured tie. Nothing would have come close to that moment, watching Manning, holding my score, feeling Whitehouse behind me at the organ. And singing, singing out loud to everyone, to that entire school and far, far beyond.

And the language, of course. With Whitehouse I had learned the aria in the original and I sang in my anglicized German. The chorales and other solos had all been printed out and learned in English translation. It was a protest, it must have been, by Manning and his Viennese origins, against the waste, the incomprehensible. Or so I liked to believe.

And then finally to Beethoven and Beethoven's life.

In my last year at that school, during Hilary Term, the choir made a start on learning *Missa Solemnis* for a performance to be given at Easter.

It was on the night of the full dress rehearsal, a black chilling night, that winter the coldest ever in memory, the first time with the school orchestra and the extra musicians from outside: kettledrums, double basses, four soloists from the University. On that night as I sat in my place in the choir stalls, not a soloist, just a voice among the altos, in our row behind the instruments spread across the nave in place of the organ of our rehearsals, on that night as Manning brought his baton down and the wonderful sounds arose, slow, solemn, as the voices of the soloists spired and twined, vaulting into piercing pleas, for intervention, *Kyrie!* For mercy, *Eleison!* For peace, in that terrible year of all years, it was on that night that I knew he would appear.

Then as the miraculous music formed and built, I felt his presence, as if he was standing on the chapel steps where I had stood for Whitehouse. His hair wild, his collar askew, his face calm but violent, holding his staff like the first performance of the Ninth.

And in that moment, just before we started again, *Gloria in excelsis deo!* after the quartet had ended, words came rushing back to me. Words that I took to be Beethoven's, words that Whitehouse had used one morning when I was learning to sing. One of the mornings when Whitehouse spoke very little, when he only played and played. One of the many days when yet more new words were being heard, Suvla Bay, Masurian Lakes or the Glasgow Boys Brigade.

'Sing, Beauchamp, sing,' Whitehouse had said. 'It's all we have.'

One of the days when I wanted Beethoven to be made Prime Minister, King, Ruler of the World. Could Ludwig van Beethoven have done any worse? In that dreadful year? In 1917?

I came to understand that I had nowhere to belong and I started to yearn. I felt that for Whitehouse each night when we discussed the performance. Each night when I wanted him to take me home, to meet his wife, his children, to have toast in front of his gas fire, to move into his house, leave that school, leave Plymouth Road, listen to Beethoven, to music, only, for ever.

7

By the end of my last term Mather loathed me, the exact opposite of his *certain type of boy*. He hated me personally, far beyond all the bleak words that he wrote in my reports.

The final break was to do with Mather's Boer War and his lies about the Transvaal.

Mather had been forced to drop all his stories. About how easy we boys had things, how we should enjoy school food without complaint. Ten times better than the army. How we had no idea what it was like to march across the *veldt* for weeks on end, with only *biltong* to eat. All his guff had ended right away and I took that as my victory.

I had discovered at the end of 1916 that Whitehouse too had been in South Africa during the Boer War. It came up just by chance. Leaving the chapel after a lesson during the last set one morning, Whitehouse had asked me, just for something to say, maybe,

'So what's for lunch do you think?'

'*Biltong* I expect sir.' The word I had learned from Mather's interminable Boer War. Bleeding and dying for King and Country on *biltong* alone. Strips of deer meat, dried in the sun for use as emergency rations, so hard that it could not even be cut with a knife, only chewed. Like school food.

Whitehouse stood with me for a moment by the chapel door. It was then that he first told me about Durban in 1901. Some idea pressed on him by his father, about widening his horizons before going up to Oxford.

'Never saw any action, of course,' Whitehouse said in his jerky self-conscious fashion. 'Shipped right home again after only two months. Hardly out of the docks. This is all I have to show for it.' Holding out his stiff little finger, allowing me to examine closely for the first time the long scar up the outside of his palm.

Whitehouse had had his ambitions to be a concert pianist after university, specializing in the Mozart concertos. But all that had come to an end with a pipe bomb.

In a camp in Durban, Whitehouse had trained to diffuse mines. His instructor demonstrated on a captured Boer device, a length of water pipe filled with guncotton and buried end-on into the ground. This primitive bomb was set off by a glass vial of detonating compound placed across the top of the pipe and hidden with a covering of sand. The bomb would blow off the foot that trod on it.

In the training hut a detonating vial had squibbed by accident, damaging Whitehouse's hand. Then an incompetent army surgeon removing glass fragments had severed some tendons, leaving Whitehouse not a concert pianist, but a piano teacher and school organist, accompanist for Anglican doggerel.

The bell rang for lunch assembly.

'I've an old friend from those days staying,' Whitehouse told me as we parted. 'Just back from German South West Africa. Would your History Society like to have him speak?' I was the Secretary.

Whitehouse's friend, Captain Addison, a former officer in the 10th Hussars, had seen over two years of active service during the Boer War. The Captain had stayed on in South Africa after the war had ended.

When war had started against Germany in 1914, Captain Addison covered the events in South Africa for the *London Chronicle*. An army had been raised by the new Union of South Africa, many of them former Boer guerrillas. This local army had invaded and captured German South West Africa in 1915, a huge colony on the Atlantic coast, twice the size of France. The victory was the only good news England had received since the War began.

Now the Captain was weak, recovering from malaria. He had returned to Europe to fight, only to find that he would never be accepted as fit.

But he was more than willing to give a talk. He had slides and a lantern and we, the History Society, would find a room in the next few evenings, before the Captain left Oxford. The Society had thirty-five members.

Then matters became out of hand. One of our members spread it around and the jingoists took over: German South West was a Great Victory, the whole school should hear about it.

The History Society was pushed aside. Soon the Warden was involved, flags were to be hung and the lecture moved to Big School. Even the hall servants and the groundsmen were to attend.

I sat with Whitehouse and Captain Addison in the school shop before the lecture started, drinking tea and trying to apologize for the fuss. The Captain seemed amused. Whitehouse joked with him about *biltong* and about Mather, right in front of me, an unheard-of breach. The Captain was interested.

'What regiment was your Housemaster in?' he asked.

'The South Berkshire Yeomanry, sir,' I answered, from Mather's flashes on his uniform on OTC days. The Captain smiled me a secret smile.

The lecture seemed to be everything they could have possibly wanted, starting with the National Anthem. The slides were exotic, all taken for the newspaper. The incredible conditions in the Namib desert, the harshest place on earth the Captain called it. Lions, elephants, snakes and scorpions; wells poisoned by the retreating Germans; the romance of a place called Walfish Bay. Our victorious advance across beautiful high ranching country around the capital, Windhoek. Through the swamps of the Caprivi Strip filled with crocodile and hippopotamus.

At the end the lights went up and the Captain stepped away from his screen to the front of the stage. He faced the entire school, the pointer in his right hand held like a sabre.

The Warden and masters were seated in the front two rows, in their gowns and striped ties. Mather with his empty pipe running across his teeth. Smiling for England.

'This is really a meeting of your School History Society,' the Captain started again, when I thought that the lecture was over. 'So it's not out of place for me to put an historical context on this little war over German South West.'

I was immediately thrilled, without knowing why.

The Captain wanted to go back for a moment to what was really the Second Boer War, the war of 1899 to 1902.

'It's fifteen years on since that war,' he said deliberately, every word plainly audible. 'And now we can see clearly that our war against the Boers was completely wrong.' The Captain paused as if to make sure that everyone had understood.

We the British were wrong, the Boer War was a travesty, a waste of lives. For nothing.

Even the start of the war was a lie, a fabrication. The Boers were not mistreating the English as the Colonial Secretary, Mr Joseph Chamberlain, had claimed. The Boers offered all-comers citizenship. And it was their country, after all, the Transvaal and the Orange Free State. They had trekked there from the Cape, they had defended it successfully against us, the British, in the First Boer War, which the Boers had won.

And it was pure hypocrisy, the Captain went on, for us to express concern for the natives under Boer rule when Britain had wiped out the Zulus with grapeshot. Genocide, the Captain called it. Then we had turned what was left of the Zulus into a subject race.

My heart began to pound. There was something very compelling but very dangerous about the way the Captain spoke.

It was simple, he said.

We, England, us, we had gone back on our solemn promises, our treaty with the Boers. Because gold and diamonds had subsequently been discovered in the Transvaal and Rhodes and Chamberlain wanted to grab them. That's all, that was the whole thing. That's what the war was about. All the rest is bunkum, simply not true.

Now surely the Captain must end, I could not bear the tension of another word. But unbelievably there was more.

'As historians,' he said, 'we can find parallels between the Boer War and the War in France. The treaty protecting Belgian neutrality, as you all know, was brutally violated by Germany in August 1914. The Germans called the treaty *just a piece of paper*. It was outrageous behaviour, sums up what we all think of the Bosche. Whatever the real origins of the War may have been.'

The Captain paused again. I was gripping my chair in anticipation.

'But in principle, our behaviour, the British behaviour in South Africa wasn't any better than the Germans' behaviour in Belgium, just further away.'

The Warden was suddenly restless, looking around at his staff. Mather's pipe stem rattled over his teeth with a new intensity.

Had they heard that right? Showing on all their jowly features.

Then the Captain was a runaway horse, beyond all control.

The conduct of the Boer War had been even more pitiful than the politics that had started it. When we were unable to defeat the Boer horsemen, Boer women and children had been rounded up and herded into places called concentration camps. Then their farms and their crops had been burned, their livestock slaughtered.

Forty thousand non-combatants had died in these camps and the *veldt* had been de-populated. Ready to be resettled with new British blood after the war. The Captain was emphatic. Forty thousand people. Women and children. White lives, real lives. Not just your local blackmen. And these concentration camps were run by British soldiers under Kitchener.

Lord Kitchener had been Secretary of State for War until he was drowned earlier that year. Our National Hero. His face was still up on posters all over the country, an accusing finger pointing at every male still in civilian clothes.

YOUR COUNTRY NEEDS <u>YOU</u>! JOIN BRITAIN'S ARMY.
GOD SAVE THE KING.

And women. Yes, we tied Boer women to our armoured trains to stop their attacks. In the scorching heat, we tied them to our locomotives.

Before all this had sunk in to the masters and the assembled school, the Captain started to describe the incompetence of the military, beyond the brutality.

As an example, did we know that whole regiments were sent out to South Africa and never used? Complete waste. Hardly even left their disembarkation point. The Captain named some of the regiments. The King's Own Light Infantry for example. Never out of Durban. And the South Berkshire Yeomanry.

I was almost unable to remain in my seat. Everything Mather had lectured me about for years, all lies. Never out of Durban. Never even near the *veldt*. Lies. I wanted to shout it out to the whole school. *Mather's brave regiment. Our Great Victory. Lies. Lies.*

The masters were now beyond restlessness and I was sure that the Warden was about to intervene.

'However,' the Captain's secret smile again, 'despite everything, there was some good to come out of the Boer War in the end. Maybe we learned how to deal with a defeated enemy.'

The Warden's moment to end it had passed.

'Once the Boers were forced to a treaty by our overwhelming superiority of numbers, the Liberals, Mr Lloyd George especially, had the courage in 1910 to give the Boers back their independence and not to look for vengeance. So now our former enemies are on our side.'

The Captain moved to the centre of the platform, legs apart. Flexing the pointer with both hands like a duellist, squared off to them all.

'And when we win this present War,' louder now, coming to an end. 'When we beat the Germans, push them out of France and Belgium, which we will, it's my hope that Mr Lloyd George's successful and generous treatment of the gallant Boers and the admission of our own mistakes, however late, will be the example to guide us in settling the future peace of Europe.'

The Captain sat down. The lecture was over.

There was an awkward silence. This was not what they had come to hear. Clapping started at the back, taken up slowly.

The Warden rose and the ragged applause died immediately. He began to lead out. There would be no speech thanking the Captain for the lecture, no school song.

I was elated as I walked up to Whitehouse, Big School emptying past us. But he frowned, motioning me to keep quiet. We walked silently towards the bicycle rack. He bent over to clip his trousers.

'Be careful,' Whitehouse said to me under his breath. 'Watch out for Mr

Mather now. He knows that you were involved. He'll never forgive you for tonight. Never.'

After that they were waiting for me, Mather and his *certain types*, for the slightest infraction. I was careful, but one day they had me. On my bicycle, off the permitted route to the boathouse. They treated my minor transgression as if I had been to a pub or off smoking cigarettes, when I had only been to Wytham churchyard to look at the tombstones. I had broken a school rule, they said, infinitely more serious than a house rule.

In front of Head of School, I twisted and I turned. But they had prepared for their final reckoning and arguing would make no difference. I shook and I started a sweat. I demanded my appeal to Mather which was a bad mistake. This was a school beating and they already had their permission from Mather and the Warden both.

Still I tried my stumbling arguments. The upper sixth, the lack of evidence, not even a name to the snitch in question. My innocent visit to the graveyard, my last term, my last month. Unjust, unfair…justice, fairness… wasn't that what we were fighting for?

At that Mather exploded, suddenly able to find the words for his contempt.

I was a snivelling little twerp. I deserved to be flogged. And a lot harder than anything that lay in store for me. He would have happily done the job himself. I had no right even to open my mouth. To think that some layabout schoolboy who knew nothing of life, messy, untidy, needed a haircut, useless, positively useless, posing as an intellectual, a worthless little toad, to think that I would even dare to talk about *fighting*. While far, far better chaps than me are out there, lying bleeding in the mud. The brave boys at Mons, the heroes of Ypres and the Somme. Had I any *idea* of the meaning of these words? Had I even *heard* of Belgium, of the unspeakable things done to Nurse Cavell? Things a little worm like me would never understand.

I had to wait to the end, standing in front of Mather's desk with my hands behind my back. On and on until finally I could go.

Head of School that year was a fully grown man at eighteen, mature and strong.

'Take your jacket off,' he said. 'Touch the bottom bar on the bed.'

I could hear the cane as it passed through the air the first time with a fierce whoosh and I knew that I had been hit hard, very hard. Cutting me through my trousers, an instant welt raised across my buttocks.

Between my legs I could see a brown shoe step back, transferring weight away then forward again, his full body leaning into the next swing.

That night I lay on my front in my iron bed, running my fingers over my ridges as I hurt, as I hated them back. And in the dark I thought that I could hear the guns across the Channel, as if Oxford was Kent or Sussex. Press censorship had not prevented me from getting a taste of the Front. Romantic, heroic, although no Old Boy that I knew had ever returned to tell the story in person. I had a picture of being in the army, of leaving England, of crossing over to the France of my imaginings. Belonging with my new friends. Men with a cause who took me for myself, not for Bow-chump, the oddity who would never fit.

The next day I saw Staff-Serjeant Yeo at the armoury and I volunteered. Then and there in his stuffy office smelling of pull-through oil and blanco. I would be in my eighteenth year in July, I told him, in two weeks. On my seventeenth birthday, which I did not mention. Yeo filled in my year of birth as 1899.

That was good enough for Yeo, eighteen or eighteenth year, he didn't catch the difference. I was of age, he said, with no consent required from my parents. Besides which my father was dead and my mother was in the power of the Chicken-Gutter.

Yeo showed no surprise which certainly surprised me. I was a useless OTC member. Level III Proficiency Test, not even a Junior Lance-Corporal after four years. Always missing some article of clothing, improperly dressed on parade every week, the odd man out again. But on that day for the first time, as I signed the papers in Yeo's presence, I felt like a man. I would be away from that school, with no house rules, no Head of School and no Mathers.

At that moment I knew exactly why I was volunteering.

Yeo would tell me when he received a PTT. Posting To Training.

A part of Big School noticeboards was headed *OTC* in faded ink lettering. In the last week of term the notice appeared.

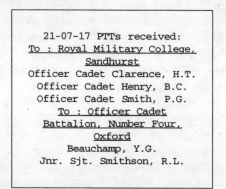

```
    21-07-17 PTTs received:
To : Royal Military College,
            Sandhurst
Officer Cadet Clarence, H.T.
 Officer Cadet Henry, B.C.
 Officer Cadet Smith, P.G.
      To : Officer Cadet
   Battalion, Number Four,
            Oxford
        Beauchamp, Y.G.
  Jnr. Sjt. Smithson, R.L.
```

Of all the school leavers, of all the one hundred or more boys leaving that school at the end of the academic year of 1917, only two were to go directly into the army.

They all had their excuses, the rugger playing shags, the cravatted cricketing dandies.

By 1917 the rush to volunteer was a thing of the past. Conscription age was eighteen years and eight months and few school leavers were that old. They all planned to wait for their papers, maybe the War would end. There was already talk of a compromise peace.

I wanted to lounge around the glass case, by the notice, lean against the bricks, jacket open, smoking maybe. No: flies open, masturbating, flagrant, leaving, untouchable, eyeing all who came to read.

From the day the PTT was pinned to the noticeboards of Big School, whatever pretence there was of school discipline between me and Whitehouse broke down completely. He called me Yves and I called him Pete.

And then the sublime moment from my nights of yearning, from my tearful, unrequited longings.

I explained to Whitehouse that I was to report to OCB four days after the end of term. Going back to St Ives was hardly worth my trouble or my grandmother's expense. I would arrive just in time for another goodbye.

'You don't want to stay on at school after the others have gone, do you, Yves?' Whitehouse asked. 'Come and spend a couple of nights with me and Barbara.'

So there it was, the bliss I had imagined. Toast in front of the gas fire with the children and meeting his wife.

And music. Whitehouse filled those days with music. A celebration of something like a feast. He played me the Bach fugues I loved the most, me sitting alone in the empty chapel. The *D Minor Passacaglia*, the *Great* and the *B Major*, a fugue with three themes and the sound of bells pealing through the Prelude. Then my modern organ favourites, Vidor, César Franck.

In Big School at the Bösendorfer Whitehouse played me Beethoven: the *Waldstein* sonata, then *Hammerklavier*. He took me to a performance of *Don Giovanni* at Oxford Town Hall, sitting in the third row, the score between us on our laps. The light and the dark in Mozart stronger than I had ever understood before.

Then on the last evening with Whitehouse, we bicycled down to the school chapel to collect all his sheet music. When we arrived he wanted me to sing my aria again from the *Passion*, from the year before. We went over the score first, remembering the breathing marks, the entries, the sustained notes. Then I stood on the steps and for one last time and to nobody but to myself and to Whitehouse, not a performance, not even a practice, for no reason other than for the music itself, for that one last time I let it out. Strong, sure now, up from the chest, out through the top of the head.

When we had finished Whitehouse came down from the organ loft.

'Here,' he said, holding a large envelope out toward me in his awkward manner, pushing back at his forelock with his damaged hand. 'I found this at Blackwells.'

In the envelope was the complete *Passion* in German. Music covering both sides of heavy pages like parchment, bound in leather, very small print and large sheets but not a thick book. Bach's name was embossed boldly on the front in Gothic script. On the title sheet Whitehouse had written: *To Yves Beauchamp from Peter Whitehouse, July 1917.*

In that moment I understood. Pete did not expect me back.

PART II

1

Before the march to Cambrai, during my first weeks with the Third Army in a quiet sector facing Armentières, I was more astounded by the obliteration of the landscape than by the war itself. This was a world beyond desolation, beyond anything that could be imagined beforehand or described later. There could be no preparation for such a scene and no forgetting it afterwards.

From our waterlogged trenches, formerly German, formerly French, now British, we looked out over a petrified storm of mud. Craters like the moon or the bottom of the ocean exposed. Ruination stretching to the horizon.

A sea of wretchedness fouled with steel and lead from shells and trench weapons, with half-buried wire, split casings, bloated putrefying mules, infantry equipment and supplies of all kinds. Hoofs, bayonets, rifle stocks and wire stakes sprinkling the surface like the tips of a field of icebergs, the bulk buried below.

An endless mudscape set in black-poxed waves swamping over blasted forests of shattered tree trunks. Forming huge ring-moulds around bomb crevasses and high slippery banks up to opposing trenches.

Without relief, without vegetation or natural cover of any kind.

There were no bearings, no references. It was as if everything I had ever learned in a distant former life meant nothing. As if all our human powers had been perverted to the destruction of everything that had gone before. On this hellish plateau, music, history, languages, art, whatever I had quaintly imagined to be the essence of civilization no longer seemed to have any value whatsoever. Survival was the only remaining credo, for that night, for that day, for my rotating periods of four days at a time in the front line.

And yet I was only on the edge of the main battlefields which had been fought over for more than three years. To the north were the Flemish villages and towns that had become infamous: Ypres, Peolcapelle, Passchendaele, Messines. Just in the summer of 1917 while I was at OCB in Oxford, it was rumoured that over two hundred and fifty thousand men had been killed or wounded for a gain of seven miles. Some said that the casualties were over three hundred thousand, but all agreed that nothing worthwhile had been taken.

In October 1917 there was little belief among the soldiers in our trenches that there could be any solution to the stalemate, to three years of bloody stagnation. An end to the Sausage Machine.

Some thought that the trenches would become a permanent part of Europe with the skirmishing set to continue indefinitely. Others had their theories about defeatism in the French army, how France would soon have to accept the domination of Europe by Germany and look for peace.

Others again were sure that the Royal Navy would win us the war eventually by keeping up the blockade of Germany along the Baltic. But this was contradicted by yet another opinion: Huns could live on turnips for ever. Or we heard that German submarines were sinking our merchant navy and England would soon be starved out.

The execution of Nurse Cavell, the invasion of Little Belgium, the library at Louvain, nobody mentioned those things at the front. The events that had seemed so important at school. Here in France all that was long ago and the origins of the war were blurred, forgotten.

Fellow officers I met or reported to would ask me the first time, as a new arrival, just for form maybe, 'So how are things in England? Are we winning the war? Don't know a damn thing out here, you know.' Then before I had a chance to answer, the subject would be dropped.

What to do now, where to march, what the men needed, what to eat, how to get dry or warm: these immediate things were the real War Aims. Whitehouse had tried to tell me that my picture of France was an illusion.

During my time facing Armentières all continued quiet in our sector except for constant trench warfare tactics which I watched with great interest.

'You'll learn all you need to on the job.' This had been Major Robinson's answer to everything.

I had passed out of OCB and received my commission but I was the shell once again. My rank was Temporary Second Lieutenant (On Probation),

Oxfordshire and Buckinghamshire Light Infantry. There was no more junior officer in the entire British Army.

My officer training had consisted of route marches with full kit and two hours' drill each day under the supervision of Staff Serjeant-Major Kempster and Serjeant Carter. These NCOs from the Coldstream Guards were exact caricatures of the drill instructor. Impeccable uniforms, peaks of their caps flat against the bridge of the nose. Every movement a drill movement. Drill was their life. Over from the wardrobe, left right, left right. Left whe-*al*. Into bed and on to the old lady, all to the count of four.

''*Shun. As you were.* Call that drill, do we, sir? What ballet school was you at then, sir? You're a worthless little individual, sir, that's what you are, sir. '*Shun. As you were. 'Shun.*' And so on. The Staff-Serjeant's beet face so close that I could see his tonsils, feel his spittle in my eyes.

There were lectures: topography, the Lewis gun, the Vickers gun, gas cylinders, how to judge distance, all given by officers back from France. Many of them distracted, perturbed. And none ever spoke to us about their own experiences.

In the afternoons my head nodded with weariness in stuffy classrooms. Enfilade, envelopment, flanking movement. Eyelids heavy from a jarring start. Staff-Serjeant Kempster stamping up and down the barracks between rows of iron beds.

'*Wakey, wakey.* Rise and shine. Yer puts yer cold feets on the warm flu-*ah.*'

Immaculate in his uniform, every surface pressed and razor-creased. Shining like a mirror. From his toe caps, from the silver edging around the peak of his cap to the brass tips of his pace stick. Perfectly turned out at four thirty in the morning.

After the first month at OCB, a small group from my intake of July 1917, including me, was added by Major Robinson to the cadets finishing their last month of the course. This had the effect of reducing my training from six months to two and a half. I missed such matters as Care of Horses, Guard Duty and the entire subject of Map Reading.

The accelerated group was made up exclusively of public school boys who had served in school OTCs. But we were still expected to sit the final proficiency test in all subjects. The test seemed impossible. A number of the questions, laid out on two cyclostyled pages, covered subjects about which I knew absolutely nothing.

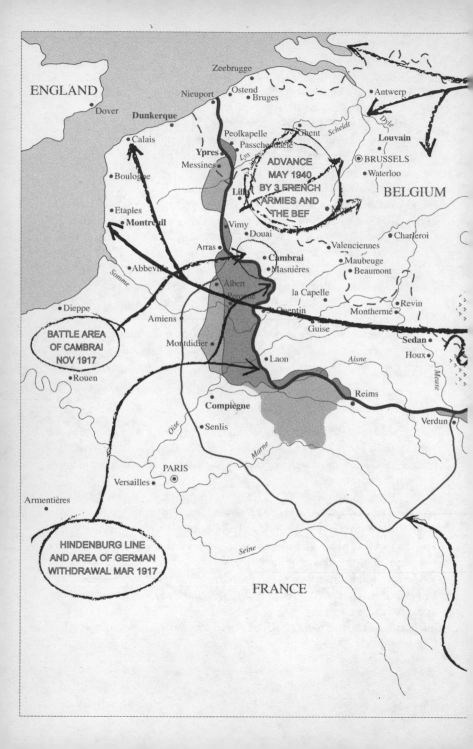

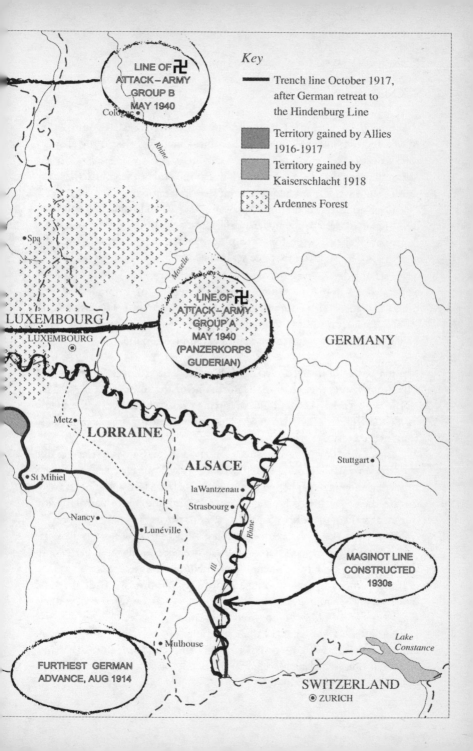

Key

Trench line October 1917, after German retreat to the Hindenburg Line

Territory gained by Allies 1916-1917

Territory gained by Kaiserschlacht 1918

Ardennes Forest

LINE OF ATTACK – ARMY GROUP B MAY 1940

LINE OF ATTACK – ARMY GROUP A MAY 1940 (PANZERKORPS GUDERIAN)

MAGINOT LINE CONSTRUCTED 1930s

FURTHEST GERMAN ADVANCE, AUG 1914

Cologne

Rhine

Moselle

Spa

LUXEMBOURG

LUXEMBOURG

GERMANY

Metz

LORRAINE

ALSACE

Stuttgart

St Mihiel

laWantzenau

Strasbourg

Nancy

Lunéville

Rhine

Ill

Mulhouse

Lake Constance

SWITZERLAND

ZURICH

Marks 10   15. What do you understand by road space?
            What is the appropriate road space of the fighting portion of the
            Division?

Where in desperation I made up my answer, I translated into Latin.
Maybe the examiner would recognize officer material even if my answers
were wrong.

I was far from ready for command, but at the end of the course the army
wanted me anyway. Staff-Serjeant Kempster understood.

'Do yer no earthly good thinkin' about it, Mr Beauchamp,' he would yell
when I paused, rehearsing my next drill command during our final days on
the square. 'They'll be up the bleed'n' town next. It's yer arms 'n' legs the
army wants, sir, not yer miserable scrambled egg.'

It was only later, in action, away from the square, that I came to understand drill. Automatic responses, pride, a feeling of comradeship with
others. All that guff and nonsense, I used to think on OTC days at that
school. But after my officer training, every time I gave an order myself, it was
as if Staff-Serjeant Kempster was standing right behind me.

My first posting was to the West Yorkshires, to a battalion re-formed out of
what was left after the battles to the north during the summer.

The West Yorks had a tradition of forcing fire ascendancy over the enemy
in all the trenches they occupied. This meant putting up an immediate
response to every German move.

German machine-guns opposite were set on metal frames to traverse our
trenches on a fixed line and sweep. Maxims raked our parapets at random
times day and night, peppering the air with whizzing lead a foot or less over
our heads. To catch us off our guard, while climbing out to patrol, during
our inspection of the wire or simply to wear us down.

The West Yorks' reply was to assemble a body of rifles as quickly as possible, as soon as the traverse started, then to fire ten rounds rapid per man in
the direction of the emplacement the moment there was a break.

If the German machine-gun opened up a second time we made the same
quick response from the other end of the trench or we tried for their
emplacement with Mills bombs fired from rifles.

Then after a few exchanges their machine-gun crew would decide that
aimless traversing was not worth the risk of being shot at in return. The same
with their rifle grenades and trench mortars. Each attack was responded to at
once until the enemy relented.

Even down to singing. If they sang, we sang louder, *Gott strafe der fucking Kaiser*, to the tune of *Onward Christian Soldiers*.

After that it was up to the West Yorks to choose, they could have a quiet time or go on the offensive. From then on we held the initiative.

I soon learned that a battalion that just accepted traversing machine-guns, random attacks and bombings had higher trench casualties than the battalion that responded. In 1917 the British Expeditionary Force was reputed to be taking over three hundred casualties each day from trench incidents alone, even when there was no push on.

Snipers were another preoccupation. The Germans were superior snipers. Their equipment and their weapons, like their trenches, were usually better than ours. German snipers were kept in each sector for extended periods of time, longer than the line regiments behind them. Until they knew our movements intimately and could catch one of us in a moment of slackness, enjoying a smoke, or back in the support lines hanging out the washing.

Having a man killed by a sniper took the wind out of a platoon for some time. A successful snipe was always a messy death and a very effective morale destroyer. Snipers got the head, the neck: there were no blighties handed out, no cushy flesh wounds to put you back home in England without too much damage.

One minute there's Private Smith and he's managed to line his head up with a loophole. Yacking away: about back home, his last leave, the missus and her problems. Then there's a piece of Private Smith's scalp on your tunic and the rest of his head is strawberry jam against the back of the trench. So fast, so final, that it brought on a numbness, a paralysis.

The West Yorks response to snipers was to do the sustained watching right back at them. Any suspicious little dark patch was carefully noted and handed from watch to watch. It was surprising how this concentrated effort could lead to a successful kill. For a few minutes at dawn the Germans were caught with their backs to the Fatherland, outlined by the rising sun before we were visible to them. In those short moments our marksmen were often able to exact our vengeance.

My platoon of West Yorkshires was run by Serjeant Thompson. A man from Coventry, not a Yorkshireman like all the others.

Thompson was splendid, I admired him from the first day. Shorter than me, but wide and brawny, a man of limitless physical resilience.

When I stood next to Thompson I felt confident, able to be what I was dressed up to be. I never saw Thompson tired or worn down, never panicked or afraid. Every situation, the whole sodd'n' war could be endured and overcome. One way or t'other.

Thompson was the most competent man I had ever met. He was forty years old in 1917, more than twice my age.

I met the men for the first time in the support trenches. I was right off the train from Boulogne and I knew nothing, nothing at all. Not even where I was or whether I should shake Thompson's hand or return his salute.

I was led to our position by a young Yorkshireman who then served as my batman and runner. I expected to be irrelevant, shunted to one side as an embarrassment. But Thompson took me on right from the start.

'Good to see you, sir,' he said with his big smile, tall gold teeth showing up one side of his mouth. 'There's been no platoon officers the last little while. Been below strength since Messines. Fine to see that's being seen to.'

A mug of tea, a place where I was expected, where at least my name was known. With A Platoon of C Company.

Thompson introduced me to the other NCOs. Corporal Higgs who worked the Tom Puddings, the coal barges in Huddersfield. And Lance-Corporal Ellington, a huge man with enormous hands, an ox. A getter from the coal face.

Then after three weeks, without any reason given, the battalion was warned for a march south, to a sector of the line opposite Cambrai.

We only marched seventy miles but our destination was like another country. Another country in the same war. Here the mud and craters were gone. From a loophole in the observation post dug out ahead of my few yards of front I could see only green open land. Like Port Meadow, the walk to the boathouse, like Oxfordshire.

We marched at night from the Armentières sector, resting by day to avoid German observation planes. Sleek Rolands coming in low over the horizon, darkly camouflaged. Faster than our SE5s, able to get away and back with their information.

The roads were congested with traffic of all sorts day and night: AEC Y-lorries, staff cars, Daimlers and Lanchesters, squads of lost-looking infantry, ambulances, pioneer work parties, mule limbers, wagons, teams of cart horses and boarded over B-type London buses used as troop carriers.

During the days we were scattered through the country to rest. Looking south I could see untouched autumn forests. A straight edge of brown parchment leaves against ploughed fields blurred by mist all day. And already some winter skeletons, rows of bare trees along a stream pocked with ivy balls like birds' nests. On the last day we were in open farm country rolling away to the south below the devastation. Real France, *la France* of my grandmother's snatches, of my schoolboy dreams.

My platoon sat in two or three circles, on logs, on packs, under whatever cover there was. Thompson said we should stay away from crossroads and Casualty Clearing Stations. He told me that these positions were shelled sporadically by German 5.9s, their artillery ranged by air spotters. Or they tried to hit crossroads blind from map references.

At one CCS a Thornycroft three-tonner was set up with an anti-aircraft gun mounted on the box.

'Shows there's been a Jerry raid, sir,' Thompson said as we passed the gun crew cooking up under their lorry. 'Just like the army. Send in the sodd'n' guns when it's over. Jerry won't be back now.'

Transport and the storemen were at the rear of our column so we had extra groundsheets, blankets and hot food every day of the march. But the men still went foraging in pairs, returning with shattered doors and window frames for firewood, a blackened cooking pot from the rubble of a house. Or a rabbit, perfect, furry and limp, shot with a catapult. Fish were massacred in the canals with trench bombs, white bellies floating up to the surface ready to go on the coals. Right under the sign, NO BOMBING OF FISH.

I inspected feet in front of our fires and I learned more names with civilian jobs to match. Miners from Nuttall and Gillbright, from Wombwell Colliery, Morley Colliery and Embley Moor. Getters, shoties and putters. Tulley was a dairyman, Barber a grammar school boy from Leeds, the closest to my age and an early volunteer like me. He told me he wanted to be a doctor, he planned to apply for a commission from the ranks.

The senior officers were with the advance party ahead and the RSM was really in charge of the column. He would tell the CSM who would give Thompson his orders. Then Thompson would tell me. Where to camp, to take better cover, when to re-form. All with a *sir* added to the end like OCB, as a nominal acknowledgement of my rank.

I just wanted to do the right thing, to look after my men.

More advice from Major Robinson. Rely on your NCOs, concentrate on your men. I was somehow learning in my stomach that I would protect myself, avoid getting the wind up, by being actively, physically, responsible for the men first.

In the days before our march, the bombardments at Peolcapelle and Passchendaele rumbled in the background. Following one battle or preceding the next. Thompson quickly became my tutor, able to name every gun.

To me at first, it was like nothing more than approaching thunder, threatening though distant. But soon I began to recognize the larger German guns, 5.9s, adapted naval pieces, Thompson told me, then their heavy artillery, Skoda howitzers. And I learned to distinguish between artillery fire and trench weapons fired from the enemy's lines, their coalboxes and Minies.

Then as bombardment and counter-bombardment started in our sector, the most important life-saving distinction to learn was between theirs coming in and ours going out.

'Soon get an ear for it, sir,' Thompson assured me. 'Then you'll know when to jump...'

As I threw myself on to the duckboards in response to an explosion which I was sure was right on top of us when Thompson had not moved.

'...and when not to bother,' he would add with a smile. Watching me struggle back to my feet, trying to brush mud off my tunic and feeling the proper shell.

Like most soldiers of all ranks, Thompson had his own ideas about how the war should be run. He had been over the top to face enemy fire ten times or more and in his opinion artillery was the answer to everything. Did the most damage, caused the most fear. Artillery, air power and planning, that was how to win the war. But, he said, none of it was ever thought through.

'When I started at Lindley's Works,' Thompson told me during the march, 'often needed three or four lathes to meet what was wanted. Passing job from one to the other. But by 'fourteen we could do same job on only one lathe and three times as fast. Better steel, better cutting blades, bosses who understood, everyone chipping in.'

But in the army Thompson had seen the same artillery methods used for three years. Only in 1917 had there been any real improvements with new fuses and the creeping barrage that moved across No-Man's-Land ahead of the attack.

'Captains of Industry,' Thompson said regularly, 'that's who should be the generals. People who can organize, get this sodd'n' war over with. Not red tabs from the bleed'n' cavalry. Then we'd soon be back to peace and prosperity.'

We had approached our new position on the fourth night of the march, moving up the Bapaume road, through Havrincourt Wood. Then into the communication trenches for the last mile to the front line.

On the way up, in a trench known as Roo Mad'laine, we collected a long list of extra equipment. Two hundred rounds of ammunition per man, empty sandbags for cleaning trench and refortification, shovels, wiring stakes, rockets, even an empty basket for a messenger pigeon. All this took a great deal of time and was accomplished against a tide of troops being relieved. We were not in position until after 0500.

But our new lines were in good condition, clean, dry and well fortified. No trench cleaning, no dead to send back to the support lines. And here No-Man's-Land was almost five hundred yards wide.

In the hour before dawn I posted sentries and the rest of my men huddled together in their leather jerkins, out of the light rain under oilskins and blankets. We had not washed for six days and I had not inspected feet in the last twenty-four hours.

After a rest the thick puttees and nailed boots came off and I made the rounds with Major Robinson's tin of ointments and bandages. Painting on tincture, smearing Vaseline on to the outside of socks, lancing blisters, advising on the cutting of nails. It was always as successful as the Major had promised.

In the night as I had marched beside them, outside the column but by their side, light without a pack, my valise with stores, I had felt some confidence for the first time. Some affection toward them all.

There was a lot of joking, about mothers and sisters, about danger down the mines, about sheep in the Dales wearing waders. About the fear we all had somewhere inside us.

The humour was quicker, harder than school, harder to catch, accents I had never heard before. But unlike school it was never intended to stick.

There were miners' songs all through the night, but always the same one first.

We are a class of working folks
With hands all hoof'd and brown'd
By getting coal with heavy strokes
Deep down beneath the ground.

After the feet I worked my way up the line along my frontage, over sleeping bodies until I found our sentry at our south end and B platoon without a sentry, resting on our right. Someone, the enemy, could have crept in between us and started throwing bombs.

Further down I came across Hodges, Second Lieutenant in charge of B platoon, sitting on a pile of duckboards in the middle of his front, smoking and staring into the trench wall. As I approached, stepping over his men, his complaints started. They had been promised a hot meal but nothing had come, the latrines were fouled and he had no trench maps. Just listening to Hodges gave me a clue as to what I should be doing.

'Public school boys', I had been told quietly before I left the OCB, 'are relied on to show the leadership that the *others* cannot. In the trenches, leadership is everything.'

I ignored his complaints. 'We'll probably find out all we need to at Battalion HQ. We're supposed to be there at 0700.' Hodges knew nothing of the briefing; he had missed the runner.

He stood up and threw his cigarette on to the ground, making ready to leave.

'Don't you think you should tell your serjeant?' I reminded him. 'You know, boundaries, sentries, gas precautions, passwords, that sort of thing?'

'Oh yes. Right,' he replied, looking around in his moony way. 'Johnny,' he addressed his serjeant. 'Gone to see bra-ass.' A grunt in reply from a sleeping body.

Battalion HQ was a reinforced dug-out built directly into the line. Hodges and I pushed in through the gas curtain and saluted. Two other subalterns were already standing in the room, helmets off and under the arm.

Major Hardcastle and Captain McAdam were sitting at a table set up on a carpet of empty sandbags. Tunics and Sam Brownes off, having breakfast, sharing a large Mowbray pie between them and drinking wine out of tin mugs. Hardcastle's khaki tie trailed into his food. A brazier warmed a tight little circle around their table.

The dug-out was deep, with the damp stale feeling of a mine, retained on all sides by planks leaking mud and water. The roof was made of more planks supported by props wedged up from the ground on fat pine shims. Like the prefects' study, Battalion HQ had all the comforts, a gramophone, dry bunk beds, hurricane lamps.

We were not asked to sit and no offer was made to share the pie. Hardcastle addressed us between mouthfuls, long moustache twitching as he chewed. He made short anxious pecks at his plate like a thieving crow.

'Where's your helmet?' he demanded of me without an introduction.

'There's not been any shelling, sir.'

Hardcastle turned to McAdam.

'What's this officer's name?'

'Beecham, sir,' McAdam replied, reading off a clipboard.

'So what do we have here, Mr Beecham? Some little hero in the making? If you know what's good for you, you'll wear your helmet.' The Major's helmet, clean and freshly painted, hung on a hook in the boards by his head.

Major Robinson had been emphatic. Standing waiting for transport on the last morning at OCB, his eye twitching harder than ever, one hand still holding mine, the other on my shoulder, as if he did not want me or any of the others to go. A last piece of advice.

'Don't wear your helmet unless there's shrapnel. You're an officer now. Wear the King's uniform not Tommy serge. Lead from the front. That's the way we do it and the way we've always won.'

I returned Hardcastle's hostile stare. I thought I saw the bully in him, the unreasonable, the things I had joined the army to leave behind.

'My name is pronounced Beauchamp, sir.' Hardcastle ignored me.

'New push,' he started with his mouth full, presuming that the four of us were idiots. Why else would we march in the dark if not to escape detection? And if to escape detection then what else if not a new push? I was rising to meet him.

'But this one will be something different,' Hardcastle continued. 'Can't tell you more than that for the moment.' Shells lived in the dark. 'We've to do some raiding and we're twenty-four hours late as it is. In daylight. Keep the Bosche guessing.'

Hardcastle put down his fork and looked up at us in the earnest and patronizing manner used by Mather. False, an act, as if he was about to start in on the Boèr War.

'One of you will have to go first. This morning. Pretty simple, really.'

Going first might mean some reward or quicker relief for my men. It was clear we would all be going sooner or later.

'A Platoon, sir,' I piped up. 'We're not in bad shape. We could give it a try.'

Hardcastle looked at me again. As one might look at an ant or a new treble. I immediately regretted that I had spoken. A regular, I thought. Ready at the first opportunity to get his knife into the ribs of any New Army type, any new junior officer especially.

'You've just come over, I suppose, Mr Beecham.' Hardcastle glowered at me as if I had been found guilty of some terrible crime and the only outstanding matter was the severity of my punishment. 'And did the bombing course at Étaples on the way through, did we? Anxious to throw some bombs, are we?' Well aware of the answer which must have been on the clipboard.

'No, sir. I was sent straight to Armentières. Then the march to here.' Leaning into the *accent grave*, not the usual Armen-tears. An unnecessary provocation.

'Well now,' Hardcastle started again, sitting back in his chair, dragging his tie off the plate. 'Here we have some kind of a Frog, gentlemen, a few days out of OCB and he wants to have at the Bosche already.'

Hardcastle peered around in a slow, half-witted, theatrical way, looking for smirks in support of his idea of humour. Two little grins from the subalterns who had arrived in the dug-out before me. Then back to the scornful again.

'Captain McAdam will be up to your line shortly. Then the others can have a turn later.' Hardcastle waved his fork to dismiss us and he reached over to cut himself another slice of pie.

2

McAdam was not a bad sort. I could not place him. Kitchener's Army or a regular? Public school.

He explained and I did my best to understand. Thompson was at the far end of the trench. I tried to remember just the words so that Thompson could tell me later what we were to do. But I began to feel windy, McAdam was saying one hour's time. We were going today, now, up and out of the trench.

Brigade Order Number 26 for 8 November. On this new push, not the one that morning, but the big one to come later, there was to be no bombardment before zero hour, the start of the attack. The guns would only start up right on zero. What we were after was complete surprise, McAdam told me.

They were finally going to try something different from the usual show, he said. McAdam was enthusiastic. There were other surprises as well, but I was only going to be given the whole picture closer to the day. There had to be absolute secrecy to this one.

The objective of the morning's raid was to fix the locations on a trench map of the entrances into the main German dug-outs. With the ramps located, McAdam explained, our guns could keep the foxes in their holes when we went over on the day.

By the time McAdam was finished I was enthusiastic too. I tried to persuade Thompson when I relayed the briefing that this would be even better than the creeping barrage, the tactic he had admired at Messines with the Second Army.

'The whole barrage at zero on the day of the push will be predicted,' McAdam had told me at the end of my briefing. 'Artillery has improved immensely. New HE that neutralizes the Bosche very quickly. Much better accuracy, better detonation, they even use barometers now to take air pressure into account. Really quite remarkable. Map shooting, they call it. Predicting a target without ranging fire first, so the enemy has no warning.'

But Thompson was doubtful.

'You see, sir,' he said when I went over it again with him, 'the usual thing is for us to race Fritz to the edge of his trench. They starts underground, we starts on this side of No-Man's-Land. The signal is the end of the barrage. Whoever gets there first fixes the other. Simple as that, sir.'

Thompson had a way of folding his arms over his chest when he talked to me. It was inexplicably reassuring, as if he had put an arm around my shoulder.

'This way, sir, this way that Captain McAdam is talking about, fine, Fritz will have no warning, but wire will still be there. Only a long bombardment can cut wire. We'll be slowed down, our guns will lift when we're close and Fritz will be set up again before we get there.'

I had no answer for Thompson, McAdam had not said anything about the wire. But that was not today. First we had to go over there, into the German trench and locate their ramps on a map. That was what this little raid was all about.

McAdam said we could cross on the double to increase our chances. Over the top and the slow walk, rifles at the high port, that was the old procedure from 1916 and before. But for this raid we could run: rip over there before they woke up. Thompson and the men seemed to like that.

There would be a short preliminary bombardment, K26, B4 to K29, A22, just to have Jerry think there was a big one coming. Then we were to go as soon as our guns lifted back on to the enemy support lines. A short pause in the artillery fire would be the signal to move.

Only three parties in the battalion were going. We would start at the break with no set time so watches had not been taken for synchronization. But it meant waiting, waiting without knowing how long.

～

Two blocks from the hospice cruisers were returning through empty streets to Vancouver Police Headquarters on Main for their midnight break. Prowling over slick pavement glowing with streetlight-amber after a gentle summer drizzle.

Morley knew where he was going from the moment he climbed into the Landcruiser. He motored slowly through downtown and around English Bay.

The West End had always interested him, a high-density residential district that really did work. The Hong Kong Chinese had moved into Vancouver real estate in a big way in the past decade and MORLEY+CHAN+WAINWRIGHT had won more than their fair share of the work.

Morley had seen over ten highrises through the entire four or five-year process. Design negotiations with the City lasting two or more years for each project, then Morley's partner Brock Wainwright had taken over construction management.

As Morley turned onto Falkland he turned off the radio. He started to look for the Jetta. His whole body beat like a drum, the ends of his fingers cold on the wheel as he crept up to the cul-de-sac at the park.

No Jetta. Morley felt encouraged. Into the lane then over a block and around past the tennis courts. Still no Jetta. He hadn't been able to find the car in more than a week.

Robert was wrong, Jane would come around if he gave her a bit of slack, let her look at the alternatives. What they had was so strong that it couldn't just disappear in the course of a few months.

Some warmth came back into his hands. He drove faster, away from the West End, over Burrard bridge and south. Up to West 12th where Jane had her little fiction.

Now Morley wasn't sure, maybe it was the truth. He used to believe her, he used to be her champion, even when there were some obvious half-truths in her stories. But somewhere in the second year that had stopped. He had become a dripping tap, she said, a big fat negative: over her accounts, her staff turnover, even the state of her car.

The radio went back on, tracks from jazz CDs introduced by a half-cut-late-nite-voice from Calgary. Coming up to one o'clock. Only nine hours until the scheduled presentation of initial design concepts to the group from Guangzhou, the People's Bureau for the Provision of Water in Guangdong Province. A treatment plant and a substantial new headquarters, big even for China. The largest job the practice had ever landed.

In those nine hours Morley had to sleep and take his run. Then he needed two hours to clean up his last drawings and another hour for printing and all the interruptions in between. Should be in there before seven.

But most important of all Morley had to know about Jane. The anxiety in his joints was an addictive drug, he hated it but it was what he had to have. He had to know.

After she moved out, Jane had told Morley that she was sharing the apartment on West 12th with a woman and her daughter, people Morley had never heard of before. The place was squalid and drab. The same question came up each time he drove by: can someone really change that much in so short a time?

Morley trusted only what the Jetta told him. And until the week before, the Jetta had told him that Jane spent her nights at an apartment block on Falkland Road.

His partner Kingsley Chan had told him the rest. Through a Chinese advertising agency which seemed to Morley to do very little advertising, Kingsley had come up with the number of the apartment, a building floor-plan, the man's name, where he worked, car licence plate, salary, prospects, even his American Express card number. It was the same man, Irish Don, *the insightful friend*, Donald Rathkin, the man Jane had met on her psycho course.

And Morley had always found her car. In the parking lot of the restaurant across the park, hidden behind a dumpster in a lane, or down by the waterfront concealed between two campers.

The Landcruiser rolled up and down the streets of McClure-style houses. The lights were out at 1345 and the Jetta was not to be seen. He covered three blocks in each direction but still no car.

The drug rose up through Morley's body again and his fingertips turned clammy. The jazz went off and he headed back towards the West End. He had missed something. *He had to have the answer.*

Morley parked two blocks from Falkland. He unloaded the contents of his pockets into his briefcase: cash, credit cards, ID. In case he was mugged in the park by a criminal. In case he was stopped as a criminal himself, the line had started to blur. Then he walked, anonymous and casual, a local resident who had stepped out for some night air. Footsteps nerve-stretchingly loud in the deserted street.

A fine spray of light rain coming in from the Pacific covered him like dew.

The path by the tennis courts and along the side of the building was the center of Morley's nightmare. From there he could see up to apartment 205. But he walked on by, up the next street and back again, a zombie, even without Robert's pills.

There were hundreds of thousands of people living in concrete canyons within a kilometre of the park. But the paths through damp foliage were as dead as the most distant suburb. As he haunted along the back lane a disturbed skunk waddled reluctantly away from a heap of garbage bags piled against an overflowing dumpster.

Morley moved into the bushes and stood looking up at the building. No lights. Maybe Rathkin was away at a Mega Sportswear Convention, or on a psycho-babble retreat. But the windows were open, someone was home.

He walked around the building. By kneeling down he could look under the sill of the garage door and into the rows of parked cars, scanning from the rubber up. Rathkin's car was there, backed in and dry. Home all evening. Morley looked around the garage, up and down the rows.

Just as he came off his knees he saw it. The Jetta, on the right, tucked into a space of its own.

Morley stood up, his heart and lungs working hard, acid pumping around his body. He walked back slowly into the undergrowth, one foot in front of the other. He looked up at the apartment again.

Here in this ordinary building, through that window, behind that blind, his wife Jane Morley was lying in bed with Donald Rathkin. A short fat balding sportswear salesman with a vocabulary full of the right words.

An idiot, a course freak. After Jane had left, Morley had found a letter from Rathkin among a pile of her papers. The writing of a Grade 10 drop-out.

'...SO OUR LIVES CAN OCCUR, TO WHATEVER DEGREE EMPOWERS US, AND TO BASICALLY INVENT THERE OWN VIRTUAL REALIZATIONS...'

Just a parking stall had made it conclusive and unavoidable as if some part of him had been removed, stolen. As if a badly damaged limb had finally been amputated and all chance of recovery closed off.

He had struggled against the advice he had received from everybody who knew Jane. Walk away, Morley. Screw her out of everything. You can afford the lawyers, she can't. A con-artist, a Blarney stone with legs, that's all she is, Morley.

But the termites in his bloodstream would not be put off so easily.

At the house Morley pulled into the garage next to Susan's Honda. Country was thumping down through the ceiling from the living-room above. The Honda had been out in the rain and not so long ago. The garage floor was wet, the car decorated with pearly drops. The music was very loud.

Upstairs Susan swirled frantically around the carpet in front of the gas fire, cigarette in one hand, glass in the other, bottle under an arm. The wholesome Okanagan farm girl who didn't smoke and hardly drank. Morley threw his briefcase onto a chair and he tried to catch her, but she pushed past him, hard. When he turned off the music she danced on, over to the stereo, switching the music back on, loud, louder. He stopped her in the middle of the room, gripping her firmly and spilling her wine onto the carpet.

Susan started to shout, blasting fumes into his face.

'You said you weren't doing that anymore.' Her strawberry hair obscured everything except wine-stained teeth. 'You promised me, you fucking asshole.' Language he had never heard her use before. Then Susan was beating against Morley's chest with the glass. 'You promised me, you promised me you weren't going round there again.' The stem broke and she cut herself. More wine went on to the floor and down Morley's shirt.

'You followed me, didn't you? You came looking for me at the hospice, didn't you?'

The phone rang, catching the scene in a frozen frame. Elaine.

'Morley, I've been trying to reach you.'

'I...er, I had to...er...whip into the office for a moment...'

'...oh, I'm sorry, I called because your old friend woke up just after you'd gone. He says he dropped off while he was talking to you.' Elaine paused. 'Look, he's not too good. I know it's late, but could you come back over for a moment? I'm really busy, Maisey's almost gone and he's asking for you.'

A silence on the line. The choice was between enduring Susan's rant or listening to some remote events that had no connection to his own life whatsoever. With little prospect of sleep either way.

'Sure, Elaine,' Morley mumbled wearily into the phone. 'I'll be right there.'

Susan was still standing frozen, clutching her bleeding hand.

Morley turned and hustled down the steps to the garage. She could go ahead and finish the job on her wrists, she could drink the whole bottle as well as the next or she could put herself to bed.

He started the Landcruiser. Then he climbed out again and slipped the keys from the Honda into his raincoat pocket. But what Susan couldn't do was drive.

The old man seemed to have weakened in only two or three hours. But when the light-blue eyes opened, Morley thought that he had only imagined the deterioration.

'Morley, I want you to tell me something about yourself.' The quiet voice seemed strained from all the talking earlier. There was no apology for the hour.

'I'm an architect,' Morley began, unsure how to answer. Why did the old man want to bother? 'I've been married twice but as we speak my second wife is in bed with another guy. My first wife remarried and is now divorced again. I have three children, one perfect, two humans. I live with a young woman though you could barely call it...'

'...yes, but what are you doing *here*?'

The old man seemed to be shrivelling down the cast. But he had once been well built, tall and handsome. Now he had the look of a very old baby, almost bald, with wisps of white hair growing from a freeze-dried skull. Only a few remaining teeth seemed to keep his jaw from folding in on itself. Emaciated shoulders rose and fell against the pillows. Taut skin over his chest bones formed patterns of fleshless hollows, partly covered by the thin gown. His spotted grey arms rested down the bed.

'I'm dying.' A direct stationary gaze searched Morley's face with a piercing light, then a hand reached out for Morley's wrist. 'But I can see who you are. You're a rogue like I was. You're fifty and you're clever. You feel washed up. You know you can't go back but you don't want to go forward. I reached that point once.'

Morley made no reply. The bony hand squeezed hard, out from the bed and into Morley's existence.

'I've not long left. People who are dying know it. Tonight, in a few days, all I don't know is when. The rot is on the move since they cut it loose.'

Morley lifted the glass from the bed tray up to the old man's mouth. He drank slowly through a straw. It seemed that even the little things were quickly becoming more difficult.

'I like you and I know I can trust you. Just from looking at you, there isn't time for more.' A smile tried to creep over the engraved face. 'So I'm going to give you some papers.' A limp hand indicated the bedside locker.

In the drawer Morley found a large manila envelope containing a black folder. He opened the cover. Leather, but supple like paper, edges frayed and corners torn. The surface scratched and battered as if the book had been retrieved from the shoulder of the Trans Canada Highway after a long winter. Many of the sheets were damaged. Staves of music at a very small scale covered every page, many obscured by stains and watermarks.

Morley turned to the title page, marked with faded scribbles and annotations. At the top he could just make out the words...*from Peter Whitehouse*...

But the pages between his fingers seemed to transform the old man's words. From some mumbling Morley couldn't piece together about Paris and a school in England, to now, to there and then in Vancouver.

'There are a few of my letters left. Some I rewrote from memory later, or re-copied over the years into English. Some I could never send.'

Morley turned more pages. Loose leaves sucked against the sheets of music, old letters razor-thin as if undisturbed for a lifetime.

'I'm asking you to see me out.' The old man was whispering now. 'Someone has to know, to remember.'

The soft voice trailed off. Morley thought he was dozing again.

'Will you do that, Morley?' The blue eyes opened. 'I want to tell you what happened. What really happened. The truth. And that's a promise, there can be nothing else left for me now.'

Emotion came sweeping in over Morley, catching him suddenly, as if pulling him inside-out through the remaining years of his own existence and into the hospice bed. Feeling under flaking skin, inside the fragile bony cage. To what it would be like when his turn came. On his back, in a brace, dying.

Acid spiked through Morley's veins again, over his knees, down to his ankles. From his heart and out along his arms with the surge of a concrete pump. Turning to revulsion at himself. That all he was, that all he stood for had come down to so little.

Down to standing in a park in the middle of the night, staring up at an open window.

Before thought or reason, overwhelmed by the need to be free, for a day, for an hour, free from the relentless forces that lived within his blood stream, Morley had given the old man his answer.

'*Yes*. Yes, you can count on it. That's *my* promise.'

～

We needed ten volunteers for the trench raid and over twenty hands went up. The men Thompson picked huddled together after we had put up the ladders, making their lottery and knocking back rum from the storeman's clay jar. Then we lined up in the trench, as ready as we would ever be. Somehow my men understood why I was taking us over first and nobody was grumbling.

My men. From a country I had never visited, speaking a language I hardly understood. Over six months since they had had any leave. Men who had lost half their number and all their junior officers.

The barrage started: huge and deafening, terrifying, even if it was ours.

The time had come for my first real action. I stood on the ladder holding a rung, a wooden bar at face level waiting to take my boots as I came up to face the enemy.

I checked for the tenth time that the feet of the ladder were firmly into the cracks of the duckboards. I had my service revolver out and in my hand, large and unwieldy through my leather glove. I had bought myself an officer's cane from a tobacconist at Folkestone but I felt awkward carrying it, a sham.

The revolver was attached to a lanyard around my neck but I was sure that I would drop the gun at the first opportunity. At the OCB range I had lost my fear of the Webley, almost learning to control the kick, but I was still awkward. I rested the revolver on the rung of the ladder in front of me. Hammer forward, safety catch off. I wondered who I would shoot, his name, or whether my name was on one of their bullets. Pointless thoughts.

I stared into chalk walls through the ladder, grain by grain. Like the side of my grave would be. It was only when waiting that I was afraid, when there was nothing left to do.

No, not like the side of my grave. There were so many dead that they used pits. We had seen one on the march, dug ahead of time, right by the road. It was only after we were past that I had realized what it was.

And lime, they used lime, like my mother, bent over the toilet buckets by the dripping washing line. Like the huge *mastaba* at Château d'Hougoumont on Napoleon's left. The engravings I had seen in the battle-field museum, vast pits of the dead after Waterloo. A man standing on the edge sprinkling lime.

Thompson came up the next ladder to me.

'We could take the lads over now, sir, lie on grass. Get going faster that way.'

Up the ladder and on to the ground, as Thompson said. Flat into wet green grass beyond the parapet. The first lines of our wire just off the end of my nose. Still unable to see anything. Bombardment so loud I could almost put my hand out and touch it.

But this was a fear quite different from school, from the beatings. This was not humiliation, not ritual. Rather it was a chance to hit back, to be better, to be brave and to score. A poor metaphor, a games metaphor, the kind I tried to avoid. I was thinking nonsense. I had the wind up.

But it was just as I had imagined, lying in my dormitory bed, backside red and ridged. Feeling the cane's smooth furrows with my fingers, over and over. For comfort, for assurance, planning my vengeance.

Whitehouse had taught me how to enter, on the note, on the beat. I could hear his voice again just before every start.

'Attack, attack, feel it, feel it,' shouted loud over my singing during our practices as he leaned back from the manuals with his arms straight out, cross-eyed between looking both at me and his music. 'Timing, breathing, weight on the right foot forward. Chest out into the sound.'

And on the night, a quick glance round at Whitehouse in his organ loft, then Manning's tight little smile just before he brought me in. My moment.

'*Ich kenne des Menschen nicht.*' I do not know the man.

I had sat in the woods during our rests on the march and followed through my score again, for something familiar and comforting. From some other Germany, not the one we were fighting. Now the leather binding sat under my tunic flat against my shirt like a breastplate. These Germans, across the way, the ones who had my name on their bullets, to get me they would have to shoot me through my JSB. Nonsense, nonsense.

Our barrage lifted but my ears continued to ring. Silence like gossamer.

A whistle blew far away down the trench behind us. I could hear shouted commands from the other parties.

'Fix by-o-*nets.*'

'Raiding party rea-*deh.*'

Now it was Thompson I looked at over my shoulder. His smile, tall gold teeth.

'God, Thompson, fixing bayonets.' I had just remembered.

'Don't worry, sir. The lads know what to do. Just get us over there and we'll be fine.'

Between the opposing trenches, toward the enemy was a meadow. Green, rough. To be crossed. Port Meadow. I was late, late for my boat crew. I had to run.

Thompson tapped me on the shoulder. We were ready.

Then I was up. Feeling my weight where it should be, leaning into the music, right foot forward but in my boots now.

On your feet, men. Double. Double.

Go like sodding hell.

I should have blown the whistle hanging round my neck but I was cluttered up by the revolver and the lanyard. I had forgotten until we were on the move. Then it was too late. Fine.

As I ran I started to sing.

Eight to a bar.

3

I had heard stories about time behind the lines that made the rest periods sound even more terrifying than the trenches themselves. About spit and polish worse than at the regimental depot I had never seen.

But by the end of 1917 so many men had passed through each battalion and so many battalions had passed through each division that many of the traditions of the pre-war British Army had been lost. Under this torrent of men and officers only the bare essentials of regimental character remained. The stories I had heard were from 1914 and 1915, the regular Army, before millions of Kitchener's volunteers, followed by the conscripts, had started to arrive in France.

Our character in the 11th Battalion West Yorkshires was formed by the current members of the battalion, by the officers and their attitudes, by just a few months of their habits together. I knew nothing of the West Yorks' battle honours or their practices. And even less of the history or observances of the Oxfordshire & Buckinghamshire Light Infantry, my nominal regiment with which I had never served.

It was like Pond House, an instant belief was expected in the Regiment which most officers had joined by a random administrative posting.

But at Armentières I had seen that trench casualties could be limited by winning the initiative. And after a short time with the West Yorkshires I came to see that discipline and spirit, even at my platoon level, led to fewer cases of minor ailments like colds and flu, to a substantial reduction in trench foot and to the total absence of suicides or deliberately provoked blighties.

There had to be a reason why some groups of men under one regimental name had more losses than the same number of men under another name. Spirit, team spirit, the hated words from that school. But for my men, spirit seemed to be a form of protection, a talisman that I could provide for them and I started to believe, to change my mind.

It was Serjeant Thompson who showed me the way, of course. I had expected the men to resent a route march, or drill every day during our stay in billets. Or me pushing to be the smartest platoon in the company. And then, it was ludicrous, to be the smartest company in the smartest battalion.

I began to be fanatical, it filled a space, occupied my mind.

But by taking these activities seriously, not resisting the training, not scrimshanking like many of the others and by participating myself, marching at the head of the platoon, wearing a pack, eating the same rations as the men on the march, I found that the men responded. In a short time we became a platoon of soldiers, not merely a group of civilian targets in uniform, fodder for the enemy's cannon. A platoon capable of defence and of attack.

But still I resisted the role of the officer even though I had volunteered. I resisted it with Hodges and his commission from the ranks, wanting not to be the public school boy with an automatic advantage over him, but to prove me, myself. I resisted it with Thompson who knew so much more than me that I had no right whatsoever, I thought, to be his superior.

But I knew that although Thompson had as much experience as any ser-jeant still alive and still on active service, he needed me to interpret army culture: messages, orders and briefings from above.

And I knew that Thompson needed me to lead. But what did lead mean? Thompson could have blown a whistle and been the first up the ladder. He was the bravest man I had ever known. Was I really needed to say *good show*, or *well done*?

Then I resisted Major Hardcastle as I had Mather. I looked at Hardcastle with contempt for treating me and the men as objects, not as human beings. For taking no interest in the effect of his orders on us, the ones who had to carry them out. I resisted him for his shiny boots, for his pressed uniform and his pristine tin hat. Even the case for his gas mask was always clean and freshly blancoed.

I tried to say to myself that Hardcastle must have been a subaltern himself at one time. But then I found that he had been a training officer at Étaples, a canary with a yellow arm band, before taking command of the battalion.

'Our Pet Frog,' Hardcastle started to call me. He felt my resistance and picked on the slightest slackness in my dress. Or he commented loudly and publicly on my second and third glasses of wine at dinner in the mess at Fins during our days in reserve.

'Our Pet Frog's at the *vino* again, I see,' he would say, shout almost, to the entire mess, red faced and slurring himself.

My conflict with Hardcastle over my helmet was endless. But I believed that Major Robinson's advice was right and I would not give in to him. After my first trench duty without a helmet, back in billets at Fins, Hardcastle had the RSM drill me in his, Hardcastle's, idea of correct procedures. Out on the improvised gravel square for an hour early every morning, pretending to enter Hardcastle's office, coming to attention, saluting, removing my cap.

'Lieutenant Beauchamp reporting, sir.' Loud, yelled out, as if to the imagined Hardcastle.

'Can't 'ear yer, Mr Beauchamp.' The RSM in my face pretending to be Hardcastle. Again, louder. 'Still can't 'ear yer, Mr Beauchamp.' Then the same procedure in reverse for leaving. None of it necessary if I would wear my helmet.

On my first trench raid as I ran across the open green field of No-Man's-Land, half crouched, skin prickling, I waited every second to be torn, shredded by bullets which I expected to be thick in the air like grains of salt from a shaker. Singing, counting to myself as I watched my boots hit the grass on every beat. But our bombardment was effective, their heads were down and I was still alive at the end of every bar.

One-two three-four-*five*-six-seven-eight. *Gebt mir meinen Jesum wieder.*

Before we reached the German main line we encountered one of their outposts which kept us out longer than the others.

This obstacle had not been part of McAdam's briefing. A new line had been dug by the Germans in the previous few days, since our last patrol report, by joining two of their saps together. No new wire defences had been constructed so we were taken completely unawares and almost fell into it, scrambling over the fresh parapet and down into the line. We found three Germans in the trench still setting up after our bombardment had lifted. We had come over in less than three minutes and they were not ready for us.

The Germans were bent double, assembling a Maxim and piling ammunition brought up from their dug-out. In the few seconds they had been out of their shelter they had posted no look-outs.

The three surrendered right away. The first Germans I had ever seen. Holding their hands up limply at shoulder height, defeated looking, beaten. Worn out, starey-eyed like wax models. Ragged almost, each in different kit over heavy grey coats, filthy and unshaven under deep helmets large like pudding basins. Just an impression in that frantic moment, but encouraging.

Corporal Higgs pushed the prisoners into the corner of their sap, bayonet aimed at stomachs. Higgs would do it, he really would. Gut them if he had a chance, lunge and twist to the count of four, rip them open from bottom to top. I saw it clearly in his face.

Thompson secured trench. Throwing bombs and charging up and down the German sap to ensure that there was no enemy hidden around corners or coming at us down their communication line.

But by then we had lost the element of surprise against the German front line twenty yards beyond and we were in the wrong place. We could not even start on marking the map, the objective of the raid. I thought we should go back but I did not want to make any excuses to Hardcastle.

After the guns had paused as we lay in the grass, our signal to begin our sprint across No-Man's-Land, the bombardment had started up again. Lifting off the German main line and on to their support trenches as planned. So by then, five or six minutes later, the Germans in their front line where we were supposed to be, would have had time to prepare.

'Can't go back, sir,' Thompson shouted urgently into my ear over the barrage as if he had read my mind. 'They'll be set up now, get us right as we climb out.'

Nothing to do with Hardcastle and saving my face. The men, we could all be killed, right now. The men. It pulled me together.

Thompson shouted to me again.

'Count to three and give us the word, sir, when I gives the nod.'

Thompson spread the men along the trench facing the parados, the back wall. Cool, efficient, walking up and down as if we were standing-to in our own trench on a quiet morning preparing breakfast. The men climbed on ladders, on boxes, on anything they could find. I could not hear what Thompson was telling them. Then Thompson turned. The man looked like oak, like steel. Confident smile, tall gold teeth.

He nodded.

'Ready,' I shouted. 'One...two...three... GO.' I had no idea what was to happen.

But the men knew. They hurled all our Mills bombs together, up and toward the German line, popping out of the trench for a split second to aim.

Then Thompson waved me on to a ladder and he was right behind. In an instant we were dancing through the German wire, over their parapet and down into their main trench.

At the same moment, under cover of our explosions three of our party left to return to our own lines with the German prisoners.

The German main trench was lined with heavy logs and very deep. I fell hard on to a wooden floor. Two bodies lay face-down on the boards next to me, victims of our Mills bombs. No one else was to be seen.

McAdam had told me that the German front line was always lightly held. It was their tactic, he said, defence in depth. To draw us in if we attacked in force, to put us in position for their counter attack from support trenches behind.

Then I was on my feet again, scrambling over the dead bodies to mark my map with the location of their dug-outs. Thompson was securing trench again.

I was beside myself, frantic, grease crayon shaking, unable for a moment to relate the map to the trench. Upside down, this way, that.

Thompson came back, he stood next to me as I finished. I felt his hand on my shoulder. He had seen my hand trembling.

'Done, sir?'

'I can remember the rest.'

'Just the run 'ome now then, sir. You'll be fine.' Thompson gave me his smile again.

We started back: up the ladders once more, through the German wire, in and out of the sap. Bracing for their fire to open up from behind with only speed to protect us.

Halfway across No-Man's-Land our bombardment ended. We should have been safely in by then.

The return through our own wire was messy, the worst part of the raid. Thompson was bringing up the rear and I misjudged the position of our opening, tangling us all up into a bunch as we looked for the way through. One of the men was killed as the Germans further up the line reassembled their Maxims and started to traverse. Peters, out on the left trying to avoid the huddle, had been caught in the wire. He was a second too late climbing in behind the protection of our revetment.

I reported to Hardcastle when the platoon had settled down. Two enemy killed, three captured, one casualty.

'You're a slowcoach, Mr Beecham,' Hardcastle said. 'The other two parties were back ten minutes ahead of you and they had no casualties.'

I did not want to say that it was McAdam's fault, or anyone's fault. There were unexpected conditions, the new sap. That was all there was to it. And the delay had cost a life, a man who was my responsibility. Laid out on the duckboards, a shape reproaching me that I was still alive. Boots and puttees protruding from under a muddy blanket.

But Hardcastle had no sympathy, no interest in my report other than in my prize, my marked map which McAdam was to send up to the artillery. And the incident gave Hardcastle another line for his attacks on me. Slowcoach. Dawdler.

~

Two weeks later I had Lance-Corporal Ellington and three men out repairing wire during the night. Before dawn word had come down the line.

Wiring party coming in.

Once the men were safely back, Ellington found that he had left two pairs of cutters out in the wire. It was still dark and he wanted to go back out to find our tools. Ellington was almost a giant, big boned and immensely powerful, a man who could reputedly pick up a cow, get fifteen tons in a shift, a man who had the strength to do anything.

We prized our inventory and the cutters would be hard to replace. We were due to leave the line the next night.

Ellington said it would take him five minutes.

Word was passed again.

Man going out.

Ellington was gone for a lot longer than five minutes and dawn began to break. Bright, cold and cloudless in the November sky. Then the Maxim opposite started a traverse. But from the middle of his sweep, not from left to right which would have given Ellington a second's warning.

A short scream. Ellington, still looking for our cutters, had been hit.

I followed our procedure, an immediately volley of ten rounds rapid from six or seven rifles. The Maxim stopped. Then Thompson wanted to call for three volunteers right away to bring Ellington back in. Through the periscope there was no sign of him. I presumed he had found cover in one of the few shell craters on our front.

Hardcastle had been emphatic at our last briefing. There was to be no unauthorized raiding. No one was to leave the trench without his permission. There was a big push coming, no risks were to be taken. Only wire repair at night was permitted and even then right by our lines and on his written orders only.

If our patrols were captured, if the Germans even found bodies, the security surrounding our preparations could be breached. The Germans were to find out nothing, not even the names of the regiments facing them.

Captain McAdam was on a visit to the artillery so I sent a runner to Battalion HQ to ask for permission to rescue Ellington.

During stand-to at dawn, while we ate bacon and drank tea, usually the best meal of the day, a sob, a sound of terrible pain, of slow death came from out in the wire. Quiet for periods, then a sudden muffled choke and cry together followed by quiet again.

'Major 'ardcastle, sir, says you t'report to battalion, sir,' the runner said when he returned. The strain of us listening to Ellington was visible on all our faces. And I could see what the runner knew. There was to be no relief.

'So, Mr Beecham,' Hardcastle started after the well-rehearsed entry, 'you think you can waste my time and yours with this sort of asinine request? Is that how you run your platoon? Want to waste more lives and break our security, do you? Didn't you hear me yesterday, Beecham?'

But Hardcastle did not know Ellington. And Hardcastle had not heard the muzzled moans, the waits, the waits that were worse, the waits between each moan. Wasn't he dead yet? *Oh God, let him die soon.*

'My orders, Mr Beecham, are to be obeyed. Without question. Do you understand me, Beecham? I'm not running some pansy school debating society, you know. Or whatever it is you're used to. And I'm not telling you again.'

Ellington would have to wait until dark. That'll make 'em more careful with their equipment in the future. Cap on, attention, salute, about turn with a stamp and the march out. As I had been drilled, but still not in a helmet.

When Ellington was brought in that night we found that he had been hit in the stomach. His uniform was black with blood to the knees. His face white, drained like a hanging chicken. But the worst was his hand. Broken, crushed between his teeth, blood coagulated through a field dressing wrapped around the knuckle. Stuck, shoved right up into his mouth to stop himself from crying out.

Ellington died at the CCS during the night. I put in another report to Hardcastle which was ignored, then I set about composing my letter to Ellington's wife. I was shaking so badly that I could hardly hold my pencil. The schoolboy to the new widow who had lost her getter, her ox.

In billets I saw a little more of the army organization which had been so quickly passed over in the lectures at OCB. Something beyond my narrow obsession with feet, with trench walls and the men's spirit.

My platoon was one of four in our company under Captain McAdam. Each platoon was commanded by a subaltern: me, Hodges with his dangerous disorganization, then Granforth and Sainsbury, Sandhurst men from land-owning families in Yorkshire. Hardcastle men, to be seen standing next to him at the mess before meals, listening intently, hollow little laughs at every boorish joke.

I should have had sixty men in my platoon divided into three sections, each under a corporal and a lance-corporal, all supervised by Thompson, my platoon serjeant. But we were never more than forty and on Thompson's suggestion we had reduced to two sections.

Then above, our battalion commanded by Major Hardcastle consisted of four companies of four platoon each, with a nominal strength of over one thousand men including HQ. Beyond that we were part of brigades, divisions and army corps that I hardly understood.

The generals who were the divisional commanders and the corps commanders were all remote figures. For me only our Army commander had a name: General the Honourable Sir Julian Byng. Byng's Boys, we called ourselves.

I had formed a picture of the General, the standard moustache, but a vigorous man with the look of a disappointed though determined bloodhound. Human, understanding, not a waster of lives, Thompson said. He told me about the General's capture of Vimy Ridge, the careful preparations then the complete success of the Canadian attack. Thompson, always superstitious, considered it an omen of good luck that the General's grandfather had fought at Waterloo.

The rest of the army composition, the relationship of General Byng to the Commander-in-Chief of the BEF, Field Marshal Sir Douglas Haig, for example, the way the artillery ran, where our supplies came from, what the engineers did, the endless organization behind us, I understood none of that.

From my first encounter with Hardcastle on the morning of our arrival I had known that a push was coming. Slowly, over the first days of November, some of the details began to emerge.

'You can see it perfectly well behind the back lines,' McAdam told us, 'but you're not supposed to know anything. Secrecy is absolutely essential for this op.'

Tanks had been coming up by rail, monstrous, ominous machines. I had never seen anything like them. In Cornwall even the sight of a steam threshing engine was enough to turn a whole village out into the street to watch.

The tanks were great steel boxes held together by large smooth rivets. Dark green or a mottled camouflage, running on continuous oval tracks like iron caterpillars, gun turrets out each side. They looked infernal, unstoppable.

I had no idea how I would stand up to such a thing if my trench were attacked by enemy tanks. German spirits had been broken, we heard, every time our tanks reached their trenches. *Devil's coaches*, the Germans called them.

But rumour was that we were safe. Popular wisdom said that the Germans had diverted all their resources to making submarines.

The new Mark IV was a big improvement over the tanks of 1916, heavier guns and better armour plating. All the same, Thompson was sure, a direct hit by even a German 77 millimetre field gun would be the end of any tank and her crew.

Each tank carried a fascine sitting over her bows, an enormous round bundle of branches and brushwood for filling in an enemy trench to make a crossing point. At night, long rows of black shapes loaded with fascines made a terrifying sight. Quiet and menacing, like poisonous frogs, I saw them sitting up on railway flat-cars stretching far down unlit sidings.

The preparations behind our lines were vast. Huge tented workshops for the tanks had been erected under camouflage nets and artillery was arriving in force every night. Track-laying teams were ready to extend our light railway into captured areas. Signallers were burying armoured cable in all directions. A row of CCSs had gone up.

Between rounds of trench duty we started training with tanks over open fields north of the Somme on the road to Péronne. The Tankodrome was a sea of mud, contaminated by petrol and oil and clouded by engine exhaust hanging low in the cold air.

First we met the tank crews. The officers of the Tank Corps were all young men, though older than me. Formerly in the cavalry, the artillery or with the machine-gunners. Their men had been bus drivers, sailors or factory workers with a bent for mechanics. Thompson took to the tanks and their crews immediately.

Then we were shown the machines. There were only two varieties of tank so the army divided them by sex. The Male tank carried two 6 pound cannons and the Female was equipped with machine-guns. The jokes were unending.

'In't 'e a big bitch.'

'Look a' *that* ol' bull. He'll foock t'un arigh'.'

Each tank carried a crew of eight men packed into hot, cramped, noisy conditions dense with fumes and cordite. Four tankers were needed merely to steer and control the engine. The motor was open to the crew like a ship's engine, right in the middle of their oppressive metal cave.

At the officers' tent during our training, the tea strong enough to stand a spoon, I talked with a group of subaltern tank commanders.

'We've been into action on several occasions,' a lieutenant told me, an officer who used to be a sailor, 'but not one of them was really successful. Lost a lot of our buses for nothing. Still finding our way.'

Then another broke in, imitating some pompous Staff officer:

'Conclusion one: tanks are unable to negotiate bad ground. Conclusion two: the ground on a battlefield will always be bad. Conclusion three: tanks are no good on a battlefield. Pretty damned simple, eh? What?' Everybody laughed.

The Tank Corps had seen action in April of that year in the Battle of Arras and again in August in the latest battle for the ruins of Passchendaele. But the tanks had been caught in the mud of Flanders, easy targets for German guns and spread out too thinly along the attacking line to be of any use. The potential advantages of speed and concentration had been lost.

Surprise had not been achieved either as the Germans had found out what was coming. Then there had been breakdowns and lack of training with the infantry. The results had been disastrous and the Tank Corps had nearly been disbanded.

'There are things we can do very well,' I was told by another tanker lieutenant, 'but for some things we definitely need the infantry. Mopping up, for instance, silencing anti-tank guns. But if we can surprise the Bosche and move fast at him across firm ground, there's no end to where we can get to.'

There was something haunted about my new friends. They all had coughs and colds from the conditions at the Tankodrome and they were exhausted. They had been through four actions in succession, McAdam told me, with a move and a refit between each, not enough rest and no leave.

Now, across the rolling beet fields of Cambrai, fields which had yet to be churned up by artillery into impassable mud, the tankers were keen to prove their worth.

We were given demonstrations of a tank's power and ability to overcome almost any obstacle. Tanks performed over a section of old German trench line, showing us how they would deal with the enemy then pass over the trenches to attack the back lines, leaving us, the infantry, in occupation of the German position. More than that, the tank itself would act as moving cover as we came out of our own trenches and advanced in the open.

But most important of all, the tanks could make a path for us through enemy wire. The answer to Thompson's doubts about the new push.

'The boys and me are completely sold on this one, sir,' Thompson told me as we watched. 'Never seen 'em as much behind a push as for this. Wire's a pancake, be just fine on the day.'

This was something different, not just more trench attacks, more wearing down, more wasting of lives for very, very little.

After the tank demonstrations we rehearsed an attack. The tanks made formations of three, one in advance and two side by side a hundred yards behind. Each tank in the second line was followed by two infantry sections in file.

As the tanks approached a mock-up of the German lines the first tank dropped its fascine into the trench, crossed over and turned left. The tank then worked along the parados of the forward trench, firing her cannon down on to the imagined defenders and their machine-gun posts.

The second tank then followed the first over the enemy front line and dropped its fascine into the second line of trench, then the third tank followed to the third trench. With all resistance broken by the tanks, our job of holding a gap in the enemy lines for the cavalry to pass through looked simple.

Two days before the attack we received our briefing. McAdam stood in front of a large map in a shelled cowshed giving us the objectives. The Third Army Plan for Operation GY, the code name for the attack.

(1) To break the enemy's defensive positions by a *coup de main* with the help of tanks.

(2) To pass the cavalry through the break so created.

(3) To seize Cambrai and the crossings of the Sensée river, cutting off the German front line troops between the Canal Saint Quentin and the Canal du Nord.

(4) To exploit the success by advancing north-eastward and rolling up the Hindenburg Line from the south.

Objective one was to capture the first trench lines of the Hindenburg system and the villages of Ribécourt and Havrincourt, marked on the map as the Blue Line. C Company was to be on the far right flank of our front line, behind the 3rd Tank Brigade.

The next objective, the Brown Line, was beyond the German support trench. Across the valley ahead of us, up to Bonavis Ridge and Lateau Wood.

Finally, on the afternoon of the same day, we were to cross the Canal Saint Quentin and capture the last line of German defences on the slopes behind the village of Masnières. This was the Red Line. Once tanks and infantry had breached the Red Line the cavalry was to surround Cambrai itself.

At Bonavis Ridge the 29th Division was to pass through our lines and take over the attack. After that we would be in support.

The Germans had retreated to their new lines in front of Cambrai at the start of 1917. To what we called the Hindenburg Line, after the Chief of the German General Staff. But named the *Siegfried Stellung* by the Germans, from Wagner and his impenetrable *Ring Cycle.*

The enemy lines had been constructed with German thoroughness during the winter of 1916 as a place of defence on the strongest ground in what then looked like a permanent war. The Hindenburg Line extended for fifty miles in the very centre of the overall trench system which ran from the mountains of Switzerland to the Channel coast.

Once the Hindenburg Line was completed, the Germans had retired in perfect order from their shallow trench system on the Somme.

The British and French had been obliged to follow the Germans back across the Somme battlefield of 1916, miles of levelled agony which was now behind our lines. An endless low tide, a lunar prairie. Old wire like a vast rusting creeper running over a root system of bones below, our dead buried in gas-filled craters and collapsed trenches.

From Péronne north, every remaining building, every tree had been destroyed by the retreating Germans to keep us exposed. Then laid with booby-traps: under a helmet waiting for a collector of souvenirs; attached to a basket of apples in an abandoned dug-out. And when our advancing line had come up against the new German defences we had dug in again while at the same time beating off their attacks.

The quality of our lines had deteriorated while the German position was much improved. Yet McAdam for one considered the German retreat to the Hindenburg Line to be an admission of defeat. Turning the Somme into a victory in the end.

The section of the Hindenburg Line facing us was particularly strong, over five miles in depth from their front position to their last support trench, the Masnières–Beaurevoir Line. The German trenches were formidable, ten to twelve feet deep as I had seen. Strengthened by dug-outs and gun positions in reinforced concrete. Cambrai to the Germans was a vital communications centre to be defended at all costs. But, McAdam told us, the strength of their defences meant that this part of the German line was manned by less experienced troops who were not expecting an attack. The Cambrai sector had been quiet for over a year while other battles were being fought further north around Ypres.

'The Flanders Sanatorium. That's what the Germans call this bit.' McAdam seemed genuinely optimistic. 'The coming offensive, I believe,' he said, sitting on a milking table in front of us, 'has the best chance of any push since the start of the War. If the Hindenburg can be breached, it may be possible to roll up a large part of the German lines east and west. Maybe even end the War.'

McAdam listed the points he saw in our favour. Complete secrecy, tanks in force for the first time ever on good ground. New artillery techniques and the battle experience of the Corps through the Somme and Ypres.

'Mopping up will be your main function,' McAdam told us, 'with the tanks taking the weight of the assault.'

But even the optimism and general expectation of victory did not improve the state of my nerves as we approached the battle. The Battle of Cambrai, as McAdam said it would be called. Only concern for my men stopped my fear from showing, prevented a cold funk from overtaking me, having me run away, or collapse whimpering into a dark trench corner. I made myself frantically busy, day and night.

Thompson could talk of nothing but the tanks and the bravery of the crews.

'Like sardines in there, they are, sir,' he said a number of times. 'An' almost cooked 'n' all.'

Near the end of our training the tankers challenged us to prepare any defences we could think of. We worked all day with the help of the Royal Engineers digging more trenches and piling logs. Nothing could be constructed which stopped the tanks. Thompson was most impressed.

'But I wouldn't never want to be caught in one of them contraptions,' he said as the company reassembled to return to the line. 'Not for all the tea in China.'

I marched to the side following Thompson's commands just like the men. 'Smartly now, boys. Lep. Lep. Lep-ri-i, lep.' Thompson always had them swinging along. With him I knew that we would always find a way, that we could handle anything.

Thompson swayed as he marched, shoulders back. Rolling slightly from side to side like a band major, proud of us all. Movements I had adopted as my own, as if inherited.

4

McAdam's briefing had not given us a date or a time for zero, the start of the battle. Finally, two days after our last tank training, McAdam had the information: 0620 on 20 November 1917.

From the moment we knew when zero was to be the men seemed to move closer to each other. Perking up, standing straighter, pushing from the back when parading for new equipment or for food. Impatient when the platoon was halted on the march. Attentive as I described our objectives. The songs were louder, raucous and we had no stragglers on our last march back to the front. We were about to do what we had been trained to do, what we all wanted to do.

Optimism was everywhere, this was something different.

Conditions on the way back from the Tankodrome were much worse than the march to Cambrai. The fields on each side of the narrow main road had been curdled into knee-deep mud by equipment on the move. It was impossible to march off the pavé so any breakdown or snarl-up had us stopped.

The road police would leave the company standing in the rain and the dark, unable to rest but unable to proceed. Rations were poor and the food was cold. Our billets when we could fall out were shelled woods or severely damaged farm buildings with no fires allowed. But a spirit of determination had come over my platoon and the hardships, usually so roundly cursed, were taken without complaint.

Eventually we marched back into Villiers Plouich, to the ruined cowsheds behind our support lines that we knew so well.

I made myself incessantly busy again. There was no time to rest or to think. More briefings, then checking the pegged tracings time and time again, the route up to our final positions during the night before the attack. An unending search for extra supplies and ammunition, for food and missing equipment. I ran weapons inspections then kit inspections and foot inspections. I tested again and again for loose respirators.

I asked the men random questions after my briefings as I painted on tincture or issued new socks. I was always surprised.

'Well, sir, objec' one be to take 'indenburg with 'elp o' tanks, then a chase 'un oot-a-Ribs-court, wi' Fifty First on left. Af'er that, on top o'ill ...'

The tanks and our training had made it all seem possible.

Before we were due to parade at the quartermaster's store to return our trench equipment, Thompson had a suggestion.

'Be out there longer than they says, sir,' he began. We had been told that the attack would last forty-eight hours and that we would then be relieved. Thompson was sceptical. 'Be relieved if all's going right sir, or if push is called off. But be stuck out there anyroads if it goes wrong.'

Thompson anticipated at least double the time expected by McAdam. He proposed that when we dropped our surplus stores forty-eight hours before the attack, that we just hang onto our Vickers which was part of our trench equipment.

'But Serjeant, how could we possibly carry a Vickers forward, not to mention all the ammunition? Weighs a ton. And the gun has to be ticked off on our return by the quartermaster.'

Thompson had a way, of course.

'That's fine, sir, but while we goes through, if you could have a word with quartermaster, sir. About 'is wife? Taken right poorly-like. Then I'll arrange the kit so as he won't notice what 'e's not got. Mostly 'e just goes through the motions anyway.'

'Well, stores is always a muddle, Serjeant,' ready to do whatever Thompson wanted. 'But what about weight? We're already loaded down with extra everything.'

'The lads, sir, would rather starve than be left in open field without Vickers. Rather take Vickers than grub or picks and shovels. An' we was all hoping that ammunition and frame could go up on top of tank when we starts to move.'

It was a complete scheme, agreed on by all of them, I was sure, before I had been informed.

'An' you don't have to worry about water for jacket, neither, sir.' Thompson grinned his big grin. 'If needs be, we line the boys up and they piss into spout by turns.' I had seen Vickers guns in components strapped on to mules. So no doubt the gun could be handled by an entire platoon and a tank. I began to see what Thompson meant.

There were sections from the Machine-Gun Corps attached to Battalion, equipped to carry their weapons on little upright trolleys like metal coffins. But Thompson predicted that if we ran into trouble the machine-guns would be sure to be moved elsewhere. We would be left to defend ourselves with only a jammed Lewis, our rifles and our bayonets. Out in some sod'n' farmer's field.

'Always got to think of counter attack, sir. Always next to come.'

Thompson had learned about carrying a Vickers from the Australians. He had seen them in action. He admired their free spirits and lack of regard for the conventional. Brave individuals, Thompson called them. Not just following orders, but each man thinking for himself.

When their attack was held up, the Australians had assembled enough of the Vickers to traverse the position ahead of them to keep the enemy's heads down. Under much worse conditions, in Flanders mud, with no tank cover.

Then after taking an enemy trench or if forced to fall back, the Australians again brought the Vickers into use for defence. Thompson warned me that even after a successful advance, we would have to hold our new positions against counter-attack, probably with no relief in sight. Something that had not occurred to me or been mentioned by McAdam.

'Won't take 'im more than a few days to find reserves for counter attack, irregardless of what the brass might say. Not daft, you know, our Fritz.'

Thompson was already three days ahead of me.

I hardly gave a thought to the consequences of taking the Vickers with us. It was not even ours, we just happened to have it for training on the last day in support. The coming attack took away any idea of life after the action. What would the Vickers matter if I did not come back? And if the attack were successful, what would anything matter?

So we had our plan, me and Thompson and it worked out smoothly. The quartermaster was preoccupied with other things. I did not even have to ask him about the wife.

And another sign of good luck, according to Thompson's superstitions, was that the tank we were married up with was commanded by the ex-sailor from the tea tent at the Tankodrome. Lieutenant Woolridge, someone I knew. Woolridge readily agreed to carry our clandestine Vickers on his tank *Helen*, as well as our SAA, Small Arms Ammunition.

During Y/Z night, the night before zero, *Helen* crawled up with the others to their start line behind us, in second speed, inching forward as quietly as they could. The trenches were ablaze that night, bombs, trench mortars, rockets. The German lines could never have detected what was happening on our side.

The tank start line was about one hundred yards from our lying-in position right behind our front. The trench where we were supposed to wait was full so we settled down in the open.

Thompson and Higgs secured our booty to the rear step of the tank: belts of ammunition, water tank, metal frame and the barrel all wrapped in two layers of blankets.

I was exhausted, taut and jumpy. Sleep was impossible even for an hour. Machine-guns were going one against the other across No-Man's-Land. Then Verylights lit up the clouds to the constant pop of rifle fire and the thud of their Minies coming in.

In the early morning there was one of those panicky episodes of intense fire between trenches that often came up quickly in the night. Nerves, boredom, anger at the whole world. But this one was edgy, threatening, as if the Germans knew that an attack was coming and we were about to walk right into trouble.

I stood with Woolridge behind *Helen*, nothing left to do but to be nervous about the din, drinking his tanker's tea, mug trembling in my hand. My muscles were jelly, fibres nothing more than pulp, as if I was suddenly a hundred years old. Earlier, before the tanks had come up, for a moment on my own in the dark I had had the wind up so badly that I could hardly stand.

One of the tank crew was lubricating track gear, feeling his way in the black with his grease gun. A familiar little routine to occupy hands and mind.

By the light of a clandestine torch with a pin-head beam, Woolridge showed me the message that all the tankers had received from Brigadier-General Elles, commander of the Tank Corps. Cheerful and straightforward: the Corps had been waiting all year for a chance like this and here it was; the General was going to lead the attack himself from a tank on Woolridge's left, in the centre of III Corps.

General Elles had even made up a flag to fly from his tank *Hilda*. Brown, green and red, the only colours he could find in the village of Fins on that afternoon. 'Those colours will just have to do,' the General was supposed to have said. 'We'll work out what they mean later'.

At that frozen moment, the story of the flag and the General's message gave me courage, something to hold on to. A man I would have liked to be following.

Hardcastle had put up a virtuoso performance on the last day. We were paraded in an open square on a field behind Villiers Plouich. I stood at the back trying to be inconspicuous in my cap against a batallion of helmets.

Time to do your duty. Excellent staff work in place, the very best. A privilege to work with a General Staff such as ours. But infantry still the infantry. Tanks just a helping hand. Catching the enemy completely by surprise this time. Cavalry breakthrough, that's how we'll win the War.

Cavalry. Fine traditions. Know you'll all do your stuff. Then he returned to his HQ.

He could not have done worse, I thought, if he had purposely set out to unsteady the men, to drive them back to the old cynicism I had heard at Armentières.

It was after four o'clock, time to get ready. Woolridge held out his hand.

'No dawdling and flirting with the girls in Cambrai, now, we're supposed to be through the town and out the other side by tonight.'

My men lay with their heads on packs, hard like wooden boxes, stuffed full of extra rations and ammunition. The smaller parts of the Vickers were slung over shoulders or attached to webbing: the lock, the extractor, the feed block and crosspiece.

Rum was distributed, much too early but in good quantity, enough over to fill my flask. Then a paltry amount of tepid burgoo and tea, hardly sufficient for a couple of mouthfuls each. After that there was no more warmth, no protection against cold and damp. The air was pregnant with moisture and we sat and shivered for the last hour before dawn.

As the final part of the complete surprise the men were ordered not to smoke while lying-in. A painful ordeal for some. Hardcastle had made a great fuss about smoking in his address. Officers, he said, had been instructed to shoot any man who was caught.

Dawn started to slink in before six, a morning of dense mist. Slowly features began to form around me: the parados of our trenches in front, a tank to each side of us, *Helen* on the left, the bulk of her fascine above. Immediately to our rear, artillery was hidden under netting, set up during the early part of the night.

Thompson's rock face, dear to me, my talisman. Alert but with no trace of anxiety. I watched him as he looked round at the men. Count'n' legs, he liked to say, then divid'n', like a sod'n' Yorkshire shep'd.

Behind Thompson, the back of Higgs' helmet. Then the shapes of my men lying on their capes.

I had no idea what the men would be thinking. Or maybe they prayed. Some of them were writing home even though there was no post. In billets many men wrote twice each day. I was supposed to censor letters but I sealed their envelopes without reading a single line. Their families were not spies. I thought that I would never be able to face them if I had read their letters.

As part of the secrecy of the attack there had been no mail permitted for the last week other than Field Service Post Cards known as Quick Firers.

```
NOTHING is to be written on this side except the date and
signature of the sender. Sentences not required may be erased.
If anything else is added the post card will be destroyed.
========================================================
I am quite well

I have been admitted to hospital
        [sick    ]              and I am getting on well.
        [wounded]              and I hope to be discharged soon.

I am being sent down to the base.

I have received your
        [letter dated _____
        [telegram     _____
        [parcel       _____

Letter follows at first opportunity.

I have received no letter from you
              [lately
              [for a long time



Signature  ]
only       ]
Date _____
```

Most of the men had written comments on their cards despite the instructions. *Thanks for woolly cap,* or, *Bearing the brunt, but over soon,* or, *Fags are always welcome. And socks.*

'If they gets that card the way it is, they thinks the worst anyway,' Thompson explained. 'So either it gets through with what's added, or it don't. And then they're not worrying except about a few days missed.' Thompson always knew how to play the system.

On his card Thompson had crossed out everything except *I am well.* Even the word *quite* had been struck out. Below his signature he had written, *Love to you my Beatrice, and to our Ben. I am fine. L.* The first I knew that Thompson had a son.

After we had moved up on the last night I walked the cards back to the Field Post Office behind Villiers Plouich and handed them to an orderly through his grille. Anything to keep busy and I hoped that the corporal would accept the cards from me as already censored and send them on without examination.

The trench firing was just a squall. Before 0500 the lines had calmed down. I started to regain some confidence. Then for an hour and a half it was so quiet that I could hear partridges calling to each other in the woods behind.

We waited, still and silent.

This time my wristwatch had been synchronized with battalion and with the artillery. At twenty minutes before zero I started to give out the minutes in a whisper. With two minutes to go I counted down the seconds.

As I reached the end, eight, seven, six... breathing hard, mouth dry, heart ripping out of my chest, four, three... the artillery barrage started and the tanks behind us fired their engines.

The noise was terrifying. Over a thousand guns so close then the roar of four hundred tanks revving together. Furious firing again from the trenches to coincide with zero. The mist itself reeling and quivering under the apocalyptic thunder of this tremendous blow.

Before we even moved I knew that the plan would succeed.

Within minutes the German trenches were throwing up rockets and SOS signals to their artillery across the length of their line, calling for bombardment support. Reds and greens shining out vividly against a black curtain of smoke behind. But the reply to our barrage from the German guns was negligible. Our massed artillery had overwhelmed them.

Under the influence of rum and the sudden passing of panic I had an urge to laugh. To laugh and laugh as we picked up and formed our two lines behind *Helen*. It all seemed to be over before it had begun.

Then we started our advance. Whistles blew, shouted commands heard faintly against the roar. After the stillness of the last hour a general commotion took over on all sides. Men were coming out of the trenches and spreading out in front of us, tanks moving forward on both left and right. While the ground shook under us with the explosions of hundreds of tons of shells fired each minute.

First a great smokescreen was being laid higher up the ridge to blind the German artillery spotters. Then immediately our six-inch howitzers were to switch to the foxholes and the machine-gun emplacements of the Hindenburg, the objective of my first trench raid. But for the first minutes of the advance it was too misty to see the full effect of our bombardment.

During the last few days we had started looking inwards at each other, at the familiar comforting faces we knew. Now it was as if the platoon was alone, cocooned in the deafening noise and fog of battle. And as dawn progressed and the mist intensified, the feeling increased, of isolation, of connection between us. By then I knew and cared for them all, each and every one.

Our crossing to the Hindenburg outposts and then on to their Main Line was a dream, leisurely and uneventful, just like training at the Tankodrome. We started by zig-zagging, moving up in rushes behind Woolridge's tank as we had practised. But we were quickly ahead of schedule, left standing halfway across No-Man's-Land until the bombardment had moved on at zero plus twenty-four minutes. Men had their rifles slung, others paused to light cigarettes after enduring hours of prohibition.

There was some light shelling and machine-gun fire from the Germans only during the first few minutes. Then our guns were dropping a cataract of devastation on to the German back trenches and artillery positions and soon all fire from the enemy stopped. The comforting smell of our cordite and artillery smut drifted forward through the last of thinning mist. A breeze was coming up from the south.

The lead tank of our three approached the enemy lines, laying their wire flat, stakes driven clean into the ground. A tanker popped out of his side door, he planted a little red flag to mark the crossing point. Then I watched as the tank bucked over the trench parados and the first fascine rolled into place. Down on to the crossing and up the other side, exactly according to plan.

As we made our way through the crushed wire the lead machine was working along the far side of the first trench, firing her six-pounder down into the hole. The next two tanks were preparing to cross the trench lines behind with no German resistance to be seen.

My platoon had arrived at the almighty Hindenburg Line without a single casualty.

'Could press right on ta bloody Berlin,' one of the men said as we scrambled down into the German trench, 'an' be there b'teatime an' all.' It was truly remarkable.

Our barrage seemed to have had its effect, direct hits on foxholes, trenches caved in up and down the line. There were signs of panicky retreat. The Germans had left equipment, food, maps and papers in every cubbyhole and dug-out.

As soon as we had secured the first line of trenches, thrown bombs and run up and down with fixed bayonets, it was time to move on again to keep in touch with the moving bombardment and with the tanks, *Helen* and our other two buses.

The second line of the Hindenburg presented more difficulty. This time there was no fire from the tanks ahead of us as they moved along the enemy parapets. When I came up to the edge of the trench I could see why.

Packed into the support lines was a dense crowd of German soldiers, their weapons on the ground and their arms in the air. They had surrendered to the tank sitting on the ridge above them. One burst from her guns and they would all have been casualties not prisoners.

The Germans were well aware of their danger. They looked relieved when we appeared over the edge of their trench. Dirty ashen faces all turning our way like a field of grey sunflowers in autumn.

'Good grief,' I said, looking at Thompson, 'now what?' I had no idea what to do, wanting to press on to Berlin, not to be burdened with prisoners. A matter not covered by McAdam in his briefing.

'Raus, you lovely-looking lot,' Thompson yelled at the apprehensive faces. 'The only German I knows, sir,' with a sideways smile. Then back to the prisoners. 'Come on, get yer bummels up 'ere,' waving his arms at them. This was better understood than Thompson's German and the group took to the ladders surrounded by our platoon, bayonets at the ready. The prisoners seemed to fall in by themselves beyond the trench, facing back toward our lines, anxious to march off to our cages, it seemed. We had heard that they were given tea and buns right away.

'Don't need much escort sir,' Thompson said, 'there's lots of units comin' up. They got nowhere to run.' There were over thirty prisoners but we risked sending them back under only two men.

By 0900 we were at our first objective, the Blue Line, beyond the Hindenburg main and support lines, with the loss of only four of our strength. A broken leg falling into a trench, an accident with a bayonet and two men with the prisoners. I saw McAdam trotting over to me, his runner behind. He stayed only briefly.

'Can't miss *you*,' he panted, trying to smile between breaths, 'without your tin hat.'

I wanted to laugh again, to hug him, still light-headed from the rum on an empty stomach and the easy advance.

The men were sitting on the grass opening their iron rations.

'No time to lose.' McAdam pointed up the valley. 'Looks like it'll be clearing fast. With the wind our smokescreen will soon be gone. Get up the ridge to the Brown Line as fast as you can. All's well everywhere, I hear. See you up there.'

By now the tanks were well out in front of us, up the valley of overgrown green fields and on toward Bonavis Ridge. Lateau Wood and the village of Ribécourt lay to our left, to our right a steep slope climbed to Welsh Ridge.

We advanced faster now, trying to reach the cover of the tanks and especially *Helen*, carrying our Vickers. The ease of our passage through the German lines, through the impregnable Hindenburg, had loosened our precision. No rushes, no zig-zagging seemed necessary.

The sun was almost through, it could well turn into a nice day.

Suddenly a row of blue smoke puffs up on Welsh Ridge caught my eye the moment before the shells landed to our front. The entire platoon was flat on the ground in the same instant. A battery of German 77s had been brought up to meet our advance and was ranging for the tanks from the ridge. We were caught in the open but we were not the target.

I crawled over to Thompson who already had some men organized to return fire even though the battery was almost over the top of the summit. There was no one to be seen on our flank between us and the guns.

'Will the tanks make the wood safely?' I lay next to Thompson watching their slow progress for a moment, eight or ten tanks heading for the protection of the trees. So far the shells were wide, spurts of dirt thrown up a hundred yards or more from the lead machine.

'Be fine, sir,' Thompson answered, surveying the valley. 'Take a minute or two for Jerry to get the down angle.'

From where I lay I could see another platoon on our left. Hodges, I thought, but we were closest to the battery. Once the tanks were into the wood we would be next.

At that moment my brain was a box of whirling cogs, apart and separate, as if beyond my control. Even under fire I could think only of Waterloo, of the reverse slope up by the monastery where Wellington had placed his infantry while Napoleon had staged his set-piece opening bombardment.

By then it was Napoleon who followed the same rigid plan, Fairy had explained, and Wellington who had become the innovator. Fairy loved those ironies of history. And when I had walked Wellington's ground with Fairy, looking back at the position of the French cannon across the valley, Wellington's idea had seemed so simple, so obvious. A place where Napoleon's guns could do his men no harm.

'How about we go under them, Serjeant? Over on to the slope below? We'll be blown to bits this way.'

'Fine, sir.' Thompson was probably about to say the same thing but for once I had said it first. He called Higgs over and we told him our plan. All of us to move in a rush, not even trying to give covering fire. We could be there before they could swing the guns around and on to us.

At the bottom of the incline we were all still safe.

I could see the ghostly faces of the tankers at Péronne.

...*definitely need the infantry. Mopping-up, for instance, silencing anti-tank guns.*

Here was the very thing we were supposed to do for them.

'I want to go up and attack the guns,' I said to Thompson, excited even by the idea. 'What do you think?'

The 77s were finding their range now as the tanks closed with the wood. More tanks again were visible on the far side of the valley toward Ribécourt. The German guns would soon be having it all their own way.

Thompson looked up at the slope above us. It was too steep and too far to take at a run.

'The lads are really weighed down, sir,' he said. 'How about ten volunteers with the Lewis and leave their gear down here? The rest could give some cover, although the Fritzes are too far over top really for us to 'it 'em.'

It was agreed. Higgs on the Lewis, the best man, knew how to fire the heavy gun from the hip with a sling. When I asked for volunteers, almost every man wanted to go. Thompson had to choose.

'I'm going up,' I told him, as if there had been any doubt. 'I need some stories for the girls in Cambrai.' Something Woolridge might have said.

Then we were moving, equipment off, only bandoleers of ammunition and water bottles, our own weapons and the Lewis. The hill was steep, climbing fast was a great effort. But by moving across the slope, right under the guns, coming up on their far flank, we caught the battery by complete surprise although we risked meeting their infantry to the rear.

There were four guns in a row, wheel to wheel. Limbers attached to horses were waiting down the far slope under a single man. The entire battery could have been hooked up and off with only a minute's warning.

In the seconds as we charged over the top of the hill and wheeled toward them, I understood how we had been undetected. Some of the gunners were crouched down behind the armoured shields of the guns loading and re-loading, others were piling up ammunition in wicker cases beside tail spades. Only the aimers were looking out, but across the valley. All of them busy, obsessed with the tanks, with trying to achieve maximum rapidity, no sentry, no small arms ready. The crews of the 77s were completely startled, defenceless against us.

We approached the guns running at full tilt. Arriving breathless, surrounding them, ready to use bayonets before many of them could even turn to face us.

The crews on the first two guns surrendered immediately they saw us, at a distance of less than thirty yards, me brandishing my Webley, the men with their rifles raised now, ready to fire.

But here there was an ugly scene.

On the far gun an officer in a peaked cap and heavy glasses tied to his ears with rubber bands, drew his pistol and fired point blank at Spollard who was moving round the spades of the guns. Spollard had been distracted for a moment by the men of the third gun who seemed undecided about whether or not to raise their arms.

The bullet hit Spollard full in the chest and he fell back without a sound on to the dirt, across tracks churned up by the wooden wheels of the guns.

But the shot was immediately returned by a volley of our own, spontaneous, angry, for immediate vengeance. Half a dozen out of the German crews fell dead, splayed back over the grey carriages, their arms still up. Hit in the head, the chest, the stomach, only a few yards now off the ends of our rifles. Killed right before my eyes. Blood splattered over breech blocks and gun machinery. Contorted, panicked faces on the living and on the dead. After they had surrendered.

The officer on the fourth gun, who had shot Spollard, was not touched by the volley. In the split second before the men could reload and fire again, I screamed.

I screamed before I lost control, while the rest of the German crews, seeing in that same fraction of a second what was about to happen, tried to press themselves on to their guns, behind the shields, under, between the wheels.

'*Stop. Hold your fire.*' Roared out like a drill command on the square.

Incredibly the order held.

In the next moment the madness receded. The rest of the crews surrendered, arms up as fast as they could, including the officer.

'Better watch backs, sir,' one of the men called out, Tulley the dairyman, now an acting lance-corporal.

We were standing there like two groups of village idiots, facing each other around the guns. Us with our weapons still pointed, the Germans with their arms in the air and their dead lying all around. We were completely open to counter attack from behind.

'No telling where t'un might be,' Tulley added, looking back across the fields toward the north as I grasped the danger.

Bristow was down with their horses and had taken the guard prisoner. The man did not even bother to raise his hands. It was over.

Quickly we pushed the prisoners off the ridge and down the slope with only two men as guards. At the worst the prisoners could run off unarmed, down into our advancing troops.

I put out sentries and started to think about defence using the guns as cover.

But almost immediately a captain came over a rise from the south leading a company in line abreast across the ridge. The Durham Light Infantry.

'You beat me to it, you rotter,' the captain said as if we were on the playing field. He smiled. 'You bloody Yorkshires are everywhere. No action left worth talking about.'

I was up on his company's line of advance, which I thought was going to turn out to be a serious sin. But the captain laughed at me. On the battlefield, he said, unlike the cricket pitch, it's only results that count. Could have lost a tank in the few minutes before he had arrived.

The captain would take over the guns and I would resume my own advance, head off down the slope again with my prisoners. The captain wrote in his field notebook and tore out a page. He smiled at me again as he handed over the ragged sheet.

> Received from 2nd
> Lt. Beauchamp.
> four × 77mm enemy
> guns captured by his
> platoon West
> Yorkshires 'C' Coy
> 6th Brig. Prisoners
> to be escorted by you.
> Signed. A. Louden.
> Cpt 'B' Coy 2nd
> D.L.I. 18th Brig.

'Not bad for a one pipper straight from school.' I had not realized how obvious my status was.

Nothing was said about the dead, theirs or mine. Our discipline had held when it was necessary. And the Fritz officer had shot first when his men were defenceless. What more should I care about?

The bodies would be left for collection by the gravediggers later.

From the edge of the slope leading down toward Thompson and the platoon, the view was now spectacular. It was almost 1100, the fog was gone and I could see for four or five miles.

To the left, back in the direction of Villiers Plouich, the Hindenburg lines were swarming with our men. The 29th in reserve behind us was on the move. Pioneers had started work building roads over the German trenches, the signallers and wire layers were busy. Support tanks pulling sleds of petrol and supplies were coming up.

Behind again the artillery was packing up to deploy forward. Cavalry was advancing along the valley toward Ribécourt, ready for their breakthrough around Cambrai. Like figures on a military model, trotting in file across open fields.

Straight ahead of me the leading formations of tanks had come through Lateau Wood and had reached the top of Bonavis Ridge, the Brown Line, our second objective, where I should have been by then.

There was some renewed shelling of the woods from German 5.9s dug in behind Masnières but it seemed that the tanks had moved on before their spotter planes could have the enemy guns relaid. Now, close to the summit, the tanks appeared to be stopped, probably making tea, I thought.

It was all so easy, so glorious.

Below to my right I could see the Canal Saint Quentin and the town of Masnières. Then the Masnières–Beaurevoir Line behind: our final objective, the Red Line and the last of the Hindenburg system.

The bridge over the canal looked to be packed with *feldgrau*. Germans in their grey coats retreating in large numbers.

Further away toward the spires of Cambrai, fragile white shapes in the clear sky were diving and pulling up sharply over enemy artillery positions. Camels and SE5s of the Royal Flying Corps.

We would be there that night. In Cambrai that night. The war could be over any day. I saw it all so clearly.

I was the happiest man in the entire British Army.

Tumbling down the slope, leaning back on to my heels, taking giant's steps, hardly able to wait to tell Thompson what a lark it had been.

5

I lay behind a scruffy hedgerow, just wide enough to protect my platoon, all of us squeezed in shoulder to shoulder from one side to the other. Like fish feeding across a river.

The hedgerow was no more than a few bushes and brambles along a farm track, spreading over a low pile of rocks taken one at a time from the fields during each ploughing season. A ribbon of ground untouched by the farmer year after year until cairn and outgrowth had formed a feature in itself. Just high enough to have saved our lives.

Flat on my stomach in the white chalk, mud like cream soaking right through my greatcoat, through my tunic and against my skin. The cover of my *Passion* damp and slimy against my chest.

I peered through the base of laurel bushes and sodden decaying grasses, through strands of brambles curling this way and that like barbed wire. I could see nothing, but in front of us was a Maxim. Accurate and deadly, spitting a flat plane of metal into our cover, bullets fizzing and whining off rocks, scything through bushes a few inches above us.

The OCB blackboard came back to me. Chalk arrows, meaningless initials for military terms I had never fully understood. I could remember some of it. I should divide my platoon into two groups, one to stay behind the hedgerow, returning fire, keeping the enemy *occupied*. The other group to work around under cover, until the machine-gun could be attacked from the side or from the rear.

But in the training example there had always been trees and hedges exactly where they were needed as cover. And in the classroom we could always count on the Germans not to move, not to see us coming, to play our game.

Our actual position in the middle of an open beet field was nothing like the classroom. I was lost, out of touch with everything, with our right flank, with the company, separated from *Helen*, out of sight of the next platoon on the left. Unable to raise my head to see, much less to return fire.

Trouble had started right after the euphoric moment on Welsh Ridge. As I lay pinned behind the hedgerow, the morning already seemed distant.

Down from the capture of the 77s we had met up with the company again on Bonavis Ridge, Thompson looking so full of pride I thought he would burst. But McAdam had been there for some time already and his mood had turned sour.

I was late, the slowcoach once more, but the story of the four field guns backed up by the Durham's receipt had qualified as a partial excuse. There was still no sign of the 29th who were supposed to take over the lead down the slope toward the canal.

By then the fields ahead of us, leading down to Masnières directly below, were littered with tanks: some untouched but broken down, some smouldering. Some black, direct hits by German artillery. Six or seven of them.

Just in the two hours since I had been on Welsh Ridge. I had no idea that the tankers could lose so many buses in such a short time.

And the crews? Where were the crews? That was Thompson's concern.

From Bonavis Ridge any visible activity to our front seemed to have ended, no retreating grey uniforms packing the Masnières bridge. No sign of the rout that I thought had started. But behind us commotion had intensified. The Hindenburg Main Line swarmed with our support troops coming across the trenches. Two long thin lines of cavalry were continuing to pour out of Gouzeaucourt.

'The 29th is still coming over the German lines,' McAdam told me. 'There's an awful lot of congestion at the back.' His bounce was gone. We were seriously behind schedule and the company had taken a lot of casualties.

C and D Platoons to the west had come under heavy shellfire in Lateau Wood during their advance up to the ridge. 5.9s from the German rear batteries directed by their spotters, looking for our tanks. Sainsbury and Granforth on the left of the company had taken a pasting. Sainsbury had been killed and his serjeant badly wounded. Granforth had lost fifteen men.

Hodges on my immediate left had skirted the wood because, he said, it was easier then pushing through the undergrowth and so in his fumbling way he had missed the shelling. From my position up on the ridge, the barrage had seemed light and inaccurate.

McAdam's answer was to push me on.

'If in doubt, advance. That's the infantry motto,' he snapped. 'The 29th will be along soon enough.'

I had hoped to rest my men. Cumulative exhaustion showed on their haggard features. Nights of marching back from the Tankodrome, the stress of the start, the continuous roar of battle.

But after the company's casualties McAdam had to move men around, consolidate down to three platoons. He was in a hurry, short with everyone. And there was a rumour that the main bodies of tanks and cavalry were held up at Flesquières.

'How many men have you lost?' McAdam asked me sharply, looking around at my platoon.

'Seven, Mr McAdam. One man killed, two injured and four back on detail with prisoners.'

'Your escorts will be lost for the day at least. How many ORs did you have at the start?'

'Thirty-eight men.'

'Well, your Thompson's possibly adequate to take some of the load. I'm going to give you ten men from D Platoon.'

'Fine, sir.'

But I had to get going right away. Shelling had started again right behind us. Our artillery was still on the move and for the moment we could give no response to the German bombardments.

'It's already after 1300,' McAdam said before he ran off. 'We're over two hours behind as it is. I'll send your new men over. If you need to, you can make someone an acting lance-corporal.' Ellington had been replaced by Tulley. Thompson had been leading 2 Section himself with Higgs at the head of 1 Section on the Lewis.

Sainsbury's men stumbled over to us looking dazed and missing equipment. Two of the men were holding on to each other and one man seemed delirious. He had that look, wild but powerless, that I had seen in the eyes of a horse sinking into Flanders mud.

Thompson tried to buck them up. He checked their kit and their rifles and he passed them parts of the lost Vickers to carry. Like a keepsake, a charm.

'Couple of holies,' Thompson said to me when he returned. 'They long to leave this lower sphere. But it's all God's will, so they're still 'ere.' He rolled his eyes.

The men ate some of their rations, bully beef and biscuits, but I had no opportunity. In less than ten minutes McAdam was back again.

'You've got to get on the *move*, Mr Beecham. The way's clear down the hill.' He pointed toward Masnières. 'Tanks are already down there. Keep moving over to your right until you find someone from the 20th. You're the far flank of the whole brigade now, you should be in contact with our neighbours. Either that or our flank's completely up in the air.'

He swept the right horizon with his glasses. 'Something must have happened to the 20th,' he mumbled. 'Caught up at Banteux, I heard.'

We set off down the slope before I could remember my questions, shooed away by McAdam like a herd of geese. And Thompson was anxious to get off the ridge. He was sure that shrapnel would be next, looking for our cavalry. Battalion would be regrouping later in the day, with Hardcastle and HQ coming up, once the balls-ups had been cleared. They would establish somewhere along the canal. Get going, I was told, you'll be informed.

But as we started walking over the fields a cold apprehension had come over me. A dread I could not shake, even walking next to Thompson.

By that time of day we should have been behind the 29th down by the canal, with the tanks approaching the last line of the Hindenburg. But we were only halfway there and still out in front. I had no contact with *Helen* or any of the others.

There was no new plan, no co-ordination with the artillery, just my platoon on our own, exposed in an open field. Thompson's nightmare. And when we did reach the bottom of the hill and the canal I had no idea what to do. It would be dark in less than four hours.

There was wide-open country ahead, then the small village of Les Rues Vertes on our side of the canal, connected to Masnières beyond by a metal bridge. The houses on the far side of the canal would be full of hidden Germans, I was sure. And no telling when I would meet up with McAdam again or find food or relief. I had not even prepared a map route down from Bonavis Ridge, expecting to be behind the 29th.

Now the trenches that I had been so anxious to leave seemed like a safe place. Something I knew, a place where I could duck, lie flat, be protected. Where relief and support were certain.

On the move down the hill toward the Canal Saint Quentin, we quickly became separated from Hodges on our left as we moved over and I never did find the 20th on our right.

Thompson spread the men out line abreast and we advanced like beaters at a farmer's shoot. Shells burst occasionally ahead and behind, sending up walls of milky brown dirt. But some distance away, still not threatening. The German guns seemed to be aiming for the ridge or for our reserve tanks coming up behind. Fritz had more pressing things to deal with, I told myself time and again, than to pick on a lonely thin platoon, insignificant dots on a bare hillside.

Up close the abandoned tanks were a sorry sight. Some undamaged, out of petrol or broken down. Then the partial hits, the direct hits, buried deep into the loam by shell bursts. But *Helen* was not one of them and there were no crews to be seen.

The descent to Les Rues Vertes was over a series of small plateaux followed by steeper slopes. Here the ground had been cultivated in furrows. This far behind the German front line a crop of sugar beets had recently been harvested.

I could see tanks down in the town, clustered like a meeting of green toads around the metal bridge over the canal. Held up by something.

I had presumed that we would have an unopposed walk to meet up with the tankers again. I did not understand about pockets of resistance left behind by the tanks, or how deadly McAdam's mopping-up could be.

We were well down the hill, off the last plateau and on to the final slope leading into Les Rues Vertes when we ran into the Maxim. The machine-gun was positioned no more than two hundred yards up from the first dirty brick buildings of the village. No more than piles of rubble and collapsed beams.

The gun itself could not be seen. At the bottom of the field, behind another thin hedgerow was a bank or a sunken road, I could not tell which. The machine-gun was well embedded using the depression like a trench, completely obscured.

The Germans, probably no more than two or three of them, had let us come half-way down the field before they opened up.

But the Maxim had started too soon. Their machine-guns, like ours, would not elevate above ten or twelve degrees and from their position in the sunken road we were too high up the slope when they fired. Bullets ripped into loose dirt at our feet, creating a line of miniature craters and dancing earth a few yards ahead. And that terrifying judder of a Maxim spewing death.

The German crew paused after their first traverse, to try to increase elevation, to clear their gun, to consider the effect of their opening burst. And in that moment the platoon had scrambled forward, down to the farm track and the low pile of rocks and bushes to our front. Retreat would have been better, but our rush ahead to the cover was instinctive, without orders.

As we landed hard under the hedgerow, now within the gun's elevation, the heavy rattle started again. Bullets smacking into leaves and stems, singing off rocks. Shards of lacerated greenery poured down on to our backs.

The machine-gun had started traversing again right to left as we made our run and two of the new men on the flank of the platoon had been wounded. Stumbling, collapsing, they had been propelled forward by the others in our headlong run.

Now we all lay flat, pressing into the ground, willing the white mud to take us in, cover us over. Bullets flying so close that almost any movement would put a backside, an arm or a head into the line of fire.

Further down the track on our left a mound of beets lay ready for collection in a long pile a few feet high. Large and brown like giant walnuts. During a break in the gun's firing Thompson detailed eight men to make a run for the beet pile. They rushed the few yards of open ground safely, leaving the rest of us with room to spread out. But that was the extent of our ability to move. Now we were trapped.

Our trap was a shallow sloping basin. On all sides open beet fields stretched up to a close horizon east, west and back the way we had come, less than half a mile in each direction. And bare to our front, down to the hedgerow hiding the Maxim.

The OCB plan simply would not work. To move, even to pull back, would be fatal with all of us exposed on the slope to the machine-gun. And in any case, I rationalized, before I asked Thompson, the enforced halt could serve as a rest, until something turned up or we could find help. We were isolated, but if we lay flat, we seemed safe for now.

I passed the word along for Higgs to make his way over. He arrived slithering in the white slime like an eel.

'Corporal, I want Barber to take this back for the tanks. Should be fifteen of them in the reserves with the 29th, very close behind.'

I had written out a field message to be given to any tank commander Barber could find.

I AM AT D22 T43. ENEMY MG STILL ACTIVE IN FRONT AT D22 T45 (ESTIMATED). PLATOON PINNED 200 YARDS TO SOUTH OF MG POSITION. BEHIND HEDGEROW. REQUEST ASSISTANCE. TWO MEN WOUNDED. BEAUCHAMP 2/LT. 'A' PLATOON/'C' COMPANY. 6 DIV/18 BRIG BY RUNNER.
1420 20-11-17

Barber worked his way over and listened to me carefully, then to Higgs who gave a second explanation rearranged in miners' order.

'Sees 'ill be'ind? Whe' we's coom over? Tha's where you's t'go oop ba-ack...'

I had to watch but I did not want to as Barber crawled away up the field. The cover of the hedgerow gave him less and less protection as he moved further away. But either the Maxim crew had not seen him or they were unwilling to elevate the gun and expose themselves to our rifles for such a limited target. To my intense relief Barber disappeared over the ridge without drawing any fire.

All fell quiet in our field but I could hear the bombardment thundering all around, their 5.9s, then our 18 pounders starting up in reply from close by. That was some encouragement. SE5s flew low overhead, dipping, weaving toward the German lines, but no other troops were to be seen within the limited boundaries of our horizon.

I would have tried rifle fire at the Germans, or a burst from the Lewis, but with our heads flat on the ground when the Maxim traversed, I could not be sure of their exact location. And any firing over the mound without a loop-hole would have exposed heads and shoulders. I wanted no more wounded, I thought, not this far from a CCS and not when we could just wait.

And as Thompson said, the Germans might move back on their own if we were quiet. Maybe the tanks behind them down in the town would make Jerry nervous about his line of retreat. There was nothing to do but wait. The Red Line on the other side of the canal seemed a long way off, unattainable. At the moment even what we had already done looked like a miracle.

'Might'ave used the Vickers 'ere, sir,' Thompson said, over by my side again after checking along the men. 'Finished 'em off with a quick burst from behind the beets.' But without *Helen* we had nothing.

We each apologized to the other: Thompson for the whole idea of bringing the Vickers, me for allowing us to be separated from *Helen*.

'That's the sodd'n' war, sir,' Thompson said into my ear. 'Hasn't been thought through. Tanks that far up and us stuck behind in the open, just like before.'

But if the tanks had waited for us at the ridge, even more would have been hit.

Hadn't been thought through.

I crawled along the platoon on stomach and elbows. The men were more than tired. Exhausted and exposed, groggy now from no sleep and over-stretched nerves. Some were too worn out even to smoke. They just lay on the wet track, heads on their packs. We would have made a poor showing against any sudden counter-attack.

We were now at forty-one men, counting Barber and the new additions. The NCOs were at full strength and all safe, Thompson, Higgs and Tulley.

At the far end of our position Davis was attending to the wounded men, both from Sainsbury's platoon. In civilian life Davis was on a Pit Rescue Brigade and he knew about wounds. One man had been hit in the face and the chest. He was unconscious and it looked bad. Half his face was covered with a field dressing. Blood thick with flesh and hair covered the rest, his cheeks, forehead and chin.

The other man had been hit in the foot and the ankle. He was conscious and in great pain. Davis was giving him morphine pills and I let him take two heavy pulls at the untouched rum in my flask. The man lay on his back covered with a greatcoat and smoking a cigarette, hand shaking, white lips trembling.

'It'll be a gonner, sir?' he asked in a stuttering whisper. There did not seem to me to be any doubt. The limb was mushy like mincemeat in his blood-soaked trouser leg and shredded puttees.

'I've asked for tank support,' I replied stupidly, my hand on his chest in what seemed like a meaningless gesture of sympathy, 'then we'll get you back to a CCS.'

Within an hour we heard the motor. A Male tank lumbered over the ridge from behind and to the right then she clanked down toward us. *Felicity* from F Squadron. I waved and pointed from my position, still flat in the chalky water. The tank commander understood the situation immediately. He made across the field toward the hidden bank at the bottom.

In desperation the Maxim crew opened fire at the tank, disclosing their location. I could hear bullets striking the tank's plates, blistering and whining off into the air in all directions.

Then from a position in front of our hedgerow, no more than one hundred yards from the German gun, the tank's cannon opened fire. A series of explosions in rapid succession and the Maxim stopped. The tank reached the bottom of the field leaving a trail diagonally across the furrows. Then *Felicity* turned right along the edge of the bank like a trench manoeuvre and began firing again, using the cannon on her far side.

It looked like an easy win, a large irate badger against two or three cornered weasels. But suddenly there was a tremendous roar from the tank engine. A wild revving, a desperate screech of gears like the last frenzied cry from a doomed animal. I watched as the tank toppled over down the bank, wanting to scream but unable to make a sound, muddy fists clenched in horror, squeezing at my temples.

Felicity had ditched, miscalculating the slope, rolling over and away from us on to her side.

Her motor stopped and all was quiet again. Even the artillery fire and aircraft engines seemed to pause for that frozen moment. I could see one tank track in the air over the top of the bank and part of her smooth belly plate caked with sandy soil from the beet fields. Exhaust smoke hung above the capsized tank like a dark halo.

From that moment, that dreadful silence in the middle of the battle, with *Felicity* over on her side, the next events were muddled. Some in the sequence seemed faster than could possibly be, others slow, agonizingly slow, never ending. And some minutes were lost, blanked out of my mind.

First there was Thompson, out from the right, on his feet, running across the field toward the tank, rifle at the trail. As fast as his legs would carry him, fully stretched like a racehorse at the gallop, suspended, not touching the ground it seemed, skimming over furrows, floating. A picture in a dream.

As he ran Thompson waved at me, finger jabbing over toward the Maxim position. The tank might have eliminated the enemy gun but Thompson wanted covering fire anyway. He was going to release the tankers, his cooked sardines. Shaken, concussed, lying on top of each other sideways in their metal box, scorched by hot pipes and boiling oil. After seeing the inside of a tank it was easy to imagine.

'Ready, aim. Two o'clock. Hedgerow. Two hundred yards. Enemy gun position. Use your own judgement. Five rounds rapid. *Fi-ah.*'

The men scrambled with their rifles as I shouted, rolling over, fixing themselves on the rocky road. Rifles cracking all around me as Thompson disappeared safely over the bank and down to the tank.

Suddenly there was a *crump*. A huge explosion as a howitzer shell landed in the field ahead, between us and the tank. Then another and another. Sheets of dirt and smoke obscuring everything to the front.

The progress of the tank down the slope had been in full view of the German battery behind Masnières up on the other side of the canal. Now they were finding their range.

Crump. crump. Again and again.

An advancing tide of brown loam suspended in the air in front of us. Deafening, stunning, the earth shaking, vision blurred. Bigger, much bigger than 5.9 shells. Now more than one howitzer was concentrated on the same target and whole corners of the field were flying at us in upside-down cones.

I was paralysed by fear, unable to move. Fear for Thompson down the bank, obscured by the spouting, cascading dirt. Fear for my platoon only yards away from the explosions, rocks and soil covering us like heavy snow.

Then an explosion like the falling sky. A burst like the crack at the end of time. Directed by the heavens at me alone, on top of me, louder, much louder than the loudest thunder. Rifting my head in two.

But then, no, I was still alive, the shell had not been for me.

The shell had hit the pile of sugar beets to our left. Beets raining through the air, split, shredded, white stars against smoke and dirt. I saw one of my men from behind the pile, up in the air, arms out, pointing back below him. Like a man in a blanket toss trying to break his fall. His outline suspended, a sprawling shape against darkened sky.

It was the very next instant, I thought, right after the thunder clap, that I was out in the field to our front. But lying face down on the furrows, halfway toward the capsized tank, coming to.

Then I was quickly back, fully awake, face pressed into the dirt. Soil like army porridge thick in my mouth, grit between my teeth, up my nose, in my eyes.

Higgs was kneeling next to me.

Looking back at the field I could see bodies higher up between shell craters, lying in fixed attitudes of violent death. The men behind the hedgerow were safe but the beet pile was gone.

The shelling had stopped.

I had been hit on the forehead. Higgs was holding a piece of metal. Twisted, grey on one side, green on the other, round not jagged.

'Tha' were a piece o'luck, sir. Must 'a' bounced first.'

I was covered with dirt, in my hair, down the neck of my shirt. My cap was gone. I could feel a large gashed lump below my hair line, blood on my scalp, down into my eyes, warm and thick. Dark red on my mud-covered fingers.

'Been out a few minutes, sir,' Higgs said as I looked around. 'On yer way over t'tank, when shell hit.' He seemed to realize that I could not remember.

I struggled to my feet. Between the time the shell had hit the beet pile and finding myself lying in the dirt, I had no idea what had happened. There were seconds or minutes missing.

Higgs and I stumbled down toward the tank, close together as if for protection against what we were going to find. My Webley dragging along the ground on its lanyard.

The scene over the edge of the bank was fascinating, searing, everlasting.

The thin hedgerow at the bottom of the field marked the bank of a sunken road, as I had guessed, a drop of five feet or more. Like a trench, the position could have been defended against three or four entire companies by a well run Maxim.

Two or three hundred yards up the road the German gun-crew lay spread across the pavé as if stretched out for a snooze on a summer's day. The slope behind them was scorched black and the remains of their equipment lay scattered on the field below: a folding chair, helmets, coats and belts of ammunition. The tank had made more than one direct hit on to their position with her cannon.

But closer to us, below where Higgs and I stood on the edge of the drop, the road had erupted into a large crater. At either end of the hole pavé stones were still linked together like a jigsaw puzzle, held together in a neat frozen ripple.

Buried in the crevasse was *Felicity*, but only her rear half, over on her back now. The remains of her muddy under-plating face up to the sky, torn across like a piece of pastry. The front of the tank was nowhere to be seen. Sections of track and jagged stars of steel lay everywhere on the road. Then smaller metal shards like the one Higgs held in his hand were scattered in a paper trail around the crater out in a wide circle.

''Owie scored right on,' Higgs said. 'Then petrol and ammo went up right after.'

I looked blank, unable to remember.

'On yer way to help Sar'nt Thompson,' Higgs added, realizing that I was struggling, still unable to recall.

No tankers were to be seen in the pit. There might have been some bits in the remaining half of the tank, some hands, feet, heads, if I had looked, a cap, a pair of gloves. I saw nothing and nobody could have survived.

But there was one body.

Lying on the pavé further down, about twenty feet away. Intact, I thought. A sleeper on his side, I thought. Head facing away from me. Quiet and motionless.

Then as we approached I could see that the body was charred, the uniform burned. Only the badge, only the rocking horse, only the West Yorks badge was untouched.

But the sleeping body seemed strangely short, shorter than it should be.

So horribly short.

It was Thompson. Thompson's torso. Just the top of his body, from his waist to his helmet which was still strapped on to his scorched and blackened face.

''E was on top of tank,' Higgs said in the quiet. ''Ad door open just as shell hit.'

Thompson had been trying to save the tankers' lives, his tinned sardines.

I stood and stared, hypnotized, vacant, unable to register what it was that I was seeing. As if that stare would go on for years and years. Fixed for a lifetime.

6

It was raining as we entered Les Rues Vertes. A fine persistent rain that hit sideways and upwards like spray from Cornish rollers off Sennen Cove. Soaking any surface not already drenched in mud. The kind of rain from which there is no protection.

We had lost all semblance of order, arriving at the first house in the village in a ragged bunch. One shell would have taken us all. We huddled down into a cellar off the main street and Higgs began to give orders, posting a sentry, having the men eat from their rations.

Higgs was a competent man, I thought, as I sat hunched on the floor with my bleeding head in my hands. Watching his boots go by, listening to his Yorkshire talk. He should have been a serjeant long ago.

Higgs was an example, he was doing something.

I picked myself up and counted. Twenty-eight of us, Higgs the only NCO remaining. Tulley had gone with the beet pile. The two wounded we had left at the hedgerow full of morphine, sure that the advance line of the 29th could not be far behind.

One of the two holies from Sainsbury's platoon wandered round the room with his arms over his head as if trying to surrender.

''Tis a temptation of the adversary who is always seeking to disturb our peace...' he wavered.

Then he was trying to get the men to sing, the thin voices of him and the other one drowned in a torrent of curses.

> Jerusalem, my happy home,
> Apostles, martyrs, prophets there...

Knock i'orf...back in't ruddy barn wiv yer...shu' yer f-ing gob.

Barber had caught up with us as we entered the village and I made him an acting lance-corporal.

Blood had washed down into my eyes with the rain. Davis wiped my face. Then a field dressing around my crown to stop the bleeding made the wound look more serious than it was.

''Elmet would've done nowt for that, sir,' Davis said. 'Right smack in the forehead.'

He gave me a big smile.

I left them trying to start a fire and walked down the outside of the village toward the canal, stumbling over little vegetable gardens at the back of a line of ruined houses, looking for someone to report to, someone to join up with, an arm around my shoulder, somewhere to hide.

The day was darkening under low cover and nightfall would come quickly.

I could see no possibility that the infantry would cross the canal that night, take the last of the Hindenburg trenches and pass the cavalry through. I could see no tanks on the far side of the canal and there was in any case no arrangement that I knew for remarrying infantry to tanks for an attack. Only the 29th would know about that, but we had arrived at the canal before them.

Angry flashes from the German artillery showed less than half a mile away now, reflected against dark clouds up the hill past Masnières on the opposite side of the canal. A battery duel had started between our guns and theirs and no shells were landing in the village.

The realization of Thompson's death began to spread through me. I could accept him being away, not there with me at that moment, not by my side for some good reason, but *never*? Never to see him again, never to hear his voice... 'would be fine, sir, but...' I could not live with *never*.

A wasting disease of *never* crept across my chest, down my arms, pulling me to lie down, there and then, to beat the ground with my fists, sobbing into the mud of the gardens. To give it all up whatever the consequences.

The true weight of *never* seemed to crush me, draw my life away, seeping out into loose earth. Numbness, paralysis. Physical and spiritual anguish all together, crushing debilitating pain like I had never known before. A sag to my entire body, a feeling of helplessness, of utter despair. Sliding on black slippery rocks against the current of a powerful river, unable to take another step forward, going to fall, falling.

But I staggered on. Looking down at my boots, one foot in front of the other through the rain. *Gebt-mir-meinen-Jesum-wieder.* Slowly, in time with my steps, a dirge now. Without my cap, bandage sodden in the rain, but cooling the throbbing lump on my forehead, water running down the back of my neck. I could not have been more wet if I had jumped into the canal.

I cared for nothing, nothing at all. Not for me, not for myself. At that moment, without Thompson there was no reason left for anything.

I came across a tank halted in a village lane leading through to the main street. *Fantasia* and two others behind were parked up on a pile of rubble, but hidden from view to the canal and the German guns beyond. A captain in a leather jerkin and cap was standing by the open hatch.

I shambled up to him.

'My serjeant's been killed...' I began. 'Thompson...the best serjeant there ever was...the best, he was like my fa–'

I made no effort to salute and I had no idea what I was saying. And now with the sight of this stranger I knew that I was going to cry. I felt like a child, unprotected, helpless, like the first night at school without my mother. Unable to go on by myself.

'Here,' the tanker captain said, 'come in here.'

He pulled me through a doorway and into the nearest house. Inside two or three tank crews were drinking cocoa. He poured me a cup from a pot on a spirit stove. He put his hand on my arm as he handed me the mug.

'Who are you with? Where are your men?'

The hot cocoa, the tanker's hand, the warmth of his body close to mine. Just for that moment even, his sympathetic look, the question about my men. I managed to pull up enough to answer.

'My platoon. We're lost. Separated from our company. In a cellar a few houses up.'

'Town's a bloody mess,' the tanker replied as if to excuse my condition. 'Bridge has collapsed. One of us from F Company, *Flying Fox*, tried to cross during the afternoon and the whole damn thing went down.'

The captain looked at me to make sure that I was listening. Then he went on.

'The lieutenant in charge of the tank lost his toupee. Damn funny. Going to make a claim for it, he says, from the quartermaster. Something special, horsehair. Evidently paid a fortune for it.'

The tanker smiled.

I stared at him as he talked on, about how ridiculous the crew of the *Flying Fox* had looked clambering out of the water grasping the girders of the bridge. Like medieval monkeys in their chain-mail tank helmets.

The tankers must have lost scores of men, I thought, but the captain had not broken down. And yet he was neither cross nor disdainful at my behaviour. He understood, I knew he did. A wave of trembling came over me and my eyes poured with tears again. These men in this room were my family, my protectors, the people I loved...I covered my face with my hands and I wept.

I started to say to myself the thing that I knew the best, like the Lord's Prayer. Or like the hedgerow: some of the men swearing to themselves under their breath after each traverse of the Maxim, *fucking Christ, Jesus fucking Christ*...Over and over.

If I got the wind up, I said to myself, if they saw me with the shakes, I said, my men would be in danger. I repeated it, again and again under my breath. My men would be in danger. My men. Danger.

I took my hands from my face then tried to wipe away the tears. Blood was still running into my eyes from under the bandage. I drank my cocoa, hot and sweet.

'Have you seen *Helen* anywhere?' I asked, encouraged by the sound of my own voice. 'She's carrying our Vickers.'

'The haitchers have headed hover to Hades,' the tanker replied, keeping up the humour. 'H Squadron are trying to get to Rumilly, by the bridge up at Marcoing. You could take the main bridge if you want, the collapsed one, it's strong enough for infantry, but I don't know if the other side of the canal is secure.'

Then the tanker started to laugh again.

It would be useful, though, if we had a few trained apes, like the crew of the *Flying Fox*. His crew laughing with him this time.

There was a noise outside, a large body of men arriving. Through the open door I saw horses groping over the loose rubble in the streets, hoofs skittering from brick to brick.

A cavalry captain burst into the room and looked around briskly. Tunic, Sam Browne and riding boots, jerkin, no overcoat. He seemed keyed up, nervous excitement ran through him as if he was wired into electricity.

The tanker captain stepped forward. But before he could speak, a torrent of words came from the cavalryman.

'Any idea what in Christ's going on? Supposed to be through the god-damned Hun lines by now, riding round Cambrai, cutting 'em off. No goddamned orders. More bloody meetings. Meetings, conferences, no *orders*. What *is* this, a railroad or a war? What the *Christ* is going on? Big hole, here to Marcoing, could have a whole division of cavalry through by now. Who the Christ knows *anything*? How many fucking chances like *this* are we ever going to get?'

The cavalry captain had a flat nasal twang to his voice. I thought that he was an American, a volunteer perhaps. He paused for a moment to draw breath. The tankers stood in a circle watching him passively, drinking their cocoa.

Th cavalryman seemed to sense that something was wrong.

'Oh,' he said, looking around. 'Oh yeah, you damned Imperials. Can't go anyplace until we've done the intros, can we.' He laughed. 'Well, I'm Captain Campbell, Duncan Campbell, Canadian Cavalry Brigade, B Squadron, Fort Garry Horse.'

Another cavalry officer came in from the street and the Captain introduced him as well.

'And this is Lieutenant Strachan, from Winnipeg.' Then the Captain plunged on. 'So?' Looking impatiently around the room, disappointed that the tankers had made no response . 'How do we get across the fucking canal and get this goddamned war over with?'

But for the tankers, the Imperials, the introduction was incomplete without a joke.

'Would you mind telling us where this Fort Garry is, old chap?' a lieu-tenant asked from the back. 'Never heard of it. Could be in Lower Saxony for all we know. And how about that What's-its-peg-place? Sounds very Bosche to me.'

The tankers must have known perfectly well where Winnipeg was but the Captain fell for it.

'Manitoba, Canada,' came the immediate reply, 'where you'll find the prettiest girls in the entire world.'

Oh, now the tankers understood, they said. The colonials had arrived so the war was as good as won and we could all go home.

Through the windows we could see the streets around the tankers' canteen filling with cavalry. Horses with saddlebags of all kinds, men in coats and gas capes, ammunition belts over their shoulders, rifles, swords. Water had been brought from the canal and the animals were drinking, noses buried in to canvas buckets.

'Awfully dangerous for you lot in the village,' another tanker lieutenant began, watching the throng of men and horses, 'all sorts of shrapnel been coming down earlier.'

'Well,' Campbell started again, 'get us across the cocksucking canal then. We're much safer galloping toward the enemy than hiding from him.'

The tanker captain produced his map. He explained once more about the main bridge and the *Flying Fox*.

'But there is another bridge, a footbridge just up from the town, by the first lock.' The tanker captain pointed. 'You could go over to Masnières here.'

'What sort of state's it in?' Campbell asked.

'Probably needs the approaches cleaning up for your horses.' Then an idea lit up the tanker's face. 'We've got this lost platoon here,' nodding over at me, 'in need of something to do. Had a bad time it seems. How about using them to prepare the bridge? There's no one else about.'

'Great,' Campbell said, 'just great.' He was ready to go immediately. 'You on for this?' Looking directly at me, sweeping me up with his magnet, just with his eyes, pulling me into his sparking electrical field. 'Ya brain still in there?' Chin out toward my bandage and a fast smile.

'Yes, sir,' I replied, my spirits returning, infected now by the power of the Canadian captain. Maybe we would see some cavalry over the canal that day, just as McAdam had predicted.

'Great,' Campbell said again. 'So, let's go.'

With that Campbell punched me on the arm, hard, enough to make me wince, then he propelled me out of the door in front of him. A hearty laugh and a *seeyalater* to the tankers.

There was no time for anything else, I was with the Canadian cavalry.

The men seemed better after their time in the cellar. Higgs had managed to light a fire and make tea. Water had been drawn from the canal, even though Higgs had seen German bodies floating against the collapsed bridge. I felt less guilty about the cocoa.

I explained to Higgs about the cavalry. He and the men were soon enthusiastic.

'We who are found were lost,' I misquoted. But Higgs knew his Bible.

''Ope they bring hither the fatted calf, sir,' he chuckled.

We were coming back.

We began to clear the access to the bridge: rubble that had spilled from the back lanes, shattered timbers and roof tiles down off the houses on both sides. We laid bricks and boards over a muddy shell hole in the pavé by the canal. Rain fell steadily but the men worked hard and well, requiring little encouragement. Even the holies were picking up bricks. Machine-gun fire could be heard flinting off walls, but too high and we were not held up.

By now the Hampshires from the 29th Division were through, crossing the footbridge in force while we worked. A Hampshire major came up to me as I stood watching our progress. Muddy and hatless, my head still streaming through the sodden bandage.

'Where's your helmet?' he asked. 'There's bound to be shrapnel soon. You'll get another one of those in the head.'

'I lost my cap, sir. In a barrage up the hill.'

'You need a helmet, you damned little fool,' he replied with a kindly look. 'There's plenty lying around. Don't want unnecessary casualties, do we?' And that was all I really needed. Some encouragement. I would find myself a helmet.

The major asked me what we were doing. He too was immediately enthusiastic about the advance of the Canadian cavalry.

'Maybe it won't be a bloody balls-up yet,' he said, almost to himself. The major looked at the badges on the shoulders of my men.

'What's the West Yorkshires doing up here? Shouldn't you be further over?'

'I don't know sir, I was directed down to Masnières ahead of the 29th and I lost contact with my company.'

'Not to worry,' the major said. 'I'm going to leave you one of my serjeants to hold up traffic as soon as the cavalry are ready to cross. Then when you're done come to see me at Battalion HQ, over on the other side. We'll find somewhere to park you.'

I reported back to Captain Campbell and his cavalry when the approaches were ready.

'Pretty good for a pongo,' he laughed. Then he punched me again, harder, right in the same place.

The Captain leaped on to his horse like a Red Indian in the moving pictures. He gave a series of hand signals. In an instant the entire squadron were on their horses behind him, moving out from the protection of the village streets.

The serjeant from the Hampshires hardly had time to get his men off the bridge before Campbell was leading his cavalry forward at a fast trot with no intention of stopping or even slowing down for anyone. Then up and over the arched structure with a little wave to me and the horses were on to the Masnières side in a tight line of nodding heads and bouncing riders. My platoon followed, mixed in with the Hampshires.

Higgs was right behind me at the head of our file.

'When in doubt advance? Isn't that infantry motto?' Higgs had heard McAdam say that on the ridge and it seemed to bring some sense to our situation.

The Hampshires had captured a bridgehead on the far side of the canal only an hour or two earlier, losing men against German machine-guns and snipers in the town. But by the time we crossed most of Masnières had been secured.

The bodies of both Hampshires and Germans lay all along the canal quay.

From the footbridge we could look over at the main bridge on the Cambrai road joining Masnières with Les Rues Vertes. Girders had collapsed into tangled wreckage covering the *Flying Fox* which lay in the remains of the structure, sagged down to the water. Like a fly in a spider's web.

Shells started falling back in Les Rues Vertes. But the German spotter planes had left the darkening sky and the range was wide.

On the other side of the canal Masnières was a ruin, much more severely damaged than Les Rues Vertes. The town was physically broken. Most buildings had taken direct hits and those still standing had been lacerated with shrapnel, tearing off tiles and blowing out windows and doors. The church spire was gone and the remaining walls of the nave were no more than a few courses high. The entire village was all the same colour, a dirty black over dark red bricks, coated with dust and smoke.

We found another cellar and we reassembled. Again I went in search of *Helen* and the major from the Hampshires.

Masnières was the battlefront. Less than one hundred yards from the last house at the end of the town was the Masnières–Beaurevoir Line, but the

Germans were defending forward from their trenches and some were still hidden in the maze of debris.

By then, in the early dark, trench weapons were flying through the air from the German lines: Minies every few seconds and coal-boxes in groups of four. Most landed in the canal and beyond us. Looking for bridges and locks to stop our advance. Machine-gun fire was coming from every side, ricocheting down the streets. Larger artillery shells were still passing overhead in both directions. The noise was tremendous.

Grime-covered troops stood in file up side alleys out of the field of fire, waiting for the order forward.

I found a group of Hampshires occupying the main floor of what had once been a large house. Now all the upper floors were missing. A captain was peering out of a shattered window, looking up and down the street as I ran in through the front door.

'If you're going to do a spot of window-shopping you'll need a tin hat,' the captain said before I could salute. 'Here,' he passed me a helmet, 'we've spares. One previous owner, looking for a good home.' I strapped the helmet on over my bandage.

The ceiling of the room menaced the occupants with two pregnant bulges on either side of a rococo ring where a chandelier had once hung. I was sure that the remains of the structure was about to come down. Killed by a plaster cornice when not wearing his helmet. That was not how I intended to go.

'So where did you spring from?' the captain asked. He agreed with me readily when I told him that I was lost, nodding his head up and down with exaggerated comic movements and smiling. I should have been a long way to the west, near Marcoing or up by Nine Wood.

'But never fear,' the captain said, friendly and forgiving like the major at the bridge. 'You've fallen in with the redoubtable B Company. Battalion HQ is off on the right somewhere. We can always use you for clearing out the town.'

I asked after *Helen* and here there was definite news. I was told that H Squadron would be back at the Masnières bridge, their next rallying point, the following day. I explained about the Vickers.

'A Vickers, by Jove.' The captain was enthusiastic. 'Now that's what I call enterprise. You'd better stick with us.' Not my enterprise, Thompson's.

The captain placed us to the rear of his company as they moved out of the side streets and north through the town in the deepening dark. We were to guard any civilians the Hampshires found as they worked along the streets, house by house, clearing out the Germans.

Small-arms fire was dying down and there was a lull in the artillery bombardment.

All night the search went on. The Hampshires could have made better progress by throwing bombs into each building, but in many of the cellars and the far inside parts of the bigger houses, there were French villagers. Huddling rag-piles of black shawls and blankets, possessions in bundles. Sacking or cooking pots over their heads for protection.

The town had been occupied by the Germans for three years. Despite the tragic circumstances, the destruction of their town, the loss of all their possessions and the deaths of many family members, the French were overjoyed to see us.

As the Hampshires passed through each building and the civilians were handed over to my platoon, there was embracing and tears, kissing on the cheeks and a torrent of explanations about the last few days, of the grief and now the joy.

I found a man who had been hiding in the attic of his house, in the dark for three years. Trying to avoid deportation to Germany. He was pale and weak, like a fish from the bottom of the deep sea. He looked over sixty, but he said he was thirty-five.

Every dirty bundle held a little cache of wine or Cognac and out it came, pressed on my men. I thought that the men, like me, were about to come to the end of their endurance, but the drink cheered us all.

During the night we had moved to a larger cellar under the destroyed *mairie*, close to the canal, which we established as an assembly point. We escorted the French back as they were found and the mopping-up of the town went on.

After midnight Barber came to see me. The thought of the bodies of our men killed behind the beet pile on the slope down to Les Rues Vertes was upsetting everyone. We had stripped two of them of some rations and the Vickers parts they were carrying. Then we had left them all where they had landed, anxious to find cover for us, the living.

'Can't just leave them all up there wi'nowt, sir. We all wants to go back and do burial, say our goo'byes or sum'at.' Thompson had hardly been out of my mind for a moment.

We set out in the early hours, during a pause in the Hampshires' operations. Me and five men, leaving Higgs and the rest to look after the French and to be available when the house-to-house clearing started again.

The night was black and very cold. Across the canal the rain intensified, beating on my new helmet like a long-drop roof. We passed back over the footbridge, around Les Rues Vertes and up the slope the way we had come.

Now the back area was alive with activity: anonymous figures dark in helmets and gas capes; machine-gunners and the artillery digging in; tank maintenance crews working on the conked out buses we had passed that morning. The hedgerows had been laid waste by traffic and the field was hard to recognize, but once we crossed the pavé road I was able to navigate.

The howitzer craters up the field were tracked and trodden in by then and the beets thrown up by the explosion had vanished. Eaten maybe, or pushed into the mud.

The bodies had gone, buried by the 29th, removed by battalion stretcher bearers, I had no idea. There were no field graves, no boots, no helmets. Nothing to say that in this place on this day, nine men had died. With their lives, their loves, their hopes and their futures.

The men stood forlornly on the black wet hillside deprived of their goo'byes. I walked back toward the crater and the tank, the remains of *Felicity*. Initials and an arrow had been painted in white on her side. What was left of her had become a convenient signpost.

But below the road, splashed with mud, surrounded by discarded gear of all kinds, I found a tiny body. A cinder, overlooked in what was now a military rubbish tip.

The men came down and we stood in a circle around the dark shape. Someone leaned down and wiped off a shoulder badge. The rocking horse glinted faintly out of the dark.

'I'm going back,' I said to the group. 'He just can't be buried here, not in this mess.'

There was no disagreement. We had brought blankets for the burials that were now not necessary. We cut off Thompson's discs and wrapped him carefully in two layers, tied up with string. He was even blacker than in the morning, almost unrecognizable. As if in a day or two more he would have melted back into the soil, been washed away in the puddles and rivulets of the field, leaving only his helmet, a muddy bump on the ground.

That was what we were promised. The body with the tag, no matter what the condition, if delivered to the rear, to a Regimental Aid Station, the body would receive a marked grave. Better than a shallow forgotten hole and half a bag of lime.

That is what they had promised us and that is what I did.

The men hoisted the body on to my back and I carried him. Hands patted at the blanket as I left, as I set off with my small load. No bigger than a child.

And this way I knew. One day, I promised. One day, I told him as we walked together back over the ridge, one day when it's over. We'll meet again, you and me. Here in a peaceful and prosperous France.

One foot in front of the other through the night, sliding on the rocks in my black river, slipping, ready to fall, falling. *Never.* With my grief and with my tears again.

By dawn Masnières was cleared except for the church where a number of Germans were holding out in the catacombs.

The Hampshire captain came to see my refugee camp. We had over twenty French in the cellar of the destroyed *mairie.* Higgs had organized water, latrines as well as food from the Hampshires' trolleys back over the bridge.

'Good,' the captain said, 'but now we have to move them to the rear. We're going for the Masnières–Beaurevoir line and Crèvecoeur. Zero for this one is 1100.'

The French had thought that their deliverance was the end of their ordeal, not the beginning. But there was bound to be a heavy bombardment that day if an attack was to go in and they had no helmets and no gas masks. They had to move but there was nowhere for them to go.

'You see them across the bridge, Lieutenant,' the captain said, 'then point them in the right direction. There's nothing more you can do.'

They could have a meal first. Using my schoolboy French I struggled to explain the situation to the few men in the group. They must find safety to the south. We must fight *les boches.* There was more wailing and more tears.

'*Le gaz,*' I tried, '*vous n'avez pas de masques. La bataille va recommencer. Tout de suite.*'

After the French had been escorted over the canal but before we headed them toward Fins, we found another hot meal trolley run by the Warwickshires on the south edge of Les Rues Vertes. A rough mess had been set up in a barn and here we ate with the French. Breakfast, lunch and dinner, all at the same time, enough for two days back and one day forward. All ranks together, off our laps with filthy hands. The smell was thick in the air: changing room, morgue, hospital and canteen all together.

The barn was crowded with men of the Fort Garry Horse including Lieutenant Strachan. He was wounded in the neck and many of his men had field dressings on arms and legs.

Strachan told me what had happened. The squadron had vaulted over the Masnières–Beaurevoir line within minutes of crossing the bridge, galloping straight at the unprepared Germans in their trenches. There was an opening with no wire where the German line met the canal further down. Then they were through to the enemy back areas before Jerry had time to organize.

There had been some splendid moments, the Lieutenant said, just like he had dreamed about as a boy in Swan River, Manitoba. Surprising their guns, charging disorganized infantry units with sabres in hand.

But almost immediately the Germans had started to encircle them. One or two machine-guns was all it had taken and the squadron were off their horses and down into a sunken road, trying to defend their position with rifles. In a quiet moment in the middle of the night after they had held off the first German attack, the squadron had stampeded their horses to create a diversion. Then they had started to make their way back on foot.

Here was the result in the barn. Only fifty remained of the one hundred and fifty troopers who had crossed the bridge the previous afternoon.

In that ruined barn the dead were all around me.

Men I knew, men who yesterday had been alive, whole, brave, capable of anything it seemed. Captain Campbell, all the others. I still had his bruise on my arm. Even the Germans we had killed, arms up in the air and panic on their faces. And my own men, men I was responsible for. Then a man I had loved, a man who in my heart I had called my father.

Dead, all gone. In that barn, exhausted figures wrapped in their coats eating without a sound, they, me, we were merely the core of the dead. The thousands and thousands of dead who surrounded us, I had no idea how many. But we were separated from them, from death, only by an hour or two, by a day maybe.

And for what? Masnières the ruined town? For that beet field? Who had made this whirlpool, drawing in a generation of men? This interminable abattoir, a Sausage Machine that ground on and on, stretching back to Fairy and that other life all those years ago.

It was at some point on that day, the second day of the Battle of Cambrai, the day I carried Thompson to the Aid Post, that my despair turned to anger. Barely controlled, boiling, driving me on when I had nothing else left.

Before dawn the Hampshires called a briefing and I took a place at the back of their cellar by the church.

There was going to be an attack on the Masnières–Beaurevoir line, ordered by Division. The attack to gain the Red Line that should have taken place the day before. But as I listened even I could see that there was to be none of the organization or the support promised in McAdam's briefing before the battle had begun.

The tanks had not arrived at their rallying point so there was no cover and the wire would be untouched. There was no communication with the artillery so there might or might not be a bombardment. There did not appear to be any cavalry ready to advance even if a hole could be opened in the enemy lines. And in any case, the prime objective of the entire battle had become a wood somewhere off to the west. Now Burlon Wood was to have priority for tanks and artillery. The objective of passing the cavalry through at Masnières and around Cambrai was no longer important.

But the Hampshires had been ordered to press on anyway, to take up the positions marked on a map hanging on the cellar wall. Detailed instructions would be issued before zero.

The Hampshire captain shook my hand when the briefing was over. I never knew his name.

Then we were handed over to C Company of the Middlesex Regiment, in support under Captain Abarth. He placed us on a stretch of canal quay just outside the town.

From our new position I could look east down toward a set of locks. The canal crossed our front line diagonally less than three hundred yards away, then curved south and out of sight. Forward we faced the main street of the town and the Masnières–Beaurevoir trenches above. The canal ran immediately behind us and the collapsed bridge was two hundred yards to our west.

My job in support was to ensure that if the Germans came up the canal, they could not circle behind us and envelop the Hampshires during their attack.

I could see a section of the German parapets up beyond the village, to the right of the shattered church spire. A formidable sight, thick wire and well prepared revetments, all uphill from the edge of the town. Only with tanks and heavy artillery, I thought, could such an objective ever be taken.

During the morning we tried to improve our position, fortifying ourselves into the ruins of a warehouse. We had only three shovels, the rest discarded in favour of the lost Vickers and our extra supplies. But it was impossible to dig through the flagged quay of the canal so we built up a parapet in rubble and timbers within the plinth of the destroyed building, camouflaged as much as possible from the air. More Middlesex in support lined the canal to our west, around the approaches to the bridge.

No tanks appeared and our barrage on to the German lines was sporadic, not even enough to stop their coal-boxes and Minies. Machine-gun fire came at us from every direction: through the gaps in the houses to our front, along the canal, singing off brick walls, thudding into the rubble in the streets.

As 1100 approached I was sure that the attack would be postponed or cancelled. Without tanks or an effective bombardment it would be the stories of 1916 all over again. It was now impossible to stand almost anywhere in the town.

But at eleven o'clock precisely I could hear whistles and see men start to appear like mushrooms on the slopes beyond the town.

I clutched Higgs' arm as we watched over our brick wall. Helmets and packs coming from nowhere to run for the wire, a few here, a few there, tin soldiers on a board.

Officers were waving their arms, running up and down their positions, mouths open, shouting but unheard against the deafening roar of the battle. Then men started to fall, some face down as they ran, others throwing their arms up to the sky with the impact of many bullets hitting at once, rifles and bayonets making wide arcs against the horizon. Some appeared to trip as if merely falling off the edge of a pavement. Within minutes the attackers had dwindled to nothing.

To our right a complete line appeared, a platoon, over forty men. They stood up in their shallow holes and started to advance, well spread out at a uniform military distance.

Through the din of the battle an extra octave joined in, another heavy edge to the constant rattle of Maxims. The line crumpled and fell. Left to right, like a drill movement for straw dolls, every single man down with a sweep of the scythe. Barley stalks at harvest time, waving then falling in an autumn breeze.

Then another group ran out from behind one of the shattered brick walls to our front and started toward the German line, darting left and right up the hill away from us. One at a time they lost men until all had sunk below the ground well before the wire was reached, drowned in a wave of lead.

I turned to Higgs. His mouth was wide open but he could not speak. I was still holding his arm, both of us paralysed by what we had witnessed.

Finally words came.

'That's England that is. They gott-a bloody stop. They gott-a bloody stop it.' Then, 'God, dear God . . .' and his words failed.

I trembled. I waited for the heavens to open in response to Higgs' unfinished prayer, for an intervention, even for an explanation. For an end, for a new beginning. But nothing came. They had died in their scores, there before my eyes. Against just the little piece of German line that I could see. There they lay, dead. And the battle, the war, that very day was continuing as if they had never been.

Over the next hour, with the Hampshires' attack repulsed by a pull on a trigger, the sweep of a frame, the Germans increased their bombardment. Looking for our reserves, or the next wave, or the bridges again to cut off the reinforcements that we did not have. The footbridge received a direct hit and the canal was filled with splinters of floating wood.

Then a Minie landed on to the right of my platoon. The explosion beat inside my head, threw me away from Higgs and hard against the back wall. The blast blew half of our ruin and five of my men into the canal. The remains of a cellar wall, used as a traverse in the middle of our position, shielded the rest of us from the blast.

Up through the froth some bodies appeared for a moment, floating, arms out in the debris like sailors in a shipwreck.

Without even another second for us to mourn or to pray again, a group of coal-boxes fell into the canal on top of them, sending up more spray, a column of foam fifty feet or more in to the air. The bodies disappeared.

And immediately shrapnel, I thought, 5.9 shells exploding in the air over the town. But I was wrong. Higgs was scurrying around between our brick piles.

'Gas,' he yelled, 'get yer sodd'n' masks on.' Thompson's expression.

The shells were harmless compared with shrapnel or mustard gas. Toxic smoke, the latest German invention, intended to penetrate our respirators. But as I had learned at OCB, our new box-type masks were fitted with cheesecloth to filter out smoke particles.

A dark cloud developed, hanging over the town, obscuring the battlefield. In goggles and masks we looked eerie, faceless and brave, like machines. The miners were used to gas mask discipline and confined spaces, they were having no difficulty. But I could see very little and breathing was an effort through the cheesecloth. I held the stem of the respirator in my teeth for two anxious hours while I watched the smoke clear and the battle subside. The German bombardment trailed off.

Limited by the mask I had not noticed the arrival of the tanks on our flank, lumbering up our side of the canal from Marcoing. They had assembled by the end of the collapsed bridge less than one hundred yards from our fortification. *Helen* was third in line.

Before I could make my way over to the tanks they started to move off again, up the main street of the town toward the German trenches. There was no opportunity for coordination with the infantry, most of whom I presumed were already casualties of the attack.

It was back-to-front, farcical, criminal.

The German bombardment started again. High Explosive looking for the tanks. In front of the section of trench I could see from my position, the tanks rolled over the wire and made their turn. But all the tanks had used their fascines elsewhere and not one was able to cross to attack rear positions. The tanks rolled up and down flattening more wire and firing into the trenches below.

But without the cooperation of the infantry and unable to deal with the support trenches behind, the tanks seemed to be making little impression on the German lines. Two tanks came to a stop, hit or broken down. Hatches opened and crews were running at full speed back toward the Hampshire lines and the protection of the town, under the cover of their machines.

Before dusk *Helen* was back at the rallying point by the collapsed bridge and I was able to catch Woolridge.

'So, the girls in Cambrai were frustrated again, eh, Lieutenant?' he said as he took off his chain mail helmet. 'This whole show after the first couple of hours has been a ruddy nightmare.'

Woolridge had some idea of the results of the Hampshires' attack. There were bodies everywhere on the hill.

'Didn't get told that we were needed here until a few minutes before the latest zero,' he said. 'We were over at Noyelles and we came as fast as we could.'

The tanks had not been able to communicate with the Hampshires to arrange a postponement.

'Now it looks as if Jerry isn't as afraid of us as he was. Their infantry are hiding until we have gone past, then out they pop again behind us. And some of them have armour piercing bullets, improved over the last lot, as well as mortars in clusters which they shove under the bus.'

We crouched down behind *Helen* but the battle had subsided once again. Darkness started to fall quickly and the tanks were safe against the German artillery.

Woolridge took me to the back of his tank.

'I believe you ordered a Vickers, sir,' he said, with a little bow and a mock smile, pretending to be a head waiter. The blankets containing the barrel, stock and ammunition were unrecognizable, crusted with mud and rubble, but inside everything was there.

'Hope it gets you home,' Woolridge said, 'because that's where we'll all be going in a few days. No sense in holding on here.'

Higgs and I set up the Vickers in a window of our demolished building, up on a platform of planks and bricks. Then we filled in around the muzzle, leaving only a slit to cover our field of fire.

Thompson was the expert. He had been a Vickers instructor during 1916. He said that the posting had saved his life. But with Higgs I could remember enough of my training to put the gun together. Water for the jacket was quickly drawn up from the canal. We did not have to line the boys up and have them piss into the spout after all.

Then Higgs fired a burst down the water. Our spirits rose as we watched the surface churn up white under a hail of lead of our own making.

All night wounded Hampshires passed us, carried slowly over the ruined metal bridge back to an Aid Station set up behind Les Rues Vertes.

The dead were also taken over the canal and laid out in a field on the far side of the village to await burial. A wooden cross was placed down each body, marked with name, number and date. My dead, whatever was left of them, had floated off down the canal. Once more there were no remains to bury.

The next day more men of the Middlesex Regiment and the Royal Fusiliers came over pontoon bridges which had been constructed during the second night. They took over the Hampshire positions, but this was no organized relief and nobody withdrew. Men of all three regiments were now mixed together under whatever officers had arrived, or the few officers from the Hampshires who had survived.

A number of days passed.

Our new troops skirmished with the German trenches. We fortified our position again and we tried to sleep in the cellars of the nearest houses.

Supplies came up every day, hot food, huge quantities of SAA, signals, but no reinforcements, no relief.

Rumour had it that there were no more troops.

Hardcastle and the battalion might have been relieved by then. Back behind the lines, having a bath, eating at a table, drinking wine, but we were part of the 29th now and we would stay.

Captain Abarth of the Middlesex treated me like one of their own and I heard no complaints from the men. The ground we had gained had been paid for too dearly just to pack up and go.

I was out in the shattered town, the ninth day of the battle, on the day the Germans came for the first time. In the early evening, checking the plan I had drawn of the canal bank. Pacing out the field of fire I had assigned to each man to cover, when the counter-attack came that Thompson had promised.

Walking back toward our fort, through a ruined courtyard, round a corner of crumbling brick, I came face to face with death.

With my own death, the death that had been prepared for me alone.

He was a large man, well nourished but ungainly. Thick like a tree trunk in his grey tunic. His rifle slung across his chest over a pouch of grenades. His face shadowed, blurred by the flare of his helmet.

In his hand he carried a short trench shovel sharpened around the curved edge like a large cheese knife. The arc of the blade glinted in the moonlight.

Immediately he saw me he lunged but missed, the shovel chipping the wall above my head. But he pinned me in my terror with his shoulder and his elbow, sideways against the bricks, while he pulled at his belt for his bayonet.

His weight was more than a match for mine and I knew that he would quickly have me down. I weakened with the inevitability of losing, watching as if from a distance as the hand with the bayonet pulled back to strike.

Behind, grey shapes were darting through the shadows, it was hopeless. Even if I could struggle free there were more, many more behind. I had met my end.

I felt his breath in my face, stale, reeking of onions and cheap liquor. This was the man who had my name. I had met him nose to nose.

In that same instant I struggled for my Webley, squirming away from him. But quickly he had me pinned again, the stab of his bayonet postponed for that fraction of a second. I could not reach my gun, but in that desperate moment I caught the man's wrist holding the bayonet above me. Then I snatched his other arm holding the shovel, from against my chest.

And with a wrist in each hand we danced. Out into the street by the light of the moon, his helmet against the night sky, the blades of his weapons two shafts of pale light. I tripped, I felt I would go over, but I held on, stumbling, contesting strength, arm against arm, prancing chest to chest.

His face came round into the moonglow and I caught two eyes burning cold under his helmet. Hatred, vengeance, determination, recognition of death. Kill or be killed. In that instant we each saw the same thing.

Then the German shrieked, head back, mouth wide, up to the sky. The cry of mortality, the advent of death and I was saved. Saved before I could grasp what had happened.

The man lurched forward, his weight limp and heavy against me, then he fell sideways on to the cobbles.

On the other side of the prostrate German stood Higgs. Like an actor revealed from behind a curtain, rifle at the hip, ready to strike again. A thick black red dripping off the end of his bayonet. Higgs had stabbed the German through the back, from a run, hard and deep, clean through, so that the tip of his bayonet on the other side had ripped my greatcoat and stained me with the German's blood. I stood and I panted. The dead German. My life. Higgs in the dark street with his narrow satisfied look.

We said nothing. We turned and we ran, bullets singing in all directions. But the dance through the doorway had kept me out of sight of the attackers for the few seconds we needed to leap into our shelter and open with the Vickers. Blazing down the street before there were any clear targets.

Soon the entire town was a cauldron of gunfire, Mills bombs and German stick grenades. *Stoßtruppen* bent on vengeance for our gains.

They came again the next morning at dawn, waves like the crashing ocean. Along the canal, across the streets that led down the hill, supported by aircraft strafing the ruins and dropping fragmentation bombs, wheels skimming ragged rooftops. Minenwerfer on trolleys were hurried back and forth across the main street and Maxims were worked forward from corner to corner down toward the canal.

There had been no bombardment to warn us of the attack but the Middlesex held. We were deeply embedded into the ruins of the town, through a labyrinth of rubbish, broken walls and cellars. Our fire was accurate and for now the enemy could not bring their weapons to bear against us.

The German counter-attack failed that day along our front in Masnières and they had lost the advantage of surprise. But Captain Abarth had no doubt: with the next attack or the one after, within a few days, our defence of the right bank of the canal would be overwhelmed.

7

It only remained to withdraw from Masnières and to acknowledge the failure of the entire show.

Captain Abarth was determined not to leave anything behind, no wounded, no dead, no ammunition. His hatred for the Hun was all consuming. He would give them nothing, no satisfaction of any kind. Nothing but an empty ruin.

The captain put life and survival above everything. Higgs had heard that Abarth had been so severely wounded in '15 that he had not been expected to live. Now, it seemed, every day, every British life was precious, even in the middle of the battle.

Before we left, the Middlesex conducted another search through the houses in the town, room by room, cellar by cellar. But this time looking for our bodies, Hampshires or their own men who had crawled under cover during the attacks. The wounded who had died alone, of thirst and starvation, unable to call for help, buried in the devastation. A few were found still alive.

Bodies were taken back over the canal all through another night. German dead were brought out and left in the streets.

In the afternoon of the final day as the search was coming to an end, the German bombardment started again. By then their 5.9s had registered the town, huge and intense. HE falling in tight groups then singles in fast succession until a pall of dust and smoke covered the rubble. As if the bricks themselves were on fire.

The pontoon bridges were the first casualties, chopped into floating tea leaves within the first half hour. But our lifeline, the collapsed bridge of twisted steel girders, was still untouched. There was no gas shelling so we knew that another attack was coming close behind their barrage. This one we would not be able to turn back.

In our fort backing on to the canal we were sheltered from flying bricks and masonry. But the impact of the explosions was so terrifying, the wait for a direct hit between each successive blast so tense, that I doubted I could survive the next. I was sure that I would start to scream, run away, throw myself into the canal. We had been in battle for twelve days.

The earth shook with each salvo. And every second or two it appeared that the rubble, the bridge, the water, my men next to me, were all disconnected from the earth. Suspended, jagged and jumbled in space.

Abarth appeared from the right again and gave me my instructions. He was clear, encouraging, hunching up his shoulders and pulling a face with every round, shouting in my ear. This time we were to pull back across the canal when the German attack started. Then I was to work my way south and find my own unit again. Abarth was almost cheerful, saying he would be in touch later, through Brigade.

'But you mustn't get caught over here, Mr Beauchamp. Jerry has been reinforced and we've got nothing. We're going to be enveloped soon through Les Rues Vertes.' Abarth's mouth right against my ear. 'You'll get the signal as soon as the main body is clear. You've plenty of SAA and you know the drill. You'll be able to get clean away.'

Abarth crawled through our defences checking my arrangements, down to Higgs on the Vickers at the end. He squinted along the jacket of the gun and out through the slit between the bricks.

'Keep 'em well back,' he advised, 'or else they'll start throwing potato mashers, or firing rifle grenades if they can get near enough.'

Abarth crouched close to me and wrote out a field order.

3-12-17. 1425 2/LT BEAUCHAMP. ATTACHED W. YORKS PLATOON TO COVER WITHDRAWAL. MOVE BACK ON 2 × GREEN VERY FROM S. SHORE CANAL. ABARTH CPT. 2ND MDLSX 18BGDE.

'Look,' Abarth yelled over the bombardment, 'you'll be good for a while. It'll take them an hour or two to bring up their bag of tricks. We'll all be gone by then except for the other rear guards on your left. But listen,' he finished, shouting louder again, 'if their artillery gets on to your position and they start knocking seven bells out of you, shellfire any closer than this, never mind my orders, the Vickers goes into the canal and you all scamper back. Understood?'

I nodded but I was unable to return Abarth's smile.

'You've been here too long,' he mouthed, 'not long now. Hold on.' Then he and his runner were gone into smoke and dust west along the canal.

I was delirious with fatigue, close to collapse, kept upright only by sheer hatred for the enemy and his HE. An unrelieved urge to homicidal vengeance. Hatred of war and those who had brought me to it. Of the Bosche in this quiet French town which their invasion had laid waste. Only that burning wick in the middle of my tallow kept me from crumbling, weeping again, burying my face in my hands at the bottom of our fort, paralysed by the shelling.

The Middlesex had completed clearing the centre of the town and were withdrawing through their flanks when the Germans appeared again for their final assault. The bombardment had lifted beyond Les Rues Vertes and we waited for them in our ambush, crouched down behind the bricks.

At first they were only shadows, dark flitting shapes through smoke, across the end of the main street, up at the top by the church. Then I saw them down side streets and along the bank of the canal. Heavy coats flapping against their knees, mottled helmets quite unmistakable, clear silhouettes in low afternoon light. *Stoßtruppen* again.

With the enemy at less than three hundred yards, Higgs fired his opening burst up between the buildings. Bullets bouncing off the walls to our front with a twang and a whine. From then it was three hours before Abarth's Verys went up. Three hours of unbroken action for every rifle in the platoon and a continuous deafening clatter from Higgs on the boiling Vickers, the floor of our fortification slippery with empty casings. And in those short hours, that lifetime, I learned in my stomach about defence.

Only vastly superior numbers of *Stoßtruppen* were going to push us back from Masnières when we had no reinforcements. But then we would establish our line again further south and their advance would fail like ours. From prepared defences even a few Vickers guns could hold off whole brigades of infantry or cavalry.

I saw it clearly. This way the war would never end.

In the war of movement during the summer of 1914 the Germans had taken Cambrai and all the French towns in the north, the population, the factories, the coal and ore mines. But there it had stopped, at the trench line. Now they could not advance against us and we could not push them out. Men against machine-guns and artillery. Them then us, us then them. It would be stalemate for ever and my entire generation would disappear.

In the seconds after I saw Abarth's Verys flaring a murky green through smoke, the Vickers was over the edge, hitting the water with a sizzle like fish into hot fat. The men scrambling between brick walls and out of the fort. Higgs had them along the quay and on to the metal beams of the bridge in less time, it seemed, than it took the gun to sink. I stayed for a moment longer to throw our belts of unused SAA on to the bubbles and rising steam.

As I ran behind them it was like my first trench raid again. Every part of my body held ready as I cut through the air. Waiting to be torn, ripped, turned into a shredded heap of bloodstained khaki. Black, without life, a former person. I saw myself lying in the street on my back, mouth open, unseeing eyes staring up at the sky. Like all the others who had died in that hell of Masnières.

Then I too was over the edge of the quay, clinging to the girders of the collapsed bridge before the Germans could take their vengeance on me, for my Vickers and for my murderous crew. We had accounted for over forty of the enemy.

I was two days on the journey back, with Higgs, Barber and the last fourteen of the platoon. Twelve of mine and two of Sainsbury's including one surviving holy. The remains of fifty-two men.

By then the German counter-attack had retaken Welsh Ridge and La Vacquerie, pinching in from the east, occupying the ground we had covered on our advance almost two weeks before. We headed west toward Marcoing then south to Flesquières.

The slopes back up from the canal were a scene of utter chaos. It was impossible to believe that this was the British Army. Both the 12th and the 55th Divisions had come close to complete collapse. Now they were retreating across cratered beet fields in a disorganized shambles, trying to avoid encirclement by the advancing Germans.

German aircraft flew low over this rabble machine-gunning at will. There was no sign of the Royal Flying Corps.

Phosgene gas lay on lower ground like morning mist on a lake. Men without gas masks who had thrown off their kit earlier in the rout crawled along vomiting into the mud.

All communications had been cut by shellfire or by retreating artillery trains and no commander from lance-corporal to colonel knew anything about the situation other than what he could see around him.

The fields were littered with our abandoned equipment: from full packs to greatcoats, from rifles to motorcycles. More shelled-out tanks surrounded Flesquières.

Bodies lay everywhere, mixed up with dead horses still harnessed to field gun limbers and splayed mules strapped into panniers.

It was bitterly cold. Snow started to fall, giving the battlefield a hopeless look of total desolation, throwing the living without a covering of white into sharp dark relief.

As we progressed we took shelter in abandoned dug-outs and shell craters against shrapnel and air attacks. We heard all the rumours: every man for himself had been declared. How Jerry would soon be back on the Somme.

A serjeant from the Guards, badly wounded in the leg and delirious, was being treated by stretcher bearers. He was muttering and looking around furiously.

'Soldiers, sir, soldiers, sir. .' although none of his officers was present, '...hardly creditable, sir, to think that British soldiers...'

We were told that the delays on the first day had been due to an argument about tank tactics. A general had ignored the tankers' battle order of three in formation, sending his tanks over the ridge to our left in line abreast. The result had been the destruction of twelve tanks by one German battery alone. Then the waiting cavalry that was supposed to surround Cambrai had been turned back for fear of shrapnel.

At a railway crossing outside Cantaing a brigadier was standing by the road, smoking and taking names. I showed him Abarth's orders. He showed me his list of over one thousand men he said, retreating in a rabble, running without orders. We heard of men threatened by their officers, pistol in hand, trying to organize defence.

I found that Hardcastle had installed himself in a comfortable dug-out, an elaborate deep hole with log walls, concrete stairs and a ventilation system.

This was our new front line: the Hindenburg Line, the Blue Line we had crossed before noon on the first day, the day of our Great Victory. We were five hundred yards from where we had started.

By then the German counter-attack had subsided and a new stalemate had resumed.

I entered and saluted, the wrong movement without my cap. For our reunion I had left my donated helmet up the trench. My wound was healing and the bandage was off.

Hardcastle looked at me in silence, for longer than seemed reasonable.

'So here's our brave and hatless Frog,' he started at last in mock surprise.

Then suddenly Hardcastle began hurling words at me as if we were already halfway through an argument. There was nothing left of C Company. McAdam had been sent to another command along the line, Sainsbury killed, Granforth wounded. Wonderful young men. Sandhurst men. There was only Hodges left.

'But now here's our Pet Frog.' Another long stare in complete silence.

Finally I realized that Hardcastle was drunk.

'They rang the church bells,' he started again. 'Rang them all over England. Boomed it in the newspapers. We were through the Hindenburg, the war could have been over. Our Division, the Battalion. Do you have any idea what it would have meant to be in the Corps that won the war? Handed to you on a silver platter, victory on the Western Front, the whole bloody war. And then what? You subalterns, no training, not the slightest under-standing of military matters, you little half-wits have let it slip through your fingers.' Hardcastle was sipping neat whisky out of his tin mug. I could smell it. I would have liked a drink myself.

'What the hell do you think this is?' Mug swaying backwards and forwards as he tried to find his mouth. 'A cross-country? A steeplechase? What goes on at those OCBs, Mr Beecham, eh? Teach you how to knit, do they? Certainly weren't taught how to read a map. What the bloody hell were you doing in Masnières?'

I had no idea how Hardcastle knew that I was in Masnières, there had been no opportunity to report or to explain.

I began to protest. This time I was going to answer. I thought I had seen too much not to answer. The impossible orders for the first day, the changes of plan at the Brown Line then again at Masnières. The Hampshires cut to ribbons. The tanks without fascines, no artillery, no support when the Germans counter-attacked. The terrible mess Hardcastle had not seen up the hill back to the lines...

Hardcastle started to bang his empty mug on the table and I was stopped in full flight.

'You, sir,' he roared, 'you sir, could be put on a charge for insubordination. We've dealt with mutineers before, you know. Oh yes indeed.' Hardcastle started to rock side to side in his chair. 'But it seems you've been out making new friends,' he said quietly and went back to his intense hostile stare, fumbling to pour himself more whisky from under the table.

There was no mention of the Vickers.

'We're going to move to billets,' he started again. 'Re-train. More training, that's what you civilians need. But you, Beecham, no, I'll be rid of you.' The hatred was out in the open now, fouling the air between us like a bad smell. 'By God, Mr Beecham, I'll be buggered if I ever have to look at your impudent bloody face ever again.'

The next day, after a night in the support trenches, Hardcastle told me that he had been on the telephone. Talking to his old friends at Étaples, he said, finding me a post somewhere out of his skirts. Transport, he said. Something insignificant, he told me before I was dismissed. There was a slot at Montreuil, at GHQ. So that the Staff can see for themselves the sort of junior officer material the line battalions are expected to work with. Just try your insubordination with *them*. And I was to take my contaminated serjeant with me. Hardcastle would be rebuilding his battalion properly, right from scratch. He meant Thompson.

By the time we moved out of the line for Villiers Plouich and Fins, for baths and clean clothes, beds and food, Hardcastle was drinking steadily from stand-to at dawn then round the clock again.

I left for my new posting with only a goodbye to Higgs and the men.

~

'I thought that was the end of active service for me. They have their little networks, those kinds of people.' The old man closed his eyes.

Morley tidied up the bed tray. Elaine was in the kitchen, long faced and exhausted. Maisey had died just after midnight.

'You're probably on the start of a death watch too, you know, Morley,' she said. Her features softened. 'You'd better take the Lay-Z-Boy from Maisey's room.'

'I promised him I'd see him out. But he's so strong when he talks. I couldn't even remember that much about last week. Do you really think he's close?'

'I've seen it so often, dying people find one last surge of energy and the important things can come back crystal clear. The sad part is that usually there's no one around.'

Morley had sat with Elaine in the kitchen on weekend nights discussing death. Point D, the fourth on Robert's list of the nine symptoms of depression. A morbid interest in death.

Elaine was developing an idea, the Recording Angel Project. The latest head-of-a-pin technology combined with Canada's army of over-educated-but-unemployed youth. Recording life-histories from the dying to ease their passage. Each departing life comforted by knowing that they had a place in the river of Electronic Eternity. She laughed. Like the Mormon Annals of the Saved, but open to everyone and way way more useful.

'How long can you stay?' Elaine looked at her watch. 'It's coming up to three a.m.'

'My ancient friend has me completely absorbed, but I'll need to leave for the office pretty early. Hectic day coming.' Morley dragged his fingers down his cheeks to accentuate fatigue.

'The day shift will look after him, he can sleep till whenever,' Elaine said. 'They can bring in an extra nurse if needs be, he doesn't have to follow any routine. But you'll probably find that he tires pretty soon. Then he might be OK for a day or two. Hard to tell.'

'I'd like to make some notes, the dates and places he's talking about. I could do some digging in the library.'

'There's a dictaphone in the office for Living Wills. Take that, your boy's the only one close now.'

Morley returned to the old man's room with another Ensure.

'Next time, Morley, bring us a good bottle of wine. I hear it's pretty potent through a straw.' The wrinkled skin around his mouth cracked a smile.

Morley had made himself tea. He sat by the bed with his mug, watching the old man draw from the Ensure can resting on the bed tray. The room, the hospice and the city were completely quiet in the small hours of the morning. Morley's heart beat slowly and the acid in his veins seemed to have lost its edge. Here, in this bare room with a dying man he could be *whole* again. *Whole and useful.*

'What about family? Is there anything I can do?'

'My wife Mary went to France before I fell down the stairs and they had their excuse to open me up. We have a house there, part of the roof blew off in a wind storm. She's on her way back but she had stomach trouble and put off her flight. I don't want to be fussed over and I asked the hospital not to notify anybody. I want to remember without being disturbed. Mary will phone when she arrives.' His eyes closed again.

'Do you want to rest?'

'Promises are so important.' Rest was not on the old man's mind. 'A promise should be like an exquisite little jewel, infinitely valuable, irreplaceable. Something you can carry in your pocket. Something you can take out and look at when you need to. But you only realize these things when it's too late.'

'This put you off?' Morley produced the dictaphone and set it on the tray.

'It was the peace,' the old man said, ignoring the machine, 'that was the trouble, all the promises that were made. And none of them was meant, not one, not by either side.'

'I'd like to make some notes later,' Morley continued. 'See where all these locations are. And I'll have my office bind the music with your loose letters into hardcover.'

'We need maps, Morley. Northern France, Germany. You can mark them up in your fine architect's hand.' He tried to smile again. His arms slithered off the tray and down to the sheets.

Morley wheeled in the Lay-Z-Boy from beside Maisey's bed. The van from the morgue had just been, the room already stark and clean, ready for the next. Then Morley sat, his hand resting on a thin grey wrist.

What was the old man's connection to Vancouver? Morley wanted to ask his questions. If he had a house in France then why did he live on the East Side, the poorest part of the city? How and when had he come to Canada? But the old man was preparing himself to start again.

8

Captain Vernon, and his superior officer Major Graves, were some of the very best types I met during the war. Straightforward and approachable, modest yet extremely knowledgeable. Always prepared to think what it was like to be in someone else's boots, even me and my drivers. They both had friendly smiles as if they had caught the habit from each other.

Vernon had run a little garage before the war and motors were his speciality. Then during two years at General Headquarters in Montreuil Vernon had expanded his knowledge and enthusiasm for mechanical things into a real talent for motor vehicle organization.

On my first day Vernon gave me an armband to wear over the sleeve of my tunic. A crude red and blue, dull faded colours like medieval stained glass.

'A sign of the ultimate source of both honour and blame,' he said as I put the band on my sleeve, feeling ashamed, my tunic blemished. A front line infantry officer skulking in Transport.

I had the usual prejudice. How all GHQ did was swank around with Red Tabs on their collars, sitting in the back of shiny cars, on a gorgeous mike with their cushy jobs. And to keep up a show of work they issued all kinds of fool orders which nobody in the trenches even had the time to read, much less to follow. They knew nothing of what really went on or what their orders meant.

I would have preferred to be anywhere in France other than Montreuil.

Vernon was anxious to change my point of view but I was an unwilling convert. I still thought of myself as one of the walking dead, with my nightmares, my faces and my list of names.

Thompson. Tears came into my eyes at all times of the day and night. Flashes of memory: Thompson's smile, his gold teeth, his arms folded across his chest leaning against the trench wall. Looking up and down the column in the dark, smiling to himself as the men sang.

But I found that it was impossible to blame Captain Vernon or Major Graves.

'Think of it this way,' Vernon explained. 'We can't sit and do nothing with the Germans occupying 20 per cent of France, with the French being our allies and the Bosche trying to dominate Europe. Once it had started we couldn't just let them win.'

Vernon was tall and thin, no curve to the back of his head, straight up from the neck. As he talked Vernon swayed from the waist, forwards and backwards like a tree in the wind. He was earnest and believable. His jokes were the same, always with a straight face.

'But whatever we do, we have to learn from scratch. This is a completely new war, the British Expeditionary Force is the largest organization Britain has ever produced. Only the London County Council comes anywhere close in size and so far their enemy hasn't resorted to arms.'

His favourite example was artillery shells. By 1918 we could fire a million shells per day. The Somme was thought of as the largest bombardment ever. But in 1916 a gun on average fired three and three quarter tons per day. Now that was up to five and a half tons.

Vernon asked me to imagine the process from start to finish. Design, manufacture, sorting out duds. Then delivery from the factory in England, shipping, distribution in France. How many times is that shell handled before it is fired? And with such vast quantities, railways had to be extended all the time, then sometimes the guns were moving every night.

'But if the shells aren't delivered, we'll lose the war. As simple as that.'

I understood. But they were not there in the mud, being shot at, going to die at any minute. *Crump*. No more life. Khaki, red, black, blankets, string. No figures on earth can explain that experience.

But in my new posting I did not want any arguments. Vernon was right in his way.

'Then in addition to running the army, there are thousands of miles of civilian railway and roads under GHQ control, half a million mules and horses to feed, twenty thousand motor lorries, their drivers, repairs and fuel. All of it under attack at various times, making alternate plans a necessity and a nightmare. Ten divisions preparing for an attack will require over thirty-three trains of equipment per day.'

I was struggling down Roo Mad'laine again, toward the front line at Villiers Plouich, the men loaded down with fresh equipment. Little of it had seemed necessary to me then, but it had all turned out to be vital, life saving. And someone had been ready for us, days, weeks before. I had never thought of it that way before.

Vernon continued with my conversion to his religion as we walked over to the mess on my first day, clean, tiddleyposh, going for a nice civilized meal.

He described the other important functions of GHQ: relations between the BEF and the government in England; relations with the Allies, French, American, Italian, Portuguese, Belgian. Decisions about strategy, plans for attack and retreat. Matching that with the supply of all types of equipment from bicycle clips to tanks and the latest field guns. Medical services, the Pay Department, the feeding of the troops; amusement and entertainment; Chaplain services; educational work.

Yes, but, but... I could not formulate my thoughts.

'And all this,' Vernon said proudly, 'is carried out by only three hundred officers at Montreuil, and a further two hundred and forty staff officers in the field.'

Vernon put the whole problem very simply.

The French had been severely damaged by Verdun, by the Nivelle offensive and by their mutinies. Events that were just a rumour in the line. But Vernon used the word openly: mutinies. Now the French had no fresh manpower left to keep their army anywhere near strength. Britain and the

Empire were going to take the weight of finishing the war just as the French had taken the load at the beginning. And if our army was not properly supplied the war would never end.

I tried to grasp that thought as something clear and bright with which I could start my new job. I was one of those officers now, those mythical Tabs, however junior.

My responsibility under Captain Vernon was to organize the cars and lorries attached directly to GHQ itself, 2I/c Motor Pool. I had no knowledge and no experience but if this was another way of fighting, I could make up for my ignorance and win acceptance by keenness.

By 1918 the distinction between Temporaries like me and the Professional Soldier had largely evaporated. There were still officers at GHQ who mumbled about *the non-military mind*. Such defective equipment being an affliction issued at birth, like Original Sin. But even among the Tabs the need to win the war had finally overcome the prejudices.

Three weeks later I understood what Hardcastle had meant about 'making new friends'. Vernon took me aside at the garage.

'Seems you've been awarded the Military Cross,' he said. 'Two commendations during Cambrai, one from the Durhams, one from the Middlesex. Not much detail, you'll have to tell me yourself. Well done, I had no idea...'

I was ready to cry again.

'It wasn't me,' shaking my head, 'it was Thompson, my serjeant. It was all his idea, everything...' My jaw quivering and the edge suddenly close.

Vernon led me outside, away from the men and it all fell out: tears flowing freely, leaning against a tree, freezing in the January frost. A toy soldier in a Christmas pantomime all dressed up in his uniform, blubbing uncontrollably.

Vernon listened to me patiently.

'Well it's too late to refuse,' he said. 'It's already in the official newspaper.' Vernon held out a copy of the *Gazette*. 'You'll find it in the middle, buried among the Flax Restriction Orders and the Companies Consolidation Notices.' He smiled at me.

I turned the pages until I found the list. I was one of three.

War Office
17th December 1917

His Majesty the KING has been pleased to confer the undermentioned awards for gallantry and distinguished service in the Field.

Awarded the Military Cross

T./2nd Lt. Yves Graham Beauchamp, Ox & Bucks Light Infantry. For conspicuous gallantry and devotion to duty on two separate occasions during an attack. While commanding a platoon he charged and captured four enemy guns, first passing through enemy held positions. Later in the same engagement in command of his platoon he remained in position to cover the movement of a part of his Division under sustained enemy fire and bombardment. He displayed gallantry and persistence throughout a trying period and his courage and cheerfulness were an example to his men. His sound judgement and quick actions were a factor in the successful action.

'Trying period ... successful action ...?'

I was about to launch into the entire fiasco.

'Look,' Vernon interrupted, 'I know what you're going to say. Take it for the sake of your Thompson if you want. But an MC is invaluable here among the Staff, help you to do your job. Thompson would have wanted us to win the war, wouldn't he? I've heard about Cambrai. But what good would it do for us to bare our souls to the frocks back in London, for them to make hay with? Our relations with the French would go down the bung hole, the Americans would lose confidence and maybe even stop the flow of new troops.'

I turned away, embarrassed by my flooding tears. But Vernon took me by the shoulders and brought me back to face him.

'Apparently there's nothing invented here, what you did was very brave,' he said. 'The best quality a soldier can have. We always need heroes to put a good face on. And since you're in Montreuil already you're on the list to be pinned by the Chief himself, next time there's a do.'

Vernon turned the page of the newspaper.

'And there was a VC awarded at Masnières,' pointing to the next page. 'Captain Campbell of the Fort Garry Horse. A Canadian. Posthumous.'

That night I wrote to Thompson's widow, tears dripping on to the paper.

GHQ Montreuil
France
2-1-1918

Dear Mrs Thompson,

You will have been informed by now of the death of your husband. I must apologize for the way in which the news was probably given to you. As his commanding officer I should have written to you before this. The Battle of Cambrai lasted into December after which I was immediately posted here.

The war has taken away more brave and dedicated people than I can comprehend, even in the short time I have been in France. But Serjeant Thompson was the bravest of the brave, the most dedicated and able soldier I have ever met, the last person in the army who should have been killed.

Serjeant Thompson gave his life in an attempt to save the crew of a ditched tank. His response was immediate and without regard for his own safety. Before he was able to release the crew the tank was hit by an enemy shell and both Serjeant Thompson and the tank crew were killed instantly. It was during the afternoon of 20 November.

I have been decorated for my part in the battle. But the actions for which the award was made were due solely to Serjeant Thompson's ideas and his coaching. I have tried to refuse but that is not possible. I am therefore going to wear the decoration, but in memory of Serjeant Thompson, knowing that it belongs only to him.

His body was delivered to an aid station that night and he is assured of a marked grave. I will let you know the location when I can. I am sure that we will win the war and find permanent peace and prosperity, the cause for which Serjeant Thompson died.

Yves Beauchamp,

2nd Lt. Ox & Bucks L. I.

Montreuil was a severe, dramatic town, an artists' colony before the war, chosen for its light and stark changes of season. GHQ occupied a former École Militaire which had the appearance of a French railway station right down to the brick and stone façade and the lace curtains in the windows.

I walked between my billet and my desk, or over to the mess, along the old town ramparts high over the surrounding country. In those few minutes of leisure each day there were views in all directions: the slate roofs of the pretty town; over downs and copses toward Crécy; west to the sea, or north over the plains of the River Canche. Wide prospects, a festival of light and colour.

Quiet and beautiful France, as if there was no war.

Life at Montreuil was comfortable in a way that I had never known. I was billeted with two other junior officers in a large house on the chausée des Capucines owned by Monsieur Laurent, the town chemist. His wife had died after a riding accident the year before and his two sons had been killed in the war. One in the first few days of August 1914.

Monsieur Laurent seemed to look to us subalterns to lift the shroud of gloom that lay over the house. With his two maids and our shared batman there was nothing that he would not do to improve our comfort. It was a daily routine of thick coffee and croissants, fresh sheets, clean laundry and pressed uniforms.

In the morning Monsieur Laurent was at the door to wish us a good day, then waiting by the fire at night to serve English cocoa and enquire about our progress in the defeat of Germany.

Monsieur Laurent spoke clear, correct French, keen to distinguish himself as an educated man from the peasants of Pas de Calais. My French improved daily under his instruction.

'*Vous pourriez considérer rester en France,*' he would repeat in his one-man campaign to repopulate *la patrie*. The three of us should stay and take French wives, the best girls in the world. After this great war France and England should be united. Then a year or two later we would have a mistress each as well. Babies and more babies, he said, that would be our next duty.

I had known only the broken down mess at Fins, a partially destroyed hotel where the food was little more than iron rations served on plates. In Montreuil the mess was an elaborate affair, occupying a very grand hotel on the north side of the town. There was a choice of fresh food from a menu typed out daily with French wines or beer from England. Served to a room full of officers in immaculate uniforms, from generals down to me and the few other second lieutenants.

There was no long mess table laid with silver to emphasize an intimidating hierarchy. The room was full of small tables for twos and fours like a restaurant. Groups came and went at different times to fit their schedules. I had not learned to smoke and mess food was cheap. I lived on less than my pay which was now 10s. 9d. per day including field allowance.

There was a convention in the mess against the formation of coteries and each day I was taken to sit at a different table. As the junior in every group I offered no conversation, but within two months I had listened to the opinions of many senior Staff officers from almost all departments.

The hours of work were extraordinary. The endless pressure of the job was in its way as much a drain as the trench sequence: front line, support, then reserve and billets. But here, at first, there was no physical danger.

No Staff officer would be at his desk later than eight and many were there well before. It was standard practice to work until after ten or all night during a crisis. Saturdays and Sundays were the same, without distinction from a weekday. Leave was unknown.

Field Marshal Sir Douglas Haig, the Chief, lived and worked at Château Beaurepaire two miles to the south. He came to the École Militaire most days on his chestnut mare across the open fields. He was a figure from another century: no papers, no briefcase, carrying only his sword.

Haig rarely came into the mess, but when he did appear at a meal, I saw the officers whom I had come to admire, stand up and pay the Chief a respect which I knew was genuinely felt. But this was the man, with his awkward inarticulate ways, looking around with his embarrassed smile, this was the man whom I had heard blamed at the front for the most atrocious massacres in the history of England. A cavalryman from the Boer War, as far as it was possible to be from Thompson's idea of a general who was a Captain of Industry.

It was a Machine, I decided as I watched the Chief walking into the mess for lunch one day, with his spurs and his wordless shy look. It was a huge unstoppable contraption for the consumption of lives. There was no one person whom I could find to blame. There was only War, living a life of its own, eating through towns, countries, through whole populations and entire generations. Without known origin, without reason or prospect of resolution.

In the dining room there was comfort and order, cleanliness and sanity. If there was to be war then all the Tabs were needed. But beyond Montreuil, I knew, there were the true Events. Men, animals and civilians caught in an inferno of destruction and death. It was an extraordinary guilt-laden contrast which I never resolved.

Vernon talked to me again about Cambrai a month later. There had been a Committee of Inquiry into the reverse, after the ringing of the church bells.

'You'll see the report, Yves, it'll even be in the newspapers. But I wanted to talk to you first. The report blames the junior officers and men for Cambrai, their lack of training, poor leadership at the lower levels, that kind of thing.'

I was stunned, incredulous. At first I thought that it was another straight-faced Vernon joke.

'We all know that's twaddle, even Pulteney and the other generals know that. The things you've told me, I believe they're all true. But if you're going to be a reliable Staff man you must understand politics. How to take a bit of a cynical attitude.'

Vernon looked at me carefully to see if my chasm would open up again.

'And of course,' he continued, 'I haven't seen any action myself. To you, probably, playing politics with this sort of thing must seem like the very worst kind of game. But look at it this way. We know that the Bosche is going to attack in the spring. He's been threatening it in his newspapers for weeks. Crown Prince Willi even plans to dine on the Champs-Élysées at Easter. They're trying to get us to give in, to compromise.'

I saw a hard side to Vernon as he spoke, utter conviction in our cause. Accepting whatever it was that had to be done.

'And this will be the Bosche's last throw, there's no question. He'll have nothing left. But to hold him off everyone must have confidence. The Chief is at a low in London and we hear every day that he's going to resign. If there was a scandal about Cambrai our chances of winning the war next year, or in 1920 would be reduced. Then even more men would die in the long run.'

It was an incredible thought. That to lie, to blame the troops for the failure of Cambrai would spare other lives in the future.

But by then it was clear to me. The General Staff had known before we attacked the Hindenburg Line that we would be exposed to counter-attack after such a long advance. Even Thompson knew it. The whole operation had been a huge gamble that the cavalry could get round Cambrai on the first day and win Haig a great breakthrough. And if that turned out to be impossible, we would be on our own without reinforcements. Fodder for enemy cannon. Then later it would all be the fault of the men.

Cambrai was no battle, it was a vast trench raid, impossible to sustain right from the first day. Not thought through, that was what Thompson had said.

It was as if I had witnessed a sniper's kill. I was numb, unable to respond.

'But Cambrai wasn't a total wash-out.' Vernon smiled as if to hold me together. 'We learned about tanks. The Mark V is coming over in quantity now. We did ride over the strongest position the Germans could dream up. And our casualties matched theirs, forty-four thousand each, which for us with our greater numbers, is a victory.'

It was more than I could absorb.

'Although,' he added quietly, 'I suppose it wasn't a real victory if the Germans didn't actually *lose*.'

Before he left, Vernon had news of Major Hardcastle, intended to cheer me up.

'Couldn't understand why he was so hard on you in his reports. Had a chum look him up in the records. Turns out he was at Étaples running training during our own mutiny there in the summer of 'seventeen. They were all sent down the line, training officers, mutineers, the lot, straight into action, only way of dealing with the situation. He seems to have cracked.'

Vernon made a drinking motion with his arm. 'He's back in England now, where he belongs. Don't let anything he said dwell on your mind, Beauchamp.'

I occupied a small office off the central courtyard, the Cour d'Honneur. My men consisted of Machinist Staff-Serjeant Jones, Anson the senior Corporal Driver and an Orderly Room Corporal for administration. Then thirty OR drivers and seven mechanics. Between us we ran three Albion motor lorries, the old 32-h.p. type with solid rubber tyres, ten Daimler staff cars and a rotating assortment of other cars and motorbicycles. The vehicles were housed in a requisitioned civilian garage below the ramparts a few minutes' drive from the École Militaire.

My job was to provide a continuous flow of vehicles and drivers for all GHQ functions. Cars for Beaurepaire complete with the right number of blankets folded to the correct dimensions and laid out precisely in the centre of the back seat. Motorbicycles for running a torrent of messages where lines were down, lorries for the transport of maps and documents between Montreuil and our armies or our Allies. Cars for staff inspections away from GHQ and a daily routine of meeting trains and collecting supplies.

Each evening after dinner, junior officers were allowed into the map room off the mess dining room. On a blackboard next to the map of northern France was a tally of the miles of front held by each of the Allies.

In March 1918 the blackboard read:

Belgians	23	
BEF	116	
French	313	
Americans	6	
Total	468	miles

My fellow officers were quick to point out that we, the BEF, held the active part of the line and that we needed twice the density of men compared with the French.

At 0440 on 21 March 1918, the German attack started and my job became a nightmare, but a different nightmare from Masnières.

The initial German bombardment covered a forty-three mile front of British and French lines. HE mixed with gas, more shells each hour than had been fired on the Somme in every twenty-four hour period. An iron carpet for their advance.

The Germans used a new technique. They presented no lines of men abreast for our machine-guns to mow down. Instead, small companies of *Stoßtruppen* with air support, mobile guns and Minies on wheels were breaking through like arrows all over our front. Reaching through to our artillery or to battalion and brigade headquarters in the rear. Then more waves were mopping up the strong points the *Stoßtruppen* had left behind. It was the greatest single attack of the war and the Allies began to lose men at three times the daily rate of the Somme.

A week later, with German advances at over thirty miles, Major Graves himself walked into my tiny office.

'Here, Beauchamp,' Graves started with a dark look. 'Need to talk to you.'

Major Graves never put on side, he was always complimentary and I tried to be the same with my men. They made a great effort under impossible conditions so it was only right to acknowledge that the frequent balls-ups were not due to their lack of spirit.

Major Graves wanted a job taken on in complete secrecy.

I was to find a three-ton lorry and have the vehicle prepared for a long journey. Then I was to staff the lorry with two drivers together in shifts around the clock. The lorry was to wait in the courtyard for further orders.

Graves said he would tell me what it was about as the vehicle was my responsibility. But it was to go no further, not even to Captain Vernon. The strictest orders.

The outlook was black, Graves explained, and the Germans could break through to the coast any day, threatening GHQ. The lorry was to take away GHQ's maps and secret documents if that happened. Even if GHQ were overrun, the papers would get away, south to Bordeaux and back to England.

But by then I had no lorries. At the start of their attack the Germans had captured our light railway. They had even put our large-gauge tracks under fire, bringing the entire railway system to the point of collapse. Supplies, shells most importantly, had to be carried by road.

Six weeks before the German attack Lieutenant-General Sir Travers Clarke, the Quartermaster General, had demonstrated why he had his job. He had started an exercise, a gym it was called, just on a hunch, it seemed. For no apparent reason GHQ began to pull in lorries from all through the BEF until we had built up a reserve of over two thousand vehicles with their drivers and mechanics, stationed at a camp between Montreuil and Étaples.

Of course Transport came in for a lot of ragging of the humorous-malicious, behind-the-back variety. We were going to fetch wine from the south, or more furniture from England, beds, women maybe.

But suddenly, when the railway system could no longer function, Motor Transport was able to step in with our reserve of lorries and keep the guns going during those terrible weeks.

Men drove for twenty-four then thirty-six hours without a break, accidents were common. But the guns never stopped for lack of shells. After that Lieutenant-General Clarke had my complete respect. I came to see that he contributed as much to victory as any field commander.

My lorries were gone as part of the gym. I sent Minns on a motorbicycle to bring one back. He was away for fourteen hours but he returned successful, the lorry following. Both Minns and Routledge the lorry driver were stupid with fatigue and had to be helped off their machines. Then I set all the mechanics under Jones on to washing, greasing and fuelling. Within an hour the vehicle started its ominous watch in the courtyard, my drivers in pairs doing shifts of twelve hours each.

Every night I watched the map board and listened to the talk. On the tenth day of the German attack I walked over to lunch with Vernon. He must have guessed what the lorry was for but he did not mention it.

'If we go down behind the Somme,' Vernon said as we walked under the magnificent trees on the ramparts, views all round as if out to sea, the war distant, non-existent, 'it'll give the Germans the coast from the River Canche to the Scheldt for their submarines. Of course we'll blow up the harbours first, the French will never give in again like 1870. They'll smash up the whole of Pas de Calais before leaving. But the Germans could rebuild in a year or two...'

'...a year or two? The war will last that long...?'

'...oh yes,' Vernon was sure. 'If Fritz gets the coast this time, the war could last another ten years. It would become a very slow process. We won't have anywhere to land the Americans. We'll have to funnel through Cherbourg, Brest, Bordeaux, much too far and too narrow.'

But even at that moment, so close to catastrophe after three and a half years of war, there was not even a hint of the possibility of failure. We only needed more time to win. Vernon liked to recite the figures, 'the simple arithmetic' he called it. Gave him comfort, he said. Together with the Americans, we the Allies had a clear superiority in men and resources.

'The Germans had their one and only chance at the very beginning because they were ready and we weren't. They had to overrun France by Christmas 1914 or not win at all. Now, even if our casualties are equal to theirs, we must eventually prevail.'

That day, walking with Vernon to lunch along the ramparts, was Black Saturday, our worst day of the War. We could hear the guns around Albert.

And that night standing in the map room, it seemed that nothing could stop the German advance to the Channel.

My nightmare now was of orders, counter-orders and disorder.

Even armoured cables buried six feet into the ground were cut by German shells. On some days the Transport Section became the only method of communication between Montreuil and the field. I started to lose men again as at the front. Messengers and drivers I sent out never returned from the advancing bombardment. Men and vehicles I could not replace.

I began to drive myself to fill gaps and I saw the state of our retreating armies with my own eyes. From Arras to Montdidier, from Chateau Thierry to Compiègne only fifty miles from Paris, it was as if all the men of Britain and France, together with every piece of equipment in both armies, with every horse and every mule, were pulling back across the plains of northern France. Filling roads, parked in fields, waiting behind every hedgerow, covering every distant slope.

And on the faces of the General Staff officers in my cars I saw fear and panic. At the destruction and confusion almost beyond command, at the open hostility of the troops we passed.

Within a week of the start of the battle the Chief and his Staff began to meet with the French. The French were sure that we were going to withdraw to the Channel ports to make our escape. And we thought that the French were going to pull back to defend Paris at all costs, splitting the front and letting the Germans through.

Then frocks began to arrive from London.

I heard that the Prime Minister, Mr Lloyd George, had taken charge at the War Office himself. And far from withdrawing he was shipping every available man to France. His representatives were to be collected from Paris and driven to Montreuil: Sir Alfred Milner, Mr Winston Churchill.

I heard someone say of the Prime Minister, 'I'm convinced that the little man *enjoys* rough weather.'

Conferences were held at Senlis, the French headquarters. Shouting matches through closed doors. Men in shock with frozen white faces climbing in and out of my Daimlers.

Up and down we pushed the cars: through surly hordes day and night, our flags flying, our klaxons wailing. Or along back roads black with jeering refugees, women wagging their fingers, men waving fists.

In April, Général de Division Ferdinand Foch was made Generalissimo of all the Allied armies and from then the road between Senlis and Montreuil became our daily race track.

But with the Australian counter-attack at Villiers Bretonneux the Allied armies finally held, seven miles in front of Amiens, only fifty miles from Montreuil. The Germans had gained a pocket forty miles deep, but their *Kaiserschlacht* was over. They had no reserves and no supplies left. Many of their lead troops were starving, more interested in looting towns and our abandoned store than in pressing their attack as our guns regained effectiveness.

Major Graves had me stand down the lorry in the courtyard.

The Bosche had thrown his last throw as Vernon had predicted. Though they were far from beaten and still capable of a stubborn defence. While we had proven it over again: against machine-guns and artillery, infantry could never win final victory, either theirs or ours.

By August we had advanced back to the Marne. Then there was talk of Fortress Germany and it was the Germans' turn to defend and to have their own Black Day. The German Army began to retreat across northern France to hold the Rhine. But still an end to the war was not even dreamed of that year. Vast preparations had been made to fight through the winter, through the summer of 1919 and on into 1920.

So when the war ended that November, it took everyone by surprise.

I was away on the day, the 11th, on my last gym for Major Graves. I did not return to Montreuil until the evening of the 12th. I found the mess having a huge tamasha. On the day before they had been too busy.

'Know how to do the can-can, eh, Beauchamp?' Vernon asked me with his mock-serious face as I entered the crowded mess, splashing his drink down my tunic. He took me by the waist and began kicking up his legs, coursing me backwards and forwards across the carpet, singing at the top of his voice.

'*Da* da dada, da da *da da* dada...'

I was the only sober one in the room.

'You'll have to do better than *that*,' he panted. 'We're off to Paris. Hotel Majestic. Will that be a single room or a double?'

PART III

1

More than a month after the night of the Café Soufflot and Le Rat Mort there was an envelope waiting for me with the FO porters. No stamp, hand delivered.

A neat female hand with a new nib. As I opened the envelope the slightest breath of a scent reached my senses. Strong and purposeful rather than sweet and inviting.

THE OFFICE OF THE PRIME MINISTER

HOTEL VILLA MAJESTIC, PARIS

16th March 1919

Dear Lieutenant Beauchamp,

Mr Lloyd George has asked me to write to you to express his appreciation for your recent assistance.

He has also asked me to inquire of you whether you could arrange to drive him to visit a number of sites in northern France, in the near future.

If so, would you be prepared to make such a journey on a Saturday and a Sunday?

Please be good enough to contact the writer at the above address.

Yours very truly,

Frances Stevenson

Assistance: that was a fine word. I wondered how much the writer knew.

On the next Saturday morning I stood in front of the car outside the address off avenue d'Iéna given to me by Miss Stevenson's secretary.

Place des États Unis is Haussmann's work in miniature. Wide although short with a park running up the centre. At the far end a statue of Lafayette embracing Washington and handing him a flag, creating a little vista, a reason. Beautiful in an artificial way.

Looking at the park, at Paris, everywhere in France, there were memories of Fairy.

In 1914 on 14 July, the 125th anniversary of the Revolution, at the end of my first year at that school, Fairy's history class had staged a little celebration. For a few it was meant, not a charade. A red white and blue banner hung outside the classroom and we sang the *Marseillaise* in French even though some boys in the class were openly hostile.

'The basis of our rights as men,' Fairy said of the French Revolution. 'And never let those Americans get away with that nonsense about their war of independence, their so-called revolution and their constitution being the first. The Americans are completely compromised, everything made into nonsense, every word, by the retention of slavery after 1776. Even George Washington had slaves.'

LG's official residence was a large suite on the top floor of Number 17, no more than a hundred yards from his office at the Hôtel Villa Majestic. Other Ministers of the Crown lived on the lower floors of the same building. The Hôtel de Crillon was LG's hideaway from them all, down at the bottom of the Champs-Élysées, provided for him by the Americans.

Right on time LG came out through the metal gate. He looked me up and down as if setting eyes on me for the first time. Then he held out his hand.

'Good of you to lay this on, Lieutenant.'

I presumed that LG could not call me *boy* again, which I had liked, because I was wearing my full uniform: old style tunic, Sam Browne, gloves and cap. Greatcoat and valise on the front seat. Some official status, I thought, which with the FO car might be useful at French road checks outside the city. LG liked anonymity. I had seen how it went at the Café Soufflet and I wanted to do it that well, or even better. The Lea-Francis suited the same purpose. A civilian number plate, less obtrusive than a Daimler and no flags.

LG climbed into the back without any instructions to me. His porter closed his door, LG gave him a friendly little wave.

'Going over to collect Frances,' LG said when I hesitated, as if I knew who Frances was other than the writer of the letter. 'Hôtel Raphaël on avenue Kléber, just round the corner. She's just back from London.'

It was a grey, wet morning. There was no traffic, the streets of Paris were deserted. I found Hôtel Raphaël and opened LG's door. Frances was waiting up the steps just inside the entrance.

Frances matched the scent, the genie of the envelope. Handsome and tall, clear features and a fine skin, white and creamy. Upright like a Victorian, that erect posture the bustle and the layers used to give. I could imagine her as a young girl coached by her mother, walking around the house balancing a book on her head.

'Head up, Frances, head up, shoulders back. Keep it on your head, even while you're eating. Come on now, Frances, chin tucked in.' Clap clap.

LG bounced out of the car and without actually embracing Frances, simply by the way he stood next to her, up against her, he managed to convey affection, pleasure and ownership, all at the same time.

Frances could have been the youthful headmistress of a good private girls' school, or the manager of a posh Brighton teahouse. Had she not been diverted by meeting LG.

But soon I saw that Frances applied those same qualities, the efficient school, the well-run teahouse, to being LG's girl. She organized LG's clothes, she ran the Prime Minister's office, she had an instinct for people and for politics. And she met the vast passions of the man, ardent, energetic, infinitely loving.

Frances was clever and subtle, she was discreet but not cunning. Her appearance and her dress were neither ostentatious nor provocative. Nothing that could ever give rise to a comment among LG's many visitors and colleagues. Lapidary but fluid, perfect from her buffed fingernails to her elegant, upswept coiffure.

If Frances had been my girl I would have seen in her, each and every day, the creature of my dreams.

Even to me the driver, the unknown lieutenant, Frances was attentive, seeming to care about my every need. My room and everything in it, ensuring that I had the assistance of a bellboy with the car and the luggage. Asking me if I was tired by the driving, ready to arrange whatever was wanted in her accurate respectable French.

Frances seemed chemically aware in the presence of a male, but in a soft and a reassuring way. Her responsiveness to me was flattering and sensuous, both together. I enjoyed being with Frances right through to my core.

Paris had influenced this quiet precision. For the drive to Nancy, Frances wore a fashion version of aviator's overalls. Grey *perllaine* with insets of red leather. Nobody could say the suit was *risqué*. Yet the originality was striking and the execution of the *mode* was carried through in all details, hat, gloves, button boots. The flow of her graceful frame through the firm lines of the cut had my heart miss a beat.

Her maid brought out two soft leather bags then a large wicker hamper which I stowed on the luggage rack and we were off.

Were they happy times, those two journeys? To Nancy and Reims, then three weeks later to Arras and Lille.

There was the conversation in the car. LG holding forth, giving his imitation of the Cabinet coming to an excruciatingly difficult decision about the funding of public lavatories. Then the voices of Wilson, Orlando and Clemenceau, expressing their national angst. Frances rolling forward with laughter, almost off her seat, holding her hat on to her head with an alabaster hand.

There were large country dinners. LG reciting poetry in Welsh, then stories of his boyhood. There were exquisite picnic lunches from the hamper. Thermoses, glasses, knives and forks from their little straps arranged on a linen cloth, with blankets to lie on. Protected from the wind by a haystack or a slate wall.

And quiet evenings. Sitting together in front of large sparking fires, the two of them touching, trusting me, warming my middle with their display of affection.

But over it all hung our mission: touring the devastation. Unbelievable to the eyes, incomprehensible to the mind, to the heart.

Along the trench line the flayed landscape had not changed. Oceans of destruction had set into congealed waves of mud during the winter. Roads were still lined with astonishing quantities of discarded equipment. Destroyed tanks were engulfed here and there and piles of casings big and small marked a former machine-gun post or an artillery emplacement. Camouflaged bunkers along the Hindenburg Line were now exposed. Incredible quantities of glowering, wasted concrete.

Abandoned lorries and burned-out transport of all kinds bordered our route interspersed with the skeletons of horses and mules. Rubbish-filled craters were everywhere and there were still some German corpses to be seen.

This was the ground defended by the German Army from July to October 1918. Exhausted, with little food or ammunition, without tanks or tank defences, yet still following Ludendorff's orders to give up France only foot by foot.

But beyond again, up toward Tournai and Mons the other side of the

Belgian border, the country was eerily untouched. As if the combatants had been taken up into the heavens without a trace. The German retreat had started toward the Rhine.

And I had seen rout before. Here there had been no collapse.

Huge dumps of German heavy armaments had been assembled at crossroads to meet the terms of the Armistice. Vast junkyards of 5.9s, howitzers and 77s were carefully arranged in wide semi-circles. Then on the inside, row upon row of Minenwerfer, hundreds and hundreds of Maxims and automatic rifles. I stared at the lines, entranced. The deadly matériel I had faced, now discarded and useless. German and Allied Armistice Officers stood around in wan sunshine, insignificant among the obscene detritus of war.

In the towns that had survived, a population of ragged refugees slouched through the streets. Old men, young boys and women. Allied flags still hung from shell-marked buildings.

There were no animals to be seen. Everything edible had been taken by the retreating Germans. Allied lorries parked in muddy town squares were distributing food and clothing. Gangs of German prisoners worked on roads and over fields, pecking absurdly at the interminable damage with mattocks and shovels.

The French had prepared readings for LG from the letters of soldiers, from the official reports of the French armies and from eyewitness accounts. LG read in the evenings, in front of the glowing logs. Sometimes out loud.

'Here's a *chasseur à pied*, a soldier in the French Fourth Army during the retreat, after the French defeat at Charleroi, in late August 'fourteen. They're holding a bridge against the German advance. The charges under the bridge have failed to blow it up. All night he watches the Germans on the other side of the Meuse, the land he has had to concede that day.'

A night of anguish and horror, watching the Saxons of van Hausen's army burning the town and shooting the inhabitants, right under our eyes. In the morning flames still rose from the village. We could see the people running in the streets, pursued by the drunken soldiers. There were shots, all through the night there were shots...

LG wound down.

We had been there that day. Revin, Monthermé. Areas to the north held by the Germans all through the War, above the heavy damage and the battlefields. We had seen black ruins, villages laid waste but set in the untouched countryside of a magnificent French spring.

By the time LG had finished we were all three of us weeping quietly to ourselves.

'King Albert wants me to visit Belgium,' LG said one morning in the car, but he seemed undecided. LG thought that maybe an official visit by King George would be better.

'Once I'd seen their damage I'd be under pressure to agree with all their demands for Reparations. I'm sure I couldn't help but shed a tear standing in Louvain and they'd be bound to have the camera men along. You've no idea what harm the wrong photograph can do.'

LG had promised Clemenceau that he would visit the devastated areas of northern France during the Conference, but privately, just following the map for himself. The visits had had some of the effect that Clemenceau intended: the bombarded hulk of Reims cathedral; the new deserts before Verdun; the ruin in Picardy and the wasteland of Flanders. But the principles were unchanged.

LG was a leader, that was his job he said. Just like being a miner or a farmer, no different. So leadership was expected of him like coal, like milk. That's how he earned his bread and butter, he would say. And his job in Paris was to establish a just peace, as he called it.

After I had first met LG, I followed every word I could find about him. I had read his speech to Parliament earlier that month in *The Times*. LG was under attack from all sides for being too lenient with the Germans or too harsh with the Poles.

We will have a stern peace, he had argued. Not to gratify vengeance, but to vindicate justice.

To make this the War to End All Wars.

How those words rang in my ears, filling my head and rippling down my spine. To have fought in such a war, to have survived. To have seen it all come true.

It was only at the end of our second journey that LG spoke to me about Frances. LG shook my hand before I left him at Number 17. The formality had not lasted long.

'Glad you met Frances, boy,' LG said. 'And she's certainly taken a shine to you.'

This was his male talk for an unspoken understanding. LG would not want to say more because that would be to admit something, while showing doubt in me. But discretion is what I knew he meant. LG was such a clever man.

Then LG put his arm around my shoulder as we walked to his front door behind the porter.

'Before Frances, boy, everything was a terrible mess. So bad I can't tell you. Couldn't find a thing. Letters never replied to, some letters never even opened and my constituents angry with me most of the time.' Now life was much better.

Even on our trips LG and Frances would be delayed upstairs for an hour or two in the mornings. Letters, they said. When they came down.

I walked around the towns while I waited, self-conscious in my uniform, never permitted to pay for anything: pastries, coffee made from chestnuts, daffodils. People trying to press things on to me from their meagre supplies: wine, biscuits, sausage.

Or I would drive to the cemeteries. LG had told me that the Empire sites were to be taken over later that year by the Imperial War Graves Commission. Permanent memorials and gardens were to be built, head-stones cut for each grave. A huge gate was to be constructed at Ypres and a monument on the Somme, both for the dead whose bodies had not been found.

During the march to Cambrai, I had seen battlefield graveyards behind our support lines and at terse mass burials after the battle. Then I saw many more again when I drove through the battlefields in 1918, during our retreat.

I had imagined that there would be huge unending fields of crosses, con-solidated by corps or by year. But I found that no battlefield graves were to be moved, only the scattered singles and pairs. The battalion sites were to remain where they were, spread like a grim necklace across our old front. Around the Somme alone there were more than a hundred graveyards, some for as few as fifty men. The rest of the bodies were still in the mud.

The grave markers made by the men in the field had been replaced with rows of temporary white crosses, same height, same width, straightened into lines. As if dressed off by the spectre of an RSM.

The hard ground was partly covered by wisps of new vegetation and that spring the sites were not so raw. Poppies and wild flowers pushing up through cracks. Putting man's dreadful accomplishments to shame.

The battle areas were being combed and the cemeteries were kept open. More corpses were found every day. At the far end of one site I saw a padre, black cassock and white surplice flapping in the wind. He was standing by a new grave reading from a prayer book. Sappers in a circle sagged over their shovels, looking morosely down into the hole and at the fresh pile of brown dirt.

As I walked by they all looked up at me with a start as if I were a ghost. Come to take away a friend, a comrade. To lift him in my arms, put him back on to his feet. Then we would set off together, laughing, into town, to a café, for a beer, for a sandwich. The whole thing gone, a forgotten dream, the nightmare erased.

The cemeteries chilled me, froze my heart again. I saw the dirt stripped away, a grid of skeletons exposed: bloody uniforms, rotting flesh, shapes bundled in blankets tied up with string. Starting on their lonely eternities. Not dead just for the duration of the War, but for them a victory as terrible as defeat.

We were too far from Cambrai for me to make my visit in a morning. And I did not want to disturb LG's route although he would have agreed readily had I asked. I had promised and one day I would make my journey back.

In the car again we dealt with lists and numbers which I found no easier. Frances had it all in a folder. France and the French Empire had mobilized more men than Britain and the British Empire. France had taken by far the greatest losses. 6,200,000 casualties, not including civilians, of which 1,400,000 were killed. The British Empire had 3,400,000 casualties of which 950,000 were killed. Canadian and Australian dead alone counted 120,000. The Italians had 650,000 men dead, the greatest loss when counted against population. The German figures were slightly higher than the French. The American dead: under 100,000.

I always remember that stretch of road between two rows of plane trees. That very place, even the sign, VALENCIENNES 22 M. One of ours from the year before. With Frances talking, softly but firmly, reciting the figures.

And then I could not see. I steered the car on to the grass verge. LG made no comment.

The figures were not a secret but totals had not been widely published at the end and I had never heard them before. And now, by then, nobody wanted to know.

I stumbled out of the car, around the bonnet and stood facing quiet fields. This part of France had been behind the German lines up until the end and the country was untouched.

My eyes flooded, my chin quivered, my whole body shook and now I could not even stand.

I sat on the running board of the Lea-Francis and it all overwhelmed me. The numbers, the incredible numbers, my escape. Men like me, millions and millions with lives to lead, families waiting, futures, their loves and their passions unfulfilled. They were all gone.

A million is a thousand thousand men.

Just a thousand men was more than my complete battalion, almost twice that entire school. Twelve thousand at the most was a full division, the same as a whole town. A million, even one million men is impossible. And behind each million, two, three million whom they loved, who loved them, whose lives would never be the same.

And for what? The question that was better left unasked. Because once war had started, we could not simply let the Germans win? Was it nothing more than that?

It was as if at that moment, on that lonely piece of road facing the open fields with Frances and LG waiting patiently in the car for their driver to regain control of himself, then and there as I sat sobbing on the running board, it was as if at that moment that I heard a great moan. Heard by me only, by me the survivor. A vast low echoing cry, up and out of the ground, floating away across the plains. Intolerable, unanswerable. Me shaking by the side of the road. LG and Frances in the car.

I climbed back in behind the wheel and LG leaned forward from the rear seat. He put his hand on my shoulder. He patted me gently.

'Never again, boy,' LG said quietly. 'Never again.'

We drove on. Frances listing the civilian damage. The battle area was 250 miles long and an average of thirty miles in breadth. The war had consumed 1,659 townships and over half a million houses. France had 600,000 widows and over a million fatherless children. Not a single square foot of Germany had been invaded.

An idea had been put to LG to preserve the trench line as an untouched Via Sacra stretching from Switzerland to the Channel. Places to sit would be built, signs and maps of the main battles would be put up, the battlefields themselves left untouched. But already in early 1919 the farmers were back on the land and the man with the idea had himself been killed in 1918.

Winston Churchill had suggested to LG that Ypres be kept as a permanent monument against war. That beautiful Flemish town had been completely destroyed, almost every building razed, the fifteenth-century Cloth Hall and the Cathedral. With most buildings not one brick was left standing upon another. But again reconstruction had already begun. The force that was rebuilding, the human spirit, that was the true memorial, LG said.

And the French had seen northern France fought over so many times that the idea of any elaborate monument was dismissed.

Influenced by Fairy I looked up to the French and soon I came to believe for myself. By the time I came to live in Paris, by 1919, the superiority of France and all things French had become a conviction. French logic for example. Real logic, tangible logic that ruled the heart when it had to. A rock to stand on, a rock I did not have.

The French had fought a terrible war and now it was over. There was the end to it. So in order to have the land back in production, life back to normal, three years free of rent was offered to farmers who would take over the battlefields. They were also promised immediate processing of their claims for war damage. A logical answer to a need.

Tin huts built by the new tenants had sprung up across the lines, painted with large white numbers to put their claims on a legal footing. The French began to level the ground. More rows of German prisoners wandered over the grading looking for metal, explosives and debris.

Farmers, old men or young boys, sold buttons, cap badges, even rusted pistols from roadside stands instead of flowers or vegetables. The process had begun, the restoration of the land that I never thought I would see.

But the restoration of the peace was the hardest of all.

The Conference opened in January 1919. In the streets of Paris President Wilson was acclaimed as a modern god. The man whose ideas would solve the problems of the world. Self-determination for all peoples. An end to the secret diplomacy that had started the War. Peace and justice in a world safe for democracy.

Hundreds of thousands had turned out to greet him. And he had acknowledged them with his famous smile.

President Wilson's Fourteen Points to end the War, it was believed, had started the move toward Armistice.

But Clemenceau made fun of Wilson and his Points right from the start.

'The Good Lord,' Clemenceau said, 'even He had only ten.'

To me, at first, Paris was a continuous rollick, an unending mike.

My motor pool under Captain Vernon had moved from Montreuil in December '18 and I was promoted to full lieutenant. But Vernon was occupied with larger transport matters, the return of the army from France, collecting our prisoners from Germany and I was left to run the show on my own.

I had the same establishment: the Daimlers, an assortment of civilian cars, a dozen motorbicycles for dispatch. A lorry for carrying bottles. And from London we added a Rolls-Royce 40/50, a seven litre six with a four-speed box, an open tourer in burnished aluminium with red leather seats. This magnificent car was called the Silver Ghost.

With this fleet, with my drivers and my mechanics, I ran a superior bus and messenger service. From the Majestic to the Crillon, from the FO on the Île de la Cité to the ministère de la Guerre on quai d'Orsay, to and from the Gare du Nord. To and from Boulogne where the Royal Navy destroyer *HMS Plucky* deposited and collected visitors from England.

And if I was ever short of cars I could call on André and his taxis from place Saint Michel, *le Club Arnaud*. André *le vieux*, my tutor, driver of the Delaunay Bellville, André in his layered *cape de clocher*, the *ancien combattant*. But from the Prussian War of 1870, not the Great War of 1914. André the lover of real Paris, of old Paris, not the Slum-Clearer's *arnaque*, Baron Haussmann's trickery that had produced the artificial show-piece that Paris had become.

The few officers stationed in Paris used the Hôtel Villa Majestic as the mess. We shared with the politicians, the civil servants and all the others dropping in on their way to and from London. The Cabinet Office occupied the rooms above.

By then the army was run from London again. The entire BEF had ceased to exist. From Field-Marshal Haig down to the humblest private, all had disappeared. At the Majestic only a handful of officers remained between me, Lieutenant I/c motor pool and Field-Marshal Sir Henry Wilson, Chief of the Imperial General Staff and driver of the Silver Ghost.

Wilson was a small man, pickled like a gherkin but quick and very sharp. Like LG, Wilson believed in power. But armed power over a disarmed enemy, not political power that could shift away from day to day, from hour to hour. To Wilson the Paris Conference was a farce. Peacemaking, he said, should be the job of the soldiers who had fought the war.

Wilson had the nervous energy of a hungry sparrow in wintertime. He hopped and pecked his way from table to table across the Majestic dining room, from group to group across the Conference floor or up and down the stairs of the ministère de la Guerre. The Field-Marshal seemed to be holding himself ready day and night, for the call. To invade Germany, to launch an anti-Bolshevik crusade in Russia, to knock heads together in Turkey, Hungary or Poland.

Wilson drove the Silver Ghost like a demonic fury, one of my drivers cowering in the back, along for the ride only to repair the Field-Marshal's frequent punctures. He rattled the car over cobbles and he slid her round slippery corners. Pedestrians fled and horses reared as he sped past.

And to the Field-Marshal, his American cousin was a fraud, a weak man under all that idealism. *Pitoyable*, he would say, a man who could not deliver on his promises. Damn well knew it too. His League of Nations was a toothless farce to protect second-rate countries with third-rate men. The US Congress would never give up their sole power to declare war. LG should play with the man, humour him until he had to leave for home, then settle everything after he was gone.

There were wars on all over the world, the Field-Marshal grumbled. Twenty-one at the last count and all the frocks could do was sit and talk: Clemenceau, LG and his cousin.

The Finns were marching on Petrograd, the Yugos were attacking the Austrians, the Bulgarians were knocking up the Greeks, on and on and on.

I soon found out that Field-Marshal Wilson was not related to President Wilson, *cousin* was just his bitter humour.

Flushed with anger and frustration the Field-Marshal would race to Versailles at all times of the day and night, often with me standing in for my driver.

Seventeen meetings the little frocks had held by the middle of April, Wilson complained as he drove. And not a single decision. Not even a single note taken of the proceedings. How do you like that? Mutter, mutter. And the Field-Marshal had visited Lloyd George's suite. Not a map in the whole place, not a single one, could I believe it?

At the palace gates he would jump from the car and flit furiously around the Grand Canal taking hurried mincing steps. Wilson was exasperated by everyone and everything, from the frocks and the entire Conference to a portrait that had recently been painted of him.

'Bounder,' he grumbled of the oil by Sir William Orpen, 'makes me look like a proper bounder. Going to keep a black book. Any woman who likes the picture will go into the book. Never talk to that woman again.'

Or, 'Peace and justice.' Mumble, mumble. 'Peace and justice. My cousin knows nothing. An ignorant academic, a self-assertive fool. Making money from disaster, that's all my cousin's men really go for.'

Wilson fumed constantly, speaking fast under his breath. I could never catch it all.

The army was restless even though pay had been doubled. Revolution was just around the corner. Paris would crash. All built on shifting sands. But, *ah-ha*. The soldier's moment was coming again, make no mistake. The frocks' writ didn't run, ignored by everybody. Who did they really think they were?

But he and Foch knew what was coming. Oh yes, they would soon be feeding the starving Bosche and then they would have to occupy. Only way to get our terms. A march on Munich, a short wait for supplies then on to Berlin. Bavaria, Württemburg and the other parts would be made into separate countries again. Defeat them properly. Only way, only way.

Old Haig would have his dream yet. Ride his chestnut mare down Unter den Linden and through the Brandenburg Gate.

One spring night with the Field-Marshal's fury calmed for the moment by a sprint around the Canal, he stopped me before we boarded the Silver Ghost for the road-race back to Paris. In the Palace courtyard we stood under the huge statue of Louis XIV, the Sun King, perfect in his boots, plumes and wig, the testicles of his horse larger than a miner's two fists.

'Look here, little man,' Wilson said, leaning his bounder's face up to mine, 'I've been thinking as I walked. Whatever we do, war must not happen again. Never. But this politics business is no way to deal with it. Everything here in Paris is exactly the opposite of how it appears. Laugh at those who cry, cry for those who laugh, that's what I say. Go back to your little room and think that one over.'

2

I was in love with Katrina from that first moment.

Outside the Hôtel des Invalides, standing in front of the cannon, the gilt horses of the pont Alexandre behind. Paris under a brilliant blue sky and the earth standing still in the heavens.

Oh, I felt on that day that I had met my other side, the missing receptacle for my innermost soul, the impossible connection for my unattached fibres. Waving, forever waving but never answered. A pale sea anemone lonely between Cornish rocks, sweeping, interminably signalling, unrequited in the flowing tide.

Katrina was the most beautiful woman I had ever seen. The most beautiful woman in Paris. It was a wonder to me that she was even in my world. I imagined her the goddess of competing suitors, heroes of myths, owners of castles, of mountains and hidden lakes. Katrina flitting between, unseen by mortals.

But she was a nurse, practical, competent, dealing with unhealed wounds, the cripples, the infinitely slow recoveries.

Katrina was tall, in her flowing headdress she was imposing. Her face was broad and open from the front, features all smoothed together by a brilliant sculptor. Strong and angular from the side, a wide tempting mouth with thin firm lips and an even nose. Her cropped hair was a dark shiny auburn, Titian's red. Startling against a white headband, stubbled, wonderfully prickly up the back of her neck.

On that first day I had not managed a single word. As if that single word might have been the wrong word. As if that wrong word might have broken the spell, made this apparition disappear. I had only been able to look, my neck contorting to follow this vision from every angle as my body continued its automated tasks.

Katrina stood loosely in her starched uniform, a wide rounded collar and a tiny cream bow tie. She was frowning, fully absorbed with the work at hand, conveying a tense impatient energy.

The task for us both was a bathchair.

Serjeant Jones had received a telephone call at the garage from the French, their transport section at quai d'Orsay. Did we have a car available that could carry a man in a bathchair? The French had such a car they said, but it had gone to Le Havre with President Wilson.

The gentleman in the bathchair, the French had explained, was a very difficult customer. Scheduled to appear before the Boundaries Commission, but refusing to arrive in an ambulance, most upset at the loss of his car even though the drive was less than a kilometre. An officer, Jones had been told, a war hero but a regular crosspatch. The senior *aide de camp* to *Maréchal* Foch.

At the garage Jones and I examined one of the Daimlers, Number 16. With the map tables removed and the leather hinge straps unscrewed to allow the door of the passenger compartment to open right back against the coachwork, we were sure that we could do the job.

We placed a chair from the canteen inside the car and had our tallest man sit in. There was certainly enough headroom. Jones made up wooden blocks to hold the bathchair in place during travel. Within half an hour the Daimler was prepared.

Then we set out to help our valiant allies, the Boys in Light Blue. Jones drove and I sat next to him on the front bench. Two men on our square-tank motorbicycles followed behind. Serjeant Jones thought that there might be some lifting to be done.

And that is how, in front of the Hôtel des Invalides, on that brilliant Paris day, 13 April 1919, that is how I met them both. Both of them together, *Capitaine* Pierre Mauduit and Katrina Combères, *infirmière de l'Armée Française.*

I saw them first coming towards me through an archway and across the cobbles of the enormous courtyard. Katrina behind, still in the shadows pushing. Pierre, his arms outstretched in a crucified shrug making some point to his *adjoint,* a young infantry lieutenant who was walking beside the chair.

Pierre was smoking. Fat offensive cigarettes rolled in yellow paper. A cloud of dense blue smoke enveloped the three of them. A packet of Celtique *maïs* and a box of matches bounced in his lap.

'*Et qu'en pense mon infirmière?*' Pierre was saying, asking Katrina to confirm whichever one of his many opinions he was delivering as they approached the car. The *adjoint* was deferential, not asked, but agreeing with everything anyway.

'*Moi, je pense que mon protégé fume trop.*' The nurse, the professional, interested not in the politics of the Boundaries Commission, but in the health of her patient. Waving her hand in front of her face at the smoke, pretending to choke.

'*Ah! le wagon lit des rosbifs,*' Pierre said as he approached, inspecting our huge car and my little squad of four.

Pierre was a serious-looking man. A tall upper lip covered with a splendid moustache sweeping down both sides of his mouth, waxed tips pointing to the ground making a caricature of an unhappy face. But his eyes had a hard edged sparkle, as if whatever the problem, whatever the obstacle, it would be faced down.

Pierre was wearing his Number Twos, an undress mess tunic of light blue twill, tall collar decorated with anchors, done up at the neck, French style. A kepi in blue to match. A simple belt and shoulder strap of light tan. Much less cluttered and ostentatious than a British uniform. None of the badges and flashes that we used for identification, for the petty distinctions on which we thrived. Small chevrons on his arm denoted rank in place of our embroidered epaulets and sleeve decorations. A well-turned-out French officer looked prepared for immediate action, *soigné*.

But the matters that caught the eye were not the parts that the uniform contained, but the parts that were missing. On the left, one narrow brown brogued boot and one leather legging. But on the right, the other leg of the breeches was tucked neatly and pinned below the knee. Dangling, empty, swaying as the bathchair bumped over cobbles.

And the hook.

Jones took a pace forward and saluted smartly as Pierre approached.

Up to his kepi in response came the hook. A metal talon, dark and menacing like the barrel of a gun. Then attached to a wooden stump which disappeared up into the sleeve.

His right hand and wrist, his right foot and ankle, both amputations on the same side. Then you started to wonder. The pressed uniform, the leather polished to a teak sheen. Then you began to ask yourself how it had all been assembled, how this meticulous dressing had taken place. You could only imagine the pain: in the past, the present, the relentless discomfort, the future. And if he slept there would be the remembering and the memories each morning on waking. You wondered how it could be all borne.

Pierre's medals were pinned to his chest. I recognized the first two. Chevalier du Legion d'Honneur, Croix de Guerre, purple ribbon, closer to blood red. And the Médaille Militaire, yellow and green in vertical stripes. The highest awards the French could give. I looked at this man in awe.

Jones explained the arrangements. Katrina spoke enough English to understand. Then Pierre was lifted into the car and Jones affixed the blocks. Katrina and the *adjoint* were ushered into the back behind the bathchair. Jones pulled away, me next to him again, our two motorcyclists following behind.

For the occasion Jones had even brought a French flag which fluttered off the mudguard as our party set off down rue de Constantine.

'*Vous êtes bien organisés, vous les Anglais,*' Katrina said as she climbed in. '*Il va être content.*' Her frown melted into a smile. Soft and beautiful.

Only later did I realize that this was French theatre that we, *les Anglais,* had produced so well. Pierre by then had crutches and a wooden foot, he could have ridden in any of the French cars. And although still in hospital and unsteady out of the bathchair, he did not need a nurse in attendance. But Pierre's chair, the dedicated *infirmière,* chosen as *une Alsacienne,* the hook, the empty trouser leg of the impeccable uniform, the ribbons, now me and my squad, all this was intended to impress. To launch Pierre's attack on the Boundaries Commission from uphill, from the vantage point of sympathy and deference due to *la France.* Wronged, damaged, owed. The furious debate over the Rhenish State.

'*Et pour za retour,* for zer ree-turn?' Katrina asked of Jones when we had unloaded in the courtyard of the quai d'Orsay. Ignoring me the dumbfounded.

Katrina spoke French and her tentative English with a mildly guttural accent. Her effort was charming, revealing something wonderfully intimate.

Jones said that the men and the car would wait. Anything for our brave French cousins.

I walked back to the FO, along the river, across pont Neuf, all in a daze. I spent the rest of the day in a daze and that night I lay in my bed still in a daze.

In the lonely stretch between 2 a.m. and 6 a.m., I squeezed out a short letter in French.

Dear Nurse to Capitaine Mauduit,

Please forgive my clumsy English manners. I became yesterday, mademoiselle, your secret admirer.

I am the lieutenant who brought the car for Capitaine Mauduit. I am with the British Foreign Office and I organize transport for the Conference.

Again forgive me, but would you consider taking a walk with me one evening, along the river? You would do me a great honour.

Your admirer.

Yves Beauchamp, Lt.

I enclosed the address card we used for our suppliers.

With the envelope marked, *À l'attention de : Mademoiselle l'infirmière du Capitaine Mauduit*, I went to see André.

'*C'est ton problème à toi*,' he said.

He, André with his palms out, him sitting back in his chair puffing on his Boyard, he was not in a position himself, he said, to advise on matters of the heart. And anyway, a taxi driver trying to find an army nurse? They were treated like *zéro!* Worse, by the military. Even after the Marne.

I was disappointed. There is a fence around Frenchmen, I thought sometimes, a fence you do not often meet, but a fence that is there all the same.

I could not go, not me myself. What if she came out? She herself. What would I do then?

But André had left me with one good idea.

'Flowers,' he said. '*Les jeunes filles françaises adorent les fleurs*.'

André told me to go to the market, les Halles, very early in the morning to buy a large bouquet of fresh flowers. And all the same kind he insisted. None of your English *pagaille*, the fussy mixed flower arrangements in the school chapel painstakingly prepared by masters' wives. Not like that.

'And,' André said, 'be careful. Different flowers mean different things. You never start with roses.'

André knew it all. Azaleas for *l'amour timide*, which, André thought, was me all over. Lilacs for *l'amour naissant*, also appropriate in my case. Or violets, he said, a large bunch, with green leaves, for *l'amour caché*.

And if she ever did merit roses, with me unable to understand what that meant, I would have given her roses right now, mounds of them, armfuls, a Daimler-full, then it must be in odd numbers not in tens or dozens. Or else the entire matter would simply go nowhere, right from the very start.

But Anson was game.

'If I can find General Gough's HQ, sir,' Anson said, 'in the dark, during a bombardment on a twenty-mile front, I can certainly find a nurse in Paris.'

When the wires to Montreuil were cut during the retreat in March '18 and our cars and motorcycles were the only means of communication with the armies, Anson had been my most reliable driver.

We made our plan. Up at four and over to les Halles by five, the Daimler and our uniforms much admired, remarked on from all sides. Under the huge glass roofs, between ornate cast iron columns, a French Babel in a hundred brilliant colours. The flower seller trying to give me the most beautiful lilacs I had ever seen. Waving his arms then wagging his finger in my face to refuse a single *sou* from his *braves alliés*.

The lilacs were lush and wonderful. I understood immediately why they represented *l'amour naissant*. The bunch filled Anson's arms. Each stem was a flower arrangement by nature herself, a profusion of tiny white heads, but erratic, unsure, *naissant* was the word. Then below, luxurious pointed leaves in dark green like shields, framing the brilliance of the contrast.

We had onion soup and beer *à la pression* to compensate for the hour, sitting among the *mangeurs de tripoux* and the market porters, *les forts des Halles*. Then Anson was on his way with the huge wrapped bundle and the envelope on the seat beside him. He was going to start at les Invalides where we had met and trace her from there.

We had made up a story if Anson were asked. About us, *les Anglais*, being late the day before, inconveniencing *la demoiselle infirmière et le capitaine*. The flowers were an apology. Any Frog would go for that.

Then, like shells from the sky in response to a coordinate. Lost, you thought, gone with the runner across muddy fields never to return. But now, wonderfully, precise at the map reference, the difference between life and death, two days later my answer came.

Dear Lieutenant Beauchamp,
Thank you for your letter and the most beautiful flowers! They are magnificent. I have them on my window-sill. The other nurses in my room are very jealous. And thank you also for your help with Capitaine Mauduit. He was very pleased.

I am walking with Capitaine Mauduit tomorrow. We leave les Invalides at 1700. Would you like to come with us? If I do not hear from you we will expect you. We will be waiting outside the Église du Dôme facing place Vauban.
Sincerely,
Katrina Combères.

I found that we were to walk to the Luxembourg Gardens, a long swing from les Invalides I thought. But Katrina explained to me that Pierre liked to practise on his crutches in private, not on the public lawn in front of the hospital and not in the gymnasium with the others.

I could be useful pushing the bathchair. Of course, anything.

Pierre held his crutches across the chair. His belt and leggings were off, he wore a fore-and-aft cap in place of the kepi and shoes instead of boots. Two of them. For his attempts at walking Pierre was fitted with a wooden foot.

I was nervous and I talked, my French stumbling. About nothing, my drivers, how much they enjoyed Paris. About André and Haussmann, about my new billet after the move from Montreuil, on the Île de la Cité, at 6 place Dauphine. The daily miracle of Madame Ballot. Real coffee made in a saucepan with fresh milk, the aroma reaching me in my room as I awoke. Fresh butter, white soft cheese, crusty hollow bread still warm. All by seven o'clock in the morning.

I pushed the chair. Katrina's cream lace-up shoes tripped along the pavement beside me. She wore a dark blue cape over long whites, a cloak with slits for the arms held in place by a tab across her chest. Katrina's headdress was decorated with a star on the forehead and a little tricolour cockade pinned to the headband on her left side. An embroidered patch was sewn on to her cape. *REÉDUCATION FONCTIONELLE POUR GRANDS INVALIDES.*

We walked through the clean quiet streets of the *7ème* and the *6ème arrondissements,* drawing looks, stares even, as we progressed along avenue de Breteuil.

'But make no mistake,' André had said to me on our first drive through the city, 'Haussmann was a clever man. How many visitors to the city today see the difference between the old and the new?'

Certainly not on avenue de Breteuil. Here it looked as if the entire street system giving such a central place to the Hôtel des Invalides and the Dôme had been built hundreds of years ago, right from the original fields. Not a mere sixty years before, the work of a band of privileged speculators. Murdered slum-dwellers, forced demolitions, the real story of Haussmann's Paris was gone. Only the most beautiful city in the world remained.

'*Mais les Français, sont comme ça,*' André shrugged. Acceptance, despite all the passion, after all the talk. Logically now, *c'est fini, non?* What else could one do?

In the rose garden behind the Luxembourg Palace, Pierre struggled up on to his crutches then grasped on to Katrina. He staggered forward, suddenly the real cripple, not the composed officer in the bathchair.

Katrina was encouraging, giving Pierre quiet instructions, worrying about his pain, walking backwards in front of him as he came toward her. Me following behind him with the chair, whole and untouched.

On the right side the grip of the crutch had been replaced with a wide wooden flange, notched to take the hook. Pierre could move forward steadily on his good leg, but to take the next step he had to hold the crutch with his hook at the same time as he took the weight on to his wooden foot.

He tired quickly. His body was weak after more than two years in bed and his recovery had been complicated, Katrina said, by a long fever. Only now were the limbs ready to try walking.

How could I even imagine the pain? In my armpits where the crutches rubbed hard, numbing my arms. Then in my joints, unused to the imbalanced weight. Ugly pressure on bone and inflamed flesh at the end of my stumps.

It was impossible to grasp. This was no recovery, this was how it would be for life. And but for the smile of some god of war it could have been me.

Pierre swore but he persevered, shaking as he moved, trembling as he caught his breath, his good hand a determined white where he gripped the bar of the crutch. Up and on to the crutches again and again after short, panting rests. Sweat in cold pearly beads glinting on his forehead.

Finally Katrina called a halt to the agony and we started back for les Invalides.

Pierre had me take a different route back, waving his yellow cigarette toward rue du Cherche Midi. Katrina raised her eyebrows at me and shrugged behind his back, a moment of private communication between us, a little flash. We were going to Pierre's café.

We sat at an outside table in cool evening air. Motors ran up and down the narrow street, pedestrians stepped into the gutter to pass the bathchair, handles out across the pavement.

Without a word from Pierre the barman appeared, a large expanse of chest and stomach in green apron. He placed two earthenware jugs on the table, two glasses, sugar lumps and a silver spoon perforated like a salt shaker.

'*Violà, mon vieux,*' with an affectionate slap on Pierre's back. Katrina rolled her eyes at me again, poised with her small coffee, the professional, still on duty.

Pierre placed a sugar lump on to the perforated spoon which he laid across his glass. From the first jug he poured a shiny green liquid slowly over the cube and into the glass, then he repeated the performance for me. Water and ice from the second jug was added into each, turning oily green into cloudy white like a medicine.

'Now we will see your real strength, Lieutenant,' Katrina said to me with her soft smile. 'We will see if you can resist *la fée verte*.' I tasted the drink, liquorice but bitter even through the sugar. The Green Fairy.

'It is against the law.' Katrina frowned her frown and shook her head-dress. 'Illegal since the start of the war. He has nightmares when he is chased by *les djinns*. And this *absinthe* slows his recovery, opens him to tuberculosis…'

'…don't listen to the stories put about by the wine makers,' Pierre inter-rupted. 'They are just jealous.' Hand and hook out in mock despair. 'This is the true drink of France. And the new imitations without wormwood are *dégueulasse*.'

He held his little glass up to the air appreciatively like a miracle cure for the flu.

'You take this drink in three stages,' he said. 'First there is ordinary drink-ing, like you and me now. Then with more, maybe *les djinns*. But after that, if you continue, there are all the things you want to see. Wonderful curious things from another world.'

'*Les djinns?*' I asked Katrina. She leaned toward me confidentially. She was perfection, a face in my dreams.

'Before the War *le capitaine* was in Algeria. He learned from the Arabs about little devils that follow those who hide from their blackest *angoisses*. They make us go mad if we will not face up to our past. Now, when he has been drinking…but I know nothing of *les Arabes*.' She smiled me her celes-tial smile. 'I like to say as *une Alsacienne*, that I have never been out of France. But still, this drink…'

It was certainly not for me, the unblemished survivor, to say that it was wrong.

On that evening, the second time we had met, Pierre's djinns saw the vulnerability of France.

'*Le Maréchal*,' Katrina explained, 'has *Capitaine* Mauduit attend at the Commission almost every day. He is the centre of the *mise en scène* for their speeches, with his amputations, his chair and his medals, the living symbol of our suffering.'

Pierre smiled at Katrina and she smiled back indulgently, a little routine between them. I felt the stab of jealousy for the first time in my life, spontaneous and unreasonable.

Pierre was quickly on to his second *absinthe*, keen, it seemed, to pass beyond the preliminaries.

'They shelled Paris, they marched up and down the Champs-Élysées.

They used Versailles to declare their Prussian state and to crown their Kaiser. They made us pay Reparations when we were the ones who were attacked. Then in 1914 Germany invaded France again. Millions more have been killed and only now have we taken back Alsace and Lorraine, after almost fifty years as the German Imperial Territories.'

Pierre was into full flight. As if it was the Franco-Prussian War as well as the Great War that had just ended.

How France would always be at a disadvantage. From equal populations in the last generation Germany now had one and a half times more people than France. Industrial production in France was declining. Villages were being abandoned because there was no one to run the farms. Now with the losses from the War and a declining birthrate, the problem had grown even worse.

'But with victory, this is our turn. We must add to France all the German lands along the west side of the Rhine. We will call it the Rhenish State. They can keep their German customs and language, but next time *les boches* must fight us through their own people first, before they can ever cross the borders of France again.'

I did not understand what went on at the Boundaries Commission and most of what Pierre said was new to me. I could make no reply.

'*Vous, les Anglais,*' Pierre continued, 'you have no idea of our history, of what invasion means. All that interests you is putting your hands on their ships and their colonies, eliminating Germany as a trading competitor. Ask Katrina about occupation. She was forced to take her schooling, everything in German. There were reprisals, brutal reprisals for the smallest thing, even for owning a French flag.'

The city of Strasbourg and Katrina's village, La Wantzenau, had been freed in August 1914 but then lost again a few days later when the French were forced to withdraw. Alsacians who had welcomed the French in those moments of liberation were severely treated by the Germans when they reoccupied.

'Like 1870 again, innocent people, women and children murdered, hundreds taken away, all the men who were not in the army forced to work in Germany. And all the local leaders, good honest Frenchmen, the mayor, the priest, the schoolteacher, all shot out of hand in town squares. President Wilson can talk of his principles, of the evil of vengeance, but next time where will America be? What are all his words really worth? Those men only care about their business.'

As I listened to Pierre I could see the devastation of Picardy and Flanders. But LG had promised me. Never again.

Pierre fixed me with his flinting eyes.

'And when they come back next time, *mon rosbif,* where will you be, *vous, les Anglais?* Clemenceau says that a tunnel will be built through to England to bring reinforcements. Do you believe that, *mon brave?*'

And I did not understand what Pierre meant by *revenir,* to come back. Germany had been disarmed and our terms were to be so definite. The Germans could have only a small army, no aeroplanes, no gas, no submarines.

'And what is this Germany?' Pierre plunged on without my answer, unstoppable now. 'It is an artificial country. When German culture was great, in the days of Bach, Beethoven and Goethe, it was a collection of three hundred small, harmless states. Now Germany is Prussian and they will be planning again for a Prussian Europe right from the first day of the peace. Of that you can be sure.'

Pierre and behind him, Foch his *Maréchal,* were proposing a system of complete security by creating Greater France. As well as adding the Rhenish State, Belgium should cease to exist. After the killing and destruction, by Pierre's interpretation brought on by Belgium's pre-war neutrality, they did not deserve to be an independent country.

'And what could be better,' Pierre argued, 'than to be *citoyens de la France?* It is what *les boches* want most in all the world...*to live like a god in France*...they say.'

Belgium should become two *départements* and not be permitted to open the way for the Germans again. Those Belgians, they have *rien, rien.*

He was shouting now, the yellow *maïs* cigarette waggling in his mouth.

'Him, *Napoléon, l'Empereur,* he never had *une foutue commission* to make his decisions for him.' Pierre's chin pointed toward Bonaparte's tomb as we approached les Invalides again down avenue de Villars.

But with Pierre in full cry I had learned little about Katrina except that she had an obvious affection for her charge. Calm and beautiful, nodding her headdress in quiet agreement with everything Pierre said.

I had resigned myself to listening to politics, pushing Pierre's chair with Katrina walking alongside again. But it was better, I said to myself, a lot better, I said, infinitely better than no reply to my letter, than no walk at all.

Katrina did tell me that she shared a small dormitory with two other nurses in the École Militaire. And on the window-sill, she said, were some beautiful lilacs. From a secret admirer, she told me with her tender knowing smile.

'*Merci, Mademoiselle Combères,*' I said when we were back at les Invalides,

Pierre wheeling away from us for a moment to talk to the sentries under the huge stone archway. The thrill of just using her name. 'I have enjoyed our walk and I very much appreciated meeting *Capitaine* Mauduit. He is a very brave man to manage such difficulties.'

I held out my hand, arm stiff, *style anglais*. And we touched. Her hand-in-mine, warm, silken, but definite.

Oh, in that second, in that immutable moment. In that momentary lifetime I could have pulled gently on that hand-in-mine, I could have taken that hand-in-mine unawares and I could have brought that *céleste* toward me.

And in that same moment, with that hand-in-mine, just in that very moment, I could have had my arms around her, encircling her sheer crisp uniform, her soft blue cape, all before she knew. Pressing her to me, my cheek against hers, taking in her scent, the beat of her heart, her very existence.

'Maybe we could meet again,' I said.

'You too must be a brave man, Lieutenant.' Katrina looked at my uniform. 'And fortunately you have all your limbs.'

I should have stopped her there, right there. I should have admitted to her right then. About Thompson, about my short life, about the ignorant wretch that was me.

But no. I walked back through the Champ-de-Mars toward the river, dazed all over again. Repeating her words, seeing her adorable look, her smile from paradise, like a clear dawn taking over a flowing landscape.

. . . you too must be a brave man, Lieutenant . . .

Chère Mademoiselle Combères,
It was such a pleasure to see you again. I am now more than your admirer.
You mentioned that Capitaine Mauduit is depressed as much by his surroundings at the Hôtel des Invalides as by his wounds. I could lay on the car again if you and he would like to drive out of Paris one Saturday or Sunday. Maybe we could have lunch together. I know a place on the Oise, only thirty miles from Paris. Would that be too far? Please let me know.
Sincerely,
Yves Beauchamp, Lt.

Then Paris became a carousel and it was too late.

A round of spring weekends, of endless lunches, whole meadows of flowers and magic evenings sitting by the river.

Too late to say: that I was only young, younger than she. That I had learned my quick façade from the war and from the good fortune of my position. That my medal belonged to another man. That I knew nothing and I had nothing to offer her other than my youth.

I went walking with Katrina and she showed me the shops, things and places she had never dreamed of as a girl in German Alsace. Paquin, Jean Patou, rue de la Paix, and rue de Berri. Katrina imitating the fast proper French of Paris as we walked, sprinkled with the latest vocabulary: *egöiste, Yankee, le baseball.*

We drove to St Germain-en-Laye to picnic in the park under dappled planes. Or we ate at Fouquet's where Pierre was a demi-god. Sitting back against the panelling as waiters scurried around.

The first question was sun or shade, Pierre said, as at a bullfight. If the roof was open they would close it, if it was closed he would have it opened.

Then: the food.

Pierre introduced me to *merlan, pieds et paquets, quenelles, blanquette de veau.* He taught me the elementary things, about sauces, cheeses, about the shapes of bottles and the wine-growing regions of France.

And after: the conversation.

Pierre undertook my re-education in French history. The real meaning of the Revolution, every man his own, belonging only to himself. The glories of Napoleon's Europe, the spread of self-determination and French culture through to the turmoil of the Third Republic. But how both left and right when faced with *les boches* had ended their arguments and waged total war joined in a *union sacré.*

'We are human,' Pierre told me, 'we French. We are open about our faults, our weaknesses. But then, when you do not expect it, we show our strengths. You can see it in our institutions, in our politics. All the things you take for chaos, that is how we move forward. We do not pretend, *comme vous, les Anglais,* to be what we are not.'

I had so much to relearn.

'*Alors, mon pauvre rosbif,*' Pierre would ask me during one of our drives, or after a meal, '*ça te plaît, la France?*'

Yes, France pleased me more than anything I had ever known.

3

In the spring of 1919 Paris seemed to be the centre of the world. And within a few weeks events in the city had decided both my fate and the fate of the entire globe.

At the beginning of May I received sixteen more cars with civilian drivers and mechanics and my responsibilities increased. In addition to the daily train arriving at the Gare du Nord and the passengers to be collected from Boulogne, an air service had begun between London and Paris which was to be met twice each day.

Then for the Sixth Plenary Session and for the Seventh we ran cars for a new round of visiting delegations and their many advisers. The French took the Yugos, the Albanians, the Roumanians and the Poles. We looked after the Arabs, the Chinese, the Bulgarians. And the Germans.

The Kaiser had missed his hanging by taking refuge in Holland. There were pictures of him in the newspapers feeding the ducks. Was he the man, this one man alone, was he the man to blame?

Now, through retreat, naval mutiny and almost a civil war, Germany said that it had had a revolution and become a democracy. A delegation from the new government arrived, the First German Republic.

Pierre wanted to prepare me for my encounter with the new Germans.

'*Une révolution?*' he asked. 'A revolution as only *les boches* could have. To return to the old order and do away with the new. *Une façade.* The new Reichstag meeting in Weimar is no different from the old warmongers of nineteen fourteen.'

'It is essential that their generals come to Paris to sign, Ludendorff, Hindenburg. Are they going to get away without acknowledging defeat? Then soon they will be blaming the politicians for losing the war.'

And Pierre was sure, it was the army that still ran Germany. All the rhetoric during the election of January had changed nothing, he said. It was President Wilson and his *connerie d'idéalisme!* Saying he would deal only with civilians. If easier terms would be given to civilians than to the German Army, then their army would arrange to produce civilians. But nothing had changed. *Il est dangereux, ce Monsieur le Président.*

There were over eighty in the German delegation, including their experts and advisers and they were assigned the Hôtel des Réservoirs in Versailles. The French said that the Germans needed protection from irate mobs. So a solid wooden palisade was erected around the hotel grounds and the surrounding streets. From the Bassin de Neptune to boulevard de la Reine no traffic and no pedestrians were allowed. *Poilus* and *gendarmes* patrolled the streets. Not even the girls from the Bois were to be let through.

Vernon thought that there might be difficulties with the French and he ordered me to attend every time we sent our cars for the German delegation.

My men were split over our new customers. Jones represented the opinion of the soldiers who had seen the war.

'Both sides 'ave 'ad their fill and now the fight'n's over. They're like bleed'n' POWs behind that fence,' he insisted. 'Peace'll never stick if they don't sit at the table.'

We had found out that there was to be no negotiation with the Germans. The Treaty was to be delivered in final form, prepared by the frocks and their committees in advance. The Germans could choose between signing and invasion.

But among the civilian drivers who had spent the war in some safe government service in England the opinion was that our army should march in. Germany should be occupied and the German leaders brought to Paris in chains.

Every visit, every contact with the Germans was awkward and ugly.

We broke the rules by delivering newspapers to their hotel. But our package was immediately turned away at the door by their major-domo without a word of thanks. We heard that the head of their delegation, their Foreign Minister, Count Brockdorff-Rantzau, knew about roses. We broke the rules again by chauffeuring the Count to the Bagatelle gardens. Then when he arrived he refused to leave the car.

On the day that the terms of the Treaty were to be delivered by the Allies to the Germans we drove their delegation through pouring rain the short distance from their hotel to the Hôtel Trianon Palace.

The Trianon Palace was the grandest hotel I had ever seen, imposing, tall, like the villa of a Roman emperor, facing the fields of Marie-Antoinette's model farm. Here the Allies had held conferences during the war and now the largest room on the main floor had been prepared for the event.

Electricians and carpenters had been busy for days installing bright lights and telephones. A dark tunnel of wood panels had been constructed through which the Germans were to pass, from a side door of the hotel directly into the chamber.

There were fourteen German delegates and five gentlemen from their press. I had detailed off eight cars and sixteen men. Serjeant Jones ran the departure and I covered the arrival. French sentries lined the route, shoulder to shoulder along the wooden barricades.

My cars delivered the Germans five minutes before the appointed time of three o'clock. But the Germans gathered at the door, huddling under a canopy out of the rain, looking at their pocket watches, refusing to proceed until five minutes after. Then they followed two French officers into the tunnel.

As had been planned, the Germans emerged into the conference room blinking under dazzling lights. Unsteadied and damp.

There was dead silence as everyone stared. Then the discomfited Germans were motioned to their seats.

A large table had been set in the middle of the room behind which rows of Allied delegates faced the sombre, stone-faced Germans.

Monsieur Clemenceau stood up. He wore grey suede gloves with his frock coat and he waved his hands as he spoke like a man sharpening an invisible knife.

'The hour has come,' Monsieur Clemenceau began, 'for the heavy settling of accounts...' He spoke abruptly in short bursts with a stern and foreboding courtesy.

During Monsieur Clemenceau's speech a far door flew open and another pair of French officers arrived carrying the treaties. Twenty or thirty large bundles each bound with red tape. The treaties were distributed to the Allies and a single copy was placed in front of Count Brockdorff-Rantzau. He pushed the bundle to one side without a glance.

When Monsieur Clemenceau had finished speaking the Count began his reply.

Incredibly he did not stand.

The room gasped in horror. There was a loud shuffling of feet and a rustling of papers but the Count continued to recite his speech, precise and hard.

'*Wir kennen die Macht des Haßes, die uns hier entgegentritt...*' The Count paused as his words were translated into French and English.

We know the power of hatred with which we are here confronted...

Monsieur Clemenceau sat quite still with his eyes closed, a large polar bear. President Wilson smiled his frozen smile showing his perfect white teeth. And he earnestly took down notes.

LG fiddled with the black tape on his pince-nez. Slumped in his chair, I had never seen him look so small. Even his lion's head seemed to have shrunk. Overwhelmed, prisoner to the leering throng behind him.

As the Count's voice rang out, metallic, ominous. As the artificial light fused to white, the gaol-birds sat upright and unmoved before the court. They were guilty before they could open their mouths. They were the men to blame.

But I knew, I had seen it for myself. Germany had not lost the war. She had given up her weapons voluntarily, accepting the terms of a solemn Armistice to end the killing. Men against machine-guns would have been stalemated for ever. LG and Clemenceau fearful of losing Europe to an American invasion. The General Staff planning for 1919, 1920.

But now, stripped of their artillery by the Armistice, the Germans were powerless to resist our vengeance, the terms of the Treaty.

Justice, fairness... wasn't that what we were fighting for?

Us, the Allies, England.

A sudden vision of Mather exploding, his mannerisms quite forgotten.

I deserved to be flogged. Had I even *heard* of the brave boys of Mons, bleeding and dying for King and Country... the heroes of Ypres, the Somme? Things a little worm like me would never understand.

The Count was clever. No nation was innocent, the imperialism and the secret conspiracies of all the European powers had poisoned international diplomacy before the war. And the Allies were still committing atrocities. Several hundred thousand non-combatants had died since 11 November, women and children starved with premeditation behind the continuing Allied blockade.

Then the Count made his arguments about the text of the Armistice and the President's Fourteen Points. Those were the only terms, the Count said, on which Germany had agreed to stop fighting. That was the only possible basis for a lasting peace.

There was to be no discussion. After the Count's speech the Germans were motioned to rise and file out. The Count was the last to leave.

I remembered thinking that I could win. That beatings came and went. But it was how one behaved, I said to myself, that was the thing that remained.

The Count paused by the door before entering the shadow of the tunnel. And with an ostentatious, an impenitent gesture he lit up a cigarette.

After my cars had left with the Count and his delegation I stood on the main steps of the hotel next to Field-Marshal Wilson as he waited for Anson and the Silver Ghost to come up the long line of official motors.

'Well, little man,' Wilson muttered at me, 'how d'you like that? Not one person had read that document right through before it was delivered to the

Bosche. And do you think the General Staff can get a copy? Not on your life.'

It was Captain Vernon's idea, after the Treaty was signed, that we move out of billets and into the Hôtel de Crillon. We both took rooms on the fifth floor, free of charge, looking out through huge stone columns across place de la Concorde and over to the Left Bank.

'Most of them have gone back to America,' Vernon told me. 'But the Yanks have paid the rent for a full year, apparently. And the ones left behind are anxious to fill the place up again, keep the party going.'

To me it was luxury beyond imagining. Rooms the same as Colonel House or Mr Lansing and the other advisers to the President.

Under the bright spring greenery of the Jardins de Luxembourg, down the narrow streets of the Marais, I moved closer and closer to Katrina. I held her hand in mine as we walked, I put my arm around her waist as we crossed the road and I looked into her candescent brown eyes over little café tables in Montmartre.

And one evening, made brave by the sharp spring air, down by the water on the quays of the Île Saint Louis, I kissed her.

Her lips against mine, her skin to my skin, her eyes closed and peaceful. Then as we kissed again, her weight laid imperceptibly on to my chest as a stockinged foot came out of a shoe and wrapped itself gently behind my legs. And it was then, in that insatiable eternity as I held Katrina to me, that I knew I was alive. Knew that I had survived and that the world could be full of love.

After President Wilson had boarded the *George Washington*, after Mr Lloyd George had left from the Gare du Nord to be welcomed by the King at Victoria station, after Monsieur Clemenceau was back home cooking his lunch in his little house in Bernouville, we had our own celebration.

By then more than twenty of my cars had been withdrawn to London or moved to our forces on the Rhine. I had less to do: only the ambassador's conferences and the minor treaties remained, Italy, Austria, Turkey. But I was short of cars.

So the arrangements for a car on that night were complicated, but in those days of ease and pleasure my men would do anything extra I asked. They thought that I kept them going in Paris, while in England over half a million men were on out-of-work donations.

On that early summer night, cool and damp, Katrina and I walked back to the Hôtel de Crillon from rue du Mont Thabor where Anson had dropped us for dinner. The Daimler had made an impressive arrival with the Union

Jack flying and five francs from the petrol fund for the doorman. With Anson pressed and smart in his suit, playing the civilian with no salute, but always a big wink.

Katrina was radiant. My head was still held in a vice and I could not keep my eyes off her: walking to our table ahead of me, standing on the dance floor with her back to the dancers, inviting me toward her with her smile. Or her glow in the candlelight as she listened to my stories, my boy's prattle after a bottle of red.

Katrina wore her new outfit from Lelong, saved for and talked about for weeks. A silk shift with a dark crushed velvet skirt over, green in one light, grey in another. A matching ribbed cape for the street with a high Napoleon collar. Pulled up against her cropped neck, protecting her beautiful face from the wind, scudding through the arcades of rue de Rivoli. A soft velvet hat down over her eyes.

After our meal, after our dancing, we walked fast to keep warm.

She talked in French, she talked in her English. Katrina talked of nursing, of Pierre and his drinking, of the shops on rue du faubourg Saint-Honoré. About Paris, the Paris we had come to know together. Then about another Paris, seen from the outside, as a German for her twenty-five years, a supposed-to-be-German with supposed-not-to-be-French parents.

But when we reached the Crillon, Anson was not waiting as arranged. There was no mistaking our cars, always parked in front, ostentatious as the victors.

I really had no plan, no clever design. I did not intend to be ambiguous or suggestive.

'I have a new room,' I said to Katrina, 'here in the hotel, the place is almost empty. You should come up and see.' It was just something to say as we stood outside, looking for a large black shape and a round friendly face.

Then the reply that I always remember, for ever like her smile.

'*Cela doit arriver, Yves. Alors, pourquoi pas ce soir?*' It's going to happen one night, Yves, so...

Her answer took me by surprise, there on the pavement looking for my car and my driver to take Katrina home. With the evening ended, I thought, with Katrina ready to go back to her cell at the École Militaire, I thought. The place I was not allowed to enter, where I had never asked to go. Blue walls, a beige tile floor and three nurses to a room. But always fresh flowers on the window-sill, she had told me with a smile.

I began to feel weak and incapable like the moments before climbing the ladder. As if unable to complete what I had started, with my letter writing, with the deliveries, our magic looks across noisy rooms and crowded streets. The feel of her body beside me, her scent through spring air.

The doorman opened the heavy glass doors, brass polished up like Beaurepaire. We walked across marble floors, through the welcoming smells of the Crillon foyer: perfume, cigars, cream sauces, but all distant and restrained.

There were meeting rooms on the top floor, above my room, so our passage to the lifts was not remarkable even at midnight. Even to some fellow officer, the nod-and-wink type, the made-out-last-night-did-we type.

We looked at each other behind the bellboy's back, Katrina calm, me nervous.

The corridors were guarded by American sentries who kept all the room keys, an over-reaction to the shooting of Clemenceau by one lone anarchist. But now the Americans no longer trusted French security anywhere. They even had their men keep watch on the chambermaids while they were in the rooms. And what could have been a regular miracle of Franco-US cooperation was probably missed entirely by the humourless Americans.

The trooper on guard duty was a man I knew and there was no trouble, he had seen all the sights come and go. But I felt his eyes following the back of my tunic as Katrina and I walked away down the corridor.

Inside the door we kissed in the dark. I felt her response, her pressing toward me, from her thin firm lips and down her silk shift, down to her knees against mine. I wanted to go forward and backwards both at the same time.

There was a knock on the door. We jumped.

'Loot'nant Bowchamp?' Katrina walked over to the bathroom and shut the door behind her.

'A Corporal *Aa*-nson's here with an *aut*-omobile, *sir*.'

Anson was bothered because he was late. Been to the Gare du Nord, he said, with some Belgian general.

'Wanted to tell me how proud he was that we had fought a war for his little country. On and bleed'n' on. Been knocking it back on the top floor I think, sir. Wouldn't let me go. Carried his bag to the carriage and everything, he even...'

'...not to worry, I won't be needing the car. Looks like my luck's in.'

More fraud than joke, a joke in bad taste, I had the breeze up. Anson smiled at me, he was the married one. He said he was on all night and he would come back when I was ready. He gave me his wink again.

The door to the room was not locked.

A pale light fell across the bed from the square outside. Katrina's head showed above the embroidered sheets. Her white silk combinations and stockings lay over the back of a large gilt chair.

She looked up at me, haloed in the recesses of the large pillows like that celestial being. Her smile, my smile, the smile for me only.

I undressed in the dark and lay against her, shaking and overwhelmed.

Slowly Katrina started to bathe me in her skin. Her hands across my shoulders, a finger running gently up and down my spine as she kissed me. Her breasts brushing against my chest, soft and wonderfully female. Then Katrina pressed me to her, enveloping me with her arms, with her scent, welcoming me against her body.

It was as if time stood still, as if there was a lifetime ahead of us just for touching and exploring. It was heaven, it was paradise on earth. There are no words for such wonderful intimacy, such fulfilment of dreams.

Katrina laid me on my back and she stroked my face. I began to float, to rise off the bed and into the sky, drifting away silently among the stars. I could look back down on the city, the hotel, the bed. At my Katrina as she began to make love to me.

Then I was inside her, reaching, loving up into her. And I was held, loved by her in return.

'Do you feel me,' she whispered, '*comme je t'adore?*' I opened my eyes but I was watching from the heavens once more. '*Oh, que je t'adore,*' she repeated and she started to kiss me all over again.

We lay still in our magic bubble, as if warmed by the flames of an unseen fire. I held her as I had imagined back on that first day. Tight against all the world, tight against everything and everyone beyond.

Then Katrina was hungry again and I wanted champagne. The Americans had left their mark on the hotel: toasted tuna sandwiches and a bottle of Veuve-Cliquot came up in under ten minutes.

As Katrina sat up in the bed with her sandwich on a plate, I put my head into her lap. Her presence overwhelmed me once again. She was irresistible, it was a starvation that would go on without end.

There must have been some sleep. But then through tall glass windows we could see the shadows of dawn turning and fading between the arches of the Palais Bourbon on the other side of the river.

Katrina lay across the bed on her front watching the light while I watched the curve of her buttocks, the line of her back and her shoulders. I moved up behind her and nibbled at her ear. I wanted her again. Again and again without end.

I knew that my life had been changed, that my torn ends had found their perfect match. Everything resolved, by Katrina's skin, by the shape of her breasts, her lips to mine. By love which conquers all.

4

I lay in bed fully clothed. The clothes the army had given me when I was demobilized as no longer required. Together with £16 3s. 2d. and my uniform folded into a brown cardboard suitcase.

After the end of the Conference, in December 1919, I had been demobbed in England and I had returned to Ethel's house, to Plymouth Road, St Ives. Instinctive, disastrous.

My room was sharp with cold, ready to grip me with raw pincers if I moved from the bed. I dozed and woke with a frantic start. But there was no danger to my men. Because I had no men. No diversions from the freezing Cornish day. No protection from wind penetrating the walls themselves. From hard icy rain that thrashed against the window.

I had lived on another sphere but now I was back again in the same schoolboy's narrow bed.

Then in my drifting memory it was the year before, long ago like a decade. The second week of November '18. Still mild, winter had yet to set in. On my last gym for Major Graves.

He had walked into my little office again unannounced.

'Can't tell you about this one, Beauchamp,' he said. 'Don't know myself.'

I was to prepare another lorry: petrol, blankets, food, tools and spare parts of all kinds. I was to take Serjeant Jones and eight men to report at 4th Army HQ, General Rawlinson's advanced headquarters near Beaumont where our right flank met the French.

The journey took all day, one hundred and fifty miles in congested military traffic. But by then conditions were different. There were smiles and cheers for us from an army moving forward.

From 4th Army HQ we were pushed up the line. The next morning we reached a battalion HQ at La Capelle, a town conceded by the Germans only the previous day. The liberation had been so fast that the townspeople were untouched in their houses. Every balcony was hung with rudimentary British and French flags.

We were only forty miles beyond the wide beet fields of Cambrai but here the country was different, filled with tight hedgerows, little valleys with limited horizons.

Finally I was taken forward on foot by an infantry captain toward his outpost, then across to his right and through the flank of the French lines. No familiar wire or trenches marked the front which was making ground every day.

A pottery factory on the road from La Capelle was being used for a conference when we arrived. A group of British and French officers was huddled around a map. Throwing-wheels and piles of shards lined the walls of the room.

'Here's the mechanic,' the captain said as we entered. A major turned toward me from the table.

'You from GHQ?' he asked abruptly.

'Yes, sir.'

He looked at my uniform, old style tunic, Sam Browne and armband. All the British officers in the room were wearing Tommy serge.

'Oh,' the major started again, almost apologetically, looking at my chest, 'seems you're pretty familiar with the business end.'

The major continued before I could reply.

'There's a cease-fire on this line,' he said. 'A Bosche Armistice Commission is coming through to meet the Generalissimo in Compiègne. Been lots of rumours about them throwing in the towel but it seems that this is the real thing. There's a group of their sappers out there now mending the road and removing fallen trees.' The major showed me on the map the route the Germans were to take.

The front was quiet, the local cease-fire had spread to the artillery.

'We don't know what state their transport is in, so we've agreed with the French to be responsible for fixing up the Bosche motors when they arrive. Can't have them breaking down behind our lines. You a specialist in Bosche engines?'

There had been a lot of needless deaths during our advance from hidden mines and delayed action shells. Even with a cease-fire, stranded Germans would have been at risk for their lives.

We brought up our lorry and we waited behind the pottery factory through dusk and into the evening. Bright lights were turned on, run from a distant generator. There was activity up the road toward the German lines. I could hear the clink of shovels on pavé, the chop of axes and the call of voices from their men working on the road.

Then after nine o'clock headlights appeared from the north. Four pairs, travelling toward our reception party at high speed. The lights were hypnotic, thrilling, holding me in frozen anticipation by the side of the road. Dust blew across the approaching glare, dramatic like theatre smoke.

A bugler on one of the cars was sounding four notes repeatedly.

Tah-ha, tah-HAAA.

Then the cars were stopped in front of us. Four large open tourers of the type used by the German General Staff, a Mercedes-Benz in the lead and three Hansa-Lloyds. The cars were filthy, but large black eagles could be made out painted on the back doors. The man with the bugle was standing on the running-board of the second car. A large white flag hung off the back of the lead car which really did turn out to be a towel, tied to a broomstick.

A circle of French soldiers in their ridged helmets appeared out of the dark and surrounded the cars. As the first German stepped down there was some ragged clapping from the *poilus*.

Voices asked: *'C'est fini la guerre?'*

Others shouted defiantly from the back.

'Vive la France!'

Immediately French officers were on to the cars checking papers and looking for arms. I found two German junior officers in the last car, the adjutants to the Armistice Commission. Almost all the others were civilians.

Oberleutnant Schimmelpfennig and Leutnant Schacht clicked their heels and shook hands. Then they stood by, rigid in their *feldgrau* overcoats and peaked caps, watching my men start work on their cars. We repaired a number of punctures and we supplied oil, petrol and water. We handed the passengers blankets and we made them tea.

Then the convoy was off again, bugle blaring, toward La Capelle where representatives were waiting from General Debeney of the French First Army.

We followed later and I found that there had been a change of plan. The German Commission had been transferred to French cars and they were then to board a train at Tergnier. I found Leutnant Schacht in the mess hotel trying to read a French army newspaper. He was to wait with their cars in La Capelle under a French guard, for the return of his Commission.

We had imagined that a cease-fire would take place immediately but the next morning small arms fire started up again across the front line. There was little shelling and it was clear that neither side was planning an attack. But the Germans were still a strong fighting force despite the collapse of their allies, the Austrians, the Turks and the Roumanians.

Three days dragged by before there was any word. I had no orders but I decided to wait at La Capelle to see the German cars back to their lines.

Schacht and I talked in the evenings, both of us nervous and suspicious. He spoke English slowly with a heavy accent. His Christian name, he told me, was Werner. He was tall and bony, not handsome, ungainly under stiff posture and polished manners.

I found that his career was similar to mine: time in the trenches then an unwanted posting to their General Staff at Spa. Although unlike mine, his escape had been arranged by his family.

Schacht had trouble with my name and he finally settled on Lieutenant Petrol-man. On the second day I saw him smile, his hollow face softer, human, as he watched me give my orders for the day to the men. Something familiar, common to both armies. Slowly we warmed up.

Then early on 11 November we heard that an armistice was to come into effect at eleven o'clock that morning and that the Kaiser had abdicated. Germany said that it was now a democratic republic.

With Schacht I walked back to the front to find a way for him to return across the lines with his cars. Their Commission had met with Foch in his *wagon lit* on a railway siding in the woods near Compiègne. Now the Germans were to return directly to Spa by train.

We stood behind the pottery factory sharing a flask of rum. There was sporadic firing. Then as the hour approached, intense bursts came from the German Maxims, but high, a long way over our heads.

A few minutes before eleven everything fell quiet.

A plane buzzed overhead, larks sang.

Suddenly there was more firing, Verylights of every colour, bright in the sky like guiding stars. Then men from both sides appeared out of foxholes, from behind hedges, upright in No-Man's-Land. Self-conscious as if caught standing naked in a bath. Just to be vertical and in the open was a miracle after years of ducking and crouching. Groups began to meet across the line, exchanging belts and helmets, cigarettes, food and drink.

A dull listless celebration started in the village behind our front lines, French and British mixed together. I took Leutnant Schacht for the conventional drink. I was almost his height so I gave him my greatcoat and cap to wear instead of his, as a disguise. In the corner of a café we drank to the Armistice but he was agitated and anxious to leave.

My men prepared his empty convoy. With the cars running I opened my arms out to him French style, wide and spontaneous on that miraculous day. Schacht and I clasped each other rigidly, our faces held self-consciously apart.

Then he was gone.

My spheres turned as I lay in my bed in my grandmother's house. Without moving, thankful merely to be warm. Turning, globes turning, one inside the other: Paris, Katrina, the Armistice, the Peace. Never still, never resolved.

In Versailles the Gentlemen on the Reparations Commission had started their meetings after the Treaty was signed. How much was the Bosche to pay? Six billions or thirty-two billions? My cars came and went. The Gentlemen were undecided while the Germans said that they had nothing anyway.

On the second day of the meetings, there was the Leutnant from La Capelle, astonishingly, standing on the steps of the Hôtel Trianon Palace. Hardly recognizable in a dark suit and black hat. I was unchanged, still in my uniform and he spotted me immediately.

'Lieutenant Petrol-man, you too in Paris? Now you must have an easier job.' But he did not smile.

His English had improved noticeably although he seemed halting and reserved. Not the same man from our short time together behind the lines.

'We should have another drink,' I said to him, without thinking of the difficulties. 'To celebrate the Peace this time.'

The Leutnant pulled a face and shook his head.

'There is nothing for which to celebrate,' he replied stiffly. 'It is not like the Armistice.'

But I would not let him go. I felt a bond between us. I was sure, two young soldiers who had survived. The bond we had made in the last days of the war. We could compare stories, I thought, about who was to blame. I would tell him about LG and we would laugh together at the politicians. I was confident that there would be no trouble at the barriers with his civvies and my FO car. French enthusiasm had fallen off since the signing in June.

Finally he said he would come although he made it sound like a favour.

That night with the Field-Marshal in London, I took the Silver Ghost from the garage. As if to confirm the official nature of my journey.

I told Katrina that I had met an old friend. I asked her to come with me to entertain him, to show him Paris. She was enthusiastic. Katrina had met Vernon, she had even shaken hands with LG at the Majestic. But this was different, I said. This man was an officer from the front. I had met him during the War, I said.

With the Leutnant in the car I made for the École Militaire.

As I drove I talked, not about politics but about Katrina. I told the Leutnant she was a nurse from Alsace, we were exploring Paris together.

'Kongratu-*lay*-tions,' he said, 'a young thing from the Imperial Territories.'

But I understood too late.

We arrived at the nurses' entrance at the back of the École Militaire. I went to the door while the Leutnant waited by the car. Katrina emerged smiling me her beautiful smile, nibbling at my cheek and feeling for my hand, laughing at the spectacle of the Silver Ghost.

As we approached, the Leutnant straightened up.

'*Leutnant Werner Schacht, Volkskommission für das Friedensheer,*' he announced, heels coming together and a small bow toward Katrina.

There was a moment of deafening silence like the end of a barrage.

Katrina looked at me.

'*C'est un boche,*' she said quietly. Her face was frozen steel.

And I knew that I had made a dreadful mistake.

Katrina turned abruptly, shoes crunching in the gravel and she was gone.

5

In Cornwall there were no reminders of war. Memorials had yet to be built, there were no cripples, no demob camps.

But here my nightmares returned. The rattle of a pane was a Maxim spitting death. Or a barn door slammed in the wind and I would come heaving out of bed, standing on the boards shivering in sudden cold, turning desperately this way and that trying to see where the shell had landed. I watched events that I could not stop: Thompson flying across furrows, men sliding away interminably, teddy bears, blankets, string. Down into muddy craters.

In Paris Katrina used to wake me on those nights then move in close behind me. A perfect mould, a suit of armour for my weak flesh. Her lips would start to play on the back of my neck, one hand lightly on my stomach. Then I would be erect and pressing myself into her, my form to her mould. As if she were my flint, the very spark of life itself.

And one night at the Hôtel de Crillon, awake and panting, blinding light from an explosion still flashing behind my eyes, well after my tearful apologies for the night of the Silver Ghost and her forgiveness, I had tried to tell her. That all death is equal. That Werner Schacht was me, his life, the death he had missed, an infinitely small part in the same huge Machine. That he was no different just for being German.

I felt Katrina tense against me in our cocoon, her breath hard against my cheek.

But I had to tell her, that was what I believed.

My head boiled with a fever of riddles. Their army had not been beaten in the field, there never would have been final victory for our infantry against their guns along the Rhine. I had watched them on the last day: firing off their Maxims, exchanging helmets and badges. Still in France. But Müller and Bell, the new German ministers, had acknowledged right in the Treaty, the defeat and the guilt of Germany. Without their artillery did they have a choice? Did that make them the ones to blame?

Alsace was part of France again but now we were causing the deaths of German women and children with our blockade. Werner had seen it with his own eyes. How many innocent deaths until Katrina felt avenged? Two hundred thousand, three hundred thousand?

But Katrina would not listen and she stormed at me for trying.

Now it was her turn to cry, face dissolving into a torrent of tears and quivering flesh. I held her cheeks between my hands and I tried to kiss her, I was wet with her salt and her spittle. But she tore away from me and around the room. She would not stop and she would not hear, she would have none of my *ignominies*.

Then she was back at me beating at my chest with her fists, her naked frame racked, swept away into an hysteria by a subterranean river that I could not see. A torrent of vengeance and frustration that flowed wide and deep within her and back through generations.

As I persisted Katrina streamed and sobbed, her body trembling as she gasped for air through froth-stitched lips.

Then she let out a shriek, as if to end it all. As if to cleave the carpeted floor and take us both down to hell together:

'*Niemals! Niemals! Wir werden Ihnen niemals verzeihen!*'

Immediately Katrina clapped her hands to her ears, fingers pressing at her temples as if in sudden terrible pain. Distorting her eyes, pulling frantically at her face, masking back tight skin, disfigured over her skull.

Then she turned and ran for the bathroom, locking the door. Katrina's unrestrained weeping echoed back to me off the hollow, useless splendours of marble floors and mosaic walls.

I had tried to tell her. Tell her what I had seen in the last few days as the War had ended. What I knew for myself.

Never! Never! We will never forgive them!

But in her extreme distress Katrina had screamed at me in German.

I stared at the ceiling above my bed in Cornwall. A patch of damp was spreading across the plaster from the far corner of the room, a dirty brown flecked with fungus. The shape could be a cloud, a map of France, Katrina's face.

Her jaw sharp, teeth clenched in rage, her skin tinged a furious bile-grey. Her head turns and she is walking away, quick fierce footsteps crunching in the gravel. Then I am running after her, but too slow. She closes the door on me, the nurse's residence where I cannot follow.

I remembered me defiant.

If she makes me choose, I'll choose. I would take Werner to see Paris without her. Did she not know that the War was over? That the Peace had been signed?

At first there was satisfaction in watching Werner as we drove. The Paris of their Bosche dreams, the place they could not have. In displaying my new knowledge, in repeating all that André had taught me.

The city came alive that July night as the sun set, orange and a bottomless blue over the Bois. Spectacular illuminations everywhere: bridges, buildings, monuments and churches, the years of darkness were being avenged.

We drove along the river then I parked beneath the Tour Eiffel. Lanterns had been hung through the Champ-de-Mars and back up to the École Militaire. Katrina was missing the sights and an exhilarating drive in the Silver Ghost. But what did I care? Werner was my comrade-in-arms. And the two of us were together, whole and alive.

We crawled through the quartier Latin, crowds thronging the streets and surging around the car. After midnight we climbed the fresh white steps of the Basilique du Sacré Coeur. And like Satan on the high mountain I showed Werner the whole tempting city, looking down from Montmartre. *All this power will I give thee and the glory.* But the future is unknowable except that the devil will collect his due.

I learned that Werner played the piano, he wanted to visit Chopin's grave. We drove along République and I parked at the gates of Père Lachaise cemetery. In the dark we walked the winding boulevards of the dead, past fantastic tombs packed in like books. Up and down under full beech trees, over cobbles large as loaves.

The simple grave was a mound of fresh flowers, just from that day or the day before: lilies, white roses and wreaths. Then hand-painted plaster statues and months and months of messages pinned to rondures or on scraps of paper held down by pebbles against the breeze.

Fryderyk, mon amour. Pour ton anniversaire. 22/02/1919. And, *A toi! Chevalier de la Pologne!*

The tomb was macabre and joyful both at the same time. While all Napoleon's famous soldiers in their elaborate sepulchres were ignored: Ney, Murat, Macdonald. Only the pale consumptive artist lived on in his vulnerable lyric trills.

'They will be dancing the mazurka in Warsaw now,' Werner said with his long sombre face. 'We tried to say that Poland did not exist, that the partition was forever. It was wrong maybe. But this *Nestbeschmutzung* the Prussian will never accept.'

We walked on in silence. Then Werner surprised me again.

'How many geniuses do you think were killed by the War, Yves, men whose work we will never know? If there is a great composer in ten million people, the War must have killed at least one, yes?'

Werner's figures included German civilians, Russians and Poles, remote peoples Frances Stevenson had not counted in her totals.

Then Werner started to tell me about the dreadful conditions in Germany. About starvation, about fighting in the streets, the powerless republic, constant rumours of a *Putsch* and the threat of Bolshevism. In Berlin alone thousands had died each day from starvation and the Spanish flu during that terrible winter.

'But I do not read of this in your newspapers,' Werner said. 'It is clear that our history will be written by those who say they are the victors.'

The value of the mark was dropping and there was no work. There was no confidence in the government at Weimar and the first election under complicated rules had produced no clear result. But he was lucky, Werner said, his family had land in Bavaria and he was to stay on in the Peace Army under Generaloberst von Seeckt.

We drove back from the cemetery through Bastille. Werner was curious about everything: the night street cleaners, the buses. Food, clothes and furniture plentiful in shop windows. Where did it all come from? Who were these people, well fed and well dressed out on the streets late at night?

'We could never have won the War,' Werner mumbled as if to himself, 'against a coalition of the whole world. With all this behind you when we had nothing left. It was a delusion, a lie even.'

We raced through the Marais and onto rue Notre Dame de Lorette. The streets and buildings a radiant blur past the Silver Lady on the radiator. The city of the gods who live in France.

I told Werner that I would take him to a place where Prime Ministers ate and I pulled up outside Le Rat Mort. We found a table amid the clatter and confusion. The same tenor and the same violin were struggling through the same aria.

'I drove Mr Lloyd George one night,' I said. 'And he brought me here.'

Werner made a frowning face to say that he did not believe me. Then he laughed showing a row of large shark's teeth.

'He told me there would be no more war,' I insisted. 'Never again, LG promised me.'

Werner ate his soup and drank his wine in silence. Then he looked up at me over his cheese-laced spoon.

'That is not what we say, Yves. What we say is that the slaves will rise again. My uncle says that beggars cannot pay.'

We had to shout to make ourselves heard, leaning toward each other across the little table.

'Here in Paris,' Werner began as I strained to listen, 'I am only the adjutant again, like La Capelle. My uncle, Hjalmar Schacht, is advisor to the Republic Delegation on Reparations. I listen to them talk, in the train, at the hotel. My uncle is a clever man who knows about money, a liberal who was against many things during the war. He asks: if we do not pay, what will the Allies do? Will their soldiers come and cut the trees, will they dig the coal and run the factories? They call it *unerträglich* and *unerfüllbar*, they say it will never work. When the treaty starts in January our people will see what a black day it was when Versailles was signed.'

I did not understand. At least it was peace. And for me the day the Treaty was signed had been the peak of my Staff career.

Captain Vernon had been even warmer than usual.

'Quite respectable for an amateur,' he said to me after the delegates and the frocks had all been driven away. Swaying backwards and forwards, pretending to be serious.

The signing at the Palace of Versailles was a French show like the Armistice. But we had over sixty of our cars and taxis to integrate with theirs: LG and our frocks; our Embassy cars; the foreign delegations on my list; visitors from England with their ladies. And the Germans.

I stood to the side, inconspicuous against the wall, checking off our motors as they arrived at the Cour de Marbre. The flow was fast, in the numbered order displayed on each windscreen, wheels bouncing up over large stones. Past the banners and the Republican Guard lined up along the Cour des Ministres. A cross marked the place where the passengers were to be landed. A rabble of diminutive *poilus* and footmen in layers of livery opened and closed doors, the cars hardly came to a halt.

Serjeant Jones was at the Hôtel des Réservoirs and Corporal Anson was at the main gate of the Palace. Our part went off without a hitch.

By then the first government of the First German Republic had fallen and the Count did not return to Paris. Now Germany was represented by Herr Hermann Müller, the Foreign Minister of the second government of the First German Republic, and by Doktor Johannes Bell, their Minister of Transport.

I had allocated the German delegates one car each and I watched them arrive at the palace. Müller was no Count, but even he stepped from the car into the intimidating splendour of Versailles, defiant and upright, winged collar and bowler hat. Like a martyr to his execution.

Unrepentant and undefeated. Just going through the motions, as Thompson would have said.

In less than an hour it was over. The Great Men came out on to the Terrasse d'Eau through the glass doors below the Salle des Glaces. Fountains sprang into life after four years of drought. French 75s thundered in the distance, the final dreadful echo of war.

In the gardens, the new celebrities of Versailles mingled with the ghosts. The frocks and their self-congratulations with the rustle of silk brocade, with the flick of a fan. With the tap tap tap of little red heels that had carried their wearer to the guillotine.

After our meal that evening I drove Werner back to the Hôtel des Réservoirs. I reassured him that there would be no trouble with the French at the barrier. I told him about the Count and the visit to the Bagatelle gardens.

Werner said that the Count was very popular in Germany after the first government had fallen. The Count had said publicly that Versailles was a trick. That he would prefer occupation to slavery. He had urged the German government not to sign. To call the Allies' bluff and then to watch as the Paris Conference collapsed.

The Allies had told their peoples that they had won a Great Victory, the Count had said, to hide the facts. So if Germany refused to sign, then the French and British politicians would be forced to admit the truth. That the War had ended with an armistice, not with the defeat of Germany.

'Our friendship is important,' Werner said to me when we parted on his last night in Paris, after another of our cumbersome embraces. 'And I know that we will meet again.'

I had felt the same thing.

6

The house in Cornwall and everything to do with it was oppressive. From the residents, the Chicken-Gutter and my mother the scullery maid, to the austere symmetry of the mottled white façade. Even Plymouth Road, a featureless cutting running in front of the house and on past Treganet's farm.

There was nothing bucolically picturesque about the Treganet piggery.

Abandoned carts, rusting ploughs, discarded piles of apple boxes and barrels littered the banks to his drive, all overgrown by thick menacing weeds. For years the roof of his barn had been under repair following a fire. Tiles piled haphazardly on blackened purlins, gave the farm the look of a small village abandoned after the passage of the plague.

A black slurry of mud and dung flowed around Treganet's farm buildings and out on to Plymouth Road, covering all who bicycled, rode or merely walked past his entrance.

The blight behind Ethel's house was no better. The Chicken-Gutting Empire was housed in a collection of tumbledown sheds. Nothing was ever done to the farm which was not absolutely necessary for that day's production. Sheets of water spewed off gutterless roofs all year round creating man-eating ponds of dirty brown slop around which the workers trailed back and forth carrying sacks and buckets, or boxes of prepared birds ready for stacking and shipping. The stench was almost visible like gas.

By the end of the War Ethel had added a second abattoir and two further batteries. Low metal buildings lit by electric light day and night, in which the hens lived during their short egg-laying life. When disturbed by an intruder bringing feed or collecting eggs they surged like demented minnows in a shoal from one end to the other, then back again. All their ugly little red heads pointing in the same direction, starting this way then that, mindless, despicable.

Then after a year or two of production, their usefulness at an end, the birds were herded into pens next to the abattoir for their final reward.

The plant was staffed by twelve to fifteen large, taciturn Cornishmen. The men who did the slaughtering were distinguished from labourers by their grey, stained whites, splattered with chicken culm, trousers tucked into large wellington boots covered in dried blood. Ethel seemed to come no higher than the navel of the shortest of the men but even the tallest cowered in her presence. If she knew names she never used any.

'*Branlaires!*' she would start. '*Chourmo de feiniantas!*' Her favourite expressions. Waving her arms in the direction of the nearest workers whether or not the men in question were responsible for the latest infraction.

'How many times have I told yer? Get that feed out o' wet.' Or, 'If 'nother 'scapes, it's *yous* for the pot.'

There was a nominal foreman who lived in the old Riley Lane house. But his function was to take the worst of the abuse on behalf of the men, not to dilute Ethel's iron control over processing.

The old smell from Riley Lane pervaded the new house, curtains, bedding and residents, the stink increasing in stale repulsiveness in the rooms most remote from the kitchen. My bedroom, at the end of the upper landing, not opened for months at a time during term, seemed for the first few days after my return to have rotting chicken cadavers hidden somewhere within the room itself.

The new furniture was worse than the old, larger, uglier, placed about the rooms in such a way as to make occupation seem transitory: wardrobes behind doors that could not be opened fully, dressing tables and mirrors obscuring windows, large chairs backing on to unused fireplaces.

And for all Ethel's expenditure on this substantial house, of considerable possibilities in other hands, there were neither decorations nor pictures.

The kitchen was much larger than Riley Lane and here Ethel had brought together all the steps of her procedure. Stained table, chopping block, slop bucket, an apple box for heads, feet and feathers. Against the back wall a line of headless birds hung across the ceiling.

At any time in the morning or the evening, to enter the kitchen could be to witness a flurry of feathers and a frantic beating of wings. A desperate final squawk and a dull thud as Ethel dispatched a special order large black cock or a petrified white pullet. Then a loud splattering would start as the shaking corpses bled into a galvanized tub.

The Coronation biscuit tin and her private customers continued to receive Ethel's daily attention, even though now, as the sole owner of the Empire, it was her own birds that she purloined. She was obsessed, she could not stop.

Two enormous Agas covered by boiling vats simmered under a stone ventilation canopy which I found had been blocked with newspaper because Ethel complained of draughts. Here my mother had taken up her old position, still wearing the same faded wrap-around pinny, frayed headscarf and matted slippers.

The vats of stewing offal had increased in proportion with the larger house and the expanded Empire. They were now so heavy that two farmhands were needed to carry each load out to the pigs. And the pig colony had grown in numbers to become a small commercial farm in itself.

Convinced that the pork butcher who bought her animals was making a small fortune with each pig, Ethel had a new ambition: to make and sell her own sausage. I knew that one morning I would enter the kitchen to find her pursuing a squealing piglet as it skittered around the table, the dripping chicken dispatcher held murderously high.

By my last year at Martyr's I had come to live at the very far end of a barren desert which separated me from what passed for my family. I posed with my interest in music, literature and European history. I wore my hair long, constantly flipping a dangling fringe out of my eyes with an affected twitch. And in the holidays I sported the coloured ties and brown shoes which I so despised during term. Worn as a badge of my superiority over my mother and grandmother and over the members of the farming community around Plymouth Road.

Maybe Ethel had expected me to pitch in and help during the holidays, raking and bagging chicken droppings, swilling chicken feed down metal troughs. But my precious, disdainful appearance precluded even the mention of work. France, the only possible point of contact between us, had been closed off two years before, with the map.

Ethel started referring to me as 'her young gentleman'.

'So, *vieue*, what's my young gentleman up to today?' she would say. Or, 'Hasn't my young gentleman got any of his school work to do?'

I made a show of reading in the unused front parlour for a while each morning to appease Ethel and stop the comments. But her creation bewildered her and Ethel had no clear idea of what should happen next.

Then in the Easter holidays of 1917, before my last term at that school, Ethel had produced her solution.

As '16 had turned to '17, until Mr Lloyd George had become Prime Minister, the government could not lead and our army could not win. The first rush of volunteers had been sent to France in '14 and '15, never to return. Now conscription had made everyone cautious. Parents heard rumours of a compromise between Britain and Germany, of peace resolutions in the Reichstag and they asked themselves if the sacrifice of more of their children was really necessary. Service was postponed until full age, or reserved occupations were found that avoided conscription altogether.

At the end of the year before, Ethel had been to see a firm of solicitors in St Ives to sign the deeds and share certificates which had crowned her fifteen years of effort, making her the sole owner of the Empire. Dalgetty, her former employer, was out, destroyed.

I was at school so I missed the spectacle: the big black car, the dead fox and the argument with the solicitors about who was to hold the papers.

'*Pèrque?*' Ethel had asked them, she told me proudly. 'What good's it do to '*av* the place if I don't '*av* the papers?'

And with that the blood-encrusted fingers had picked the documents off the solicitor's desk and deposited them in to the Coronation biscuit tin.

I could imagine the horrified solicitors and their exaggerated protestations, waffling and mumbling as they realized that with the deeds and share certificates out of their safe Ethel could take her next legal business elsewhere without even so much as an explanation.

'I mean to say, Mrs Stoat...' Or, 'Well, er, really what? If you insist, Mrs Stoat...'

So faced with Ethel's determination, the upper hand, the solicitors had been ready to accommodate her suggestion about her grandson.

'There, yer can start July,' she said to me. 'First off yer'll be making the tea,' she added, before I understood. 'And yer won't be needing no new clothes neither,' she went on as her scheme began to dawn on me. 'Yer can wear yer old school suits.'

In early '17 awareness of the scale of the casualties in France had reached even the Cornish countryside. Just the endless flow of names each week in the local paper told the story. There was talk of *leaving the Hun where he is*, and of *getting on with our lives*. Little Belgium seemed less important by then. And our huge shipping losses to U-boats in the Atlantic at the same time as the defeat of the Russians all seemed to add up to an impossible situation.

Ethel, for one, was quite ready to make peace.

'Never 'ad any of them Germans round 'ere bothering me,' she said.

They could have been in the next county so long as her processing continued undisturbed. Nor did she want to see me, the product of her ambitions and her expenditure, going to waste. Ethel was confident that she could arrange an exemption for me as an agricultural worker, necessary on the farm for the War Effort. And of course, she said, there wouldn't be no one round checking. Then with my farm papers in order I could start work for the solicitors.

But making tea in my three piece suit, starting as a shell again just as I thought I was about to free myself of Martyr's, it was unimaginable. I refused to her face and the talons came out immediately.

'Well, yer can't just 'ang around 'ere when yer's out of school, yer know. I'm not supporting any little toffee-noses with nothing to do all day.'

The world had seemed to have me cornered and I had joined the army.

But now after the War, lying in my bed again, nothing had changed.

I imagined the solicitors: Cairns & Young was the name of the firm. Offices upon offices full of fatuous, self-important pipe-smoking Mathers and Hardcastles, ready with their dull-witted training for the new junior. Five or six years, just for a qualification.

'Tea, Beecham? You call this tea? Never make a solicitor at this rate, you know.' Or, 'Fine woman, your grandmother, she could teach us all a thing or two. You should try to be more like *her*.'

I had written to my mother from OCB but I had not been able to explain why I had joined the army a year and a half early. Reasons that blurred Plymouth Road with Pond House, Mather with the unknown solicitors, their tea urns with Ethel's buckets of blood.

My mother had replied, stiff, formal, as if she had already said her final goodbye. I wrote again from France, after Cambrai. From Montreuil, trying to say that I would survive. Survive when my drivers were going missing, sometimes one a week during the final German attack. When I was up three days at a time without sleep, driving, riding the motorcycles, terrified, stupefied. Our line bulging, ready to burst. Trying to tell her what I did not believe, that the worst would not happen. But that things between us would never be the same again.

By the time I returned to Cornwall I was all those wonderful things: a full lieutenant, I wore an MC on my chest, I had seen the great events of the world with my own eyes. And above everything I loved the most beautiful woman in Paris.

The break with Ethel came on Christmas Day 1919.

The break came over money, but that was just the effect. The cause was my defeated mother, my dead father, my absent grandfather. The life I knew that other families lead. The mistakes they make, but their human existence together in which they find some meaning. Their love for each other.

By December 1919 I had used up all my back pay from Montreuil, even in devalued francs. I was under daily pressure to regularize my account from the Orderly Serjeant at the Majestic.

On demob I had been obliged to carry the debt over into civilian life. I had arrived at Plymouth Road in immediate need of three hundred pounds, then and there and a regular allowance thereafter like some of the others had. Ethel wanted a gentleman for a grandson. Gentlemen cost money.

I had come out with what I needed and a quarrel had started immediately.

'Didn't yer get paid in the army?' Ethel asked. 'War's over, yer know. Yer could be doing something useful.'

Did I need to grovel or was the answer really no? It was not clear and I did not like either alternative. There was Katrina and the whole world waiting beyond Plymouth Road.

With Ethel gone, my mother had tried to explain, trying to bring it all back to normal. To what passed as normal. How Ethel had worked so hard over the years. The first five years as a slaughterman in Dalgetty's abattoir, how would I like to do that? Then big debts to buy into the farm when Dalgetty had needed money for his horses. And always the fear of sliding back to Botchergate, of dying poor.

Ethel asked Treganet over for Christmas dinner and my mother spent the day at the Aga. Chicken in place of turkey, roasted with greasy gravy and overboiled vegetables as only the English know how. One of the big black cocks from the pen behind the house and Treganet's bitter farm brewed cider.

My mother asked me to wear my uniform and she changed into a dress, the first time that I can remember other than for the excursions. Production had stopped and the labourers had grudgingly been given the day off. Ethel had fed the birds herself that morning and collected the eggs. She was still wearing her stained whites at the table.

'Go try tell *'em* it's Christmas,' she said, nodding out toward the batteries.

My mother had set and decorated the table in the front parlour with holly from the lanes and two red candles.

We were a morose group. Ethel and Treganet exchanging stories of their hardships all told in short surly statements framed as questions.

Did 'e know this and did 'e know about that. With Treganet asking in reply, had she ever thought 'a zis or ever really counted 'a cozt 'a zat.

My mother running backwards and forwards from the kitchen, hardly sitting once during the entire meal, never saying a word. I had expected to be asked about the War or about Paris, bracing myself with a joke as a deflection. But my grandmother avoided subjects in which she did not have the upper hand, while Treganet hardly recognized my presence. I listened to the talk, helping myself to cider out of Treganet's reused ginger ale bottles. Always at the bottom of one, always looking for another.

I began to understand what they were talking about. They saw the end of rationing and wartime profits. The end of control over their workers with the threat of declassification.

No more pony traps sent to the train for their private customers in London. Cream, eggs, calf and chicken, all prepared in the barns out of sight of the Food Act inspectors. My mother had explained the boxes to me when I had asked one day, as *special orders.*

Even without black market rates, food prices had doubled during the war, with no control on profits and not many of Ethel's costs had increased.

LG had said to me a number of times, 'Have to sit with them, boy, round the table in the Coalition, hand them OBEs, call them Sir This and Lord That. I'll giv'em any Ruritanian title they'll pay for. But profiteers are the one breed I can't abide.'

How does a man justify to himself, LG had asked, making huge windfall profits? When others, his neighbour's sons say, were all off being slaughtered in France or drowning in the Atlantic. What went through that man's head?

That was how Ethel had paid for Plymouth Road, that was how she had doubled the size of the plant. Some scheme she and Treganet had cooked up over Dalgetty's prostrate body.

I became more and more drunk. Until I was on my feet, swaying and reeling.

'I know what's been going on here,' I started. 'You've been profiteering, while so many good men have been dying to, to...' Why *had* so many good men been dying? '...you're filthy profiteers, both of you, this whole house, this entire farm, stolen...'

Ethel and Treganet looked up at me from their dealings as if I had just popped through the floor.

'Si'down, yer dunnow what yer on about,' Ethel screamed. 'And half stewed.'

She turned to Treganet.

'Born a little bastard 'e was,' Ethel said. 'Right on the platform. Didn't even have a ticket. And a little bastard 'e'll always be. Just like 'is gran'father.'

'You've probably been upping your prices,' I continued, 'every time you hear of a U-boat attack.' Registering Ethel's words through the drink, but not understanding what she had meant about the platform and the ticket. Or the bastard.

'Siddown,' Ethel screamed again.

'No,' I shouted back, 'I'll not spend one more dreadful minute, eat one more shameful bite. The two of you should be in gaol.'

Then about my father and Canada. My grandfather. Where was he? She didn't even know if he was dead or alive. Her own husband. And my mother, look at her, just look at her, the scullery maid. And a lot more that I do not remember.

Upstairs I started to pack. My mother came in and sat on the bed weeping, her face in her hands. I continued to fill my case, red-faced and furious, no stopping me now. Anything, anything was better than this. This *taudis*, this slum of a chicken-gutting hell.

As I left into the cold night in my greatcoat, cap and gloves, carrying my suitcase, as I made through the door, my mother pressed a little bag into my hand. I looked at it later when I could see, when I could breathe. After the white light had gone. In the bag were the few remaining pieces of my mother's jewellery from Carlisle, from the good days.

And a note in her large simple writing.

Dear Yves. I am very sorry this is how you were told. It is true that I never married your father. There was nowhere to go. That is why we let Mother give you her family name. What Mother says is right, you were born on our way to Cornwall, at Exeter station. Love from Mother.

I had no idea where to go beyond Jowett's pub. I could think only of Katrina. I would hop a train, steal a boat ride. I was going to marry her, I had already told her so. I carried her last letter with me as my proof.

Yves, my darling, my intended, lover
Isn't the written word *wonderful!* You can sit on the steamer tonight, reading something I wrote early this morning, so that even if I had to work today, I can talk to you still.

I love you very much this morning. Deeper than I can find the words to explain, is my passion for you. All the feminine parts of my heart and my soul are lit up by you...as if you have a torch to light all the corners of my secret room.

It is possible to love more than one man in a lifetime, but not like this. And how is it possible that you found me, across the war, our different countries and histories, that we found each other?

You are so clever, and you will do so well in London. Of course I don't mind starting at the bottom. I have good training from Alsace, and I am sure that I will soon find a way of working with the wounded again. Life must be wonderful in London, like Paris. The concerts that you can explain to my ignorant ears, the new cinema, the drives into the famous countryside.

Oh! Yves, how can this all be true!

Yves' very own Katrina

In the last months at the Crillon my work had trailed off to nothing. I had watched only Katrina. I had dreamed only of her on the rare nights when we were not together.

I could see her, the bathroom door open a crack, dressing to go out. Me lying in the large bed: our corvette flying us across an endless sea under bright-edged clouds; our roan galloping us through leafy spring forests.

I could see her standing at the basin in her stockings and her underclothes, her corset embroidered with black owls. Shiny black shoes with large tongues like a pageboy. Then her Beer gown pulled over, black and lilac. A find we had made together at a Samaritaine sale. And her smart blanket coat, loose sleeves. Her shiny red hair slicked back. Katrina was all ready and I was still in bed.

Oh, where did we have to go?

Nothing, nobody could be as important as then, as that moment, as making love over again. Slowly once more from the start, supreme, consuming, unquenchable.

Vernon had told me to look him up and Lieutenant-General Clarke had given me his address. Vernon and a friend had an idea for modifying Morris tourers. They planned to rename his place Morris Garage, MG for short, he said. But I knew nothing about mechanics and the General lived in Newmarket. There were better things to be done, I was sure.

We had sat around sometimes in '17, in billets or in officers' cafés during the rest days, between spells in the trenches. We had a picture of how it would be after the War. You would think of the profession you wanted, you would be given some address in town, in London, smart in a new civilian suit and tie. You would mention your name to the receptionist and the Managing Director would come out of his office right away.

'Oh, *ssso* good of you to come, Lieutenant Beauchamp, we're truly honoured, *ssso* glad you chose *usss*.'

Then you would be shown to your desk and you would start work. Organizing men and supplies, seeing chums for lunch, going home at five o'clock to your pretty wife in a nice modern flat.

It had been so clear. *Usss* the returning heroes.

The NCOs and ORs had their own versions of the same picture: Thompson running his lathe shop, Jones driving his taxi cab.

Winning The War was all that had stood in our way.

PART IV

1

There was no doubt. I had the right pub.

'The Clarence,' he had said. 'D'you know the Admiralty? A building like a country house, but wires all over the roof. A row of niches for statues of famous admirals along the front wall. But of course they can't think of any, so they're all empty. Ha ha ha. Right opposite, on Whitehall, at the corner of Great Scotland Yard. You know, The Clarence.'

Wordy. Been drinking. Thinks he's funny.

Me with my big silver tray, black trousers covered with grease, dirty white shirt, striped waistcoat like an apprentice butler. All borrowed from Phillip, f-f-flipp'n'-f-fillip, d-d-damaged beyond my comprehension. Staff Officer for kitchen jobs, half a head and less of a body.

Me standing in the middle of the corridor leading from the kitchen to the private dining rooms. Holding out the tray so that Green could not get past without a scene.

Him looking down at me, not fully understanding what he was seeing.

The little boy from the next bed.

Yes, I had heard him correctly. The Clarence, but Green was nowhere to be seen.

I had decided to wear my old uniform. To help Green along with the good word, to make Green feel better about the little bit of help he was going to give me. Then as the idea grew, as a cover for what it was that I really planned to do.

I had no greatcoat against the March cold. I had taken them up on that offer as well, like the hostel and the queue for meals from Haig and his Officer's Association. Hand in your greatcoat at the left luggage office at any station and they paid you a pound. I needed the pound then but I needed my greatcoat now.

No gloves, cap out of shape from months in the suitcase, buttons tarnished, my good brown leather shoes leached in white patches by slop on the kitchen floor. Hair long and matted. One good look up and down and Staff-Serjeant Kempster would have had me in the guard room.

A penny three farthings for the beer and a penny for *The Times*, both to wait with. Enough for fish and chips for two days. I fiddled in my pocket with two thre'penny joeys, passing them through my fingers, one over the other. Feeling the worn surfaces like a blind man.

The last two joeys I had. The last two anythings. For dinner, for the next day, for the day after that, unless Phillip let me in to work another night. Or unless I broke my promise to myself and queued up again. And there could be no going back. Vernon, General Clarke, it was too late, there would have to be too many admissions.

But Green would give me a bit of help. With just the right little word. Because he's someone who does that, I thought. That intimate thing, that borderless thing, I said to myself, they would help, wouldn't they?

Yes. I would get a good word put in somewhere. With an estate agent's in south London, or with a removals company maybe, running men and vehicles again. Green's father might be a director, helping them out with his City connections. All for a small and quite manageable director's fee. Two hundred a year. Enough to pay the assistant gardener.

Just mention me. That is where I had started. The former soldier: full lieutenant, on his feet at the end, the MC, time in Paris as a transport organizer, a leader of men. A job to get me away from four nights a week at the hostel where no permanent residents were allowed. Away from my two nights under the bridge before I could go back. Away from the Savoy kitchen, from the comments of the kitchen clan.

Phillip they could take. So knocked about that cleaning was all he was good for, whatever rank he had held before. But me, the ex-officer with all four limbs, me with my stories of other kitchens, of being on the other side, me they could not tolerate.

Letting it slip after a few cups of their kitchen punch, all the leftover drinks and fruit juices mixed together. They drew me out and then they had their fun.

Would you mind, sir, very much indeed, sir, would you mind at all, sir, if sir was to get his tiny little bollocks sweaty and move it a bit faster there, sir?

Some had been soldiers and they thought it was a laugh, the roles reversed. But most had stayed in the kitchen all through the war: Reserve Occupation, or Unfit for Duty.

I tried to explain myself to the soldiers to justify where I was. Not that I was unusual, there were a million men out of work.

But to curse the other group. Coming up to the word, thinking about it, but holding it back with a big effort. *Conchie.* The worst thing a soldier could say. We all objected conscientiously to being shot.

You go, sir, *you* put in an appearance for us all at the private dining room, *you* let 'em know, sir, that there's really some class working back 'ere. More to us than just a load of navvies, sir.

With that I had been dressed for the part, the part they did not like. Being polite, putting on an act the other side of swinging doors, balancing huge trays.

And that was where I had recognized him, white tie and tails. Half a dozen bottles of Bollinger's over ice on a silver salver. From there it had been easy. Wait for my moment, step out into the plush corridor with my large dirty tray as Green came back from the crapper. Then I had him. Looking down at me with contempt, pulling on his cigar.

We had stood there facing each other, the privileged senior and the junior occupant of the adjacent bed.

Separated from his company. Under the old gas lights between flocked red walls, unable to get past my tray. Obliged to deal with me.

That was when he had suggested lunch.

Then for days I had planned it, hours over a single cup of tea somewhere out of the cold. Thinking forward to how I would put it.

And backward to that moment. The big white bed in the Crillon. Katrina bathing me in her skin, fingers slowly over my chest and my boy's hairs soft and sparse. On to my quaking stomach, feeling me, down, down again. In and out of my navel, down, and down again.

Oh the god of lilacs, he had also made a hand. Cream, perfect, cold, hot, mine.

But then the hand was changed, suspended. Now it was Green's hand I felt working under bedclothes. A ferret in from the cold. Large and uncontrollable, with a life of its own. Wild. From the woods. Doing what it wants. Taking what it will.

Then the ferret was on top of me, a bull now, large, scrumming in my bed. But quiet, not to wake the others. This weight, his sandpaper face in mine, intense animal breath in my nostrils, him pushing, working into my hands, me holding them where I was shown.

The warm mess and the ferret's retreat, me turning over, trying to lose the sticky on the sheets. Disgust but a secret victory. A digested sense of power. Power I was going to use.

Then I was back again to Cornwall: out of the house in a blind white fury and a stolen trip to Paris on my mother's fake jewellery. I am standing shaking in the linen cupboard at the École Militaire. And all the while Katrina is looking at me so steady and so lovely. Looking at just me. Me the *ingénu*, the unable to perform, me the broken-down liar with nowhere to sleep.

Then it was no longer just a little bit of help. Then I wanted more.

The ferret had committed a crime, I came round to saying, a repeated crime. A crime for which men went to gaol, I said, subjected to shame and ridicule beyond imagining. Like Oscar Wilde, I said.

In the pub, sitting with my beer, it all became clear. My Katrina waiting, my Katrina believing, trusting, lied to. And then I wanted my vengeance, on Green, on that school, on them all.

A crime for which Green would pay. Pay me the starving *plongeur*, survivor of the War, hero, lover of Katrina. Me the penniless and unconnected. Me the defeated.

Then to my campaign. Force ascendancy over the enemy trench. Catch one of them through the lens, suspended over a hole and sucking at his pipe?

Crack.

What did I care? It was not me that had started it.

But there was no enemy to be seen. Green was late. I had worked my way through my pint, through my *Times*.

Don Giovanni at Covent Garden, Schnabel playing *Hammerklavier* at the Wigmore Hall. Oh, how I wished. The opening: magnificent, pum-per-pum-perdi-um-pum, up a third, pum-per-pum-perdi-um-pum. And the fugue, Beethoven's fate-crazed rats scurrying in and out, up and around, driven to the far, far ends of where a fugue can go.

Ludwig knew Fate. Ludwig made me bold. Ludwig and my pint would see me through.

Four columns of Situations Wanted.

Gertrude Elliot and her company in *Come Out Of the Kitchen*, Dorothy Burnton and Daisy Elliston in *Baby Bunting*. Things I could not even afford to think about.

The Court Circular for 21 March 1920. What we had fought and bled for.

Still no Green. Still no enemy to be seen.

I needed food even though I had taken leftovers off the washing-up trays in the middle of the night. Scoffing furtively behind the door to the outer scullery.

'Time, gentlemen, please.'

Three o'clock. Enemy has the wind up.

I walked along Whitehall.

My step had lost the bounce of '19, a lift from the ball of the foot that had propelled me around Paris. Now I trailed purposelessly along past the Privy Council Office, past Downing Street.

I turned into King Charles Street, between the India Office and the Foreign Office. The pickings from Greece and Rome hanging over me, reworked for the glory of Empire. A classical canyon between the two buildings, meant to intimidate, to show might and invincibility.

I looked for frocks I might know: from the Majestic, from the Île de la Cité, my privileged position. Having such fun with them in Paris. Now this was their fortress.

But my uniform, even down at heel, gained me an answer.

'Oh, Mista Green, sir, well 'e goes 'ome at five thirty sharp. Catches the 6.05 from Charin' Cross.' Back to that rubbish. 'Know Mista Green do we, sir?'

Security on his mind maybe, my wild look. Maybe he recognized me from Paris. I had my answer but there was no being allowed in.

Down the steps past the statue of Clive and toward the Serpentine.

A salute from two Irish Guards. Returned by reflex. Me the fraud. Not there on duty, no longer commissioned even. Permission to wear my uniform had expired one month after demob, except on *ceremonial occasions of a military nature.* Blackmail did not qualify.

I walked on and into the park.

Trees along Birdcage Walk were contemplating a start on a new season. Bare brown limbs tinged with a pregnant green.

In Victoria the pubs were open again. I found another pint for a penny, cheaper by the station.

The publican was talking to two men in worn suits, shirts without collars, scarves tucked into lapels. Buyers and sellers with their trolleys and their barrows, not soldiers. Having no trouble putting their brass down on the bar.

'Attack on frift, that's wha' i' is...'

'What's right abart taxing a man wiv only two fousand a year, when the bleed'n' profiteers are at the race track every die, women, jewellery, 'orses, cham-pain. 'Ow we supposed to live if we're taxed li' that then?'

'Man oo's stinted hisself all during war, now has to face bleed'n' taxes...'

'Spread panic, that's what it'll do. Won't 'elp us recover from the ravages, no' at all.'

The rounds had been fast, I had consumed at least another three pints and two of the rounds had included brandies. I made to leave, fumbling in my pocket. A penny and a joey. I brought them out.

'Tha's all right, guv,' the publican grinning the self-conscious grin of those who never went. 'I knows 'ow 'ard fings are. An' I knows what yer wearin' on yer chest an' all.'

I wanted to protest, maintain my dignity, weep for Thompson right there in the man's arms, maudlin and half-stewed. Not accept the admission that I had drunk without being able to pay. My 'ard times.

'Thank you,' I said, 'I won't forget your kindness.'

Now I wished I had eaten as well.

As I walked back, light-headed through Parliament Square, desperation and drink overtook me.

By God he would pay, the sodding little ferret would pay. You'll pay, Green my friend. Yelled into the cold evening air, shaking my fist at the trees.

Per-der per-der per-der. The end of the first movement, the theme again. Fast, faster. Schnabel pounding it out as only Schnabel can. *Pum pa pa pum pumdidi pum pum.* Oh yes, Ludwig and I would get the bastard.

Back on King Charles Street I waited, trying not to lounge, trying to look like an officer. Even if I was a criminal in the making.

Frocks began to emerge into the dark street in ones and twos: long black overcoats, gloves, scarves and top hats, some still in spats. A few in motor cars with drivers, a Lanchester, then I thought I recognized one of my Daimlers.

Five-thirty sharp. And there he was, heading off toward Whitehall with a purpose. To catch the 6.05 home. Home to Lettice or home to Penelope, home to somewhere warm, with a meal waiting.

I followed, it was easy. Green had no reason to look behind.

Up toward Trafalgar Square.

Then he started to cross Whitehall, planning to turn into Great Scotland Yard, I thought, past The Clarence. Then over to Charing Cross station. No case, swinging his umbrella like a walking stick.

As he crossed Whitehall, out in the middle of the wide expanse of macadam, waiting for an omnibus to go by, out there in the centre, traffic going both ways, unable to get away, just like the Savoy corridor again, I came up to his side.

'Hello, Green.' Cheery tone helped along by the drink. It took Green a second to recognize me in my uniform. Then restrained horror from under the rim of his shiny top hat.

'I thought we were going to have lunch,' I continued, swaying slightly, beaming at him in his discomfort.

The omnibus went past, the whining gearbox of a troop carrier. Then up into third speed and rumbling away on solid tyres.

I saw jerkins and rifles. I waited for cheers from under tin hats.

Wan' a ride? Tuppence an 'ead. Other troops riding by, shouting from the platform, us marching.

How come *we* never get to ride, Serjeant? I thought you had pull with the army.

Oh, so sorry, sir, turns 'em down every time they offers. Knows how much you likes to take a little stroll. Big smile. Gold teeth.

We were still in the middle of the road. The drink, the feeling of advantage and surprise. The way Green looked. Perfect timing.

'Let's have that drink, now, at The Clarence,' I said. Just as Green was casting around for his way out.

He opened his overcoat to consult a silver pocket watch attached to his waistcoat by a silver chain. After a quarter to. He could not both deal with me and catch his train, but now he could not avoid dealing with me. The missed lunch, my uniform, the totally unexpected, the sway, a premonition of difficulty, a scene.

'Right,' he agreed with a grim little smile, continuing quickly with his explanation. 'Called to a conference this morning, unexpectedly. Tanganyika. Dragged on most of the day. Sandwiches.'

2

Green had no idea of my purpose.

A little chat about school, about what had happened since, my uniform. All that and off again to his train. Then me and the whole set of incidents put out of his mind: the dormitory, the ferret's needs, the ferret's needs satisfied. Just part of school.

Green bought me a pint which made it six or seven that afternoon plus the brandies at Victoria station. And without food all day. He settled down and started to talk, the decision made to take the next train.

'Julia doesn't necessarily expect me until the six forty,' he explained earnestly. 'Often delayed by significant events.'

I knew Green's father to be a wealthy City type in the way that boys gain knowledge of other boys' backgrounds over the years by some hidden but accurate smut conduit. His mother bred Dobermann pinschers, always two of them with clipped ears straining against short leads when she visited the school.

But City type was not good enough for Green, he had been after something better. He was keen to tell me. It all fell right into my lap.

Green stood at the bar in his overcoat not intending to stay for long. From an inside pocket he brought out a silver cigarette case, matching the watch. I accepted one and stored it in my tunic pocket for a skite, a swap for something else later.

He was dressed fastidiously. Clothes handmade in tight gleaming wool, white shirt and high starched collar. Sculpted knot to his silk tie held in its perfection by a pearl-headed pin. Under the topper his hair was combed back strand by even strand. The groomed appearance from society pages of *Tatler*. A silver lighter to match the case.

He was confiding in me.

'Dash'd lucky thing that, meeting old Julia at the May Ball. Last year at Emma. She was with some other chappie. Took to her right off the bat. Lovely girl, just adores me. Shouldn't be the least surprised if we heard the patter of tiny feet in the near future, eh what?' Thinking that I was drawn into all this.

After school Green had gone up to Cambridge, Emmanuel College, to read sciences. But he had developed an ambition to be in the Foreign Office. Policy, government, not commerce, trade. Launched by Papa's good luck.

But the FO entrance examination had been a bit of a hitch. No languages, not enough travel. Really, really competitive. Well, along comes old Julia, fished off the other chappie. And you'll never guess, but Julia's father's something important in the Home Office. Well suddenly the exam didn't seem so difficult did it? And now here he was: natural diplomat, born policy-maker.

So three years at Cambridge while I was at school, '14 to '17, he could put the War off for that before conscription. And by the time conscription came along and he was due late in '16 he had almost finished his degree so he could avoid the combing out. Then of course, the FO was a Reserved Occupation. Needed all the little frocks they had, could not spare a one for the front.

Then 1918 to 1920 he had been at King Charles Street. But not in Paris, Green was in the Africa Section. I understood it all so clearly.

He was still talking.

'Awfully nice group of chaps I work with. So, so much to do, with the world being made anew at Versailles and all that. And the Colonial Office, of course, knoweth not *what* it doth. Taking over old German South West, for example, the Cameroons. Complicated stuff, that.'

Intended to impress. But I knew about the German colonies that had meant so much. For prestige, to say that they too had an empire like the British, like the French. When all along colonies were of no use at all.

I remembered Werner wrestling with his strands of molten cheese.

'Ten times more Germans have moved to America than to our colonies. And all they do, those places, is cost us money and men. But we want them all the same, Yves. And taking them away from us will be useless for you too.'

Straining to hear him against the roar of the *soupeuses* and the screech of the tenor.

'This was not in the Armistice. This was not in President Wilson's Fourteen Points. And where is your Self-determination for all peoples? Have you asked the tribes of Tanganyika about this? Taking away our colonies was just spite, Yves, spite when we had been tricked into giving up our guns.'

Green was on about his cosy arrangements. And the really nice little house Papa had bought for them in Wandsworth.

Finally to me.

'So what have you been up to, Beauchamp?' Not really wanting to hear. Another glance at his watch then smoothly back into his pocket.

I looked at his face: square and handsome, strong chin, dark eyebrows. I felt carborundum against my boy's cheeks, his pushing prick and big hairy balls in my hands. The ones Julia handled now. Well, maybe not actually handled.

How it had all gone badly for me at that school. Enough for him to think later that I fitted nowhere, had nothing to lose. But not the whole truth: Mather, the beatings, the hate, what I had thought was my vengeance and the wrong reasons for the army. Emphasis on the Upper Sixth, the School Choir.

Then the army, the right reasons: King and Country, our great victory at Cambrai. He could see the MC for himself. Paris: skiving, playing the driver, my closeness to the great. Nothing about LG or LG's girl, of course. LG was still the PM. Then to demob and nothing: Haig's Fund, the Savoy where he had seen me. And sleeping under the bridges which I did not mention.

All of which brought me around to the little help and the good word.

I asked nicely first.

Green started to brush me off.

'Tremendous lot of chaps having a hard time of it.' He tried to appear sympathetic. 'And Papa says it's only going to get worse. Especially with that Bolshevist Welshman Lloyd George. The loss of markets for British goods, the cost of all his ludicrous promises: health, electricity, housing, pensions. No end to our troubles.'

Rehearsed, as if he had known all along what I was going to ask.

'Papa says that the old staples aren't going to see us through any more. You know: coal, textiles, shipbuilding, that sort of thingy. War's eaten away our markets. And then those incredible increases in income tax, over a shilling in the pound now, you know. They're taking away everyone's capital.'

Green smiled a self-satisfied smile. Papa was sure to have some plan to make money from any conditions. Buying disused armament factories for shillings on the pound, maybe, or war surplus at a fraction of cost.

'So I can't see what I can do for you, old chap. Just got a job myself y'know.'

He laughed again. Ha ha ha.

'And don't have a market garden or anything like that where blokes are needed. Take you in a flash of course, Beauchamp if I did. In a flash.'

Time was running.

I was an ordinary soldier. Only one weapon, only one chance. As I looked at Green I fixed my bayonet, that particular unforgettable deep metallic click. I swigged my rum and over I went.

'Unless you get me a job, Green, I'm going to write to the Foreign Office about what happened at school. About you being a homo. And I'm going to write to your wife, I'm going to write to your mother and father in Brighton...and...and...' I trailed off.

But it was out.

Green looked at me with renewed horror. The benign gone immediately. Then his eyes narrowed and I thought I saw his upper lip curl like one of his mother's prize Dobermanns.

'A job and two hundred pounds in cash,' I added weakly.

It had not been very sophisticated, not very spy-like, but it had done the job.

'Nobody would give a damn what you have to say, Bow-Chump,' Green replied slowly, now that he had the measure of what was happening. 'You're just another out-of-work ex-soldier, petty thief probably, a bloody dishwasher.'

He paused, inspired.

'Why don't you join the volunteers in Ireland? Black and tans. Just pop a police belt over your khaki tunic. Bunch of thugs I'm told but doing a very good job. Going around threatening people. You'd do well there.'

He was not taking me seriously.

'I meant it, Green. I've done all my fighting. And I've drafted the letter that'll go if you don't do it for me.' I pulled out my handywork, written before I even knew that he had a wife. Looking the more genuine for being crushed in my pocket and smudged by rain.

I put the paper his way up on the bar.

Dear Mrs Green,

You don't know me, but I was at Martyr's with your husband. Have you ever heard it said that a desperate situation calls for desperate action? I am certainly desperate. There are many others in my situation I know, but every one is doing the best they can to get along.

I was in my first year when Andrew was in his last. He was the dorm prefect for Dorm Three and I slept in the bed next to him. I won't go into details, but Green was a homo and it went on for a year.

I don't believe that the Foreign Office knew everything about Andrew when he was accepted and I think that it might make a difference to their attitude if they were to be told. Proof of something like that would certainly have put an end to an officer's career in the army, even in war time. The Foreign Office is probably the same. I am looking for work, almost anything, and I know that Andrew can help me.

'I'm not completely finished. I was going to say something about your father. His reaction and so on.' Feeling more confident.

Green looked as if he was going to slap me. Like a child that had done the very worst it could. Hand into potty, proceeds rubbed on the wall.

The prospect of disruption in his smooth oiled life. This madman rampaging around in his career, his marriage. From the little talk about how swimmingly everything was going. To this, this muck.

Facing the shabby object of his forgotten desires. Not really a homosexual desire, I had to admit to myself, more an imperative to do something with his fit rearing body. Something he would have done with a girl had there been one around. But there I was, at hand, so to speak.

I could understand how he made the transition later. With another boy it had never reached under his skin. Never meant much. He was not the arty type like some of the others who had started and never let it go, bent, furtive and guilty.

Maybe he had tried out the real thing in London before Julia, with a girl in Soho. Or off place St Michel to keep it really quiet. I had seen how easy it was and how the girls liked the rich young men looking for *l'éducation sentimentale*. English gentlemen especially, paid for by their fathers. The gents brought out the mother in their little tarts' souls.

Green was no homo. But what did I care? A Hun innocently taking a bath still wearing his helmet?

Crack.

They were the enemy.

Green was packing away his burnished cigarette case, purposeful, as if responding to a sudden summons to an urgent meeting.

I had expected an answer, I had expected to win, to win that easily.

'That's enough of that nonsense,' he muttered without looking at me, finishing up his drink. 'And now we know what kind of little rat you are Bow-Chump. But I have a train to catch. Lots of men did that sort of thingy at school, just part of growing up. You wouldn't stand a chance. There'd be no one left to govern England. *Goodbye.*'

The ferret to the rat. Slamming his glass on to the bar.

Green had already paid for the drinks. He could make his immediate exit. He headed for the side door on to Scotland Yard, turning a loathsome look at me as I made to follow.

Did he think I was going to stay at the bar and order another drink? Take no for an answer?

Outside he put on his top hat, adjusting the brim as he walked briskly away, feeling himself somehow unassailable in the street. Maybe he thought he could call a policeman.

Ah, Constable, Green's the name. With the Foreign Office y'know. This man here is bothering me, loitering outside The Clarence and begging.

Not in my uniform, not with Thompson's medal.

'Get away from me, Bow-Chump,' Green barked as I fell in step with him coming up to Northumberland Avenue. But I knew he was rattled.

'You're blackmailing me and I'll call the police.'

'A pal of mine has a copy of this letter.' Untrue, but firming up. Tasting alcoholic venom. 'And if I'm not back at the hostel he'll be over tonight and deliver the letter to your wife.' Bluff, but Green started to walk faster. 'You're a homo, Green,' louder now. Past The Sherlock Holmes and heading into Craven Passage. Mist wreathed around gas streetlamps, a fog was developing. Our footsteps rang in the alley.

'And I was the lush,' I continued from behind. 'I want you to make amends, Green. Now when I need it.'

We were up Craven Street toward the Strand, soon he would turn into Charing Cross station. There would be crowds, my opportunity would be lost. I would never get at him again. All this demonstration of the rat within, it could not just come to nothing.

And my Katrina waiting patiently. Confident in my connections for a new life. The confidence of love. I wanted to force the answer, to shake him like a rat with a chick. Like the rats I used to watch eating their kill under the henhouse: beak, feet, feathers, the lot.

'I've nothing to lose, you know...' breathless now, up the hill toward the Strand. Green was pulling ahead, just short of running. Taller, more athletic than me, better fed.

...*I'll ruin you*...I wanted to shout but he was too far away.

I held on behind, up to the station. Into the courtyard, weaving between taxis and buses, under the ridiculous Victorian façade of the hotel. Wild and desperate, trying to be French, Italian, foreign, like me. Ending as a joke, like me.

Green made for Platform 5. He was three bodies ahead of me at the barrier where passengers were squeezing to get through a narrow opening between the railings and past a ticket collector in his wooden booth.

I tried pushing on to the platform giving the ticket collector a cheery little wave, ready to duck away through the crowd ahead. Run to catch up to Green before he boarded the train. Catch his sleeve, be the rat, make him listen. Turn to pleading and I did not know what.

But the ticket collector had seen them all.

'Ticket please, sir,' squatting on the front of his stool and holding out a pudgy little hand. Ready to hold up the entire crush until I had given him my ticket, the ticket I did not have. Maybe the uniform had been stolen, maybe I had been stealing rides on trains for weeks and now he had me.

'I'm just seeing a friend on to the train.' I turned my chest so that the collector and those pushing behind me could see.

'You'll need a platform ticket then, sir,' the ticket collector said calmly, not infected by my hurry or by anybody else's hurry.

'A ha'penny,' he said, holding out his hand again.

'I only have thre'pence.' If I looked dejected, perhaps my lack of change would let me pass on to the platform for free. But the ticket collector began to fumble in his bag.

'Yer supposed to buy ticket from slo'machine,' he said, still burrowing, the others behind stamping and snorting like a herd of horses.

I looked down the train.

Steam was wisping from beneath the train. I could see Green's long coat disappearing behind the door of a first class carriage. The guard was standing away ready to wave his green flag. Southern Railway, always on time.

From his gropings the ticket collector was eventually going to produce a platform ticket. Then he was going to look for his clipper. Then he was going to dig again for change.

'I'll get my change on my way out,' I said, placing my joey on to a little ledge on the side of the booth while the ticket inspector's back was turned. As I moved away the gate was immediately inundated by anxious passengers.

'Oi. Oi, oi,' I heard behind me. Spluttering, wanting to come after me but kept in his place by a forest of arms and tickets.

I pushed into Green's coach and along the corridor looking into compartments, struggling around umbrellas and attaché cases, making for their comfortable reserved seats. Green was sitting in a window corner in the last compartment. Tapping a cigarette against the silver case, catching his breath. I had been disposed of.

I rolled the door back.

Faces looked up at me resentfully, as if I was going to sit down and disturb the commodious arrangement the four of them had made out of six seats. I stood at the door.

'Green,' I said, leaning into the compartment, eyes meeting his and ignoring the others, 'Green, you're a ho...'

But before I could complete the word, spit it out at him, Green was on his feet. Pushing violently toward me across outstretched legs and neatly turned-back newspapers. Past startled then outraged looks, crashing into me and propelling me back into the corridor.

The train began to roll along the platform and the corridor had emptied. Green pulled the door to the compartment closed behind him.

'I'm staying,' I said, before he could speak. 'I'm coming home with you. To tell your wife what you really are.'

I had no idea how I would accomplish this but it sounded adequately manic. I wanted him to think I was on to him, that he would never get away. Me the rat. The War, the shelling, I would start on about Waterloo Bridge. I wanted him to think I was insane. Unstoppable.

The train slowed then jolted, couplings taking up their slack. Then we began to pick up speed to a brisk walk. I had no money for a ticket, not even to the first stop. The complications were unthinkable, being found on the train by a ticket inspector, being charged or imprisoned. My Katrina, my promises, me in gaol, penniless, trying to explain.

But at the moment that I was going to concede defeat and head for the door, turn on him, mouth some empty threat but let him go, just at that moment Green said,

'I'll see what I can do. Same time tomorrow. The Clarence. Five thirty.'

I looked at him waiting for the sting. After all that cold and harsh, the rat within exposed, could there be warmth? My bridges chopped to tea leaves. And watch out now for the counter-attack.

I turned and lurched down the corridor grasping at window railings and door knobs. The train had accelerated to five or six miles per hour. I let myself down on to the last of the platform at a fast run, thin soles slapping as I slowed to a walk.

The ticket collector was gone with the train. Gone with my joey. I felt in my pockets. One penny left.

Back at the Savoy and let in for work again, the insults were more bearable. How nice of you to come, sir. Some of us thought that you might not make it, sir, thought you might 'ave got yer old job back, the one with Daddy at the bank. Or maybe you was going for dinner, sir, with the PM.

Just because I was a few minutes late.

The next day I put on my uniform once again with a shilling from the night shift in my pocket. *The Times* and a beer. What would I say? Sorry, Green? Thank you, Green?

The answer to my questions was Mr Harris. Or from his bearing, erect like a smoke stack, it had probably been CSM Harris or RSM Harris. But now it was just plain Mr Harris. Dark three piece suit, smart but serge. When you looked carefully you could see where he fitted in. Waxed moustache like a comedian, friendly like a walrus.

Mr Harris, my answer. Mr Harris said that army ranks were over now, just names on their own, thank-you-very-much.

'You'll get the hang of it,' he said with a smile, before I knew what was to hang where.

Mr Green had sent him.

Mr Green himself? Well, he couldn't come today, very busy. Some official pow-wow or other. So he, Mr Harris, had come in his stead. And no beer, if-you-don't-mind, just a cup of tea.

He, Mr Harris, was in a different section from Mr Green. Mr Harris was in the Transport Section. And Mr Harris understood that I knew a thing or two about transport myself.

I began to take it in and I launched into Montreuil, the War, all the dangers and all the difficulties. Then Paris and another set of problems.

Mr Harris let me ramble on for a while.

'There won't be any of *that*, you know,' he said finally. 'No shelling, no panics, no make-it-up-as-you-go-along, not like over *there*. Over there in France. Everything at the FO is done methodically, no misses.'

So this was my good word, my little bit of help. Not with the moving company, not with the estate agent's but with the FO itself.

I cast about with questions What training would I need? Would I have to take an exam like Green? What about clothes, a frock coat? I was prepared to do anything to find myself a job.

Nothing-quite-like-that-I'm-afraid. But if I wanted it I could start work the following week on the first of the month. As a driver. A driver on a delivery lorry, a route around London with a swamper, picking up, putting down, envelopes, FO boxes, that sort of thing.

Did I want it? Not much money. And, of course, not what I was used to, what I might be expecting. Decorated officer, public school.

He, Mr Harris, he would quite understand if it wasn't suitable. But short hours and government security.

Did I want it?

Mr Harris clearly did not know what I was used to.

Yes. Yes, I'd take it. Right now.

'And oh,' Mr Harris said after he had discussed when and where and after I had discovered that Mr Harris himself was to be my superior, 'Mr Green said to give you this.'

He slid an envelope across the table.

I could not believe my eyes. In the envelope was two hundred pounds.

Mr Harris wanted to know nothing about it. Just the messenger, he said.

Yes, Mr Harris, CSM Harris, RSM Harris or whoever you are. Clever Green, clever, bought and paid for. How could I start my threats again when I was working right under him somewhere in the building. I would immediately lose my job.

But it was all too easy. I knew that there would be more to come.

3

I was sure that Werner would be at the conference, valuable as an English speaker with his experience of Versailles. The awkward soldier-diplomat and his shark's smile.

But from my observation post on the driver's bench of the Daimler Eight parked in the courtyard of the Palazzo Reale I had yet to catch sight of him leaving or entering the conference hall. Twice each day delegates poured down shallow marble steps and out through the palace loggia. Huge but delicate, our century and its barbarities invading the setting for an Annunciation.

And twice each day delegation motors lined up on the pebble surface of the courtyard waiting to make the impossible manoeuvre out through narrow gates and into the busy street.

The gates of the Palazzo opened on to Via Balbi, the main street of Genoa. Carriages, steam-driven buses, motors, carts, the life of the whole swarming city poured along this confined alley.

As the Daimler emerged, crank handle, huge chromium headlights, rolled bumper bars leading big black mudguards, all were pushed out blind between obstinate pedestrians and into the clip of traffic.

I thought of Mr Harris every time.

At the garage in Croydon he wore a long white technician's coat on top of his serge waistcoat. Starched and ironed like his shirts, immaculate. An RSM born not made.

During the days before I had left London I was sure that Mr Harris was going to burst into tears at any moment. I thought I could see his eyes bulge and his chin wobble when he came to watch me preparing the car. His new

Eight was going to foreign parts and his face confirmed the worst. They might just as well have told him to push his precious motor off the dock and into the sea. He knew that he would never see her again.

'Aren't those Eye-ties the 'osts?' he complained. 'Don't they 'ave any cars of their own then?'

But that was Mr Lloyd George for you, twenty conferences in the three years since the end of the War and still nothing was settled. Now-it's-my-cars-going-over-*there*-if-you-please.

Mr Harris warned me constantly of the dangers facing a driver in distant lands. I was to be on the look-out for Bolsheviks approaching our motor, long black coats and bombs in brown paper bags. And Mr Harris gave me a glass beaker wrapped in cheesecloth: I was to check all Frog petrol for dead snails before I filled her tank.

Mr Harris even had me believe that it was a driver with his guard down who had started the War.

'That's right,' he said, 'Sarajevo. June of 'fourteen. Idiot of an Austrian driving a chain-drive Steyr. Lost his way and stopped to turn around. That's when they got him. Seven Bosnian assassins been trying all day. Then with the car come to a stop one of the little buggers jumped on to the running board, emptied his pistol point blank into the Archduke. And, well, you should know, Driver Beauchamp, the rest is history.'

Mr Harris left no room for any disagreement. He succeeded in scaring me. Millions dead, my savage memories, all the fault of a driver. I was always nervous making the slow turn out on to Via Balbi.

I knew a much better war-story about a driver.

About August 'fourteen the first month of the War. And about Joffre, the Generalissimo of six French armies during the German invasion.

Joffre was always calm and taciturn, even after his counter attacks had failed in the first few days and the Germans were pouring across the frontier. And to his staff, it seemed as if he could be in three places at once. Behind his bare desk at GHQ, or eating one of his three-per-day-proper-sit-down-meals at a remote country inn. Or almost simultaneously, it seemed, *le Maréchal* would appear at the front, standing motionless behind one of his army commanders, watching him fight. Assessing his *cran*, his guts.

Then finally after a month of patient retreat Joffre found the right place to seize the moment of German overconfidence, their weakness. And Joffre turned them, he held them off Paris and pushed them back up to the trench line. His Miracle on the Marne and the Prussian's one chance was lost.

All accomplished with his driver, Georges Bouillot, three times winner of the French Grand Prix, who drove Joffre everywhere at seventy miles per hour. Bouillot and *le Maréchal* were *complices*, a team.

His Britannic Majesty's Delegation to the Genoa Conference on Peace and Security in Europe had taken over the Hotel Savoia Majestic. A sad place, a poor imitation of the sumptuousness of Paris or Cannes.

I decided that Harry, the head porter for our Delegation was a spy for Mr Harris. Suspicious like Mr Harris and forever muttering about Reds. I could imagine him making up his reports, stabbing with two fingers at his big black Regal.

10th April 1922. Your Agent begs to report that Driver Beauchamp takes a great interest in the delegate lists. He asks me every day for unpublished information with regard to the Delegation of the First German Republic...

Harry had claimed for his own a stretch of the hotel reception counter where he kept a set of the delegate lists, to be thumbed through by anyone. For the German Republic twelve delegates were named, Doktor Walther Rathenau their Foreign Minister, then other politicians and diplomats. No military attachés.

In Versailles there had been no lists, just a group of downcast Germans in their pre-war suits and spats, two to a room at the Hôtel des Réservoirs.

'How much staff do we need for us to be tricked?' Werner had asked me. 'Or to say we cannot pay? Just one to two civilians. That is all. Yes? We always bring too many.'

Now conferences were even more complicated.

In Genoa there were twenty-five Delegations of at least ten Delegates each with advisers and support staff behind. Our Delegation alone consisted of over ninety people. It seemed impossible to find just one individual.

And how could the problems of Europe and the world beyond be solved by such a crowd? In Paris the Council of Ten had been unworkable, LG told me. Then the Big Four could hardly agree. Meeting as the Three in the end after the Italians had walked out.

But in Genoa, for the first time, the German Delegates were being treated as equals. Whatever the French were saying under their breath. No wooden fences, no tunnels and bright lights, no barricades.

I watched the Germans in a tight group entering and leaving the Plenary Sessions every day. Dark suits, winged collars, very serious in two black Italian taxis.

And the Russians: the first time they had ever been invited to a conference or had even been seen in Europe since the Revolution. And there were no long black coats, no brown paper bags. Just five or six modern-looking men with goatee beards who arrived at the palazzo every day on foot arguing passionately among themselves.

This was LG at work, the biggest challenge of his career, he told me. The chance to put Versailles right, to get Europe back to peace and prosperity.

But there was resentment, I knew. From the French and from the FO brass, even from RSM Harris. Probably from the Belgians and certainly from the absent Americans.

LG was doing it all himself, they said, ignoring Lord Curzon and the experts at the FO, the professionals. LG was going far too fast, they said. Planning to compromise with Germany on guilt and Reparations, or recognize those Bolsheviks as the government of Russia. How ever would that help our men at home who were on out of work donations?

They criticized LG in *The Times* every day even after three years of misery.

I did better with Matthew, Harry's second. A corporal from the Coldsteam Guards, a man who understood war friendships. Even from across the line.

'Could always send 'im a telegram, at their delegation,' Matthew suggested, after the third or fourth time I asked, 'if you're sure 'e's 'ere, that is.'

Persistence. The only word Haig ever spoke to me and from then on a word I liked to use about myself.

On the grass in front of Beaurepaire, the band of the Black Watch playing *The Black Bear.* The Chief singled out the word from my citation, grunted in a low, strangled voice as he took the pace toward me holding the ribbon and dangling cross. Captain Vernon behind, smiling as if he was giving away the bride, clutching the little blue box. Me trying not to cry. Haig's cap in my face as he fiddled with the pin on my chest.

'Come back after twelve tonigh',' Matthew suggested. 'No one'll be 'round.'

In a little porter's room off the deserted foyer Matthew let me write out my message on a block of telegram forms. He would have it sent that night and he would be sure to tear up the original.

TO W. SCHACHT GERMAN REPUBLIC DELEGATION STOP HM CAR
AVAILABLE FOR EXCURSION TO LIGURIAN COUNTRYSIDE STOP DRIVER
NEEDS FEEDING STOP SIGNED BEAUCHAMP HM DEL STOP

The next night Matthew had my reply.

TO BEAUCHAMP HM DEL STOP DRIVER TO MEET RAPALLO TRAIN GENOVA STATION STOP ARRIVAL 1805 APRIL 12 STOP SIGNED SCHACHT HPT DR DEL STOP.

Schacht, *Hauptmann, Deutsche Republik.* Captain, coming up in the world.

My play-acting in Paris, holding the door of the Silver Ghost, my mock salutes and the driver's cap. Werner could have no idea how true it all was now.

At Genoa station he stepped from the train, heartier than Paris, new flesh filling out his tall frame. Werner had prepared himself for a *Bummel*: green velvet suit with a leather waistcoat, plus-twos, stockings and walking shoes. An Alpine hat complete with feather and a long overcoat in matching green over his arm. All for an outing in the soft Mediterranean spring.

Beyond the old city and port, cherry trees were in an advanced bloom of pinks and whites along wide boulevards. Flowers evoking the peak of summer decorated squares and gardens in honour of the conference. The sun shone bright and warm as if my frozen London winter had never been.

I was much less prepared, in a white shirt and corduroy trousers like an out of work cricketer.

'No one could possibly mistake you for a German,' I laughed as we made another awkward northerners' attempt at a Latin embrace. 'Good thing you're not in the spy service. You'd have a lot of trouble blending in.'

'Don't laugh, Yves,' Werner replied in a stage whisper. 'There is such a thing you know. It's called the *Abwehr*. They had your telegram and asked me what was the code.'

Mock serious, arm around my shoulder.

'Anyway,' as if to bring our opening formalities to a close, 'no work for the rest of the day, Yves, no army talk. And we start with a visit to the tomb of Herr Giuseppe Mazzini.' He gave me a dramatic Italian wave of the arm.

I explained that I did not have a car.

'We brought just two from London,' I said, which was only part of the truth.

'We take a carriage, then. It's not so far,' looking around as we came out of the station into Piazza Verdi.

'Yves,' he began, as if we had been together for hours debating this topic, not apart for over two years. 'I say, that if these Wops can make a republic, so can us good Germans, don't you think?' More laughter.

In France Werner had always been keen to learn English slang and to understand expressions in the London newspaper. He made careful notes in a little school exercise book, kept ready in his pocket.

I had my picture of him in his dark Berlin apartment studying at night, preparing for the next day when he was to speak English. *A Wop, an Italian. Wop. A Wop*, reading aloud from his notes, trying to bury the V sound, but whistling instead. Then I could hear him with his Delegation, bringing the conversation around so that he could display the new addition to his vocabulary. *These Vops look happy today. You agree, no?*

We climbed into a shabby black landau pulled by a sad-looking grey. Then along the river to creaking springs, the clip of hoofs and a strong smell of horse.

'But why the grave?' I asked.

'It's not a grave, it's a tomb!'

'Well why the tomb? Did you play better after visiting Chopin?'

'Yves, I say that if I can see that there really was a Mazzini, stand by his tomb, understand that one man can make a republic, I will have hope for Weimar.'

The sun had begun to disappear over high hills behind the city on the left. Beyond the last buildings, round a bend in the dry stony bed of the Torrente Bisagno, a sloping vista of cypresses came into view, black and sentinel in the shade. Sombre cones of dark green pointing into the sky. Strikingly different from the natural cover beyond: laurel, oak, *cárpine* in a bushy spring green.

~

'Have you ever been to Italy, Morley?'

'I studied for a year in London in the sixties. I made the student trek to Florence, but that was it.'

Morley had warmed up some chicken soup from the back of the hospice fridge. Adding cream, salt and chopped onions, but the old man showed no interest. Holding up a wobbling hand in protest at the second offered spoonful.

'You really should go. But not the tourist Italy, the other places. The back streets of Naples, the Roman and Greek ruins on the remote side of Sicily, or across to Bari and the Gargano peninsula. And Genoa, the largest port on the Mediterranean. Real people, a real city, wonderful food and the most incredible cemetery you have ever seen. You would get more from it than me. I'm just a drywaller, a boardman, I'm not an architect like you.'

Morley stirred the soup listlessly. He could see what the old man saw, nothing could transform hospital food. The bowl fixed them both with a colourless stare. Back to the present, to reality, death.

'I haven't had any decent food since my fall.'

A pale hand took Morley's wrist. Translucent blue eyes swept Morley's face as if looking for a ship on the horizon. Yes, but what are you doing *here*.

The answer to the question was death. *Here* so as not to miss it, experience death close up, through another, skin to skin. Someone even Morley's arrogance had begun to recognize as an equal.

And life. *Here* to have death drive him to consider his own worthlessness, what Morley would see when it was his turn. To have death reveal the shallowness of his own existence. A trail of Janes and Susans, of perfect meals that turn to shit in the bowel, money without value earned and spent, trendy transient architecture. His intolerable life.

And over there on Falkland, where did she go in her mind lying in that other bed? More Morleys and more Donalds, fashion that came and went. But on the very inside, right in her middle, what did she really see?

The old man let go, slumping back against waiting pillows.

'In the late afternoon, as you approach, columns of white and grey marble can be seen between the cypresses. Then brick and stonework in different pastel shades caught in the last rays of the sun. Columns slowly resolve into a bizarre display of every design and period, every spire and *campanile* imaginable. From Sicilian Norman, to Lombard, from Renaissance to Romanesque. Through Flamboyant Gothic, High Gothic and every other Gothic variation there is. The known, the unknown and everything in between.

'All the necromantic nightmares of generations of architects past. Architects beyond all hope of a church commission pouring into these structures the depths of their spurned ecclesiastical talents.

'From a distance, coming up the river, the scene is other-worldly. Like a canvas stage-set for an Italian melodrama: the trees too tall for the landscape, the hill too steep, the structures too distant. The entire scene unattainable as in a dream.

'Then as you cross the creek, with a little shiver it becomes clear. You see that every one of these phantasmal structures is a crypt.

'Tombs of infinite variety and size. The hallucinations of a whole regiment of draughtsmen. Demented in their determination to preserve for all time the memory of their client's beloved, through this display of their wildest fantasies.

'Or the vista is the work of an army of crazed sculptors. You imagine them fingering through leather bound tomes covering the entire history of art and architecture. You can hear them gibbering to themselves as they chisel and scrape in their ecstasies. "One of these, one of those, yes, *haha* and two like that..."

'This marvel is without end, ranging upward in rows toward an unseen summit beyond. Heavily planted terraces like a Tivoli for the dead. Each level competing with the next for macabre prominence.'

The eyes flickered and closed.

'I tried to write a description of the cemetery once,' the old man said with a sigh. 'But that is one place where a picture is worth a thousand words. I remember it clearly. Back when death was for the unlucky, the weak, for the old. But never for me.'

Silence.

'You know, Morley, you shouldn't be afraid of dying. You should be afraid of not living. A comfortable death, when you finally arrive in exhausted old age, seems like a very sensible arrangement, a privilege. It's when people never live. Those are the real tragedies. Things that could be prevented. Short wasted lives, endings of excruciating pain, despair, lost loves...'

The old man seemed worn out by his efforts. His head rolled sideways.

'Do you want to sleep?' Morley asked.

'No no, I must go on. There'll be lots of time for sleep. It's remembering that's important, passing it on, my promise. And I'm coming to the hard parts, Morley. The things that didn't have to be. The truth I promised you, the events that I might have changed.'

He paused. Morley could almost interpret an expression through deeply wrinkled skin. Something infinitely sad, he thought. Sad but not for himself.

'This remembering used to be impossible, Morley. My djinns were waiting, they would rush me from all sides. I had to stop. I couldn't face the truth. But now? How can I avoid them now?'

There was silence again, then the story resumed.

~

The landau stopped at the main gates. Werner pushed boldly through, as if he came every week to visit his ancestors. The driver settled down to wait, the grey with her head lowered in the heat, a sagging skeleton outlined in mangy skin.

Behind the cemetery walls, hidden from outside view, a plain opened up at the foot of the hill of tombs. Rows and rows of shrunken plinths stretched away in crescents, the graves of ordinary Genoese. Small, as if for dead children. Placed closer together than seemed physically possible. Many slanted, heaved by the roots of well-nourished trees.

Family rituals attempted to preserve a physical connection with the departed. Copper lamps holding half consumed red candles were everywhere. Yellowing photographs of the deceased reproduced as enamelled medals adorned many headstones. Fresh flowers on most graves. The fatuousness of the gestures was clear for all to see.

Werner was already leading the way up the hill. Close to, the sheer diversity of the monuments was miraculous. Even in death, the endless expression of our inextinguishable human individuality.

Each crypt bore the name of a prosperous Genoese family. *Famiglia Viganego, Famiglia Astolfi, Famiglia Trucchi.* Within, an occasional empty shelf or hollow sepulchre gaped at us from behind an intricate iron gate. Standing sinisterly ajar, waiting patiently, confidently, for the inescapable arrival of the next member of the family.

'I want to say,' I started, as Werner paused to look at the view over the graves and down to Genoa, 'how stupid this all is. But the Menin Gate they're planning at Ypres is the same really isn't it? Just at the opposite end. Military and Anglo-Saxon. We all want something to be there for evermore.'

'No war today, Yves. Today we think only of the future!'

'But isn't that what all this is for? To make the future better by remembering the past?'

Werner was intent on climbing the stairs following a small sign. *Tomba di Mazzini.*

'Aren't you supposed to come out here on a Sunday and say, *thank you Grandfather. The firm's still in good hands. Doing even better now than when you left us.* Or won't you go to Ypres and say, *your deaths are not forgotten. I really am doing all I can for peace and prosperity.*'

We had reached the tomb. A cave for the hero of the Italian Republic dug into a rock face. Theatrical Greek columns and architraves resolutely holding an entire mountainside off the dead luminary. On the terrace in front, Signora Mazzini lay in a bulky sarcophagus, insufficiently worthy to join her husband in his marble splendour for an eternity together.

'There,' Werner said, his jäger hat in his hand, 'there he is.'

Mazzini's tomb itself was not to be seen, only the sealed entrance to the cave.

Werner stood in silence for longer than I thought necessary. Being neither Italian, nor a veteran of the Risorgimento.

He looked up from his contemplation.

'That is what we need in Germany, Yves, a great man, a leader like Mazzini. You have Lloyd George, the French had Clemenceau to lead, to explain. Someone to make our lives good. Good and with a purpose.'

Werner stood silent, at his crossroads once again: the dutiful officer wanting clear orders when there were none. The patriot intent on harnessing the wasted power of German ability.

Then Werner put his hand on my shoulder and we walked back toward the stairs.

'And now, Yves, women.'

We had completed our pilgrimage and Werner had his plan.

Genoa was a large port. When the boats came back the women were waiting, it was like that in all big shipping cities. All we had to do was to go down to the harbour and make our choice. We were much better than any sailor, us soldiers.

I protested. About being married, about syphilis or even worse diseases from overseas, but Werner was having none of it.

'And what about Inge?' I asked ineffectively. 'The girl you were going to marry?'

'But it is more important still when you are married, Yves, no boredom, yes?'

Werner's smile took over his face. A nervous giggle, long hollow features alive and expectant. Then back to his reserve, arrogant almost.

'And as to disease,' he countered, 'you look first. With a candle.'

Werner made me laugh. I thought that he was about to show me his whoring stores, German Army, for the use of: candle, some matches in a damp-proof container, a tube of tincture, a bottle of disinfectant, all in a little *feldgrau* bag marked *Whorenmongerzurvivialishekit.*

'*Al porto!*' Werner commanded the driver, '*Avanti!*' he shouted, standing up in the landau like the Captain in an operetta off to some charade of a war.

At the harbour there was no sign of Werner's women.

Ships filled the skyline. The angular make-believe shapes of the Italian navy. Passenger steamers, cargo boats with tall funnels billowing black smoke, then a few masted clippers. Silos, cranes, warehouses behind.

The landau pulled up at Palazzo San Giorgio. A palace from the thirteenth century that had once been the Banco di Genova, then the richest and most powerful in Europe.

We let the driver go and circled the building, Werner ahead.

From around a corner, after we had admired the facade I heard a surprised German oath. *Gott in Himmel!*

'Look,' Werner said when I caught up to him. He was standing back from the flank of the building, arms folded, a stance of theatrical amazement. 'All the architecture, it is only painted on.'

His voice was shrill with indignation as if he personally had been deceived.

A delicate fresco covered the entire side wall, brimming with colour and light. Woven with pastel flowers and loaded vines, imitating the classic façade but on a single stucco plane.

'It is just a flat wall, Yves, which has been painted over to look like columns and plants. This is a lie.'

Werner made me laugh again.

'No, *Kamerad*, not a lie, decoration. Even the parts that you think are missing are not real.'

But the Italian fresco could not penetrate the Bavarian cranium.

'Just painted on,' he repeated, 'the picture could be of anything.'

'And so could the columns on the front be of anything, even if they are stone and not paint. They too could be square, round or even left off altogether. The columns do not hold up the building. It is all illusion, either way.'

Werner was not listening or could not hear.

'In Germany, if an architect did this the people would come from all around, just to laugh. But in Italy this is art? So much difference?'

There were occasions during our times together when I could almost hear the crash of cogs. Sprockets which for twenty-five years had made a smooth Teutonic mesh.

4

Italy in the 1920s, from London, was an exotic and far-off place.

Even France was a most foreign country.

Genoa matched the image. A vast port facing a dense rats' nest of a city. The poorest quarters I had ever seen. Little shops no bigger than market stands cheek by cheek with great palaces from the sixteenth century, tumbledown tenements packed around tribal churches of concupiscent baroque.

Then above, on the steep hills of Liguria, large mansions, *hôtels* the French would call them, of the successful merchant class.

The entire unsightly metropolis was pervaded by an atmosphere of frantic activity, as if there were only today in which to get things done. Quite different from the picture of lazy Italians cherished in England. But impoverished for all the bustle.

And as with most male sorties the comfort of alcohol slowly replaced the illusion of women.

Our unsuccessful search had started under the crumbling porticos and arcades facing the port. Decrepit rubble structures revealed through flaking plaster missing in large patches like lepers' skin.

We walked into a pedestrian maze behind. The stinking streets becoming narrower and narrower until we could no longer walk side by side. So narrow that the sun never penetrated to the damp and slippery cobbles below, running with urine, fish scales and grey slimy water. The buildings above us so close that facing shutters clashed. Washing lines blocking out any residual light.

Yet alive, I thought, teeming with Italian life in its harsh echoing cheerfulness. Their inside lives revealed, lived on the outside for all to see. Poor but not in poverty, simple but provided for.

Werner saw conditions differently.

'Is really this a nation of the victors?' Almost to himself, like a man from the moon in his elaborate green suit peering into smoke-filled hovels.

We stopped for rounds of draught beer in cubby hole bars filled with grunting fishermen and gesticulating porters.

Weimar. The word had passed by me at the cemetery. We leaned against another high wooden counter, our third or fourth. By then we had started to drink grappa with each beer or beer with each grappa. Werner choked back his little glass in one throatful.

'Slowly, Werner, slowly. This is liquid sunshine. Not schnapps from boiled potatoes just to get drunk on in the mess.' We laughed.

The grappa at every bar was served cold. An innocent-looking texture like iced paraffin. But the taste of nuts, of harvest, of late summer and all that lay behind: full granaries, loaded carts jolting over bleached fields of stubbled straw, fresh manure, this year's fruit laid out carefully in planked lofts.

'It is a town on the River Elbe. A pretty town. There is a small university, some traditions. Bach lived there, where CPE and JC were born. And the town for which Schiller and Goethe planned their perfect enlightened state. Where music and joy would reign supreme.'

Werner smiled me his shark's smile.

'At this town a constitution for the First German Republic was made to replace the Kaiser's Reich. Weimar was away from Berlin, a symbol of the new, of peace and prosperity.

'Weimar seemed good. By which the old independent states, Bavaria, Saxony and Württemberg became parts of the German federation. From the

War and from your Versailles we are more of a whole country now than even Bismarck could make.'

Werner's smile turned into another grim laugh. Fairy would have enjoyed the irony too.

'But it has been chaos, Yves. The election in nineteen-nineteen had no answers, so many parties, so much squabbling, no leadership, no Mazzini. Threats of *Putsch* from left and right. Us Germans cannot stand that.'

We took our glasses out into a small square dominated by a Romanesque facade and an octagonal *campanile*. The rest of the church was obscured by crumbling buildings. Five and six storeys of slum decorated with more washing lines and strings of salted cod.

Haussmann's nightmare. The Baron and his dragoons would have had their grand town plan for Genoa's narrow streets.

A small patch of waning sunshine found its way between the buildings.

'But behind the Republic is the Army. At the end of the War, after the Kaiser had gone to Holland on his train, there was a pact made on a secret telephone line between Spa and Berlin, between the Army and the Republic.

'The Republic would send civilians to sign the Armistice if that was what President Wilson wanted. In return we, the General Staff, would bring the Army back from France in good order and protect the government from revolution. This way the civilians become dependent on us. Only we can raise up a leader. Only a government can rule that has the confidence of the German Army.

'We used irregulars, Freikorps, to deal with the revolutionaries. Old soldiers with their frustrations and their hatred, still carrying their rifles from the front. They killed tens of thousands of Bolsheviks and strikers in the streets. But then these men turned to politics and called themselves Nationalists. They became assassins. Liebknecht, Luxemburg, Eisner the President of Bavaria, they have all been shot. Even Erzberger who was head of the Armistice Commission and was at La Capelle, he was shot last summer, just for signing. Walking with his daughter in the woods, the act of cowards.

'Now these Nationalists say that the Republic at Weimar is to blame for Versailles. They say that the army was winning the war in nineteen-eighteen when the politicians drove to Compiègne and capitulated. *Dolchstoß*, they call it, stab-in-the-back. They hold parades, they march in the streets with banners.'

We moved on again, following Werner's tour from his memorized *Baedeker*.

'There is a lift, Yves, to take us up to the top of the hill. From there we can see the complete city. We must find this lift.'

Werner asked of the barman, *ascensore?* A long explanation we could not understand: further up.

At the next bar, drinks again ready, Werner continued. I was losing count.

'I will always remember you, Yves, standing in the lights. Looking so happy, smiling face like a schoolboy under your officer's cap. You too knew that you had survived the War when you saw our cars arriving.'

The grappa was beginning to have an effect. Tears shone in Werner's eyes. People pushed past us to the ornate bar calling to the barman, jabbering at each other between us. But we were an island.

'You were the peace, Yves. You, the first Allied officer I had ever met. You in person, the sign to me that the war would really end.'

Werner began to talk about Spa, the German GHQ. How on that November day, the ninth, when the Armistice Commission was preparing to leave in their four cars, how Herr Erzberger had had his doubts.

Doubts about leaving for the French lines, his doubts about signing.

And how Generalfeldmarschall Hindenburg himself, the Wooden Statue, the Greatest Man in Germany under God, how Hindenburg had climbed down from his train and grasped Erzberger by the hand, tears streaming down his miserable jowly features and into the sweeping white moustache.

How Hindenburg had beseeched him, Erzberger the civilian, to undertake this terrible task. For the Sacred Cause of the Reich.

'There was no *Dolchstoß*, Yves. The story of stab-in-the-back is a lie. Generalfeldmarschall Hindenburg personally gave the order to sign the Armistice. To preserve the army, the country. This lie is to preserve honour. For Weimar to take the blame in the place of the General Staff. But from this blame our new Republic is doomed.'

Werner remembered the drive. Bright lights, our petrol, my tea and blankets, then their Commission climbing aboard the French train. And the civilians signed. In a month we had pushed them back all the way from Chauny to Hirson. The German Army had given up most of their French soil since their Black Day in August. In one day alone during October they had lost 20,000 men as prisoners and 10,000 dead.

Soon the Allies would be on the borders of Germany itself. And behind, the Americans were arriving.

'What the Nationalists say is not true, we were not winning the war. *Dolchstoß* is a lie. But neither were we defeated like the words of Versailles. You would never have crossed the Rhine, Yves, millions more would have been killed. You and me, maybe.'

Our names on each other's bullets.

My lorry in the courtyard and our line ready to break. Vernon saying ten more years. But finally our defence holding and then it was the Germans who could never win. Their *Kaiserschlacht* was over, they had thrown their last throw and our advance had begun. But over a defended Rhine? Now it would be us who could never win. GHQ planning for war into 1919, 1920...

Werner remembered the large white towel flapping on a broomstick from the lead car. The silences between them as they drove toward the Allied lines. The dreadful thing they had been sent to do.

Tears were rolling freely now down Werner's bony cheeks.

But had not President Wilson made it clear that if the Allies had to deal with the military or the monarchy that war would never end? Was not Erzberger therefore saving lives by signing, saving honour even, allowing the orderly return of the Army to Germany?

'I do not know how the War started, Yves, only that it must never happen again. Never. We were encircled, they say, or the cynics talk about the train timetables. After the assassination in Sarajevo first Russia mobilized then Austria, then by treaty we had to mobilize. And the schedules for the troop trains were so complicated that we all ended up at war without meaning it. An Imperial war game that went wrong.'

Werner tried a smile through his tears. He swallowed another grappa then sank his lips into the froth of his beer. He slumped against the bar.

Before Little Belgium, before Nurse Cavell, we were never told. We had just hated. The reasons were never discussed.

'*Das weiß ich wirklich nicht,*' Werner said. 'Truly I do not know. But we had fought bravely and no German soil had been occupied. And hadn't we made huge gains in the East? I understood our reasons so well.'

Werner looked around the tiny bar as if aware of his surroundings for the first time. Coming back to the present.

'And what did it say, this Armistice?' Out loud, talking to the whole room. Blank stares from uncomprehending *lavoratori*. He counted the points off on his fingers.

'End to hostilities, repatriation of Allied prisoners, evacuation of Belgium and France, of Alsace your Katrina's country, pay the civilian damage. We pull back behind the Rhine, we surrender all our artillery, many machine-guns and our submarines.'

Werner took a long pull at his beer.

'Yes, it was one-sided, the Armistice. In your favour because we were on the defensive. And conditions were bad at home, hunger under your block-ade, revolution sweeping in from Russia. If Bolshevism from the East had taken over Germany behind us what would we have been fighting for anyway? That is why we signed.

'But we had President Wilson's Fourteen Points. Both sides accepted his terms by telegram before the Armistice. I read the English for myself at Spa.

'And our heavy weapons? Wouldn't we also have protected ourselves against new attacks if we had been in your position? Yes, of course. We understood military matters, Yves.

'But there was nothing in the Armistice about guilt, about how the war started, about Reparations, about paying the total cost of the war, even your army pensions. Nothing about complete disarmament for Germany. About the loss of our colonies, all our ships, the making of Poland from Prussian lands, the end of the General Staff. Millions of Germans now living outside of Germany. Nothing. Nothing.'

Counting on his fingers again.

A long staring silence as more drinks were set up. Short frosted glasses of grappa and overflowing golden beers.

'And Versailles?' Werner started again. 'President Wilson and his wonderful ideas. What was the result?

'A slave treaty prepared in secret or we face invasion. Is this open diplomacy? And after we had given up our weapons with the Armistice. When we were still starving behind your blockade. So many German people put into new countries without any voting, not even discussion. Into Czechoslovakia and into Poland. Is this Self-determination for all peoples? Austria wants to join Germany but it is not allowed. In this a world safe for democracy? Even Alsace was not asked about becoming French. Were they afraid what the answer would be?

'In this Versailles we Germans are made the guilty ones. We are told to pay until the end of the century when we have nothing. But we did not start the War alone, Yves. And this is not peace and justice.'

The value of money in Germany was falling even faster than in '19. Werner gave me an example. A family with 50,000 old marks saved was very comfortable before the War. But now that same money was worth the equivalent as one old 20-mark note. Good for a single meal. This was ruination. And Reparations were to be set by the Gentlemen on the Commission at the equivalent of 300 old marks per person each year.

Werner's voice was rising.

'That is why we call it slavery, Yves. My uncle says the German people are now so poor that they have lost their course, like a ship in the fog. He says they will support anyone who comes along with an easy-sounding solution.'

Werner tossed back another small glass, ignoring my advice again.

'Do you think, Yves, that we would have signed the Armistice if we had known the terms of Versailles? Do you think that we would have given up our weapons? Allowed our artillery pieces to line the boulevards of Paris, as if you had captured them from us in battle? Don't you know that we would have defended the Rhine to the last man? *Sie haben uns "reingelegt!"*'

Werner gripped my arm with a ferocious drunken intensity. Now he was shouting.

'But in Versailles without our heavy weapons we had no choice.' Holding on hard, as if with his cries to me he could reach every one of us. Past or present, dead or alive. 'I have made my admissions, Yves, about *Dolchstoß*. So now it is time for you to make yours. Your Great Victory in your Great War is a lie and your Treaty is a trick.'

I remembered Vernon at Montreuil, the morning after the big party. Holding his head and drinking his tea without milk.

'You've been at school since me, Beauchamp,' he mumbled. 'What did Wellington say about Waterloo? Closest run thing he'd ever seen? Not how we see it today. But that's the way this war has ended. If the Bosche had defended the Rhine we would have had to let him go. Keep his guns and his Kaiser.'

The bar began to swim around me.

I was a worm who deserved to be flogged. But I had seen it for myself: *le vrai lion* shrinking down his chair, hostage to the leering crowd behind. The German gaol-birds in their damp black suits under the white lights of the Hôtel Trianon Palace. Humiliated but unyielding. Judged to be guilty before they could even open their mouths.

Justice, fairness, wasn't that what we were fighting for?

Mather suddenly finding his contemptuous words as I stood in front of his desk. All his mannerisms quite forgotten. Would have happily done the job himself. And a lot harder than anything that lay in store. For the brave boys at Mons, for the heroes of Ypres...the Somme...Had I any *idea* of the meaning of these words...?

Cambrai...the Peace...Versailles. A battle...a war...a Great Victory we had never won. A treaty by a trick. By our great lie that had made their lie, *Dolchstoß*. Their about-to-be-victorious army stabbed-in-the-back by the civilians of the doomed Republic.

Things this worm now understood.

Barmen merged then separated again, coming and going through the drink like moving targets on a range.

'But my General,' Werner started once more, moving unsteadily toward me along the bar, 'my General says we will neutralize this poison of Versailles. He says that we will have a war of liberation one day. Generaloberst von Seeckt is a Prussian, he believes in *Abmachungen*, co-operation with Russia to eliminate Poland. Poland has our land and many of our people. And Poland came to exist only through your tricks.'

Werner called loudly for more, rattling his glass on the solid wooden counter then hanging his head as if ashamed.

'And now I am sent secretly to Rapallo because my life also is in danger.'

Slow and serious, mouthing at me in his drunkenness so that I could see that it was no joke. He was not to be seen at the conference in Genoa. He was to hide in Rapallo like a fugitive, like a coward, he said. The incomplete Delegation list.

'After Erzberger, who is safe? When the Nationalists on the right hear what we are doing here, negotiating with Bolsheviks, I will not be able to leave Zossen. Doktor Rathenau will be assassinated. I have already moved my Inge to safety inside the camp. I was with the Armistice Commission, then in Paris, now Rapallo. To them I am a traitor. Even to come today, to see you, was a hard decision.'

There was more.

Werner took from his wallet an elaborately printed visiting card, flimsy stock of the kind used by a masseur or a piano tuner. He handed the card to me.

GEFU
Gesellschaft zur Förderung gewerblicher Unternehmungen
Moscow   *Berlin*

Werner M. Schacht
Export Manager

I looked at the words carefully, making the name to mean *Company for the Promotion of Industrial Enterprises*.

'Aren't you in the army anymore?'

'Yes, Yves, yes I am in the Army. But I have two jobs like most people in the Army now. Because our Versailles army is so small.'

Werner sank his head into his hands. He looked as if he was carrying an invisible weight made ready to slip by the drinking, by our bond, our differences. A safe place to talk.

'Of course I am in the Army,' facing the floor, almost inaudible. 'In the War I was not a civilian carrying a gun like one of you English, but a sworn member of the General Staff. For my life, Yves, for my life. I follow the orders I am given. You do not understand, you English, what that means, our Officer Class, our General Staff. *Kadavergehorsam*. Obedience to death. Obey, obey, that is my life.

'Clemenceau, he understood. In Paris he said, *They will never forgive, but only work for the day when they can come back.* Your Tiger was right. We are preparing to come back with this company. In Rapallo we are preparing also. And like my General I have a clear conscience. Everything from now on is justified by your tricks and your lies.'

'So what's in Rapallo?' Unnerved, even with the alcohol. By Werner's tears, sure that he should not be talking and that I should not be listening.

'It is sixty kilometres down the coast. There is a beach, a pretty bay, a little fishing village and a small castle in the sea of which no one knows anything. Not even to whom this castle belongs.'

Werner looked dazed.

'That's it?' I asked. 'You're in Rapallo to see a little castle, when everyone else is here in Genoa at the conference? Even the Roumanians with no reservations and no hotel. Wandering around the streets with their black beards and their valises.' Trying to make a joke.

'No, Yves, not to see a little castle. There is a big house in Rapallo. A big house full of Russians.'

'Russians? Your difficulties are with the French and Belgians, with Reparations, with economics. Not with Russia. They were not even at Versailles. What can the Russians do for you?'

Werner was going to reply. But suddenly I wanted to stop. Talk about women, even the War, have a laugh. Werner's look, the talk of his life in danger. My feet on slippery black rocks again, losing my balance against the river of *never*.

'This is politics, Yves, everything backwards from what you think. Our Delegation came to Genoa to make an agreement with the Allies on Reparations. One big payment over just a few years and it would be over. Europe at peace again.

'But instead the French will not even talk. And they invite the Russians to claim Reparations against us as well. In return Russia would repay to France the old debts of the Tzar. Then our Reparations would stretch beyond the end of the century.

'So we make our own agreement with the Russians to eliminate all debts between us, to have no Reparations and to start to trade again. Peace and prosperity without slavery. To show that it is possible.

'The Russians want industrial machinery. They can get nothing from the West because of the Revolution. So in this treaty we make our protest about your Reparations and the Russians protest also because their government has not been recognized by your governments.' Werner smiled me an intoxicated version of his shark's-tooth smile. 'And of course, the Russians like to shock the world.' He laughed, a loud drunken bray. 'The Treaty of The Two Outcasts.'

Some of Mr Harris's prejudices had rubbed off on to me.

'Be careful, Werner, they only want revolution, those Bolsheviks. They are not to be trusted.'

But Werner dismissed my comment with a wave.

'Bolshevik means nothing, Yves, the Russians want power and strength like every nation. And after all, it was our General Staff who sent Lenin to St Petersburg from Switzerland in a sealed train. To start the Revolution, to take Russia out of the war. So that we could move all our troops to fight you in the west.

'I see their military and they tell me the truth. As soldier to soldier. There is nothing to worry about for us. They have a full job just keeping the peace inside Russia, just feeding themselves and stopping counter-revolution.

'To my General, they could be Sun Worshippers or Voodoo Men. The name means nothing. But this agreement rebuilds the Army, Yves, that is the important thing.'

We came up to Via Garibaldi, lined on both sides by enormous palaces. Raked stonework in huge blocks formed massive entrances through which could be glimpsed a Renaissance world. Inlaid marble floors, forests of columns, frescoed ceilings in startling fluorescent blue.

Werner's *Baedeker* had told him that this was the most beautiful street in Italy. Designed by Alessi in the 1560s at the height of Genoa's fame as a city of merchants and bankers.

Above Via Garibaldi we found the entrance to the lift. Then down a dark tunnel lined with tile, echoing like an enormous public lavatory. Heavy cast-iron machinery clanked and ground its way up through an enclosed tube to deposit us on a paved terrace two or three hundred feet above the city.

It was now early evening. Below us lay Genoa. The old city appeared from above to be one continuous edifice topped by a single multi-faceted slate roof. Punctured by towers and domes which marked the locations of pocket squares. Jetties pointed out from the harbour in to the Mediterranean beyond, shadowed by the remains of a pink glow in the western sky. The city gave off a light scent into sea air: cooking, ships, brine, burning woods, pine, mimosa.

We sat on a bench and surveyed the scene.

After a long time Werner spoke.

'They say we will find our leader, Yves, our Mazzini. And my General says that our army will be ready, hidden under the chains of Versailles. The whole country will be ready. Every German knows that Versailles was a trick.'

Then Werner sat silent again, slumped on the bench.

The noises of the city carried up to us. A muffled rumble broken by the braying of a mule, the cry of a street vendor, clock towers striking the half hour, intermittent clanking from the *ascensore*.

'Lies and tricks.' Werner looked at me with a dull stare, hunched as if the full weight of the words was pressing down on his body. 'Can this ever lead to peace?'

We walked on through tree-lined streets, past quiet terraces of *hôtels*.

We found a *trattoria* where we were served an endless meal on a scrubbed wooden table. Without comment and without choice. *Vino, antipasto, primo, secondo piatto con contorni, formaggio, dolce, frutta e caffé.*

'Now, *Kamerad*,' Werner said over the remains of our food, the last of the wine, the table covered with bread crumbs, 'now I will tell you of our secret Rapallo.'

Out in the hushed street he put his arm around my shoulder as he had at the station and we started back toward the lift.

5

Cannes and Genoa as driver abroad were my counter-attack on Green and his vengeance. The start of my own way back.

On my first morning in 1920 it had been a sad wet walk along the Embankment to the FO. Half-truths to Katrina about my uniform, the hostile porter at the front gate.

'Side door ain't it,' he snarled when I explained that I was to see Mr Harris.

An hour's wait in a cellar corridor. Only to be told, and not by Mr Harris, that there was no lorry, no delivery run. Just the Motor Pool if I was still interested.

With two hundred pounds in my pocket I had asked Mr Harris if I could postpone my start for two weeks. To get married, I said, which was hard to refuse. But I had lost the job on the lorry.

Now I was to get fitted for a uniform and start off on the bench next to a more senior driver. Open doors, close doors, stand smart, wait. Insignificant little frocks coming and going. Green's vengeance.

How could he have heard about my bit of fun with the Silver Ghost in Paris, pretending to be a driver. From the porters? From me after seven pints? I could not remember.

Green's vengeance was that I should become that driver. No more play-acting. But in 1920 people were starving, sleeping on benches, under bridges. And I had a wife, the most beautiful woman in Paris. For her, for my Katrina, anything, even if I could not tell her the truth.

Then one morning in 1921, after a year as a footman then as a junior driver, at the garage in Croydon while I was washing one of the Lanchesters, Number 27, Mr Harris called me into his office.

'Driver Beauchamp, I'm thinking of sending you to Wales.' Sipping on his tea. 'Our Gentlemen on the Reparations Commission are arriving home Sunday morning. A party of four. You'd be taking Number 22, meet the boat at Portsmouth and drive them to Wales, to the Prime Minister's residence at Criccieth.'

But there was something else.

'Driver Beauchamp, do you smoke cigarettes?'

'No, Mr Harris.'

'It says here, you was seen smoking and lounging against your car while on duty.'

'By whom, Mr Harris?'

'Ah. That I can't say, Driver Beauchamp.'

'Where was this, Mr Harris?'

'And that I can't say neither, nor when. And I didn't see it myself, Driver Beauchamp. But it's a complaint in your file and there it will stay. I should be keeping you under my eye, not letting you go running all over like this.'

Mr Harris paused as if undecided, but weekend work was not popular. He sighed.

'Draw your maps and your vouchers,' with a resigned shake of his head. 'You'll be gone at least three days.' Then as I turned to leave his office, 'Me, myself, Driver Beauchamp, I don't have no complaints or you wouldn't be here. But somebody does so you'd best watch it.'

I was the misfit again, the one they never liked. Only Alf Barnes took an interest in me, showed me the ropes. Both his sons had been killed in the War.

My resignation would have been a relief to them all. But I did my job, better than any of them, I thought, and without being chased. Though there was a grudge somewhere.

Then in Wales, standing smart in my suit and cap, holding the door for the Gentlemen on the Commission, LG out on the gravel to welcome them, the wind blowing his mane forward and his cape around his shoulders, LG had recognized me.

'*Beauchamp*,' he called out to me, 'what a pleasant surprise.' One of the gentlemen thought that LG was addressing him and there was a moment of confusion. I remained in my place at attention, holding the car door.

'Who are you with now?'

'I'm a driver with the Foreign Office, sir.'

'Well, how about that.' LG turned to one of the gentlemen. 'This officer drove me all over the battlefields in northern France, 'nineteen.'

The gentleman looked at me disbelievingly. Then to me, LG said, 'How good to see you again. Still listening to Mendelssohn?'

But LG had turned back to his guests before I could answer.

And there, I thought, it had ended. LG never came out of the house again in the two days I was in Wales and the Gentlemen on the Commission climbed back into the car for the return to London without LG seeing them off.

Our paths had crossed, the Wizard and me and now times had changed.

But Great Men are great men in many different ways. Not just for the reasons seen by the public. LG was a Great Man for his energy, for his talent at getting things done, for mobilizing arms production, for Winning the War. But in my opinion LG was also a Great Man for his memory and for his interest in men and women as people, not just as objects for work, objects for war.

In December of that year, 1921, more than six months after Wales, Mr Harris sent for me again.

'FO's going to a conference, first in Cannes, then in Genoa,' he said. 'And it seems you're going as well, Driver Beauchamp.'

He shuffled his papers waiting for his kettle to boil.

'You know, Driver Beauchamp, this kind of thing gets talked about. Do you no good in the end.' Mr Harris looked at me carefully, chewing his biscuit. 'How did *you* get the job?' As if everybody wanted to go, which I realized later, they probably did.

'What job, Mr Harris?'

'You know perfectly well, Driver Beauchamp,' thinking I was putting it on. 'Driving for the Prime Minister in the south of France. Then Genoa.'

'I really don't know anything about the job, Mr Harris.' Mr Harris with a mouth full of crumbs, still not believing me. 'I drove Mr Lloyd George in France, during the Versailles Conference,' beginning to feel excited but without knowing why. 'And he said a word to me in Wales earlier this year. That's all.'

'And even if I *was* to let you go,' seeing me light up, 'what am I supposed to do about the complaints in your file? Am I really supposed to let you go traipsing off over there, to France, with all these against you? How will I look, later on? When there's trouble.' Picking up and dropping the file. Mr Harris always was the pessimist.

He read the list out like a charge sheet.

'Smoking and lolling about again. Not at his car when needed. Seen driving on Curzon Street without his cap. What about all that, then?'

I had no idea about the complaints either. I was not guilty on all counts. But protesting did no good.

'Though I suppose,' returning my smile now, 'since the PM's asked for you by name, there's sweet F-all I can do about it, even-if-I-was-to-be-so-inclined.' Mr Harris turned away to make his tea.

And that was how it started. My second career. As Driver Abroad, OHMS, On His Majesty's Service.

In Cannes, at the preliminary conference for Genoa, LG was always friendly. I was Georges Bouillot and he was General Joffre. We were *complices*, a team. Every day he had a word or a nod for me, a little smile. Even after I had let him down.

He said it was not my fault. But that was not what I thought.

I let LG down because I did not say to myself, though it was there inside me wanting to be said, I never said to myself, simple though it would have been to say, I never said: I'm driving LG, I'm looking after LG. I must keep a look-out for LG at all times.

I loved LG. From Paris, from '19, the Wizard was my Hero, standing in a shining place, alive, up on my hill, near to Beethoven.

But on that day, the day when LG needed me, I sat in the car and read my book.

Of course, to myself later, I tried to blame Mr Harris and his warnings: Bolshevik bombs in brown paper bags, the assassination in Sarajevo caused by a driver. Telling me to stay with the car and not to be away from her at any time.

And where were the Frog police? Drinking coffee in the club-house. It had been an early start for them.

But I knew that I had failed him.

To love. To love is to be ever watchful. To love is to fix the heart, to fix the eyes where the heart is and never, never to let go.

LG was always polite about Sundays. Asking me, never presuming, but in Cannes I had nowhere to go, no one to see. Katrina did not even reply to my letters.

On that Sunday I washed the Wolseley in the early dawn and I collected LG from the Hôtel Martinez at eight o'clock sharp. Then we called for Monsieur Briand at the Hôtel Carlton, back along the promenade.

Monsieur Briand was short and stocky. A never-ending smile hidden under a bushy black moustache.

'I am stay-een *au Carlton, être sous les roberts...*' he said to LG as he climbed in, me holding the door, the Carlton doorman upset and the Frog police grumpy in their Panhard behind.

'What's he saying, boy?' LG asked. The Wolseley had no division between passengers and driver, a *conduite interieur* as a closed car used to be called. The Wolseley was intended as our second car for the Delegation staff, not for the leaders. But more suitable than the Eight, I thought, for a Sunday outing to golf. And Tom, the Wolseley's driver, he was in his room nursing his head.

'He says, sir, that he stays at the Hôtel Carlton to be under someone's, er, t-t-tits, sir.'

'*Oui,*' Briand picked up enthusiastically, '*teets,* zat ees zer eengleesh word.'

Then Monsieur Briand explained what he was talking about.

'Zer two black cupola on zer roof *du Carlton,* zay are representing zer teets of *la Belle Otéro, courtisane aux rois.* I am waiting for 'er evarie night, but, *hélas,* she is never com-ing.'

Briand's smile was all-knowing and disreputable. LG looked back at the two black domes on the hotel roof and he roared with laughter. *Le vrai lion.*

Just the joke for LG, lover of womankind. Lover of the species as a whole. He had his girl, Frances the handsome, Frances the efficient, once the creature of my dreams. But for LG, I thought, Frances was just the tip, the little tip to an iceberg of undiscovered femininity below. The women of the entire world. LG loved them all, each and every one.

It was going to be a good day.

At the golf course at Juan-les-Pins, sunny and mild for mid-January, we were clearly expected. Breakfast had been prepared and the course cleared of holiday-makers. Managers down to porters were on hand for the two leaders, *le Premier Ministre de France, et son collègue, le Premier Ministre de Grande Bretagne.*

After breakfast in the clubhouse the Great Men appeared on the first tee. I took off my jacket, I sat in the car and I started to read. The Great Men would be gone for two hours or more. I had not been asked to follow but I could easily have tailed along in the background. The car was safe.

Suddenly, only minutes later it seemed, through the words on my page I heard the familiar booming voice:

Boy. That man, get that man. Stop him. Quick. LG, but in extreme urgency, frantic, running up toward me. A man ahead of him close to the car, coming within my reach, sprinting like the wind, chest out, tie flowing over his shoulder, clutching a large box camera and tripod.

But in that moment, LG coming up at me through the car windscreen, the man with the camera running ahead, I was back behind the hedgerow above Masnières. I saw everything clearly.

Through the curtain of dirt, the ploughed field itself heaving and twisting, through explosions, smoke, split beets falling like luminous hail, I knew that Thompson was in mortal danger. There were eight sardines, eight trips into the tank, eight times Thompson would have to risk his life.

I had to go, to help him, get him away, something, anything. More than my own life I had to be by Thompson's side.

Then I was running, streaking across the furrows.

Down sir, down. Frenzied, shouted from behind.

And at the same instant a heavy blow from the heel of Higgs' hand on my shoulder, pushing me, striking me hard from behind, down, flat on to the ground.

Higgs had heard the next howie shell in its immeasurable crack of approach.

And as I struggled up to run again after the explosion, not registering that the shell had made a direct hit on to the tank, scrambling to my knees, to my feet, then up, springing forward, released like a demonic sprinter, fumbling with my pistol, no bayonet, no Mills bombs, meaning to kill, to tear, dismember with my bare hands alone, as I came to my feet I felt Higgs' short powerful arms around my legs, grappling, closing like a vice.

Too late, sir, they bought it. Hissed from below as I hit the ground again, hard, desperate. Dirt still flying through black smoke, showering on to us, then clear for a moment over the wreck.

The man with the camera was right by the car. But I was frozen to my seat. Higgs holding my legs tight like a rugby, me unable to move.

Then the next fraction of a second. Even with my face pressed into the dirt, dirt in my mouth, dirt between my teeth, in my throat, up my nose, in the next moment, even facing the ground, there was the searing white light of the Second Coming. A thunderclap as the tank magazine exploded less than a hundred yards in front, bursting as if inside my chest.

Sod, rocks, the tank itself was in pieces, small like fractured shrapnel, some round some sharp. Up, over, down on top of us like a blanket of death.

In that same flash I was hit and there were more minutes missing.

Higgs had saved my life.

I flung myself out of the Wolseley. The man was up ahead now, down the clubhouse drive and off through the pines.

I had no idea of what or why. I ran hard, pelting to my utmost after him. But as I came over a rise in the road the runner was still ahead. With his load he bounded on to a waiting car, on to the running board as the car sped away.

Hispano Suiza, burgundy. Long strapped bonnet, driver with goggles, windscreen down.

They were gone, obscured by dust, even the number plate was clouded and too distant to read. I walked back to the clubhouse. LG was breathless standing by the Wolseley.

'Did you get him?' Hopefully, but knowing the answer.

'They had a car waiting, sir, I'm very sorry, I ran as fast…'

LG bent over, arms supporting his weight on his knees to catch his wind. 'It may come to nothing but if they had a motor waiting they knew what they were doing.'

He paused again, drawing large heavy breaths.

'I was giving Mr Briand some tips on his swing. They could do a lot with a picture like that to publish in France. Even in England.'

I knew that LG feared the newspapers, wanted them always on his side. I had even heard people say that LG cared more about newspapers and their proprietors than about the people who had elected him. An easy and a superficial thing to say.

'Anyway, it's a nice day, boy, so we'll have our game all the same.' Still recovering from his run.

LG turned and walked away. But I knew that I had failed him.

And in the next few days it was over, the government of LG's friend Monsieur Aristide Briand, Prime Minister of France. Now it was Monsieur Raymond Poincaré, Prime Minister of France.

I knew of him. Hero to Katrina. From Lorraine she said, the only people, the Lorrainers, who had it worse than Alsace. Not heard about much because Lorraine was so small. But here is a man, she said triumphantly, here is a man who would make *les boches* pay. *Ils payeront tous!* Not one of your *voyoux*, your *débiles de la gauche*. LG, Briand, me, she had us all lumped together.

LG had described Poincaré as a little terrier of a man. Dour, more Flemish than French. LG had met him in Boulogne, between Cannes and Genoa. Glazed staring eyes, he said. But with an inner eye, his mind's eye fixed on one thing and on one thing only: *la revanche.*

The photograph had been published in *Le Monde* the next morning, on a Monday. LG with his arms around Monsieur Briand from the back, making the swing for him showing Monsieur Briand how to play golf.

The caption under the picture read: *Mr Lloyd George, British PM, coaching the Prime Minister of France for the coming Genoa Conference.*

No Frog PM could survive that.

LG told me the story on the drive back from Genoa to Cannes. The only time I can recall when LG and I were ever alone together.

He wanted to see the coast: the fishing villages and the wild mountains of the Riviera rolling down to the sea, a pearly green stretching out into African haze.

And he wanted to avoid an official send-off from Italy and an official welcome back into France. Just two British passports at the barrier, a quick salute from an Italian customs officer dressed like an admiral and we were off again. Anonymous.

The French Delegation provided the car, much to Harry's disapproval. A DeDion Bouton Torpedo in an astounding white. Eighteen horsepower, eight cylinders and a top speed of over seventy-five miles per hour. But the car was open and upright, comfortable like a coupé, not harsh and noisy like a racing car. A complete joy.

And what was Harry to do with the Daimler, me traipsing off to France like that with Mr Lloyd George? Did I think that Tom could drive two cars at once?

I told him not to worry, I would take the train back to Genoa from Cannes, then drive the Daimler home to London. And railway tickets? And a temporary garage? I left him with it all. Even LG's luggage, which was to be sent to Cannes by rail.

20 May 1922. Your Agent begs to report...

LG was beside himself with pleasure. He admired the car, walking all round.

'Trust the French.' That said it all. 'This'll get us back faster than the train.' He climbed in next to me and settled down for the ride.

Soon LG started to talk.

The road was slow, winding around a barren coastline. Outside the towns there was no macadam. But occasionally I could open her up, adjust the spark back, pull the cut-out and then LG's talk had to stop.

The wind seemed to blow a faint smile on to his face, silver mane streaming out long behind his head. Clearing the cobwebs in the veins he called it. Cobwebs from drink and from smoke, cobwebs from small minds. From impatience when the way forward was so clear but all around him were blind.

'That was a waste of time, boy. Pity we didn't catch the photographer.'

But LG tried to resign himself to the outcome of the conference. The underlying current of events cannot be changed, he used to say. All a politician can do is deflect, manipulate, he does not create the forces.

Whatever the Genoa conference might have agreed, even with Monsieur Briand as Prime Minister of France there would have been difficulty with ratification in the National Assembly back in Paris. LG saw that now. He couldn't control Poincaré, he said. If the French want to invade Germany for vengeance, collect their Reparations with bayonets, just let 'em try.

The reproach that I was waiting for never came. But I knew that Genoa was my fault. And Rapallo would never have happened if Monsieur Briand had been there.

'The Frogs have every right to be resentful,' LG continued. 'I know that. However much we try to pretend that it's not so. We wouldn't agree to their Rhenish State, no matter how many times Foch and his man with the medals and the bathchair appeared in front of the Boundaries Commission.

'Instead we bought the old boy off. We promised Clemenceau complete security by treaty. Me and Woodrow.' He laughed, LG was never going to get used to that name. 'But we didn't deliver. American Senate wouldn't agree. If Clemenceau had known how it was all going to turn out, Foch would have won. The map would look quite different today, boy.'

We drove into the little village of Savona, narrow dirt streets, donkeys and carts blocking the way, buildings that looked like whitewashed rubble. Not a single other motor to be seen.

'But there are enough resentments on the Continent already,' LG said, as I slowed down for the town, 'without a German population twice the size of London held as hostages by the French.'

LG wanted to stop to take a walk on the shore but I was sure that a crowd would form right away. The DeDion Bouton was like a chariot from the heavens in a place like that. Savona was poor and destitute in a way England had never experienced in my lifetime. Even compared to the smallest most remote fishing village I knew in Cornwall.

We drove on a few miles further then LG had me stop by the edge of the water where the road was little more than the beach itself. Here, LG thought, he could see the line of the old Roman road linking Rome with Marseilles and Provence, Via Aurélia. Only the railway line next to the road would have changed this wild uninhabited landscape since the days of Hadrian.

Back in the car LG continued about Clemenceau and the French.

By the Genoa Conference Wilson was gone, had a stroke, not even considered by his own party for another term. And America, President Harding had declared, wasn't much interested in the Treaty. Wasn't good for business. Didn't play well in Peoria. And definitely not any League or any guarantees of borders. Wha-at? All the way over *there*? In Fra-ance?

On 25 August 1921 the United States signed a separate peace with the German Republic. Every word, every single thing that the Americans had said and done in Paris had come to nothing. Nothing at all.

'Wilson wouldn't change one comma in the Treaty to get it through the Senate,' LG said. 'Not a real politician. An academic. A tragic man. He alone has divided the Powers, Britain, France and the United States.'

Then with the wonderful logic of gentlemen sitting on committees, if America wasn't going to guarantee the French borders, they asked, why should Britain? And as to the tunnel? It was never heard of again.

France saw herself facing Germany again. Again and alone. Even the Reparations were unpaid. In 1921 the Germans said they could not pay and they had stopped.

LG was silent for a while, sitting well down in his seat.

'But boy, the other solution, the hostages on the Rhine, that wasn't going to work either. The Germans in that Rhenish State would have been no happier than the French in Alsace had been under German rule. Constant turmoil. Way for another war to start.'

A few days before Genoa, Poincaré as the new Prime Minister had threatened that the French would not attend the conference unless LG would agree not to discuss Reparations. The Germans were in default and that was how Poincaré liked it. There could be no compromising with *les boches.*

'But that's what it's all about,' LG said. 'Economics. We *must* get the Germans back to work. If I had my way I'd cancel all payments tomorrow between everybody. Get us all back on our feet.'

LG was even more sure of that now than he had been in Paris.

And what was his big conference in Genoa going to achieve if the French would not agree to discuss economics? It had all come to nothing. All that work, all those people. Nothing. And the little frocks at the FO laughing behind LG's back.

'So, boy,' LG asked, perking up, wanting to change the subject, 'what did you get up to in Genoa? Women? Wine? Song?'

'I have a friend, sir, from the end of the War. A German officer. I met him during the Armistice and we were also together in Paris. He was the adjutant to the German Delegation in 'nineteen. We went drinking together.'

LG and I had started early and we had made good time. LG seemed reluctant to arrive in Cannes: to telegrams, to dispatch boxes. Frances had already left for London.

We had climbed up from the shore on a dusty trail of hairpins to the border-crossing on the main road. Now we started down again on another loose road on the French side. Through Eze and La Turbie, looking down on a big fishing harbour and a castle beyond, transfigured in the bright sunshine.

'How about some lunch down there in Monte Carlo?' LG asked, rhetorically. We had come unprepared, without Frances and her picnic basket. I had made no plans other than to drive wherever LG told me.

But LG had another of his spots. The Grill Room on the fifth floor of the Hôtel de Paris. Set among tropical gardens opposite the Casino. Once again LG was recognized, but once again it was all so discreet that I could not tell whether or not he was known in his official capacity.

And as at the Café Soufflet, as at the country hotels where we had stayed in Nancy and Lille, places which LG affected to calls p*u*bs with a working class *u*, the meal at LG's spot was superb.

'Now there's *teets* for you.' LG pointed as we entered the splendour of the hotel. A detail of four unadorned mermaids decorated the exterior façade above the second floor. The lawns in front of the hotel were perfect, as if maintained daily, a blade at a time, by the entire citizenry of Monaco on their knees with nail scissors.

Across the huge foyer decorated in *style empire*, we made for the lift accompanied by one of the hotel managers in a morning suit. The DeDion Bouton was parked conspicuously outside the Casino under the care of a small brigade of uniformed doormen.

Old English dears sat around in twos and threes, loaded down with pearls and diamonds. They had been for their walks and now they were on to their teas and their cream cakes.

'Not really Empire style,' LG said, looking up at the gold-encrusted ceiling. 'No bees, Napoleon's personal symbol. Nap Three doesn't really count.'

The lunch was beyond my believing.

Légumes de jardin de Provence mijotées à la purée de truffe noire.

Poitrine de pigeonneau et fois gras de canard grillé sur la braise.

Gratin de fraises de bois.

Red wine: Gigondas.

I cannot remember it all and I could not even begin to guess at the cost.

You always dine better with a Liberal. That was another of LG's expressions.

'Well then?' LG asked, arms stretched out across adjacent chairs, pulling on a huge cigar, turning it between his lips, his little intimate trick. 'What did you and your Fritz get up to?'

'We talked mostly and we drank grappa, sir. Or rather Werner talked and I listened. He told me about Rapallo.' LG was immediately interested.

'Just the damnedest thing,' he said 'The Bolshies and the Germans getting together like that and just down the road. Should scare the pants off France and Poland.'

LG wanted to hear everything I knew.

I put Werner's card on the table. But I kept most of it back: the extra men over the Versailles limit training in Russia so that the Disarmament Commission could not count them. The General Staff calling itself the *Truppenamt* and pretending to be a civilian defence ministry. Everything justified from now on. The secret manufacture of tanks, aeroplanes, gas and submarines on Russian soil. What went on in the head of Werner's General: that one day he would be ready to strangle Poland like a chicken? With Russia holding the legs.

I was nervous about being disloyal. But I did not know to whom.

LG knew some of it anyway.

'In late 'nineteen,' he started, 'a Junkers transport, the latest model with a full load of important passengers from the Junkers factory in Berlin, had to make a forced landing near Kovono, in Estonia, on the way from Berlin to

Moscow. One of our officers with the Military Mission in the Baltic States captured the lot of them at the point of his pistol, together with all their papers. Turned out the pilot was ex-German Air Force and that the group was off to establish a Junkers factory in Russia, on orders from the German General Staff.'

LG paused, twisting his cigar again.

'No one made too much of it at the time and the story didn't get into the papers. It was before Versailles came into force on 1 January 1920. But it certainly worried me.'

LG learned toward me confidentially. 'I think something is going on between Russia and Germany behind all that nonsense about Cultural Exchanges and Economic Agreements.' More puffs at his cigar. 'We'll never have real peace without the Russians. Ignored them at Versailles and that was a bad mistake. But the dukes won't have it.'

Winston Churchill for one, Lord Curzon for another, they were all implacably opposed. Rather get rid of LG than recognize the Bolshies. And here was the result.

'We all deserved Rapallo,' he said, 'and the French certainly brought it on themselves, trying to get their money back from Russia.'

For once I knew what LG was talking about.

LG thought I was right, being friendly with a German. And a German soldier at that. Personal diplomacy, he called it. Every little bit helped.

I asked LG about what Werner had said about the Fourteen Points and about the Armistice being so different from the Treaty. That Germany had not started the War on her own, that all Germans believed Versailles to be a trick.

LG looked uncomfortable, playing with the tape of his pince-nez as he had on the day of the presentation of the Treaty to the Germans at the Hôtel Trianon Palace.

'The old Tiger said it best. On the last day at Versailles, one of those German schoolmasters they sent over to sign, asked Clemenceau what he thought history would say about the Treaty. Quick as a wink the Tiger replied, *bien monsieur*, but history will certainly not record that Belgium invaded Germany.'

LG laughed. Hard, too long.

It was time to leave. LG rose from the table, he shook the waiter by the hand and we stepped into the lift. No bill was brought, no mention was made of payment.

Outside, the vulnerable spring light was fading. The sun was an opaque film, heading for soft dimples of mirrored blue. It must have been after five o'clock but Cannes was only an hour away. In front of the Casino LG pointed down the hill and we walked toward the harbour. Still he did not want to leave.

My questions had followed us out into the Mediterranean air.

'I suppose your Fitz is trying to tell you that they were about to be victorious, until they were let down by the civilians.'

That was not what my Fritz had said. The impossibility of us winning against a Rhine defence. An unending Masnières, barley fields scythed down by machine-guns, howitzers chopping bridges into tea leaves.

LG continued.

'In June of 'nineteen when we gave the Germans five days to sign the Peace and the whole Delegation went back to Weimar, we know that they made an assessment of their chances if they were to start fighting again. And we know that Hindenburg told them that there was no hope.'

LG took another puff on the cigar.

'Of course,' he mumbled, 'by then, I suppose,' his lion's head hidden by smoke, 'by then Foch had all their heavy weapons.'

LG looked out to sea in silence.

But the north, the trenches, the War, *Never Again*, obscured our view.

'I've done my best, boy. The new boundaries aren't perfect but they're as close as we could get them. And God knows I've tried. Feelings are even worse now than in 'nineteen.'

LG turned to me directly, LG to me. The port and the palace behind him, sun a misted glaze. In my memory for ever.

'Maybe you're too young to understand. The will to vengeance. Stronger than life itself, boy. And maybe you can escape it. I thought that I could deflect it later, see the passions cool down a mite. But I didn't have the power.' LG was almost whispering. His favourite word had lost its three-syllable glitter.

He put his hand on my arm. Even after all the food and drink he was white meat: hair, skin, moustache. Drained like a well-bled bird.

'You won't always be a driver, boy. You'll see for yourself how hard it is to change the forces of history. You'll be involved in all of this nonsense one of these days.'

I could not possibly see how.

'And when you are I want you to think of solutions. Forward, not backward. The War was terrible, the most terrible thing that has ever happened. But we have to ask ourselves, *what's the answer*, or, *how do we prevent another one.* Not, *how do we get even.* Vengeance is mine, saith the Lord.'

Back at the car there was a doorman for each door then a half dozen left over. Like the first night in Paris, I did not look like the driver in my suit without my cap.

We drove through Nice round the old port, past the villas I now recognized as Genoese but here ochre not mustard. Dusty red like the rock of the surrounding cliffs.

LG was coming back to reality, gloomy as Cannes and the islands came into sight round the point of Cap d'Antibes.

'I'm just one voice in a coalition, boy. And Britain's only one country among the Allies. I'll be gone soon, coalition's split. I was good at the War but they're going to want one of their own for the peace. Genoa was my last chance. Last chance to change.' LG smiled a sad smile, wistful puck. 'So now it's up to them, the Churchills, the Simons, the Chamberlains. And The Lord help 'em all.'

At the Martinez there was immediate commotion as I pulled the Torpedo up to the front steps. Doormen, gendarmes, a Permanent Under Secretary in his frock coat. It seemed that there had been an international manhunt under way for the Prime Minister of Great Britain.

With his door held open by a fresh set of doormen, LG put a hand on my knee. I understood that I was not to get out. He was well attended to.

LG looked at me again, into my eyes, holding me fixed beyond and above all the commotion around us.

'Pan-Europa, boy, that's what Briand called it. That's the real solution. See if you can sell that one to your Fritz.'

The first time I had ever heard the words.

LG climbed out of the car making a show to the crowd of being stiff.

'Looking for me we-*rr*-e you now.' Putting on his frothy accent, a cross between a question and a statement. He ran impatient fingers into his long hair as he walked away from the car.

Then he was gone. Through a pair of enormous glass doors.

6

Katrina put a good face on everything at the start. Her parents had suffered much worse hardships.

Did I know, for instance, that living in Strasbourg, away from the farm, working in the city during the hard winters to keep themselves alive, that her mother and her father had shared a fork? Shared the only, tiny fork they had.

After the fourth or fifth telling I began to recreate the scene for her.

Jeanou forks his mouthful. And while he chews, Patouche fills her mouth. Then, while Patouche chews in her turn, Jeanou again has use of the little implement. Passing the bent fork back and forth between them, without complaint in a frozen Strasbourg garret.

I imitated them with little forking motions and exaggerated chewing.

Enjoying it in fact, positively revelling in their shared deprivation.

Mais oui, that was true love, Katrina would say. Complete devotion, *l'engagement*. A French word, she told me, in case I had not guessed, which means a lot more than some shared surface life, some shallow English *cohabitation*.

It means an undertaking, she would say, something serious with no way to proceed other than forward. Like taking a horse and cart down a narrow Alsace lane. Worn wooden hubs barely clearing stone walls on either side. Simply unable to go back.

Vous les Anglais, we had no idea what such a word meant between two people.

How was I to respond to such a story, told and retold, a sharp and bloodstained weapon used against me on so many occasions?

None of my inadequate actions, my stumbling words, nothing could match the intense visceral connection between her loving parents. Us in Paris, our times together, the walks, the flowers, little boxes, letters every day: *eh! superficiel*.

And we had our own hardships in a broken-down world: London 1921 and then into 1922, recovering from the Great War. A short boom which I had missed then a severe slump.

Why was I to be compared so unfavourably to Jeanou and Patouche? Wasn't our squalid room, the humiliation and crushing boredom of my job, Katrina's impossible struggle for respect in the hospital kitchen, me sleeping under bridges, a misfit of a dishwasher at the Savoy, stealing boat rides, blackmailing a little frocked homo at the Foreign Office, wasn't all that enough? Us, ourselves, now, together?

But the worst parts I had not told her. The parts that did not match with Yves of the Hôtel de Crillon, Lieutenant Beauchamp and his Silver Ghost, confidant to LG, lover of the most beautiful woman in Paris. Two hundred pounds that I had made to look bottomless in her ruined Alsace village, my mess bill still unpaid.

My punishment was the fork.

'And a knife?' I would inquire, unable to let it be. 'Did they also share a knife?' Or in the complete absence of knives did they mash their food with that same little fork like two teething babies?

Katrina fumed, she blew her furious blue smoke, seeing me making my fun. Smoke in English, smoke in French.

Their diet must have been very limited, I suggested with a serious frown. Only food that could be eaten without a knife. Let's think... what would that have been...? Peas, of course, beans, rice, very small potatoes maybe? Something cheap, obviously not *amuse gueules*, probably not *petits fours*...

Suddenly, up on her feet, Katrina would be swearing and weeping in German. Pounding round the little room, fists clenched.

A picture I had of A Platoon resting at the Tankodrome, Thompson's smiling face over to one side, the only picture I owned. Flung against the wall. Smashed glass all over the bed and on to the floor.

I had no idea of the hardships of Alsace, I had no idea what love was. I was a cynic, a dripping tap, my pathetic attempts at some perverted English humour were completely intolerable. What were we, we Englishmen?

Then back into French.

We had no idea how to appreciate a woman. It was all show and pretence with the English. And underneath there was *rien! Nichts!* We were all *pédés* as she had heard. Oh, yes, her friends had warned her that all educated Englishmen were homosexuals. If you could even begin to call all that *merde* and pompous German music an education.

Katrina had a way of finding enough of the truth to hurt, to wound and to draw blood. Enough to make me indefensible, to plunge me into silences, dark, interminable. Into resentment and withdrawal.

But still I would not relent. Over the little things, the little things especially, over the fork and the knife.

Then it would be my turn. I would start on her German, the core of it all.

Up and at her around the room, my driver's boots powdering the smashed glass, pressing it into the floorboards as hard as I could.

How come German was her ranting language? What of all the brave talk about speaking only French and English? How she wished, she had said, that she had never learned this *langue de boche*. How she longed to be free of it, have it amputated, she had said, be normal, *équilibrée*.

Then on to the aunts at the front of the church, not a word of French between them, I said. And they had lived in La Wantzenau all their lives. You call that a French town? Back at the little farmhouse on the river, nodding at me in wonder during the wedding lunch. Me in my uniform. From another planet, a foreigner. Speaking *French*.

I wanted Katrina to admit that she could never turn her back on German, on German things, on German thoughts, on German ideas, on German expressions that came to her in her rages.

I wanted her to see, to admit, to swallow. To gag on her artificial French views. I wanted her to tell me, to get on her knees, even, as I had done for her, to tell me that she was wrong. Wrong.

That there are no absolutes, there is good in German, that it cannot all be black and white. French perfect, German the root of all evil. A devil buried in the soul of every one of them, man, woman and child, just because they were born across the river.

But what really hung over us was the ghost of Paris. The spring of 1919 and into the winter, the fabulous conditions under which we had met and first made love.

My stories of the Inuit and how they had over forty words for snow. From a book my father had sent me from Northern Ontario: snow in a dark cloud rolling toward you from a distance; snow blowing at ankle height; snow in gentle flakes like Christmas; snow whipped horizontally by the wind, freezing the skin. I could remember only some.

And how I was going to invent my own equivalent language for her smiles. Her distant reassuring smile, both of us in our uniforms, separated across a Committee Room; Katrina in my bed smiling at me from below, strong but intimate, firm but soft; the quick smile, displaying inside nerves as we arrived at quai d'Orsay, part of a throng moving up the wide stairs, Katrina in her green Chanel, shining like a star on a clear winter's night; her smile for Patouche, slow, indulgent, infinitely patient; her smile on the dance floor like the smile from the pillow, showing her handsome profile in the candlelight; the smile for her young niece, like a little playful cat, bright, sparkling; the smile for Pierre at Fouquet's, his chair back up against the panelling, showing her admiration for him, the love that my heart knew was there between them.

In June 1919 the Treaty had made the world anew and we saw ourselves as the irresistible force for good. France would be rebuilt, the League of

Nations would take over international affairs. Katrina and I would marry, we would have children, *babies and more babies.* Strong assured young adults, citizens of both France and England, two languages, two cultures. Europeans of the future. Free of past hostilities, free of dark tribalism.

We would be the same, Europeans, not just French or English. In Paris and London regularly, living in St Germain-en-Laye or on the Sussex downs. Expanding commerce between the two countries or whatever it was to be. Prosperous, rising in a new order.

We would visit America and Canada. With Katrina's love I could do anything.

Yves Darling,
This is an *event* isn't it? I truly feel as if something magic has happened in my life, that I am loved in a way that only Yves can achieve. We are so close, I feel we might at times melt and fuse like a wonderful new kind of steel.

Do you know how I see things? This will not be an ordinary marriage, just as it was not a 'love affair' comme ils disent les Américains. Your past, my past, our year of knowing and loving each other. I see our pasts as a combination of choices and luck, that has concluded with me in your arms. For that I do thank the god you have lost, and his universe, every morning.

Do you know that there are days I can barely keep the delight inside. I want to pull Laurence or Béatrice by the sleeve and say 'Sais-tu que je vais devenir l'épouse d'Yves?' That I am going to care for him, be his woman. That he will be my only man, and that we will have a child? How can people think that marriage is boring?

Oh! Yves, I have feelings inside me that you will see in flashes, in poems that I will write for you, in my eyes, and in the way my body reaches for yours, and my mouth searches for your lips. The way my back arches when you penetrate the soft wet place between my legs.
Love,
Yves' very own Katrina.

Our room above the King's Arms was a long way from the picture we had developed so strongly and so easily. The pub was down a claustrophobic lane leading from the Borough High Street to the refuse bins at the back of Guy's Hospital. To a dark ramp down to the entrance of the morgue beyond.

The pub was black on the outside, bricks and copings impregnated with London smut. And black on the inside, stained by cigarette smoke and sticky spilt beer. Low ceilings, tiny doors and windows like a doll's house. All decorated with a faded Edwardian jollity like the waiting room of a railway station.

Our wretched upstairs cube was relieved only by a window looking out on to the lane, across to another building less than ten feet away.

The alley echoed with the comings and going of drinkers, hospital orderlies, men and women who ran the barrow market. Unemployed who somehow had sixpence in their pocket. The effect was to magnify the coughing, the greetings, the drunken singing and vomiting. So that in bed, facing away from the window, it was often easy to believe that all these activities were taking place within the room itself.

At first we walked in the evenings along the Embankment and over to Trafalgar Square and Piccadilly. Like Paris, Katrina tried to say cheerfully, when London was not and never would be. Or over Tower Bridge and into the City.

But the walks were quickly casualties of the same conflict.

I could not say that I knew where they lived, those hobbling hulks from under bridges. Those creeping cadavers emerging in the evening to beg for scraps, moved on by the police from the Strand or Temple station. All I could do was to show my useless sympathy for them all.

The better men had been taken up by then, by the late summer of 1921 and those who remained were the double and triple amputees, the irreparably shell-shocked and the gassed.

We watched a man, no legs and one arm, hunched on a makeshift board fitted with piano casters. He pushed himself along the pavement, humming, and grumbling crazily to himself. His remaining good hand, wrapped in filthy black rags, sweeping the pavement, pushing his trolley along like a grotesque punt.

I stood at the Embankment wall and looked across the river, tears streaming down my face at the sight, at what I knew to be the cause of his hideous maiming.

A deafening burst directly above the trench. A noise all of its own. A thousand Christmas crackers right in the ear at once. A bursting noise from the inside, as the casing splits into a hundred blades, each one looking for its own piece of whole pink flesh.

Then the scream, the terrible scream. Someone not under cover.

God. Oh God of Battles. Not one of mine. I beg of You.

There that moment, shrapnel, that deep infinite crack, there, over the pavement, over the river. Ear-splitting, racking my body, the report so loud that the flagstones shook under my feet. The Embankment wall moving under my hand.

Dolphins around the street-lamps swimming this way and that, the obelisk swaying. The Savoy behind us falling back then coming forward again, as if through sights on a misty morning.

Oh, the obelisk has been damaged by the burst. Quickly I am on my knees, scrabbling at the holes, fumbling over the chips like Braille, like spouting wounds I cannot staunch. Blood is everywhere. Everywhere.

Then I am lying on flagstones staring up at the sky. Black, khaki, red, blankets, string. The entire pinnacle ready to topple, fall on me and end it all.

I read the words as the stones come down.

THIS OBELISK

PROSTRATE FOR CENTURIES

ON THE SANDS OF ALEXANDRIA

WAS PRESENTED TO THE

BRITISH NATION AD 1819 BY

MOHAMMED ALI VICEROY OF EGYPT

A WORTHY MEMORIAL OF

OUR DISTINGUISHED COUNTRYMEN

NELSON AND ABERCROMBY

Then I was back, eyes flooding. The wholeness of my own body, the ghastly mutilation on the makeshift board, the inescapable unhappiness of our lives, that we...

That I alone had created.

Katrina helped me to my feet. But she had no sympathy, I had all my limbs. She turned me from the river grasping me by the shoulders.

'Look at these men carefully, Yves, these are the ones you are hard on while the Germans you forgive. There should be *boche* labour here, rounded up from their unspoiled countryside, like they took our men, whole villages in cattle wagons. Bring them over here to England, to build nursing homes for these men. The Huns should be cleaning wounds, making beds, scouring lavatories, cleaning arses with their tongues.'

Now it was Katrina who would not let it be. Her face cadaverous, her jaw clenched so hard that the skin under her chin was pulled taut, pulsating and angry like a toad. Her clothes hanging off her like a set of worn curtains.

Me and LG, that Bolshevik, playing golf, eating our wonderful lunches in Monte Carlo while these men are living under bridges. While La Wantzenau, while her home village is still a ruin. While Patouche is still carrying buckets of water up from the River Ill on a wooden shoulder yoke.

Our walks were ruined. This was marriage, I said, this was how marriage became. The romance was over.

But I really wanted to say, oh how I wanted to say, beyond all my pride, all my humiliation, beyond my own life that had escaped the shrapnel, beyond all my lives, all my lives still unlived, I wanted to say, more than my life itself, I wanted to say, there on the Embankment, tears streaming, the soldier on his board pushing off down the pavement without his farthing, oh, I wanted to say, 'But Katrina, *chérie, attends, arrêtes-toi un instant!* I am Yves, your husband, I love you, we have jobs, we have our limbs, our health, we are together. We have a bed for making love, a fork with which to eat, two wages coming in. And together, *mon amour*, love of my life, together we can make a success.'

I wanted her to stop, hold me, let my tears fall on to her face, trickle down her beautiful soft neck. Take me back even to that room, have me make love to her gently, beautifully, as we had done in Paris. To press myself into her until our biblical flesh was one once more.

But it was too late. Already it was too late. I could not. I was struck dumb and my arms were filled with lead, unable to move, unable even to reach for her.

I used to think, before I was married I used to think, before I had ever made love to a woman, looking at couples who were together, lived together, made love every day, I thought, that impossible, inside, extravagant, boundless thing, I used to think that if two people did that, that wonderful transcending thing, then surely there could surely be no quarrelling after. A couple who did that, overcame everything to do that, their days, their happy lives must, must be strengthened. That is what I used to think.

Katrina's first day at Guy's had been worse still.

I had told her that she would have to start as a junior nurse, even though the job had come through Major Graves whose brother was a surgeon and a Director on the Hospital Board. For Katrina I had gone back and asked for help, for her alone, the job had been found against all odds. And on the first day she had dressed in her full uniform, the *Ordre des Infirmières de l'Armée Française* complete with her stripes.

Katrina was confident in her abilities and in being offered a fair British chance to prove her worth. But she had immediately offended some battle-hardened Head Matron by her mere presence.

The Head Matron had looked at her papers, first in German then notarized in French. And knowing nothing of Alsace, nothing of French history, secure in her ignorance she had launched herself off, 'Can't think why we're taking on bloody Germans, for goodness' sake, when there are so many qualified English girls out of work. And in any case,' pushing the papers away from her across the desk, 'I wouldn't even take *Frog* Registration seriously.'

Katrina was made to change into cleaner's overalls and she had been assigned to the kitchen.

She screamed at me that night, so loud that I thought she would drown out the pub below.

'Don't they know, these stupid English, that France had three dead for every Englishman killed? That France has five times more wounded than England? That even in the first weeks of 1914, that France lost more men, many more men than the whole of your useless little British Expeditionary Force put together?'

Round the room again, fists clenched tight, beating on the walls.

'Don't they know that France has made more progress already, with nursing, with artificial limbs, with treatment for shock, for gassed lungs, more progress than England will make in ten, twenty years?'

I could imagine her every day in the kitchen, jaw set, her strained, agonized look around the eyes. Trying to be the most efficient, working at twice the speed of the others, trying to prove herself and her obvious worth. To the insuperable taunts of the staff and the sniffing of the Head Matron.

But once the German tag had been placed it was impossible to remove.

She was French, she said, quietly now, furious. In all that time, in all the forty-seven years of German occupation, France had never let down her citizens in Alsace and Lorraine. They were nationals, by French law they were entitled and in French eyes they always had been entitled. They always were.

No one in Alsace and Lorraine had ever stopped being French. Not the slightest shadow had fallen across their belief in their true nationality, for all the *boches* who had been moved in. The French still knew who each other were.

Jeanou's father, Katrina's grandfather, had been obliged to change his name in the 1870s to a German name without a French accent and so he had chosen Comberg to replace Combères.

But even that name was a defiance. *Berg* which the grandfather had added meant mountain, when *combe* in the ancient French root meant valley, the opposite. Herr Valleymountain, ridiculous. And every time the grandfather said it to a German, or every time a German used the name to him, he could have a little inside chuckle.

And immediately in October 1918 the name had reverted to the French, Combères.

But among the staff at Guy's, to the Head Matron, Katrina's German name on her German papers from before Versailles meant that Katrina had changed her name to cover a German past.

Her accent in English was guttural, there was no denying it. And in the kitchen, in shops, in the pub, Katrina was a Bosche.

But if Paris was the shadow over our marriage, the Peace was its grave. A shaky marriage based on an unjust peace. Versailles: a trick in France, slavery in Germany, scorned in America, misunderstood in Britain, cursed among the Arabs, insufficient to the Italians, unfair to the Austrians, the Hungarians, the Czechs and the Poles with the Russians ignored.

But to the French, to the Alsacians and to Katrina personally, Versailles was a fraud. *Une arnaque*, she called it. Like a card trick. After all the promises, France had no guarantees, no security and no Reparations.

It was Monsieur Poincaré who ended it. In Paris, sitting at his huge Louis XV desk in the Hôtel de Matignon. Did he know that he was ending my marriage over in London with a flick of his quill pen?

In January 1923 it happened. Poincaré ordered the invasion of the Ruhr, demanding full payment of Reparations. Belgium went in with the French. Britain refused and America was already out.

'Didn't I tell you?' Katrina was beside herself with excitement.

There were pictures in all the newspapers: the French in their firemen's helmets, divisions at a time, marching through the streets of Köln, singing and smiling for the camera.

'Now there's a *man* for you, not some useless politician, some conchie like your MacDonald. You will see, Poincaré will extract every *sou* we are owed.'

'Katrina,' trying to take her hand, 'this is a disaster. The Germans will stop work, they will pay nothing and this will make France poorer, ruin the franc. The tricks and lies from Versailles will never end.'

Non! Jamais! I knew nothing, I was just a parrot for all those Bolshevist ideas of LG, that *jobard*, the womanising *vantard* and his *putain*. Pushing my hand away.

I had told Katrina about Frances, about how happy they had seemed and what a comfort Frances must have been to LG during the dark days of the War. Then during the tensions of the conference.

I had opened myself to another torrent.

Jeanou, Katrina told me, had taught her that married people behave in a certain way. That there were things that married people just do not do.

A married man or woman simply does not allow a situation of temptation to arise, much less ever reach the point where a temptation has to be resisted.

Fidelity once promised was complete, a condition of life. Not just for as long as things were good.

LG was married and Frances was a whore, that was all there was to it.

How come I could not understand such simple things?

I felt inferior for having no such inheritance. I just loved Katrina, enjoyed so much being with her and more than anything else in the world I enjoyed making love to her. The intimacy, her body, *juste pour toi.*

But Katrina had made it clear, there were definite rules.

Then as the invasion of Germany proceeded we battled every day. A French *Régie* was established to run the German railways, saboteurs were being executed and the Rhenish State was to be proclaimed. Taxes were to be collected by the French Army at bayonet point.

France had fought a terrible war, France had been attacked without provocation, millions had died. And if winning had brought France nothing then she must fight again.

What did I mean, Germany had not been defeated? What lies were these? She had married a Bosche-lover, a Bolshevist, *un collaborateur*. And what did I know? Living over here in this undamaged country? And during the war with my safe job behind the lines? My medal to cover over an English *pagaille*. Now I pretend to be affected. Falling about in the street like a common drunkard.

'You and your useless little English Army, your *bay uh eeffe*. Really, of war, of loss, *vraiment*, what do you know?'

I could only ignore it for so long.

'How the *fuck* do you dare to say a thing like that?'

Anderson, McDough, Minns, Peters... out of fifteen men at Montreuil I had lost seven in five months. And I had filled in for some of the missing drivers myself. Making more trips than anyone. Not boasting, not brave, just had to be done.

Not to mention Cambrai: Thompson, Tulley. Ellington and the trenches before that. These were lives she was insulting, dead men, brave men. Men who had given all they had for France.

Could she not see that we could have stayed out of their war games in August 1914? France and Russia in their stupid Entente. Of course we could. The Germans would have fallen over themselves to make an accommodation with us after France was beaten. *Then* how would her precious Alsace have been freed?

And the BEF, while we're on the subject, was destroyed in France in September 1914 and Paris was saved. The core of our army gone in a month.

And after that we raised a new army of millions. All for France.

This is not just some lovers' quarrel. These are truths.

You bitch. You *fucking* bitch.

And when were you ever at the front? Or anywhere near it? You and all your ignorant, sodding talk about war. Treating German soldiers in a safe hospital back on the Rhine. You've never heard anything worse than a fire cracker on *quatorze juillet.*

Your brave *fucking* Alsace was really a German province, Kraut and happy to be Kraut when they were winning. Why? Go on. Tell me why there was never a referendum in Alsace. Well, I'll tell you why. Because even in 1919 the vote to stay German would have been a landslide.

White bile, khaki face, her fists again. Objects thrown, the room looking as if Beethoven himself had lived there.

We grappled, we cursed, then she slapped me hard. Very hard across the face, a shock.

That blind spot, that searing white moment and the force that comes with it. I pinned her arms, I propelled her to the door and I pushed her out. Out, stumbling down the narrow dirty stairs. She fell headlong. I shut the door and locked the bolt.

Soon the banging started. The cries, rage, tears of anger, of frustration. I covered my head with a pillow and I sobbed.

'Only the English,' Katrina had said in Paris after our first row, about Briand, 'only the English could make a swearword out of making love. That shows where your brains really are, *vous les Anglais.*'

I did not know where she went that night nor did I care.

The next morning I left the door open and took my bag. Mr Harris had some important American visitors. I was to drive.

No note, no explanation, no apology.

I was right and Katrina was wrong. I stuck to that.

7

I was away for only a few days, driving the Americans to meet the gentlemen on the Reparations Commission, but in that time Katrina had constructed a wall. Huge and sheer between us. No doors, no windows, neither flaws nor handholds in an even glinting surface.

Part of the wall was night duty.

By volunteering to work at night, Katrina had said, she could escape the kitchen and make a start even as a junior in the operating theatre. From there she might find her way back to the treatment and long-term care of amputees, prove her superior French abilities.

How could I disagree with that? Moving closer to a position where she could use her training and her proficiencies. The opening we had both hoped for.

Katrina began returning at all hours of the night or in the early morning, engaged by new, outside matters of which she did not speak. And matters about which I did not inquire. Not wanting to confirm the wall, to give the wall recognition by asking questions which previously would not have been necessary.

And to avoid me further, to build the wall higher still, to avoid any chance that the wall could be demolished, Katrina slept in her clothes. She would arrive tired and drawn, she would perform some nominal bird ritual at the sink and climb into the bed without undressing.

I was angry, I boiled. It was my turn.

Then from behind the wall I was told that Katrina was taking baths after surgery at the nurse's residence. She took her kit with her in a little black bag.

Her dresses would disappear and reappear from the wardrobe. She would smell of a new Katrina, of chloroform, of sterile soap and pipe tobacco, not the Katrina from the kitchen. And sometimes, to the silent piercing of my heart, she would smell of the Katrina from Paris.

But still I did not inquire. Words had been said, things had been done and the wall had been built.

And as to her time-off shift? Again it was hard to fault. A course in surgery procedures and post-operative care, she said. A chance to get to know the surgeons, she said. The way to a permanent appointment.

Then on Sundays something else with the surgeons. Sailing with the GHYC, she said, on the Solent, she said. Or watching a cricket match, the GHCC, she said. Playing away against another hospital.

I thought of myself as a tolerant man who neither dictated nor possessed. I thought of myself as a man who could win against a mere wall.

Life followed a new and hard road.

Even in our terrible conflicts there must have been some hope of resolution, of finding an answer, of resuming our love and our happiness. But now, separated by the wall, all chance was gone.

I had even forgotten the words, the words I had never spoken. Katrina, *chérie, attends, arrêtes-toi un instant, je t'aime . . .*

And if we did have to speak, it was in English, the language of contest and division. French was our language of love. And certainly not German. There was no ranting any more, the wall had ended that too.

Then one morning, with Katrina just back, me dressing, her sitting up in bed wearing her petticoat, her bra, her nurse's stockings and only she knew how many layers beneath and below, reading an old copy of *L'Art et la Mode* she had found in a second hand clothes shop in Lambeth, idly flicking the pages, drinking the coffee I had made her, grey, khaki, the same colour as her face, looking tired and annoyed at the entire world, Katrina said to me:

'I have met another man,' she said. 'A surgeon at the hospital who is going into practice. We plan to start a new life together. His name is David Althorpe.'

I knew about him. From after the start of the wall.

Dear Yves,

I thought I should tell you where I have been for the last two weekends. I went on two courses – called the Surgery Forum – because David Althorpe who is a surgeon at the Hospital took me to an introductory meeting some months ago. I met him when I applied for a transfer to the theatre.

The last time I can remember truly loving you without any reservations or restraints is a long time ago. And yet when I asked Dr Lange who works on the gas ward, a Belgian, very knowledgeable, 'doesn't anyone just fall in love anymore?' he replied, 'not unless they're sixteen and have an intelligence like *un singe*. You use logic and analysis in your work', he said, 'and you should use the same in your marriage.' But a big part of me says *no*, Yves.

I went to see David a few weeks ago and I joined the programme. It is intended to improve how the teams work, especially in the operating theatre and with the patients.

The course strips away all the personal restraints and mannerisms that build up in people. They are amazingly rigorous and disciplined about the process. The world would not need policemen or wars if everyone had to go on two weekends like this.

What choice do I have but to be cynical (learned from much exposure to you) and say you care nothing for what I have to say, or what I feel. Your behaviour makes me in my turn behave in a way that I do not like. I do not like myself when I am with you.

I do not love you any more because there is too little trust left, and too little tenderness, too many cruel things said. How can I ever love you again when you think that all the problems are mine? You simply ignore the pain you cause. If

you have stopped thinking I am beautiful how can I make you say it? You no
longer feed my soul.

I know that if you were the one doing the leaving in our marriage I would be
terribly terribly hurt. I am not leaving you for David or any other man. And I am
not leaving because of some revelation I think I have had at the course. I am just
not comfortable.

Katrina.

P.S. This letter is nothing to do with the course.

There was no one to hold my legs. Powerful forearms clamped around my
thighs, then the urgent hiss, *Down, sir, down. Get us all kill't.*

And without Higgs to restrain me my anger was without limit, an urge to
vengeance stronger than life itself. But there was no white light, no bitter
words. *Manger froid* is the French recipe for revenge.

Katrina had spoken up too early. And after a few days it was clear: she
had nowhere to go. Conventions were not that easily broken in the early
twenties. Her new life was not as ready as she had imagined.

Each night or each morning when she came home, whatever the time,
whatever she had been doing, especially if I thought she had been with him, I
made her perform to my command. It was the price.

I would decide in advance, prepare the scene, sort through her wardrobe
in a clouded gibbering craze. And when she entered I gave her not a
moment's pause. She was to dress in her full uniform, just as she had looked
on the day we first met. Or her pink Molyneux from the last Conference
banquet, shining like Venus in a perfect evening sky up the steps of the
Grand Palais.

She was to exaggerate her make-up, sitting in front of me at the ugly
kitchen table, facing the chipped bowl. Paint her nails, the final drops of her
scent from Samaritaine. Every movement to my plan, relishing her pathetic
efforts to apply mascara to her flowing eyes.

Then I would have her stand and read to me. An early love letter or the
words she had written about David and her new life. An article from *L'Art et
la Mode* in her thick French: a happy young Paris couple choosing colours
for their nice new flat in the *seizième*. Katrina's voice shaking, her chin riven.

Until I would fall upon this mockery, this *pot de peinture*, every crease and
orifice. On the floor, back to the bed, against the wall, tied to a chair with one
of her scarves.

Smudged and dishevelled I would have her start her preparations again while I resumed my watch. Finally I would move across the room at her, take her violently against the wardrobe or up in her heels halfway through her fresh dressing. Exhausting myself into her, thigh bones smacking against hers like a set of raging toothless gums.

The performances took an hour, more. Carried out in complete silence.

Then I would climb into bed, face the wall and will myself to sleep. To the violent knocking of my heart that now knew only raw hatred. To the pulsing in my ears, behind my eyes, out to the tips of my fingers.

Or if it was morning I would dress in my uniform and leave Katrina weeping in a corner. Pound away to work, down hollow stairs in my driver's boots.

It was my right, my reprisal, the reparations I was owed. Consuming me all day, blurring my vision as I drove.

What of the hours I had spent listening to the story of the fork? What did I know of *l'engagement*, she had asked. When her *engagement* was not even up to surviving an argument. An argument in which I had been accused of hiding during the War.

And all the promises in her letters. This will not be an ordinary marriage... the magic, the fusing between us... I am going to care for you as your woman and you will be my only man...

Just over a year since our wedding and she was fucking with a doctor. Now I understood, why we *les Anglais*, why we use that word to swear.

I was not Katrina's first lover as she was mine. Out of loneliness or the hope of love, she had told me. From being pressed, she said, her beauty, her poise, a magnet for men, but with no lasting result, she said.

But with me, *oh! que tu me fais mouiller,* or, *oh! Yves amié, juste pour toi pour toi... non, oui, non...oui...* with a cry, a groan up from inside her chest, her head flashing from side to side on huge embroidered pillows.

Katrina lasted three days. On the fourth day when I came home she was gone.

8

I could not keep away. I would have to be dragged.

From outside the grimy building, the dirty alley and the ramp down to the hospital morgue.

Above me my Katrina making love with the surgeon in his rooms.

Again. Say it again for my deaf ears: my Katrina making love with Dr Althorpe. Twice is not enough. A thousand times is not enough.

First it was the little things. Her bicycle hidden in the entrance hall of Copley House, innocent behind the statue of Keats. Althorpe's letters under the lining in her black bag: brash, half baked.

...I am, by the way, quite comfortable about spending some time in eternity with you for a while...

I remained confident in my contest with a mere wall.

I saw them in his new tourer, Katrina hardly recognizable in headscarf and goggles. Off to boating or off to cricket. An AC 1921 model, dark green, nine horsepower, the type made famous by S.F. Edge the racing driver. Equal to ten years of my salary.

Althorpe was short and already bald. He knew nothing, I could see that right away, a puppy dog who wagged his tail every time she appeared. Nothing of Alsace, not a word of French. Nothing of my Katrina's inside, her conflicts, of Jeanou and Patouche. Give it time, I said to myself as they drove by, then we shall see.

But still I could not grasp the edge, the razor edge between my waking dreams: I was just away, no, she, Katrina was away, coming back today, tomorrow, tonight. But then the truth, there in front of me in her little mirror.

The disease of *never* filled me once more. I could not live with *never*. *Never* pulling me to the ground again, to lie down in the road, scream, roll into the gutter, washed away, khaki, black, blankets, string.

Across the hospital quad I followed. The two of them side by side. Through the cloisters, black and white tile echoing with their footsteps, theirs together, theirs clicking together. Past statues, past shadows on frosted window panes, under a reeling sky and into Copley House.

Behind the building I found a fire escape. Balanced and weighted so that the panic-stricken, pounding down the metal stairs away from the fire, would be pivoted to the ground as if guarded by an angel. But without a fire the first rung hung ten feet up in the air: so that thieves, criminals, deceived husbands would all be kept out.

A real felon would have been more circumspect. He would have tried later, given up for some safer mark. But I was desperate and reckless. I stole a rake from the groundsman's shed behind the hospital lodge. Never returned, concealed for the future, the many futures. I snagged the bottom step.

Then I was up and over open gratings, on to metal landings. Past windows, squalid rooms and unmade beds, smells of cooking. Bright lights burning, past rooms never meant to be seen. Then to the landing behind 7A.

But for 7A there was another fire exit over a far balcony and through a locked building that I could not enter. Every other window of Copley House I could see and touch, press with my face. But their window was beyond my reach, out of sight around a chimney stack.

But now I knew, I had the map reference. The light on the ceiling that we could both see together: me from the shadows of the alley, her from his bed. I knew the place where I could be close to her. The only place in London where I knew she was going to be.

I wore a path to that perch, my place of agony. I went to the lane every day, twice a day, all day in my desperation. To know, to feed my distress.

Then one night as I stood blind on the fire escape but less than ten feet away from her, I saw. In the dark curtained window on the other side of the lane, reflected in the glass, I saw them both. Motions slow as if against a wind, blurred, reflections undulating on wavy glass. A mirror, the curtained window opposite was a mirror.

I found a mirror of my own, Katrina's hand mirror left behind. And then I could see. Around the chimney stack, the mirror held out in a shaking hand as I balanced on the edge of the landing, precariously over the lane.

I could see the room. Two faces together and no evasion possible. No other explanation.

Absences: Katrina out of the door then back again. It was cold, the gas fire was on, a glow. Appearances: Katrina entering again in her dressing gown, white, tied at the waist, stolen from her from the Crillon. Her hair in a towel to dry, his towel, David's towel.

She sits on the floor by the fire on the floor. Pudgy David is reading, absorbed by the newspaper in the single chair. My Katrina ignored.

Oh, I would now, this moment, now, take her home, fix the eyes where the heart is and never never let go. I would now, now, the world, anything.

Katrina combing her hair by the fire, motions I knew like my own.

Out of the room again, back without her dressing gown, towel thrown over the door, her tall slim body. Every pore, every hair I knew. Armpits and thighs still damp from the bath.

Finally David is looking up. Will he or won't he, now, then, that night? He can't decide. He prefers the mornings maybe.

I shook. Pete and my entry, counting, breathing. Up on to the wet grass with the men. Running toward the salt shaker, the air full of lead. Singing out eight to a bar as I watch my boots hit the grass. Dancing the dance of terror with the storm-trooper who had my name.

It all meant nothing, nothing compared with this.

Carts rattled below me at the end of the lane, taking bodies down to the morgue. Down on to the ramp and into a long black corridor. There was room down there among the shrouded cadavers. Room for one more, for two, for three.

~

A long silence.

Morley thought the old man had fallen asleep again. He reached over to take the empty Ensure can off the bed tray. But a bony hand stirred, grasping Morley's wrist, hard, shaking.

'But then I got lucky, Morley,' he said in a whisper. 'And we were all saved, all three of us. By Mr Harris and by General Dawes, they dragged me away. But what about you?'

~

I wanted to dislike General Dawes. I planned to ask him about peace and justice and the failure of Versailles. But he was not the man to blame.

The General had a Tartar's face, narrow hooded eyes, then all his features drawn down to a wide flat jaw, as if his chin were resting on an invisible shelf. He wore civilian clothes, immaculate but loud like a character in a play and he parted his hair straight down the middle.

Plain speaking and fair dealing were his style, the General said.

I held the door for him outside their Embassy in Grosvenor Square and even on the very first day, he spoke to me as he climbed into our Daimler:

'I hear you'll be driving us in Europe.' The General was to take the boat-train.

'Yes, sir.'

'And you're supposed to speak the lingo, know your way around?'

'I try, sir. I know France and Paris.'

'How about Berlin?'

I had never been more than a mile into Germany. Had I been in the army? Seen action? So in that case he didn't have to fuss. He had been in the American Army in France, he told me. But he'd never faced enemy fire. The Military Board of Supply, hardly even heard the guns. I liked him saying that.

'What's your name?'

'Beauchamp, sir.'

'No, your real name.' The General sounded impatient as if he had come across this problem before. 'Your first name. What do you people call it over here? Your Christian name.'

'Yves, sir.'

'That's better, soldier. I don't go for titles or any of that hyphenated stuff. Well, Yves, we're going to have us some fun with this thing, right?'

It seemed that we might. General Dawes was to head a Committee of Experts and lead the Gentlemen on the Commission out of their fog. He was going to settle Reparations once and for all.

By the end of 1923 resistance to French occupation of the Ruhr was costing the Germans five times more than the Reparations payments they refused to make. And the invasion was going no better for the French. They found that they could not dig coal with bayonets or cut trees with sabres. Their Rhenish State was failing against German strikes and sabotage.

Now both sides were looking to the General to find a way out. For Germany to back down and start work. For France to withdraw with the appearance of victory when she had achieved nothing except the end of my marriage.

Germany was once more on the verge of revolution. Conditions were terrible. The mark had lost all worth, falling to one billionth of the value of 1914. The country was destitute. And not just the workers, this time even the middle classes were facing complete ruin.

A determined attempt by the Bolsheviks or the Nationalists during the first months of 1924 would have overwhelmed von Seeckt's model army and ended the Weimar Republic then and there.

And once again American power had the opportunity to establish peace and justice. Wilson was dead: this time their man was the General, a Captain of Industry, a prominent banker and lawyer. A Republican with ambitions to live in the White House.

~

The old man's whisper trailed off and he drifted away, mouth open, face frozen in some silent supplication to the ceiling. But his breathing was even and Morley sensed that the end was still some time off.

Through the window of the hospice kitchen dawn had begun. Dimming the security lights of the container port, creeping through stacks of cubes in random patterns. Back to Vancouver on a pitilessly wet morning. And to

Jane and Donald, so close, so cosy in their bed just a short drive away on Falkland Road.

Morley poured the hospital soup away. Where did the old man go in his dreams: back to the 1920s or forward into nothing? What illusion was there left for the dying? He had worn himself out again with the narrative of his marriage, his skeleton body trembling with an orgasm of grief as he came to the end.

The story had filled Morley with a satanic dread: that lost love could come to haunt a deathbed over seventy years later. They were the same, he and his dying friend. Morley felt himself overwhelmed, more and more with every hour that passed. Love, betrayal and vengeance. An endless ramp down into the dark, down then down again.

When he awoke the old man seemed to be weaker, smaller in the bed and less light in his eyes.

'There are two letters in the book of music, Morley, right at the back,' he whispered. 'I retyped them not so long ago, late '60s I think. Maybe he read them over my shoulder, or maybe he already knew it all. It's hard to remember what the world was like back then. We were all in a trance.'

Morley searched through ragged pages, to find a package of sheets held together by a rusting paper clip. He started to read to himself.

'Read them out loud, Morley, it's your turn to do the talking.'

Dear Thompson,

I think about you so often. This is the ninth anniversary, 20 November 1926.

I am here in France with your Beatrice. Ben has started as an apprentice at Lindley's. He's stopping with his aunt while his mother is away.

I was already on the Continent so I met Beatrice off the boat train. We are at the little hotel in Fins that used to be the mess. She is in her room asleep as I write. I think I've made her tipsy pouring wine and talking too much.

It's been such a trip for your Bea, never been abroad before and says she hasn't stayed in a hotel since your honeymoon at Ramsgate. Apart from that she's in very good health.

We visited Villiers Plouich although I have been before, to the sunken road behind the trench line up on C Company's left. The Commonwealth War Graves Commission has done a fine job even if the stone cross is a bit much. Just a little plot inside a hedge, part of the landscape now. Only 65 of you in this one so there are a lot missing. There's certainly not 44,000 accounted for in all the grave sites around the battlefield. Then Cambrai was fought over a second time in October 1918 and there were a lot more again.

The whole place is almost unrecognizable now. The trenches are gone, even the deepest parts of the Hindenburg and all the concrete. But there are still traces on the ground, long narrow shadows across the furrows and a few church spires that have yet to be rebuilt. Rusted casings are piled up in the corner of every field, more come up each time they plough.

We walked the route of our advance, me and Bea, right from our trench line to the farm road where the Maxim was and where Felicity was hit. Weather was about the same, foggy then sunny. It all seems smaller, not such long distances as in my mind and flatter.

Bea has been very touched by the visit. She told me she had always wondered what the place was like. 'So this is it, this is where it was,' she said. Then she just looked around quietly for a long long time. The breeze carrying the last of the morning mist blew at her hair below her hat and her walking shoes were covered in that same light brown dirt. I gave her your big smile, I put my arms around her for you and I tried not to cry. It was so very good to come here together.

I am taking Bea back to England on the boat tomorrow. I'll be able to drive her home to Coventry before I have to be back at work myself. Government car of course.

I brought the MC with me and I gave it to her still in its little blue box, as a keepsake. She didn't want to take it at first, but then I think she remembered what I had written to her at the time.

I told you in my last letter how I managed to progress from being an infantry officer in the victorious PBI to a nobody of a government driver. Well, I'm still at it. Life post-war is nothing like we imagined.

The work hasn't been that bad. As a single man, which I am again, I can live on the pay and even save a little. Especially as I am on the Continent most of the time, at conferences, with a special allowance and all my meals paid for. I even enjoy driving the senior people who are at the centre of events. I told you about my times with Mr Lloyd George. Nothing quite like that has ever happened to me again.

For the last two years I've been driving for Sir Austen Chamberlain, the Foreign Secretary. Son of the man who set off the Boer War! Joe the Screw-Maker. But Sir Austen is quite different. Started pretty stand-offish, though once I got to know him he turned out to be a good bloke. Very much against war and I think secretly he feels guilty about not having been at the front himself.

The peace has been quite the balls-up so far, not thought through at all, as you would say.

I saw some of the German Army first hand at the time of the Armistice. They were being pushed back all right, but we hadn't beaten them. We wouldn't have crossed the Rhine with our cavalry or our tanks in a big hurry. Their howies and their 5.9s would have had our floating bridges registered in no time, HE, shrapnel, gas, smoke, the works. You never saw the canal at Masnières, only a small show, but even that was a proper mess.

Everyone I know says that Versailles is wrong, but no one will do anything about it because of popular opinion. But then the press didn't tell the truth about what happened at the end of the War in the first place. The new Parliament of '18 was full of jingoes, bloody cavalry officers who said at all the public meetings that they were going to squeeze the Bosche until the pips squeaked. LG did the best he could. He thought it could all be changed later. Genoa proved how wrong that was.

The lies in the newspapers have been repeated so often now that they have become the truth. I suppose with so many dead we had to tell ourselves that we had won. A mess and a cover up, like Cambrai all over again, but the whole sodding war this time.

I've come around to thinking that it was really our fault, us, England. The Count was right, back at Versailles we should have sorted it all out before the Treaty was completed, not deluded ourselves.

Since 1920 Fritz has kept up a constant trench warfare against the Treaty using every tactic he knows. They have not accepted the outcome of the War one little bit.

The Germans feel completely justified in doing what they can to avoid the Treaty because of the way we treated them. They certainly haven't reduced men or equipment to the required levels. Then there's another army of Brown Shirt volunteers, the SA, who could be put into the ranks tomorrow. And I know for a fact that they have tanks and aeroplanes in Russia.

And even though Hindenburg is President of Germany there is still a lot of dissatisfaction. That cry of 'Dolchstoss' just won't go away. A couple of years ago Ludendorff even tried to overthrow the new republic, he mounted an unsuccessful coup together with a former infantry corporal called Hitler.

The Germans have worked everything they can to get around Versailles. On the financial front they let the value of their currency drop so badly that even billions of Marks wouldn't buy a meal. You needed a barrowload of notes just to buy a loaf of bread. Fritz blamed the French invasion for the mess and said he couldn't pay anything more.

It's the Reparations and the guilt clauses that seem to be the worst. But then as well there's six million Germans on the wrong side of the new borders, in Czechoslovakia mainly and Poland. The Germans really hate Poland, a lot of that country used to be East Prussia.

My Fritz asks how we would like it if Liverpool was given to Ireland just because a lot of Irish navvies live there.

All the governments have changed in the last year or two. We had our first Labour Prime Minister, Mr MacDonald. Can you imagine a conchie as PM? He was even threatened with Dartmoor during the War! But at least he understood that there will be no peace and prosperity while the Germans are starving.

But finally there's some good news after all the troubles since 1918. My Fritz's uncle, Hjalmar Schacht, became President of the Reichsbank and he stabilized the mark in only a few months flat. It shows what Fritz can do if he wants to. Now their industry is achieving wonders. Not daft, are they? Just like you said.

Their Foreign Minister is Herr Stresemann. He says Germany wants to co-operate now. He's another Captain of Industry. Stresemann's opposite number in France is Monsieur Briand whom I know from being with LG.

Between Briand, Stresemann and Sir Austen there seems to be a real friendship and some hope at last.

There's even been progress with Reparations. A Commission of gentlemen had been meeting for years trying to fix the amount for Germany to pay but they could never agree. I drove an American General in 1924, General Dawes, to Berlin, Paris, everywhere, a very clever man. I admired him no end. He made all sides settle on reduced amounts within a very short time. You would have enjoyed the General, no bull, very straightforward, 'I'm all business,' he used to say. The result was that the French and the Belgians pulled back from the Ruhr. It was a wonderful moment, the Germans even seemed happy to start paying.

In 1925 I was in Geneva all year. I drove for more conferences both there and in Paris. Then in October all the diplomats and the conference staff moved to a little town called Locarno on Lake Maggiore near the border between Italy and Switzerland. A new treaty was signed between Britain, France, Italy and Germany as equals and the first big hole was made in Versailles. Germany agreed to keep the Rhineland disarmed and accepted her western borders which mostly means Alsace and Lorraine being French in perpetuity. And all voluntarily this time.

I couldn't believer that it really had happened. On the last day at Locarno I saw tears in Sir Austen's eyes. He and Stresemann hugged like a couple of bears. Even Mussolini, the Leader of Italy came across the lake for the dinner. The townspeople sang and danced in a square by the water. It was quite the sight, flags, rockets and Roman candles.

No more War. Never!

Now Germany has become a member of the League of Nations and to cap it all, Briand, Stresemann and Sir Austen were given the Nobel Peace Prize.

Then last month the three of them wanted a private meeting to take things even further. But in Geneva that is impossible. The cars are followed by the press day and night. They never tire of photographing the three gentlemen who are, I suppose, at the centre of the world at the moment.

They are a funny-looking trio. Briand and Stresemann are short and stout while Sir Austen is tall and something of a dandy with slicked back hair and a monocle. Herr Stresemann could be Mr Winston Churchill's brother while Monsieur Briand you could take for a lecherous schoolmaster on a dirty weekend in Paris.

The French cooked up a plan to out-fox the gentlemen of the press. In the end Sir Austen couldn't come and a little frock was brought in from the FO (actually they've stopped wearing the old frock coats now). The frock said nothing all day but Sir Austen has full confidence in Monsieur Briand anyway.

We put the motors on to a barge at Geneva. The gents from the press set off at high speed north and south around the lake trying to guess where we were going to land for the conference. But as soon as their cars had left, the barge came back to the dock and we made for France, to a little village called Thoiry at the bottom of the Jura mountains. Gave them all the slip.

Because the plan had worked so successfully Monsieur Briand wanted the drivers to have dinner with them. We were seated at the back and had the same meal as the great men.

It was just a small pub really, low ceilings with heavy beams, wonderful smells. Only six tables so I could hear it all. The food was marvellous and the conversation became quite raucous. I've often thought that a good meal can solve a lot of problems.

We had baked trout, roast partridge with rosemary, duck with oranges, morel mushrooms in cream sauce, all sorts of wine, then champagne at the end. I have to say that since the War I have developed quite a taste for French food.

It seemed to me that the Foreign Ministers moved further forward in those four hours over dinner than they had in all the years since the War. Germany with her industry working again is going to buy back the Saar and two towns the Belgians took. Reparations are going to be ended with a final lump-sum, so many billions in gold. In return the Allies will leave the Rhine next year, many years early according to Versailles. Germany is going to get some colonies back but most important of all, Germany's war guilt will be wiped out formally, in another new treaty.

So it's all progress and right now everything looks just fine.

Must get some sleep or I won't be safe with your Bea tomorrow.

Yves Beauchamp. (Lt. Retd!!)

P.S. You would be very proud of Daimler. I am driving their 1924 model now, Number 31, four-wheel brakes, 35 h.p., the same as the cars supplied to the King's Garage. Cylinders lined with steel, hardly any engine noise at all. They call her the Silent Knight. A real achievement for British engineering. I went to collect Number 31 from the factory in Crewe myself and I was taken through their museum. I had to laugh: Herr Gottlieb Daimler, the original designer of the cars, still owned a part of the English Daimler company right until the War. Royalty's favourite motor, the only car Haig would ride in, designed and owned by Fritz!

The next letter in the package was handwritten. Morley read the first few lines to himself.

'Are you sure you want me reading your love letters?'

'You must hear it all, Morley, to understand what happened in the end. You must read on.'

20 November 1926

My dear Katrina,

I don't know how many times I have written over the last three years but not one of them has ever been posted. I don't even know where to send a letter to you. Isn't that something, for a husband not to know where his wife is? I see Pierre from time to time and even he has heard nothing of you.

My sense tells me that there is no point but my heart will not stop. A spell cannot be recreated, I say to myself, but then I think... only by persevering can anything be achieved.

It's another riddle, one of many I cannot answer. But there must be millions of people around the world trying for another chance at happiness. Are they all to be denied?

And what of you? Can you have found happiness with David Althorpe so quickly? Is he so good and am I so bad? Oh the many many questions, they ring around my head like an unforgettable melody.

I was at a dinner in France just recently, sitting at the back as the driver but listening to it all. This is not 'I told you so', this is genuine good news. You must have read in the papers by now that in the Treaty of Locarno Germany gave up any claim whatsoever to Alsace and Lorraine. And there are preparations being made to go a lot further, to remove all the other contentions between European nations. Now maybe we really can have peace and prosperity.

Monsieur Briand was there with Herr Stresemann. They are talking about Pan-Europa. A sort of higher state above all the separate countries so that we could cooperate on economics, on reducing customs barriers and improving health and transportation. It made me so happy and so sad at the same time. 'To unite so that we can live and prosper,' M. Briand said.

This is the place where we were going to live, my Katrina and have our family. You and me. Now it's going to start without us.

So silly this, my writing to you about politics when that was one of our big troubles.

I went to a series of concerts in Geneva, all the Beethoven sonatas in seven evenings played by a pianist from Chile, a man younger than me. On the last night the applause was deafening and so he played again, a Bach chorale prelude. Oh Katrina, after all the Beethoven and all my thoughts, my life, you most of all, the War and all the deaths, I went outside by the lake and I cried. Cried as I have not done for years. Not since the battle that took place on this day in 1917.

Katrina, I have done nothing without you, just the same job for the FO although I am on the Continent a lot, which is a bit of a compensation. All the things that I could have done. For you, for us, to make the life we wanted...but there is no point in finishing this thought...I know it will never be. All gone in such a short time, my one chance for happiness. Oh it hurts, it hurts.
Love. K's Y.

9

By the early thirties Pan-Europa was dead, buried under the weight of the Crash. It started in America but depression soon spread to Europe. Then the biggest bank in Vienna failed and we were back to the conditions of the early twenties, worst of all in Germany. I heard that the French were to blame for starting rumours and spreading panic. They wanted to stop the proposed customs union between Germany and Austria. But nobody really knew who or why and misery gripped Europe once again.

In 1932 and into '33 I was away from Croydon for over nine months. I did not understand at the time but when I returned it was the end of an era.

At the garage Mr Harris was in a good mood. Even though there was bad news, he said.

'While you've been abroad there's been a little accident,' he began. I could almost see a smile, a wobble to his cheeks below the walrus moustache as if he was sucking a gobstopper.

'One of the cars, Mr Harris?' My face dead straight like the parade ground, not understanding the joke.

'No. A friend of yours, a certain Mr Green. Electrical wire came down while he was walking his dogs in a thunderstorm. Killed instantly, he was, stone dead.'

'I'm sorry to hear that, Mr Harris.'

Mr Harris looked at me carefully, as if waiting for the merest flicker. He picked up his kettle and went to the garage tap for water.

'And in addition to that,' he continued when he returned, bending over his gas ring then leaning back in his hard wooden chair, 'there's a reorganization coming up.'

I could see my file open on his desk. Mr Harris removed the clip and started to divide the loose pages into two piles like so many used banknotes.

'Your file has always been a puzzle to me, Driver Beauchamp,' Mr Harris started again after a long pause, sheets in his neat piles now, side by side. 'There's nine years' worth here now, you know.'

He fiddled with the pages, squaring off the corners.

'But if I do this,' he said, picking up the smaller bundle, 'there won't be no puzzle no longer.' And with that he tore the sheets of the smaller pile into tiny squares and let the wad fall into his wastepaper basket. A little flourish and his serious walrus look again.

'So *now*, in this here file,' he continued, returning the rest of the papers on to the clip, 'we have this Driver Beauchamp. Coming up to a decade of service and no complaints at all. Knows the Continent, they say, speaks the language like a Frog they say, letters of request and recommendation from Mr Lloyd George himself, from Sir Austen Chamberlain. And even from a transatlantic personage, a certain General Dawes.'

Mr Harris gave me a broad smile as if I had won some kind of prize.

'But now Driver Beauchamp's driving days are over.'

His kettle boiled, he disappeared down behind his desk, spooning black tea into the pot as he talked.

A new foreign post had been created. His Majesty's Ambassador to the League of Nations. They were going to have their own cars in Geneva. FO motors would only be running from Croydon, no more jaunts on the Continent thank-you-very-much.

'But you'd be wasted here at the garage, Driver Beauchamp.' Mr Harris smiled at me again as he put his pot of stewing tea on to the desk. 'So I'm taking you with me. I'm being moved up, responsible for the KMs, the King's Messengers. Just-the-cat's-pyjamas. And looking for one more, it seems. So you can consider it done, you'll be at King Charles Street starting Monday morning.'

He lifted the lid of his pot and stirred the brew with a teaspoon. He offered me a cup, then a biscuit, then the milk, the sugar. The first time in almost ten years.

It was one of those arragements, those nod-and-a-wink jobs that has happened before you know it. Before you know what you think about it yourself.

There were only forty King's Messengers to cover every British embassy in the world. We were a mixed crew: dispossessed RSMs, older junior officers from the regular forces on early retirement and the best of the senior FO porters who were too young for pensions.

KMs were a separate Corps, operating from a basement corridor, jealous of their position, jealous of one another and the routes to which each man claimed ownership. For the older men the longer routes by steamer were the prizes, where embassy bags were delivered monthly: Shantung, Tokyo, Buenos Aires, for example. The main capitals of Europe with the pressure of bags once or twice each week were the places where a new man started.

There was no training.

'Wouldn't have you if you needed training,' Mr Harris said, as if he had been running the Corps for a lifetime. 'Character and reliability, that's what we look for.'

Within a month I was travelling every week to Berlin or to Paris, occasionally to Rome. Now it was me who was being driven, from King Charles Street to Waterloo station and back again wearing one of my new suits, carrying my portmanteau and a big diplomatic case. Behind my lapel I wore a brass badge, a greyhound at full stretch and underneath the letters, OHMS KM.

At our Embassies, from the moment I arrived to the next day when I left, everything seemed to revolve around me and my bag. Examining what I had brought from London, then rushing to complete what I was to take back to King Charles Street.

Oh yes, I had moved up in the world. Always a sleeper on the *wagons lit*, no quibbles with expense monies, excellent meals. A position of responsibility.

~

Elaine had snuck into the room like the start of wan light through blinds. She leaned over the back of the Lay-Z-Boy and felt for Morley's pinch muscles. He sat forward sharply, jerking out of reach then on to his feet.

'...I'm sorry...' they both said simultaneously. But Morley recognized some new instinct. An electric flinch away from the touch of fingers, away from any new start, down on to another ramp and down again.

Elaine moved over to the bed.

'I'm going to make up the morning pills and do my paperwork before they all start to wake.' She felt for a pulse, looking at her watch. The old man's eyes flickered open.

'I feel as if I've gorged myself when I've hardly eaten a thing,' he said.

Stick arms crept down the covers and crooked fingers weaved together over his stomach.

'I'll start you on a course, very low dose. See if we can loosen you up a bit.'

Elaine reached for Morley's shoulder again as she left. His hand came up and covered hers for a brief moment.

'...I'm sorry...' they both said again.

Elaine returned with her pill tray. Morley began to break the old man's tablets into fragments, posting them gently between grey lips, alternating with pulls through the straw.

'You were telling me about the 1930s, as a King's Messenger.'

The past was right there for the old man, as clear as yesterday. Words began to come quickly, but no stronger, not much more than a whisper.

'At first, in my new position I didn't see much of Werner. A little bit when we were both in Geneva, we went to concerts together. He still played the piano, very well by then. In 1932 he was sent to China for three years to organize training for Chiang Kai-shek's Staff.

'When he returned he was Adjutant to General von Witzleben, Commander of Wehrkries III, the Military District of Brandenburg surrounding Berlin. Staff Officers couldn't stay at the Bendlerblock, their HQ, or out at Zossen for very long. Their army was still small so they kept moving Staff men around to make room for others. Fourteen years after the War and Werner was still only a captain. But then I was just a messenger.'

The old man's head turned toward the bedside locker and he nodded.

'There are two more letters, Morley. I can't talk any more, I need to save what strength I have left.'

Morley started to read again.

Dear Thompson   20 November 1937

The twentieth anniversary of Cambrai and we're thinking about war again.

Peace and prosperity have vanished, pushed out by economics, by the politicians and the dictators.

I thought that I had kept my promise. You and me meeting again in good times after the War, Beatrice and our visit to Villiers Plouich. But I spoke up too soon.

All the lost opportunities since the War are like those nightmares that I still have. Everything going wrong at once, you racing over the beet field, men face down in the mud, blankets, string. Nothing I can do to stop it, nothing.

In the late '20s and early '30s I used to think of it as a circle, all the problems linked together:

–World recovery depends on European recovery, but

–European recovery depends on German recovery, but

–German recovery depends on resolving Reparations, but

–Concessions to Germany depend on French security, but

–French security depends on Germany's acceptance of Versailles, but

–Germany will never accept Versailles because they were tricked.

Once it seemed that all we had to do was to settle everything at once around a big table or at the League of Nations. An offer, a fair counter offer, like LG said in Paris, as he tried at Genoa.

But no, we each have our pet solution. Britain passed the Peace Vote, the Americans have isolated themselves across the Atlantic and the French have built a wall. The Germans have their leader, Hitler, the corporal from the failed Putsch of 1923.

It's a story that hardly bears telling by the living to the dead. I haven't been back to Villiers Plouich recently. The headstones themselves would reproach me. We are the dead. Why?

First there are Reparations. Like the guilt, right at the middle of this problem. I thought General Dawes was a great man but he turned out to be nothing more than a salesman for the American banks. He piled debts on to Germany, huge loans, that's how he did it. He loaned Germany four times more money than was owed in Reparation payments, so of course the country boomed. Germany has never paid a penny of Reparations that was not a loan in the first place.

Then the crash came on Wall Street. The Americans immediately tried to force repayment of their loans from Germany and within a year there were five million out of work and rising. That's when Hitler got busy, stirring people up against the Republic again, back to the old cry of slavery and stab-in-the-back. He has a party called the National Socialists, Nazi for short. But it was the Americans who gave him his soap box to stand on. I'm sure that the Americans will never get their money back from Hitler and I for one won't be crying.

Then when Hitler came to power we said nothing while he renounced Reparations altogether. Just like that. If only they had made some real concessions when poor old Stresemann was in power, how different things might be now. All that wonderful talk in the pub at Thoiry came to nothing back in London and Paris. The dukes wouldn't have it.

Germany's Nazi government is something that our old-fashioned FO types can't understand. Even the Count was a gentleman, but these new Nazi men are professional villains. Within a few months of coming to power they had Germany out of the Disarmament Conference, out of the League of Nations and they started threatening us from the brink.

During the Disarmament Conferences in Geneva I attempted my own bit of diplomacy and a real disaster it was too. I've told you about Pierre, my friend in the French Army who was wounded at Verdun. He lives with his mother in Évian now, just around the lake. We had a dinner, me, Pierre and Werner my Fritz, just before Werner went to China. It was a beautiful August evening by the water. But I was sorry I tried: they were like two dogs and Versailles was the bone.

All Werner can see is the humiliating 'diktat' based on trickery, how Germany wasn't the only one responsible for the War and shouldn't pay for everything. How they lost all that land in Poland and all the Germans who were put into Czechoslovakia. I know the list so well. Werner says that allowing all the Germans to be together again is the only way to ensure real peace. Many people in England agree but no one has the courage to speak.

And Pierre? There's his foot and his hand of course so he remembers the destruction of northern France as if it was yesterday. The War has already made Germany bigger and more powerful, he says, while France has become weaker. And now some comic opera corporal is demanding that we make Germany stronger still by adding more millions to their population and forgiving their debts.

Pierre says that the attack on France in 1914 was unprovoked, but Werner answers that it all started with Russia, France's ally, mobilizing against Germany and Austria. Germany only came in later and was not the aggressor he says. The discussion became very heated.

Afterwards I drove Werner back to Geneva and he hardly said a word while I felt anxious and nervy, like the night before the battle. No one seems to know how the War really started, the truth I mean.

Then there's rearmament. Hitler is quite open about what they have built up. He has an air force, tanks, submarines and a general staff, all since Rapallo. Recently, when the French increased military service from eighteen months to two years Hitler decreed the same in Germany. The German Army is now almost twelve army corps with forty divisions.

Herr Hitler is becoming stronger and stronger. He marched his troops into the Demilitarized Zone across the Rhine. Quite illegal of course, although it was his own back garden, as they say. Then after that it was the Anschluss. Austria is now part of Germany, another thing that was not supposed to happen.

We can't seem to find the right answers and Hitler is always calling the tune. We could never enforce Versailles through war after twenty years and Hitler says the Treaty is deader than a doornail anyway. And Locarno too just for good measure.

This year Hitler is demanding the German part of Czechoslovakia and who knows what beyond that. But the Germans have a case, that's the whole problem. If the Austrians, together with the Fritzes living in Poland and in the Czech Sudetenland want to be in Germany again, why shouldn't they be? Wasn't Versailles supposed to be based on self-determination?

It's the helplessness that is the worst. How easily this could have been solved but how impossible it has become. I carry messages every day, more and more useless pieces of paper creating bigger and bigger misunderstandings.

We've had a rotten crew recently. There just doesn't seem to be a single effective man in the entire FO. Sir John Simon as Foreign Secretary is an international calamity and Eden is a featherweight. Sir Austen has died and his brother Neville is a real disappointment. He's only interested in reading his name in the newspapers. Believe me, I see all this close up.

I was going through *The Times* on the train yesterday. There was a very clever letter to the editor. The writer quoted Machiavelli: a victor should either conciliate his enemy or destroy him. We have done neither.

Yves Beauchamp. (Lt. still Retd!!)

P.S. Had a meal with Werner at the Hotel Adlon in Berlin. He told me that when the German Army entered the Rhineland their troops were only issued three rounds each. That was all the SAA they had! It was a complete bluff. One good push from the Frog battalions and they would have gone scurrying back to where they came from in a big hurry.
YB.

And a second letter to Katrina.

20 November 1937
My dear Katrina,

It's been years and years now. I suppose that I have healed over a bit and I get through each day, but I'm still raw underneath.

I saw Pierre at his mother's house in Évian recently, doing my bit for three-way European diplomacy with him and Werner. He had news of you through les Invalides. He told me you had a son in 1923 or 1924 but that you left England to live in Strasbourg again. A big hospital has been built there I've heard. What's your son's name? You will make a wonderful mother, but it hurt me all over again as if it had happened only yesterday.

I took Werner to meet Pierre but it was not a success. My punishment was to be in the middle translating, able to agree with both sides. Pierre went to bed very drunk and very angry.

Werner played the piano. Chopin as I had never heard him before. Fast and loud, rests where I did not know breaks existed, then sudden jagged runs. Trills detonating out across the lake that brought tears to my eyes. Melodies from the heart arcing up into the night sky. Werner had a Polish piano teacher who told him that Chopin was not a romantic, rather he was a man who wanted things that were not possible. Werner said that those words were like a blinding revelation to him and that his real love of Chopin's music had started from that moment.

It's a terrible thing to face, that my life is full of regret, but it is. The past is so painful and the future is unbearable, knowing that we will repeat our mistakes over and over again. Is there no way ever to put things right? Why *is* that, why?

I remember writing to you about Locarno. What a joke that seems now, the same useless clauses from Versailles wrapped up in different paper with new ribbon and sold to us a second time. Were we blind? But yet what action can be taken? Do we really go to war again? It's unthinkable.

I could post this letter to Jeanou at La Wantzenau, but I don't know if he is still alive. I could come to Strasbourg myself but what's the use?
Love, K'sY.

~

'A tormented edge that will not heal, a loss that can never be made up. Those are the hard things, Morley. When you know what you should do but your little black heart won't let go. With some things I understood so clearly: my mother, that school, I never went back, never. There was nothing there for me. But other things I carried for life: a few months with Thompson, a little longer with Katrina.

'Through the early thirties I kept myself to myself and I watched, hypnotized like the world around me. Walking the streets of Paris, back to London, getting to know Berlin. And I paid sometimes, I admit. Ugly little scenes in stale boudoirs of worn plush. Though my money never bought me anything except sharper loss and more emptiness.

'I was watching and waiting, available. But for what I did not know.'

PART V

1

From the first day I met Tricia she asked me questions of a kind I had never before heard from a woman. Was I angry like her? Did I have a lover in London? How often would I be in Berlin? How could she be sure?

Tricia lived in an attic looking out on the Tiergarten through a tiny dormer window with a high sill. She worked in a flower shop on Leipzigerstraße. Both the room and the shop were an insult, she said, adding to her bitterness.

We climbed five flights of gloomy stairs to her room after lunch on a beautiful Sunday afternoon. It had to be a Sunday, she told me later, for her to enjoy her vengeance.

'I would sit for hours with them, listening to all their stupid crap about heaven and hell. All that Calvinist shit about who is already good, who will always be bad and what promises mean. And the hymns, oh the hymns. Yes, I knew them all by heart. Hours and hours every Sunday just to please him and his brainless family. Now what is his religion? Blood and soil. His blonde floozie and her pigtails.'

Tricia spoke English with an American accent and a vocabulary to match. A nasal drawl then her words clipped off at the end German style. She had lived in New York, she said, but for some time she told me nothing more.

Werner and I never spoke of my marriage, it was as if that one evening had told him the entire story. Katrina's look of frozen steel, her shoes crunching in the gravel as she walked away toward the École Militaire. But I knew that he had not forgotten and that he blamed Katrina's French side.

'You should find a good German girl,' he would say. Like his Inge, a respectable officer's wife, a presence behind him. Not a film star like a French girl.

Werner and I had established an easy routine, we met nearly every time I was sent to Berlin. Practising our friendship again like a half-forgotten duet: from the Armistice, from Paris, Genoa and Geneva, now Berlin. But here there were rules: no use of the telephone, walls have ears.

Berlin in the late thirties was a drearisome city, grimy and dark. Brooding Prussian façades competed everywhere with new Romanesque columns topped by stylized golden eagles. Copies of copies, obsessed with the connection to Charlemagne and the First Reich.

Werner had discovered that some of the newest monuments were made of wood. Permanent stone would follow later, during the Thousand Years.

He would rap furtively on walls as we passed.

'Another German fresco?' His shark's smile. 'I liked Italian illusion better.'

Scaffolding as if for public executions had been erected over statues and steps along the main streets, but only to be mounted by a succession of state visitors to the New Germany, in order to review the troops. Double headed bronze lampposts marched up and down pavements like an unending military parade. Red and black banners hung against public buildings as if to proclaim some national mourning. There was no sign of joy or anything spontaneous. Paris could have been the other side of the widest ocean.

There had been some life to Berlin in the early thirties left over from the golden twenties. The bright centre of light around the Memorial church, *bistrots*, small hotels, a few shops that opened until late.

But then the raids had started. Brown Shirt bullies from the SA looking for *Dreckjuden*, loud and drunk, demanding free liquor in all the bars. Or secret policemen searching for anyone they could arrest to fill quota, as a communist, a homosexual or an habitual criminal.

Taking down names in a cabaret was all that was needed. The next day the establishment would be locked, windows covered with stickers and posters, rubbish blowing in lazy circles outside the front door.

But Germans seemed to be fulfilling their destiny, I thought, all working together to recover from the past. There was none of the economic uncertainty of Britain or the political instability of France. Announcements were made almost daily: the start of a new motor-road or an airport, laws extending working hours or establishing enforced savings. The chaos and the wasted energies of Weimar were over as well as the hardship of ruinous inflation and party violence on the streets.

Yet crowds watched the demonstrations of the Third Reich in a sombre mood, I felt, as if under orders. And there seemed to be little enthusiasm for military displays.

Women were still smartly dressed, elegant but plain, as if every one of them was off to some vital employment. Despite cloth rationing femininity was there to be seen for those who were interested.

And off the main streets there were even a few places left to sit outside. Werner always wore his uniform: it improved the service, he said with a humourless smile. By early 1938 he was back at the Bendlerblock south of the Tiergarten. He was Major Schacht now, with a new desk in an expanding organization. The Armed Forces had been renamed the Wehrmacht and the Army General Staff was now the Oberkommando des Heeres, which Werner called the OKH.

My job was to be unremarkable. With my clothing allowance I took to wearing double-breasted suits with wide lapels and full trousers. I bought a German trilby, I had my hair cut short and I grew a wisp of a moustache. Sitting at a table outside the Hotel Adlon we could have been taken for the Party man and his Wehrmacht counterpart.

If we were alone we would talk about politics in Europe or Werner's experiences in China, the sinking of Franco's cruiser *Baleares*, the mass treason trials in Moscow. Or more rarely, new appointments to the Reich government, Generalfeldmarschall Göring as Plenipotentiary for the Four Year Plan, Herr von Ribbentrop as Reichsminister for Foreign Affairs. The very best men in the whole of the Reich, Werner said, laughing a mocking laugh. His uncle had resigned as Reichsminister for the Economy earlier that year.

But slowly, as the spring of 1938 turned to summer, even Werner's hollow laughter seemed to fade. He made terse comments without explanation: the Old Man turning in his grave, Oskar Hindenburg, his son, regretting what he had done. This experiment, Werner would say, has gone far enough.

Then quickly as the next table was occupied or a waiter appeared, we would go back to women. Werner watched women as other men might watch birds. Deriving pleasure from subtle variations of colour, the set of a head, a glimpse of a life in the wild then taken further by the imagination.

Tricia was an exception, flesh and form with a name, a woman who was not content merely to be observed. Werner introduced us on the steps of the Adlon on a wet March afternoon.

'*Ein Kriegskamerad von mir,*' Werner told her, baring his shark's teeth, as if about to take a bite from her clear white neck. To me, 'I present Frau Tricia Boch.' Then he kissed her gloved hand.

She addressed me in German. I understood what Werner had said but not Tricia's words to me.

'No, he is British.' Werner replied for me. 'He is visiting their Embassy.' Then in English. 'But where he was born is not his fault.' He gripped my arm and gave me a playful shake.

Tricia looked at me with noticeable interest like a jockey examining a fresh mount.

She was short and slight, pretty in the way of a window dresser's mannequin. But through the mask there was a cleverness and a ruthless determination.

Tricia followed fashion with the desperation of an addict and her appearance showed an almost military obsession. Her hair, like her clothes, was strictly *à la mode*, a skullcap of fine streaked strands ending in clouds of permanent waves around the back of her neck. She wore hats of all descriptions, usually forward like a cadet, down over one eye, colour and texture contrasting with her artificially pale make-up and exaggerated red lips.

Tricia stood upright and defiant as if she could increase her height by will-power alone, her stance and expression defining her character. I would watch her in front of a mirror shaking out her bleached frisée with the snort of a pedigree filly, red tips of her pointed fingers running impatiently through curls. Or wrinkling her nose behind her menu, choosing the very dish that Captain Boch particularly disliked.

My time in Berlin was always tense and rushed. Events were always *on the edge*, or, *the balloon was about to go up*, an expression that I did not understand.

The volume of diplomatic paper seemed to grow with every week. And after Mr Neville Chamberlain moved into Number 10 Downing Street when Mr Balfour retired, a new kind of communication was added to my routine.

Now I was instructed to keep my distance from the Embassy, to be in the building only to deliver and to collect, to find lodgings outside so that they were used to my absences. I was not to sit in the staff lounge nor to discuss my routes and schedules. I soon understood that personal letters to the Chancellor himself or to Ministers of the Reich were being used by the Prime Minister and some Ministers of the Crown to circumvent Sir Nevile Henderson, His Majesty's Ambassador in Berlin.

I came to know the government buildings and who was to be found where. The back door to the Old Chancellery on Wilhelmplatz, hidden behind a new office block cold like a factory. Or the offices of the Reich cabinet, temporarily in the Hotel Kaiserhof while a new Chancellery was being built on Voss-Straße. Then the modern Air Ministry building on the far side of Leipzigerstraße.

I learned my way past sentries in black, through sombre corridors and across marble halls filled with elaborate Hohenzollern replicas. My instructions varied. Sometimes envelopes were to be delivered to a particular person or returned to London unopened. Sometimes to a personal private secretary or to a deputy. Often I was to wait: *the sender requests a reply by the same hand*, I was to say, or, *a reply may be forwarded at the Minister's convenience.* I had my little speeches memorized in shaky German.

On the day after my introduction to Tricia I returned to the Hotel Adlon in the afternoon, at the same hour that we had met. I was to leave for London that evening on the train then by overnight steamer from Bremerhaven.

Every afternoon, Tricia had told Werner, Frau Karen allowed her half an hour off to walk to the hotel for coffee. Just a little taste, she said, of the life she had known before.

It was as if she had been waiting for me. Before I could ask, she had me seated at her table and she was pouring me a cup from her silver pot.

'So how is your visit?'

'I'm a diplomatic courier, not a visitor.'

'Already lies,' she said without a smile, as if she had expected nothing less. 'Is that high or low?'

'The job is important, but not the individual.'

'I myself, I am just a flower girl,' she said, with an empty little laugh.

'You don't look like a flower girl.'

'Oh, you like this?' She looked down at her skirt, clearly pleased with the slightest compliment. 'It is Mainbocher. My wardrobe is all I have left.'

Everything Tricia said always led back to the same festering wound.

Tricia's Mainbocher was a calf length cream dress, a moulded crêpe silhouette wrapped over her small frame. The provocative cling of the cut was partly covered by a dark green summer coat, almost khaki, falling behind her like a shadow. Then the same green was picked up by her hat, her shoes and gloves.

Gloves were a national obsession. Worn by every woman in all seasons as well as by most officers and many civilian men. As if hands were too shameful to be shown in the new Germany.

Many of Tricia's questions I could not answer, even saying that I was a courier was a breach. How did I travel? What was my bag like? What was in it? If I was a courier, why did I not wear a uniform? Was I not proud of what I did?

We talked of politics and at first that was my main attraction. With me Tricia could let off her frustrations and know that she was safe. And it was usually Herr Hitler himself who was the object of her rages. She told me how he came to power as *Adolf Legalité* using the old Weimar constitution. She mocked him as an Austrian with a thick accent, she made fun of his origins, calling him the Bohemian Corporal, or Herr Schicklgruber, which, she maintained, was his real name.

From then on we would refer to Hitler in our conversations as Mr S, as a code between us. Tricia taught me the Nazi salute which was used everywhere, in shops and restaurants, at the post office or boarding a tram. A quick flick up of the right forearm, palm facing the front without moving the upper arm. And a mumbled *Heil Hitler.*

'That is how we show that we are loyal,' with a mock stern look from her handsome profile. 'Do it when I do and no one will notice you.'

It was from Tricia's sour monologues that I began to understand what had happened to Captain Boch.

Inge was her best friend at school in Bavaria. And by the end of the twenties they were both married to career soldiers in the *Truppenamt,* von Seeckt's illegal General Staff. But Captain Boch had been more ambitious than Captain Schacht and in 1936 he had launched himself into a fresh career on the rising tide of National Socialism. Frau Boch had been offered no place in this new future.

Tricia said that restaurants or cafés were not safe, especially when speaking a foreign language. So when she wanted to talk we would walk through the Tiergarten or the diplomatic area beyond. She said that we looked like a *good couple,* and *well-to-do.* Appearances were important to her.

Rendered over the white heat of her anger Tricia's opinions came down to a few stories, short and bitter.

She had admired von Seeckt: the Army above politics. Holding the Republic together against *Putsch,* inflation and invasion. But she detested von Schleicher, his successor, trying to manipulate the Reichstag by playing the National Socialists against the Communists.

She knew the Army, she would say. She understood it well.

'Then in 1932 von Schleicher himself became Chancellor to keep Mr S out. The Commander-in-Chief as head of state. It was the end of the Army's independence from politics. Now Germany lives with the results of von Schleicher and his scheming.'

Tricia let out her brittle, contemptuous snort.

'They all thought they could control Mr S. Like a mad dog on the end of a rope. They said that he would be their captive in their coalitions after he had delivered to them a majority in the Reichstag. Ha! The industrialists wanted the unions suppressed and the Army wanted rearmament. They were all innocents. While Mr S is a ruthless gangster who carries pistols in the pockets of his overcoat. And when von Schleicher failed they had to make Mr S the Chancellor, legally. Then he out-manipulated them and took absolute power. Mr S can make events follow his will.'

On our first weekend together we walked along the River Spree below Königsplatz. Many of the buildings in the diplomatic area were deserted, doors and windows boarded over. It was a beautiful spring day but the streets and the embankment were empty. I asked Tricia what was to happen.

'The tenants were given only twenty-four hours to leave,' she said, 'and it was not much different for owners. To make way for the diversion of the river and another monumental building, the Great Hall of the People, but work has not yet started.'

Tricia gave a wave of her gloved hand as if to dismiss Mr S and all his works.

'They will all be puppets in there anyway. The place itself just for show. A dome bigger than St Peter's, a pinacle taller than the Eiffel Tower. But nothing original, only that it must be more.'

Toward Bellevue a wide road was being pushed through the Tiergarten: pits, trenches and fallen trees scarred the park in all directions. A new East–West axis was under construction Tricia explained, to be ready for the birthday parade. Mr S, his fiftieth, the next year in 1939.

'It is important, Yves, that you understand how these things have been done, how Mr S took his powers only after he had been legally appointed Chancellor. He had no need to try another *Putsch*.

'First there was the fire in the Reichstag. That is five years ago now but still there is no proof that the Communists were involved as we were told. But the day after the fire the Communists were banned. Then a few days later there was the last election we ever had, with the Communists still on the ballot paper.'

We sat in a park café out of earshot of anyone, surrounded by rows and rows of empty metal chairs and tables. A melancholy brass band wheezed interminably in the distance. Tricia rummaged through her handbag.

'I have this piece of paper from that day, I carry it with me always. It is like a leaf in the autumn wind swept away by euphoria for the Nazis. But on this leaf is written the end of my marriage and the future of Germany.'

Tricia produced a scrap of folded newspaper, a cutting from the

Allgemeine Frankfurter Zeitung. On an empty page in her diary she wrote out the words for me in English.

Results of Reichstag Elections 5 March 1933

PARTIES	SEATS	PERCENTAGE OF VOTES
National Socialists (Nazis)	288	43.9
German Nationalists	52	8.3
Centre Party (Catholics)	73	11.2
Social Democrats	120	18.3
Communists	81	12.3
Others	33	6.0
	647	100.0

'There,' Tricia said, 'now you too have a leaf,' tearing out the sheet and handing it to me.

'So who became the government?' I asked. Although the answer was obvious.

'Mr S was already Chancellor from the coalition. And now he said that the Communist votes were invalid so he removed them from the list. Though only after the election. *Ungültig*, that was a clever word. So without the eighty-one Communist seats Mr S had a majority of five and he was appointed Chancellor again. But this time, with his *Law to Remedy the Distress of the People and the Reich*, Mr S gave himself the power to rule by decree.'

The end of the doomed Republic, blamed for Versailles. For *Dolchstoß*.

Tricia snapped her fingers in the air.

'Just like that, no objections, not a word, just a few hopeless votes against. By then Brown Shirt camps had been set up. For riff-raff and perverts, they said, but really for opponents of the government and in order to threaten rich Jews. Everyone was so terrified of disappearing that all the other parties liquidated themselves voluntarily.'

She sipped at her coffee glassy eyed, mesmerized by her own story.

'Then shortly after the election old Hindenburg died, the President of the Republic and only Mr S was ready. He made himself both President and

Chancellor together, the very next day. So by a trick Mr S had become our Führer with forty-three point nine per cent of the vote. Now they say that his referendums are approved by ninety-nine and something per cent. Do you believe that?'

Tricia hated Sundays. Lonely and dull. Even working in the flower shop was better. She wrinkled her nose as she spoke, as if confronted by something obnoxious on the pavement. But it was a little gesture of admission, I thought, the start of an affinity between us.

Within a few weeks of our first meeting I changed trains in order to return to Berlin for a Saturday night. I left Waterloo on Friday evening and travelled in my own time. Mr Harris had no objections.

'You're only on immunity between the station and the Embassy, of course,' he said, moving his teacup around so that I could lay my new itinerary in front of him. 'But where you choose to spend your own time is up to you.' Mr Harris never could understand my interest in foreign parts.

The Embassy received the bag early on Monday mornings which suited them. And with my new distance they asked no questions about when I had arrived in Berlin or where the bag had been during the weekend.

On our first Sunday together Tricia and I had lunch on the Kurfürstendamm in a restaurant hung with heavy lace and scenes of boar hunting set in peeling gold frames. The room was large and loud: safe, I thought. I began to talk about the Olympic Games, about what I had seen as the courier on the day that Jesse Owens was to have been presented to Mr S. But still Tricia worried about ears. She silenced me with a little wave and nipped at her Schaumwein, talking about the Captain but without mentioning his name. She had heard that he had been through an operation, she said. The same one as his Führer. She patted her lap below the table. It was rumoured that Mr S had only one testicle. Now *there* was true loyalty for you. Her malicious laugh.

Then we walked back through the Tiergarten and she put her gloved fingers through my arm.

'How do you English say it?' She paused, searching for the right words. 'You will do very nicely,' pursing her lips and trying to imitate an English accent.

We climbed the stairs to the attic. A small sitting-room with simple furniture, a few pictures, tired flowers from the shop left over at the end of the week. As Tricia said, she had salvaged very little.

The bedroom was an alcove under a low ceiling, filled by a divan up high between elaborately carved posts in Germanic baroque. The best part of the flat was an old-fashioned tiled bathroom, through a tall door inset with an oval panel of etched glass. A governess or a housekeeper had been the original occupant. The place was something better than servants' quarters, whatever Tricia liked to claim.

She moved around the room while I sat. Taking off her summer coat, pinching dead-heads from the flowers, in and out of the bathroom, straightening newspapers. Then she stood over by the narrow dormer, looking out at a bolt-bright sky, an elbow up on the high sill. A pose, as if following stage directions in a play.

Without turning from the window, she spoke.

'You may make your English love to me now.'

I was startled by her lead, but immediately aroused like Pavlov's dog. I walked over to kiss her, exquisite and small like a very expensive doll. But she held me back with ten determined leather fingers against the lapels of my jacket.

'No,' she said quietly with a toss of her curls, 'I have changed my mind. What do you English know? It is I who will show you what Captain Boch is missing.'

She tapped my chin from below, as if choosing me for her purposes from a line of eligible gladiators.

I stood close to her: the salon perfume of her permanent, the tiny painted creases around her mouth as she gave me her look. Bored, impatient, carnal. Breasts rising and falling under tight crêpe-de-chine in the narrow canyon between us.

Tricia took off her gloves then her hat.

She started to undress me, jacket, waistcoat, laid over the back of a chair.

'I used to like his uniforms,' she said, as she folded my trousers. 'And maybe the pink-faced whore likes his new black suit. Who knows?'

I wanted to be done with Captain Boch, I wanted to kiss her, to push my way up her skirt and into her, there against the wall, lift her doll's frame on to me and make her mine. But still she held me away.

'We are all going to die,' she sissed at me like a snake. 'Mr S is going to kill us all. So what reason is there left to be holding back?'

Tricia's red fingertips prodded me across the room until I lay naked on the bed. She began to caress me, cool hands down my cheeks, wide open blue eyes staring into mine. An intensity of looking and feeling, of anticipation, of breaking down barriers. Her face to mine, eyelashes like giant palms flickering against light from the window, her skin moist and creamy against my cheek. The smell of her perfume intensifying as she leaned over me.

But still she would not let me kiss her. She held me down with one persistent finger, tapping on my chest like a piano tuner plumbing a note. While her mouth ran over my chest, down my legs, holding my toes between her lips. Brushing me lightly as she ran her hand back up to my cheek. It could have been five minutes or an hour, I was lost, carried away by her fingers, by the touch of her lips over my skin.

Then from nowhere she had a scarf wrapped tightly over my eyes and tied hard against my temple. I started to protest, but she tapped my chest again and whispered into my ear,

'No complaints or I will plug your mouth as well.'

I heard her walk around the room and into the bathroom, the door opening and closing, the lock engaging. Her heels clicking on the tile floor.

My heart pounded patterns of purple light into my blackness. A light breeze blew in through the window, a phantom passing over my tingling skin.

Tricia moved back toward the bed. I heard the bathroom door, the rustle of her skirt, her heels on the wooden floor. Her scent over me again. Then she took a wrist and tied me with a band pulled tight to the bedpost. I lay still as she worked her way around from wrist to ankle, from ankle to wrist until I was secured to the gothic carvings. Splayed like Leonardo's man.

Tricia untied my blind and she resumed her pose by the window, admiring her handiwork from across the room. She was radiant, perfection itself, a little she-devil of untold wickedness. She was the betrayal of my deepest feelings. But there, that minute, with my past suspended, the thing I wanted most in all the world.

'I kept the Captain's best neckties,' she said. 'But he wouldn't be wanting them now.' She laughed out loud.

Tricia walked back slowly from the window. She started to caress me again. Making as if for a kiss then lifting her painted lips away, beyond the range of my straining neck.

'You are helpless,' she whispered fiercely in my ear. 'Now only I decide.'

Still I pulled at the stays, tightening the knots around my flesh, popping at the air toward her like a goldfish out of its bowl.

Slowly Tricia began to feed me. In no hurry. A glistening finger carefully run around my lips, the momentary touch of her tongue against mine, her musky curls in my face. Always a tease, drawing back from each contact.

Then she was on the bed, over me, her knees pressed against my ears and her skirt covering me like a tent, settling herself down on to my mouth.

'So now you may kiss me.' Low, under her breath like a dangerous threat. Followed by her short malicious peal.

I lost myself to her: unending like pain, unrelenting like a storm at sea.

305

Finally she laid her trim little body down mine, skirt around her waist, fitting herself tightly over me like a hand into one of her fine kid gloves, heels scraping down my shins. She held my face between her hands, smothering her captive in kisses. Bearing down on to me in a terminal fury, panting, humming to herself as I detonated upwards, engulfed by her, squeezed, emptied. As if her body would suck me dry of every drop I had.

2

The taxi had been waiting for some time, lights off, inconspicuous on the side street by Café Holtz. While we sat packed into the bar, camouflaged and unremarkable among Berliners.

Werner looked out of the window every few minutes at the lights in the street, then back at the front door reflected in a long mirror behind the bar. PILZNER etched into the glass distorted his face into an unfinished jigsaw puzzle. Gaunt and anxious.

He was dressed as a civilian, but unlike Paris or Genoa, here he blended well. Brown suit, leather waistcoat and another jäger hat.

Werner seemed to be counting heads, who had been there when we had arrived, who had come in since.

'Be ready to move, Yves,' he said quietly, 'like the army. On the word of command.' He flashed his shark's teeth. Our old joke. Two small cogs in the same military machine. Sides were not important now, Werner told me many times. But soldiers still had work to do.

Then his long grey face quickly lost its smile as he resumed his careful watch. I finished off my wine sitting expectantly on my stool, twiddling the stem of the empty glass between two fingers.

Werner was a better man than me, a better soldier certainly, professional. A lead I could trust completely.

'*Jetzt*. Now. The side door, follow.' Command and automatic reaction. No coats, no possessions, our bill paid ahead, just out through the door. Lively across the bricks in dim light and into the taxi. The heavy thud of an electric solenoid, engine firing first turn.

I looked back: within a few seconds our glasses had been removed from the packed bar, already the crowd had filled our space by the window. Blink and we were gone.

The taxi driver knew Werner and knew his business. He might have been waiting for hours but not a word passed between them. An upright Berlin taxi and an upright Berlin taxi driver, grey uniform and peaked leather cap like an engine driver. Clipped hair up the sides against a wide black moustache flowing across his face like a miniature longbow, a former soldier. From the *Stoßtruppen* I thought suddenly, a storm-trooper from Masnières maybe. Huge like a tree, the blade of his shovel reflecting the moon. The man who had my name, face smudged and blurred under the flare of his helmet.

Older now, traces of grey through his stubble but as determined as ever.

Here he was again in a black Stoewer Eight from the 'twenties, the good times. A limousine converted into an anonymous taxi: cage added on top for trunks, high windows, plush interior, stuffed and stitched for passengers other than us.

The car pulled away still without lights before I had the door closed. Werner turned to look out of the tiny oval back window. There were yellow headlights in the distance but not the lights he was looking for.

The road from Café Holtz curved left and right between blocks of modernist concrete flats, rounded, plain and bleak, three and four storeys high. The café was rowdy, close to a large hospital, but this part of the city was *kleinbürgerlich*, quiet and respectable. Streetlights glowing bright orange between beech trees along the empty boulevard. A few cars were parked on the sides of the road, Opels, DKWs, the transportation of a revived *Mittelklasse*.

We turned on to a busier street, buses, army lorries, more cars, shops shut up and people queuing outside a cinema. Now the storm-trooper turned on his lights. I recognized the road to Magdeburg where the Embassy had a country house.

The taxi turned a second time, smartly, so that I rolled over against Werner. Fast into an alley where we stopped behind a pile of timber next to a construction site, a rehearsed routine. Engine off, lights out. The driver looking back in his wing mirror. Still no words between them though the glass division was wound down. Minutes passed.

Finally the driver spoke.

'*Alles in Ordnung, Herr Major.*' Nothing had turned in behind us, or maybe the driver had recognized the car they were looking for as it passed the end of the alley, missing our turn.

The taxi started off again down toward the end of the lane.

I wanted an explanation for this hole-and-corner ride, for our bar crawl. A reason, a briefing to stop my nerves.

All evening we had worked slowly out to the west from Anhalter Terminus, past the Sportpalast on Potsdamerstraße, lost among the crowds pressing in to a rally through the front gates.

I had followed Werner's instructions: buy a ticket as if you are taking the last train to Bremerhaven. Leave your portmanteau at the luggage office. That is not unusual, yes? You do not always have your diplomatic bag. So now you are going for a stroll, then dinner, until the time of departure. You buy a newspaper, you wander the shops in Potsdamerplatz, this is easy.

I was looking at jewellery and thinking of Tricia. Obsessed with her dramas, her demonic imagination, a fantasy life flowing from her like a secret river. Sweeping me along, out of my depth, drowning.

Then a quiet familiar voice next to me:

'Why do you choose the only Jewish shop in the whole square?'

At the end of the long display window two young toughs in black shorts and khaki shirts stood by a sign plastered on to the glass.

PROTECT YOURSELF – BUY ONLY GERMAN MADE!!

One of the boys brandished a rubber stamp, menacing passers-by with a marked face if any dared to enter the shop. The other rattled a collection box. Hitler Jugend, no more than sixteen or seventeen.

Werner pulled at my sleeve and we walked away in the opposite direction.

'Old friends who have just met by chance, you shake my hand.' He held out his arm and we made a big show.

From there we were furtively in and out of bars, hiding together in lavatories like guardsmen. Suddenly ducking into a *Konditorei* pretending to buy cakes while Werner looked back through the shop window.

But Werner was intent as the taxi started off again. This was not the moment to ask.

Out of the bottom end of the lane and a hard right without stopping. We moved through more traffic and into another residential street.

There had been little talk. In the first few minutes, in the first bar, Werner had asked:

'Tricia? You told her you were going to London?'

It had occurred to me more than once: Werner had been interested himself.

'Yes,' I replied although it was not true.

From that first Sunday afternoon Tricia had set the rules.

'You have done well,' she said to me without a smile, 'you may sleep now.'

'I must have the bag by the bed,' starting to get up.

Tricia picked up the heavy case and moved it toward me.

'Do you have the key?' she asked. She gave me a wrinkled nose.

'I only have one, the Embassy has the other. But Tricia, I cannot discuss this with you.' Feeling suddenly vulnerable standing naked by her bed.

She handed me my shirt. Her first rule was no nudity without a purpose, nothing familiar or habitual between us. If I wished to spend the night I was to bring pyjamas from London. Tricia would be sleeping in a long night-dress, from her neck down to her ankles. And when she occupied the bathroom she would lock the door.

'It is far too important,' she said, 'to be worn down by routine. What is it that you think? That we are married? There will be none of that strength through joy, no swimming in cold lakes, no boat cruises.' It was all to do with the Captain, I was sure.

Und für unsere Begegnungen? Tricia would let me know, she alone would decide. When and how, following one of her many scripts. She would count my days and be prepared. Time to London and back. Then if I did not appear on the due day, I must be in Paris. So three days for that and another calculated day for my arrival in Berlin. Followed by the weekend, followed by two days for the Embassy papers and back to London again. Tricia liked to know where I was at all times.

'You must think of me on the train,' she would scold without a smile, 'then you will be pleased when you see me.'

That morning I had started to pack.

'But you are not leaving today, Yves, today is Monday, their returns will not be ready until tomorrow.'

'Today I have an appointment,' I said, feeling annoyed, still the bachelor. Not used to having my movements examined.

'Already secrets,' Tricia retorted quickly. 'Soon it will be like Captain Boch all over.'

Half a mile up a quiet street the storm-trooper pulled sharply over to the kerb. Werner started to get out before the car had come to a halt, scrambling across my feet.

'*Raus. Raus. Schnell.*' No jokes this time, through his teeth, spitting and pushing, sinister almost.

As Werner closed the car door behind us the Stoewer drew away and down the street, but slowly now as if asking to be followed, a decoy.

A cobbled pathway ran between two blocks of flats, high wooden palings on each side. Werner set off at a brisk pace into the black beyond. I hurried after him. My turn to look over my shoulder, my turn to worry about the unknown followers.

We came out into a park, heavily treed with pines and oaks, gravel pathways, grass and shrubs to each side, dark. Distant lights from surrounding buildings made the inside of the park blacker still. Werner slowed down and I walked beside him, the anxious outlander, quite drunk in the evening air. Werner started right away.

'I know you do not understand, Yves. But there is a war that you cannot see, everywhere can be as dangerous as No-Man's-Land.'

Even after months of Tricia's stories I still saw Germany through the eyes of a foreigner, a united country with common goals and a single-minded determination. Held back all these years by our weakness and our indecision.

And like most Germans I knew, but not Tricia, Werner seemed to have abdicated. Events were beyond his control, even talk was pointless. But now a torrent of words boiled from him as we paced through the night.

'Divide and rule, that is how he keeps power. It is everywhere, in the diplomatic service, the economy, now against the Army. Party bosses building dominions like animals in the jungle, but each owing personal allegiance directly to Hitler. It is even more chaos than Weimar. Though this time nobody complains.'

Germany had found her leader, the poison of slavery had been swept away. The General Staff had emerged from under the chains just as von Seeckt had planned.

The size of the Wehrmacht was increasing. Many new divisions had been added to the Army since the occupation of the Rhine Garrisons and the Anschluß with Austria.

Hitler had come to power as a reaction to the tricks and lies of Versailles: the imposition of guilt, our Great Victory, their endless Reparations and new borders. But the long-awaited leader had brought with him the beginnings of a new destruction. Germany was now a country run by gangsters, gutter-boys driven by ambition for power and conquest. Leading to war again, Werner was sure.

'And we have met a coalition of the whole world before,' he said. 'In the war on two fronts we know what will be the result.'

National Socialism was now the new poison, Germany's new chains.

The Party had formed its own force, the SS, to neutralize both the Army and the SA which had not been under Hitler's direct control. The SS were the worst men in the country, old Freikorps, psychopaths, murderers who had taken control of the concentration camps and all the police forces. The men the Army had used in 1919 against the strikers, grown to become a state within a state, beyond the law, thriving on conspiracy and race hatred.

'Did you know,' Werner asked, 'that they pulled down Mendelssohn's statue in Leipzig? Just because his father was Jewish. *Mischling*. Half-caste they call it now.'

The little things that say so much, the things I had ignored. A book bonfire on the newsreels, a face I knew so well, broken in pieces on the pavement.

We crunched along in silence then Werner started again.

The SS had grown out of Hitler's protection squads, Schutzstaffeln. And the SS security service had become very powerful, the Sicherheitsdienst. The SD was everywhere, as many as fifty thousand informers across the country. Here were to be found all the unbalanced misfits from the middle class: the dismissed schoolmaster, the unemployed clerk, the ambitious little policeman. And behind them were the enforcers, TVs, Totenkopfverbände, Death's Head Formations who had learned their trade as camp guards, Gestapo, Sipo, Kripo and Einsatzkommando. Men ready to carry out the dirty work.

Only the Army stood between the Nazis and absolute power. This was the war I could not see.

Already that year the SD had won a major victory against the General Staff. General von Blomberg, the Minister of War and General von Fritsch, the Commander-in-Chief had been forced out. The first by allegations that his new young wife had been a prostitute, the second by stories of homosexual acts in a railway station. Later both stories were found to be completely untrue.

'Such hypocrisy,' Werner snapped, 'from those degenerates. But the result is that Hitler himself becomes Minister of War and increases his control over us. Soon they will have the Army totally in their power.'

I could see lights at the far end of the park. Werner slowed down, not wanting to arrive.

'I watched it with Boch,' he said. 'A hard thing to endure, a close friend becoming a Party man. As if he had been issued with a new SS brain. Everything from before meant nothing. A good staff officer, I thought of him as a *Kamerad*. Now we do not speak and he looks after training for the *Allgemeine SS*.'

Werner paused.

'And he was issued with a new woman. From the SS stable, picked for their Aryan looks and clean backgrounds. Taken to special officers' clubs to make babies for the Führer. Then in the Lebensborns the mothers even compete for the highest milk production. They are objects like prize cows.'

We had come to the end of the park but Werner was not finished. A stone arch led out on to another street of beech trees and orange lamps. Werner stopped me undercover, in the shadows. Now he whispered.

'Tricia was gone in a month. To me and Inge they were the perfect couple, very much in love, we thought. Something was found against her I am sure, something that stopped her from objecting. But possibly there are still feelings left with him, dangerous even.'

'Feelings?'

'Jealousy maybe.'

'Jealousy? Dangerous?'

'Jealousy. Of you.'

'Of me? Would Boch know about me?'

'For the moment there is our own security service, the Abwehr for our protection.'

Werner looked up the street ready to move on. *Jealousy, dangerous*, these were words I understood well. I hung behind, suddenly riven with fear. For Tricia, for me, so far from my protected route. Involved with matters and forces about which I knew nothing.

'But why would they follow you, a major from the OKH? Where are we going?'

We were still huddled under the arch.

'You are going to meet my General,' Werner replied. 'It is for him to explain.'

Then he led me out into the bright light. We started to stride along the pavement like a route march without the songs, with heels ringing in the silence. Decoys. Further up, before the lights and the houses came to an end, Werner caught my arm and held me tightly. We stopped abruptly. He pressed me against a garden fence, into shadow once again under a lilac bush tumbling over on to the street. We stood dead still without breathing.

'Last chance to be sure,' Werner mouthed.

The street was deserted. Not a sound except the beating of my heart. Except a ghost rustling through late summer trees. Foreboding, dangerous, a sign of changing weather. Then we trod quietly like burglars on tiptoe past the end house and we turned into an unlit gravel driveway. The street ran on into the night where the suburb became dark ploughed fields.

We were blind for a moment, walking into a void between more beech trees. Then I could make out a mansion, a *Herrenhaus* from before the expansion of the city, set back into its remaining handkerchief plot. Faint light from between heavy curtains defined the bulk of the tall stone building.

We climbed a few steps on to a porch. Werner knocked lightly as if expected. A movement inside then a brighter light went on behind stained glass panels in the front door. An elderly maid opened up, scullery clothes, worn slippers and her hair in a net, peering into the dark but not seeing us.

'Anna, it's me, Werner.'

Anna stood back opening the door wide, trusting, without a word. Werner led the way into the house, a quick grimace to me meant as encouragement. We placed our hats on a chest in the hall. Heavy panelling hung with embroidered regimental colours lined the walls like a long-established mess.

Anna stood hunched, mumbling to Werner at length and wringing her hands.

'*Ja, Kaffee bitte,*' he replied finally. Then to me, 'You must excuse us, Yves, this house is one of my Staff duties. There are many old residents and always problems.' On cue a lavatory flushed and a precarious skeleton emerged on to the landing above us, tapping his way along behind the banister with two canes.

Werner opened the first door on our left. I walked through behind him.

We entered a long formal dining room filled with an enormous polished table lined by twenty or more high backed chairs.

And there was Werner's General. Standing against a rock fireplace that ran to the ceiling, decorated with the mounted head of a chamois ram. He seemed to have been waiting, hands clasped behind his back, impatient.

The General took a step towards us, down from the hearth.

'*Sind Sie in Sicherheit?*' he asked Werner.

'*Jawohl, Herr General,*' Werner replied, standing to attention and nodding his head. Then Werner turned back to me.

'*Ich möchte Ihnen Leutnant Beauchamp vorstellen,*' with an arm on my shoulder, '*ein Kriegskamerad.*'

The General smiled at the word, used so unself-consciously between two former enemies. He held out his hand. When I took his he put the other hand on top of mine like a priest greeting a long-lost sinner at the church door.

'*Je suis General der Artillerie Franz Halder, Chef du Quartier Général de l'Armée Allemande,*' he said, his eyes looking directly into mine.

Halder was a small intense man I judged to be in his late fifties. He looked like a diminutive Prussian, hair shorn tight like a grooming brush, perfect bearing. But he was Bavarian, Werner had told me, a devout Protestant not a Catholic even though his mother was from Lorraine.

Halder's head was completely round, shrivelled and creased like a desiccated prune. But his eyes flashed penetrating green daggers from behind rimless pince-nez. And there was something else, I thought, far at the very back, something ready to erupt.

Halder continued in French, still introducing himself.

'It has not been announced yet, but Colonel-General Beck resigned last week and I have been chosen to replace him as Chief of the OKH, the General Staff.' He let my hand go. He spoke solemnly. 'But it is not any honour. The resignation of General Beck was a matter of principle. I should have gone too.'

Halder pointed me to a chair at the table and he sat opposite. His peaked hat lay between us, red piping and the gold rosette of the General Staff.

He took the hat by the rim to move it down the table. Underneath lay a chromium-plated pistol, small and shiny in a pool of its own reflection on the glossy wooden surface. Halder picked up the gun and flicked the magazine clip out of the stock, muzzle pointed to the chandelier above.

'Beholla 7.65,' he said. 'I have carried this since 'fourteen. They will never take me without a fight.' With another metallic smack he replaced the clip, checked the safety catch and tucked the gun back under his hat.

No further introduction was needed. I was fascinated, terrified. From an evening out drinking with a friend I was in a battlefield again. I had not seen a bullet for almost twenty years.

'Major Schacht speaks highly of you, that you can be trusted,' Halder began again. The conversation was going to be awkward, Halder to me in French, Halder to Werner in German, Werner to me in English. But Werner spoke very little in Halder's presence.

'The Major says you were awarded the British MC during the War and that you are now the link for England between Berlin and London.'

I was going to protest, about being only a courier, about the medal, but the General rushed on before I could find my words.

'I do not have long, Lieutenant. I believe my movements are watched when I am away from Zossen. They think at this moment that I am visiting my mother.'

Then Halder was back on his feet and over at the fireplace again as if propelled by an unseen force, by the importance of what he had to say. Bursting for some action he could not define. I turned to look at him up on the hearth.

Halder was wearing his *feldgrauen Waffenrock* loose without a belt. High collar overlaid with gold leaves on a red patch. Riding breeches of a coarser material, a different shade from his tunic. A double stripe in bright claret ran down the outside seams, disappearing into glossed riding boots. Spurs shone on his heels.

An Iron Cross First Class from the War was clipped to his top pocket and the Knight's Cross of the Iron Cross hung around his neck. In German style he wore no campaign ribbons on his Number Twos.

'I will tell you briefly, Lieutenant. There is little time to elaborate.'

Halder made a visible act of self-control, squeezing his hands together as if to stop shaking. He seemed as nervous as me and talking fast.

'We have made a pact with the Antichrist. And now the time has come for the truth.' He held one finger up in the air like St John the Baptist. 'From the days of von Seeckt only the Army has held power in Germany. Only we make or break governments. With Hindenburg as President our control was complete. The Army above politics, standing for the restoration of honour and the end of Versailles.'

Halder turned to Werner and spoke in German. Werner nodded.

'You know about these things, I understand, Lieutenant. Major Schacht says that you were in Paris in 'nineteen, then Genoa.'

Again before I could answer Halder was off like a galloping horse under his silver spurs.

'We had dealt with politicians before, Conservatives, Catholics, Social Democrats. We thought that Nazis meant no different, that they would work with the others toward the objectives we all desired. Once in government, we said, they would be moderate.'

Halder started to pace around the table, his head facing me from every direction, eyes looking for mine. Words pouring out like Werner through the park.

'In the early thirties we were afraid of the SA and Röhm their leader. He was more powerful even than Hitler. Röhm had millions of Brown Shirts when we, the Army, were only two hundred thousand. The worst people in Germany. Their leaders were homosexuals, drunkards, the membership were the illiterate unemployed. In comparison we thought that the Nazis themselves were nobodies. Hitler would be in our power we thought, if he did not have Röhm to protect him.'

The door opened and Anna shuffled in carrying a tray, coffee in a tall china pot and squares of black bread carefully laid with sliced sausage. Werner quickly pushed Halder's hat along the table so that Anna would not uncover the pistol. Then he poured the coffee and the General sat down next to him.

Holding his cup in mid-air, Halder started to tell me what had taken place on a battleship, during the spring manoeuvres of '34. Hitler was Chancellor after the elections of '33 and President Hindenburg was dying. A pact was made as the battleship *Deutschland* ploughed through grey storm waters in the Baltic. When the time came, the Army would support Hitler for President. In return Hitler would put an end to the SA.

And why not? The Army would have raised him up and with the SA taken care of, the Army could bring him down.

Halder tapped his chest.

'But you see this?' he asked. 'The Party symbol. That was when we had to start wearing it on our uniforms. After the *Deutschland*.' Halder pointed to the Nazi eagle and gold swastika above the right pocket of his tunic. 'We had no idea how powerful such a small thing could be. We are soldiers, not brain doctors.'

Hitler had quickly delivered on his side of the bargain. The Brown Shirts were a threat to him and his SS as well.

That year, on the night of 30 June, a pistol in each hand, Hitler had surprised the leadership of the SA in their beds. Röhm and two of his male lovers had been shot through sheets at an inn on Weissensee. During the following weekend hundreds of others were stood against prison walls or strangled in police cells.

But Hitler's purge went further than just the SA. The Nazis took the opportunity to settle old scores and to remove men who stood in their way. Those who knew the truth about the Reichstag fire, for example.

Halder paused to see if he needed to explain.

Among the dead was General von Schleicher, former Chief of Staff, former Minister of Defence and former Chancellor. Von Schleicher had been scheming again. This time for the restoration of the Monarchy.

Halder started to shout.

'And the Army did nothing, when we knew it all, everything. So that we became accessories to murder and to lies. About how an SA *Putsch* had been prevented. The SS did the actual deed, so like Pilate we washed our hands. Even after the murder of one of our own. We were no better than the criminals themselves.'

Halder was wringing his hands again.

'Just a few hundred lives, nothing compared with the War, maybe. But that is only the beginning. We have released an evil on the world like a poison gas.'

Then in August of the same year Hindenburg died and Hitler called on the Army to deliver on their part of the pact.

To the funeral march from *Götterdämmerung* the Field-Marshal was carried to his grave. Hitler became President as well as Chancellor. *Führer*.

And the very next day, on every barrack square across the country the troops were paraded to take a new oath: *I swear before God, to give my unconditional obedience, to ... Adolf Hitler ...*

Werner spoke for the first time.

'You remember Genoa, Yves, when we spoke at Mazzini's tomb? How sure I was?' He smiled at me: grey, ironic. A strong leader, the Army waiting under the chains of Versailles. 'Now we have found him, but he brings with him our next destruction.'

Halder did not understand Werner's English. But he looked at our faces and he smiled a grim little smile with us.

'Now most officers below the rank of colonel are Nazis,' Halder continued. He tapped the badge on his chest again. 'We in the General Staff are losing our power to stabilize the state. The Army has become just a fire brigade, only to be called out when there is a need. Soon we, the old generation, we will be eliminated as well.'

He looked at me across the table, fingers drumming impatiently. The imperative need for action.

'For years you democracies have let things go well for Hitler, the Rhine Garrisons, Austria, conscription, the Luftwaffe. Now Hitler plans a war and so comes our chance to act. This is where the man's romance with the German people will have its end. It is even in the newspapers that we are planning an attack on Czechoslovakia, so I am not troubling you with any secrets. But what is not well known is that this attack cannot succeed.'

Halder walked around to my side of the table and pulled out a chair. I thought that he was going to sit again. But from a briefcase he produced a map of Europe overlaid with numbers, letters and arrows carefully drawn in India ink.

'You can see for yourself, Lieutenant,' he said. 'Czechoslovakia is linked by treaty with France and Russia. Britain will always come to the aid of France. Germany has forty divisions, many of which are not fully trained. France has one hundred divisions. Czechoslovakia alone has thirty divisions and the Russians many more behind that. In addition, Britain's navy can blockade us within eight days of mobilization.'

Halder laid a hand on either side of the map like two advancing armies. 'If Germany attacks Czechoslovakia it faces a war on two fronts. The result will be *finis Germaniae*. The OKH has no doubt about the outcome. Even our fortifications in the west are not complete. *Der Gefreite* and his tantrums cannot change the facts.'

Werner smiled at me again. 'That means junior corporal,' he said, 'the lowest above soldier. That was Hitler's rank during the War.'

The General explained the Division and Corps symbols on the map, giving a short summary of his vulnerable military situation. The Chief of Staff to the former Lieutenant. When he had finished he sat down heavily on the chair next to me.

'You were a soldier in the War,' he said despondently, turning to face me, 'so you know what destruction is like. And this time would be much, much worse. Weapons have made great advances since 1918. The bomber, the tank. And even though Germany is destined to lose, when war starts we will all have to hold to *unsere verdammte Pflicht.*'

Werner leaned across the table toward me again.

'Our bounden duty,' he translated, making a motion like tying a noose and pulling.

There was silence.

Halder looked at Werner as if for some reassurance before he continued. Halder's hands working faster now, one with the other by turn as if he had caught them both in a door.

'We are Secret Germany,' Halder said quietly. 'We are civilians and we are military men. I will not give you names but we are resistance. Our group has members of the government and senior army commanders including many who are retired. We are the Germany of Beethoven and Schiller, of Bach and Goethe. The old Germany of peaceful states and free cities, of decency and Christianity. These lies must be stopped. Our country must not be destroyed again.'

Another long silence. It was like the central moment of a Mass. A transubstantiation, a mystical change between us. I was drawn in but frightened. Lacking faith in flesh and blood, confronted by an abyss.

'What do you plan to do?' The first words I had spoken since Halder had started.

Again he was off round the table.

'Do? We can do little without Britain,' his voice rising again. 'That is where we need you, Lieutenant. Our plan is to make the German people see the true character of their Führer. Over Czechoslovakia Hitler will face either a war he cannot win or the humiliation of retreat. We know that he will choose war and then our event will see the end of him.'

Halder paused.

'We have sent envoys to explain. But from your government nothing, nothing.'

He gave me the names of the people his Secret Germany had sent to London as if I might have met them: Ewald von Kleist, Hans Böhm-Tettelbach.

'But in reply we have only a letter from Mr Winston Churchill and there is talk of you recalling your ambassador, Sir Nevile Henderson.'

Halder stood facing me from the other side of the table, pitching backwards and forwards in his boots. He seemed about to fulminate with tension.

'I must have a fresh message delivered, Lieutenant, of the most urgent kind, from myself as Chief of the General Staff. The moment is now. There have been two meetings between the Führer and your Prime Minister Chamberlain but nothing was settled. Hitler made more and more demands and threatened war. Soon even you British must understand that only resistance will be successful.'

Halder took an envelope out of his briefcase.

'The moment is now,' he repeated. 'We believe that the attack is to be ordered for 1 October. Five days.'

He placed the envelope carefully on the table, upside down so that I could read the address: THE FOREIGN MINISTER. THE LORD HALIFAX. LONDON.

'I ask you to go to him, the Lord Halifax, he will remember me.' Halder picked up the letter again. 'This will be welcome in the right places.' Nervously tapping the envelope against the back of his hand.

Halder nodded to Werner and they both stood.

'Now we must leave.' Halder placed the envelope on the mantel below the ram's head.

I could not move.

'If you believe that you cannot be of help,' Werner said looking down at me, 'for loyalty, for your position, whatever your reason, we will understand.'

He smiled me his grey smile again. Warm but distracted.

3

Anna has my clothes. To be ironed by the night staff, she told me. But now I am not so sure.

I am lying naked in the vast bed. The bedroom door is locked. From the outside.

The *Herrenhaus* is large like a castle, wide corridors run in all directions on three or four floors, thick red runners centred over polished oak. Portrait upon portrait along the panelled walls. All bigger than life, the forgotten soldiers of the Prussian Army.

The bedroom is like a grotesque museum to the nineteenth century but there is no gold rope to keep the sightseers back. This is where I am trying to sleep.

I can still smell Tricia on me, up from my body between starched sheets, out from under my fingernails.

It is Tricia who is the gladiator. She has thrown her net over me, fine but infinitely strong. Or she is a miner, she has tapped a concealed seam and now her molten river flows out of me. Traitor to my deepest memories, I write no more letters to the dead or to the lost.

But there will be no talk of love.

'It is forbidden,' she says with a wrinkled nose. 'If you speak the word you go to my KZ. Into the cattle car, still in your pyjamas.' Then her empty clatter.

There is no future, no plan, nothing but now. Mr S is going to kill us all. Six months of nows.

Thinking of her I am immediately erect.

A different bed, Tricia perched on the edge of the mattress. She is wearing her Chinese Schiaparelli, legs crossed. I lie back, holding a suspended ankle lightly in my hand, then I run a finger down to a stockinged foot, a shoe falls to the floor. We are going out to dinner. Tricia has chosen the place. She avoids my eyes, working with her pointed tips like a mortician over a slab. Red on red.

Then, she says, when we make it back from the restaurant, it will be my turn: I will give her Brooklyn Bridge.

I always laugh at her American expressions, but one day she tells me. About the Bridge.

And about the man who took her to New York. Herr Stenner of the

Hamburg-Amerika Line. The man who had chosen her personally, he said, from all the other stenographers in the company. For promotion, for travel, responsibility, he said. And the head of the company? Herr Cuno, Chancellor in the days of inflation after the War.

'They had their offices in the Woolworth building ...' Tricia is talking, calmly, no emotion, we are walking as usual with her gloved hand through my crooked arm, '... a building decorated like a cathedral to business, the tallest structure in the world. I had never seen such a thing. Incredible. Sixty storeys.'

But in this building Tricia had no desk, no chair even, her work was not what she had expected when she came to America. And instead of office memos or accounts, Herr Stenner would send her letters, suggestions, pictures. Then the doorbell would ring at her smart little apartment on Water Street.

Tricia had become a princess, the best that money could buy.

And once each week there would be a different performance. To the bank to collect a small leather bag then a taxi down to the boat ready to leave for Hamburg from South Street Pier. The First Officer usually. Tricia was to watch while the dollars were counted out on the wardroom table.

Those were the days, she says, when a hundred thousand dollars would have bought you the whole of Schleswig-Holstein. Stenner and Cuno became very rich. Coal, iron, timber, bought in Germany for nothing, sold in New York or Chicago for dollars. They laughed when the Mark fell to a million. Then they laughed a thousand times harder, she says, when the Mark hit a billion. For them it was made of gold.

Tricia turns to look at her reflection in a shop window, she adjusts her hat with a little frown. I want to go back to the attic, now, now.

But Tricia is telling her story. And I must control myself.

In New York she learned a lot: about currencies, making deals, about what men want. About being pregnant.

At first with Boch, she says, Emmanuele was not a problem. Tricia was a catch, her looks, her dollars, experience, ambition. Stenner paid the bills, Emmanuele lived with Tricia's parents and went to a good school, grew up a nice little girl. Stenner's name and a clean neat story. But later, she says, after Stenner left Germany, after the money stopped, after the divorce...

Tricia does not finish her sentence. She has been sold Brooklyn Bridge.

Or it is the morning, I am dressed and ready to leave. But Tricia is a she-devil: she can make it suddenly evening. I am sent out on to the stairs, told to count to fifty. Then I am to return home from the Embassy.

So here I am, back early from Wilhelmstraße. But strange, the door is not locked. Oh, I have surprised Tricia face down and naked on the settee. I open my coat. There are no preliminaries, those will come later.

I am her slave. I do not need her to tell me: the train is my torture, thinking of her, speeding along the lines as smoke races back over the coaches and wisping out across the Heath. Clickety click, clickety click, the bag between my feet.

I am her slave. For her I could be dismissed, the bag in her flat, her post smuggled to London in thick letters. Quickly on to the top of the pile, quickly extracted as the bag is opened at the other end, all with a nod and a wink. A conscientious correspondent she says, an American girlfriend from New York, she says, now living in London. Then there are more envelopes to bring back. Their secrets exchanged, she says, filled with cuttings from the newspapers, she says. Tricia pretends to giggle. I wonder what she writes about me, I want to read her reviews of my performances. But I do not look.

'The *Reichpost* is searched. This way I may say what I please.' Tricia dabs the end of my nose. I am her slave.

Now it is Werner who is leading me upstairs from the dining room. I do not know why. Halder is doing his rounds below, along the corridors and under the colours.

'*Wie geht es mit der Gicht, Oberst?*' I hear him say.

We climb the wide staircase. Werner tells me that the ambulance has arrived and they must leave. There are many old soldiers in the house, he says, mostly Staff officers. He laughs. I could probably find an officer from Group Caudry, from Prince Rupprecht's Staff right here in this house. Maybe the very man who directed the successful counter-attack at Masnières. The British gained only 400 metres and lost 300 tanks. Not to mention Allied artillery losses. For both sides Cambrai was a Great Victory. Werner laughs again.

At the top of the stairs we find Anna shuffling around in the room, opening windows, turning down the bed. She leaves a tray, a water jug, a glass and an unobtainable orange. A dressing gown is laid out on the bed, heavy like a blanket and embroidered like a quilt.

Still I do not understand.

Werner stands facing me, we are awkward in his world and he too is nervous. I have never seen him this way before. His tall frame is stooped, he smooths his hair with two hands. Grey showing through black. Werner is my *Kamerad*, I want to put my arm around his shoulders as he did for me when I was drunk and adrift in Genoa.

He thinks that I will resent what is happening. He apologizes, saying that he could give me no warning. But he wishes to reassure me so he tells me that his uncle Hjalmar is one of the civilians of Secret Germany. He hands me a copy of Halder's letter to Lord Halifax, the letter that is waiting for me on the mantel. Then the original English version of the letter they have received from Mr Winston Churchill. I am to read what is written.

I see that Werner wants me to argue for them in London. Because once I was an officer he cannot understand that I am only a courier. That I am afraid.

I tell Werner that it is an honour to have met General Halder to show him that I am not angry.

That is when Werner tells me that I cannot leave the house, that I must spend the night. In the morning they will be told if the envelope has been taken, that is how they will know of my decision. But any doubts ... any doubts and I must not do this.

They have guards outside. I must remember: the war I cannot see.

I am shaken.

Arrangements have been made for the morning, another ambulance. Somehow to the Embassy and then I must go directly to the station. They will protect me until I am on the train, more people I will not see. If I return as we intend I will walk the streets, look at the shops, have a drink. Contact will be made. I have the wind up. But any doubts, any ...

I am in Secret Germany.

This is their house. I will be told only what I need to know. The less I know the better for me. I am asked only to be the messenger. But already I know names.

When we said goodbye outside the dining room Halder told me that I will not be involved in the Event. If I am in Germany I will be warned to leave. Because if the Event fails there will be blood. The SD have their list. Halder laughed like a cough. *Il y a pire que la mort*, he spluttered.

I had caught my breath.

Werner explains the event as we stand facing each other in the bedroom. He moves his weight from leg to leg. It seems that I must be able to describe to London what is planned.

Operation Green, the invasion of Czechoslovakia. All is ready, only the final order is missing, from Hitler. But Operation Green cannot succeed. Apart from relative troop strengths there are the Czech fortifications, strong like the Maginot Line. The OKH considers the Czech border to be impregnable. The Czechs are well armed. Do I remember the Skoda howitzers which were so effective against our tanks during the War? A Czech piece, he tells me. Yes. I remember. The gun that killed Thompson. But I do not tell Werner what I am thinking. Only prolonged bombing, he says, or a flanking movement through Ostland, the old Austria, could eventually be successful against Czechoslovakia. And for this Germany does not have the resources, quite apart from the counter-attack that will come from France in the west. There can be no escape from defeat.

So when the Führer Order comes to invade, the OKH will replace Operation Green with their own plan. The Berlin Garrison has already been relieved by regiments of the 2nd Panzer Division, troops that are completely reliable under the command of General von Witzleben, a man Werner knows and admires. Werner tells me that we shook hands with the General one day when we were at the Adlon together, but I may not remember. Now Werner's smile seems more confident. With General Halder as the Staff Officer and with General von Witzleben as Commander they have the best condominium in the entire Wehrmacht. The event has been planned right down to the last gaiter button. But very few know the real objectives.

Halder will give the final order.

Werner is the senior adjutant, he has the complete picture.

First the Transport Section. A convoy of Henschels rolls into Berlin at three o'clock in the morning. Metal barriers are unloaded as if for a military parade. Wilhelmstraße, Albrechtstraße and Potsdamstraße are quickly sealed off. Almost immediately there is a distant rumble, then a roar. A first wave of over two hundred half-tracks. Detachments of the Panzer Rifle Regiment speeding into the centre of the city from Charlottenburg in the west and from Zossen in the east. Traffic up and down the main streets has already been cleared by the Motorcycle Battalion.

Simultaneously assault squads pour out of the Henschels and rush the main buildings: the Reich Chancellery, Göring's Palace, the Zeughaus, the Gestapo and SD Headquarters. There is fire from SS guards, some are killed. Hitler is captured. Himmler, Göring, Goebbels and Hess are taken prisoner or shot.

Other reliable divisions deal with the outlying areas: the *SS Leibstandarte Adolf Hitler* at Lichterfelde, broadcasting stations and telephone exchanges, the SS barracks at Sachsenhausen and at Munich.

Hitler is brought here, to the *Herrenhaus*, in an ambulance. A panel of doctors is waiting. The Führer is pronounced insane and immediately committed to a military hospital. Badly gassed during the War, the story has already been agreed. The other Nazis will be tried as accessories to plotting aggressive war.

The General Staff announces to the German people the details of the planned attack on Czechoslovakia and their prediction of the outcome. By then Britain and France have broadcast warnings that invasion will lead to hostilities.

There is euphoria throughout Germany that war has been avoided. By eight o'clock that morning the streets are crowded, the troops are embraced by the population. Any doubters, the Kriegsmarine or the Luftwaffe, are carried along by the success of the action.

Elections will be held, a new civilian government will be formed. The Republic will return. Negotiations with France and Britain will take place. All matters will be solved. The era of Pan-Europa will dawn.

Werner leaves me, we embrace. Like two Frenchmen, like La Capelle and the last day of the War.

Overwhelmed, I sit on the bed. I read the letters.

The letter from Mr Winston Churchill is useless. For this their messenger von Kleist has risked his life, Werner says.

A messenger. His life. I have no idea what I am doing. I know that I should leave.

The letter from Mr Winston Churchill quotes from a speech by Prime Minister Chamberlain: '... England and France are devoted to the ideals of democratic liberty and determined to uphold them...' Then his predictions of civilian slaughter from the air, of a war lasting three or four years, a grim fight to the finish. I see that Mr Winston Churchill relishes his descriptions, for him War is the highest aspiration of mankind. A quote I remember from Fairy. Nothing that would help Secret Germany. Nothing for the here and now.

The letter from Halder.

OBERKOMMANDO DES HEERES
DER CHEF DES GENERALSTABES   Zossen, den 25/9/38

The Lord Halifax
His Majesty's Minister for Foreign Affairs
London

Dear Lord Halifax,
You may recall that we met in Berlin last year at the International Hunting Exhibition from which Britain gained the most prizes.

From last month the writer of this letter is appointed Chief of the General Staff. The Announcement is planned for later with certain other changes in the personnel of the Government. In our position in this letter the Opinions of all the Senior Members of the OKH are represented.

On the instructions of the Supreme Commander and Minister of War, Adolf Hitler, the OKH has prepared a plan for the invasion of Czechoslovakia. However we are aware that the implementing of this plan will lead to European War. An alternative plan has therefore been devised for the removal by the Army of the present Government of Germany. This will be followed by a public Discussion of the International Issues facing the Signatories of the Locarno Conference. We believe that all matters can be brought to a satisfactory Ending within a very short time.

It is certain that War is strongly opposed by the German People.

We ask for no direct help in this enterprise. But we however urge that an unconditional Statement from the Governments of Britain and France be made to the effect that the invasion of Czechoslovakia by Germany will be responded with a General Declaration of War. Only if there is outside Resistance can our plan be made.

As an earnest of our good intention we are prepared today to provide a Military Representative of your Government with full details of the plan of attack against Czechoslovakia. This information will include the Date and the Disposition of all German Forces.

This Communication is of the greatest urgency and importance. You are asked to reply to the Writer immediately in addition to making the Announcement that is asked.

This Letter is sent to you by the hand of a Person we both trust. Reply could be by the same hand.

Faithfully,

Franz Halder
General der Artillerie

My copy is unsigned. Werner made the translation. He says that I will think the letter to be treason. But in Germany now, he tells me, it is treason to follow honour and decency.

The images of Tricia are gone.

In the dark my bed is invaded. Little Arab devils. I find that I too have djinns. They rush out from behind black shapes around the room. A chest of drawers like an Etruscan shrine, a wardrobe from the Hall of the Gibichungs.

The past washes over me, jagged and ugly. Small things become large.

Large things are meaningless: the War, England, the Peace. Gaol-birds guilty before they can open their mouths. Things this worm now understands.

That our Great Victory, that our Great Lie ... could come to this.

My life is examined and I watch the djinns' images. I follow scalloped shadows and circles around the ceiling. I surrender myself to the darkest corners.

Katrina walking on the dyke by the Rhine. Her hair is longer, streaked now, her natural colour maybe, blowing in the wind. She pushes a perambulator. A baby with a large nose looks around at the world from big believing eyes. He plays with his sunhat, chewing on the brim.

But this year the child will be fourteen or fifteen, my devils are out of date. In two years the boy will be in the Army.

She has a new smile, just for him. I can hear her teaching him English, I can see her cooking for him after school. Her looks are rounded, blunted but deepened by motherhood.

I am in the tumbledown barn in Villiers Plouich.

The men are gathered around on the remains of a straw pile. Thompson is sitting with his legs out, stripping our stolen Vickers. He is very fast, the instructor. Metallic clicks and slaps and the gun is down to its components. That is when he tells me about the counter-attack. To watch out for the unexpected.

Thompson has taken off his helmet. Underneath he is balding from his crown outward in a soft ring. I am standing over him looking down as he divides the parts between the men. He wraps the barrel and the stock in blankets. Then he looks up at me.

'That's the thing about our Fritz, sir,' he says with a smile. 'Smarter than 'e looks.'

He pauses. The men know the chorus.

'*Which i' joost a' well for 'im.*'

All join in together. Laughter every time.

Oh, I loved Thompson. And sometimes I can miss him as if he was once part of my body, I feel pain in the amputated limb. Peace and prosperity, he said, that was why we were fighting. To be rid of the old and to bring in the new.

To stop the lies, Halder says.

Thompson would take the envelope with two hands.

Then I am with Jeanou.

1920. He is walking me through La Wantzenau, up from the little farmyard on the river. Feet turned out, scuffing the broken pavé in his *pantoufles*.

By now the rubble has been piled up on to the plots where houses once stood. The streets are clear, a fraudulent appearance of order in the shelled town. Here, Jeanou says, *la famille Bernard*, all killed together by a *boche* shell. And here, pointing to another pile of broken bricks, the family of the mayor. The mayor himself was shot in '14. And that one was a French shell but they are all equally dead.

LG's hand on my shoulder. Never again, he says. Look forward not backwards, he says. Slumped into his chair as he recites:

> *... but I am bound*
> *Upon a wheel of fire, that mine own tears*
> *Do scald like molten lead.*

Blinding white rage, my face smarting. She looks shocked, as if it is my hand that has hit her.

My cold cunning to discover her movements. Paralysed horror at what I see in her hand mirror, watching as she combs out her hair in front of the gas fire.

Our sordid room over the pub, Katrina dressing in her uniform and her heeled boots, my body red and angry, hard and ready. Taking her, forcing up into her against the wardrobe door. What I love most in all the world defaced, demolished. Vengeance. I have taken what belongs to the Lord.

A soldier whose Great Victory is a lie, a husband who violated his wife, an educated man, privileged, with every opportunity. A man who turned to blackmail. A son who cannot stand the sight of his mother.

My life is examined: it is worthless.

The Schutzstaffeln could take me now if it would stop war. Quick and neat, no pain. I would do it myself.

Brave words but I am too weak. Too embarrassed by the mess, blood in the bathroom, pistol fallen to the floor. Or the train stopping, passengers watching as a body is carried away. A failure of a man, they say to each other, a man who could not cope.

I am condemned to live.

It is dawn, dissonant clocks chime the hour, six. I doze. Anna knocks, I call. *Entrez.* She has brought coffee and my clothes. I wash and dress. The soap is candle wax.

And the dining-room is a scene from Bedlam. Old men in bathchairs, on sticks, some in uniform, some in dressing gowns, some a mixture of both, one wearing his *Pickelhaube*. Some are muttering, others shouting, a few sitting quietly masticating their *Butterbrot*.

Anna mumbles to me: the ambulance has arrived.

I take the letter from the mantel.

The ambulance is large, armour-plated like a tank on wheels. I am hidden, swaying to and fro, sitting on a stretcher.

'*Wie alt?*' I ask the driver.

'*Siebzehn Jahre,*' he replies. His eighteenth year.

This is the boy who will drive Mr S.

Hitler's threats against Czechoslovakia were a laxative to the British animus, stirring the nation to action in a way that he cannot have anticipated.

In Berlin the mood was dark. Thin crowds watched unmoved as artillery was drawn through the streets. Self-important Party men were ignored as they sped past in their Großer Mercedes convertibles, grim arrogant looks behind pairs of flying red swastikas. Now there were no *Führergrüßen*, the forests of extended arms I had seen in the streets after the Anschluß. Only in Nürnberg was there a reaction from the faithful at the Party Rally.

Hitler's speech was broadcast live, every pause, every rasp. His dripping hysteria echoing through the city from ten thousand wireless sets. After the newsreels I could imagine the searchlights, the Wagner and the wooden columns. The spasms of the Führer's right arm shaking out over the crowd as he comes to each frothing climax. Then a moment of silence followed by an explosion of sound.

But in Berlin the cheering came only over the airwaves. Down empty streets there was no matching enthusiasm for the call to war.

In London it was all cheer. The prospect of standing up to Bully-Boy Hitler had converted the country into a huge national side, out to win the Cup.

Most of the drivers I had known at the garage were gone: into retirement, a few posted abroad. But Alf was still there, content to be driving year after year, still saying that the old cars were better than the new. He was duty driver when I telephoned and he collected me from Waterloo.

'That'll be the last trip, then?' Alf asked.

'Why ever do you think that?' Guilty before I had started, as if Alf knew what was in my pocket.

'Their nibses were back to Hendon on Thursday from Germany, Bad Somewhere. PM and Lord Halifax together. We took the big cars down to meet them. Anyroad, news is pretty grim I heard. Czechs are mobilizing, fleet has been called out, talk of war next week.'

This was the second time around for Alf, he was more interested in the small things.

'Don't see as the PM's up to it myself. Sixty-nine and never been in an aeroplane before.'

From the station Alf took me past all the preparations. Outside London County Council women with prams thronged the steps to claim gas masks for their children. On the Albert Embankment an anti-aircraft gun was being assembled. Half-dressed Territorials stood about in an unorganized shower surrounded by open boxes, equipment in a shambles and shells in haphazard piles like spilled matchsticks.

On the King's Road and on New Scotland Yard recruiting stations had been opened. Both were besieged by young men from banks and government offices anxious to relieve their boredom and Win the War.

But most amazing of all were the Royal Parks and the sacrosanct preserves of London's privileged horsemen. Along Rotten Row and opposite St James's Palace turf had been dug up like allotment gardens. Rows and rows of men in braces and shirtsleeves were preparing trenches as if England was about to be turned into Flanders.

'Goes on night and day,' Alf said as we drove slowly along the Mall. He nodded up toward Marlborough House. Next door the new German Embassy looked out over the entire scene of operations. 'You'd think Jerry would have got the message. We're going to give him a proper fight this time.'

I had decided to tell Mr Harris the whole story, right back to Werner and the Armistice. We sat in his windowless dungeon sharing sugared biscuits as his kettle came to the boil. When I had finished Mr Harris wanted to take the envelope.

'There are channels, Mr Beauchamp, and diplomacy is not our game.' He held out his hand.

'I accepted the letter for personal delivery, Mr Harris. And I have a bounden duty.' I made the same motions as Werner, a noose and a pull.

'Duty?' Mr Harris repeated quickly. 'Bounden duty?' He looked at me wide-eyed, stroking his moustache. 'Hold-on-half-a-mo. Duty? To them Germans, Mr Beauchamp? Just whose side do you imagine you're on then?'

But Mr Harris was soft underneath and he picked up the internal telephone.

We came up the back stairs, past the Tube Room and across Homer's quadrangle. The Empire was at its largest after Versailles but our prestige had been on the decline ever since the building was completed seventy-five years before. And each day that passed made the laboured Victorian structure seem more and more ridiculous.

Then up the Grand Staircase, a classical folly worthy of Musso himself.

Saints and Evangelists blessed our cause from the cupola, Muses inspired us down corridor walls. Justice, Honour, Truth, they were all there.

'None of your insolence now, your war's over,' Mr Harris said as he left me. 'Seeing Sir Andrew Bilsen is as far as the likes o' you will ever get.'

There are no grander offices in Whitehall than the top floor of the Foreign Office looking out west over St James's Park toward Buckingham Palace. Rooms the size of storehouses, oak panelling, decorative plaster, Axminster rugs deep like mown grass.

I was taken into Sir Andrew's office and I stood in front of his desk like a schoolboy in corduroy shorts. He held his hand out for the envelope without looking up from the important papers on his desk.

'I would like to deliver this letter to Lord Halifax in person, sir,' I said.

At that Bilsen raised his head.

'Frankly, I don't care whether your damned letter is delivered or not. It's quite by the by. And in any case neither Lord Halifax nor Sir Robert Vansittart is in.'

Then he looked at me again more carefully.

'Weren't you a driver at Palais Wilson in Geneva?' It was the little frock from the dinner with Stresemann and Briand. Grown up, thinning hair, but still a little frock.

'Yes sir, I drove you to Thoiry.'

'A driver, eh?' he said. 'A driver with an important message.' He chuckled as if he had said something amusing. An oxymoron.

I handed the letter over to Bilsen. There was no time and no choice. He sat back in his red leather chair and slit the envelope with an ivory paper knife.

'There you are,' he mumbled after a few moments, 'not even the right title. It's not His Majesty's Minister for Foreign Affairs, Lord Halifax is His Majesty's Principal Secretary for Foreign Affairs. Those Jerry amateurs just can't get anything right.'

He finished reading the letter then he looked up at me:

'Where did you get this?'

I thought it was an opportunity to explain: Halder and Werner in the *Herrenhaus*, the detailed planning for the *Putsch*, the terrible urgency for an immediate response.

But that was not the answer to his question. Bilsen cut me off.

'You're a KM,' he burst out, ignoring my avalanche, 'what on *earth* do you think you were doing in some Jerry hidey-hole?'

I had been caught in Wytham churchyard again and nothing else mattered: not the letter, not my story, neither bluff nor deceit.

Bilsen leaned over his desk at me, elbows on his important papers, affecting a frankness and an earnestness.

'This entire building is devoted to the management of relations between His Majesty's Government and the rest of the world. We are diplomats and we do not deal in letters off the street brought in by a driver. Our files are bulging with this kind of conspiratorial nonsense. My God, it reminds me of those poisonous Jacobins in the Court of France in good King William's day. We can't go taking sides with every damned *fronde* that comes along, you know. Herr Hitler has the full support of his people, elected by a clear majority. And as far as we are concerned he *is* the German Government. Dictatorship is just the natural order of thing for some countries. And if any ultimatums are to be handed out, it will be to the Czechs. We have Herr Hitler's word that once their present little nonsense is settled, then that will be that and Europe can settle down. If we go fomenting civil war in Germany the Bolsheviks will overrun the whole place. And how would you like that, now?'

Bilsen took a pause for breath but he did not intend that I answer his question. To silence me he held up Halder's letter by one corner as if it were smeared with something fetid.

'And your General? You can bet your driver's boots that he's a monarchist and a reactionary, with big plans for both himself and their General Staff. And you know what happened last time we had a Kaiser in Germany. These army men don't stand for peace and justice, you know, they just don't think that they can win. What have they done, for instance, about controlling their hotheads who torment the Jews and criticize the churches?'

I stammered, not knowing where to start in response.

'But, but ... there is a Secret Germany, decency, free cities, the land of Ludwig van Beethoven ... everything will be ...'

'I've had enough of this nonsense,' Bilsen snapped immediately. 'Secret sodding Germany, Ludwig bloody Beethoven ...' His voice trailed off in disgust. My explanation had failed before I had started.

'You've been away too long, all that travel has affected your brain.' Bilsen tapped his forehead. 'Forgotten what it is to be British.'

He looked past me at the open door behind.

'Mrs Miller,' Bilsen called out, 'give this man a pass to the Stranger's Gallery, so that he can see how policy is decided in this country.' He gave me a patronizing little smile. 'Democratically,' he added.

Bilsen returned to his important papers. 'The PM is making a statement this afternoon,' he said without looking up again. 'Quite a privilege for a man in your position.' He dismissed me with a little wave of his hand.

Every seat in the House was taken and many MPs sat on each other's laps. The Peer's Gallery, the Press Gallery, the Speaker's Gallery, all were full to overflowing. Even with an FO pass I had to sit on the steps in the Stranger's Gallery.

After an hour of procedures and wrangling on unrelated subjects, Chamberlain stood up to speak. He arranged his papers carefully in front of him on the Dispatch Box and started a recital of the facts. The House was restless as the ashen-faced Prime Minister grated through recent events concerning Czechoslovakia. Pages darted about the Chamber delivering and collecting papers and pink slips.

As Chamberlain reached the previous day, Tuesday 27 September 1938, in his dry chronological narrative, a page carrying a white envelope walked solemnly down the middle of the green carpet between facing benches. When the page reached the Dispatch Box and proffered the envelope, the Prime Minister paused in mid-sentence. He tore open the flap and appeared to read over the contents.

With the self-satisfied smile of a churchwarden after a record collection, Chamberlain announced,

'I have now been informed by Herr Hitler that he invites me to meet him at Munich tomorrow morning. He has also invited Monsieur Daladier and Signor Mussolini.'

There was an instant of complete silence, like the empty airwaves on a million German radios as the Führer runs out of froth. Then it broke: a roll of thunder, both sides of the House rising from their pews as one man, cheering and waving their Order Papers.

The men in cloth caps had dug the trenches but their betters were giving in.

Mr S had won.

4

I had no idea how long we had been walking but it was growing late in the wet summer evening. I was completely absorbed with Beethoven, the tiny, tiny, yet the immense question at hand.

By the time we reached the drive again my good black shoes were heavy with clay from the fields, soles like toboggans cascading down the slick grass bank. Like 1914, the summer of 1939 was unbroken perfection, a sadistic gift from the god of war. I had picked the only wet day in three months.

I was soaked through, hair plastered to my scalp, rivers running into my collar. The jacket of my suit stiff with damp, trousers scuffed with mud. But I was beyond caring. I wanted only to make my delivery, force him to take what I had brought.

Chamberlain was prepared for the rain, though he said that he too had only just arrived from London. The famous umbrella that he never used, a fishing hat, his gaberdine and wellingtons all incongruous against a starched wing collar and black tie with a faint silver stripe.

I still felt Alf's eyes speaking to me. Sharp glances in the mirror between gears as we had made our way through Friday evening traffic. Past evacuees in long lines and sandbags everywhere. Past more Territorials deploying another ancient ack-ack, still larking in shirtsleeve-order. And here balloons really were up in the air.

What had I gone and done now? Fixing me from behind the wheel of the Wolseley as I sat sandwiched in the back between my keepers. Asking me to stop whatever it was, trying to tell me: *you can't win.*

Alf had driven straight to the kitchen, an experienced man who knew where his passengers belonged. My head keeper inquired at the tradesmen's entrance and came back out to the car.

'Prime Minister's comin' round,' he said, pointing his words artificially, as if in deference to the house. Chequers, the ho-fish-hull country residence of the Prime Minister.

We waited by the car, permeated with drizzle. Fine droplets like tiny jewels covered every surface. I had thought that it might clear.

I recognized Chamberlain at once walking toward us from around the house. I was still taking him in when he was standing in front of me.

'This is Mr Beauchamp, sir,' my other keeper said, the *Mr* emphasized, an obvious irritation. A prisoner would not be a *Mr*, a driver would not be a *Mr*.

Chamberlain looked at me, his face close like a drill sergeant. But his voice was soft, no word of command although no hand out to take mine.

He was not a magnet like Sir Austen. He was old, withered like an undertaker worn down by his corpses and with the breath of something rotting inside, billowing out from under a contaminated moustache. His face had a lost, defeated look, a faint abstracted smile staring into the middle distance as if entranced away from the present. An impression of preoccupation rather than of thought.

He knew why I was there.

'Ah, Beecham. Vansittart tells me you're in Berlin a lot. Brought some kind of a message. Caused a lot of fuss and bother, apparently.' He paused as if sizing me up, undecided about what to do. 'Just off for a stroll,' he said. 'Care to come along?'

I had expected to be received in a hall then shown into his study. Somewhere I could get it all out directly, eye to eye. The venom, the story, my insistence, what I had planned. Not in the open like this, not standing in the rain. I had no coat, no boots, but I had no choice.

Chamberlain moved off, looking over his shoulder for me as I hesitated, me wanting it all to be different. To go back and start again.

My keepers were not happy either.

'You men go and get some tea from cook,' Chamberlain called back when he saw them following.

I wanted to make an immediate attack, some veiled menace. Get his attention with a display of my knowledge. Lady Ivy's stories of the sisal farm in Jamaica. Or what I had heard about the old Czechoslovakia after Hitler had taken it all. Bodies piled against brick walls in muddy farmyards outside Plzen. While the German Army rolled on ahead, up the road to Prague, pretending not to see.

To shock him, force him out of his superficial patrician talk. Remind him of Highbury: marquetry panels, gold and white plaster, brass grilles, the nouveau riche mish-mash mansion of Joe the Screw-Maker. Putting on airs, changing classes in one generation just as the Chicken-Gutter-in-Chief had planned. I had driven Sir Austen and Lady Ivy, I knew it all.

I had seethed in the Wolseley during the hour from London, a razor-sharp panic wiring up my joints, ringing in my head like a tocsin. Big and small tumbling together again in a tangle that could not be resolved. Tricia's wrinkled nose, Halder at Zossen, tears dribbling untouched down his grey cheeks as he handed me his second letter, TO THE PRIME MINISTER OF ENGLAND. My picture of Katrina and her son by the river, his schoolbooks in a battered case. My hand on the gate through the hedge, leading to the little cemetery at Villiers Plouich.

Now the impossible thing that I had to do.

But with just one tiny word, *innig*, I thought that Chamberlain had understood.

We are a lost tribe, I used to think, a brotherhood but hidden from each other. We who have felt Beethoven's presence, have heard him speak.

Chamberlain started first, asking about Berlin: what was it like inside Herr Hitler's Germany. He had been to the south he said, but never to the north.

'What do you do, as an Englishman,' he continued, 'when those big parades are on? Do you make that awful salute too?' As an island of British sanity and decency he meant, in a land of hysterical madmen. Every German a Nazi.

Like the year before, the march through the streets to celebrate Munich. After Chamberlain had created Hitler as Wotan himself.

The route down Saarlandstraße had been announced over the radio that morning, the day I returned to Berlin. A national holiday was proclaimed. Tricia immediately had her plan.

'This visit you will move to the Excelsior,' she ordered. 'You take a room on the front. Mr S will walk right past. We must celebrate his great and bloodless victory.'

There were few visitors to Germany that summer under threat of war. I could choose any room I liked and pay with Travel Marks.

'We must leave right away,' Tricia insisted when I returned to collect her after my mission to the hotel, 'I will need time to be ready.' She started to fill my portmanteau with her possessions.

From the room I watched the regiments assemble. Tricia came over to look past my shoulder out through the balcony window.

'Yes, I have time for my soak, I think.' She disappeared into the bathroom, the door locked behind her.

The preparations took over an hour.

A line of Army helmets dressed off on both sides of the street. Every few hundred yards an Honour Company was drawn up, proudly clutching their Gothic paraphernalia and accompanied by a brass band. Tasselled standards were unfurled against huge vertical swastikas flapping off all the buildings up the street. Then the roadway was cleared and dense crowds jostled behind the soldiers.

It was sunny but cold, the day that war should have started, the day of the coup. The day that Mr S should have ridden in the ambulance. The first of October 1938.

I called on Tricia to hurry as the first black SS battalions marched up from the east. Mesmerizing drill, the smartest troops I had ever seen, high-stepping, sixteen abreast. There was no response so I knocked on the bathroom door as the street filled further down. Caps and uniforms in a group, braid and insignia of all kinds walking up toward us, still at a distance. Göring's outline unmistakable, waving his Field Marshal's jewelled baton.

And in the lead a lone figure, small in his brown greatcoat and high peaked hat, arm out sideways acknowledging the frantic crowd.

At last Tricia came out of the bathroom, wrapped in a sheer silk dressing gown that I had never seen before.

'Are you sure he's coming?' she asked, standing over by the bed. 'There are often delays.'

'Yes, yes, he's walking past the Anzer now.' I turned toward her, away from the window. Excited despite myself. 'He'll be right outside in no time.'

I had never seen him in the flesh.

'This is good, our timing is perfect.'

She bared her doll's shoulders then let the gown ripple to the floor behind her. The crowd below our window started to roar, breaking into a rhythmic chorus.

Sieg-*Heil*. Sieg-*Heil*.

Tricia stood naked and motionless smiling me her she-devil's smile from across the room. She mouthed some words I could not hear, swallowed by the insistent thunder from outside.

Ein *Volk*. Ein *Reich*. Ein *Führer*.

Then slowly she laid herself back across fresh white sheets, one foot still touching the floor, hands above her head gracefully like a ballet dancer, legs wide apart and toward me.

Her flawless cream skin glistened with bath oil. She had shaved off all her hairs.

Chamberlain was still looking at me, expecting my answer. About the awful salute.

I was intoxicated, as if seeing him off in the far distance.

'I'm not much out on the street, sir,' I replied quietly.

But on about Berlin. Yes, sir, I know Berlin quite well, KM to our Embassy for four years. And I have a friend in Berlin, a soldier from the War, the Great War, a man I have known for twenty years now, a major in the OKH, senior adjutant to Generaloberst Halder, Chief of the Army General Staff. An officer like me but German, no different, a man who hates war, a man who gambled his life last year, a man we let down, a man I would fetch from No-Man's-Land at the risk of my own ... a man, Werner Schacht is his name, sir, this man is the real hero of my ...

But Chamberlain interrupted my story in mid-flight with another question: all this nonsense about officers and late War. He wanted to find his bearings, he said.

'I thought Vansittart told me you were a driver with the FO. Didn't you meet LG while on duty and some old connection got you into Van's rooms yesterday?' As if I had somehow misrepresented myself.

Yes, sir, I had been a driver before a KM. But first I was an officer, the Ox and Bucks, full lieutenant at nineteen, on active service from '17, in the trenches, the Battle of Cambrai, the MC. Then I had been kept on in Paris and by chance I had driven Mr Lloyd George through the battlefields in '19. And yes, sir, I had been to see the old gentleman and he had arranged for me to see Sir Robert Vansittart. Then to be brought here to Chequers to deliver my message in person. As General Halder had asked. As I do with our letters to Ministers of the Reich.

I was impatient. How long did I have? I wanted to go on: describe the last meeting with my friend and his General, the OKH headquarters in Zossen, my second meeting with Halder. After the failure of the first letter to Lord Halifax, after Munich.

Halder facing away from me toward windows looking out on to an empty parade ground. Tears of rage and frustration. Your Prime Minister, your Mr Chamberlain. He is the man to blame. Tears of sorrow for the future, at the crash and devastation of Germany that must follow Hitler's incredible rise.

'Oh, yes,' the Baptist's finger in the air again, 'oh yes, Hitler can make his peace with Stalin, that man Ribbentrop can fly off to sign whatever piece of paper he wants, but the two-front war will come, it will come.' Shaking his head in disbelief. Werner next to him, a colourless frame. Long arms dangling by his side as he sat, shoulders slumped in defeat.

'I do not have troops under my command, Lieutenant,' Halder said quietly. 'I am a Staff Officer. What am I supposed to do? *You*, England, *you* have made this man.'

Now on the vast map table there are two pistols under two hats. The war I cannot see is being lost.

Then Halder was wiping his eyes and telling me about the day of the failed event.

Thursday 29 September 1938, early morning in von Witzleben's command post at Charlottenburg. Fifty Henschels are assembled in the barrack square, one hundred half-tracks are lined up around the perimeter road. The rest are waiting here at Zossen. The two Generals stand in a small cubicle off the situation room, a portrait of von Seeckt hangs on the wall above them. Von Witzleben is tall, the natural leader, beaknosed like a proud eagle. Towering over Halder, the worried prune.

The radio room is adjacent. Voices, crackles, whines can be heard through the open door.

Halder and von Witzleben have little to say to each other, the decision has been made, Hitler's Trimotor has arrived back in Berlin from Obersaltzburg.

Only the timing of the final order is missing. They have one remaining worry, whether England and France will stand firm. I have taken the first letter from the mantelpiece in the *Herrenhaus* but they have heard nothing, there has been no announcement by the British.

They synchronize their watches, the order must go out within the next two hours. The two men look at each other. They know the risks.

A sergeant comes into the cubicle holding a message board.

'*Herr General, eine Meldung vom BBC. Herr Chamberlain wird in München für eine Konferenz mit dem Führer zu erwarten sein, um unmittelbar die Tschechische Krise zu lösen.*'

Chamberlain is in the air, for Munich.

Chequers is a concealed valley enclosed by soft ridges of mottled greens, every species of tree in southern England all mixed together. The outside world is imperceptible, only the Boer War Monument up on Coombe Hill is a reminder that this groomed paradise is an illusion.

We walked past the rose garden, through a field of plump picture-book sheep and on to a wooded pathway. Even the magpies were the size of cats.

While I plunged on with my story, the manic edge of my voice muffled by the dense forest floor under foot. Chamberlain walking impassively by my side, nose in the air. He had agreed to see me, for Van, for old LG. Now he was just going through the motions.

I told him how a written reprimand had been placed in my file in '38, for unauthorized contacts with the German military, for carrying a letter which Lord Halifax had never received. A letter to stop a war.

But not dismissed, I had had another year of travel since Munich. To Berlin: burnt-out synagogues and halls after a night of shattering glass; walls defaced by slogans and stars slapped on in white paint; Jewish shops under new management but the stock has disappeared; churches boarded up and draped in red and black; streets deserted at night. A population with their heads down following the cracks in the pavement.

And lies, bigger and bigger to hide the rot within: German Martyrdoms in Moravia; the vicious attacks on peaceful German farmers by Polack thugs; Goebbels' impressive figures for national production; the need for Living Space for the Underprivileged Germanic Peoples. But there's no coal at Christmas and they can't eat the Sudetenland for dinner.

And to Moscow recently, this month, August '39. Six days there and back in the train to deliver a portfolio. In the splendour of the Spiridonyevka Palace, His Majesty's Emissary, Admiral Sir Reginald Plunkett-Ernle-Erle-Drax, faces Marshal Voroshilov. And sitting with him is the Chief of the

General Staff of the Red Army, the Commissar for the Navy and the Chief of the Air Force. But our Admiral has forgotten his credentials in London and discussions cannot start until I arrive. Then by the time I am back in London, Sir Reginald has left Moscow. The Russians have lost patience with months and months of British waffling and Polish obstinacy.

Now it is Ribbentrop who is in the air, for Moscow.

Then two days ago to Zossen at six in the morning, to the OKH *Lageraum* which Halder says he cannot leave. Until war starts.

How I had pretended to take the Bremerhaven train, slipping off at Hamburg as if to buy a paper, hiding in another lavatory. Back to Berlin by the fast train, attempting to swallow my accent at the counter.

'*Heil Hitler! Berlin, einfach. Wagon Lit.*' Gruff, the Party man.

And hailing a taxi at Alexanderplatz station to find the storm-trooper in his Stoewer. We drive without a word to Spandau Military Hospital. The storm-trooper comes in with me, an uncle, a friend of the wounded man's family, nodding and smiling this way and that. Out to another ambulance at the back parked between the rubbish and the morgue. At Zossen Halder is waiting for me with his second letter.

I have it in my jacket, sir.

We came out of the forest with Chamberlain leading, down the edge of a muddy field toward the home farm. A crop had recently been taken off, chalky stones thrown up to the surface like a vineyard. Along the hedgerow poppies seemed to be watching. Shaking their heads at us, heavy and sad with raindrops.

I took Halder's letter out of my pocket, moist and creased like a bar of melting chocolate. I handed the envelope to Chamberlain. From the front, face to face.

Into his gaberdine pocket without so much as a glance.

'Do you know what's in the letter, Beecham?' he asked.

'Yes, sir,' I said. 'It's about *Blitzkrieg*.'

Lightning war, chapter and verse. Real Wehrmacht divisions, no bluff this time, not like Czechoslovakia. There on the border, right now, while the Poles have only their horses. *Blitzkrieg*: all available force concentrated into one surprise attack, devastation by land, sea and air simultaneously. Tanks, motorized infantry, the new Luftwaffe, bombardment from battleships of the Kriegsmarine on the Baltic. *Blitzkrieg*: what the Germans have developed in their year of breathing space since Munich.

I knew some of the names, the new aircraft, the Ju 87s, Do 17s, the Ju 88s. Then the fast tanks, *Panzer Kampf Wagen*, the incredible Mark IV. Artillery towed by half-tracks that can cross a ploughed field at thirty miles an hour, even motorbicycles and sidecars with mounted machine-guns. All-wheel drive troop carriers each with twenty rifles, an entire division moving as the wind, crashing on to the enemy like a tidal wave.

And in his letter General Halder asks about Poland. No natural frontiers, this is not Czechoslovakia, he says, protected by a line of strong fortifications. Poland will be smashed in a week. Halder knows. The OKH has planned it all. But this is the country Mr Chamberlain has chosen to guarantee, the General says, the place where Britain has chosen to stand and fight.

Will Mr Chamberlain take Europe to war just because he was tricked at Munich? For vengeance?

Beyond Halder's understanding. Poland is not even one of your democracies, he says, there are race laws for example, like Germany. An artificial country with an artificial corridor leading to an artificial Polish port. A compromise by forgotten Gentlemen on a forgotten Commission back in the days of Versailles. Surely not a reason for war.

And how will Britain even get there, the General asks? And what will they find if they ever do arrive?

Beck, the Polish Foreign Minister, with his unconditional British guarantee is as dangerous as a child holding a loaded pistol, the General says. Britain has handed to the Poles alone the power to decide between war and peace in Europe.

Then Chamberlain asked another question to stop my tirade, all this rubbish from a driver who doesn't know his place.

'Ever go to concerts in Berlin, Beecham?' he asked. Cheery, as if the rest was irrelevant.

I was meant to say *no sir*, or, *can't say I have, sir*, bewildered, on the wrong foot. Then Chamberlain would mutter, *pity*, or *shame* and move on to something else, trivial, irrelevant, till we reached the house. Then he could be done with me.

But the answer was *yes*.

'Oh really?' Chamberlain replied quickly, his staring teddy-bear eyes settling on me with an amused air of disbelief.

'So what's Furtwängler up to these days? Still sticking up for Hindemith?' Mock intense, sure that he had me now. 'One hears that he's gone over.'

I took it as a sign like a secret handshake and I started off again.

About the new gallery on the river, to Germanic Art, opening a Golden Aryan Age. Robust peasants in pastoral scenes, lifeless statues in perfect proportions, nude goddesses looking like bored housewives. And next door,

Degenerate Art, how *Kultur* had been saved by the Führer: Klee, Metzinger, Chagall, side by side with dabbings and blotchings by inmates of an asylum; old soldiers by Otto Dix begging in bandages on the streets in the early twenties, hung under the label MILITARY SABOTAGE.

But at the doors the Berliners passed their own judgement, with their feet. *Consummate Madness* was the winner by three visitors to one.

And Furtwängler on the radio, yes, still conducting the Philharmonic, part of the Fiftieth Birthday celebrations. No martyr, perhaps, but there are Jews protected in his orchestra and he's never once given the salute.

We follow one of Tricia's scripts as Goebbels makes his speech over the wireless before the concert starts. All three of us at climax together, '... *er soll für uns bleiben, was er immer war, Unser Hitler!*'

Then I hold her still, both of us panting, as he starts. Without a break, almost on top of the words. The supreme maestro of timing, brilliant white light brought out from behind a black eclipse, Beethoven's music, Furtwängler's one man resistance. De-dum. De-dum. De-dum. The opening bars of the Ninth. Eradicating the speech, the words, the speaker, Our Hitler. For that moment eradicating the Reich itself as if it had never been.

As I described the concert I saw Chamberlain smile, but in a different way, from another place.

Then it was his turn to talk. About Beethoven, about a little book of criticism Chamberlain had written on the quartets, the last five he told me. I was impressed. But far from satisfactory, he said, the introduction could have been quite a bit longer, he thought. Starting further back with a comparison between *Eroica* and the *Rasoumouffskys*. Beethoven's New Way. How many people really understood that properly? And he had wanted to include a story about Goethe meeting the great man in a Vienna park and his description: *innig*, Goethe had said of Beethoven. The untranslatable word that I loved. Profound, intimate, calm but violent, distraught but beautiful. The face I knew and the words,

Sing, Beauchamp, sing. It's all we have.

Chamberlain would take my message, he would act, I knew, after that I was certain. Our Secret Germany had gained a new member.

The biscuit-tin mansion came into sight again, perfect. A perspective of Georgian roof lines, bull-topped gables and wide brick chimneys.

Chamberlain pointed with his umbrella. If we were to cut across the next field we could be back in under ten minutes.

Then we were sliding down the slick bank behind the gatehouse and on to the gravel drive. Beethoven, the tiny tiny, yet the immense question at hand.

Further up I could see the Wolseley with my keepers in the back, Alf having a smoke outside the kitchen door. There was no time, the most important part was still undelivered.

'And General Halder asked me to say, sir...' I had to break the spell. Chamberlain started to walk faster, as if he had not heard, '... about the Non-Aggression Pact with the Soviets...'

Still no response.

'... the General says you might be thinking that the Pact cannot last, that Russia will end up fighting Germany over Poland, tearing each other to pieces while the West laughs.'

Now it was a race. We were by the wall of the kitchen garden, Chamberlain crunching along the drive as fast as he could, as if to catch a bus. The bus that he would miss. I had less than a minute before we reached the car.

'Then General Halder says to tell you, sir, that if that's what you are thinking, that you should know that there is a Secret Protocol to the Ribbentrop Pact. For Russia and Germany to partition Poland between them at the River Vistula. There is no protection for Poland now. With the Secret Protocol, Poland will be off the map within a week. We have it backwards the General says. Czechoslovakia was the time to fight. Before Munich. Now is the time for the aeroplane, now is the time for a real Munich. Danzig, give the Corridor and parts of Silesia back to Germany, have a referendum if it makes it easier. Self-determination, it used to be called. A railway line to Gdynia, an Autobahn across to the east. Simple things, changing the buttons on the tunics of the customs officials if that's all it would take to stop a war. And a futile war, the General says, all that Britain would be left with would be a war of vengeance...'

But my minute was up and the rest remained unsaid.

... vengeance is Mine saith the Lord. Millions dead for a country that has already disappeared. For the lies and tricks of Versailles.

The sun had come out just in time to set. Fractured orange rays fusing through rose trellises. Smouldering back at us from a hundred leaded panes in the upper floor windows of the great house.

My keepers sprang out of the car as we approached, buttoning the jackets of their shabby dark suits, pulling down waistcoats, straightening ties and crumpled collars. They took their places on either side of me.

'Well Beecham,' Chamberlain said, close to me again, facing our little rank. 'Quite the dreamer. Be babbling on about Pan-Europa next. But interesting talk. Nice to know that people in all walks of life know a bit about Beethoven. Very, very encouraging.'

He gave me a cheery little wave, a sort of mock salute and he turned away. I moved out of line to follow, to protest, but my keepers each took an arm. I had had my fun, it was their turn now.

'But sir,' I shouted after him. 'What's the answer? To General Halder. The answer to his letter.'

Chamberlain took the few paces back to me.

'Beecham,' he said, bored now, ready for his tea, 'you get me your Secret Protocol, the one that you say divides Poland between Germany and Russia. Then I'll answer your General.'

You say, *your* Protocol, *your* General. I was already counted among the enemy.

Chamberlain turned and walked away looking pleased with himself, swinging his umbrella. He had disposed of me with something clever, something clever and final.

I had thought we were a tribe, that old man and me. But I was left standing by the car, soaked and alone. Alone in my broken-down brotherhood of one.

5

Clickety click, clickety click.

I watched smoke billow out over the empty train, then away across the heath and marshes of Lüneburg. Further and further from Bremerhaven. From safety. Where the docks were crowded with anxious fugitives with their boxes and their bundles. Me going the other way. It seemed that all the foreign residents of Germany were trying to pack into a single customs warehouse, overflowing along railway lines leading to the pier. Trying to get to England, to anywhere, away.

I would visit her at the flower shop, but just to watch, there was no time. I must not lead her into danger. The war I could not see. Small white hands wielding chromium scissors, clipping stems, trimming leaves. A red tip tapping the till, counting out change.

'*Danke, bitte kommen Sie wieder.*' Her artificial shop smile.

'*Heil Hitler!*'

I was her slave, she blocked my senses with her presence. The trip of her shoes across floorboards from the bathroom, a condescending look for her captive, elbow up on the high window-sill. A leather finger dabbing at the end of my nose, feeling for my ring.

One evening after Munich, after Prague, I had tried to talk about a plan. We were walking across the canal and into the Technical University, flawless grounds, sculpted oak trees in a perfect forest.

'Plan?' Tricia repeated indignantly, as if I had used a dirty word on a Bavarian Sunday. 'Only Mr S makes plans. When will you ever learn?'

I had thought of America like the poets and the films stars. A boat from Rotterdam and leave them with it all, two new Republicans for the isolationist cause. My savings would get us across then I would work. Tricia knew New York, we could start there. Just the two of us. Before I knew that we were three.

'You're a dreamer,' she said contemptuously, withdrawing her arm from mine, 'and what dream ever came true? Ha? Tell me of even one.' That was tomorrow not now, it was a whisper of lo ... Dismissed with a wrinkled nose.

I had to play the part, the KM with my bag and my greyhound badge.

Mr Harris had leaned off the end of his chair to attend to his gas ring and his whistling kettle.

'You know, I suppose, that if you don't come back this time there'll be no search parties being sent out?' But reluctantly he had to agree. Even if the bag was empty except for the London newspapers and a bolt of silk from a wholesaler in Covent Garden. Even if I had been suspended from the Corps, even if Mr Harris and Sir Robert Vansittart were the only ones to know that I was in Berlin again. Even if I had no idea what to do.

'Be-sure-to-take-your-gas-mask-with-you.' Mr Harris had given me his sad walrus smile as he patted me on the back.

I walked Potsdamerplatz and Leipzigerstraße, I drank coffee and I ate my lunch. Berlin was hot. I stood outside the flower shop, trilby down over my eyes watching her with Frau Karen through reflections in the window. White, red. Shiny blades reflecting the sunlight. Then arranging a few roses, red on red.

I returned to the Embassy as if waiting for the bag. Then Potsdamerplatz again, slowly, slowly.

Pitiful displays of nothing in the shops, cheap leather goods from the old Czechoslovakia, now the Protectorate of Bohemia and Moravia. Clothes like paper or cardboard, their good cloth was needed for a higher purpose. Werner's story about the man who wanted a perambulator for his newborn son. Not to be found anywhere. Finally the man obtained a kit through a friend of a friend who worked in the perambulator factory. But the bundle of defective components had to be returned. No matter how many times the man followed the instructions the result was always a machine-gun.

Our Imperial halls had been filled to their ornate ceilings, half furniture showroom, half lost-property office. The possessions of the Embassy staff and all the English residents of Berlin deposited for safety before they ran.

I stayed at the Excelsior and in the evening I walked through the Tiergarten or along the river in the blackout.

Another visit to the Embassy.

Then the second day hotter again. Other shops, other streets, slower still, time in front of each window reading the prices. Over then over again, converting the figures into pounds: first at the official rate then at the Travel Mark rate. But at the tout rate I could have had the whole shop for less than a month's salary.

Military vehicles in groups, every make and description in endless grey convoys passing through the streets to the east. Rows of *feldgrau* sitting impassively in transports. Citizens on the pavement with their eyes down, following more cracks.

Finally I heard a voice, an old man, a few simple words at a time. Making sure that I understood.

'*Augen auf das Fenster. Eine Botschaft von Major Schacht. Nehmen sie Taxi Lehter Terminus um sechs Uhr. Sechs Uhr. Zählen bis Hundert bevor Sie gehen.*'

Then the speaker was gone.

I followed my instructions, staring blankly at the window while I counted to a hundred. Then I walked slowly to the station, still arriving an hour early. There were no evacuees leaving Berlin. Their trains too were being put to other uses. I sat drinking more coffee, conspicuously reading a German newspaper. I understood only the headlines. *POLISH OUTRAGES. FULL DETAILS.*

At ten to six I stood under the arch at the main entrance and watched the taxi rank. There was the Stoewer with the storm-trooper driving, moving up, innocent among black NSUs and upright Maybachs.

I timed my approach to the rank to coincide with the Stoewer coming to the head of the line. But as I moved to open the car door, a large woman towing a small shuffling man appeared from nowhere. She had her hand on the handle ahead of me. The taxi suddenly lurched forward, door swinging back against hinge straps with the woman left trying to climb into a void where the car had been. I rushed for the open door and quickly climbed in.

'*Gangster*,' I heard her shout at me, '*Dreckjude*.'

I fell as I entered the compartment, tripping over a pair of high black boots. Sent sprawling as the car moved off again.

'Lieutenant,' said the body on the floor beneath me, 'I am so pleased that you could come.'

We tried to laugh, brief and nervous, two amateurs.

'You take the seat,' Werner instructed. 'You look out of the window, not at the floor. We have very little time.' Werner sat on the carpet obscured from outside view, his back up against the far door, his head resting between shiny handles.

At first I thought that he was drunk. The car lurched left and right as the storm-trooper drove us round the Memorial church and then south toward Schöneberg. Werner rocking despondently to and fro. His *Waffenrock* unbuttoned exposing a cotton vest. He looked tired and weighed down, worse than the last meeting at the *Herrenhaus*. He had not shaved.

A long silence even though there was little time.

'Things are very dangerous,' Werner said finally. 'As war approaches, *die verdammte Pflicht* starts. Even for General Halder. When lives are committed and the plan of attack is engaged, responsibilities change. It becomes impossible to disobey orders, to think of any independent action. Soon we will all be agreeing that only the Führer knows best.'

Berlin passed by the window, millions of lives, millions of futures, waiting, helpless. London the same, Paris, Warsaw.

Werner's ruined look down on the floor, our world in a trance.

Even without saying why I had come, it seemed that we had reached the end. That Werner could do no more and our Secret Germany was over.

'But you have come a long way,' he said, after another pause and trying to smile. 'You prove yourself. We are *Kameraden, ja*?' He put his hand up on my knee.

Together in the tumbrel, a moment of complete connection between us, the condemned of the old world swaying along together. As steel banded wheels jolt over cobbles toward the new.

'I saw Mr Chamberlain and I had help from Mr Lloyd George,' I told him, rigidly watching the road straight ahead past the storm-trooper's cropped head. 'But I received no answer. We talked about Beethoven. He's quite the expert, I thought that he…'

Werner smiled a tired smile. I had thought the impossible. He understood. The rest seemed hollow, but I continued.

'… Mr Chamberlain told me that if he could see the Secret Protocol, if we could prove that Poland was lost from the start, then he would give an answer to General Halder. In England it's not like 1914, Poland is not Belgium, there are no crowds in the streets in London. Mr Chamberlain could make a difference with another conference, the British people would support him. But there is no trust left. And he talks as if I am a traitor.'

'Then we are both traitors, Yves. Neither side wishes to know the truth.' Werner spoke quietly. 'We have been working day and night. The attack on Poland, Operation White, could be tomorrow or the day after. But it was postponed once so who knows? After your government said that you and France would fight this time, it was expected that Chamberlain and Daladier would both fall. When this did not happen *der Gefreiter* had cold feet. Even Italy withdrew from us.'

'I need the Secret Protocol,' I repeated, 'or else they will think they are being bluffed again like Munich. Chamberlain has it backwards. Last year when we should have stood our ground we conceded, now when only talk can save Poland we are threatening war.'

'We hear many things,' Werner replied despondently. 'That Poland would send a plenipotentiary if it was not for the British guarantee, that Hitler has lent your ambassador his private plane to speed negotiations, that Mussolini will arrange another conference. That the Russian Pact is a sham and once war starts Poland and the Ukraine will be settled with Germans. It is the extremists who will make the gains. They are the ones pushing for war. We need your Prime Minister, now, here.'

Werner called to the storm-trooper.

'*Geh zurück zu der Siegessäule und zeig' dem Leutnant wo die Statuen zu finden sind.*'

The car turned back toward the centre of the city, up Potsdamerstraße and into the Tiergarten.

As part of the new works through the park for the Fiftieth a triumphal circle had been built. Rows and rows of clipped cypress trees, marching lamps and imperial monuments had produced a harsh regimented look, like a year-round Party Rally. At the focus stood a stone column over one hundred feet high. Decorated with cannon and oak leaves, a golden goddess flying on the pinnacle.

Werner looked up at me, pale and worn.

'That is the Siegessäule. It commemorates Great Prussian Victories. Granite not wood or paint, but illusion all the same.' He had no energy left for another smile.

The taxi slowed as if to show me the sights.

'We will make a plan anyway,' Werner said, 'just in case. But the other side is more powerful with every success. We are losing the war you cannot see.'

Pauses between his words as he thought, like the first rehearsal of a play.

'It is possible we have the complete document ... through Hitler's High Command, or by an intercept of the Abwehr. But we cannot meet again, Yves ... I am being watched, right from the gates of Zossen. My uncle, everyone ... they cannot touch the Army with war coming, but I put you in danger ... even with your diplomatic papers ... once Operation White starts there will be nothing to hold them.'

The car had come to a stop further down Charlottenburger Chaussee.

'And this is where the Siegessäule used to stand, until this year. You will see a pathway leading around the statue of Bismarck,' Werner made to point from the floor. 'Down the path you will find other statues, Beethoven and Goethe. Let us say you are deficient in *Kultur*, so your punishment is to walk along that path twice each day, east to west...'

Still no smile. He looked at his watch.

'... half past nine and half past twelve ... newspaper under your right arm. Slowly through the park, before and especially after ... whatever happens ... you are waiting for your bag, you have little to do, you are in no hurry. But only two days then you must go home ... two days...'

I glanced down at my friend. Much greyer again, just in the last year. Tall hollow face, long pianist's fingers lying motionless along the floor, the calm look of a man who is prepared for his future. His future on a strip of celluloid.

'Keep looking out of the window. You have your orders, Lieutenant.' I thought I saw his face soften.

The car started to move again, driving slowly through the park next to the kerb. From the corner of my eye I caught Werner buttoning his tunic and picking his cap off the seat next to me. Then he tapped on the partition.

'So this is goodbye, *Kamerad*.' He put his hand on my knee again.

The taxi made a sudden hard turn into a treed lane, to come to a dusty halt. The door on the far side opened and closed before I realized what was happening. Then the storm-trooper was reversing out into the street again, changing directions, leaning out of his open door to look back like a lorry driver.

A ghost at the crack of dawn, Werner had disappeared.

For two days I walked by the statues. Beethoven's eyes followed me as I passed in front of him. His themes flooded my mind. Little black dots on a piece of paper, mere sound waves, just moving air. But with these notes he could take on the whole world, with his scratchings he would defeat the Reich.

At the Embassy again I pretended to be engaged on some covert delivery or collection, but I drew little notice from the skeleton staff who were lost along cluttered corridors and through piled-up rooms. All the familiar faces were gone and below stairs the staff lounge and canteen were also being filled with boxes and large awkward objects covered in sheets.

At the Excelsior I made a point of taking my meals right on time while complaining about the delays in my return to England.

'*Verdammtes Bürokratie*,' I commented as often as I could.

And in the Tiergarten I lolled on benches, I walked along the river appearing to enjoy the sunshine. I sat by shady green ponds among the others on folding park chairs, all of us looking for relief from the heat. Gossamer hung everywhere in the air. Even the trees looked tired.

I searched faces for my followers but it was impossible to tell. The park was full of Berliners intently enjoying August, a last respite from the universal God of War. Already rationing had started and cars were thin on the roads. Tearful wedding ceremonies were being held every hour in Wittenburgplatz, bridegrooms in uniform ready to leave.

Anti-aircraft guns and searchlights were deploying across the city. Long grey-blue barrels up to the sky. Crews purposeful and efficient, putting our shambling Territorials to shame.

On the second day at half past twelve I started down the path again, toward the statues, toward Beethoven's reproachful eyes. East to west, breathless, scrutinizing every person walking toward me. My heart beating in my ears like a snare drum, hands tingling. One foot following the other along the gravel. Telling myself that I was on immunity, that I was on the route.

In the seconds before the collision I realized the obvious, that it would be another old man, another retired office from the *Herrenhaus*. He came toward me along the path, leaning on a cane, looking up at the statues. When I had almost passed him, right under Beethoven, he changed direction into my path and in that moment I was ready. He fell against me, then he clutched at my shoulder as if to stop himself from falling. In the fumble I was holding an envelope which I slid into my jacket pocket.

'*Guck hin, wo Du läufst*,' the old man said loudly as if it had been my fault. '*Platz genug für zwei*.'

'All right?' I asked, making a show of being concerned.

'*Jaja.*' The old soldier staggered off, waving me away with an annoyed gesture.

I continued to admire the statues, my heart now timpani. Then I sat mesmerized on another bench and unfurled my newspaper. I bought a coffee at the park kiosk, hand shaking, unable to swallow. I made my way back to the Excelsior. I ate my lunch as slowly as my anxiety would allow. The fast train was not until two.

I packed my portmanteau and made a show of leaving. I paid with my Travel Marks and I shook the *concierge* by the hand.

'*Kommen die englischen Bomber?*' he asked. I pretended that I did not understand and I walked out into the street.

In the bathroom I had looked in the envelope. The entire treaty in German, typeset, printed like a book. A short main body and twelve appendices including three maps. I could make out the heading I was looking for.

APPENDIX N
FIRST SECRET ADDITIONAL PROTOCOL

I was exhilarated, lifted off the pavement as if I could fly back to London just by spreading out my arms. I collected my empty bag from the Embassy and I was ready to leave. I had become omnipotent, I held the answer to war in my hands. I trembled with excitement, hardly able to walk without running.

At Potsdam Terminus I wanted to grasp the railwaymen by the hand, put my arm around them, call each one *Kamerad*, assure them that there would be no war. Our Prime Minister would be coming, I would say, in his aeroplane. Peace was assured, for them, for us, for their families. The course of the world had changed, from now, from that morning in front of Beethoven's statue.

But at the ticket office the news was bad.

'*Reisebeschränkung. Reisebeschränkung*, I was told. I showed my pass but there would be no civilian train to Bremerhaven until six o'clock that night, in over four hours' time.

I could have waited at the station kiosk, on the platform, sitting on a bench, anywhere. But I knew where I was going even before my feet started to walk. Following cracks in the pavement, out of the station across Potsdamerplatz and along Leipzigerstraße, a bag in each hand.

Tricia acted surprised and annoyed, both at the same time. I watched her frown then wrinkle her nose. But she concentrated on wrapping a small bouquet for a customer at the counter. Not even a second glance in my direction.

She was the flower girl: white shirt, long dark skirt and striped apron. Her hands were wet and stained with green, she was perspiring through white make-up.

'This is a good time to arrive, no warning, no notice,' she said when we were alone, hands on her hips like a gym instructor facing a lazy class. She seemed nervous, out of breath. 'You know, I can never say where you are these days.'

'I am leaving, not arriving,' I replied. 'There has been no chance...' Worse than two strangers.

I looked around the shop. All the pots and vases were empty and the shelves were bare. A few sprigs of green and some tired daffodils lay on the counter.

'We are shutting the doors,' Tricia said before I could ask. 'Flowers are not needed in wartime.'

'So where are you going, what are you going to do?' She shrugged at me, even now she seemed to have no plan.

But I had mine. I put down my bags and moved close to her, my face brushing through her frisée. She smelled of my enslavement, hot like the bedroom.

Tricia led me to the back of the shop through a set of hanging beads. Empty boxes and used packaging filled the small room. A work surface was arranged as a desk, covered with papers held down by a telephone. A stained sink full of dirty cups and bowls hung on the far wall. There was no stock of any kind. Tricia held up her palms in mock despair. It was obvious that the shop was about to close.

'I was looking forward to seeing you again,' she said, 'but not like this.' It was an unusual remark, a sign of affection or returned feelings. Something that I had hardly heard from her before. I took her words as the invitation I wanted.

'My train does not leave for four hours.'

Immediately Tricia was bustling the keys to the attic into my hand.

'There will be no customers on a day like this and we have nothing to sell anyway. Frau Karen has already gone, I can lock up in a few minutes.'

I picked up my bags and left her in the back room. But before I stepped into the street I changed my mind: the door to the alley would be safer. From the war I could not see, from the reproach of cracks leading back along the pavement, back to the station where I should have been.

In the stockroom Tricia was dialling with a swirling red nail. But the moment I entered she hurriedly replaced the telephone handset. She looked as guilty and as flustered as me. We stood and stared at each other for an instant. An instant in stone, stones who could not see, could not speak.

'Frau Karen is not home,' Tricia said quickly, turning her face away as I started to clear boxes from the back door. 'I'll be there real soon.'

The flat like the shop seemed empty. A picture in a silver frame was missing, Tricia and Inge hiking against snowy mountains. In the cupboard two bags were packed, few clothes remained. I had no idea how Tricia was to be evacuated.

I tried to read the Pact again using her dictionary. A striped map attached to Appendix N showed clearly that Germany would occupy Poland to the Rivers Narev, Vistula and San. Russia would take the rest.

I was unable to sit or to stand. I paced the small flat, frantic to be at the station, on immunity. I had made a mistake. Frantic to sit by the rails, caress them, watch over them. Joined, forming a long elegant arrow, pointing into the far distance, the bright future. The rails that would prevent war.

Then I heard Tricia on the stair and she flew in through the door, out of breath, eyes flashing.

'There will be no war,' I burst out, 'I know it for sure.' Tricia had started to take off her hat and gloves as she entered the room. I tried to embrace her.

'No war?' she repeated, as if disappointed, pushing me away. 'No war?' Indignant. Then she put a stained finger up to my lips.

'But first there is you.' She disappeared into the bathroom.

I wanted to talk, to give her the silk I had brought. Tell her that I would return from London again in only a few days. I wanted to blow open my secrets, my meetings with Halder. Tell her that I had been carrying messages, for us, for them, for the Army that she knew. That now we could make our plans, enjoy peace and prosperity in Europe together. That I would marry her. That I loved her. But the latch had turned in the door before I could bring myself to begin.

I heard her shoes click on the tile floor, drawers opening and closing fast and hard. In a moment she was back, no apron, fresh lipstick and washed hands.

She moved behind me impatiently and started to remove my jacket. Rushed, awkward, I felt nothing except some primal apprehension, communicated instinctively like a doctor's waiting room. But I allowed her to continue, perfunctory, routine and limp, until I was naked and the Captain's ties had me secured to the bed. It was the relief of no war, the summer heat, the waiting rails, my unexpected arrival, events. The magic would come back.

Then I watched her walk across to the window, but there was no she-devil in her. I was about to tell her not to, to stop, to talk to me, when she began to shake. Her shoulders heaving as she took big gasps for air. She turned to the window-sill and buried her face in her arms as if she had just witnessed some terrible scene.

There was a noise on the stairs, footsteps and voices. Tricia broke into hysterical sobs, her face streaming. Then she was running for the door.

'Stenner ... New York...' she shouted between spasms of drawn breath, her back to the door as if to shut out some wild beast. Words reeling from her as the door handle started to rattle, overwhelmed, desperate in those last few seconds to tell me something that I could not grasp.

'Herr Stenner, *Jude*, I never knew, I was young, but Boch knew ... the divorce ... Emma, Emma will be at the border to meet us ... I have made a deal, Yves ... but you are safe, we will all be safe ... in America...'

The door burst open, sweeping Tricia effortlessly to one side. Three men came into the flat. A tall thin man with black hair slicked straight back from his forehead, two bulls behind. Civilian clothes but formal like uniform: the thin man in a black leather jacket with a silver lapel badge, black gloves, the keepers in dark suits.

I was instantly terrified, my stomach a knotted void. My body ice, my crotch open and vulnerable like a raw wound.

'Who are you, what's this...' I started. I pulled at my ties but I was unable to move, knots tightening around wrists and ankles as I struggled. Exposed, tied to the bed, the treaty and maps spread out on the table, my bags over by the bathroom door.

'*Halt's Maul*,' one of the keepers ordered without looking at me. I was still fumbling with my words.

I heard the leader address Tricia as Frau Boch. He knew her, she seemed calm. Standing still and unafraid as if she had been expecting his arrival. But as the leader began to bark, an immediate change came over Tricia's face, more tears streaking her cheeks, lips quivering, hands up to her head in panic. She looked very small, suddenly shrivelled like an old woman.

This was not the army that she knew.

Then I saw the whip. Held in a black leather glove, tapping against the back of the leader's leg as he shouted at Tricia. The whip was suddenly my centre of the room like a loaded gun aimed at my chest. My mouth was parchment, ceiling and walls revolving. Close, away, close again. There was a momentary chasm between reality and what I saw. As if this were a dream: suddenly the door would slam behind them and there would be my she-devil again, poised, ready and wicked by the window.

The keepers looked in the bathroom then out of the window.

'*Alles in Ordnung, Hauptsturmführer*,' one of them said. I recognized the rank, an SS Captain, like Boch himself.

The Captain caught Tricia's shoulder and pushed her toward me. More rough commands and Tricia was sitting on the edge of the bed. She put her hand on me as if trying to cover me up, her touch a moment's relief. A glance, terror in her eyes, everything overturned by the swing of the door, by faces that she thought she knew.

Tricia tried to speak but nothing came.

Another bark from the Captain and she took my shrunken penis in her hand, less than the size of her small palm. Now she was weeping, choking, her hand clammy and cold.

When the Captain was satisfied with the tableau he opened the door again. Another man entered carrying a huge camera. I could see more men through the open door, out on the stairs. Three flashes in fast succession blinded me, then the cameraman disappeared. The keepers stood at the back of the room and leered.

Snapped orders from the *Hauptsturmführer*. My straps were unknotted from the bedposts. I was pulled off the bed and thrown hard across the room and into the bathroom, ties flapping off my wrists and ankles. Then one keeper held my neck from the back with a large powerful hand, smearing me against the bathroom door while the other secured the ties. I was helpless, face against the etchings in the glass. I could see the other keeper's outline, sitting on the bath behind, holding me with the ties under and over the door. My wrists and ankles drawn hard against the top and bottom edges of the door, cutting into my skin, circulation stopped by the knots.

Behind me in the room Tricia began to scream in English and in German.

'*Keine Gewalt.* No violence. Yves, they promised me. Expulsion, no more of your messages, I made a deal. We were safe, the three of us. Across the border, Holland. *Aber keine Gewalt, Sie haben es versprochen … versprochen*.'

There was a scuffle and the sound of the room being searched. Tricia was brought into the bathroom. The Captain moved her round so that I could see her face; there was blood on her lips. He grasped her savagely by her frisée and held the whip to her face. Tricia stopped crying and took on the terrified look of a pullet at the end of its usefulness. Eyes popping, jaw clenched.

'This is the whore of the Jew,' the Captain said in thick English. 'So how does that feel now?' he pointed the whip toward my groin. 'And there is a little Jewish *Mischling* as well. Did she tell you that, messenger?' The Captain knew all about us.

'I am under diplomatic immunity, from the British Embassy,' I stammered, 'and she is innocent.'

'Innocent? Innocent?' The Captain shouted at me like an actor working himself up to a scene of self-righteous rage. He threw Tricia to the floor. He took off his right glove and reached into the pocket of his leather jacket.

'Innocent?' he shouted again. He held up a handful of envelopes, letters I had brought for Tricia from London in the Embassy bag. From one of the envelopes he pulled out a small wad wrapped in silver paper from a bar of chocolate. He opened the package to reveal a fold of American twenty dollar bills. He passed his thumb across the edges of the notes like a pack of cards.

'Innocent?' he repeated, quietly now. 'Good business, no? Smuggle our marks to England, buy dollars at the official rate, smuggle dollars back, trade Marks as a criminal on a street corner. Start again, the money increased five times each journey. Good business for the Jew's whore and her messenger, ha?'

Tricia started to cry again from the floor.

'It was to leave, to leave ... to pay them, Yves, they promised ... they told me how much ... my plan ... I had a plan, a plan...'

The Captain snatched her by the hair again and threw her out of the room. Tricia started to scream, '... for my Emmanuele, for you, to pay, no, no, Yves, they promised...'

Her voice receded down the stairs. The other bull had taken her away.

The Captain came back to me and pointed the end of the whip into my face. Thin and long, very finely plaited strands of leather ending in two frayed cords, forked like a snake's tongue.

There was a silver ring on the last finger of the whip hand. The design matched the badge on his lapel. A skull, a death's head.

Then the Captain ran the whip softly over the back of my neck, down my spine and on to my buttocks. Admiring my unblemished white skin. Gauging his distance.

'So,' he said softly, 'there will be no more talk of diplomatic privilege.'

I started to tremble, violently and involuntarily, fear spreading like a virus into every pore and muscle. I had learned to win, the worm who would show them nothing. The man with the cheese knife and the bayonet who had my name. But here it was the end, here I had lost, I could not hold. Gangsters not gentlemen. Life or death, kill or be killed.

Only the ties kept me upright.

My mouth opened and began to plead. Words coming before thoughts were formed: I would do anything, I would sign a confession, I would leave for England immediately, I would never come back to Germany, never. I would resign as KM...

Then he hit me, three times. In the bathroom mirror I could see his arm move high above his head and a downward cutting motion on to my back like the swings of a hammer, with all his strength.

The pain was electricity, intense and mortally shocking, as if my back had been scored by a razor and the bones exposed. I felt blood seeping down my spine.

I was a man trapped inside himself, drowning, hands tied together, feet, in water, scalding now, struggling frantically with a strength beyond my own. Until suddenly there was a release up toward the surface. As I screamed. A shattering bellow from my stomach, scouring my throat like a flame.

'Names,' the Captain said. 'And not Schacht, we saw him in the taxi, we know all about the spirit of Zossen. Their turn will come. After victory.'

I made no reply, breathless from the cut of the whip and my bawling pain.

'How did you get this?' he demanded, holding the Pact up to my face. 'What messages have you been delivering? Who for?'

Still I could not reply.

'We have been following you, how did you get it? And this?' He held up a scrap of paper, my autumn leaf. They had been through my bags. Tricia's writing, the results of the election of 'thirty-three.

'We will have to teach you to stay out of our business.' Quietly again, like an afterthought.

'Ludwig.' I forced a whisper: in front of the statue, the old soldier, ready to tell him everything. The *Herrenhaus*, the civilians, Halder, whatever I knew. Make it up, anything to avoid more strokes. I could not survive another one.

'Ludwig?' the Captain repeated, suddenly interested 'Ludwig who? Is he a Wehrmacht officer?'

'Ludwig van Beethoven ... there's a sta...'

The Captain stood back, dark, angry, tight lipped and he started again. Lash after lash across my back and shoulders, then further down toward my buttocks.

It was a death, an agony of incomplete death. Death that I wanted but could not have, continuous unsustainable pain.

My head flipped from side to side like a lunatic fit. To the ceiling, neck arched back, frantic screams ripping up from my bowels, out through the top of my head. Unable to form even the words of betrayal.

Then the Captain was peering into my face and the strokes had stopped. The whip was held against my quivering chin. Covered with blood and flesh as if from a shrapnel wound.

'So, messenger,' he hissed, 'what message will you deliver now?'

I gasped for breath. I shook like the fever.

'No, no. It's not...' The Captain moved behind me. The smell of his lavender hair oil.

I felt the handle of the whip between my cheeks as he whispered ferociously into my ear.

'Here is a message for *you*.'

I tensed when I had nothing left.

'From Boch.'

It was a sensation of being filled, then compressed violently, a piston. An edge of tearing pain, all the intimate organs of my body battered from the inside.

And before I passed over into a cascading white void, a wave of utter degradation, of unbearable revolt, at myself.

Of the whole world defiled.

PART VI

1

Percy the purser was the humorous type. Everything reduced to a joke and a flashed smile.

'My, my,' the first impression. 'You looks like you's seen a ghost.' My keepers unmoved on either side. By then, day eight, I could stand without help.

Fat and round, bald and shiny, Percy had spent all his working life on passenger ships. Although as he said, he was not a real sailor.

He kept talking as he signed for me like supplies from the chandler.

To Percy the declaration of war was a distant event. He imagined that his ship, the *SS Uganda*, would soon start carrying troops, but from where to where he wasn't sure. Then regular service would resume: after we've won. Colonials and their families again, farmers on leave, safari groups, neatly divided once more between his upper and his lower decks.

Then silence like the back of the Wolseley again as we made our way in file down a long passageway to an end door, another cell engraved with the same word, SANATORIUM.

My reception had been carefully arranged. They had been told how to treat me: needs medical attention but not a passenger; can't leave the boat though not a prisoner. But the key turned in the lock of the cabin door after Percy left.

The ship's doctor came aboard that night and my treatment continued. He showed no interest in the origin of my wounds. He too had been briefed, working in a rough and confident way.

'If you were going to croak,' he mumbled gruffly when the dressing was off, 'you'd have done so by now. Men in Nelson's navy usually lived, once they had survived the shock. Salt water and lemon peel was all the treatment they ever had.'

And as to the other damage, he would keep me on laxatives but there was little more he could do. He certainly did not intend to look.

I was asleep when the ship left Southampton and the next morning England had disappeared. Over the horizon, behind the hypnotizing wake of rhythmic propellers.

At sea I was moved into a crew cabin away from the passengers and I took my meals in an unused wardroom. I could promenade on the cargo deck then around the stern on B deck behind the galleys.

On the third day at sea Percy came into the wardroom while I was eating my lunch. Bangers and mash with gravy.

'We were never properly introduced,' he started. 'You probably know we're headed for Mombasa in Kenya Colony.' I had found out that much from the Ceylonese cooks, worried about U-boats, relieved to be passing Gibraltar without any trouble. 'I'm always busy the first few days out and on this passage even more so. Under the prevailing circumstances.' His quick smile and wink again.

Percy emptied the contents of a paper bag on to the table.

'I've brought you a few things.' A bottle of gin, a bottle of orange squash and a few books. John Buchan, Rider Haggard, as if I needed adventure or stimulation.

I had no wish to mix with passengers or crew. I was a ghost, I wanted only to rest, to have the sea air do its work. To feel the Mediterranean sunshine on my face. Watch screeching gulls diving against the wind for kitchen scraps. To discover if there was any life left. And if there was any reason to continue that life.

I looked over the side of the boat alone in the night, or into grey dawns when sea merged with sky. When the railing seemed no higher than my knees. Pulled, ready to sink into the dark blue spume sweeping by.

I could disappear from my cabin without a trace, slide under the restless chop. The ship churning away into a starry void, across an inky sea.

Then I was lying in the bed in the *Herrenhaus* again. Or I was following the cracks in the pavement as I left Potsdam Terminus. Her betrayal that was a plan, my plan that was a betrayal. Two stones that could not talk, could not understand.

The temperature rose as the ship sailed east, turning hot as we passed through the Canal, past Suez and into the Red Sea. Two days later the SS *Uganda* docked at Port Sudan and a few passengers made their way down the gangway in operatic colonial costumes.

Looking out from the stern at the adobe town of sandy streets and at the desert behind, Africa came into my consciousness for the first time. Endless, inviting like the sea, another place to disappear.

Then past the Gulf of Aden, around the Horn of Africa and into the Indian Ocean. We sailed along the coast of Italian Somaliland. Luminous cliffs crumbling into the sea like an interminable sandy glacier.

By the time the coast of Kenya came into sight, almost three weeks out from Southampton, the dressings were off and I could wear my fatigue jacket over hardening scabs. Or on a hidden part of the cargo deck, I could stand with my jacket off and my back to the sun.

In a small mirror in the crew ablutions I had been able to examine myself for the first time. Alive but damaged, whole but marked for ever.

Individual weals up near my neck and down across my tail bone. Then a mass of cuts in between, a molten tissue of scars. The tips of fifteen or twenty lashes licking out of the central crust and around my ribs under my right arm. And filling in any unmarked skin, a deep purple, a violent bruise that ran below the surface like squid ink on white stone slabs at Falmouth market.

The air thick with lavender hair oil. The Captain's voice, smooth and dreadful. Creaking leather against me as he whispers in my ear.

... so messenger, what message will you deliver now?

And I saw my hand reaching across Bilsen's desk, holding the first envelope. His voice nasal and impatient. *We have Herr Hitler's word that once the Czech's present little nonsense ...*

My hand out a second time, nervous under perfect elms. Chamberlain's fingers slipping my bar of damp chocolate into his coat pocket. Halder's second letter, unopened, unread.

Eyes on the mirror. The sight of my failure holding me fascinated, unable to look away.

Percy had told me that he would be busy again at Mombasa. Most of his passengers would be disembarking, returning to their posts after home leave, by which he meant England.

In the early afternoon, after we had been tied up for a number of hours, he sent for me.

'I was to give you this in port.' A five pound note and a travel voucher for the train journey from Mombasa to Nairobi was pinned to a sheet of FO stationery on which had been typed:

On arrival in Nairobi, report to:-
A. M. Quale, Office of the Chief Secretary,
Kenya Colony

I was besieged by rickshaw men and sellers of carvings as I walked out of the gates, the only white skin in a sea of curious black faces. Bodies parting on the pavement as if by command to let me pass, followed by stares and comments. Children walking next to me for a few paces, looking up with bright faces.

'*Jambo bwana*,' they said, '*jambo*.'

The town of Mombasa was absurdly British. Official buildings a cross between Lutyens and Inigo Jones, familiar cars in the streets. White faces here and there, European, they liked to call themselves.

But then other cultures. Warehouses and shops belonging to Indian traders, godowns and *dukas*: Hamamjee Brothers, Importing Generals, and Hethabhai Company, Importers and Fitters of All Sanitary. Turreted mosques and ornate painted temples. And Africans, unobtrusive but every-where, bare feet through the sharp perils of the town, slow moving under the fierce sun.

Mombasa station was a group of low metal buildings like the harbour. A roof against the sun but open sides to the heat and an occasional breeze. Every surface cleaned, swept or polished.

A large sign board on the platform read: Mombasa 44 Ft.

Surprisingly my travel voucher produced a first class sleeper, even though I had no reservation and I was given no ticket. Walking the platform the length of the train before we left, I found the reason. First class was for Europeans, second class for Asians and third class was African.

The dividing lines were rigid with coaches to match: first class sleepers well appointed with carpeted floors and panelled walls, toilets clean and shining, maintained like the boat; second class a poor cousin of first, older coaches overflowing with Indians and their families. Third class was a row of overcrowded charabancs without compartments, lined with wooden slat seats like park benches.

Already Asians and Africans were cooking in their coaches. Strong smells of turmeric, onions and garlic overtook the platform odours of Africans hawking fried chickpeas and grilled bananas. Then a sweet smell from the tangle of black and brown humanity knotted at each doorway. And the tang of the sea in the distance, mixed with the sweltering town.

The train began to move exactly on time but at walking speed through mud and thatch villages in the low hills behind Mombasa. Naked children lined the tracks to wave up at the tall train, close enough to see the expression on every smiling face.

On the equator dusk and dawn come quickly and at the same time every day: six o'clock in the morning and six o'clock in the evening. After a brilliant pink moment as the train climbed from the coast out into the African bush, all below us turned black.

With each bend in the track I could see the length of the train ahead. Pulled by two huge locomotives, outlined in the dark by tongues of jagged flame down on to the rails. Furnaces roaring and breathing fire through the African night. A smell of some exotic wood burning.

A barefoot African steward in a white uniform worked his way up the corridor of my coach playing a hand-held xylophone. For first class, dinner was served.

The dining car was a perfect colonial scene: tables for two and four against the windows on either side of an aisle, starched white tablecloths, place settings and little Pullman lamps. Africans serving, Europeans eating.

By the time I entered the dining car almost every table was occupied. There was a halt to food and talk as I appeared on the footplate. Pink faces looked up at me as I stood rocking with the train. Men in khaki jackets and cricketing cravats, women in long dresses or khaki suits matching their husbands. Cheap jewellery and a sense of the proper.

Among the kitchen crew of the *SS Uganda* I had paid little attention to my appearance. Now I was a sight, still wearing cotton fatigues from my nights at Aldershot, from day six or seven.

My army shirt had come to pieces on my washing line on the cargo deck. The back of my tunic had worn down to threads with constant scrubbing to remove pus and blood. The laces in my brown plimsolls had broken long ago and I had thrown my woollen socks overboard in the heat of the Red Sea. My hair had grown out since the recruit's haircut in barracks, standing straight up and more grey than I remembered. A straggly salt and pepper beard covered my face.

Another African in whites stepped up to me and the moment passed. Conversation resumed to the rhythmic sway of the train.

The steward sat me at the last table and handed me a menu.

'*Bwana? U nakunwha kitu gani?*' I looked up at his smooth wide features.

Intensely matt black, not brown and buffed like the African playing the xylophone. The steward was waiting for my answer.

'What's your name?' I asked. 'Do you speak English?' The steward looked uncomfortable, shifting on his feet as he bent over me.

A European at the table across the aisle leaned over from his chair.

'The boy wants to know what you want to drink.' The man was neatly groomed, hair parted straight. A flabby face with a slack jaw. He and the steward stared at me, both waiting for their replies.

'I asked the steward for his name.'

'You must be new, old chap,' he said, leaning back in his chair, enjoying his advantage. 'We don't bother with boys' names out here. Just give boy your drinks order.'

I looked up at the steward.

'My name is Yves,' I said slowly, 'Yves Beauchamp,' palm to chest. 'What is your name?'

But the steward was intensely embarrassed. He looked around at the table across the aisle, unwilling to answer such an extraordinary question even if he had understood. I relented before the incident escalated. Feeling suddenly exposed, hunted. My name a dirty secret.

I asked for wine but there was none, prompting more fuss and more patronizing looks. I settled for gin and orange squash like the boat and the steward began to bring my meal.

The engines roared on, pulling steadily uphill from sea level toward the high plains of Nairobi.

The cadence under me was even and loud. A gin-lubricated rhythm creeping back into my head for the first time since Berlin. Distant music in time with the rails, from a world that had disappeared. Against a bathroom door, down five flights of stairs. The measures of my shame.

Yum-per-da, yum-per-da, yum-per-da, yum-per-da. Ripe for the madhouse, Weber had said of Beethoven after the first performance of the seventh … *yum*-per-da, *yum*-per-da, *yum*-per-da, *yum*-per-da … oh yes, I was ripe.

Clickety click, clickety click. Frightened faces packed together on the ride of oblivion. *You must think of me when you are on the train.*

I sat eating my meal to the sway of the dining car, tears running down my cheeks.

At Nairobi station the first class passengers were met by other Europeans attended by their servants, quickly dispersing into waiting cars. The Indians had a chaotic Indian version of the same ritual. While Africans with cloth bundles, tin trunks and cane baskets on their heads left the station by a side entrance, blending into the black-faced crowd outside.

I walked up toward the centre of the town in search of my contact.

Nairobi in 1939 was a clean and well organized town. Wide streets, heavily treed and planted. Roads and pavements meticulously maintained, almost to a military standard.

The board at the station read: Nairobi 5,382 Ft.

In this horticulturist's paradise, altitude, frequent rain, daily sun and regiments of cheap labour had produced an amazing variety of vegetation. The city was a continuous lush garden, splattered with dazzling colours. Rows of decorative palms and exotic herbaceous borders, tunnels of jacaranda trees shedding luminous lilac bloom, all set off by lawns of perfectly trimmed coarse green.

I found Quale's office by late morning in a large government building. More *style Empire britannique*, a poor cousin of Greece and Rome via India. A Sikh clerk in a brilliant pink turban and khaki suit ushered me through a door marked A. M. QUALE, DEPUTY ASSISTANT CHIEF SECRETARY.

Quale and I looked each other over. He was ordinary in every way. Hair combed over balding patches, harassed and scruffy in a baggy white shirt and twisted brown tie. An amateur: vacant smile, whisky and soda in his fist at half past eleven in the morning.

'We seem to get nothing but the misfits and the unwanteds out here,' Quale began after I had handed him my piece of paper. Then he peered into a grubby manila file folder brought by the clerk. 'The remittance men. The embarrassing bankrupts. But this really is a first, I must say. Simply nothing on you. Just an FO reference number over the wire. I suppose it's the ruddy war.'

Quale wound down, expecting some explanation from the apparition of the dining car. All my possessions in the world stuffed into a grease-proof paper bag from the ship's galley. My sandwich lunch prepared by the Ceylonese against the unknowns of Africa: lions and tigers, headhunters and witchdoctors. Now the soiled bag held a used cake of soap, a splayed toothbrush, a small flannel and my *Passion*.

I looked at Quale with a dull stare. Insolent, it would have been called in the army.

But he waved me into a seat. A deep leather armchair, flat wooden arms suitable for a glass.

'*Boy*,' Quale shouted. An elderly African scurried in through a narrow door at the back of the office. '*Latea whiskisoda kwa bwana wageni*,' Quale demanded. '*Sasa heevi*,' he added. Right now. I soon learned. Words of command were the first.

Boy returned immediately bearing a jingling tray. He wore a long white *khanzu*, armoured chocolate toes protruding from beneath the hem. An Egyptian fez and a matching red cummerbund distinguished the garment from a nightgown.

Nothing was said as boy attended to the filling of my tumbler. A lifetime of useful training, soda and ice brought up carefully to an exact if invisible line.

'So, let's begin at the beginning shall we, old man?' Quale started again, confused, out-of-his-depth. Afraid-he-might-look-a-damn-fool. Maybe I would turn out to be the illegitimate son of some minor royal. Maybe I had been cited as a co-respondent in a nasty political divorce.

I could have helped him. Something about having had responsibility at the FO, always pretty much worked on my own. Involved with Munich, then with Poland. Change of policy and my presence now a bit of a tribulation. Made it sound important. A lot of more important jobs than messenger could be described that way. And what was more important than peace?

I said nothing.

'Who are you? What *is* your name?'

Did I indeed have a name? Or maybe I had been travelling under an alias and now it was time to come clean.

I felt only anger. Rising up in me like poisonous sap. From my extruded bowels, up the crackling on my spine. I hated him, his kind, this sodding pretentious place. This middle class Botany Bay.

The Mathers and Hardcastles, the Bilsens and Quales. This Beecham who had ruined the world.

About my name and who I was. Quale was waiting.

Didn't even have a ticket. Little bastard 'e is, born right on the station platform ... yes, right on the platform at ... at ...

'Exeter,' I answered. 'Graham Exeter.'

2

Some time after six o'clock in the morning, Morley sat in the hospice kitchen, glazed over.

Sleep had come and gone as he had maintained his watch in the Lay-Z-Boy by the bed, but the nightmare lingered. He couldn't recall the scene in detail. Repulsive, undermining everything he thought he stood for. Peaceful, liberal, tolerant, Canadian. Not violence-prone, not American.

But seductive, the lure of some total dream solution.

A gun. A revolver like Graham had described, but without a lanyard around his neck. Smaller, more compact, not much kick. The beginnings and endings were a blur, but somewhere in the sequence Morley had felt vastly relieved, his veins flowing again with pure thick untroubled blood. He had fixed her, he had fixed them both, her stupid course, her half-truths and her double-speak, their Irish nonsense. She certainly wouldn't look good in Rech any more. Or ever hike Macgillycuddy's Reeks.

Then screaming, running. The Landcruiser was crossing Lion's Gate Bridge like the wind, swerving this way and that at oncoming cars. Apprehension, panic at being caught. Into the back of a police cruiser. No, officer. Me, officer? Why, I've been in bed all night, officer. Haven't I, dear? Ten fat policemen looking at him through the bars. A large native vomiting on the concrete floor behind.

But back at home he had Susan, his alibi, the truck parked three blocks away to cool down. Too drunk to drive, officer. Into bed, warm and secure against his snoring alibi. And in Canada these things weren't possible. There were laws, gun laws.

Now the start of another day of nameless dread, *whole and useful* gone into the void. Dread so strong again, a physical presence. A constant flow of debilitating acid through his veins and over his joints, interspersed with short bursts of the necessary activities. Then at night, when the necessary activities were over, he would start wondering again. Imagining and remembering.

So, Mrs Morley. And you're under oath remember. I'd like you to tell the court what it is about Mr Rathkin. Exactly what does he have over Mr Morley? Superior male equipment, for example? His prospects as a

367

sportswear salesman, maybe? Or is it Mr Rathkin's all-purpose-pseudo-psycho vocabulary?

But Morley knew that his divorce would be nothing like his daydreams. There would be no answers, not even the satisfaction of confronting her. Nothing except two or three years of expensive agony.

Tim Wilson was already charging him $400.00 per hour to play the game with Jane's lawyer. And every communication from the other side seemed to Morley to undermine further whatever chance there might have been of turning it all back.

Jane's evangelical fervour after her course at Quorum, about making the everyday things of life softer and better, *humanizing reality*, had become a series of hard-edged affidavits with his most intimate love letters attached.

Clause 22. In support of the Petitioner's claim for an interim maintenance Order pursuant to the *Family Relations Act*, in the sum of $15,000.00 per month, and for the immediate sale of the Respondent's house at 692 Beckley Drive, Vancouver, with equal division between the parties of the proceeds of sale, the Petitioner states that a binding financial obligation was indeed entered into by the Respondent in favour of the Petitioner, as evidenced by Exhibit 'A' hereto.

Exhibit 'A' to the Affidavit of the Petitioner Jane Catherine Morley

Jane Darling,

I am thinking of you and loving you a great deal this morning (5.15 a.m. Dallas time). You must be able to feel it on the airwaves between Texas and B.C.

I was very tired yesterday when I arrived, but what a worthwhile cause! You are the most wonderful sexy creature ever. When I think of our incredible dinner, and you saying you are mine and mine alone, for ever, it sends shivers up and down my spine at all times of the day, even in the 110 degree heat! Three times in one evening, not bad for 50!

Darling, don't ever worry about money. This office in Dallas is doing well and Vancouver is growing fast. I promised at our wedding to 'support you in your endeavors', and that I will do with all my heart and everything I have.

Must go, the guys from Bechtel will be waiting at 6.00 for our first site meeting. I will have this couriered, together with the fashion insert from the NY Times you wanted.

Love and more love
Jane's Morley.

The night before that trip to Dallas, almost a year before but like yesterday, Jane was to have collected Morley from the office for dinner. But instead there had been a limo driver at the reception desk with Mrs Morley's instructions, he said, to chauffeur Mr Morley to the Oceanic Hotel.

In the Pacific Bar overlooking the harbour Morley was poured a glass of his favourite Italian red and handed an envelope by the barman. The imprint of a pair of red lips glistened in the middle of a sheet of hotel stationery. Below Jane had written, *not before 7.30 – L.J.*

A magnetic door card fell out of the envelope.

Room 1001 was a suite. There was no Jane in the sitting room; Morley walked into the bedroom. Through the door he could feel Jane up behind him, the swish of her skirt, her perfume in the air. Before he could turn round she had his eyes covered with a silk scarf tied tight behind his head.

'Shhh,' she whispered in his ear, 'you're under arrest.'

Cool fingers removed Morley's clothes then he was led naked to an arm-chair. The blind came off with a flourish and Jane was walking away from him, trailing the scarf across the floor behind her.

She turned toward the window, pretending to be absorbed by the view of Lion's Gate Bridge caught by the setting sun. Jane was wearing an evening dress Morley hadn't seen before. Obviously Rech, plain black crêpe with a halter neck, back open to below the waist. She had prepared herself carefully as if for the runway at one of her fashion shows, her hair, her make-up.

Morley sat completely still. The cares of the practice evaporating as if he had swallowed some magic elixir. She was the most perfect woman he had ever known, at the height of her beauty right then maybe, on that very day. He walked over to her, turning her back from the window. Jane quickly put a finger up to his lips, holding him away.

'Did you know that there are three different restaurants here? We're going to have a bite in each. And I'm going to bring you back up and show you parts of our new summer collection between courses.' A mock serious face. 'Could last all night.'

Then there was the old man with his battered book of music, a connection back to the beginning of the century. As if to question which story was reality and which fantasy.

The daytime staff arrived. Making coffee before the start of their shift while Elaine was busy on her handover round. Graham still asleep, in the same position on his back, only his eyes had closed. On the medication board Morley had written his phone numbers for when his promisee awoke: office, mobile, restaurant and home.

The head day-nurse was at the opposite end of the care-giving scale from Elaine. Wide and officious, unwilling to stop her fussing around the office for two minutes to listen to what Morley had to say. A mere volunteer, she had a hospice to run.

The necessary activities pressed in on him. The presentation for Guangdong, Susan dead or alive. He reached for the kitchen phone and punched out Susan's number.

She answered on the first ring.

'Susan?'

'*Morley*. Don't you realize...'

'... I spent the night with my old friend, here at the hospice, I was phoning to apolo...'

'... you big bastard ... have you taken the keys to the Honda? You know that my office is going up to the Kelowna site today. In under an hour we're going to have missed the plane. And I have all their tickets.'

'Oh jeeze, I was with the old man. Forgot completely. Be right there, run you out to the airport.'

He rushed to find Elaine.

'This is Alyce...' Elaine began.

'... sorry but I really have to run, forgot about my appointments, my numbers are on Graham's board. Please don't wake him, he's been up all night.'

Alyce ignored him, Elaine blew him a kiss.

The street was a sudden roar after the insulated quiet of the hospice. Thick with impatient traffic pouring into the city from across Second Narrows bridge.

Morley saw the tow truck at the same moment as he remembered that metered parking was prohibited on Powell Street during rush-hour, 6.30 to 9.30 a.m. The tow truck was at the kerb facing into the flow with the Landcruiser hooked by the back wheels. A row of orange lights rippled above the cab as the driver waited for a break to make his U.

Morley ran.

'I'm real sorry,' he mouthed through the glass. 'I was at the hospice, forgot about the time.'

The driver rolled down his window. Loud fuzz and a booming bass reverberated out into the street, competing with the bark of diesels and the surf of speeding tyres. The driver was a large bearded man in a soiled T-shirt and oily overalls. Eating a dripping hamburger with one hand, holding a big slurpee with the other, eyeing the approaching traffic.

'It'll be at the pound on Second,' he snarled.

'No, no.' Morley held on to the cab door. 'I need it now, I'll pay the freight, whatever.'

'Didn't you hear me? The pound on Second.' Like a badly treated Rottweiler straining to break his chain and avenge himself on the entire world.

'I don't have the time, I need my truck. I'm late as it is.'

'And I don't give a flying fuck how late you are buddy, it'll be at the pound. Now step out of the way, I'm comin' across.'

There was a gap coming up in the traffic. The tow truck was about to pull away, but the last car before the break was moving slowly. Morley ran for the Landcruiser fumbling for keys in his jacket pocket. Before the tow truck could move Morley was behind his wheel with his foot hard on the brake. The tow truck jerked to a halt. Morley started his engine, crashing into four-wheel low and the clutch out with a bang.

The back wheels of the Landcruiser spun in the air while the front tyres squealed against asphalt. The tow truck rocked violently, front suspension jerking off the ground.

Then the driver was out of his cab banging on Morley's window. Morley locked his door. The driver mouthed every obscenity known to the breed. He kicked hard at the side of the Landcruiser then disappeared back into his cab.

Morley stopped pulling at the tow truck, engine idling. Then in his side mirror he could see the driver talking on his mobile.

Almost immediately a police cruiser wailed around the corner, separating traffic with blue and red ripples. Headlights flashing alternately side to side, as if a hostage taking, a rape and bank robbery were all taking place simulta-neously. The hospice was only a block from Main Street Police Station.

The police car pulled up with a shriek of rubber.

Morley was relieved. The police would sort the situation out, then he would buzz Susan to the airport and phone in his instructions to the office on the way back in. He could change later and he had missed his run. But only three hours remained until the meeting with the Chinese. Out along his limbs sleep privation and acidic anxiety edged against each other.

In contrast to the drama of his arrival, the policeman ambled from his cruiser. Past Morley to the tow truck, then back to the Landcruiser.

'Step out of the vehicle, please, sir.'

'I'm really late,' Morley began through the window. 'I'm a volunteer at that hospice, I was ...' nodding towards the door.

'Step out of the vehicle, please, sir.' The policeman stood back. A large man, bursting out of his blue shirt and black trousers, both front and back. His face a jaded frown, as if he had been on shift for two days straight and he'd seen it all.

Morley climbed down from the suspended Landcruiser, searching unsuccessfully through his pockets for a business card. But there was no interest in Morley's explanations, or in his card even if he could find one. And no effort was being made to lower the Landcruiser off the hook.

'Driver's licence,' the policeman drawled, holding out his hand.

'I don't have it on me.' Morley's briefcase with his cards and ID was back at the house. He had emptied his pockets, the criminal-proof criminal. 'But this is a simple parking matter, officer, I'm happy to settle whatever the fine is but I must get to work.'

The law remained unmoved. Bored thumbs were squeezed in behind a tight belt, spaced between nightstick and flashlight.

'First off I'm gonna give you a ticket for not producing your driver's licence,' the policeman said. 'So I'll need your name and date of birth.'

'I'll just get a cab. This is completely ridiculous.' Morley looked around as if a cab was to be found waiting conveniently down the street. But it wouldn't be easy in the East End at that time of day.

'In that case the vehicle will be impounded at Main Street Police Station until this is cleared up.' The policeman was obviously in no hurry and under no pressure to see things Morley's way. This could happily take up his whole weary morning.

Morley relented; it would clearly be worked through quicker by co-operating.

'Alrighty. Edward J. Morley. 5 July 1948.' The policeman strolled back to his cruiser, started talking into his radio. Morley waited by the Landcruiser. The tow truck driver sat in his cab finishing his hamburger and licking his fingers.

The policeman returned.

'Are you Edward James Morley, 692 Beckley Drive, Vancouver?'

'Well, yes,' surprised that dispatch had provided so much detail so quickly.

'Turn around,' the policeman said.

Morley obeyed instinctively. Before he realized what was happening, the policeman had Morley's wrists handcuffed behind him.

'There's a warrant out for your arrest. I'm going to take you now to sit in the police vehicle.'

The policeman held Morley's arm and started walking him over to the cruiser.

'Arrest? Arrest for what?' Morley asked, voice rising. 'You just don't understand, I've got to ...'

'They'll tell you all about it back at the shop,' the policeman answered, even more bored than before.

The door slammed. Morley started to shout his protests, but it was useless. The back seat of the cruiser was a metal cage, designed to withstand anything Morley could do. He could kick at the sides, he could scream, he could vomit, he could piss on the floor, it had all been done before.

Morley could hear the tow truck moving off. Through bars on the rear window he caught a glimpse of the Landcruiser fishtailing away backwards through traffic.

The policeman returned, the cruiser started to move.

Morley was familiar with Main Street Police Station and the Provincial Law Courts building in the adjacent block. An office team under a promising associate partner had recently designed and supervised alterations to both buildings, but Morley had not been involved. And he had certainly never evaluated the buildings from the perspective of a criminal under arrest.

Elaborate security procedures started as the cruiser pulled into the garage. Distant voices blared incoherent orders through speakers, closed circuit cameras covered every movement from every angle. The policeman in the cruiser was met by others who took Morley from the car and pushed him roughly into a large elevator operated by a key attached to the belt of one of his protection squad.

On an upper floor the handcuffs were unlocked. Morley's shoe laces were removed, he was body-searched and his jacket was scrutinized inside out by yet more policemen wearing surgical gloves. The sixth, seventh and eighth in the chain. Morley watched his belongings being put into a plastic bag then thrown onto a heap behind the counter. He was locked into a holding cage thick with the stench of urine and vomit, overwhelming a faint trace of disinfectant.

Time seemed to stand still and all connection with the outside world was at an abrupt end. No ID, not even a prison number. Without dignity or definition, he had become nothing and nobody.

Morley asked the same questions of each new face in front of him.

How long will this take? Why have I been brought here? When can I make my phone call?

Responses were snapped back each time.

No talking in the elevator.

Just stand over there, will yer, get to you later.

Can't you see we're busy here?

Policemen wandered back and forth outside his cage, slowly, like men under water. Trailing broken down prisoners in handcuffs, some white, mostly native. Or the captives hovered like shadows in the corridor while their escorts stood belly to belly drawling blue jokes and spinning hockey bravado. Completely comfortable in their harsh fluorescent claustrophobia of barred windows and frosted glass.

After what seemed an hour or more Morley was taken out of the cage and put in front of the counter again. A policeman was standing at a typewriter facing him.

'What's J stand for?' he snapped.

Morley started to ask his questions again. But the answer was another blank look, as immune as all the others. The policeman repeated his question.

When the form in the typewriter had been completed, Morley was walked down the hall and pushed toward a large metal door.

'When can I make my phone call?' he asked of the policeman holding his arms.

'Look you. What the hell do you think this is? Some kind of a coffee shop? We'll let *you* know when you can use the phone.' The policeman propelled Morley through the door and shot the bolts.

Metal bunkbeds three high lined a large room of boarded windows and artificial light. In the corner a tapless sink next to a seatless toilet, recently occupied by a heavy pockmarked native who was struggling with his jeans. Bodies were sleeping on the mattressless cots, curled up under worn leather coats and lumber jackets. Dirty sneakers without laces and battered cowboy boots stuck out below the heaps. Someone had recently vomited onto the floor. The stink competed for prominence with the recent contents of the native's bowel.

Morley was beside himself. Anxiety and fatigue now bursting along his arteries. Limitless anger, a clockwork unwinding violently, pushing him to break his bones against the metal door or plunge his head into the unflushed toilet.

He paced up and down breathing deeply. Loose shoes dragging the floor, palms wringing against each other damp and hot. The events taking place outside the prison could hardly be imagined. Susan waiting by the front door until it was too late for her to phone for a cab and make her flight, her entire office stranded. His design team mooning around, unsure which drawings were complete or how to assemble the packages. His partners approaching panic, phoning all over the city. The Chinese delegation in their cardboard suits preparing to leave their hotel. Graham opening his eyes to find that Morley had disappeared.

One of the bodies stirred then sat up.

'What the fuck time is it?'

Morley's watch had been taken at the counter, he showed a bare wrist. He shrugged, unable to speak. The man dragged himself off his bunk and over to the blocked windows. He stood on the sill, his eye to a crack.

'Coming up to nine.' The man loped back to his bunk. Morley had the impression that this was not his fellow prisoner's first incarceration. 'When the hell are those motherfuckers going to take us over for court?'

At that moment the bolts on the door were pulled back and another heavy-set policeman came into the cell holding a clipboard. One of the small army required to protect society from these few lost scarecrows. The policeman began calling out a list of names which did not include Morley.

'I have the right to make a phone call,' Morley began. 'I demand to use the phone.'

The policeman started as if Morley had slapped him. He raised the clipboard like a weapon with a menacing pace forward as if to retaliate for the imagined blow.

'Look buddy, time you just backed off. You've been watching too much American TV. We have twenty-four hours to get you to court. *Habscorpse*, that's the law. You've never heard of it, I bet.'

The prisoners whose names had been called herded themselves wearily toward the door stepping around the vomit. They were led away and the door was bolted again. Only one sleeper remained.

Morley had walked through a mirror and he had emerged into a secret totalitarian empire. An unseen world where all the conventions and pleasantries of normal Canadian life were unknown. Within an hour he had become just another face in a gulag of the lost dregs of society who formed the clientele for a group of psychopaths in uniform. Locked into the unbreakable cycle of a continuous nightmare.

'You sure the fuck won't get nowhere like that,' the remaining body mumbled, rubbing at a battle-scarred face. 'They send all the prickheads on the entire force in here as punishment, so they take it out on us. If you want a call, you'd better the hell kiss some ass.'

The door opened again, a different policeman started calling out more names, still not including Morley. With a deep breath Morley began again.

'Excuse me officer, would it be possible for me to make a phone call when it's convenient?'

'You been printed?' the policeman asked.

'Printed?'

'Fingerprints. Have to be printed first. What's your name anyway?'

'Morley.'

'I'll see.' Bolts were shot into place again.

Morley resumed pacing the floor. The door reopened almost immediately. A younger policeman entered, the first one Morley had seen who fitted his uniform.

'Morley for prints.' Morley stepped forward and was led across the hall into a small room reeking of chemicals like a blueprint shop.

'Been printed before?' the policeman asked.

'No.'

'Pretty simple. Take your jacket off.'

On a counter the policeman prepared a board of black ink. He worked Morley's fingers into the ink, then rotated each in turn onto squares printed on a form.

'Nice hands,' he said with professional interest. 'What work do you do?'

'I'm an architect.'

'Oh really.' The policeman looked at Morley in clear disbelief. If you're a god'amned architect what the fuck are you doing in here.

When the printing was complete, Morley was given a cleaning compound to wash his fingers, standing over an inkstained basin. He started again.

'Do you know why I was arrested?'

The policeman read from the form attached to the fingerprint sheet.

'Harassment of a Victim Jane and a Victim Donald,' he read. 'But charges aren't my job.'

While Morley was absorbing what he had heard, the policeman continued. 'See a lot of it in here. Women having their husbands arrested, pretty common these days. Quick way of getting their alimony jacked up. Judge'll believe anything if a woman says she's being victimized. Female judges especially.'

Morley was led out of the print room.

'Make your call.' The policeman pointed to a wall phone. Morley hesitated, then he dialled the hospice. Life or death, he reasoned, but he knew that he was only putting off the moment when he had to speak to his office. Alyce answered.

'Powell Hospice, hold please.'

After a wait the impatient voice was back. 'Yes, hello?'

'This is Morley, we met this morning. Could you tell me how Graham is?'

'You family?'

'No, I'm a volunteer.'

'Can't give out any information except to family.'

The policeman was standing behind Morley again.

'Make it quick, pal, I've got other things to do.'

'Look,' Morley said to Alyce, 'I'm visiting with Graham, I was there all night. How is he?' Still no answer. 'I had a run-in with a tow truck driver outside the building when I left, I'm at the police station. Could you call my lawyer for me? His name is Tim Wilson, Wilson and Shaw, in the book. My name is Morley, would you please ask him to come to the Main Street Police Station right away.'

'You in trouble with the law?' Alyce asked. 'Didn't you go through interview before they let you volunteer?'

'I probably only get one call and I wanted to know about Graham. Please talk to Tim for me. It's really urgent.'

Alyce started to protest at the same time as the policeman gestured impatiently for Morley to hang up. Then reaching over to do it for him.

After another hour or more Morley was transferred to the courthouse, handcuffed and padlocked into a bulletproof van for the two-minute ride. Then into a holding area, shuffled from cell to cell among prisoners sleeping on benches or sitting in defeated heaps on the floor. His stomach told him it was lunchtime.

Finally his name was called, the handcuffs were taken off and he was thrust through a door to find himself in the prisoner's dock of an elaborate courtroom. Out through the mirror again.

Morley looked around. Tim stood on the far side of the court, smart in his buttoned jacket. A female judge in black and red robes sat up on a raised dais.

'These cases are to be taken very seriously, Mr Wilson,' she was saying. 'There's far too much maltreatment of women in society these days for the court to make any exceptions. Either the accused signs an undertaking to the satisfaction of the two unfortunate victims in this case or he will be remanded in custody for psychological evaluation.'

Tim squeezed out his most deferential smile.

'My client will sign, your Honour.' He sat down. The judge turned to Morley.

'Do you agree?'

Before Morley could reply or ask to read what it was he was to sign, Tim was on his feet again.

'My client agrees, your Honour.' A sheriff tapped Morley on the shoulder and opened the door to the cells. Back into the looking-glass.

By early evening Morley was in Tim's Porsche, laces in his shoes and watch on his wrist. Tim pulled up outside his office, and consulted the dash clock.

'No problemo,' he said, 'the vivisectionist will still be in her office.'

Morley was silent in the elevator, trying to concentrate on the menu waiting for him at La Piazza, pushing away at black anger. *Away, away,* Jane's new mantra during their arguments, accompanied by a dismissive rowing motion with her arms.

To Tim it was all routine. He explained Morley's situation quite casually like the dissection of squash tactics over a beer.

'They've a no-brainer now that you've signed the undertaking not to contact Jane or go near. But otherwise you would have been in there for days, proof or no proof. So from today on, Jane can call the cops any time with your file number. All she has to say is that she saw you or that you called her and they'll come and take you right back to the cells. No questions asked, no evidence needed. A woman under threat and all that. You can't practise architecture with this hanging over you. And your dear wife's lawyer will tell Jane to keep on making the calls until you pay up.'

In the office Tim hit the speed dial on his speaker phone.

'I'm not supposed to do this, amigo, but you can listen in if you sit on that chair over there and you don't say a single word.' Tim pointed like a policeman. The phone started to ring. Jane's lawyer came on the line.

'Mary Cullen here.' Tim chatted for a moment about another case and made his cluttered desk the excuse for the speaker. So bad that he needed two hands free.

'So, about Morley versus Morley. Seems we're getting quite bitter.'

'Nothing bitter about my client, Tim, she just doesn't want to be bothered by your Mr Morley any more. Did you receive my last documents? You'll see that your client has resorted to criminal behaviour, in addition to penalizing my client financially.'

'The Crown has yet to prove anything, although Mrs Morley is already referred to as the victim I see.'

'Of course she's the victim. Does your client think he owns his wife? She saw him two nights ago outside her bedroom window. My client is petrified.'

The pitch was rising. 'You can stretch this out, of course, Tim, but it has to be in the best interests of your client to settle. Basically all we want is the clothes shop and clear title to the building it's in. As well as half the proceeds from the sale of the matrimonial home. Plus the fifteen thousand monthly, of course.'

'But my client paid a fortune for that building in order to keep Mrs Morley in business. And your Mrs Morley was on the rocks before they even met.'

'That's a gross insult, Tim. My client's shop has always done very well, it's only Mr Morley's weird and expensive tastes that have put the business at risk.'

The argument was on. Tim ready to justify his $400.00 at every break.

'And if I remember rightly the business no longer even belongs to Mrs Morley. She handed her shares over in return for the last round of loans from the architectural practice. I seem to recall that she agreed to repay my client before the ownership of the business reverted back to her. Never mind the building for the moment.'

'Did you draw up that agreement, Tim?' The shrill voice had achieved lift-off. 'I have the document in my file and I'm going to give you my opinion of your draftsmanship right here and now.'

A ripping sound came over the speaker as Jane's lawyer tore up the agreement into her phone.

'This isn't just another one of Mr Morley's business deals, Tim. This is marriage, commitment, meaningfulness, things you just can't put into *monetary* terms. We're entitled to a lot more, but Mrs Morley wants to take on a new partner and get going again with her life.'

'And if Mr Morley doesn't agree?'

'Then we'll be coming after the practice as well as the rest. My client deserves a large part of Mr Morley's ongoing income. Do you know, just for one example, that my client has been to China and Hong Kong five times with Mr Morley? Really put herself out, even went to Africa to support him. She's done as much as anyone in that firm to land their jobs abroad. And she had her own successful business to run at the same time. I call that true dedication. For which my client should be recognized and by a substantial and generous settlement of...'

The indignation screeched on. There was one of Jane's letters that Morley knew by heart.

Morley, darling,

This is for you to read on the plane.

Thank-you for my Hong Kong and China holiday. I enjoyed myself so much –
the day tours to the mountains and the harbour were wonderful. Missed only
you, but I know you had to work.

You've taken very good care of me in the past two years. You're a very clever
guy with great talent and excellent people smarts. You should remember that
when times are tough.

I'll care for you to the full extent of my love and my little Irish ability –
especially that lovely silky hard bit that I like so much. But you should take stock
of what you have accomplished recently. The new work on the Chinese
Mainland especially, quite apart from your latest elegant highrises back here. It's
not just Kingsley and his contacts, it's *your* design and organizational ability that
has won the work.

About our conversation on the plane (isn't First Class *marvelous*, never done
that before!!) I do hear you when you say … 'I'm your husband and I really do
care about you…' I know you and Kingsley are busy intelligent men, and I
should be really flattered that you take so much time out to look after my
business.

It keeps a relationship very romantic and special when the day-to-day things
can't break through. You set me a good example, my love.

Morley's very own Jane.

P.S. Cash flow still v. tight. Might need a bit more loot, darling. I'll go over the
figures with you when you're back from Dallas. LJ.

3

'So your lawyer's got you out of jail, I see.'

Alyce was standing behind the Lay-Z-Boy with Graham's lunch tray.
Morley made no reply, he didn't trust himself to speak to her without losing
his temper. Only Tim's friendship with Crown Counsel had prevented
Morley from spending the night in police cells. It had taken Alyce three
hours to make the call.

'And I thought you only came over in the evenings,' Alyce continued, as if
thoroughly suspicious now of everything to do with Morley.

'I don't need the lunch.' Morley didn't turn. 'I brought Graham some restaurant soup. It's on the stove. I'll feed him in a moment.'

When Alyce left, Morley opened his briefcase.

'And I brought you the wine you asked for,' he said, putting Graham's glasses on for him and holding the label up to his face. 'Hope it mixes with painkillers.'

'What *are* you doing here in the middle of the day, Morley?' Graham asked.

'I'm supposed to be at the Dallas office today but I'm taking the day off. I'll go tomorrow.'

'And what did Alyce mean about jail?'

'Oh, a little quarrel with a cop yesterday. All my own fault.'

Morley went for the tureen he had brought from La Piazza. Three-dimensional minestrone under a thick mat of grilled *parmigiano*. He started to feed the old man spoon by spoon. The dark soup went down with silent approval.

Graham's hands felt warmer on Morley's wrist.

'The arrogant ones,' Graham began in a whisper, 'they're the really dangerous people. The men who know it all. I saw it with Henderson, the ambassador in Berlin. Came crashing down in the end.'

He lay back against the pillows while Morley fitted a new tape into the dictaphone and set the machine running.

'It was all backwards, Morley, neither side meant it. The mistakes and the lies, right back to Versailles. Then it couldn't be stopped. We had ignited the evil that floats over the world.'

~

Back from falling nightmare white.

Down narrow stairs, five flights. Held between the two bulls. Wrapped in the cover from Tricia's bed then my jacket over my shoulders. To make me look sick, to hide the leaking blood, as if I was being helped by considerate friends. Faces at each landing looking up, my screams must have pierced every room. Tricia before me. Then one glance at the suits and silver badges, the haircuts, the set jaws and the faces were gone, doors closed. They had seen nothing and they had heard nothing.

Standing next to my angel, as if observing from above. Into the car, bulls in front, me pushed through the rear door and on to the floor. The Captain sitting back and smoking, watching the city go by.

Only a short ride and the doors were opened again.

More steps, stone, shallow like a bank. Falling face down on to my elbows, caught in the ends of the bedcover. I heard car doors slam, the engine revving and they were gone.

Another jumble. English voices, I was at the Embassy on Wilhelmstraße. Looking up at summer sky, at faces. Then at Imperial chandeliers, plaster ceilings, carried past shrouded furniture and between piled boxes, through more rooms and into Henderson's study. On to the settee and other faces above me, Lady Henderson.

When the bedcover came off and they saw what they saw, I was moved to the floor face down. Dust, floor wax. Ohs and ahs and ohmygods.

'*Tricia, Tricia, Sie haben sie mitgenommen,*' sinking again, rising, back to be with my angel.

'Must be a Kraut.' From near my head.

I heard Henderson's voice as he pushed through. Down close to me fumbling with my jacket.

'Isn't that a greyhound behind his lapel?' Then, 'By God, it's the KM. This robbery? Where's Percival? Did anyone see the car? Where's his bag?' Commotion in the crowded room and I do not remember the rest.

People in and out, on to a bed face down again, soft hands on my back. Turned over, strong arms holding me this time, water. Splashed, dribbled, some into my mouth. A man. I whisper to him. It's not just my back.

Then Henderson's face again and it must be later. Saying nothing, holding a large photograph. Me and Tricia.

'They sent these. This you?' Roughly now.

Lady Henderson in the background.

'Give the man a chance, Nevile, he's been out for two days. And it might be one of their tricks, you know.'

'That's him all right,' ignoring her. Then to me again. 'How dare you. Creating incidents. Disturbing good relations, after all the time and trouble I've ... What nonsense have you been up to? Eh? Disgusting little man.'

Then later again, after more ins and outs, more white light, ups and downs with the angel, as I tumbled and cascaded, Henderson said,

'Your bag was delivered at the same time as the photographs. Lock broken. Empty. What was in it? What have we lost? And what's *this*, for heaven's sake?' Holding up my *Passion*.

I tried so hard to warn him: the day that Beethoven needed me, our Secret Germany, face to face with Chamberlain under perfect elms, just going through the motions. The River Vistula, right from the gates of Zossen.

But he understood nothing.

'The man's delirious.' Henderson impatient, back over to the door. 'And he's not to leave the room. Going back on the boat. They'll be wanting to talk to him in London.'

But in the car it was different. After his last interview with Hitler.

Day three. Out of Berlin in convoy.

I lay on the back seat of the Embassy Rolls, clutching my *Passion*, covered with a blanket. Her Ladyship had insisted. Still thought it was one of their tricks, she said. Henderson on the occasional seat like an equerry.

Stopping by the side of the road, a laxative, I tried to say, I need a laxative. Squatting among the heather flowers, full summer still, held up by porters, unreachable inside agony and wishing to die again and again. Tearing off strips from the *Deutsche Allgemeine Zeitung*. Reading the words over and over as liquid squeezes out, as falling white comes and goes.

Then through my pain and my slow tears, a curled foetus bouncing on the leather seat, I heard Henderson sob. He would be in all the history books, the Ambassador to Berlin at the start of the war. Blamed for generations.

Then later he started to ramble.

Munich was right, those rotten little Czechs had it coming with their stinking treatment of the Sudeten Germans. And the Poles, my God, this time last year almost, they weren't even a country at all. What the hell right did they have to Danzig in the first place?

It had started with his operation. The PM used to listen to him before his time away.

He understood H and he understood the PM, both of them. Then all those negative staff reports while he was in hospital and that damned idiotic Polish guarantee. And the Cabinet was in direct touch, that was a lot of the problem. Someone had been delivering letters from London straight to Ministers of the Reich. Even to the Chancellor himself. Couldn't possibly do his job properly with all that going on behind his back.

We don't *mean* to fight, the Germans don't *plan* to fight, the Italians *can't* fight, the French will *never* fight. Could have found the answer, give a bit, take a bit, save H's face for him ... I knew him, I knew him. Nothing wrong with him. Man of great internal tensions, simply had to bear that in mind when dealing with him.

Mile after mile of it across Lüneburg Heath.

Had H convinced. Got him to pull the troops back from the Polish border, rattled he was and only six days ago. Even told me, after Poland he'd guarantee the British Empire.

All we needed was an envoy from Warsaw. Make H an offer, the one he was waiting for. Didn't want war, didn't, *didn't*. Only that snake Ribbentrop and the real extremists were pushing. He understood, he understood it all only too clearly.

But what can you do when your own people are swimming in the other direction? Wasn't his fault. Wasn't, *wasn't*.

That warmonger Churchill and his damned Focus, telling the Poles not to give an inch. Just a way of undermining the government for his own purposes. Couldn't those stubborn Poles see even that much? Personal ambition. Good two fisted drinker, all that bloody man really is.

Then north toward Bremerhaven, nightfall. Roadblocks inspecting papers.

'*Sie können weiter fahren. Heil Hitler!*'

And the Americans investing in Germany left and right? Cars, electricity, coal, all their big companies are over here. Who would believe our threat of war with all *that* going on? And huge debts still owed, right back from the 1920s.

If only he'd been left alone to deal with H. by himself. Göring had invited them all for hunting in October. October. *October*. Personal invitation. And Nürnburg before that. There wasn't the slightest *intention* of going to war in September, not the slightest.

Could have done it, could have done it.

'You know that's not so, Neville.' Lady Henderson sitting upright on the other folding seat. Not a move, not a hand toward him. 'Your job was to convince the little man that we meant business this time and you couldn't do it. He called you the Umbrella Men, the Worms of Munich. He was never going to believe that we'd stand up to him whatever you said or did. Now look at the lovely mess.'

Neville was finished, so was she. Thank God he'd already got his K. Hardly even worth a look-in at King Charles Street. Cancer was spreading into his jaw, operation hadn't worked. Curtains. And *her* name would be in all the history books as well.

The Ambassador sobbing into his hands. Her Ladyship's fine horse profile unmoved, reflected in dark glass. The heath speeding by.

The boat reached Harwich during the early hours of the morning. I was to be taken ashore by stretcher but none could be found. I struggled down the gangway between two porters. At King Charles Street my keepers were back and the sanatorium was my prison.

A nurse was brought over from St Thomas's. Dark blue stripes and a Florence Nightingale headdress. I asked her what was going on, even what day we were.

'I'm not to talk,' she said, looking at the watch pinned upside down on her sloping chest and feeling my pulse. 'So there.'

The next day was a Sunday, I could hear bells ringing, the Abbey, Westminster Cathedral.

Must be day five.

After the nurse had changed the dressings for a second time my keepers cleaned me up. A macintosh smelling of the country over fresh pyjamas, socks instead of shoes. Then they held me by the arms, one each side like a murderer to the scaffold. We made for the Grand Staircase. Past Virtue and Honesty, past Bilsen's office, along to the end of the ringing corridor.

Sir Robert Vansittart was polite but I could see two large shiny photographs on his desk. I had let him down, the world had let him down. The event that he had been predicting was taking place.

Sir Robert was quiet and superb like some of the senior officers at Montreuil. Tall, a pale benevolent buzzard, he could have been General von Witzleben's twin.

He started without introduction.

'I have no sympathy for you,' holding up a large bony hand to stop any explanation. 'But I have admitted to some involvement in this matter so you have been given a choice. Either face charges under the Act or you resign quietly and there will be a transfer. Either way you are no longer with the Service.'

I tried to ask.

Where was Mr Harris? He knew where I was and why I had gone. I wanted him beside me. Well now, here's-a-fine-how'd'yer-do.

Charged with what? who would defend me? I had held what Mr Chamberlain had asked for right between my hands. Showing two useless empty palms. I could remember the words, the map, I could put it back together from memory. Despite what had happened, what hadn't, I could still remember, for ever, for ever...

Vansittart cut me off.

'Look out the window, Beauchamp.' He called in a keeper. I was helped around his desk to face the raised sash overlooking St James's Park.

Through the trees I could see the Mall crowded with coats and hats. Going-to-church clothes. Everywhere below, on Horse Guards Road, down Birdcage Walk, people were converging on the Palace. Drawn irresistibly as if by some celestial beam. Quietly, no cheering, not like 1914 had been, even in St Ives.

Reasons, Whys and Wherefores had immediately been forgotten. No trial, no revelations from a messenger would change their minds. The Sovereign, Britain in time of need would receive the unconditional support of her people.

The next generation was of age. A man who had survived the Great War, who had married in '20 or '21, his son would be seventeen, eighteen. A man who had been killed and left a son, that son would be twenty-two, twenty-three.

'Our ultimatum expires at eleven,' Vansittart said. He took out his pocket watch. 'In ten minutes' time we'll be at war with Germany. Then what chance would you have? As the first spy.'

He was next to me, hands together behind his back. But I saw him through a shadowy lace.

I stood trembling, I was defeated, beaten.

Silence until we heard Big Ben strike the hour.

The Sausage Machine had started again.

'We all make our mistakes, Beauchamp.' Vansittart was still facing the window. 'And you're not the first man to come under the spell of a woman. But don't go making another one. They'll find you a place in the colonies. Just disappear.'

My chance had come and gone. Events had taken control.

~

A long silence in the shadowed room. Muted light through blinds.

'That's how I came to be Quale's ninny,' Graham said quietly. 'Cannon fodder, a specimen again. It was no less than I deserved.'

4

We drove out of Nairobi towards Thika, then the road turned north up to Mount Kenya.

We passed through European coffee plantations after the veldt country had become foothills. Then through *shambas*, tribal smallholdings of the Kikuyu Land Reserve, every inch of steep ground cultivated, even the edges of the road along narrow red banks. Land to work for someone who had none.

Progress was slow. We were off the end of the macadam and on to dirt soon after we left Nairobi. Grinding up monotonous inclines toward the highlands, I began to take stock of the Bedford, her crew and our journey.

During the first few weeks after the declaration of war, near panic had taken over the city. African askaris were everywhere, guarding government buildings, manning barriers at crossroads. Ready day and night to beat off an army of valiant Italians from Abyssinia who could attack Nairobi only after first crossing hundreds of miles of desert undetected.

In their panic the colonial administration had abandoned two government bomas on the border: Mandera in the east close to Italian Somaliland and Moyale on the northern border with Italian Abyssinia.

District Commissioners and District Officers, their police, their Asian clerks and African staff had been hurriedly withdrawn. But as even the messenger knew, Italy was not going to go to war over Danzig. She had no tanks, no artillery, her best troops were still in Spain. And once at war all her ships would be bottled up in the Mediterranean, exposed to the Royal Navy. Musso would not jump until he saw which way the wind was blowing.

But the ridiculous nervy conditions had suited me well and it was Quale who had been frustrated.

'IGS have signals to London swamped,' he had threatened, 'or I'd be finding out a lot more about you.' Looking up from his desk and shaking his finger, the mock friendship gone now. Grim, resentful that I would not tell him myself. The answer was dirt, he was sure.

Then Quale had found his use for me and he no longer cared to know.

Transport, like everything else in Nairobi, was being requisitioned and hoarded. No government vehicle was available to take me to my new post. Even the KAR, the King's African Rifles had used all their vehicles in the first weeks of the war, mobilizing for a revolt by German farmers in Tanganyika that never came, or transporting supplies to Wajir in preparation for an attack that the Italians would never make.

After a week's wait in a shabby Nairobi hotel I had been assigned the Bedford. A short wheelbase tipper. Meant for nothing more than fetching gravel and repairing roads around the city.

In addition to Njeroge, my driver, there were unexplained passengers who appeared the following day. A group of Africans in torn clothes standing in the box, leaning forward over the cab, peering toward our distant destination.

Watu, they were called, *people*, *bodies*, but they did not seem to mind.

On the first evening we reached Nyeri. I spent the night at the Outspan, a settlers' hotel now turned into a fortified camp, sandbagged gates thick with more armed askaris.

Inside the hotel more colonial life. Africans behind the bar in *khanzus* and

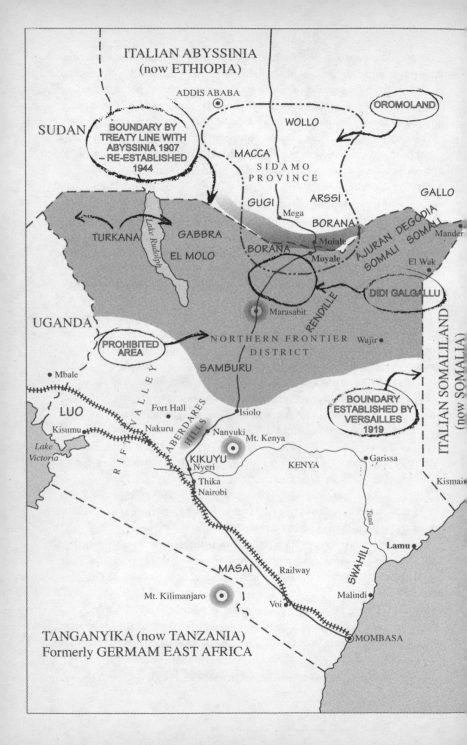

Arab waistcoats serving whiskys and soda to a range of European officers in uniform: KAR, Kenya Police, even the RAF in a khaki shorts version of their blue. More servants lit log fires against an evening chill. Nyeri was at almost 6,500 feet, cold at night during the rains. Another small army prepared the rooms and served dinner.

The talk among the Europeans was inevitably of war, the Italians, theories on an invasion.

'We had the Ice Cream Merchants last time, only fair the Huns get 'em this.' Banter, uninformed and meaningless. No concept of war, of destruction, of incalculable damage, the empty mistaken reasons. In this bar and around the world I imagined the momentum of war building, starting to lead a life of its own again. A monster already, quickly beyond the control of its breeders. I longed for morning, for Njeroge and the tipper, to be away, lost in the desert.

At dawn the most amazing sight in all of Africa, the snows of Mount Kenya from the lawn of the hotel. Unimaginable, shining for a brief hour before rain clouds obscured the peak. Delicate but supreme against an unending sky, set on a shallow purple base as wide as the horizon itself.

We climbed again out of Nyeri and through Nanyuki. On to a magnificent high savannah rolling from the forests on the slopes of Mount Kenya on our right, down and away further south, miles and miles. Then on the far side, up again to the tree line of the Aberdare Hills. Patched with small woods, quilted by squares of sunshine playing on to golden fields, alternating with dusty beams of rain from silver clouds. Sharpening colours, transfiguring paradise.

Settlers' homesteads were visible in the distance, a metal windmill, a stand of decorative trees surrounding a corrugated iron roof. A secret utopia, a hidden valley, a private treasure chest of virgin soil.

Driveways and farm tracks led out of sight. I read names painted on a plough disc or on wooden boards nailed to fence posts: McGregor, Black, Trevellyan, Davies. The land of the colonist's dreams.

Assured of their mission, their important white lives. Summoned by open spaces: Scots in Australia, middle Europeans in Canada, the English in Kenya. The harrows in their deadly romances slicing rich humus like bacon. Prosperity and contentment unlocked, falling into our Aryan hands. By a grant from the Crown at five pounds per acre.

By an Allocation from the Rasse und Siedlungshauptamt.

A farm in the east for every SS family.

August in Zossen to collect the second letter. For Chamberlain: delivered under swaying elms and slipped unopened into the pocket of his gaberdine. An age ago, it seemed. Before the *Hauptsturmführer*, before the bathroom door.

Halder's pince-nez lying on the table between us, part of his face like false teeth, changing his look with them off. Weaker, more vulnerable. Rubbing at red impresses, eyes closed, head down.

The Army had done its job, securing town halls, railway stations and telephone exchanges. There had been some formality, some saluting. Honour had been saved, Halder thought, as the installations were handed over. And the Czechs hadn't put up any unpleasant resistance, hadn't cost Halder any lives.

But behind, the next day, had Halder known what had followed? The Berlin Embassy knew, the Prague Embassy staff had told them on their way back through. Even the messenger had heard.

SS Einsatzkommando, long black coats against the March cold, down over high boots. Silver *Totenköpfe* glinting from collars. Squads from Section III/225 working from a long card index, Lugers out, ready in a gloved hand. The mayor, the priest, the schoolteacher, the intellectual, the ideological enemy, the Jew, the resister: behind Halder's army there had been no saluting and no honour. Just heaps in the mud against farmyard walls.

The Protectorate of Bohemia and Moravia had been created in one short day from the rump of Czechoslovakia that had survived Munich. Her armament factories incorporated into Göring's war economy, her valuable German blood formed into keen young regiments. Her farms occupied by the new settlers.

The dirt road was lined with gum trees, small pale leaves glinting in the wind against blue trunks of ever-peeling bark. Here there was a smell to the air: dust, the brine scent of grasses on Mount Kenya carried down on the breeze, like Exmoor, like Scotland, but stronger. Arousing, suffused with unfulfilled primitive longings.

Halder had described meeting Himmler on his way to the front.

'Front? What front? We broke our word. After all the promises, all the deluded cheering at Munich. We just snatched the rest of Czechoslovakia. They were to sign or we would flatten Prague with the Luftwaffe, kill all their women and children. Our brave Luftwaffe. There was no front.'

Himmler's big Horch, Gläser model, 5 litres, I could see it over there, now. There, speeding by that line of blue gums.

Wide like a Mercedes 770, but Halder had been explicit, Horch, the SD car of choice. Hood back, passengers protected by a glass division. Good Germans all, enjoying the fresh air, high peaked caps visible over the large leather hood pouch. Chromium spokes twinkling in early spring sunlight, chromium windscreen and hood arms glowering against dark grey bodywork. The gangster car, Halder called it.

Suddenly the big car comes to a rapid halt and Himmler is out in his long grey coat. Tasselled sword held steady by his side, striding, running almost across a ploughed field. Another *Hauptsturmführer*, Himmler's adjutant, in imitation dress and sword follows nervously, looking back at the car, unsure why the *Reichsführer SS* is dirtying his polished boots.

'The sword. Ha! The SS as an Order of Teutonic Knights?' Halder was openly contemptuous. 'Himmler used to sell fertilizer. And Ribbentrop? He used to sell champagne.'

Then Himmler is crouching over a furrow, glove off, sword behind him, the hem of his coat trailing. He picks up a handful of dark earth, he walks back toward the Horch kneading the dirt in his fingers, out in front of his face like sign language for money.

'The rich soil,' Himmler says to the passengers in the Horch as he stumbles back, his little dimpled face transported. 'This is where our Teuton blood belongs.'

Halder had started to shout. Hadn't anyone told your Mr Chamberlain? Even British Intelligence. Did they really think that informing your Prime Minister was *my* job?

And now Poland? Can't your government see for themselves what is about to happen? You say that Hitler mistreats a few German Jews. Wait until your Mr Chamberlain lets him into Poland, where there are millions.

Then despairing, defences down. Dagger eyes bulging, trickling his defeat on to parchment cheeks. *Housecleaning*, he whispered. *There is nothing that I can do.* The last words that Halder had spoken to me. The words he had written in his diary. The words that I did not understand.

Kenya. Our own blood. McGregor, Black, Trevellyan, Davies. Our own Lebensraum, the Kikuyu as our own *Untermenschen*, a number on a *kipande* hanging round every black neck.

The beauty of the scene, the ugliness of the world: bringing back those salty blood-warm tears that I thought were all used up. Quietly shaking in my corner of the cab.

Conversation was difficult against the continuous blast of the engine. The dirt road racing under us, sandy brown through a rust hole in the floor-boards. Tyres rumbling on the loose surface like ripping canvas. By mid-morning the road surface had dried and a long plume of dust clouded up behind us, drifting off slowly across fields as we passed.

Then the first words of Swahili between me and Njeroge, one word at a time, shouted, thought about and maybe understood. *Ghari. Sirikali. Bwana Dee-oh. Siku kunajoto sana.*

From the secret plateau we descended north into another world: untouched Africa in all her prehistoric beauty. The land left for the Africans, unwanted desert free of our imperial dreams. The sun like a close fire now, burning into my arm on the window.

We arrived at the barrier at Isiolo in the afternoon. I was given a smart salute by an African corporal just for being European, then escorted to a tent behind sandbag fortifications. An officer sat at a trestle table. Captain Browning, 2nd Battalion KAR, was short with me, the sightseer. There was a war on.

The Captain was very smart, as if he had come straight off the parade ground at the depot. Starched uniform, khaki tunic and shorts. Slouch hat Australian style strapped under his chin, decorated with the KAR flash and a black ostrich plume.

The King's African Rifles were the regular troops of East Africa: European officers, volunteers from British regiments. African NCOs and ORs recruited from the smaller tribes with warrior traditions, turned into military fanaticism by the British Army.

A polished rocking horse shone on the Captain's shoulder. *Nec Aspera Terrent.* Hardships Do Not Terrify.

Someone leaned down and wiped off a badge. The rocking-horse glinted faintly through the dark. Face blackened, helmet still strapped on. But the body short, too short, oh, so horribly short. Charred, shocking like a burned toy.

'The West Yorkshires,' I said to the Captain as I held out my hand civilian style. 'Exeter, Graham Exeter,' almost used to my new name, 'DO Moyale.'

The Captain's manner changed, a smile came over his tanned face behind a thin boyish moustache. He stood up and took my hand. The African sergeant behind the Captain's chair and the corporal who had escorted me in maintained their rigid positions, chests out, shoulders back, eyes to the front, expressionless black faces.

'I was seconded to your 11th Battalion in 1917,' I said without thinking. Then wondering how far this would travel, whether this bit would lead to more bits. 'Near Ypres then at Cambrai.'

'Good Lord,' the Captain replied, looking straight at me now, 'the battle honours for Cambrai are on the wall right where I sit in the Mess, back at Imphal Barracks in York. But I've never met anyone who was actually there.'

Captain Browning looked about twenty-five years old, certainly under thirty. Tall and well built, confident in an untested way. Cambrai was twenty-three years ago the next month, November.

And with this introduction, a few words, a long ago battle, Browning became my ally, my plank in a storm.

'Not much honour,' I said. 'Forty-four thousand lives for a gain of five hundred yards. Lost more artillery than we took.'

'That's not the story we got. First successful use of tanks, straight across the strongest German lines.' He smiled at me again. 'Things haven't changed much then.'

We walked outside to look at the Bedford and her crew.

'Did you say Moyale?' Browning laughed. 'You'd better spend the night, you'll need a couple of full days in that rattle trap, just to Marsabit.'

The KAR looked after the Captain in style.

His company HQ had been established at Isiolo only a few days before, when Browning had taken over the southern boundary of the NFD. But already he had a well-equipped mess tent, a covered latrine, shower, bar, barman in whites, all set up on the banks of the Isiolo river. The other officers of his company were out on patrol.

With my *watu* settled in the African lines, we sat on camp chairs drinking gin and watching the flood waters of the rainy season. A milk chocolate torrent splashing over grey boulders. Little birds filled the trees like leaves, grey monkeys played at working their way up to the tent until chased off each time by a steward flapping his napkin.

'Just one wireless message and they were gone,' Browning started. 'The entire Moyale boma, like a troupe of gypsies flitting in the night. The sahibs running away in their *gharris*.'

Made him ashamed. Us, the British, turning tail before war had even been declared. Granted there were more of them, but what sort of troops were the Italians anyway? It had taken them a whole year to defeat the Emperor of Abyssinia and his horsemen. The Germans had made mincemeat of the Poles in just eight days. And what about the British tribes up there with no protection. Tribes we had colonized, who took us for the Great White Bwanas.

'So how did you become the ninny?' Browning asked. 'Sent up to Moyale to show the flag again.'

By then I had a cleaned-up story: used to be in government back at home, enrolled by Quale as a District Officer because someone was needed in the north to relieve a younger man for active service. Been sick but regaining my strength, taking my quinine regularly now.

I showed Browning my letter, produced in less than a day after my first interview.

Quale had found his ninny.

ON HIS MAJESTY'S SERVICE

Office of the Chief Secretary
Kenya Colony
Room 299
Government Buildings
Nairobi   18th October 1939

To: Graham Exeter
Ref: MO/5/39

This will confirm your appointment as Acting District Officer (Cadet) posted to Moyale District with Third Class powers under Special Ordinance, effective this date.

A. M. Quale
Deputy Assistant Secretary

Sworn in the next day, part of the system now by authority of God and the King.

Then I was given an empty office and six bound volumes to read, the political reports for Moyale District going back to 1902.

The reports were a history of Kenya Colony told by a succession of DOs and DCs. Men dedicated to Empire, free of doubt about their calling.

After the turn of the century the railway line from Mombasa had pushed inland toward Uganda. Then Kenya Colony was expanded north to take in Mount Kenya and the Kikuyu tribes, the desert beyond and more tribes, Samburu, El Molo, Turkana. And in the far north we had come to the Oromo people, peaceful nomads migrating with the rains over the hills of Sidoma and back on to the plains below.

The British move north had been resisted by the feudal Abyssinians and in 1907 a border was agreed by treaty, between the two Empires. The larger Oromo tribes were split along the new frontier: the Galla, the Borana, their clans and families, their traditional routes not even considered.

But the two Empires were not the same. The Abyssinian side became a refuge for *shifta*, Somali bandits of all kinds. They raided into Kenya for cattle and slaves which they shared with the ruling Amharas of Abyssinia in return for protection. A frontier war continued for years, a number of DOs had been killed and countless natives, but slowly order had been established by the KAR.

Then it was Musso's turn, strutting and pouting on his balcony in Rome, not wanting to be left out, dreaming of his *Impero Reale d'Africa Orientale.*

He finds an excuse for war with Abyssinia, he sends tanks, his Alpini, gas left over from 1918 and soft nosed bullets. But it takes him an embarrassing year to defeat the Amharic cavalry and reach Addis Ababa. A vicious skirmishing war still goes on.

The Italians burn villages so in return the Amharas castrate their Alpini prisoners in public. The Italians recruit native troops on the coast, their *banda*, the worst types they can find, the Freikorps of Africa. They fight fire with fire. In retaliation the Amharas supply the *shifta* with arms. A four sided war starts.

Finally by the late 'thirties the border has stabilized again. British rule brings some benefits: a dressing station, locust control, roads, water allocations, courts and Indian traders. The Italians appoint a *Residente* in Italian Moiale opposite the British DO. There is peace. The reports start to count heads, both cattle and human. Taxes are collected.

Then Danzig, war, panic and our unnecessary flight.

'So you can see what a mess it is up there,' Browning said. 'Us running away has let all the genies loose again. The Amharas are still fighting the Italians, the *banda* and the *shifta* are competing to see who can be the dirtiest brigands. Armed deserters from both sides roving around. If we go to war with the Eye-ties that'll make five sides fighting. With our tribes and their herds exposed to the lot of them.'

But with war in Europe at a stalemate and Italy still not in, Nairobi had become ashamed of their panic. Someone should be sent back up there, at least make a show of government, something to put in their reports. And if that someone just disappeared? Well, it wouldn't be the first DO they'd lost in the Northern Frontier District.

'The right man at the right time.' Browning laughed and slapped me on the shoulder.

The steward returned with his tray and poured us both another drink. Gin and orange squash.

5

Soon after daybreak the barrier was raised to another smart salute from the corporal, arm snatched back to the side like a Guardsman.

The Northern Frontier District is a magnificent place. Away to the far distance flat in all directions, until little tufts of cloud meet the horizon in a perfect purple and silver line. The earth rising and the sky falling in exactly equal proportions. Perpendicular mountains like faraway ships on an ocean. Then further on, outcroppings of monstrous rocks, lunar shapes against the sky. Memories of cathedrals and castles across other plains. Laon. Les Baux.

The road changed from white to red, then to sharp loose rock, reducing speed to twenty miles per hour. Our treads were no match for the road surface, well worn before we left Nairobi. The nightly camp-site was determined by where we had the second or third puncture of the day.

The dust-choked *watu* would climb down and set up on hard earth between thorn bushes. I had scrounged what equipment I could in Nairobi with Quale's requisition: a tent, two camp chairs, a folding table and bowl. Eating utensils and a valise, Gibbon's *Decline and Fall* found in a missionary shop. A Webley revolver and 200 rounds from the KAR. My new European's outfit: khaki shorts and shirt.

A meal was prepared, ground maize, lentils and gravy. I ate as they had planned in my separate camp. But when I had finished my food I tried to squat like them, over by their fire, feet flat on the ground, hunched down with my backside suspended off the earth out of the way of columns of ants. Digging into their common *posho* pot, my presence embarrassing them, restraining their talk. I was a European, expected to behave to a code understood by both sides. A common meeting ground was not a part of the arrangement.

Swahili words kept coming, joining together now. A simple language with no irregular verbs in the 'up-country' European version. Just a series of imperatives and nouns. The way English can be used for talking to animals: *bad dog, supper ready, heel.*

I relished every mile, every hour. The cord spinning out thinner and thinner until surely it must break.

Fires were kept going all night. Not for fear of *simba*, lion, nor *chui*, leopard, but of *fisi*, hyenas, menacing and unstoppable in packs.

Another African world took over from the sterile heat of the day. A frescoed ceiling in gold and silver, close, touchable, the Milky Way as a shining wall of light. Stars as I had never seen before.

And sounds, blurring into a background din of unseen life. Crickets, cicadas, locusts chaffing in higher registers, frogs below. Pierced by the shrill call of a hyrax, the laughing of hyenas. And from close by, a huffing and stamping, as if buffalo were about to nose into my tent. Bats' wings flapping by against the rustle of night wind through the bush. Then a muffled word from the watchmen and a whoosh as more logs went on to the fire.

In the morning the commotion disappeared as if it had never been. Bird calls for a new day starting up before dawn.

In the centre of the NFD a series of extinct volcanoes form a high plateau of green grass and dense forest. An island massif in a surrounding desert sea. Misted during the rains, trees hanging with beards of moss, dripping like Compiègne in November. A place where at least some rain falls every season, where a herd can be sustained. A retreat for big game in the harshest years.

Njeroge drove into the Marsabit government boma, stone buildings with thatched roofs in a fenced compound, metal sheds for vehicles and African lines behind. All to a colonial order: swept roads, pathways edged with whitewashed stones, imported plants and stencilled signs.

The boma was crowded with the African staff from Moyale. Some like Njeroge were Kikuyu, considering themselves to be among the primitives, as unable to communicate as me.

The Bedford was immediately surrounded, men, women with their naked children looking for news or fresh supplies, the chance of a ride south. We began to unload pressed by the mob of black flesh, to the curses of the *watu* on the lorry.

Then more curses, understandable English curses from the back of the crowd. A European appeared. Quickly the throng parted to let him through. He pulled roughly at two old women in skin wraps who came between us. Then the man was standing in front of me with an outstretched hand.

'Saunders,' he said, 'DO Moyale. Or former, I should say.' A vacant toothy grin and an asinine laugh.

The DC's house was overflowing like the compound. Suitcases, boxes and *kikapus* everywhere, papers and files strewn around the living room.

'There's four of us here,' Saunders explained as he poured me a gin from a tray. 'But the DC is in Nairobi, Inspector Roberts has gone on safari to Wajir and Browning I haven't seen in a week.'

'Browning is at Isiolo, seems pretty settled to me. You should take him his belongings when you go on down.'

'But I thought the KAR was coming up here. God knows where those bloody *banda* are by now.'

'Browning's going to send a platoon to Moyale,' I told him, 'as soon as he can. To meet me.' Saunders was taken aback.

'You mean to say, old chap, that you're thinking of going on, up to Moyale? My orders were to wait here, not even try to go back.'

Saunders began to describe the dangers, his justification. *Banda*, *shifta*, Mohammedan fanatics. Exaggerated for my benefit, I was sure, when I had hoped for some insight.

'How much of the local language do you speak?' I asked him. 'Maybe you could help me with a few words.' Saunders had been in Moyale for five months, in Kenya for two years.

'I mean to say,' he protested, 'what's the ruddy point of learning Boran? If they can't speak Swahili, it's damn well not my fault.'

The next morning I made my arrangements. I would continue to Moyale with Njeroge. Then Njeroge would leave me in Moyale and drive back down to Marsabit for Saunders.

'This is all tommy rot, old man,' Saunders maintained right up to the moment the Bedford pulled out of the compound. 'You'll be back. The place can't possibly be held. You'll need a fully company of askaris at least.' Both hands clutching the lorry door as if to hold us back.

North of Marsabit the plains become complete desert. Strewn with volcanic boulders, black rocks lying dense on the surface like seed scattered by a giant sower. Stone shoulders thrown up here and there, split then packed together, octaves of huge piano keys.

The road ran straight out to a dancing horizon. One puncture, two. After the third we prepared for our first night in the Didi Galgallu. No firewood, no hot food, no protection from *fisi*. My tent could not be erected, pegs refusing against enamel ground.

Behind, Marsabit brooded under dark evening cloud. In the far distance ahead, the purple shadows of the hills of Abyssinia. To east and west endlessly breaking surf: a chimera of camels, a line of men, then I thought I saw Antibes, the ocean.

On the fourth day from Marsabit the Bedford whined off the desert and up a long steep hill toward Moyale. We were an easy target and I had no idea what to expect. Through the rear window of the cab I could see the *watu*, no longer peering over the roof, sitting down behind the protection of the metal box.

The Webley bounced on my lap, safety catch off, hammer forward.

British Moyale stood at the top of a ridge. Beyond, the land sloped down again to a river bed, the border between Kenya Colony and Italian Abyssinia. The town was a cluster of square mud huts and a few *dukas* fronting on to a single sandy street. Italian Moiale on the other side of the river was a more substantial town, clustered around two large stucco buildings fitted with awnings and shutters like the villas of Sorrento in high summer.

Our town was deserted. Stray chickens pecked around unconcerned, a goat trailing a frayed cord bleated into the silence. Houses had been burned down, their charred contents blocking the street. *Dukas* had been forced open: broken bottles and split sacks of posho strewn across the sand. Boxes and furniture had been axed into fragments and papers had blown everywhere. Inside, shelves were bare, counters ransacked, the floors littered.

The government boma was up a slope behind a cactus hedge. The sentry box had been pushed over, a symbol of toppled authority. The gate was unlocked and swung open.

In the centre of the boma square stood a mature pepper tree, dense and shady, weeping down to the ground. Calm and dignified, an import planted at the beginning of the century by the first Europeans. But all around the tree was devastation. The boma buildings had been destroyed. The DC's house was a blackened box, only the stone walls remaining. Metal vehicle sheds had been pulled down and the African lines torched. Next to the pepper tree, furniture had been piled into a bonfire which had now burned out. In the middle of the fire was the post safe, taken to red hot and back in an unsuccessful attempt to force the door.

In the radio hut the transmitter had been attacked with axes and hammers, the metal casings beaten out of recognition, tubes, wires and fixtures crunching under my feet. The wreckage was covered with little piles of human faeces crawling with flies and larvae. The stink reached out into the boma.

Animals had been slaughtered, stripped of meat and left to putrefy in the sun. Even the unripe fruit growing in the *shamba* had been slashed.

Four hours of light remained. I made Njeroge understand. He should unload the stores under the pepper tree, then he and the *watu* could leave. Off the slopes and out to safety before dark.

With the work complete and my tent erected, Njeroge stood in front of me. Engine running his escape route clear.

'*Kwaheri bwana,*' he said with a sad smile. I held my hand out as I would to a European. He took my hand in his, but with a quick upward flick his palm enclosed my thumb. In automatic response my fist came around Njeroge's thumb and we each held thumbs in turn up in the air between us. Just a brief moment, something that would only pass between Africans. Then he was gone.

I sat under the pepper tree. Flies were thick from the rot all around. Lizards with sharp blue bodies and orange heads were already on my stores. Motionless, as if fixed by the fading sun. Overhead, I had not noticed before, vultures turned slowly against a creamy sky.

I lit a fire and faced my possessions in the twilight. My service revolver and two .303 rifles. Supplies of all kinds: ammunition, flour, dried beans, quinine against malaria, gin against boredom, my *Decline*, my *Passion*.

I had reached Moyale, the far end of Empire, separated from the world by a desert. Sandy streets and desolation, my chance to be away from them all, to re-build.

Back before I was a driver and a messenger, I had been an officer responsible for men. I had been taught how to lead. SMELS: Situation, Mission, Execution ... a tag to help you recover yourself and your men. But I could get no further than S Situation. Staying alive obscured all the rest.

After dark I carried my camp bed over to the prostrate vehicle shed. At one end there was enough room to recess myself like a crab into a shell. Revolver in my hand, a .303 beside me on the dirt floor, right by my hand. A round in the chamber, safety catch off.

I dozed and woke then dozed again. Beyond the night chorus of crickets and frogs there was singing in the distance from the Italian side, dogs barking. Later a lone cock was crowing. The compound fell completely still.

Suddenly I was fully awake, grappling between nightmare and reality, struggling to remember where I was and what dreadful danger had my heart pounding. One hand a vice on the revolver, the other flailing over the floor by the bed searching for the comfort of the rifle.

Beyond the pepper tree the tent was moving in the moonlight, bulging as if two or three men were rummaging inside. Instantly, without thinking about my flank, about crossfire or enemy positions, I was off the bed and on my feet. Racing across to my camp, revolver out at arm's length, cocking the hammer as I ran.

At twenty yards I fired into the wall of the swaying tent. In my anger at the looters, murderers, disrupters of the peace. Then moving up cautiously until I could pull at the tent with a hard jerk, jumping away simultaneously, ready to fire again.

The canvas ripped open and a head appeared, startling, large, tongue out like a butcher's window, eyes fixed like marbles. I had shot a calf. Through the head, through the neck, through the ribs and hindquarters. The animal was stone dead and there was gore everywhere. My cooking equipment, my tilly lamp and dishes had all broken or bent under the weight of the falling carcass. The smell of paraffin mixed with dung and fresh blood.

I dressed and patrolled silently, like No-Man's-Land. But my shots had brought no responding movement.

Dawn broke as I returned to the compound, the branches of the pepper tree thick with little yellow birds, twittering and busily exchanging places.

Thin grey light illuminated the ruination. I blew on the fire, adding window frames and shattered doors. Then I sat sipping tea and eating tack biscuits, the survivor of the first night.

I started again with S, Situation. My longing to be away. The rail of the boat under my hands, ready to sink into dark blue spume, disappear from my cabin without a trace. My disdain for Saunders, for them all, that had taken me on recklessly past Marsabit without orders or armed support.

Flies crawled over the calf's snout. A line of ants was carrying away shards of bully beef spilled in the dust the night before. Africa the pitiless, the unstoppable.

Then as I began to contemplate M, Mission, I could hear voices, the clink and stamp of men. A group of soldiers was coming toward me up from the boma gate, but not in any military formation, more like a football team sauntering on to a field. Africans, but tall and light skinned. Extraordinary uniforms, long wrinkled tunics, trousers tight like riding breeches down to bare feet, pith helmets shaped like pork pie hats. Carrying ancient rifles, long-barrel Mausers from the days of the Austro-Hungarian Empire, held any way they pleased.

I stood still in my ruin as the troop approached, holding out my tea mug like a sentry without a rifle. Behind, a short stout European was endeavouring to keep up, a large layered topi in one hand, the other mopping his bald pate with a red kerchief. He wore the official white suit of a colonial officer, fastened up to the neck. Gold tasselled epaulets, matching gold buttons. Around his waist a green sash drew attention to his stomach. A pair of dusty white canvas shoes completed the ludicrous apparition.

The soldiers shambled to a halt. The European pushed his way through. He walked toward me, putting his topi back on to his head and the kerchief up his sleeve.

Close up his bright little face showed a quick nervous smile, shaded now from the piercing light of the sun. He gave me a mock salute, a comic opera gesture with two fingers to the topi. The gaggle behind took no interest. Some had already started smoking, picking their teeth and spitting *miraa* fibres.

By then I knew what *miraa* was. Njeroge had put a green bundle on to the seat between us after Isiolo, after he had my measure. He had chewed all day, green leaves and red stems like new shoots from a hedge. I lacked the patience, a whole morning to build up any effect.

'*Monsieur le Day Cay?*' the apparition inquired. '*Est-ce que j'ai l'honneur?*'

It was a moment of high farce: wrinkled brow, trimmed and oiled moustache like the caricature of an Italian barber, black and pointed, twitching in expectation of my affirmative answer. Eyebrows working up and down like a pair of wings. Me in my dirty shorts and bare torso, the ruins of Empire all around. The dead calf by my feet wrapped in my torn tent.

'*Je suis le Day Oh, en fonction temporaire,*' I replied with a slight bow. '*Et je vous souhaite la bienvenue à mon bureau administratif.*' The troubled little face broke into a big grin then he laughed, we both laughed. The apparition held out a hand of real flesh and blood. 'Exeter.' I said. '*Graham Exeter, à votre service.*'

'*Cavaliere Giovanni Marconi,*' he began, '*Primo Capitano di Terzo Reggimento degli Alpini di Como, Residente di Moiale, Impero Reale Italiano d'Africa Orientale.*'

Then Marconi turned toward his men with a quick gesture, hand out, palm up, like a museum guide hardly needing to identify a famous masterpiece.

'And these,' he said, continuing in French, 'are my *banda.*' The group had a hostile, brigandish look, already bored by this lack of rapacious action, this absence of throats to slit.

'You have KAR with you?' Marconi inquired. One eyebrow high up his wrinkled forehead.

'No, I brought some men up, Kikuyu civilians, but they didn't want to stay. The KAR will be here in a few days.'

'You are alone?'

I shrugged, it went with the French.

'You English,' topi off again, kerchief out, shaking his head as he mopped. 'Incomprehensible. First you leave for no reason, now one man. Just one man.' Rolling his eyes upward as if appealing to the heavens for British Reinforcements.

'This place is dangerous. *Pericoloso,*' he said, louder, as if I had not understood his French.

We moved to my camp chairs under the pepper tree and the *Capitano* started to tell me of his troubles, my troubles, our troubles. While the *banda* lounged on the ground like a pack of menacing guard dogs. Mausers on the ground in a dusty heap. Close to their master, docile for now.

Marconi had attempted, he said, to explain to Signor Tatton-Brown, the previous DC, that while Italy was Germany's ally, Italy was a long way from declaring war. Italy was not even mobilized, her army was not equipped. Marconi knew about such things. He had been in the army before being a *Residente*. And *il Duce* himself, Marconi had heard on the wireless, had made every effort during August. Even prepared to cut short his summer holidays in order to have the Polish question settled by another conference.

'Sensibly,' Marconi added emphatically, 'between civilized people.' Leaning forward in his chair, expecting that I would share his point of view. Just like Munich.

And he had promised, he, Marconi, not Roma, not *il Impero*, but he personally had given his word. If there was to be an invasion of Kenya by Italian forces, the British would be given ample warning. Arrangements would be made. Civilized, he said again. Between two Empires.

But still the British had left. And now look at the result. Signor Tatton-Brown, did he not trust Marconi's word? A hand over his heart and a stricken look of physical pain.

And the day of the evacuation the Ajuran and the Borji, Somali riff-raff Marconi called them, had begun to loot the town and the boma. Everything the British had abandoned had been taken or destroyed. The Indian traders who had not left with the column had kept the crowds away from their *dukas* with shotguns. Two or three looters had been shot dead.

Hearing the shots the *Capitano* had come over to our side with his *banda*, thinking that the British were under siege by *shifta*. Signor Tatton-Brown had not even had the courtesy to say goodbye.

Marconi had been horrified by what he had found. The DC's house was burning. Against the flames, the shadows of looters darted from one building to the next. Marconi had made arrests and the *banda* were turned loose. Marconi himself had broken the butt of his rifle swinging at Borji. It was hard to imagine, but Marconi demonstrated his very motions to me with great vigour.

Then the next morning Marconi sent a European lieutenant and another force of *banda* over to help in removing the contents of the Indian *dukas*. Lalji Mangalji, the most substantial of the local traders was still locked into his shop. When Marconi's officer arrived he was firing panicky volleys out through the windows. Lalji had been persuaded to come out only after a long discussion through the bars. He and the other two merchants were then moved safely to the *Residente's* boma on the Italian side during the second night.

The following day the town was sacked again.

'I sent my *banda* over once more,' Marconi protested with another gesture of topi and kerchief, signifying that by then it was all beyond his control. 'But I cannot always spare an officer,' Marconi said with mock innocence. 'And without an officer, my *banda* can be ... *violenti*,' he added softly.

We did well under the pepper tree, me and the *Capitano*. Civilized and sensible, as Marconi liked to say. Settling everything he raised without any interference from Roma or London. Customs agreements, the problem of deserters, of tribes sharing wells, things I did not understand but to all of which I readily agreed.

He would let me have the prisoners arrested on the British side as my labour and he would lock them up again for me at night. He would lend me a *banda* guard and send over a carpenter to supervise the rebuilding of the DC's house.

'*Tutto bene*,' Marconi said, slapping his knees to show that the interview was over. 'Now my men will take the calf. And I will expect you for lunch at one o'clock.' Marconi's best proposal yet.

Within an hour two *banda* returned herding a group of downcast Africans in prison smocks and ragged shorts. My prisoners: fourteen men with two shovels between them. I chose a man at the back with sharp intelligent features and an earnest expression.

'*Wewe mijikenda.*' I tried in pidgin Swahili, meaning to appoint the man as foreman. His face brightened, I had communicated.

We walked around the compound. With signs I managed to explain where to start: burying animal carcasses, clearing debris and faeces from the radio hut, pulling dead pigs out of the wells.

Marconi's residence was a veritable *palazzo*. Unmistakable Italian style, even in local materials. High ceilings and tall windows, a curved end to the building which gave the dining room a panoramic view of the town.

The meal was the same. I sat down at Marconi's table, revolver and .303 on the polished wood floor beside me. A white tablecloth, shining silverware, Ampolla plates, Cristallo di Murano, delicate fragile stems which had somehow survived the journey. And wine, thick and strong from Lago di Garda, brought standing in a bucket of cool water. There was soup, there was salad with onions followed by *trenette*. Then the marauder in the tent as *scaloppina di vitello con contorno*, as if by magic.

I managed very little conversation as I ate and drank. Marconi smiling benevolently at me from the other end of the long table, his face obscured in lined shadow against the louvres. While his servants strode silently in and out: tall Somalis made more impressive still by stacked wiry curls, white jackets, long trousers, white gloves. And most amazing of all, white canvas shoes.

Finally there was grappa. Hay, grapes and the harvest of Chianti. Elixir from a bottle opened at the far end of the earth.

Marconi lit a cheroot.

'So good of the British to send up a French speaker.' Marconi blew a thin stream of smoke through pursed lips. 'You must have lived in France.'

'I have been in France many times for the British Government.'

'*La France*,' Marconi began slowly, '*ah, la France*. My family is from France. From Nice, before Garibaldi gave it away.'

There was a pause. I had nothing left for politics or for history.

I began to pick up my weapons and thank the *Capitano* for the fine meal, but Marconi was up before me and out through the dining room door, returning with a large map pasted on to a board. Galla-Sidamo Province of Italian Abyssinia and down to the northern part of the NFD in Kenya Colony.

'Wait a moment. Please sit down, *monsieur*,' he said, setting the board on to a chair and preparing to point with a silver knife. 'I must show you where your tribes have gone. We must approach our problems sensibly, together.'

The large airy room, the remains of a meal. Crumbs, wine stains, from across another table, as if listening to another voice, far far distant. Genoa, from the past when there was a future.

Africa through the louvres, across the valley to my new career. M for Mission, a fresh chance that I did not deserve. I sat down.

The *Capitano* poured me another grappa, beyond my power to resist. He showed me my District, names and details, more coherent than anything I had read in the DC's reports.

Marconi held opinions on every local subject: Somalis, his *bêtes noires*, with a little chuckle, people who do not understand certain words, honesty, trust; the ridiculous head taxes levied on nomads, either we can afford an *Impero*, or we cannot; his *banda*, I say kill and they kill, but tomorrow they could be killing for someone else; the Borana, the best tribe of all, I would soon come to appreciate *Nagaiya Borana*, the Peace of the Borana. They are their own government, they do not need us. All we have done is split them in two.

Marconi had three years' experience, a significant achievement. British

Moyale was considered a hardship post with four DCs during the last three years.

'I have some information,' Marconi said, businesslike now. 'Your Borana were attacked by Ajuran Somali. No serious losses that I have heard. But the Borana have left the slopes around Moyale where they should be at this time of the year after the rains.'

Marconi paused while I located the tribes on the map.

'The trouble in your town was caused by Somalis. The Borji, the Ajuran and *surtout* by the Degodia.' Marconi had prisoners as proof. He also had the names of others and he knew the villages they were from.

'But the Borana,' he said, 'the Borana are the tribe you must deal with. If you have them on your side you will be able to bring order back to your District.'

Finally Marconi showed me through his enormous residence.

'I take you for *un uomo d'onore*, Signor Exeter,' Marconi said earnestly when I was ready to leave. 'I know I can talk to you in confidence.' Marconi paused as if to see whether I would object to my new status. 'Monsieur Tatton-Brown, and his young assistant, Monsieur...'

'Saunders.'

'... *oui, oui*. Monsieur Saunders, they treated the Borana very badly, even the name they have wrong, Boran. And the language, there is no Borana language, they are Oromo speakers. From Saunders there was slapping and kicking. You cannot understand what a terrible thing that is for a Borana, Monsieur Exeter, terrible. They want to be a British tribe, your Borana, they even know the name of your king. Show them one thing, that you are a man they can trust. Just one thing and you will have their *rispetto* for ever.'

I left Marconi in his *palazzo* and walked back across the border. My new headman was keen to show me what little had been accomplished. Reconstruction was going to take a considerable time.

The two *banda* guards had become four, spread across my camp picking their teeth. They made no move as I approached. I felt threatened and uneasy, no longer sure about who had sacked what. One of the *banda* pointed languidly over to the town. The traders had emerged from their hideouts on the Italian side.

Lalji was a little rabbit of a man with nervous bulging eyes, neatly combed black hair and a coffee coloured skin. An Ismaili, a follower of the Aga Khan, he told me. A born trader, but it was difficult to understand how he had found the courage to start a *duka* in Moyale.

'The go'ment is mad, sahib, mad I am telling you, mad,' Lalji said as soon as he too realized that I had no KAR with me. 'I am paying go'ment taxes for five years,' he protested, 'and what am I getting? What am I getting from go'ment, sahib?'

The *banda* and the prisoners in the boma had given Lalji a bad scare.

'It is those robbers, sahib,' he started again, not differentiating between the *banda* and their prisoners, 'those robbers who are stealing our *dukas*. And now you, sahib, you are to be bringing them back. They will be slitting our t'roats, sahib. And I will be dying,' Lalji ended unhappily, his singsong voice trailing off, sure of his imminent demise.

I tried to assure Lalji that I, Exeter, was camped in the boma. That I, the representative of the British Government, had established relations with the Italian Government. That I was guarding his property, me, personally, with my Webley and my Lee Enfield .303. But the mournful look was unrelieved. He had no confidence left in any go'ment or in me its humble servant. He would still be taking his sleeps with the Italians.

But Lalji spoke Swahili and Somali and the next day I was able to re-establish the sway of Empire.

I arranged my camp table under the pepper tree, I put on my good felt hat from the Nairobi outfitters and tried to look as much the colonial official as the surroundings made possible. The prisoners assembled and I sat Lalji in the other chair as Official Court Translator.

I asked each man in turn for his tribe and his name. The first man, fidgety and nervous, answered in a mumble, looking down at the ground.

'He is an Ajuran Somali, sahib,' Lalji translated, giving me the man's name and where he belonged.

'Ask him if he will accept my judgement as DO today, or as an alternative he has the right to a full trial in Isiolo when transport is available.' A long discussion ensued between Lalji and the prisoner, Lalji's voice rising and his arms waving, enjoying his exercise of the reflected power of the British Empire.

'The prisoner need only answer yes or no.'

'This Somali man, sahib, he is wanting to be knowing, sahib,' Lalji said, affecting boredom for the benefit of the prisoner, 'he is asking, what is his sentence?' Lalji had probably been bargaining with the man.

'Yes or no to the question,' I repeated slowly and solemnly, looking straight at the prisoner.

'*Ndyo, Bwana*,' the man mumbled in reply.

'I am charging you,' I began again, trying to remember the legal language more to impress Lalji than the prisoner, 'with taking part in the sack of

Moyale, on the evidence of the Government of Italian Abyssinia. How do you plead? Guilty or not guilty?'

For a moment there was a misunderstanding between the Bench and the Official Translator. 'Sack sahib? What is it this man has been putting in sack, sahib?'

The prisoner was guilty. He admitted it sullenly.

'My judgement,' I intoned again, 'is that you return forthwith to your tribe, that you seal with a thumb a Bond under the Special District Ordinance to keep the peace and that you are not to be found within the town of Moyale for the next two years.'

The men came up one at a time. All were guilty. Men from the tribes Marconi had listed. And following Marconi's advice I sent the Somalis home and retained the Gabbra and the Borana in my work party. But as of that day they would work at government labour rates to be paid when full administration resumed. In the meantime they could eat from my stores.

'And me, sahib?' Lalji inquired when we were finished. 'Go'ment will be paying me? Have you been seeing, sahib, the sacks in my *duka*?'

The last man up was my headman. He was Borana. His name was Dambala Sama. But he said that he was known as Girreh meaning black, pronounced with a soft rolling *rrrr* from the front of the mouth. Girreh because his skin was very dark, an impenetrable midnight black.

'Ask him,' I said to Lalji, 'why he is not with his people.' A discussion, then Lalji turned back to me.

'Sahib, this man, you know, sahib,' with another disdainful flick in Girreh's direction, 'this man is not speaking Swahili very at all. But he is saying, sahib, that the *shifta* stole his family's cattles. And he is coming to the town for working.' Lalji flicked his wrist again. 'But I am not believing, sahib.' Turning away in his chair with a sour look.

'Ask him if he knows where the Borana are.'

More discussion followed.

'This man is saying sahib, at that mountain's bottom, sahib,' Lalji translated, bored now that the exercise of power was over.

The court rose and poured itself a gin and orange squash. The slow task of reconstruction began again. Drudgery under a blinding sun.

6

Slowly life returned: to the boma, to the town. To me.

My labour force increased to over thirty men, volunteers appearing from the bush looking for government wages. Girreh had become the complete foreman, striding around in mis-matched wellington boots issuing orders, goading them all along.

I lived in my torn and scrubbed tent on dwindling supplies. I promoted a labourer to cook/houseboy and I slept under a mosquito net donated by Marconi.

Within two weeks the lines had been rebuilt and the *watu* and their families moved in. A community developed, structured by tribe, by function, date of indenture, I was not sure.

On the day the KAR arrived and the unwelcome cord of dominion was reattached, I was sitting with Lalji and the Gentlemen on his Commission, the other traders in the town, Mohammed Noor and Savan Patel. This was not the first time that the Commission had met, nor was it the first time that the Commission had adjourned without making progress. And at each meeting the list of Reparations grew longer and the sums higher.

'I'm going to give you new names,' I said to the three serious dark faces. 'Clemenceau, Foch and Poincaré.' Mohammed Noor wanted security, absolute and guaranteed, for him and for the hut used as a mosque. Now and for ever, by order of the King of England.

Savan Patel wanted territory behind his *duka* to establish a secure boma of his own. And Lalji wanted money.

'I'm not knowing those p'rtic'lar sahibs, sahib...' Lalji looked at me sadly, his voice trailing off, sure it was a trick to reduce his claim.

Sheets and sheets of invoices in a laboured hand were presented at each meeting. A second set in pink made through magnetic carbon paper. Some were legitimate: nails and paint for repairs, destroyed inventory, the cost of storage and transport to the Italian side. But spread through the list were entries which, I tried to explain, would undermine the entire claim when eventually the matter was considered by Nairobi.

44.	I, Lalji am suffering	Shs 2,000/-
45.	Mohammed Noor, he is suffering	Shs 1,750/-
46.	Savan Patel, he is suffering and hitting head	Shs 1,500/-

Back at the boma I found the gate fastened by wire.

'Girreh,' I yelled, rattling the gate. A little power had gone straight to his soot-black head, he had appointed himself camp commandant.

In response to my shout a fully armed askari popped out of the sentry box and took up the on-guard position, fixed bayonet, full battle order.

'*Simama*,' the soldier shouted at me, '*Halta*.' Then before I could answer he barked again. '*Passa-ward, semma passa-ward*.'

The askari's saucer eyes rolled. Big features, large flat nose and huge mouth. At the same moment a European officer and two more askaris appeared over the rise leading up to the pepper tree.

A young man, a second lieutenant. A scornful look from under the brim of his slouch hat.

'I'm Exeter, the DO, this is my boma.'

The Lieutenant eyed me: my filthy clothes, beard fully grown, rifle and revolver. He consulted a notebook from his tunic pocket.

'No,' he said smugly, 'there's no DO up here.'

'My letter of appointment is in my office.' We stared at each other for a moment then the Lieutenant nodded toward the gate and the askari let me in.

In the middle of the boma more askaris with fixed bayonets stood guard over part of my labour. Twelve or fourteen men squatting on their haunches, crowded together, hands on their heads.

'These wogs, are all under close arrest,' the Lieutenant announced. 'Caught looting the government post.' I strode over to my office in the restored radio hut. Back at the pepper tree I pushed Quale's letter under the lieutenant's nose.

I could see Girreh's upturned face among the squatters and I beckoned him over.

'The askaris didn't know,' I explained to him. Girreh pointed to the bush behind the lines. The soldiers had surprised them from the far end of the boma.

'*Kazi ingene*.' They could go back to work. Girreh turned to the men and they all stood up. Neither the Lieutenant nor the askaris made a move.

But we would be living in the boma together, Lieutenant Warner and me, for the foreseeable future. He was Browning's promised support.

It was shortly after noon.

'Would you care for a drink?' making a considerable effort. 'Gin and orange squash. All there is.'

Under the pepper tree Warner began to talk as if to cover his embarrassment. And I could feel the war again, almost forgotten for a few weeks.

Behind him, Warner said, the KAR was being rapidly expanded. Soon there would be over twenty thousand Africans in the ranks. Strategy was being taken very seriously indeed, he explained intently, with the SSG, the Senior Strategy Group, meeting every single day.

Beyond, India was mobilizing and a Gurkha Mountain Battery was already disembarking in Mombasa. The Gold Coast and Nigeria were sending troops. The South Africans and Rhodesians were at sea as we spoke.

Warner's platoon sergeant marched up and came to an elaborate parade ground halt with a matching salute.

'Prim-tah sucuah, sah,' he shouted, staring straight forward, out over our heads. 'Ready t'advance trans'pt, sah.'

'Carry on, Sergeant Ogaye,' Warner replied, so languid that he must have practised daily in his shaving mirror.

'Silly clot,' he said to me, affecting officerly ennui, 'they could have had the lorries up here an hour ago, had their grub by now. I'm not holding him up.'

'Lorries? But you came into the boma from the bush to the west.'

'Oh, yes,' Warner replied, 'but that was part of our tactical advance. One section moves, one covers. Military strategy. There's no actual war on yet, but we don't want to get flanked, do we? Been doing that all the way from Marsabit. Bringing up the transport at night. Taken us about four weeks.'

They could have driven up in two or three days now that the roads were dry again. I was almost out of gin.

That night with Warner's wireless crackling through to Isiolo we sat in front of his tent spooning mulligatawny soup, attended by a steward in whites.

'I'll introduce you to the traders tomorrow,' I said. 'Then I'm going to leave the town with you and go looking for our tribes.'

'Wouldn't do that if I were you. Damned dangerous out there. We could send out patrols, bring their headmen in.'

'I'm told the Borana don't have headmen.'

'Damned waste of effort, if you ask me.'

When my tour of the town with Warner was over, I had Lalji explain to Girreh about our safari. Lalji was of the same opinion as Warner.

'Sahib, before you are going, you must be signing our bills on those matters we already are agreeing, sahib, because, you know, sahib...'

After another breakfast from the new stores, spam fritters and biscuits, I set off with my section of five porters. The *watu* had my supplies and equipment balanced on their heads in boxes and bundles. My camp chair and tent, a spare rifle, ammunition, rice, gin and orange squash. I walked at the head of the line. It was a scene from the silent pictures: *The Adventures of Doctor Livingstone.*

With the end of the rains the rivers had stopped running. Brown ponds between rocks were the last moisture from a disappointing season. Heat had started to build under a cloudless sky: eight months to the next chance of rain.

Along a river bed we came to a tall full tree, a naturally round shape with large fleshy leaves like a laurel, but bigger, translucent.

'*Od-a*,' Girreh said. Under the tree a shallow hole had been dug, which had filled with water. Girreh pointed to the tree again then at the water and back to the tree. I understood: beneath the *oda* tree water was to be found. But the surrounding ground was bare, no trace of the Borana nor of their herds.

For four days we marched south. Game was plentiful and we ate well: warthog, ringed waterbuck, kudu. The men were expert skinners. Then we passed through thinner bush until we were out on the lava field. Girreh shook his head.

'Didi Galgallu,' he said respectfully. Lalji had translated the name for me as Desert of the Night. We turned east.

In the afternoon of the second day there had been blood on the back of my shirt. I had fallen down a small rock face in the river bed, tearing the brittle crust in the centre of my wound. On the march Girreh touched my shirt and looked at his fingertips. Blood, thick and dark against his black skin.

I could not dress the wound myself and infection would put me back in Nairobi. Caught up in the war effort, moved from here to there like labelled baggage. I had no choice but to show them. I stopped the march and took off my shirt.

I sat on the stores with my back to them. I felt Girreh's finger trace over the highest cuts up near my neck then down the sides around the raw open centre, smarting now in direct sun. Girreh let out his breath.

'*Heee-ya*,' quietly to himself. '*Kidona.*' Then a long question in Oromo I did not understand.

'*Shifta*,' I said, '*shifta ya inchi yango.*' *Shifta* from where I live.

Girreh put the joint of a finger between his teeth and a soft clicking came from the back of his mouth. As if he would have taken some of the pain himself if he had known how.

I showed Girreh how to apply disinfectant and powder from the first aid box. Then I stood while Girreh wrapped a bandage around my ribs and diagonally across my chest.

We moved on, continuing the search. But from then on, between me and Girreh, there was a shift in our relations. A barrier had come down.

On the sixth day out of the boma we crossed tracks and droppings. Even I could tell that the Borana were not far away. Within hours we caught up with the back of a herd through a fog of dust and the heavy sweet smell of animal. Flies like blowing snow.

Borana cattle are their own breed. Short tough-looking creatures with a large bony hump like a bell where neck and body join. Stocky, well proportioned, a deep chest and large head. All of a single solid colour: a dirty white, shades of brown and jet black. Adapted along with the tribe to desert life in the years since the Borana had been moved from the hills of Abyssinia to the great desert plains of northern Kenya.

Borana cattle walk with a particular gait. Stumping along determined, sceptical of humans. Their eyes would widen at a herdsman wielding a light stick. But not in fright, I never saw a Borana animal maltreated. More a bovine resentment that the business of walking, finding food, of survival, was to be made harder still by some futile human demand.

Biblical sheep and goats completed the herd, jostling together, indistinguishable at first glance.

Unlike animals in their fields in France or in England, Borana herds were always on the move. Constantly searching for food with heads down, investigating every tuft of vegetation, mature sheep and goats reaching high into the bush on hind legs.

Borana warriors wore simple leather breeches tied with a beaded belt under dirty white wraps. Many kept their hair long, arranged in knotted rows. They carried long and short spears in a cluster and wore swords in simple scabbards.

The men were like Girreh, black and fine featured. Quite different from the large open Luo faces of the KAR, or the unreadable tight Chinese faces of the Somalis.

A *manyatta* was being erected, the men responsible for constructing an animal boma of thorn trees piled into a dense prickly fence. Women were assembling *warra*. First two primitive beds were placed at the chosen location. Then long supple sticks were fitted into holes dug in a circle around the beds and bent over to form a lattice dome. Donkeys stood patiently by as more sticks and roofing skins were unloaded and the bell-shaped huts went up, covered with skins.

I greeted a group of women but they answered with flat stares. There was immediate hostility from the tribe toward me. Men, even the boys looked away as I passed and my greetings were not returned.

NuBorana ... Marconi had said. We the Borana ... superior, exclusive of outsiders. Even more so when there is trouble, *gaaf daaba*, the time of the stop.

The curve of a river bed protected the settlement to the north and east. To the south, the lava field made escape for raiders impossible, leaving only the west to be defended.

And in this location there was plentiful water. An *oda* tree grew among the fever trees and doum palms along the dry river. Between the roots of the *oda* tree, down at the level of the river bed, a cistern had been dug. The well was filled with water, almost clear.

A line of warriors stood in a human chain up from the cistern, each man a few inches higher than the next. The men passed up woven buckets full of water hand to hand to fill a long trough dug in the earth. The line swayed and chanted, buckets moving fast without a break. Other men out of the chain took the empties back to the end of the line, clapping, leading the song as they walked to and fro.

More herdsmen were bringing groups of animals up. Cattle, sheep and goats together, some donkeys, mouths sunk into the water, silently drinking their fill.

One man stood apart watching the entire operation, holding a wooden bat shaped like a solid tennis racquet, issuing orders but not participating.

As I walked round to face the line of men, the singing stopped and the flow of buckets slowed.

'*Olin naga nagaa*,' I tried, the evening greeting Girreh had taught me. Blank stares in reply. Then one of the men picked up the song again and the chant and the flow of the water resumed, as if I did not exist.

Saunders had told me how he stood for no nonsense, '... some of them get *stroppe* from time to time. But I don't stand for any cheek, old man. Oh no, I hit 'em for six when they get like that. Nairobi doesn't give a damn what you do up here, just to long as everything is quiet...' A Boer word: uppity, insolent.

Even my men seemed to have been affected. My camp was put together but the porters' rolls had disappeared. Another man arrived bearing a bundle of firewood. He was dressed like a Borana but he carried no weapons and his hair was unplaited.

'*Waarta*,' Girreh explained. A nameless man assigned to look after me. From a lower caste, a *waarta* not a warrior. Then Girreh too was pulled away by the magnetism of the tribe as they gathered.

On the fourth morning at my camp I put my plan into action. My plan as *un uomo d'onore*, to show them what Girreh had seen. My plan to bring the barriers down.

For three days as I waited, I had let camp routine expand to fill the time. Warthog was plentiful, my favourite dish. The bandage had come off and my wound was healing over again. In the afternoons I drank my gin and orange squash, I read my *Decline*:

> *I have reserved for the last, the most potent and forcible cause of the destruction of Rome, the domestic hostilities of the Romans themselves.*

And each evening I peered out into the haze, into the dust of returning herds through a mirage of gin.

Yes, I was sure. We the invaders, warring among ourselves, we would decay and disappear. The Oromo would become one nation again, free of our divisions and our borders. All the Oromo speakers together. Oromoland: proud, African, peaceful.

Self-determination for all peoples. How those words had rung along the halls of the Quai d'Orsay, out through open windows and across place des États Unis. Like the meaningless doxology of some long-forgotten sect.

On that morning I was up in the dark. The sleepy *waarta* scrambling for a fire as a pale shadowless light moved across the camp and a dawn wind rippled over dusty ground. I set off with my canvas chair. I chose a place two or three hundred yards beyond the *manyatta*, a barren piece of red earth trodden into powder by the coming and going of the herds. I was in their path, a place littered with droppings and flies like a plague.

Facing east I sat: legs forward, ankles crossed, hands folded across my stomach, elbows resting on flat wooden arms. Completely still.

The uppermost tip of the sun appeared. A tiny curve against pale blue heavens, bright orange, glowing along the straight blade of the earth. Then it grew, larger, larger, visibly gaining speed until the sun had formed its full burning round, hanging stationary above a purple earth. On and up, over toward me, turning into a formless dazzle of sheer white light.

A long time passed. The sun moving overhead, beating me down into the chair. Around me the sounds of the settlement: low voices, clinking, milk gourds knocking together like muffled bells.

But there were no calls or whistles from the herdsmen opening bomas, preparing to drive the herds out to pasture. An unusual quiet settled over the *manyatta*, broken only by the cry of a baby, the bleating of goats like question and answer.

Slowly they came up. Stopping at a distance at first, looking, talking quietly. By the time the sun was on the back of my neck, burning as if through a glass, I was surrounded by the clans. But I remained still, completely motionless. The heat was breathtaking.

I could see them in front of me, six deep or more. I could hear them to the sides and round the back: spears rattling together, creaking leather clothes, feet moving in the dust. A hundred or more, males mostly, but some elderly women, small children old enough to be away from their mothers.

Flies were black sequins on faces, legs and arms. Large menacing reptiles, luminous blue wings, impervious to temperature, indestructible. Crawling on my sweating pink skin, then stationary, rubbing their front legs together, repulsive, feeding on dirty pores. But I held still, still.

Finally I stood up and unbuckled my belt. The jingle of the crowd died away. Slowly in a crushing sweat, deliberate leaden movements like wading through deep water. A performance in a play, fastidious, ridiculous. Until I was standing up straight between them, wearing only my shirt.

The circle tightened around me. Warriors with handsome impassive faces. Matted, decorated hair and metal earrings, no more than three feet away. The group gave off an overpowering stench of rotting leather, of putrefying milk, of fresh dung and the sweet decaying smell of African bodies.

I dropped the shirt off my back.

Black, blue, cloudy red. Shocking, angry, now exposed to all the world. Criss-crossed welts that were becoming permanent grooves in my skin. Long narrow flicks up the edges of the healing pulp.

On the *SS Uganda* I had started to tally my stripes. I had lost count at thirty-three.

I lifted my arms straight out from the shoulders, weight unbearable in the stifling air. I began to turn within the circle. Slowly, slowly, staring out, beyond, in a trance, bare feet padding in the dust.

No sound came from the tribe other than a rustle as those at the front shuffled back out of the line of my outstretched hands.

Still I turned. Every surface, every crevice. My body hair, the lines where the sun had tanned my legs and my arms below my shirtsleeves and shorts. My weak and vulnerable whiteness, my frail humanity beyond race and origin.

My humiliation, my defeat and my scarring.

My inferiority: unable to survive like a Borana, barefoot in this hostile country; unable to protect my herd from a lion with only a spear; unable to find a lost animal, out for days with just a pouch of water. Unable to read the shining stars in a desert sky. Unwanted by my own tribe, a fugitive.

An old man came through the ranks, weak and slow but resolved in his movements. Staring eyes but he could see. A detached tranquil smile, soft and all-knowing. A stubbly beard, the pale silver of pearls, a halo over his parched black skin. White wiry hair under a loosely tied turban.

The crowd parted and he stood in front of me. Without his stoop he would have been as tall as the tallest warrior. His tongue flicked out and round his lips as if to catch something that was not there.

Slowly a big twisted hand came toward me, held out European style. I extended my hand in reciprocation but his palm brushed mine and his fist encompassed my thumb. Then I held his thumb, our hands stationary, up in the air between us.

'*Ngaa...*' the old man said, '*ngaa*'. He smiled around his eyes, dark, shot with blood from a life of driving sand and constant dust.

Then the crowd started to press in around me.

'*Ngaa, ngaa,*' they mumbled.

Others held out their palms and their thumbs and I turned again in the tight circle, holding thumbs on all sides, meeting eyes and returning smiles, my thumb held and squeezed in return. I felt fingers behind me run lightly over ridges and scabs, down my back and across my buttocks.

'*Nganaga, nganaga,*' I replied, as Girreh had taught me, '*nganaga.*'

Then the old man was standing next to me, the backs of our hands touching down by our sides. He took my wrist between two fingers.

'*Ulcho waa li kalenaa...*' he began, Oromo words that I did not understand.

When the old man had spoken a warrior came through from the back of the crowd carrying a white cloth. The old man covered me, crossing the cloth at the front, top corners knotted behind my neck. Then a leather thong was tied around my waist.

Holding my wrist again the old man led me through the crowd, between the *waara* and into the centre of the *manyatta*. It became a procession, women with small children watching from the entrances to their huts.

The men began singing. A slow gentle rhythm. Da da da de *dah*, da da da de *dah*. A song of hope, of peace, I thought.

In the middle of the settlement the circle formed again. The song continued, the men shuffling and stamping where they stood swaying to the rhythm.

A bed was carried out of the nearest hut. The old man sat with two others, older and frailer still. My camp chair was brought. I sat next to them facing the standing tribe.

Without any word from the old men a ceremony began. I was poured water in a wooden gourd, then milk into another, thick and frothy, red like the earth under our feet. Milk mixed with blood. Heavy and fatty, smelling like the cow herself.

Two goats were led into the circle and a warrior straddled each animal. In a unison of movement they drew their short swords. Holding the animals' muzzles from behind, they reached down to slit through deep meaty throats. There was an instant when the goats seemed unaffected, eyes open, still standing. Then the animals collapsed, legs kicking and twitching. Blood spurting everywhere: on the warriors' white cloths, their legs and faces, sprayed out in a circle making black balls in the dust, splattering on the three old men, over my shins and bare feet.

Before the spasms had ended, one of the swordsmen had the larger goat on its back. With another single pass of his sword the animal was opened from chest to stomach, blade slicing between testicles and deep into the bowel. Innards pouring out like a slit tomato, like spilled quicksilver, sliding, slipping on to the ground. Greys, blues and reds, twisted organs, heart still beating but all strangely free of blood.

The warrior stood back as the smallest and weakest of the old men walked solemnly round the gutted carcass. The killing and severing had taken no more than five seconds.

The little old man hunched down to face the goat's entrails. He passed a twig back and forth over rounded, perfect parts. The cut had been skilful, the stomach neatly parted by the same single stroke, the sword penetrating the goat's belly to exactly the right depth. The result was clinical, every part of the goat's insides laid out in order. Stepping up from balls of half-digested leaves lying on the ground, past a tangle of exposed tripe and back to the gaping stomach wall, ready for a lecture at a veterinary college.

Then the little old man stood, holding his stick in the air over his wizened head. There was a hush.

'Ngaya,' he croaked. 'Ngaya huu!' Peace. All was well.

There was a mumbled response like grace before a meal.

Live coals were brought and a bundle of sticks. The goats were skinned and prepared for the fire.

Discussion started and I tried to make myself understood by drawing a map in the dust. Before the sacrifice the women had disappeared. The gathering was now all male.

Law and order have been re-established, the KAR have arrived. Your tribal area will be protected. The European war, the Italians, the Germans. Words I did not have, explanations that I could not possibly make. That I did not understand myself.

Then we ate. Meat in handfuls was passed from the fire out into the crowd to be consumed standing. The women reappeared with water for washing and drinking. Milk and blood was passed again. I missed my gin and my orange squash.

'The Borana have a saying,' Marconi had told me. '*Gurra egen dubii duga*. The ear and the tail of a discussion shows the truth.'

I understood better now his respect for the tribe.

'For a Borana warrior, to bring back the ear and the tail of his kill is his proof that he has been brave and successful. Without them he cannot tell his story. So with a Borana discussion. The truth must be found, the ear and the tail, the final proof. The discussion will go on until all is known.'

The warriors spoke in turn. I understood the procedure but none of the words. The old men were not chiefs but seekers of the truth. Upholders of the peace of the tribe. I felt confident and I trusted the outcome.

Through late afternoon and into the evening the discussion continued. I could hear the animals being milked again as the sun began to set, dropping fast and even.

After dark the talk ended. The old man spoke, quietly but with emphasis, more words that I did not understand. He was Yabbo, at the end he spoke for them all.

Then the fires were built up again and two bundles of *miraa* appeared. I rose to leave, to return to my gin, to my book and my camp bed. Burned by the sun, exhausted by the strain of the unknown.

The next morning there was a group at my tent. The old man who had read the goat's omens with a crowd of warriors, Girreh and my porters. The little old man produced a small cloth bundle. He said a few words and took my wrist. He slipped a bracelet over my hand, a section of elephant tusk decorated with a leather braid. Then he and the warriors turned to leave without waiting for my reaction.

In ten days Moyale had become a military metropolis. As I led my little line up the hill we were challenged by pickets from behind newly sandbagged positions. Lorries ground past loaded with askaris and supplies. A group of sappers was laying a culvert across the road packed with explosive.

In the town, soldiers off duty wandered in and out of the *dukas*, sitting around aimlessly on improvised benches. Lalji, the good Ismaili was selling beer. I could already hear him singing his song: 'Well, sahib, my customers, they are demanding this beer, sahib. And it is being your law of demanding and supplying, sahib...'

From desertion in September to invasion in December.

The KAR in Moyale was now up to company strength, six European officers, three hundred men. The Kenya Police had arrived, a crew from the Public Works Department was running a grader drawn by oxen up and down the landing strip. Preparations for war had taken over my town.

But there were some immigrants with useful skills. The dressing station had been rehabilitated and two orderlies began to treat over two hundred outpatients each day. A young man from the Kenya Regiment introduced himself without rank, Nigel Hunt, an irregular attached to the KAR, the son of a local farmer. His job was to engage scouts and interpret for new European officers.

Hunt spoke fluent Swahili. The KAR officers had no interest in African languages and I was able to use Hunt every day. My speech improved rapidly with his coaching and we both set ourselves to learning more Oromo words.

My boma was now run like an army camp, a town within a town, larger than Moyale itself. A town of tents. Khaki canvas stretched out in all directions, up to ridges, down to ropes and pegs. A large tent for the European mess, individual tents for officers.

C Company 2nd KAR was commanded by Major Gourley. Lieutenant Warner had become just one of a number of European officers who marched about the camp in starched uniforms, waving canes and giving orders.

Gourley was the keen moustachioed type. In my absence he had detailed police patrols, he had established work schedules for the PWD and he had issued directives to the civilians in the town: *From the Military Commander.*

At our first encounter Gourley had talked about *checking up on the headmen* and *putting some fighting spirit into them.*

I tried to explain about the Oromo and the split tribes. But Gourley had no interest. He wasn't all the way up in Moyale, he said, to worry about the wogs. He was there to lick the Eye-ties.

And in the first months of 1940, before the real war started, while Italy was still neutral waiting to join the winners, while France sat smug behind her Maginot Line, while Hitler waited for his next perfect moment, Moyale continued to grow. I was where they had sent me. At the end of the earth, the remotest corner of Empire where I wanted to be. But now I was caught up in war again.

The boma was made stronger and stronger. The slope of the hill facing the Italians was covered with a series of trenches, protected by wire and anchored by concrete pill-boxes. Cement, timber and labour that would have built a school, a cattle dip.

And every day there was the Meeting of the Liaison Committee, for the Civil Authority to meet with the Military Authority and for my venom to rise.

My *watu* for example: they should be strictly confined to their lines when not working. How else could we prevent the locations of our fortifications from being given away to the Italians? How *our* tribes should be obliged to spy on *their* tribes when grazing close to the Abyssinian side.

Or Gourley's plans to parade his entire company, together with the Kenya Police Detachment, the Signals Corps and the Pioneers. All in full dress, the Major on a camel. Every Sunday with the tribes called in to watch. To demonstrate, Gourley said, the invincible might of His Majesty's Empire.

The Major would never listen to my replies. Wasting my breath, he said. But the Wops had tanks and his trenches were useless.

'And some of us,' he would repeat, 'do seem to spend an *inordinate* amount of time over there with the Spaghetti Merchants.' Reorganizing the world over Marconi's endless supply of *rosso di Riviera del Garda Bresciano*.

I wasn't a military man. I was a civilian and a defeatist at that. And if it hadn't been for the war, by God, the Major would have had me taken down a peg or two. Oh yes indeed. A cattle dip when there was a war on. The most preposterous thing he'd ever heard.

And as to dress, did I have any idea at all what it was to set an example? The loincloth and the bangle. Did I have any *concept* of what a sight I looked in front of the natives?

The break between us came early in 1940.

The Yabbo had told me, he said, down on the plains, when I had visited him in his *manyatta*, that he would come to visit me, up in my *manyatta*. Return the honour. I had not understood and now here he was, splendid in his white wrap and accompanied by fifteen warriors. Unannounced as I had been.

The Yabbo had welcomed me, spoken for me in front of his tribe. Now I would do the same for him.

We sat under the pepper tree, me, the Yabbo and Hunt. Girreh and the warriors squatted around. Between us we began to overcome language.

I had the mess corporal in his starched jacket bring a soda syphon and a tray of tumblers for the water greeting, each warrior holding his glass with two hands like a gourd. The corporal looked around anxiously, swatting at

Borana flies with a white-gloved hand, hoping that Gourley would not emerge from his tent and catch him in this sacrilegious act.

Then I had gin brought and I poured a shot into every glass. Hunt followed with orange squash, enjoying the scene as much as me.

I called *mpeachie* out and ordered food. A meal for sixteen, *style Empire britannique*. *Mpeachie* was as nervous as the corporal. He returned with a mess chit book, he wanted his orders in writing. Solemnly I wrote out:

> 10 bottles Gilbey's gin
> 5 bottles orange squash
> Lunch for 16. Visiting delegation
> G. Exeter, DO

We started to do our business. The Yabbo's name was Guyo Galma Boru, his own name, father and grandfather. In return the Yabbo made my name into Gramama, the name I too had taken from my father.

We talked haltingly about grazing lands, about wells and the movement of Borana herds, *durri durri*, the same since time began. About the tribe now split in two by the border. The bad treatment of the northern Borana and other Oromo tribes by the Abyssinians. Slaves taken, animals driven off, women and children hunted down by Amharic cavalry.

The gong sounded. My brother Europeans trooped into the mess tent from all directions, slouch hats off as they ducked beneath ropes.

Then the food arrived under the pepper tree, three trays, sixteen plates of meat, gravy and potatoes. Hunt refilled glasses. The warriors started to eat hungrily with their fingers.

I took the Yabbo by the wrist. I walked him under the canvas flap and into the mess.

The group in the tent was ten or twelve strong. They had finished their sherries and were seating themselves down the table, neatly laid with mess silver and bowls of bougainvillaea bloom.

As they took their places, Major Gourley at the head, the others in some jealous order of rank below, I stood the Yabbo at a spare chair. He faced Gourley at the opposite end of the long white tablecloth.

The red face at the far end and two rows of pink all looked up together. Shock then outrage spreading over their features. I stood next to the Yabbo still holding his wrist.

'Gentlemen,' I said, slowly and clearly, 'I introduce to you Guyo Galma Boru, Yabbo of the Borana people. He is my guest.'

7

The old man was weakening. His dozes were longer and breathing seemed harder. His hands hardly moving when he spoke. After the two nights Morley had been away in Dallas it was quite noticeable.

Two nights and three days away from the protection of the hospice. Out in a world where Morley had once been *whole and useful*. Before flowing acid in his veins, before the grip of impulses that invaded his reason. But now time had disconnected once more. Day or night blanked out by blinds, no regular meals, following no schedule. Graham was talking and dying simultaneously, the rest was inconsequential.

The rest. From his partners, whose very reasonableness and understanding was worse than the white-faced anger he knew he deserved. To his flight south and all the overwhelming irritations that had never seemed to be able to work their way under his skin before.

Even up in Leader Advantage Class. Why go to all the trouble and expense of creating a new name for a service when very little had changed. There was still nothing first class about it. Morley had found his seat covered with breakfast droppings from a previous occupant on the earlier flight into Seattle-Tacoma and the cabin had a background aroma of vomit. Eau de Holding Tank.

Passengers were loading into the back through the forward cabin. Festooned like sidewalk displays outside a discount luggage shop.

A stewardess fought her way to Morley's seat in the third row through the surly crush. She handed him a leaky cup which dripped onto his silk shirt. The contents were cabin-temperature and sweet, colour unidentifiable against the airline's logo.

'Ya-*ca*-*a*mplimentary-fresh-squeezed-juice.' Welcome to the US of A.

Morley's lost day in the gulag had cost him his seat on the only direct daily flight Vancouver to Dallas-Fort Worth. Then to save a three-hour hub change in a four-hour flight he had driven down to Seattle-Tacoma airport to catch a non-stop at noon. He had justified the wasted day and the drive each way by resolving to work over the weekend in Dallas. Two twelve-hour slogs back to back and a visit to the Chilliwack site on the Canadian side of the border on his way back up on Sunday night.

An overdressed widow in the next seat had started telling Morley her life story. Zero to seventy-five in under three minutes. On the in-flight screen the world was unfolding. An all-female British rock group had been visiting LA. Two buzzed teenagers were recounting their experiences in the crowd. 'So she's like, hello, and I'm like, I mean gag me, so she goes, beautiful day, and I'm like, can't speak, so she goes again, hey, you're all so happy, and then I'm really on it and I'm like...'

Morley wanted to bellow at the bulbous men dragging backpacks and garment bags against him as he tried to take refuge behind the newspaper, at their ugly women treading on his loafers with their combat boots. Run amuck from the cabin and down the runway. Mown into a rubber smudge.

Before he had left the house for the airport an envelope had arrived from the office on a courier hot from the evening before. He couldn't read the letter while driving but once the plane was in the air Morley had no more excuses. He tore open the flap.

Morley+Chan+Wainright
Architects

800-800 Beaumont St., Vancouver, B.C. Canada V5Z 4K3

From the desk of Kingsley Chan MAIBC
Direct: (604) 662 7191
Fax: 662 7155

Dear Morley,

I know you have to be in Dallas, so I am committing this to paper, which is in any case probably more effective than taking a meeting on your way out the door.

Morley, you know that my relationship with you and Brock is the best thing in my life second only to my family and my marriage to Peggy. So what I have to say has to be seen as starting from there.

We blew the biggest chance of our fifteen-year career on Tuesday and I ask you to hear me out on it. We have too many important clients and too big a staff counting on us for our personal lives to prejudice the firm. I know how much you have been involved with the Jane thing, but I have to tell you, my friend, she is not worth what is happening. We welcomed her because she was your wife, but that is as far as it goes with me and Peggy. I have to share that honestly.

As to the firm, the People's Bureau for the Provision of Water in Guangdong Province will be going elsewhere. The real trouble in China is that the functionaries who appear to make decisions only have responsibility. The parallel government, the Party, has the power. They are the real ruling class in the background. So far we have done well with the bureaucrats, your Harbor Development Plan for Zhuhai especially. But in Guangdong Province, because we are small and operating from Vancouver, we have not met the Party bosses while our rivals have. The head of the Water Bureau was under pressure to give the job to a well connected Hong Kong firm and our performance on Tuesday gave him the perfect excuse. Brock and I made a good show, lunch at La Piazza and a drive around some of our bigger sites. But the designs were not ready and that fact could not be obfuscated.

They were all very polite of course, but we've screwed up. We are carrying $0.61 mil in office costs and overhead against the project to date, which is now a full write-off.

I had a long talk with Tim on the phone. He is an excellent guy and you are lucky to have such a good friend as your lawyer. He told me what needs to be done off the record to beat out Jane's claims. I am sending a crew in this morning with a bailiff to close down Jane's shop, remove the inventory and prepare the premises for re-leasing. I'm not supposed to tell you, but her 'new partner' is the same fellow she's living with. He was going to sell sports goods out of the other half of our shop. Nifty little plan on our money, hopefully we'll get there just in time!

As you know we overpaid for the building and my guess is that we will end up with a market lease rate that does not even cover the mortgage payments. This is not a complaint, just fact. You and Brock helped me enormously when I was in trouble with my professional liability. It's just part of being committed partners.

The talks with the guys at Partners 2001 have come a long way. I was in Toronto last week as you know. What they really want is to take us over, put one of us on their board and say that Partners 2001 is the first truly Canada-wide architectural firm with offices from St Johns to Vancouver and Victoria. We have to consider it very seriously, Morley. Our constant cash-flow grind would be over, the big Federal projects would open up from Ottawa and we could start a full-time office in Hong Kong.

Personally, I think that for you it would be a good thing too. You are under more pressure than anyone in the office and frankly, given the Jane episodes, you seem to be cracking.

Needless to say, Partners 2001 has five or more design hot-shots in Toronto who are keen to move to the West Coast. What I'm trying to say is that you could slip away for a while with some ready cash and get your head sorted. Brock and I are agreed on Partners 2001, it is really you we are waiting for.

Have a good trip to Dallas, and tell those guys at Bechtel from *me*, that we need our invoices turning round a lot faster than 90 days!

Ever yours,

Kingsley Chan

~

Graham woke again, Morley felt him stir. Then the light blue eyes opened.

'Alyce has discovered who you are,' Graham said softly. 'Your design for the new city library was considered to be the best. She read in the paper that the Council already regrets taking on some international superstar and his ballooning budgets instead of your firm.'

Morley brought the tray table up the bed. Graham reached for Morley's wrist.

'So what was a man in your position doing in jail?'

Why did the old man want to know? He was dying. Morley's shoulders sagged. Defeat, exhaustion, acid and despair. He had lost his way. But he had to answer, there were no barriers left. The closeness of death, the depth and intimacy of Graham's story. His struggle to tell it all.

'I went following my wife and she complained to the cops. She and lover-boy say that their lives are in danger.'

Graham's eyes swept Morley's horizon.

'And is that true, Morley? Are their lives in danger?'

'I'll fetch you some more liquid.' Morley carried Graham's tray to the kitchen.

Elaine was drinking coffee at the kitchen table.

'I thought he wasn't going to wait for you to get back from Dallas,' she said. 'He's very weak. But he says he's made you a promise and that's been keeping him going. A promise to his Recording Angel.' She smiled, then she frowned as she looked at Morley's face. 'You're pooped,' she continued quietly. 'This is why we need volunteers, I couldn't get involved like that, there'd be nothing left of me to do the nursing. So death inevitably becomes routine, slipping in and out of the rooms, handing out painkillers. Some hollow encouragement that avoids reality. Exactly what we're trained not to do.'

Morley smiled back at her. One tenth his earnings, work that was ten times more valuable. Thoughts, places, people he would never have known in his other life.

'It's a three-day weekend isn't it?'

Elaine nodded. She pointed to the clock. Past midnight and into holiday Monday already.

'I don't think he'll last much longer,' she said. 'I'm on nights for a while. Looks like we'll be going through this together.' She reached out for him with her eyes. The professional to the amateur.

~

426

Marconi made me laugh, a man without delusions. A man who had joined the army in 1919 only when war was over. And then, he said, simply because he liked to ski. A man who had left the army in 1936 for the *Servizio Imperiale e Reale* because, he thought, another war really might be coming.

I liked Marconi. Or maybe it was the compliments.

'Signor Exeter, such a pleasure to have a civilized discussion with a Frenchman. And to find one here, among *les Anglais. Vraiment.*'

And Marconi was well informed.

'The banquet with your Borana in their *manyatta*?' One eyebrow halfway up his forehead, 'are you planning, *mon ami*, to be canonized maybe, the first Borana saint? *Santo Gramama ya Borana.*'

Marconi made me laugh again.

'And now they are calling *you* Yabbo and the tribes are expecting peace and prosperity under your rule. You will make it impossible for us mortals.' Eyebrow again, twitching smile. 'And this wound? What is this wound they talk about? You have stigmata already?'

But war between me and my friend was only a matter of time. By early 1940 Chamberlain was going, Poland and Norway were gone.

Even Marconi's attitude had changed. I heard more about the *invincibility* of the Germans, of the *inevitability* of history. Of *la merde* caused by politicians and their *soi-disant* democracy. The need in a complex modern state for a *strong leader*. For the good of *all* the people, not just pandering to *cliques*. We would come to the same conclusion in Britain, Marconi assured me. It was progress, unstoppable. I would see.

We made a pact, Marconi and me, our own Anglo-Italian Pact and we drank to ourselves in his *palazzo*. There would be no unexpected attacks. If the military men on either side planned a raid before war was declared, each would inform the other and surprise would be lost.

Yet still we assessed each other's chances and we spied.

Our spying started in a way I could not prevent. By the Yabbo at lunch with Major Gourley in the mess tent.

In the moment of appalled silence after I had introduced my guest, two mess stewards came through the tent flap as if following a script, carrying soup. And before the red face could burst, a steward was at Gourley's side with a tureen and Gourley's chance was lost. To stop it before it began.

In that moment as Gourley turned, automatic, picking up the ladle, good mess manners, the old man sat down. Then the Yabbo, his due as guest, received the other tureen first. The steward's eyes rolling and popping all over again, white on black, but following his drill.

The Yabbo was a dignified, elegant man, aware of events around him. He saw what to do and calmly he ladled soup. I picked up my spoon to show him how and the old man picked up his. He began to eat his soup.

By the time the stewards left, Gourley had found his lost wits.

'Mr Exeter,' loud, soup spoon waving in the air, 'this wog you've brought into my mess is a god-damned disgrace. A bloody insult. To me and to my officers.'

The officers looked at me down the table, two rows of choirboys: unison of thought, unison of expression and dress.

And before Gourley was finished I was at him.

'This wog, Major Gourley, is my guest. I am still the DO here. And this is still my boma.'

Then we both started shouting at once, the Major pounding the table.

'Mr Exeter,' deep livid purple, 'you get that bloody wog out of this mess or I'll call the guard and have my askaris put the two of you out.'

And across him I was shouting.

'My guest, Major Gourley, is the Yabbo of the Borana people, the largest, most loyal tribe in the NFD. The Yabbo has come to show us his confidence, after we...'

At that moment the old man stood up. Straight and commanding, stoop quite lost now.

'*Islaa, ne Kingi Georgi nucho infafa ya nItalee...*' slowly and deliberately as if standing behind the fire in the *manyatta* facing the tribe. There was silence as he spoke. Then the Yabbo sat down, he picked up his spoon again and he continued to eat his soup.

The stewards were through the flap once again to offer more soup, right on cue. Hunt filled the gap.

'I think the Yabbo said, sir, that the soldiers of King George have nothing to fear from the Italians. They have no fuel for their tanks and they are under constant attack by Tasfayo, son of the Wolde at Mega.'

Then one of the choirboys broke in and Gourley's last chance was gone.

'Gosh,' a lieutenant said enthusiastically, 'how awfully interesting. Absolutely the sort of stuff we've been trying to find out for yonks. But can you ask him,' he went on, 'who this Wolde chappie is?'

Through the rest of the meal Gourley sat in a trance while his choirboys chattered on self-consciously. Trying to cover over the awkwardness of having a bloody wog lunching with them in their mess.

The Yabbo ate quietly, working his way through the cutlery following my signals. Then before coffee was served the Yabbo was on his feet again. After another short speech, thanking *Kingi Georgi*, the Major and the KAR, he left for the pepper tree, for my gin and orange squash.

The next week it all came to an end. My war with Gourley, my friendship with Marconi and the reconstruction of my town. Winston Churchill became our leader for the great event that was going to make him a Great Man.

I sat with Marconi in the evenings, listening to the BBC. Away from the choirboys and their rooting. *How's that!* or, *Knock 'em for six!* Like a cricket match, at any fragment of good news the BBC could scrape up. As Panzers rolled through the Ardennes and into Sedan. Around the Maginot Line, across the Meuse, Rommel plunging headlong to the sea. As another British Expeditionary Force retreated to the Channel, too few and too late again.

Then more Germans were coming through Belgium, over the Dyle, down the Oise. The British and French Armies were trapped.

On our last night together there was no need for me to translate the news. Marconi had received his own message. We sat quietly by his huge upright wireless, a piece of furniture in itself.

'This is the Overseas Service of the BBC,' the voice began through the crackle. Short wave coming and going through the ether, composed and unruffled as if the news that day was nothing out of the ordinary. 'Here is the news for Tuesday the 10th of June. Italy has declared war on France and Great Britain. Hostilities have begun immediately. In the south east of France, Italian forces have attacked French border posts at...' *Il Duce* saw France weak, his chance to take back Nice.

'You must go Gra-ham.' Marconi stood up, suddenly forlorn. 'They will want to do some shooting tonight, right away.'

We embraced. Marconi held me hard for a moment, then he walked me down the hill, through his pickets to the empty customs posts facing each other at the bridge.

'Look after your Borana,' Marconi instructed as we parted, 'then when the soldiers start fighting, *je serai tranquille.*'

Two weeks earlier Gourley had declared his defences complete. Then C Company had been relieved by A Company 2nd KAR under my friend Captain Browning.

'It's the usual balls-up, Exeter,' Browning had told me the day he arrived. After his company had been installed, as we sipped gin and orange squash under my pepper tree. 'We were going to make a stand up here with support from the South Africans and 4th KAR from Buna and Marsabit. But that's all changed. Now we can't be reinforced so if the Italians attack we're to pull back.'

The evacuation of Moyale started again. My Goan clerk and his files, the dressers and their hospital supplies. Most of my labour evaporating with their last pay packet. Lalji and his stores, everything was sent south again.

'Acts of War, sahib,' Lalji cried out of the cab window as Mohammed Noor's lorry pulled away. 'I am to be claiming Acts of War.'

Bombing and small-arms fire had begun on the first night. But harmless Italian fire, not German, deadly.

A Junkers Trimotor flew low over our position. A passenger aeroplane of Al Littoria, fully lit cabin, identification lights flashing. The passenger door was open and I could see an airman in a leather flying helmet clutching the door frame with one hand, throwing hand grenades and bombs with the other. Most of the grenades exploded in the air, narrowly missing the plane's tail. His bombs were no more effective, falling off into the bush, many with an audible thud and no explosion. I could have picked off the man in the flying helmet like a warthog. But really, what harm was he doing?

Soon our war started to drift. Their tanks were not ready and the *cara-binieri* had little stomach for an assault on our wire and our trenches. The KAR carried out offensive patrols, capturing four *banda* and an Italian officer, blowing up the customs posts which the Italians were using as cover for snipers. But only to maintain morale among our askaris.

After ten days the Italians brought up reinforcements. And by the end of June, Browning's single company faced three enemy battalions, thirty or forty tanks, eighteen field guns and enemy air superiority.

On the night of 2 July the Italians advanced. With a lot of revving and clanking, shouting and waving of lights we were immediately surrounded. The road was cut behind us and our water supply fell into enemy hands. The next day we were shelled, after which two half-hearted attacks by *banda* were repelled. But we had five askaris dead and three wounded including one of my porters.

The Yabbo had been right. The Italians had no fuel to continue their advance and no lines of supply to cross the desert. Besieging my boma was the best they could manage.

The time had come to leave. The following night we crept out of our fort abandoning everything but small arms. Askaris with bare feet, Europeans in plimsolls, the wounded left doped and propped up, visible to an approaching patrol.

The retreat took all night, one hundred and twenty men in single file. Covered by a section of fearless Luos under their European lieutenant, a volunteer farmer who stayed in the boma until the last, blazing away at the African night as if we were still defending.

One of my Borana porters was the guide. He appeared at the departure point resplendent in white cloth, hair in newly plaited rows.

'He'll have to take that bloody thing off,' one of Browning's officers said quickly, 'be seen in an instant. Give the whole game away.' I translated but I knew the answer.

'If this man is to die, he says he's going as a Borana warrior.' I laughed at the worried look. There was little danger. At midnight it would be Sunday, Eye-tie day off.

We crept down the hill, each man a few feet behind the next. We could hear the Italians on each side in their bivouacs, playing cards and singing songs.

'*Oh! che culo, che tieni!*' and '*Maronna mia!*' distinct against crickets and hyraxes, through the bush symphony as we passed.

Down on the plain before dawn, Browning's transport was waiting, six lorries and a car. There was tea, bacon, *posho*, whisky and water.

I sat with my food on the running board of the car. A Buick, rounded and ornate, American, from a different future.

Other cars, other open spaces, across another world. VALENCIENNES 22M. LG and Frances in the back seat waiting patiently for their weeping driver.

> *... but I am bound*
> *Upon a wheel of fire ...*

A lunch could have solved it all. In Marconi's shaded dining room. His military men and my military men, puffing on cheroots, sipping from little glasses, horizontal light and shadow from the louvres masking their faces.

'Well, *signore*, here's our offer.' Unsteady on my feet, trying not to slur. 'You are far stronger than us, so we're just going to pull back to Marsabit. If you think this little piece of Africa will make your *Impero* grander, your *Duce* a greater man, then you can have it. Border's artificial anyway. Better that the Oromo are all together. Wander on over when you're ready. No fighting, no casualties.'

I down my grappa. One of Marconi's Somalis silently refills the glass.

'But just one thing, *signore*, just one thing. With all the matériel and man-power you will save by our sensible attitude, you must make some improvements. A cattle dip. And a school. Yes, a school. Two classrooms. And teachers ... teachers. How many teachers...?'

Browning was standing in front of me anxious to get moving.

'Those Junkers will be out looking for us soon. We'll be pretty exposed on the Marsabit road.'

But Browning knew what my answer would be before I spoke.

The birds were a full bush choir as the sun came up over the plains. Already shafting across red earth, cracked like a burned pie.

'No place for a white man,' he said. 'And with the war on there won't be anybody coming back for you.' But it was only token resistance.

We loaded up, Girreh and four porters. No tent, no chair, my hat and boots abandoned in the pill-box. A few packets of biscuits, water flasks, six bottles of gin, ten rifles, my Webley and five hundred rounds of ammunition. A KAR map and a compass, binoculars. My *Passion* had come down the hill chafing and sticky in the front of my shirt.

Browning held out his hand.

'Bad news over the wireless,' he said with a grim face. 'France is a gonner. While we were up the hill. They've surrendered to the Germans in the north and to the Italians in the south.'

There was more.

'You won't believe this but Hitler brought out the same old railway carriage Foch used for the Armistice in 'eighteen. The same clearing in the same woods. Can you imagine that? All of them sitting in the same places around the same table. But France doing the capitulating. Now *that's* vengeance.'

I set off south-west into the bush. My little troop in a file, bundles and boxes on their heads, rifles over shoulders, two per man. France a gonner.

The Borana *manyatta* was much tighter this time and bigger again. Huts only a few paces apart, cattle bomas in the centre for complete security.

We were met enthusiastically, the water greeting then blood and milk, thumbs held in all directions. Fingers feeling for my bracelet like a charm.

I drew my map in the sand again facing the warriors. But now, slowly, a few words at a time, I could make myself understood in the Oromo language.

The Italians had invaded Moyale and could come no further. But from where they were they could let the *banda* loose. And with the KAR back in Marsabit the *shifta* could be anywhere. A five-sided war was about to begin.

'You the Borana must choose,' I said. 'You go up the hill and make peace with the Italians and I will leave. Or you move south to Marsabit until war is over.'

A warrior spoke up, standing at the back, black parched skin. A face that did constant battle with the elements.

'But to go to Marsabit,' he said, 'we must walk the Didi Galgallu.'

There was a long silence. Then the discussion started and on into the night. Would the Italians stay in Moyale? When would the KAR make war?

Where were the KAR now? Why were they afraid? The decision had to be reached by them all.

Finally the Yabbo stood up and gave his short address. If Gramama would come with us, *nuBorana*, across the Didi Galgallu, that is where they would go.

I slept without a tent under a thorn tree by the river bed, open to wind and mosquitoes, the *waarta* materializing out of the dark to make a fire. No longer a visitor, no longer a European with a boma to return to. Exposed to Africa without privilege, without resources or protection.

In the morning I asked the Yabbo for ten men. Men with no duties other than to protect the tribe under my orders. I would train them with rifles.

There was no word for gun in the Oromo language. I used Swahili, *bunduki*. The Yabbo looked down at the dust and dung under our feet, pearl halo against his jaw. Bowed over further with the weight of my request.

'*Bunduki*,' he said softly, his mouth to my ear, '*nuBorana* have no *bunduki*. If *nuBorana* have *bunduki*, how will young men learn to be patient and brave? The ear and the tail, it means nothing with *bunduki*.'

The curse of *bunduki*: killing would be easy, without skill, without courage. Animals, other tribes, each other.

Then the old man hunched down on the ground, trying to resist the inevitable, white cloth wrapped around his shoulders as if against an imaginary cold wind. I squatted next to him, waiting.

'Gramama,' after a long silence, 'you will promise me. When your war is finished, even if I am gone to live with the lizards, that the *bunduki* will go back where they came from.'

That morning the women started to dismantle their *waara*, women's work, *hui jin naddeeni*. The men led the herds further down the river bed where another shallow well had been dug under an *oda* tree. Gourds were being passed along the chain. Men's work, *hui jin diira*. But slowly, conserving their energies, without their songs. They brought their animals to the trough in the order set by the *konficha*, the supervisor of the watering, the man who carried the bat. A position of great respect, as close as the Borana came to an individual who could give orders.

The stubby cattle looked thin and vulnerable, heads and long straight horns too big for their bony bodies. In 1940 the long rains had been poor, May and June less than half the annual average. Taken by Gourley as divine intervention for the completion of his trenches. Now July would be the hottest month of the year.

My men arrived, five young warriors. The average age was under twenty.

Mature warriors were needed for the herds. I was to use Girreh and my porters to make up my section of ten.

I began weapons training. First a demonstration of the power of the rifle: a bullet pierced into a tree at six hundred yards, which, to a man with a spear is as far away as the pale day-moon. We cut the tree down and removed the bullet, comparing flattened lead with spent shell then with an unused round.

Disassembly, re-assembly, repeated and repeated. Then with each man blindfolded in turn while I counted aloud and the others watched: bayonets, magazines, bolts, sights. Into pieces and back together again all in under twenty seconds. Cleaning, oiling, use of the pull-through. Followed by firing, the men lying flat, kneeling, standing. How to hold the stock tight into the shoulder, squeeze not pull. Rapid fire, aimed fire. Then safety and last of all ownership: matters that the army puts first.

On the fourth night of our training, in front of my fire, away from the tribe, I lined them up. I moved along the line, presenting each man with his rifle and twenty rounds.

'This is your *bunduki*,' I repeated solemnly to every one. 'It is only for the protection of your people. You guard it with your life.'

We stood for a long moment, ten black faces shining, reflecting leaping flames. Rifles clutched tight in both hands. I knew that they understood.

The Didi Galgallu is a desert without sand, without oases or palm trees. A desert of rocks. Sharp rocks, brown and red, packed into a hard impenetrable crust like a road. Then spent cannon balls scattered over the surface, jagged black lava, so thick in places that humans and animals must pick their way carefully like walkers in deep snow.

The next day the tribe and the herds moved down a long shallow slope and off the Sigiso Plain. Out of the last of the vegetation and on to the lava field.

My training continued dawn to dusk. We moved through the bush in file. We advanced line abreast spread out across open ground, each man maintaining contact with the next.

Defensive tactics were the hardest. I could see it in their faces, thrilled and keen. They thought only of attack with their awesome new-found power.

My orders were emphatic. No shooting without command, surprise is everything. If an intruder was sighted, the cry was to go up. '*Ga-ara!*' Acknowledged and passed on. When the right moment came I would fire the first shot. Then we would charge, bayonets fixed, shooting from the standing position, making every bullet count.

But before this was fully understood the *banda* attacked.

The herd was split into two that day. A man on our far east flank caught sight of *banda* creeping along the dry river bank at the edge of the desert. In his excitement he started to shoot. Then the others thinking they had missed the signal for attack, began to charge through the bush firing in all directions. In response, dull pops from Mausers could be heard, the *banda* returning fire from the river bed.

By the time I regained control, over two hundred rounds had been used without inflicting any casualties, two cows were dead and the *banda* had been warned that we were armed.

The Yabbo looked silently at the animal carcasses then at me and my *bunduki*. The *banda* had been repelled but war had started, they would be back with reinforcements.

Night was falling as we reassembled. I wagged my finger at a row of contrite faces as they cleaned rifles. Then we set out in single file, attack the best form of defence. Round in the breach, safety catch on. Due north, back into the bush.

Without a moon the march was slow. Only an awning of starlight made a faint horizon with thin vegetation, outlining the man ahead. But within an hour we had found the *banda* camp. Meat cooking on rocks around a bright fire, ten or twelve men chewing *miraa* and talking loudly. Slack, not expecting any trouble from primitive Borana. A sentry no more than fifty feet from the circle, facing inwards, listening to the talk. We moved silently around their position until we found an anthill two or three hundred yards away with a clear view.

I placed Girreh and two men flat on the mound. Beside each man a few rounds of extra ammunition. I adjusted their sights. With the rest crouched behind, waiting in the bush, I gave Girreh his instructions.

'You count out loud. Thirty cows. Slowly on your fingers. Then three shots only, three shots, three cows between each.'

Girreh nodded. The lost cows of his family, he still remembered every name.

'Dubarr ... Dalach,' I heard Girreh start as we left, 'Girreh...' the black one like him, 'Obol...' Thirty cows, five seconds each, two minutes to work around through the bush, firelight and voices kept on our right.

It seemed more like half an hour before we were in position, crouched down, line abreast. Then Girreh's first shots spat through the night. The *banda* sentry twisted and fell. Aim, squeeze, reload.

There was a tremendous commotion around the fire. In their frenzy a pot was knocked over into the coals and a cloud of steam obscured our view. There was cursing and swearing as *banda* tumbled over each other looking for their Mausers. Three cows, fifteen seconds and another volley cracked into the panic.

My men looked at the confusion, eyes bright, their enemy vulnerable. I held out my arms to keep them back, glowering left and right silently but emphatically, pistol in my hand. Do not move.

Within a few seconds the first *banda* had found their Mausers. Out in front of the camp, throwing themselves on to the ground, aiming in the direction of the shots as Girreh's third round whipped through the bush. Wide, poor aim under pressure.

Now eight or ten Mausers were concentrated on returning fire. The *banda* were ours.

I motioned and we stood. I wheeled them right and straightened them up again. Agonizingly slow against heavy thumps from the Mausers, now only fifty yards in front. As if we would surely lose the moment.

But against the Borana the *banda* had not thought of their flank. Lying in a group on the ground, rifles firing fast, intent only on out-gunning Girreh. Khaki uniforms, belts, puttees, visible by the remains of the camp fire. We had achieved complete surprise.

I signalled to the section to bring their rifles up, aim. Another long second as positions were taken, safety catches off, left feet forward, heads cocked down over the sights.

Fire.

The splitting crack of seven rifles almost together. The Mausers stopped immediately as if by order. Then two or three *banda* were scrambling to their feet in panic at our charge.

As we overran the camp most of the *banda* on the ground did not move, only a few running wildly into the night. I jumped bodies in pursuit, emptying my pistol in the direction of fleeing shapes. Behind me bayonets were being used in every direction on bodies dead or alive.

I saw one of my men leap through the smoke and on to a startled figure crouching behind an ammunition box, bayonet taking the man through the neck. Others were behind me on the far side of the fire, rifles grasped by the barrel, butts held high over heads with two hands like an axe. Instinct, not learned from me.

Then, as I stood watching the scene, only seconds after I had passed through the *banda* camp, not knowing how many had escaped and whether or not they were armed, thinking about defence, in that moment I heard shots. From Girreh's anthill. My orders had failed.

I knew before I shouted, '*Girreh, simama. Simama.*'

I knew before I saw the body, white cloth lying over heaps of *banda* khaki. Girreh's section had fired a fourth round after our charge, in the excitement of the moment. A Borana lay face down, head between a pair of *banda* feet.

I turned him over. The bullet had entered his chest under the arm. Through his wrap, through the ribs and out the other side. A jagged hole from shoulder to waist, red, black. Eyes closed, blood filling his mouth.

I walked round the fire and counted bodies. Eight *banda* dead without searching the bush. And one of ours, Damballa, from the Yabbo's family.

I felt no satisfaction, only anger. At the *banda,* at the dead bodies, their fire, their meat still sizzling, equipment lying all around. In this remote stretch of bush far distant from Europe, in peaceful Oromoland. At the Italians, at us the British. For our fortifications, for our retreat. For the pastoral Borana forced to *bunduki.*

Damballa's blood-soaked body lay arched and awkward. He was Thompson, he was Ellington, he was every useless death in every useless war.

Girreh arrived with his two men, waving their rifles like spears ready to start a dance, beaming faces looking at me across the fire. I pointed silently to Damballa.

But their sorrow was short: Damballa had died the death of Hokoba Borsa, a brave warrior of Borana legend. We must all die. And Damballa had not been married, there were no children.

I said nothing to Girreh about the shots. Damballa was dead, it was over.

I decided to act, to be as ruthless in my cause as *banda,* as barbaric as *shifta.* In the name of the innocent tribe I could be as evil as the Amhara.

Dawn again, creeping white light, an orange arc, the bush symphony and chorus. Then a bird with a single clear note echoing like a repeated key from the xylophone on the train, *boing, boing, boing . . .* Africa unmoved by any mere human event.

We buried the Mausers and *banda* ammunition in the river bed, covering our tracks back across the sand. We moved off with the bodies from around the fire and a ninth from the bush. Damballa ahead, carried high on crossed rifles, shrouded in his bloodstained white.

The tribe went into a frenzy: warriors cheering, women jumping and ululating.

But there was no time for a *baraaza.* Damballa's body was laid on a bed and one by one the men in my section came forward to recount his heroism. His family, twenty or thirty people, stood around the bed, enjoying the stories it seemed. Only the Yabbo appeared to think that a high price had been paid. Nine guilty bandits against one innocent young life.

Damballa's family took the body back toward the dry river and made a covering of rocks, tightly packed like a jigsaw puzzle in three dimensions. They sang a song, quietly, mumbling almost, first the men, then the women. Damballa had gone to live with the lizards.

I posted sentries again and we followed my barbaric plan. Women stripped the *banda* bodies, uniforms, hats and equipment distributed among the tribe. I took a belt, SERVIZIO IMPERIALE E REALE cast around the buckle and a *banda* kepi complete with cloth flap for the back of the neck.

I chose a bare piece of ground in the middle of the trail left by the herd as they had moved into the desert, where we were sure to be followed. Here we laid out the naked bodies in a line a few feet apart.

It was an inhuman, putrid job but I was carried along by my hatred. How many unarmed Borana would the *banda* have killed? A hundred? Two hundred? With their herds driven off and the rest of the tribe left to starve and die in the middle of a war.

The bodies had already started to rot in the sun, stinking like a charnel house, quickly losing their features to the heat. White ants and a cloud of flies worked into ears and up noses. Dust and dung covered the bodies like joints of meat rolled in flour.

We cut poles from the trees along the river bed, Ys and Ts, then we strapped the bodies on. One by one, they came up, a Roman crucifixion, a Golgotha. Until all nine hung in a row. Limp, unidentifiable. Heads hanging left, right, forward.

I found the swordsman, expeditious dispatcher of goats, precision slitter of stomachs. I took his short sword out of its sheath, handle toward him.

'Now,' I said holding his wrist, turning him to face the line of suspended bodies, 'do like the Amharas do.'

The swordsman walked to the nearest corpse.

Deft certain movements, genitals like fresh sausage falling bloodless over his bare feet. Working his way along the line while we all watched in silence, until a purple gash defaced the front of each cadaver.

The bodies looked shocking, female.

So, messenger, moving close to me, my mouth wide open, slobbering tongue splayed against etched glass, shoulders shaking like a man taken from the coldest sea. Moving round so that my blurred eyes could see him. Undisturbed black hair, coagulated lavender strands combed straight back from the forehead. A point to his hairline like a Dracula in the pictures. *So messenger,* hissing quietly, creamed crop caressing my quivering chin, *what message will you deliver now?*

The days in the desert became one. Overpowering white heat followed by a long black night of exhaustion and death.

Water and food were carried by donkeys and women. A supply of water for only a few days of normal consumption. Each night warriors drank first, sharing with their bulls. Then young men and donkeys. Women were next, dribbling precious drops of moisture down to their children. Then milking cows, sheep and goats. Calves, kids and lambs were given a lick at first, the moist edge around a gourd, a suck on the fingers of a child.

Then as the time for the journey seemed interminable, the tribe caught for ever in the centre of a burning ring of unbroken horizon, young animals were the first to be excluded.

Food was not a crisis even after the cows dried. A gourd of preserved meat lasted a family for five days or more and donkeys carried as many as ten gourds.

No feed was brought for the animals. In the first few days, sheep and goats turned up tiny caches of grey dry grass or herdsmen pulled at roots dormant between rains, a handful here and there to a prized bull or a donkey. Then the desert turned completely arid.

There was no wood. Without wood there were no fires and there were no bomas for the herd. Warriors slept standing like their animals, leaning on their spears, unable to be off their guard day or night. No *warra* could be erected in the rocky ground, the tribe slept in the open.

After I had lost track of days, but before the Yabbo said that forward was as far as back, we met Rendille tribesmen. Crossing our path east to west, camels in line, noses slanted against the inferior cattle herders. There was an elaborate greeting, water we hardly had, camel milk in return.

Warriors gathered around and discussion started. I looked at faces. Dust in their hair, fair against black parchment, white eyebrows and eyelashes accentuated like actors, very early old. But still standing straight against their weapons, passive, each waiting his turn to speak.

The Rendille were resplendent in ochre. Traditional allies of the Borana, the group speaking a mixture of languages I did not understand.

The Rendille knew of water which could be dug three days east. A place, they said, where a river could be found underground.

The discussion went slowly, round and round, one voice at a time. Five or six days more waiting in the Didi Galgallu against a new supply of water. And after the wait the worst was to come. *NuBorana* came to their decision, the Yabbo spoke. They would halt while the strongest warriors and donkeys made the journey.

The worst that came after the Rendille water was a hell of one foot in front of the other. Of hour after hour almost defeated by the sun. A hell of nights, of restless exhaustion between jagged rocks. Unable to understand how women, children and unwatered animals were still alive.

I watched them as they passed. Beyond determination and resignation, stumbling forward like an army from the other side, glazed eyes set on a mystic inner goal.

By the time Marsabit mountain came into sight through the haze, the dead had started to fall behind us in a continuous trail like beans from a leaking sack. As if the inner eye had seen the purple hills and the flesh could take its leave.

Across the desert my section had kept to its position, patrolling day and night in an arc behind the tribe. Against an enemy who had been warned and did not come. Now we became undertakers, consignees of the dead.

At first the death of an animal was observed, owners standing silently by, counting the loss. The death of a tribe member was a ritual, an event that affected us all. But by the last days, with the end in sight, animals and humans fell together under the feet of the advancing herd, unnoticed and uncounted.

Cattle collapsed forwards then sideways often bringing down others with them. The living animal unable to stand again, panting and dying by the corpse. Children slipped silently from their mother's arms and the old dropped face down, nothing more than shadows by the time we came upon them. No lingering death, no delay. The dead on the ground and the living moving forward. Only the flies multiplied and strengthened.

We covered each body with rocks. A desolate trail of forty or fifty cairns marking our passage. Animals were left to the scavengers.

From the first days of the crossing I had watched in my glasses as vultures and hawks circled our last camp, swooping on to the bodies of the *banda*. Eyes would be first, then stomachs, bowels.

Out in the desert as our weakest fell, the huge atrocious birds began to follow, gliding and wheeling on suffocating air off the desert floor.

I built up a fury for vultures: for every death, for the suffering of the tribe, every tottering skeleton in the herd. For war, for the state of the whole ugly world. Irrational, demented in the desert haze.

I hunted them, ten and twenty at a time as they hopped toward their defenceless prey, as they ripped at leather, at fleshless bones, many victims not yet dead. I shot them as they flapped away from picked carcasses, so full of carrion that they could not fly. Then, repulsively, others arrived, beaks pecking and stabbing through the shabby brown feathers and flayed bare necks of their own dead: brothers, sisters, uncles and aunts all at the feast. I shot them again and again, magazine after magazine, until I was surrounded by ejected casings and piles of corpses, by heaps of tatters spread by the scalding wind.

Then closer to Marsabit hyenas came, howling and laughing in the night. Pairs of luminous orange eyes glinting in the moonlight as they looked up at me from their banquet. Or they came in the day competing with jackals, running at vultures, then scattering like frantic rocking horses as I started to pick them off.

But for all the scavengers I might kill I could bring nothing back to life.

The Yabbo who understood everything, even my *bunduki* and my vengeance, he told me one night how the world was made. Hoarse, words very slowly into my ear. About the heavens and the earth, the power of creation.

Grass is the gift of the earth, water from the heavens, the life from which the Borana had sprung. From *horro*, the word for well, for moisture, for ancestor, the word for fertility, for the animal wealth of the tribe. The same word for all life.

It was an admonition to the destroyer, diseased by vengeance. And I stopped my killing.

Domine Deus, Creator coeli et terrae. The Yabbo knew it all.

Our journey had no defined end. A grey parched thorn bush at a time, a tuft of white grass then another, vegetation started again. But we moved on for two more days after we had passed the first stunted acacias and occasional sprigs of mimosa, up the slopes of Marsabit toward green. Recovery had to be slow: a little grass that day, a few leaves the second.

On the third day off the Didi Galgallu the lead herdsmen came to a Rendille well cut deep through lava and limestone, cool and dark, the promise of plentiful water. The Yabbo and a group of warriors examined the find. I was anxious to start drawing water. But the warriors held back.

A discussion started. How would watering be done from such a deep well? Gourds could not be passed. As the Borana had not dug this well, there must be purification, a bull sacrificed, whipping sticks laid down, spitting.

The men were gaunt, lifeless statues, women staring, stumbling to the back. Animals beyond, bones so sharp that brittle skin must surely rip with any movement, each carcass folding into a pile of bleached bone.

But their lore held. There would be no water for anyone, warrior, mother, child, until the tribe had come to their decision. Each speaker having his say: slowly, many words lost, croaking, beyond speech. Flies buzzing and flicking on leather clothes, on heads, lips, arms and legs, triple in number after only two days off the desert.

I became desperate. Discussion about moving on, searching for an *oda* tree, about the benefits of shallow wells. I spoke: there was a way for the well to be used. But I wanted to scream, shake them, threaten them with my revolver, make them start, now, draw water for the women, for the children, for me. But I stood, I had no energy to do more.

Then the Yabbo came forward, a living corpse, as if unwrapped from his shroud and balanced on his feet just for that moment to speak to us from the dead.

'*NuBorana*,' the Yabbo whispered, 'make you Gramama, *konficha*.' A warrior brought the *konffi*, the big bat. The Yabbo tried to hold it out to me, shaking, unable to lift the weight.

I stood next to him holding the bat, the loose skin of his wrist crumbling between the fingers of my other hand. If there had been a drop of moisture in my body tears would have swelled my eyes. But I was dry, *bachaa*, like the lizards.

I issued my orders. The well could be purified by laying down whipping sticks and by the spitting ritual. But there would be no sacrifice of an animal that had survived such a journey.

A man was lowered down the well. He wedged two boughs across the shaft at the waterline as a platform. From there he could sink the gourds as they arrived. At the top water was splashed into a trough, slow and shallow, barely adequate.

Then I started my triage, my judgement between life and death.

Best attention to the strongest, the least damaged. Then to those who could be patched up for the front in a day or two. The severely wounded left to die.

Thompson had told me, on the march before Cambrai. But I had not understood at the time.

'Triage, sir,' he said, as we swung past a CCS, ambulances coming and going, men on stretchers lying outside. Row upon row, a parade ground for the horizontal.

Invincible, immortal I was then.

'That's what goes on in there, sir. Must be the hardest job in the whole sodd'n' war.'

8

After Jane had left, but a month or two before the hospice. Before no-name-brand had moved in. Morley panicked at four o'clock in the afternoon. Cellphone ringing, stepping onto the quay. Granville Island market in the background would give him away.

'Brock, I'm sorry. I've already left you a message. I have to be out at Delta Municipal Hall.'

Was that the first time? The first time he had lied to his partners.

'Morley, listen, you know how important Friday nights are. You've got to be able to put Delta off. Keeping the guys revved, talk about what's coming up. Do you really want your best draughtsmen drifting off because they're in the dark about the future?'

And maybe that was the first time for them as well, that night. Brock picking at a skirmished cheese tray, only the boozers left at the office party. Kingsley's fingers reaching for a sprig of parsley. They had to face it: they had to find themselves a new partner or else sell out.

Morley's menu would be a touch of everything she had liked from all the places they had been together. *Crudités* with anchovy sauce, seared spring rolls with chopped cashew nuts, curried lentils, sherry over crushed ice, then Tavel rosé. Flowers, black candles, a Ronnie Hawkins CD as a wrapped present complete with bow. Only three hours to go, Morley hustled from stall to stall down the market aisles.

A dedicated evening was all he had asked. To sit and talk, nothing coming in from the outside. To ask why, to go over it, live it again, back to when everything used to work. Find the crossroads where he had taken the wrong turn, scrutinize the signboards over again. Understand. Now make the *right* decision.

To concentrate on her alone. Tell her what he thought she knew, what he thought did not need saying every hectic day. That he loves her, that she is more beautiful at forty than ever before. That he is only what he appears, nothing less, nothing more. A confused bear, a Morley who dearly needs his Jane.

He unpacked and cooked at the same time, listening to the radio then Coltrane on a CD. But the happiness, the assurance was missing. There must be something stronger: *real conviction, comfort level.* Always back to Jane's new words.

Two hours of preparation, hot for her like a red pepper seed.

The first time she had promised him, the evening hadn't stood a chance.

'Oh Morley, that's just lovely, just exactly right, be off the rotten phone in just another second,' as he takes his tricks out of his oven one at a time. But her voice empty, forced warmth like the young volunteers in for a day. All good intentions toward the dying.

Upstairs after the meal and Morley bursting, Jane avoiding him, into the second bathroom.

Then, 'Morley darling, would you mind if we made love in the morning. Terribly terribly tired.'

A worse night than alone, padding the house, calculating, fretting. In a glass box: she can't hear him, she's looking the other way. Shouting, waving. *Reconciliation*, isn't that why you came? Beating on the see-through walls, I love you. I love you. Over here. I'm sorry. I'm sorry. For everything.

Her black bag on the spare bed and he can't help himself. The letter is at the bottom.

HI JANE. I REALLY ENJOYED OUR LUNCH AND WHIRLWIND VOYAGE TO EXOTIC SNUG HARBOR. IT'S REALLY WONDERFUL THAT YOU ARE DOING SO GREAT AT THE STORE. WE ARE GOING TO HAVE AN EXTRAORDINARY ADVANCED COURSE IN TRANSFORMATIONLAND. GREAT THAT YOU'RE GETTING COMPLETE WITH MORLEY. YOU HAVE MY PERMISSION, THINK OF THAT REALITY AND WHAT YOU HAVE TO ACTUATE WILL BE SOMEWHAT MARGINALIZED. LOVE DONALD.

In the morning he'll bring her coffee and fruit, magazines, they'll sit and talk. What he had read was a nightmare, not real, doesn't exist. Make love to her, lie her across the unmade bed, every pore, Jane, just Jane. Concentrate.

But she's up while he's still in the kitchen waiting for ever for water to boil. She's wearing his dressing gown, back into the spare bedroom and hunting through her black bag.

Pale, right out of bed, the Jane he loves the most.

'Forgot to tell you Morley … my god, is it that time already? Two of the girls are sick … rotten flu about … must be there to open up. First customers are getting earlier and earlier on Saturdays. Have a bath at home. Bye-ee.'

Home? This is your home. That's what your vivisectionist's documents say: the Matrimonial Home. Sell it. Give me the money.

Now another chance at a dedicated evening.

But at eight o'clock the risotto went from the table back into the oven to dry up, candles burning down. Morley sitting with the newspaper but not a word taken in.

The phone, answered in one ring. Jane on her cell.

'So sorry to be late.' No *darling*, no *Morley dear*. 'I'm at the accountant's. They're after my PST returns almost by the day now. Miss once and you're a criminal. Should be there by half past. Bye-ee.'

Even then he could have felt it coming if he had listened. No call at half past, next call at nine with the food over the top. Still fussing with this paperwork, she says.

Then finally:

'Look, I'm dreadfully sorry, but this has gone on much longer than it should. Really tired and I wouldn't do you much good anyway. Better I go home and get a good sleep. I'll call you tomorrow or you come by the shop. You haven't done anything special have you?'

Noises off like a bar.

'No, I thought we'd go out.'

Do you much good. She knew him, it was a sign, a hopeful sign. Anything.

'Where were we going to go?' Playful, teasing. It was coming to the house she didn't like. Morley and Jane's house.

Fitful sleep, images of Brock eating cheese. Of buildings, strikes, no cement, steel frames like rubber bending in the wind. Libraries with no books, sheer walls like a prison, snap ties hanging, a danger to the public, danger, *pericoloso*.

One o'clock, up and sweating, tracksuit on, down to the Landcruiser and over the bridge.

Heart smacking like an air wrench in a tyre shop. Ten cylinders clutching the wheel, more Coltrane and the late-nite voice from Calgary. Turned off.

Starting three blocks away, down the rows. Would it be on the street or in the garage? His eyes could recognize the car before his mind registered, from a fender, from a sliver glimpsed three cars up, hitting his body like a high dive. He knew it by heart, every dent, every scratch. Up and down then around into the park. Slowly, veins running acid, eating away at his limbs. Arteries bored out to the size of water pipes. Hatred, strength, weakness, love: the far extremes of every emotion he had ever felt.

By the tennis courts, on its own. All the others gone, windows dewed in all round. Wiped away with his hand, cold, wet. Papers and samples falling off the back seat and onto the floor. The Jetta.

Why wasn't the car in the garage? In her designated stall?

The passenger door was open. Control, he was a dripping tap. The one she needed. Even nags me about the state of my car…

Morley sat in. Jane, Jane's scent, Jane's mess. He started searching, glove compartment, floor, back seat. Then with the tips of his fingers he felt what he was looking for. Far under the front seat, wedged against a decaying orange, behind a discarded coffee cup. The remote control for the garage door of the apartment block, he knew there had to be one. Lost in the rubble on the floor. That was why the car was on the street. Into his pocket.

Terror like a murder, anger like a bad drunk, body out of control, world without meaning. If he had a gun…

They all say that, but nobody actually does it. This is Canada.

Memories, memories within memories, no nows, no todays left.

Morley pulled the Lay-Z-Boy up to the bed and took Graham's wrist. But here he was safe, far from Falkland Road. Safe in Africa, the past, in Graham's past.

～

The bulls began to look stronger. I held the *konffi*, watching as they came up to the well for the third or fourth time. But each morning when the herd moved out of the boma they left their dead behind, victims of my triage. Those who could never be returned to the front. Shrunken heaps lying in the fresh dung that had come back with new grazing.

But with the tribe I followed a different order and we lost no more children. Legs thin like crutches, little old faces over stomachs bloated by hunger. Mothers sagged and dry.

The Yabbo came up the hill to visit me in my camp. The *waarta* skinning warthog by the fire. Stooped, one foot carefully in front of the other, leaning heavily on a stick. Without moving he seemed to explore me, outside, inside, reading me and all that I was. I did not have to tell him that I was leaving.

'We are strong,' he whispered. 'You Gramama, now you are strong.' The journey across the desert, their lost lands. After so many deaths? 'We are strong,' the Yabbo repeated, 'we who still live.'

The Yabbo was silent again, searching to understand the incomprehensible. By leaving the tribe I was giving up something of infinite value, of endless continuity. In return for a desert chimera, the life of a European.

I felt closer to the Yabbo than to any other person in the world. With my life, my defeat, my small victory across the Didi Galgallu. Finding here in the desert that there was life still to be lived.

'*Kingi Georgi*,' the Yabbo said with no more than a breath, 'he will send you back. We will wait for you, Gramama.'

The DC's post at Marsabit was a shock, ordered and absurd, painted stones and swept earth. The DC had changed since October of '39. Exeter, my name and my posting were completely unknown to the new man.

From the verandah of his office he watched me approach across the compound, smart in his administrator's outfit, bush jacket, pressed shorts. Older than me, probably ready for early retirement before the war had come along.

He faced our little section: filthy white wraps, leather aprons, *banda* kepis and a covering of flies like scales on fish. Carrying all the *bunduki* to be returned.

I held out my hand.

'Exeter,' I said, 'DO Moyale.'

'Merry,' he replied. 'I'm the DC here.'

Then a silence that seemed like half an hour while Merry's pipe levered up and down between his teeth. He spoke again.

'However do you manage *that* trick?' staring down at my motionless arms black with flies.

Within a week the summons came. To the office of the Chief Secretary in Nairobi. Merry looking smug. There had been talk on the wireless. Letting the side down, moving tribes around the Colony as he sees fit. Asking the Rendille, if you please, for grazing. Ignoring him, Merry the DC.

Quale was now Assistant Secretary, no longer the Deputy. Promoted to an even larger office, an even deeper verandah. I sat through an hour of bluster and accusations.

I'd gone native. Oh yes he'd heard, looking at my bracelet. Exactly who did I think I was? Africans expect leadership from Europeans. Where would they be without us? Back swinging in the trees.

Judicial proceedings in excess of my authority. No Poll Tax, no Hut Tax, not a single shilling collected, no Customs Duties. Insulting officers of the King's African Rifles. Consorting with the enemy. Playing Dr Livingstone. Prisoners found castrated and mutilated. Formal complaint from the Italians via the Red Cross, but, luckily for me, no proof of who.

I sat as if still covered with flies. He could do as he wished, the Borana were safe at Marsabit.

But then Quale started to talk about OETA, Occupied Enemy Territory Administration, us replacing the Spaghetti Men. The Wops were going to be licked and Quale would need every man, no matter what his record. Frowning, opening and closing my file, wanting me to think that he might change his mind and make me a hospital clerk somewhere out of his hair.

Now it was our turn, we were going to attack them. And behind the advance of our army Quale would need administrators to run the captured Italian colonies. Experienced men. I had almost a year's service.

Then he stood staring out of the window pulling at his whisky.

He would send me back up-country. He had no choice. But the Colony was going to hell, that much was quite clear. Used to be a decent place once, with the show run by solid reliable men.

The next month, November 1940, a regiment of South Africans arrived in Marsabit to prepare for the invasion of Abyssinia. European troops from the colonel down to the private soldiers, but they called themselves *white*. They all spoke Afrikaans or a rough aggressive English if they had to, with a clipped nasal accent.

To the South Africans the others were *blacks*, *kaffirs* to be kicked and sworn at with no place in their schemes.

They themselves were a tribe, the Afrikaaners told me, of white Africans. Every black tribe had, after all, originally migrated from somewhere.

The South Africans looked down on my type. Europeans in Africa. Temporaries. Ready at the first sign of trouble to *voetsek* back to England. Probably planning my retirement in Brighton already, a stuffed kadu head on the wall and all the stories.

And certainly, they bellowed, as the arguments heated up, certainly they were African. Just as white Australians were Australians and just as white Americans were Americans. Just as entitled to their land as all the other Europeans who had put natives into reserves and occupied the great open spaces of the world. I was a hypocrite like all pinkos. They would have had racial separation by law in Canada years ago if the coloureds there had outnumbered whites.

The South Africans were keen to fight. Against the Italians, against the British again if necessary. But not fight because of European War, but as part of their own African war, for territory, for domination of the continent by their white tribe.

The campaign was underway on New Year's Day 1941: the KAR through Mandera, the South Africans up to Moyale.

Our convoy crossed the Didi Galgallu in four days, a straight line up the stony road, a motor grader working ahead of us. Hurricanes in support, so low they blew up dust.

There was no Eye-tie morale and there was no Eye-tie defence. Without rations, fuel or ammunition some of their fortified camps gave up without a single shot: Wardeglo, Afmadu, Kismayu. And within a month the Italians had crumbled on all fronts.

On 22 February 1941 the South Africans entered Moyale and on 6 April General Wetherall entered Addis Ababa. The KAR had advanced 1,687 miles against the enemy in under three months, which they claimed as a record.

The Second Reconstruction of Moyale was more complicated than the First. Shelling aimed at the boma had destroyed the town. Then after our withdrawal our own planes had bombed the boma buildings and the airstrip to prevent anything useful falling into the hands of the enemy. Even though the Italians had matching facilities of their own which were left untouched.

Then for a year the ruins of the town had been occupied by the Italian Army and the *banda*. The water system had been blown up, fires set, unexploded ordnance and charred vehicles blocked the roads.

And in the few days between the departure of the Italians and the arrival of the South Africans, *shifta* had pillaged the remains.

For the first year of OETA I lived in Marconi's *palazzo* which had been protected by his Somalis, but out of self-interest rather than loyalty. I ate Marconi's food, I drank Marconi's *Lago di Garda* and I slept in Marconi's bed. Mamma Marconi's picture admonished me each morning from his washstand.

After the rains with everything green that year, the tribes returned. The Sakuye from Wajir, the Gabbra from North Horr, the Borana from Marsabit, supplied on the move by lorries with fresh water, fodder, firewood and sacks of food.

Twenty-two years after the first Abyssinian treaty, all the tribes were reunited, north to south, under our rule. The border was gone and the era of Oromoland had dawned. *Nagaiya Borana*, the Peace of the Borana. I remembered words from Fairy, *Pax Britannica* and I was proud.

The resources of the Colony were available to rebuild the town. I dug my cattle dips and I built my school. The dressing station reopened with medicines for smallpox, malaria, conjunctivitis and jaundice. Without the border for their protection the KAR pushed the *shifta* back to the east. The old nomadic routes were followed again and the herds fattened and multiplied.

During 1941, with the Second Reconstruction of Moyale well advanced, the Italians began to return. Not in their Lancias and their comic uniforms, but standing in rags, packed on to convoys of KAR three-tonners.

Prisoners of War and interned government officials, some women and children, all on their way to camps in Kenya. There had been no Decline and Fall to their New Roman Empire, only complete collapse.

From the second convoy to pass through I heard my name shouted out, a familiar call.

'*Signor Eekse-tear, Santo Gramama ya Borana,*' from the back of a lorry.

It was Marconi. A slim, worn-down Marconi, but the same eyebrow halfway up his forehead, the same arms outstretched, about to glide down to me like a piazza pigeon.

'*Signor Cavaliere Marconi,*' looking up at him, holding my hat to my chest, as if ready to receive his field benediction, 'what a great pleasure to see you safe.'

Marconi looked around at his countrymen in the lorry. You see, he seemed to be saying, I really am what I say I am.

I had Marconi brought down and I signed for my friend as my personal prisoner. To be put back on the next convoy following. And Marconi himself did not want to stay any longer than a short time.

'I too have my responsibilities,' he said. To see his defeated tribe across the desert.

I started with my guilty occupation of the *palazzo*. But there was no bitterness.

'Who better than you, Grah-ham?' Arms out again. 'We declared war on you and your house was destroyed. So it is one thing, just one thing that I can offer you.'

Marconi's Somalis were sullen, sensing defeat and blood. I had to chase them for drinks, for his bathwater. And Marconi was nervous and exhausted, more than I had seen at the convoy.

With food and wine he began to rant, his French failing under the strain: Italian, English words all jumbled together. Flailing his arms like a signaller. The Italian retreat, a rout, it had been terrible. Nobody had been prepared for the speed with which the *Impero Italiano* had crumbled.

Right away the *banda* had turned on their masters or they had deserted. Many *banda* had changed sides to fight for the Amhara who were now supporting the British.

For the Italians, staying out of Amharic hands became much more urgent than running away from the British. Did I know that there were some Amharic tribes that used the skin of an enemy's scrotum as a facial decoration? And that the skin, to achieve real cachet, had to be taken while the enemy was still alive? Then there was another tribe that pickled their enemies' genitals. For presentation to their brides on their wedding night as an omen of fertility, a spare set.

Outside Addis, Marconi had been able to arrange for the surrender of the two southern provinces with immediate British protection for the Europeans. But still a number of Italians had been captured by Amhara, who achieved surprise many times by approaching the Italians wearing looted *banda* uniforms.

'And those who were captured, their ending,' Marconi said quietly, 'their ending would be unspeakable.'

I had seen those endings often. In my nightmares of the swordsman.

Marconi fell forward on to the table in a twitchy mumbling sleep, calling out, pouring sweat on to the tablecloth. With a reluctant Somali I carried him to his bed.

The following day I showed Marconi around the Second Reconstruction. But by noon the next transport had arrived and I had to give him up before lunch.

'Be careful, Exeter,' Marconi warned me, back up on the lorry. 'Take it from one who knows. You are an innocent, a saint. But Nairobi, London, like Roma, they will have other ideas. *Tu vas voir, mon ami.*'

Marconi was right.

They put on a good show down by the bridge between the two towns, between the two Empires.

The earth was swept, stones were painted and flags were hung. Strings of little Union Jacks, long pennants for Abyssinia, now the Ethiopian Empire. A black lion on a bright yellow background holding a Coptic cross under a paw.

The KAR sent a band and a Guard of Honour. There was a March Past and a General Salute, the officers awkward and unrehearsed with their swords.

For the Crown there was the Officer in Charge of Occupied Enemy Territory Administration, Lieutenant Colonel Reece, OBE. In by air, sweating and dusty in his Number Ones, unused to the large KAR hat and thick leather chinstrap.

And for the Emperor, Haile Selassie, King of Kings, Lion of Judah, there was Fitaurauri Damisi, the Emperor's son-in-law, Governor of Ethiopian Borana. With him was Ras Abeba Adegai, Ruler of Galla-Sidamo. Splendid on their chargers, in their white embroidered blouses and leggings, black silk capes flowing out in the breeze.

Behind them a squadron of mounted Amharic lancers on matching black Arabs from the bodyguard of the Emperor himself. Jostling, jingling, impatient in their lines for the hunt to begin.

Then our Empire handed over to their Empire: the Wollo, the Macca, the Arssi, the Gugi and the northern Borana. All the Oromos from above the old line, my tribes under OETA, under *Pax Britannica*. All given over to the Amhara, the slavers, the raiders, the protectors of the *shifta*.

Words were spoken, hands were shaken, the band played and the deed was done.

The border was put back and Oromoland ceased to exist.

After our Great Victory we delivered them up and we washed our hands. *Festgeknebelt* they call it in Germany: bound hand and foot.

It was Marconi who decided me on what to do, on how to leave.

I was not a colonist.

PO Box 6,
Lamu,
Kenya
5th July 1944

Caro Gramama ya Borana
You are still in Moiale?
I am the English writer now, but I sure one thing. You are still no learning Italiano.

I ask your government to send this letter.

One hotel is being mine in Lamu. It is being burned. Me as well maybe.

You will be needing holiday mon ami. Come to stay in Lamu. I am making grappa from sugared canes. Write to me in the box on top.

Your friend,

Giuseppe Marconi

Nairobi made it easy. They were happy to see me go. All my back pay, a glowing reference, a passport: Graham Exeter and no questions. I went back up, for one last time.

The Borana gave me a *baraaza* before I left. All my clothes off again, turned in a circle then another white wrap. They sang, they drank a lorry-load of beer.

Then I sang for them from the steps of the DC's house in front of the fire by the pepper tree. From my *Passion*.

Mache dich, mein Herze, rein,
Ich will Jesum...

Holding the score with both hands. Breathing, counting, the sustained notes. Up from the chest, out through the top of the head. Singing to the old and to the new. With the fresh life that they had given me.

9

Morley had been away for three nights, two in Dallas and one at the hospice. But Susan wasn't going to speak first. She watched him climb the stairs with his suitcase.

'Been sleeping in?' Morley asked. It was almost noon.

'And why not, it's a stat day off, isn't it?'

'What difference does a long weekend make to a UI team member? Every day's a holiday, right?'

He dropped his bag into the small bedroom. The bedroom he had been moved into on Gulag Day.

He had returned home late the evening he had been released from jail. After dinner with Tim, after recovering the Landcruiser from the pound, to find Susan moving. But not moving out of the house, things weren't going to be that simple.

'I lost my job, Morley, all because of you,' Susan greeted him. She had been at the Chilean red again. Her tongue was a luminous purple. 'You gave them the perfect excuse to can me without a nickel of severance pay.'

Susan was so angry she was spitting as well as lisping. Most unattractive.

'Landscape design is very slow. I waited a year from my last job. But this time you're going to be supporting me. It'll be six weeks even before my UI cheques start rolling.' As she talked, Susan ferried armfuls of Morley's clothes from his dressing room into the second bedroom.

'What are you doing with my stuff?'

'It's over, Morley, whatever it was. You're sleeping in here now,' pushing past him with another load and into the second bedroom. 'Then you can come and go all night for all I care. Go stalk your wife, I don't give a hoot any more. In fact I hope they catch you and you're put away.'

Susan dropped more clothes onto the floor of what was now Morley's room. She went for another load. Picture of herself: *Co-dependent no longer*.

'This is purely financial from here on, Morley. One-way street. Have you ever even heard of UI? It stands for Unemployment Insurance, you snob. And UI has a ski team, they have a jogging team, a horse riding team. And I'm going to join them all, Morley. All at your expense.'

Morley started to pick his clothes up off the floor and organize his new closet, lobotomized by the tirade, a Susan he had never met before. When Susan had finished her deliveries she retreated into the large bedroom, now her private domain. The door had slammed behind her.

Morley returned to the garage to collect the rest of his things. The overhead door had closed and the ceiling light had switched off.

Morley sat in on the passenger side of the Landcruiser. He opened the glove compartment. Then he leaned back, eyes closed.

Immediately his nightmare returned, the prequel.

A face comes into focus. Stepping toward Morley but on the other side of a glass-topped counter. A small shop, heavy security fittings round the walls, bars covered by chains and padlocks and more bars under the glass counter.

'How y'all doin'? Can I help ya with something?' The face belongs to a huge white man with arms like Italian hams, tattoos on massive biceps disappearing up into rolled sleeves.

Morley stands at the counter stammering.

'Personal security, is that it?' The man wants to be helpful, he's the store clerk. Morley nods inanely. 'Every citizen's right,' the clerk adds in a reverential tone as if quoting Scriptures. 'Probably yer first piece? Recently moved into the Lone Star State? New to our fine city of Dallas?'

'I'm a Canadian,' Morley replies defensively as if to excuse his nerves. We don't have these sorts of places in Canada, he wants to add, we're civilized.

'Allow me to show you this one. This is a .38 snubnose. Fits in the back of ya briefcase, or down a coat pocket.'

A short revolver comes out of the show case, grey-black metal. Like a toy in the large meaty hand. The gun is repulsive, attractive, a dark irresistible magnet. The clerk flips the chamber out to the side, a bullet goes in and the gun closes again with a steely click.

'Real nice 'n' easy. Stop a man dead at fifty feet,' the clerk says proudly. 'Do a lot of damage at two hundred. One hundred and fifty smackers.'

'But I don't live here,' Morley replies realizing what he is about to do if the clerk doesn't stop him.

'Y'all don't be worrying about that now, even makes it a *who-ole* lot easier. The gun going outta town in the next few days?'

Morley nods again.

'I'm heading for the airport at five o'clock.'

'Well, that a-way,' the clerk drawls on, 'there won't *be* no wait'un period, there won't *be* no background checks and there won't *be* no State of Texas Firearm Ownership Card, will there?' He grins Morley a big sinister grin. 'Know what I mean, jelly bean? Don't think you're the type who *needs* to cool-off, are yah?'

There is a pause and in those few seconds Morley has bought himself a gun.

'I'll charge you fifty dollars for the case and the trigger lock, so for two hundred bucks yer on ya way.'

Morley tenders his credit cards feeling like a virgin in a motel room.

'Best you don't pay with the card,' the man says. 'You never know what weirdo can get a-hold of the record. Fact, yer shouldn't even be out on the street in Deep Ellum with all them cards on ya body. Certainly not after two in the afternoon when them gangbangers wake up.' The clerk grins his repulsive grin again. 'And in any case, no records is what the fifty dollars is for.'

Morley takes out his billfold and hands over four fifties. Within minutes he is back on the street, half instructed and fully armed.

At Dallas-Forth Worth airport the answer to his question should have been self-evident. Morley feels naive even for asking as he lugs his suitcase out of the shuttle and over to the check-in desk at the kerb.

'Not right with you in the cabin, sir, but there's no restriction on firearms in checked luggage on domestic.' And to Morley's astonishment his suitcase slides onto the carousel at Seattle-Tacoma airport. Innocent, as if containing nothing more lethal than dirty underwear.

Another irony of life in the United States. Something that should be straightforward, a signature on a piece of paper to start a hole. An excavation for a thirty-million-dollar building, an addition to the Baylor School of Dentistry, all approvals in place, every ordinance duly adopted and signed. But that last piece of paper is one big six-week problem at the County Judge's office with no reasons given.

But take a loaded gun around the country by air? Ain't no problem there, mister.

And Canada? Oh, Canada is so nice. Customs officers, young boys looking like bus drivers in their light blue shirts and their clip-on black ties.

'How long have you been out of the country, sir?'

'Three days in Dallas on business.' Did the shaking show?

Morley's British Columbia driver's licence is handed back to him through the booth window with a little smile.

'Have a nice day.'

But don't you want to search my truck? There's a gun and six bullets in the spare wheel cover, don't you want to find them? And I didn't plan this, I really did miss my flight on Tuesday, that's why I had the Landcruiser at Sea-Tac airport and that's why all this has been so easy. And the gun shop? I was just walking past. It all happened so quick. But I could well be unbalanced, you can't tell by looking at me. And my wife, she could be screwing with...

He's through. Into Canada with the revolver.

Morley sat up with a jerk and started to fumble through the glove compartment for the key, then he unlocked the cover to the spare wheel at the back of the vehicle. The gun was there, safe and sound. Carefully Morley wrapped the case into his rain jacket. A triangle in heavy plastic like the container for a jumbo-sized processed-cheese sandwich. He would hide it in his new closet, under his socks and underpants.

Suddenly a deafening blare pulsed through the dark garage. Morley jumped, case on to the floor, gun and bullets spilled. The noise was half-police siren, half-industrial-strength smoke detector. The horn connection to his carphone. Site-Alert, for drawing his attention to a call on a job site, switched on automatically with the keys in the ignition and the engine off. Morley rushed to the phone on the console, hand shaking.

'H'llo, h'llo.'

'Morley, it's Tim. What are you so nervy about, amigo? I've been trying to reach you. Your office had told me you'd be back last night.'

'I was at the hospice all night, my old boy is sinking.'

'Well, don't answer your door, the cops have another warrant.'

'Another warrant? What the hell for this time?'

'Apparently your partner did a first-class job on Jane's shop last week. Cleaned out the stock as well as the bank account. Got it all covered. But I've had the vivisectionist screaming at me for two days. I'm going to start charging you danger money, I can hear her sharpening up her scalpel with every call.'

Morley was still shivering. He expected Susan or a policeman to open the garage door the next moment and find the gun lying on the concrete floor.

Tim was still explaining.

'So Jane has retaliated by reporting to the police that you were outside her address on Falkland on Thursday night. It's a standard ploy, have you taken in on a Friday or a Saturday and spend the long weekend in gaol waiting for court on Tuesday. Soften you up for the coming financial settlement. Anyway, mucho problemo.'

'But I was in Dallas on Thursday night.'

Tim paused.

'Well now. Isn't that interesting. You've still got your boarding card and hotel bills, I suppose.'

'Oh yes, part of my expense record. You know what Kingsley's like.'

'In that case, amigo, I suggest that we head down to the copshop together right now and put all that on the counter. Demonstrate that they're the ones with the teeny problemo. Show Jane up for the lying little bitch she is.'

PART VII

1

Lamu is where the Northern Frontier District meets the Indian Ocean. Where Arabs in their dhows from Oman and the Yemen came to trade and to take slaves from the interior. Where Islam and the Qur'ān made their first conversions in black Africa.

After Italy capitulated to the Allies in 1943, POWs in Kenya were released. But even for those who wanted to go home there were no passages. Italians with nothing began to work: in kitchens, in makeshift factories, as foremen labouring on roads under the burning sun, next to their *watu* man for man. The extraordinary spectacle of Europeans performing manual labour.

Marconi could have chosen anywhere in Kenya for his hotel: in an up-country town where agriculture was expanding for the war. In Nairobi, booming like Johannesburg and Salisbury.

But Marconi had chosen Lamu, a remote island town of the coast Swahilis, a tribe as well as the universal language. Close to the Somaliland border and accessible only by dhow.

My KAR transport pulled up at the end of the road. Where bare plains, baobab trees and red earth merge flat with the sea through mangrove swamps.

On the opposite side of a wide channel the town was an African Savona: a concentration of upright white buildings set against a tropical forest. Blue in front, green behind like different shades of the same colour. Two and three storeys, flat roofs mixed with steep pitched *macuti* tight along a timbered quay. A dramatic contrast to Borana sticks and skins.

A dhow arrived manned by two Swahili sailors. Light-skinned Africans with fine features wearing bright red and yellow *kikois.*

The dhow is the timeless boat of the Indian Ocean, the Red Sea and the Persian Gulf. Related to the first craft on the Nile and the Euphrates, connecting present dhow sailors with the beginnings of civilization.

Dhows large and small share the same high prow deep like a primitive cutter, a rising flat stern and a forward-sloping mast for a single sail. A work of simple genius to the desert dweller.

The town clustered against a huge fort, dense and rounded like a child's sandcastle. Cornered by sloping turrets pushing up to over a hundred feet high. This massive structure was fortified with Arab crenellations and decorated by a row of ogee archways. Features which were repeated and varied through the architecture of the town.

Details of the buildings came into focus as we met the pier: heavy wood doors defended by rows of brass spikes, the intricate patterns of Islam tooled into roof beams, painted on wooden doorposts and set into plaster.

'*Waltalee.*' The helmsman pointed. The hotel was narrow and deep, no more than two rooms wide facing the channel. *Albergo Lamu* carved like the gunwale of a dhow along the railing of the first floor balcony.

Hands from the boat carried my kitbag down a narrow alley at the side of the building. The foyer was dark and cool. Italian rustic merging with Swahili materials, lime white against red tiles and carved *mvouli* wood ceilings. Birds of paradise and fan palms framing a window of deep blue coast sky and a view across rooftops to the pointed minarets of a mosque.

'*Santo Gramama di Borana.*' From behind the reception counter like an oath of good fortune, then arms out wide.

I spent over a month with Marconi, days and days of talk, of eating and drinking, watching the slow pace of the Swahili people. An Africa that looked outward, living off the sea and the natural products of sandy soils and predictable rains. Spices, bananas, cashews and coconuts.

Marconi told me about the rest of his war. He had filled out again and his face was alive, twitching with a newly expectant smile.

He had been unscrupulous in the interests of survival. Marconi had promoted himself to *maggiore*, claiming successfully to be the senior officer at a large POW camp in the Rift Valley. Then as *il Comandante* Marconi had negotiated an agreement with the British which he put to a vote.

'*Democrazia,*' shoulders hunched and palms up to the mangrove rafters. A comedian's gesture of resignation. 'Gra-ham, you would have been proud of me,' he laughed. 'The vote was even secret.'

The camp agreed to co-operate with the British in building a road up the side of the Rift Valley. Stone barriers, hairpin turns, places to pull off and admire the view. Like his village on Lake Como, the road up from Fagetto di Lario. Same eyebrow up into his forehead in anticipation of a joke, same moustache bobbing again like a pair of well-oiled wings. A job that needed one thing, just one thing. Superior Italian engineering, there in the middle of British Africa.

And when the road was complete they built a tiny church to *la Maronna* at the foot of the escarpment.

In return Marconi's men were well treated. Reasonable food supplies, a wage, better camp conditions, a still for making grappa from sugar cane. His collaboration had been completely vindicated by Mussolini's fall in September 1943.

In Nairobi after his release, Marconi had taken up with a former diplomat, Count Alfredo Cacacce, the pre-war Italian Consul. The Count had suffered little through the war in Kenya, interned at the Muthaiga Country Club.

Then the Count had become a dealer in war-surplus, buying wholesale from the British and selling retail in South Africa, in Mozambique or to local farmers and contractors. The merchandise consisted of everything that we had imported for the Italian campaign. From corrugated iron buildings to three-ton lorries, from galvanized steel fencing to cases of tinned spam.

In the course of his business the Count had bought, sight unseen, a burned-out hotel in Lamu. Marconi, who enjoyed remote places, took on the hotel with the carpenter from Moiale as his contractor, the Count as his partner and a loan from an Italian syndicate in Durban.

Marconi had been promised a flow of customers from among the Happy Valley crowd looking for something out of the way, not civil servants who preferred the Mombasa Club and not competing with Nyali Beach Hotel for the new settlers on their holidays. So far business had been slow. But the Count was to send Marconi a *motoscafo* then Albergo Lamu would offer marlin fishing.

Marconi had no visitors, only two permanent residents. Elderly English sisters, the Misses Albright, retired missionaries who had given up on the human race. Devoting themselves to a donkey sanctuary on the edge of the town.

But even without customers Marconi was all enthusiasm.

He had studied the history of the coast and he was ready to give his guests the benefit of his knowledge. Did I know, *per esempio*, that the Periplus of the Erythrean Sea, a guide for Greek sailors written in the years Before Christ, describes the East African coast as the land of Azania made up of prosperous city states ruled by benevolent merchants? All this when England was merely an Italian colony.

And the Frankincense and Myrrh of the Nativity? Marconi was sure. The fragrances had started in Lamu, by dhow to Oman, by camel across the Arabian peninsula to Jerusalem and Bethlehem. Where, I might remember from my history, the Jews were also a subject people of the Italians.

We walked through the town together, down cool narrow streets between *gofu*, large solid Swahili houses built of coral rag. Elegant interiors of simple Arab furniture behind billowing cotton drapes.

Finally we talked of Europe, of the future. And of going back.

'There is an *épuration* taking place in Italy,' Marconi warned me. 'In France as well. Terrible and bloody. Those who say they were patriots killing those who they say were collaborators. While here in Lamu there is peace. And economics? Only the Americans can revive Europe. Just think of it, *Signor Eekse-tare*, the marvellous irony, *tutto capovolto*. All those poor Calabrian emigrants coming back as rich Americans, as the *nuova aristocrazia*.'

His mother would visit Lamu as soon as the Germans had been driven out of Italy. His sister would find him a good Italian girl. Or maybe he would choose a light skinned Swahili, untouched and perfect behind her *shuga*.

He was young, he said, fifty-two that year. Ready for an entirely new life.

When I left I gave him my belt buckle. SERVIZIO IMPERIALE E REALE. And my bracelet as a charm for his new future. I was not an African.

Marconi put me on a larger dhow for the voyage to Mombasa. A *sambuk*, Persian captain and crew, over one hundred feet long, dwarfing the Lamu craft.

'What is it that you expect Grah-ham?' Marconi shouted after me from the quay as the dhow drifted slowly away. 'There is nothing to see, no reason to go. Forget them all.'

The *Aziz* had no engine, taking all day to clear the sand bar at the end of Lamu channel, scimitar sail hanging slack, as big as a small field. The monsoon was over.

She was loaded with mangrove poles for Salalah in Oman but first the master had a hundred carpets and twenty Arab chests from Kangan to sell in Mombasa. The voyage lasted two weeks tracking the outside of the reef. Days of dragging fishing lines, of time marked by the arc of the sun and the saying of prayers, by sleep on an open deck. The crew smoking water pipes while I rationed my supply of sugar cane grappa.

The day before the start of Ramadān we ate the goat I had brought on board for good luck. And on the eighth day of the Fast we were gliding into the old port of Mombasa.

The Count also owned a shipping line, Marconi told me. And Marconi had arranged for me to work my passage. But in Mombasa I found that the fleet consisted of a single rusted tub no bigger than a mine-sweeper with an Italian crew of ten. My work was to be her owner. I could make her a British ship, Mombasa registered, when Italians were both enemy and ally in the confused waters of 1944.

It was very good business. Coffee from Uganda sold in Durban, war-surplus drums of oil from the Cape sold in Dar-es-Salaam. Then as the Count became bolder in 1945 we shipped coffee to Italy. In and out of British ports and through the Suez Canal. All questions answered by my new passport, by my ship's documents and a wad of American dollars from the captain's pocket.

I was well paid even before we left Mombasa, just for my signature. And with every delivery there was another generous distribution of dollars.

In Genoa during our first unloading I walked the same streets, drank in the same bars. Even poorer than before, now a nation of the vanquished. The city was occupied by France and there was no work. Italy had no trade.

Across Via Garibaldi, up the steps winding around the broken-down *ascensore* to the terrace overlooking the city.

And there I could see him, stooped limbs slumped on to the bench, staring eyes. Werner's sad concentration framed by the port below, the lines of his face etched by an African sun dying into haze.

Tricks and lies he had said. But us soldiers still had work to do until there was peace. The war we had not won, the war they had not lost. Our treaty by a trick. Before they had found their leader, before Poland became their chicken with Russia holding the legs. When I lived with Katrina and the world was still new.

Europe destroyed by a golf game and a runaway cameraman, an unopened letter into a coat pocket. By four hours to wait for a train. Another woman and another child. War reaching to the edge of a flat world. A bundle of rags slipping from a mother's arms, tiny shadows evaporating between black rocks.

From Genoa I could go anywhere. My talents as an owner were well known among the Italians. Marconi was right. Away. Forget them all. Across the Atlantic, through to the Pacific. These djinns could not follow me right around the world.

The East End of Vancouver on a long weekend.

Neat little yuppies climbing out of their shiny Bimmers, unstrapping plump pink children from car seats, off for an ethnic shopping experience. The old and beaten-down discharged from care by budget cuts shuffling along the sidewalk searching through garbage bins or through bundles of out-of-fashion clothes dropped-off outside charities. Trying to scrape up three dollars in empties for a quart of Velvet. Natives snoring in doorways, reeking of excrement, barricaded in by rusting grocery carts overflowing with plastic. But the relentless passage of time will level us all.

Tim pulled up to the kerb outside the hospice, motor running. The impatient rattle of a Porsche flat six.

'That's about the best I can do for now,' he said to Morley. 'But there's no doubt that the Crown will have to vacate their warrant on Tuesday.'

The desk sergeant had been sympathetic.

'Some women think we have nothing better to do than sort their crappy little lives out for them,' he grumbled after Tim had explained the situation. But the sergeant himself didn't have the authority to cancel the warrant. All he could do, he explained, was add a note on the computer file to the effect that the accused had presented himself voluntarily and his counsel would contact Crown after the weekend.

Jane's writing on the police form, the way she made her capitals, some letters joined but not others. Morley's life, his marriage, his innermost desires. Almost a moment of spontaneous detonation as he watched the sergeant's fleshy fingers running over the words, there between them on the worn police counter. The writing that used to say other things. A barely resistible force to vengeance. Stronger than life itself.

'But you're still a wanted man,' Tim warned as Morley prepared to climb out of the car, 'so no speeding tickets. Your name will come up on their screen, they'll take you in and call the tow truck again.'

Tim looked up at the stucco building through his sunroof. Trendy imitation California, a completely unsuitable finish for the Pacific North-West. Streaked and grimy after only two or three years of Vancouver rain. Sheltered housing, subsidized housing, handicapped housing, with the hospice on the fifth floor. A people warehouse for the misfits and the dying.

'Nice place to spend a long weekend,' he said. Tim obviously had better plans: his boat, his latest conquest, both at once maybe.

'According to the nurse my old boy doesn't have long. He's telling me about his life. And I made him a promise, I suppose you could say we're looking after each other.'

Tim pulled a face. Rather you than me, amigo. He was a handsome devil, practising law wasn't the only thrust in his life.

In Graham's room time was swallowed up again by filtered light through closed blinds. Streetlights or a cloudy day, it made no difference. No clocks, television off, no connection to the outside world.

Morley sat on the Lay-Z-Boy and reached out for Graham's hand. The room had been tidied up and the bed remade. Graham was lying completely still. Like a corpse made presentable for viewing by the family. Then bony fingers stirred, feeling for Morley's wrist.

'What's up?' Graham asked. 'Your face is dark and your pulse is racing.'

'I've been with my lawyer. That's enough to upset anyone.'

Graham's far arm inched across the bed and he took Morley's hand between his. It was as if the old man could read the entire story right down to the police counter, down to Jane's writing under pudgy digits. To boundless anger and despair.

Morley's voice wavered.

'Tell me where you went on the Italian boat.'

'Through to the Pacific, up the coast.' Between breaths, slowly. 'Then back to Italy and over to America for a second voyage. Not the Count's rust bucket. I transferred to a proper cargo boat with a few passengers. Owned by some rich Genoese. I was the Administrative Officer, dealing with cargoes, handing out bottles and envelopes in port, signing off our manifest and bills of lading. The Yanks were pretty surprised to find me on board and I made it easier for the boat. After 1945 the Americans had no time for foreigners. Lost a lot of their boys in Italy. The only good Wop was a dead Wop.'

~

I left the ships on my second voyage through to the Pacific. I had a little sack of dollars saved, my *Passion* and my few possessions from the cabin. I was not a sailor.

At the Legion, a drinking club for old soldiers, I was called *oddball* or *screwy*. They laughed when I inquired about Swan River, Manitoba or about the Fort Garry Horse. But I was welcome, I was still a veteran even if from a forgotten war. The West Coast of Canada was generous and sincere.

Soldiers were returning from Europe by the thousand. Happy and confident, swilling their brew to fast talk about good work and boom times. Survivors from the Pacific were not so hearty: thin and frail, standing uncertainly outside the circles.

Vancouver in 1945 was a raw unfinished place, as if only recently cut from the forest. Spreading out at the foot of sharp blue mountains like an illuminated octopus. I was told that this was the city with the most neon in the world, now that Shanghai was lost.

Full of expectations for timber and mining in a world that was rebuilding. Exuberant and ready in a way that I had never seen anywhere else. There were plans to build thousands of houses. The biggest hotel in the city was being demolished and replaced, just because it was old fashioned. A highway was under construction right across Canada from coast to coast and City Hall was changing the rules to allow taller buildings, over six storeys high.

I asked about the Indians, thinking of the South Africans and the White Highlands. But I was told that they lived in the north. There was nothing in the way. It seemed that expansion would be for ever. I was welcome to a place in their new country.

I started at the bottom with a broom and a shovel in the immigrant tradition. Working with a plaster crew, loading board, carting scraps and sweeping out. Living in a rooming-house in the East End.

Then I moved into a different life. As advertised on the Legion noticeboard.

～

The hospice looked especially ugly in bright light. Detestable sunshine.

Morley had decided that each resident who had passed through had bequeathed a favourite piece of furniture. And here they all were, jumbled together, a testament to those lives, to how those lives really were. A small bookcase on splaying spindle legs, packed with complete sets in phony leather. Bought on time, never opened, never used. A sentimental verse from Revelations hanging on the wall, burned into a scalloped wood shield and preserved for endless lifetimes under half an inch of lacquer. Two hard looking sixties sofas in chocolate brown.

Maisey's room had a new resident, bright scarf covering the effects of her chemo. She riveted Morley as he passed. They had not been introduced. Tell me that I am still beautiful, her eyes demanded. Hug me, kiss me, take me to bed. Now, as I am.

At the end of medicine only prayer is left. Condemned, starting out bitter in her last room with flowered drapes and cuddly toys. In the corridor Morley had been taken for a doctor before.

On Falkland Road branches would be swaying gently outside windows. Voices keeping score, gentle plunks from tennis balls on racquets. Empty grain ships anchored in the bay turning imperceptibly with the tide. Warm bodies waking up against each other. Another gift of a day for questing the moment.

And at home, what was once home, Susan would be waiting. Fruit of the Loom Y-fronts tantalizingly concealed under a stained bathrobe. Ready with her complaints and a newly discovered cache of his possessions to be dumped onto the floor of the small bedroom.

A dramatic house, Morley and Jane's house. A repainted bedroom couldn't change that. Vertical raw cedar turning silver, echoing the Pacific landscape of mountains and tall trees. From the front only a single narrow window. One long slash of white revealing a Bauhaus metal stair, blue and green paper birds on a flying mobile. Wedges of Haida motifs in red and black under bright pencil lights.

Drawers of clean folded clothes, meals planned a weekend in advance, an infinite reserve of toilet tissue and San Pellegrino. Up to date with the bills, with dental hygiene and Pap smears.

Now the Art of Living Museum was holding a different exhibition: DEPRESSION 50. Green garbage bags lined the walls of the living room. Jane's possessions packed in a blind fury after the no-show dinner, but never dumped. Now an innovative nihilist furniture, covered with coats, with sweaters and old newspapers.

Surfaces everywhere were decorated with empty bottles, mugs and plates. A wide red stain surrounding Susan's broken wine glass still disfigured opulent white carpet. The fridge was running its own experiments on a replacement for penicillin.

Now a filthy house. But what really worried Morley was that he hardly noticed.

That morning, waiting for Tim and the ride to the police station, Morley had fallen onto his narrow bed. Exhausted, out immediately, fully dressed. Then half-awake, twisted in his clothes, self-analysis through alpha consciousness. Checking off his symptoms against the shrink's list of nine.

Another day of dread. With no name, no face and nothing to fight. Gnawing, gripping. Gravity so heavy that he couldn't breathe, couldn't swallow. Grief, numbness and back again. A list of symptoms from one of Robert's handbooks. The book that did not explain how a body can hurt so badly and still be alive.

The thought was always there: that some wonderful event would snap him out.

Like Jane in Kenya. Less than a year before.

Nairobi and Mombasa. And just as all roads led to West 4th and to

Falkland Road, the lane behind the shop and the tennis courts, so Morley's life ran parallel with Graham's life. The two could not be shaken.

Kenya, but not the same country that Graham had described.

Nairobi today: a city of uncounted millions, of muck and squalor. Prematurely old like a young hospice patient with a wasting disease. Morley stepping over bones outlined in taut bags of black skin. Ribs heaving, boys panting and dying in the gutter. Walking when he had been advised not to, turning down the hotel car. Scrutinized, jostled by surging waves of dirty ragged bodies. Sidewalks heaved and cracked as if by permanent earthquake.

On his first day in Nairobi, his body still in Vancouver, fourteen time zones behind. On his way to meet a large man in a shiny silk suit. They had walked into the restaurant at the same time, Morley on foot following a map, the large man stepping out of his black 500, a driver in uniform holding the door. Parked up on the broken kerb outside a smart two-storey trattoria, part of a glass tourist hotel, as if on a different planet. Barefoot pedestrians struggling around the polished car. The man's bodyguard already standing by the till, his shoulder holster bulging his jacket. Lunch for twice the country's annual per capita income.

The large man smiled at Morley through meaty liquorice lips, missing nothing with his red-veined eyes.

'So-ho,' he says in an awkward open-voweled accent, 'Mr Arajay wants to build another hotel in Mombasa.' The meal is over, talk about difficulties with the floating Kenya Shilling and falling coffee prices. Canada's aid cut back every year. Distortions in the Western press. What police brutality? Had Mr Morley seen any personally?

In Vancouver, before he left, Morley had told Ari that his services would be useless. Ari needed a bagman not an architect.

'Your trip will be worth every dollar.' Ari smiled. 'A top professional, a pristine Canadian. The price to you will be less than half what it would be to me, an Indian. And quicker too. Mr Kimau will have trouble admitting to you how things are done.'

Ari was smooth, passing easily for a rich Italian. But to an African he said, he would always be a *kalasinga*, a small shop owner, a *duka wallah*.

Morley and his expenses away from the partnership for ten days had cost Ari more than twice Canada's per capita income.

'And take your lovely wife,' Ari added. 'It'll make you less impatient.'

Kingsley had told him not to refuse even if it wasn't all architecture. Ari was well connected with the Aga Khan Foundation, he said. The Ismailis were quickly becoming another powerful new force in the West Coast development community. Kingsley had laughed. Morley's turn to brown-nose it.

A city where tourists and expats lived in luxurious prisons behind barbed wire fences, protected by security patrols carrying bows and silent poisoned arrows. Hotels that were little pieces of the first world parked in Africa to catch the sun and a few remaining animals. Hotels where even the elevator technicians were flown in from Frankfurt.

And less than a quarter of a mile away: squatters on a lesser planet. Crowded up and down the banks of a river which had become a frothing khaki sewer. Out beyond the last crumbling buildings of the suffocating city, out onto dry plains where dust tracks came to nothing.

Cardboard boxes and metal drums flattened into shelters as far as the eye could bear to see. Alleys between the rows littered with putrefying garbage. Shit festering in stagnant trenches, flies by the billion, rats like small dogs. Bodies of naked children lying where they had fallen.

A country where the President had started as a teacher at a mission school. Now he was one of the wealthiest men in Africa. A country where a building permit for a hotel would cost a seat on the board, a salary and car for the Minister's representative. And three hundred thousand US into a bank account in Botswana.

Then Morley had spent five days at the coast in Mombasa, inspecting the site, interviewing local architects to find one capable of implementing his design, of looking after electrical, structural and mechanical. More boozy expats living charmed lives, earning twice their worth in London or Toronto.

And Jane by the pool at the Norfolk Hotel in Nairobi. Then in Mombasa, walking along a white beach, wide and long like a runway. More guards following. Or she was driven to a game park for the day while Morley worked. Then later in the afternoon, with Morley exhausted, sitting next to him under a baobab tree at the edge of the beach, reading her magazine.

A tan had become sinful. But Jane took on a mesmerizing glamour after a few days in the sun. Hair in a bold wedge. She looked good wet, she looked good dry, she looked good anything in between.

He had plans for the long journey home. A short flight from Mombasa to Nairobi and back to the Norfolk Hotel where they had started. Straight from the sea and onto the four o'clock plane, her skin still smelling of salt, of French blocker, of baked Jane. Sand in all her creases.

Into a cool sumptuous room by six o'clock in the evening. Birds singing as the sun goes down. He would peel off her safari outfit the moment the bags had been delivered, breathe her in, taste her, feel her beautiful brown back arch up against him.

Then eleven o'clock at night: onto the London flight, asleep in the nose on large leather seats. At Heathrow, a car to the Hilton, it's seven o'clock in the morning. Now she's wonderful, barbecue fumes rising. Sex, Jane, *Satyrus Africanus*.

Back onto an afternoon flight to Vancouver, reading the Canadian papers, watching a film, champagne and lunch.

Then home by 8 p.m. Pacific time, jazz program just beginning. Jane in bed, exhausted but still waiting for him as he brings her tea. Under the familiar duvet and body against body. Holding her tight, starting again with a slow slow kiss.

Three times on three continents in twenty-four hours. Morley expected to be presented with a certificate.

Jane put down her magazine.

'I know your mind's still on your work. So I'm going for another swim. Bye-ee.'

Morley staring out toward the constant roar of the reef.

Two days later she was gone.

Dear Morley,

I called the shop and they're having troubles of various kinds. I'll need to talk to you about cash flow. You may want to stay longer and I'm probably adding to your distractions, so I thought I'd head back early. Very nice East Indian girl at the desk was able to change my flights. Let me know when you are getting in and I'll try and pick you up. J.

Every memory contaminated, reflected in a cracked mirror of black glass. Was that before her course? After the first Rathkin lunch? Nothing left unpolluted.

Elaine was sitting in the kitchen smoking when Morley arrived. She seemed to smoke as a matter of principle, puffing defiantly, denying the death that was all around. Then jumping up to lose her ash down the sink. There was a smoke room for the lung cancer cases; in the kitchen was definitely not allowed. But cancer wasn't going to happen to her. She shrugged: it just couldn't, she was the care-giver.

Elaine read from the day-shift report. Graham had slept for some of the day: blood pressure down slightly from the night before. Breathing hard but satisfactory.

'If he's quiet he could plateau for a while,' Elaine said. 'If he wants to talk, go ahead, but don't let him get stressed about anything, or ...' She shrugged again. Death, neither hasten nor postpone. Her job.

~

Another bed. Already mine, only a few weeks after the hand-written card on the Legion noticeboard. BASEMENT SUITE FOR RENT. Dipped in the middle, taking the shape of my body like a pall. Hands parched and joints stiff. Hair thick with plaster dust, coarse up the pillow like a toothbrush.

As a bwana, as a ship's officer, I never had to work. And for many years I had not been in the cold. A soaking Vancouver cold, worse than northern France.

Each night I was tired, every muscle ready for my bed. Lifting, sweeping, banging. The noise and confusion of a construction site. Our crew at work: bursts of energy then long, unproductive breaks with sweet black coffee. Wilting by three o'clock in the afternoon, looking for someone's watch and feeling my age.

That was when the beer came out. *Get'uhr fi-nish* with two cases of twelve and a string of Québécois I could not understand. I left when the horn blew, confident that I would not be behind, that they would have little progress to show by next morning.

Mary cooked something different every evening and wine now, not Legion beer. With my rent to help pay the mortgage things were already better than they had been. We ate and we talked while the children played next door. Until they came back breathless with their new words: Italian, Ukrainian, Portuguese. The world levelled out by the kids of the East End. Then I would put them to bed with stories of Africa, or ships and the sea, a blood-promise before uncorking another bottle.

When the door opened I found that I had been expecting her. Hanging her head uncertainly against the light at the bottom of the stairs, trying to smooth out her crumped nightdress.

I lifted the bedclothes without a word like a well-practised routine. She filled my shroud: cloying detergent, Germolene, kitchen smoke in her hair. She put her face under my cheek and into the pillow, buried against my neck as if hiding from what she had done. I held her frail light body against my nakedness.

Arms by her side, tall and thin in my embrace. Surrendered but not giving in, to be comforted but not responding. Dipped down together into the middle of the bed.

She had no breasts. Nipples, long and meaty sprouting from the chest of a young boy. Bony and flat, quivering under her nightdress. Chicken feet cold and clammy. A couple of unused basement rooms looking for a tenant, a bag of rattling bones hungry for sustenance.

We lay still and quiet. Rain beat on the window, pelting and sustained as only the West Coast knows. My hand stroking her swan neck and her short curls. Board counts, boxes of ring nails, my crew, trying to form a picture of Québec. Worrying about production, our cash and our cheques. Her apparent frailty, my apparent strength, all churning together.

She lifted her face from the pillow. Tears wet and warm on my face, salt in my mouth as I kissed her cheek.

She ran her hand over my chest, pinching my skin lightly between her fingers.

'I don't even know what happened,' she said, as if she would find the mark on me, her fingers into the wound. Make him better, whole again.

I knew what little story there was. I could see him parachuting safely then lynched by a mob driven mad by nights of terror and days of propaganda. Or I could see him in his leather jacket, falling free through the air like an expended comet. Or fighting with his harness, struggling through a flaming tunnel as the ground comes rushing up at the howling frame.

Mary talked about his letters: flying in the dark, one tour done and halfway through the second. The crews that worked the hardest to avoid the night-fighters and the flak, changing altitude and heading every few minutes, they were the ones who stood the best chance.

She asked me about death. The RCAF had told her nothing. Whispering her secret fears. Was it merciful and swift like in the Bible? Was he brave?

She had not been there to catch him, angel's wings beating in the raging night sky. She had failed.

'Stu was only twenty-three and I was the same. Now he'll be that age for ever. I don't even know who was there. I don't know a thing. I'll never meet anyone who saw what happened, who talked to him. I'll never see the grave, even if there is one. Just a piece of paper and the children, that's all I'll ever have.'

She started to feel my chest again.

'I think of it every night. My fingers pressing into a ragged hole like preparing food. His guts under my nails.'

I would watch her cleaning, cooking, with her children, all of it held inside as she worked. She was silent again, fresh tears rolling down on to the soaked pillow.

The schoolgirl from Victoria. What did she know? Just an ordinary marriage. Now it seemed like a miracle.

Mary rambled, then down to one word at a time and drifting into sleep. My body against hers, my tears mixed with hers, silent and unseen. Four of us in that narrow bed, five.

I felt like an imposter, a mountebank sent by the Canadian Legion to the requisition of a young war widow and her three children.

A book with turning pages. A new chapter word by word. Without schemes or betrayal: sentences, paragraphs, whole pages of happiness, intervals and cadences perfect to the human form. Love as a building, brick by brick, earned, constructed.

Mary sat up and I changed the wet pillow. Sleepy, propped on her elbows, eyelids flickering. Smooth young face reflecting a waxen glow from streetlamps, white light bouncing off rain drops and in through the high basement window. Soft and beautiful in silver shadows. A life to be revived, a life still to be led.

She presumed an entire history for me that had never been detailed, but that I had not denied. What was unfinished never explained. My djinns perched on ragged furniture around another room. Following me from continent to continent until I would return to Europe to face them.

Now the light was too dim for her to see. Maybe one day I would show her. Maybe tomorrow, maybe never.

∼

Elaine had come back on night-shift, making her first round with her tray. Ensure, water and pill pots. She stood by the bed holding Graham's hand, smiling down at him. She turned to Morley.

'He must sleep for a while. His plumbing is giving him more of a problem than he lets on. He's to take the pinks, then the blues a half at a time. Then there's three white ones if he wants them later.'

'What are they?' Graham asked.

'The pinks are more looseners and the blues are to keep down the discomfort, maybe help you to doze. Nothing heavy.' Graham nodded.

Morley began to break the tablets, slipping small pieces into Graham's mouth one at a time, followed by a pull on the straw.

Then Elaine was back, but very busy she said, couldn't stay. The others had started dinner.

'Must watch the exhaustion level,' she said to Graham. 'From talking as well as the main problem.'

Shé gave Morley instructions as she left.

'Sit with him a while but he must sleep. If he's not out soon the white ones are stronger, knock out an elephant. They'll dissolve in his water.'

2

1946. France as a black and white photograph.

Beauty stark and empty, villages from before the War, the Great War. Horses and carts on pavé. Stone farms like lost settlements, no plumbing, no electricity. France untouched for generations. In the small towns only a few cars, a cinema or a 1914–1918 memorial had changed the streets. More chiselled names than survivors.

But in the cities it is different: bomb damage everywhere, Europe's heritage in ruins, buildings shelled to rubble. Bailey bridges, tanks, not much food and very little work. GIs crowding cafés. Here it had been the Second World War in the Twentieth Century.

Across wheat fields, out of Paris towards Orléans, sheaves leaning into each other merry like a dance. Bowed down with grain in the first full year of a slow recovery. Through the Jura mountains the train was an explorer in an undiscovered land of primal forest over and over to far green horizons.

Then into Switzerland and along by the lake, hazy summer mountains in the distance without snow. Caravans pulled by a metal-wheeled tractor or a baker's van, I recognised a '20s Peugeot. Swimmers as dots in the water, a sailboat beyond on reprieve between winters. Back into France. Through Thonon and on again, no damage. A paddle steamer from the Swiss Navy pulling up to the pier. There are seagulls on Lac Léman, I had forgotten.

The station at Évian-les-Bains has a panoramic view high over the water, across to Lausanne and the Vaud beyond. What I had once thought was the centre of a civilized world.

I walked down the hill with my kitbag over my shoulder. Footsteps slapping on the pavement, familiar sights, the sounds and smells of France making my heart race. Wanting to catch every overhanging branch, run my hand over every door, walk into every café. Stand, sit with Frenchmen, listen to them talk. The sharp cut of a young wine over a zinc bar, an aroma of musty walls and Gitanes flavoured by a stone pissoir.

Flags hung for *la Révolution* had been left up into August. Lush boulevards clipped and edged, decorative palms still alive and geraniums planted out for the season. Ceramic signposts had recently been erected in front of faded army stencils. HQ (EA) 2ND DIV next to GENÈVE 44.

Boulevard Pétain had been changed to avenue de la Libération but the numbers were the same.

Number 16 was a cloud of wisteria over the wall and out into the street, tapping wild into plaster and tile. Slate roof and upper windows almost obscured. The gate had been blanked with a metal panel but left unlocked. Squeaking open against flaking rust.

The garden was a private ruin, brown against the green boulevards of the town. Grown over like an abandoned orchard, apple trees spreading out into bushes and decorative bushes pushing up to become trees. The pathway down to the boathouse was thick with twigs and pine needles, dead grass, rubbish, tubes from spent fireworks. An uninhabited house with crumbling edges. Paintwork flaked like parchment, a caricature of itself like stage scenery.

I remembered a mosaic foyer, dark grainy panels up to blue flowered paper above. Beams of morning light through red and green glass on to embroidery and banana trees. Madame in a silk bodice, long skirts, hair drawn back. Fussing with her sewing.

'*C'est vrai qu'il pleut tous les jours en Angleterre, monsieur?*' Always the same question.

I knocked but there was no reply, the bellpull came away in my hand.

At the back door a row of rusted laundry tubs had once been oval herb gardens. Now mint like a hedge was taking over, root-bound soil still soggy on a hot day. The garage roof had come down. Through a crack I could see a rafter collapsed into the windscreen of a Citroën Quinze '37 or '38. Her black paint turned grey with plaster dust and pigeon droppings.

The scullery door was open, sand floor laid with wooden boards. Then a kitchen I had never seen before: stone sinks and terazzo counters, an ornate Aga, French version. Dirty plates, glasses and cups littering the tables, flies buzzing. Dust like flour, cobwebs like lace, times past as lost history.

Two grey cats patterned like mackerel skittered for a broken window.

The dining room had become a tunnel. No bow window and inlaid wood floors. No Utrillo hanging over a fireplace of green tiles patterned with oak leaves and acorns. No Steinway in the far corner beyond the table and chairs, facing the lake through open glass doors.

Long white fingers darting over keys, Werner's perfect octave leaps. Chopin played as *never, never. Art* showing the way but us unable to follow. The angry drunken cripple climbing his stairs to bed.

Nocturnes as anthems to what could never be. Trills exploding out over the water like the first fusillades of war.

No dinner, no talk could have saved us that night. We were Europeans.

Now only a narrow passageway led through piles of boxes, through bundles of newspapers and stacked rubbish, past tiers of rotting sacks filling the living room to the ceiling like a storehouse. Potatoes that had sprouted and died leaving ghost grass through fabric and the gas of decay throughout the house. The next room and the next the same, a series of rat-runs through a dark depot of decomposing trash high above my head on either side.

Across the hall and into the study, following the trail. Here there was a clearing like a forest lair. More cats sped for unseen holes and boarded windows. Two chairs faced a fireplace filled with charred remains, a table of stub candles was piled with used dishes and dirty glasses. Cigarette ends covered the floor like shavings in a carpentry shop.

A bottle rolled toward me set off by a panicked cat. Picked up at my feet and set down on the table.

Through the rot I smelled smoke. Celtique, bitter with an edge of pure burning tobacco against the thick humus of the house.

And a voice, low, almost delirious, a rumble from nowhere.

'*C'est terminé la guerre, non? Vous ne pouvez pas me laisser tranquille?*'

I moved through the debris round to stand in front of him. A cat in his lap looked up with yellow-eyed malice.

More black and white. Fingers black with nicotine. Nicotine stained moustache drooping down to white at his jaw. Hair and skin white like an *omble chevalier* from the bottom of the lake. White like a man experiencing permanent shock, sucking on his life and speeding the disintegration of his bones.

His open mouth was another shade of black from smoke and wine. His teeth seemed to have grown apart, one from the other, each into a separate character. He was sunk into his chair, workman's blues merging with the upholstery and cemented in with ash.

'*C'est moi...*' not knowing where to start or how to finish. But me, my new name, any explanation was unnecessary.

It took minutes: saying nothing, a lost look, ashamed, left then right, coughing that racked his chest as he gasped for breath, dull eyes coming to focus. I thought that I could see tears. Then he struggled up, pulling with his left hand on a thick rope hung from the ceiling and down over the chair. He balanced himself on a large knot tucked tightly under his right arm. Cat twisting to the floor.

'. . . where is your hook, your limb? . . . your crutches?' It was an agonizing performance. He wobbled on one foot, empty trouser leg flapping through the debris. The arm securing the rope had no hand below the sleeve.

'*Ah, mon pauvre rosbif, tu n'as encore rien compris.*' Hoarse, from the depths of his chest. As I moved toward him he took a lunge with his free hand at a stack of boxes on the far side of the chair. '*C'est l'heure, non?*' Holding a bottle out between us as if to keep me away. Suspended from the rope, swaying back then around and toward me again.

Unlabelled red from the farm plugged with a lead cap. I took the bottle and he fell hard into the chair. Cat back on to his knee.

The glasses on the table were milky with use, dark rings of evaporated wine down to congealed sediment. I poured, then carried his glass over to the chair. Close up I could smell him, sweet like stale piss, putrid like soldiers' feet.

He lit another Celtique. An elaborate procedure using his knees to hold the match box, leaning forward. A cough that shook the chair.

'*Et même maintenant, pauv'con..?*' Pierre looking up at me through the smoke, more black in the dark room, '*... et même maintenant? ... ça te plait, la France?*'

~

Morley was on the phone.

'Hi Susan, it's Morley. Remember me? The guy in the small room. I'm back at the hospice. Holiday Monday evening, after 6 p.m. My old boy isn't too good. He needs some rest, didn't sleep last night, then a rough day. Me too. But I thought we might grab a meal, haven't been to La Piazza recently. And I know I really do owe you an ap—'

Too wordy, the machine had cut him off.

Through the kitchen window the day was burning off over Vancouver harbour. A summer evening of sugared orange sliding down purple mountains.

Humor that he didn't feel, an act. Dinner that he didn't want. Morley hunched over the kitchen table, acid running past his ears and down his arms. They would be walking along the sea-wall holding hands, talking their new language. Love conquers all, Morley used to say to her. Now it was *letting the reality of their oneness actualize at its appropriate termination.*

Exeter dying, Jane on Falkland Road.

The end of the last day of a long weekend, cloudless cool and perfect. The end of their first summer together. Trees in the park would be displaying everything they had after two weeks of rain, lush and heavy. The West Coast exactly, right out of the guide book.

An echo of tennis balls early. Waking up that morning: a day off, no sportswear to peddle, reaching out for her. He runs his finger gently down her vertebrae and moves himself over against her.

Morley sank forward onto the table. Something that would make her understand, see what she had done. Make her come back, start again. No consequence, no new present could be worse than the one he had.

Unending anger, overpowering strength that could not be used. Thrashing heart that could not escape its cage. Sweat pouring through his shirt. Face and hands red and damp.

Elaine was calling.

Morley jumped up from the table. They met at Graham's door.

'We've had an accident. I'm going to change his bed. He'll need you.' She sped past Morley and away down the corridor.

The room had become an emergency ward. Bedding and catheter thrown over the chair and the stretcher ready. Graham uncovered, lying in his green gown. Blinds up and the window open. And a choking stink: sulfur but animal, chicken manure but human. The bottom sheet a swamp of khaki ooze, soaking the hem of the gown and down thin speckled legs. His fragile arms heaped over his face like sticks.

Morley sat on the Lay-Z-Boy swallowing, breathing through his mouth and trying not to gag. Graham was barely audible.

'His legs. Oh God, when he turned. Down his legs. He was running, running. Smeared, everywhere. God. No, no. My *Kamerad*, my *Kamerad*.'

Morley lifted the old man's arms gently off his face. His jaw was trembling and his eyes were closed.

'Elaine will have it right in a minute,' trying a joke. 'It's all part of the service.'

As Morley spoke, Elaine was back.

'Three swabs and we'll be done, OK Graham? Nothing to be upset about. Day shift doubled the dose and I went along when I shouldn't have. You were the other way around when you arrived.' Talking as she worked with a large sponge and two bowls. Then she was out through the door again.

Morley held the old man's hands. The face was a mask of wrinkled flesh, hard to read, but the state of the bed was causing Graham severe distress, as

478

if gripped by a nightmare. He shook, chest rising and falling, twisting where he lay, inconsolable like a weeping child, out of proportion to the event itself.

Elaine returned with two clean bowls and a fresh rubber sheet.

'We're going to have to move him,' she said to Morley, lining up the stretcher next to Graham's bed and adjusting the height. They reached over together, Morley at the head, his hands under Graham's cast at the shoulders, working the old man gently off the bed. Morley wheeled him across the room while Elaine changed the mattress cover and sheets.

'Just one more wash and we're done,' Elaine told Graham, back at the stretcher. Working with the sponge again, then fitting him with a clean urinary tube and a fresh bag.

Between them Elaine and Morley slid the old man off the stretcher and back onto the bed. He was still breathing hard.

'This must be agony.' Elaine rested her hand on his forehead. 'I'll get you something.'

'All done,' Morley said, trying to raise a smile. He covered the old man's cold fingers with his hot palms. Their hands rested together on clean sheets.

Graham's eyes flickered up at Morley and across his face.

'I can feel you,' Graham whispered, 'I can feel you hot. What is it?'

Morley cleared up the room, closed the window and dropped the blinds. He followed Elaine back into the kitchen.

'I can see what *you* need,' she said, holding her arms out. Morley sagged against her, she had a scrubbed smell, reassuring. She wrapped her arms around him. It was a moment of pure taking, without complications: companion, comfort, friend. Words he had forgotten in a woman's embrace.

'You going to make it?' Elaine asked. 'Bowels going is always hard.' Morley nodded, his chin digging into her shoulder so that she knew the answer. 'That was a lot of strain,' Elaine added, 'it's going to weaken him more.'

They went back to the room together. Elaine took Graham's blood pressure.

'How's the pain now?' she asked. Graham nodded, then shook his head. He didn't want any more pills, he still wanted to stay awake for a while.

'What would it take to turn me right over?' Graham whispered. 'Could you do that? Take this cast off?'

'One hell of a lot of agony,' Elaine said, 'could be fa...' She caught herself. The old man's head drooped.

3

Nous sommes tombés des nues.

Asking for explanations wherever we went. Of a war we had both missed: bridges blown by an advancing army? American bombs on to French railway yards from fifty thousand feet? More houses destroyed than trains? More French civilians killed than retreating Germans? Shoulder flashes on the Armée Française that Pierre had never seen before, all claiming a brave history of resistance.

Or the meaning of a wall slogan: *L'ARMÉE ROUGE POUR LA LIBÉRATION!* Did they really expect another war?

We knew nothing. As if we had fallen from the sky.

The American Army occupying every city. Wasn't France one of the victors?

Even on the morning of the day Pierre had refused. Didn't have his jacket he said, couldn't leave without it. Had told me *mille fois* that the journey was not a good idea. But by then there was no use him arguing, I knew all the places to look: under the lid of the piano or carefully folded inside-out and hidden by the cushions of his chair.

We should have a lunch, I had said. For old times, I had suggested. When all the work was finished and all the cleaning done. To end his four years in the house.

To see France in her humiliation? *Jamais, jamais.* No, he would never, never go.

But one morning, the cleaning as far as the upper floor, he had given me his reply: if there were to be a lunch it should be cooked by the best chef in France. To celebrate the Great French Victory. Yellow stub waggling, his eyes squinting in the smoke. Over honour, over bravery, to mark the end of all those fine words.

So that is how our journey started: with a lunch.

And it was understood without being said, that lunch could take a few days. I packed our bags with two new spare sets of workman's blues which was all there was to buy in the town. With our shaving kits, soap, then petrol and cigarettes in exchange for my dollars. With more wine from the farm. Supplies for a plan to have no plan.

The local bar understood as well, that a meal might take some time. Word had spread and they all turned out to see us off before nine o'clock in the morning.

Jacques and his father from the Mauduit farm. Pierre *le propriétaire* now, his tenants equal but deferential. There was laughter and handshakes but no embraces. Ikki their giant farm horse had come too, with her coarse white mane and her big blue cart. Eight loads piled up like hay just to clear the main floor, out to a bonfire behind the cow shed. Then Jacques' two sons who had pruned apple trees and dug flowerbeds. Paulo the Italian-Swiss who had rebuilt the Quinze, fitting her with a new windscreen and new tyres, smuggled across the lake. The other way.

The painter and the carpenter were there, but without their wives, the real workers, *les femmes de ménage* who had tackled four years of accumulated filth back to the day of the funeral. The last day Pierre had been out of the house.

And *monsieur le maire* arrived with his *premier adjoint,* claiming to have turned the police station inside out until, they said, Pierre's hook, his foot and his crutches had finally been found.

No no, *monsieur,* it was the Germans who had taken them, the Germans. *Pardonnez-moi,* but you quite misunderstand, *monsieur.* So that is the only reason, *monsieur,* the *only* reason why the items had not been given back long long before. Not even returned for his mother's funeral. Such terrible treatment. But, luckily, *les boches* threw nothing away. Although, of course, by the morning of the liberation, all record of German relations with civilians had disappeared.

Désolé, vraiment désolé.

And to smooth things over, a new folding bathchair had been presented. From what was now a grateful council.

Then the rest of them in their happy group, the postman, two firemen, a few others. Men with positions, immune from labour deportation. Men who had lived through, almost unaffected.

A bottle of rosé clinking into tiny glasses to wish us *bonne route.* Always on the winning side.

Pierre emerged from the house, standing by the gate like a freed prisoner blinking into the sunlight. Then he staggered forward on his crutches, the beginner again from the rose gardens of the Luxembourg. The crowd round the car watching tensely, knowing not to help.

'*Vive la France!*' from the back. Then clapping echoed off the garden wall and another moment when I thought there might be tears.

The mayor was a large man, fat like a butcher when rationing had ended only the month before. Far from my picture of a communist. With an earnestness that did not ring true, that teased at the unasked question. You were in a Spanish prison, you say, *monsieur le maire*, during all those years? Or was that a Swiss chalet?

'You will always be welcome, Monsieur Eek-set-aire, in Évian-Les-Bains,' the mayor had told me. Only after he understood that I lived on the other side of the globe. 'We should have discovered him ourselves, a long long time ago.' An enthusiastic nod from the *premier adjoint*. 'But then you came, *vous, un sale étranger*,' the mayor muttered under his breath.

'Now *le Capitaine* is our living monument. To the true spirit of our *Résistance*. A real hero. Fifty lives, maybe more, including some of your fliers. *Les boches* knew something but never what. We would have helped sooner ... but without the records...?' Beaming at the town asset and rubbing his meaty hands together.

The mayor, of course, he had never doubted. It was a front to keep the Germans away. The mayor had always known that. And now, he said, those who had doubted were feeling truly ashamed. But I watched as Pierre hobbled round the car avoiding the two of them and their outstretched hands.

'They are happy now,' he said as we drove off. 'They can start again with their *petite politique*.'

The Quinze pulled past everything on the road. Six large piston pots eating hills for breakfast, *traction avant* putting hairpins away like an express train on her tracks. Ugly until she started to move, a mechanical insect, black shell, yellow eyes out on stalks. But on the road, sloped back as if by the wind, then she was the most beautiful car I had ever driven, a car that was a revolution.

Pierre's new chair was packed in behind us, held steady by a row of jerry cans. We rattled over pavé and across Geneva tramlines. Petrol *noir* slopping to and fro, wine bottles clinking in metal milkcrates. Flat rubber floor littered with bottle leads, with stale *pain bis* and deep in Celtique fag-ends. Ebbing away then flowing back toward me at every turn, under the pedals, stuck to my shoes. The military-trained driver and his dissolute passenger.

Pierre read the map, *la carte de France*, a large leatherbound volume open on his knees. But he ran us on to ·farm tracks, he stopped us dead facing canals. What kind of a map was this? The best, he assured me, the best. Jean-Dominique Cassini, prepared on the orders of *l'Empereur* himself. If canals had been dug since 1820, how was he to know? Hand and hook thrown out in a gesture of desperation.

And why was I laughing? Did I not understand that in July 1940, during the first month of occupation, that maps had been the first things to be taken? After the patriots had removed all the road signs, maps were even more important to the Germans than finding a few farmers' shotguns. This was all he had left.

We were seeing the old France, from the days of her glory, he said. Turning pages expertly with his hook.

But we gave up Cassini's shortcuts and kept only to main roads, unchanged since Napoleon. Through the Défilé de l'Écluse then south through the hills of the Réverment. Above Vienne we joined the Rhône, wide and fast. The Quinze wolfing down empty straights in high third, long legs stretched to a gallop, flashing between rows of *platanes* and along stone quays.

In Vienne we turned away from the Rhône on to a street of shuttered villas. We parked by an obélisque standing in the middle of a small square, mounted on a stone base with four legs like a giant's coffee table. A turn marker for Roman chariot races dug up as the town expanded. The town council had erected their find on to the plinth of a royalist statue swept away by the Revolution. And knowing little of history, or of geometry, they had renamed the square, place de la Pyramide. The restaurant had followed.

Pierre was a customer of the Restaurant de la Pyramide from before the War. He and Madame Mauduit were well known to Monsieur Point, he said, famous chef and renowned editor of Larousse. The only establishment in the entire country to be awarded *une étoile* in the first post-War Michelin of 1946. Pierre was very proud of his friend Monsieur Point.

But at the door there was a scene: Pierre's undershirt, pantaloons and slippers were not welcome. His jacket over my arm, two unshaven tramps.

'*Vous avez réservé?*' the doorman asked stiffly, barring the way to our lunch. Looking around for our means of transport which was obscured behind the obélisque.

Then the maître d'hôtel came up behind the doorman, peering at us over his reading glasses, leatherbound menu held at his chest like a hymnal. The tight little smile of the *petit bourgeois*.

Pierre surveyed them coldly, wobbling on his crutches. I started to explain.

'*Mon collègue était…*'

'*J'ai froid,*' Pierre said loudly, cutting me off, sweat in patches where the crutches caught under his arm. '*Ma veste,*' he ordered. I draped the jacket over his shoulders, loose like a toreador, worrying that he might be falling ill.

But the garment had magic powers, dissolving the two guardians of *haute cuisine* into summer air. So that now we faced an open doorway, abject gestures of welcome and a smile that knew its place. The magic of green and yellow, of deep blood red. Out from the buttonhole and around the lapel, Pierre's two ribbons cut across his cheap workman's blue.

Then there was Monsieur Point himself striding out of his tiled kitchen, a huge man in a stained apron the size of a window curtain hanging down to the floor. Seating us at a large table covered in a peach tablecloth embroidered with obélisques. A bottle of champagne as an apéritif, regrets about Madame Mauduit, concern for Pierre's health and discussion about the coming crop.

Then the event began.

Terrine de lapereau royale.

Gratin de queues d'écrevisses.

Poularde en vessie.

The wines of Condrieu and Tournon. Goat cheeses.

Carameline à la mangue, fresh fruit.

Another bottle of champagne. *Marc de Châteauneuf-du-Pape.* Real coffee.

The dining room was quiet in the early evening, all the tables relaid and the staff on their two hours off. Shining cutlery and panelled walls. A *commis* shuffling by the kitchen door, apron and white shirt, told to stay to fill our glasses and empty Pierre's obélisque ashtray after every puff.

We were talking about his mother. Born in the house and died in the house at ninety-four without ever entering a hospital. Then the great Point was back sitting at the table, making conversation before his work began again.

'I must congratulate you, *mon brave,*' Pierre broke in. 'You have started again so quickly after the Occupation, just like before, even better.'

He was looking away from Point, busy with the lighting of another *maïs* and he missed the stiff smile. But as the famous *chef de cuisine* rose to leave for his kitchen without another word, Pierre understood. The restaurant had never closed.

There was a long silence.

Pierre gazed into his smoke, the *omble chevalier* in melancholy relapse. The first customers of the evening were arriving. I watched them through the window, the new army of occupation. A group of officers in a khaki Chevrolet, light trousers and dark tunics, fore-and-aft caps and cigars. Dinner promptly at six.

The Americans settled into their seats two tables away. A drawl in the background. Non de rye? Hell, they had been told that this was just the very best lid'ul ol' spot in the whole of go'dam Fra-ance.

I did not think that Pierre had understood.

'Now I know why we came,' he said. He smiled me his hard-eyed smile. 'And we must be courageous, *mon pauvre rosbif.* We must drive until we find them. It is time to look them in the face, to stare them down. You will see. We are stronger than any djinns.'

We made for the door, the maitre d'hôtel levitating, bill on a silver tray stamped with another obélisque. Pierre hobbled right past on his crutches. He turned at the door.

'*Tu dois payer en dollars,*' he shouted to me so that everyone could hear. 'They will need dollars to buy *rye noir* for their *nouvelle collaboration.*'

The maître d'hôtel took my money.

'*C'est le système D,*' he explained, voice controlled and lips pursed.

Pierre was pegging away down the steps, I could see his back through the open door. Cursing the doorman, his crutches, the entire world. Out toward the obélisque.

'*D?*'

'*Débrouiller.*' To get by, to keep living. It was everywhere, he said. It was how France had survived.

First it was the Meuse. Pierre wanted to stand on the river bank, at the precise spot. We drove north for two days until we were pushing through herds of cows on muddy roads along the river, looking for the village of Houx.

On the west bank I wheeled him to the edge of a wood, looking down over the water flowing wide and fast around a small island. On the east side the German approach would have been across a flat bog of black soil. Our position seemed impregnable. Immediately below us the river poured over the rotting gates of a weir.

Pierre sat with a bottle between his knees telling me the story of the fall of France. There had been trials of those involved, men he had once known: Laval, Riom, Pétain. The facts had come out.

Sunday 12 May 1940. A bath of sun, the air sweet. Warmth starting to rise from the ground carrying the dry flavour of summer crops.

'Here is where they removed the first stone.' Pierre pointed down at the island and the weir. 'A few enthusiastic German motorcyclists with light machine-guns exploring the east bank, then pushing across the river during the night.'

Rommel's advance guard creeping up on the French 39th Infantry Division which was defending the river. This was the west end of the Maginot Line, opposite Belgium and the forest of the Ardennes, with no attack expected. Only a few reservists were facing *Blitzkrieg*. And many had marched over one hundred kilometres only the day before.

By dawn the next morning Rommel had a bridgehead on the west side. Then he was burning houses and crops to cover his crossing. By the end of the day he had fifteen heavy tanks across the river.

For two days there was no counter-attack by the French. It was impossible they said, for the Germans to cross in force in under five days. Even if they could come through the forest, their artillery support alone would take four days to bring up. And in any case, the High Command was sure, the main German attack was coming over the River Dyle much further north, down through Holland and Belgium.

Times for a French counter-attack were set, changed, then aborted. Reinforcements were misdirected, Staff work failed. The French artillery had no shells and their tanks had no fuel. Commanders in the field were confused, they waited for confirmation orders.

Then rumours started: a French artillery battery commander reported German tanks in force on the heights of Marfée. A divisional commander decided to move back for safety. Soon soldiers were filling the roads toward the rear in terrified waves. Efforts by some brave officers to stop the rout could not even slow the flight. All had their stories about Panzers over the river by the hundred, by the thousand, about whole divisions being encircled. The size of the disaster magnified with each telling.

But up and down the river, as aerial reconnaissance would have told, no more than a handful of tanks were across. On the day that the French were breaking, Army Group C HQ was trying to hold Rommel back. He was out too far in front.

Then from the motorcyclists in the night, those few loose stones, the avalanche of collapse began.

The next day Panzerkorps Guderian came across the Meuse in force almost unopposed and the panic spread up the French chain of command. The General Staff at Château des Bondons stood a paralysed night's vigil round the map table. Like a family at the bed of a dying member, General Georges sobbing in his chair in the dark. French calculations were wrong, the Germans were not waiting for their artillery. They had Stukas.

And by then it becomes clear, there are two German attacks. In the north as well as across the Meuse at Sedan. Now Panzers are streaking across France, carrying their own fuel and ammunition. Their way to the sea lies open. The French armies and the BEF have been sent to the wrong place, they are about to be surrounded.

Panic in Paris, Paul Reynaud, Premier of France, sends an SOS to Churchill: *our front is broken*. Paris is made an Open City to avoid destruction and the government is moving to Bordeaux. Churchill flies to Paris, a last desperate attempt to galvanize the French into resistance. He proposes the unthinkable: France and Britain will unite, Frenchmen will become British citizens, the British will become French. The fight will go on.

But Reynaud's stand is voted down by his cabinet and Pétain climbs aboard the *wagon lit*. The same places around the same table in the same railway car in the same siding. Only the text has changed.

Germans in shiny boots pull their chairs up to Monsieur Point's table.

As we left the Meuse there were two hours of deep silence between us as I worked my way up another American convoy, vehicle by vehicle and into Verdun.

I knew that Pierre had never returned between the wars, despite the requests and the offer of a staff car to collect him from Évian. Despite the promises: flags flying, a new uniform and a guard of honour.

'But a part of me will always be here.' He held up his hook with a big laugh that ended in a choking cough. His left hand slapped me on the back of the neck, then his arm coming around my shoulders to grip me hard as I held the big grey wheel.

The battlefield of Verdun had been turned into a national shrine during the 1920s. The razed villages were marked with stone crosses or tiny chapels. The identified dead were laid out in rows and rows of graves. An ossuary topped by a Deco belltower contained what had been found of the rest. And further into the forest we came upon a German graveyard of dark Teutonic crosses.

The bell had been silenced in 1940 but the memorial had survived German occupation. Now as Pierre limped the rows, crutches sinking into the grass, the knell of *never, never*, rolled out again over barren countryside. Sewn with so much steel and lead that even thirty years later vegetation was no more than knee high.

We read some names. The markers were much simpler than British stones: no regimental badges, no inscriptions, no dates. A plain white cross bearing a small metal plaque: *MORT POUR LA FRANCE*.

Then Pierre took me into the fort of Douaumont. An endless underground structure of concrete caverns and deep stairwells like a vast upside-down factory. Uncertain grey light came in here and there through turrets and ventilation shafts. Rusting machinery or dismantled gun emplacements filled most of the rooms. Cold even on a summer's day.

Moisture running down walls and floors oiled with a thick slurry, acid effervescence lining every crack and joint.

Pierre hobbled in front of me through the abandoned galleries. Like crypts for the dead below an endless twentieth-century cathedral that we no longer had the faith to complete. He rested every few steps and our voices boomed through stale air. A place to lose one's mind.

A place to lose a generation of men into a German trap.

1915. If the Germans could not win the war by direct assault on French trenches, they would bleed France to death. They chose Verdun, a chain of impregnable forts. The symbol of Republican France, rebuilt, invincible, after the débâcle of Napoleon III and the defeat of the Second Empire in 1870 at Sedan. A symbol that France could never ever give up.

For ten months through into 1916 the Germans kept coming and the French kept defending. Until both sides had achieved a greater number of dead per square metre than any battle in the history of the world. Until the French were broken and mutinous, relying on the British to finish the war. Until the Germans were on an irreversible slide, down to Ludendorff's last throw of 1918.

With the first surprise German attack the great Douaumont had fallen. To just a small group of Brandenburg Pioneers entering through a gun turret by building a human wall up the battlements like a gym class, while under fire from their own guns. The Germans had found the fort almost empty, at that moment purged of men, ammunition and guns for a French attack elsewhere in the line. The few French defenders had been taken at the point of a pistol.

Behind the fort the effect on the town of Verdun was immediate. The Meuse bridges were prepared with charges, the population was told to leave. The Germans brought up their artillery and close shelling reduced defenders to panic. There was looting, drunkenness and total disorder. The Prussian Crown Prince claimed to be within a stone's throw of the Champs-Élysées, hungry for his lunch.

Pierre had arrived in Verdun the following week with General Pétain. A marble statue of command, unforgettable in perfect horizon blue. The right man for that terrible moment. An unbreakable defender, a man who could distinguish between the possible and the impossible. A saver of men's lives. But once he had uttered the fatal words, *ils ne passeront pas*, the man to preside over the greatest slaughter in French history.

'He is a man,' Pierre said, 'who thinks too much about the French and not enough about France.'

We reached a long narrow cavern under Casemate B.

'That is the doorway,' Pierre whispered, leaning against the opposite wall. In the dim light his face stretched into a look of long pale horror. A man facing his djinns.

'We had been defending for a few weeks from a trench line between the town and the fort. Douaumont was still in German hands.'

Finally a dawn attack had brought the first French troops back into the fortifications from the south. Pierre and his platoon were among the leaders.

'You can have no idea, *mon rosbif*, of the exhilaration of that moment. We thought that all of France was watching, we believed that the entire war, our whole civilization turned on this one action.'

There was furious hand to hand fighting along dark corridors, up and down stairs, running feet, shouting, pistol shots as if right against the ear. It was hard to describe the events in any order.

Then a break. Pierre regrouped his *poilus*, twenty men right here in this room. They lined the walls, reloading, preparing for the German counter attack, quiet as mice.

Then suddenly Pierre realizes, through an open door, down a short corridor, a German section is doing exactly the same thing. Right in the next room. They too are lined up around the walls in complete silence. Glances back and forth down the passageway as both groups consider the situation. Who will rush whom. Who will surrender, who will retreat. Pierre is standing next to the door.

Then there is a whoosh like a huge match being struck. A pause. But Pierre has it in an instant. A German has stripped his potato masher but he is counting to the last second before he throws.

The next moment the sizzling stick is bowling toward the French along the floor. Twenty petrified faces as if illuminated by the bomb approaching up the corridor.

Pierre puts his foot out beyond the protection of the wall, he reaches down with his hand to take the handle, to return the grenade to its legitimate owners.

He has it ... he has it ... he is going to throw ... send them their possession back. Back among those to whom it rightfully belongs. He has just let go ... the stick has just left his hand ...

Blinding light, shock like a breaking rock wave. Then black, screams in the dark and Pierre is bouncing through the corridors of Hades on the back of one of his men. He feels nothing. But there is something very wrong, he cannot hold on. Others have him held up from behind.

Then the morning light is on his face, he feels straps being applied to his arm and his leg. But he has lost too much blood and the rest is gone.

Pierre put his good arm around my shoulder and we struggled across the stale cave, crutches abandoned against the far wall like the approach to some miracle cure. With him leaning against me I lit a match, then another and another. But there was nothing to be seen, no chips, no fragments. Neither blood nor bone.

'And that was my war,' he said softly into my ear as I held him to me in the middle of the dank room. St Cyr, years of training, learning the attack, deployment, the enfilade. His first posting in Algeria, guarding endless sand that only the Arabs wanted. Then as a junior officer: waiting, marching, conflicting orders in static trenches all accomplishing nothing. More marching. Six weeks of foxholes outside Verdun and then the night of the attack. One blinding moment followed by a succession of field hospitals, a year in a converted château in the south, then at les Invalides.

Nothing gained, nothing. Medals and glory to cover over the unthinkable losses.

Paris as a cripple and still only a young man, twenty-nine when we first met. He had seemed a lot older.

A woman he loved. But the thought, even the thought, his scarred shocking stumps pointed like two carrots. Just looking down the hospital bed had filled him with disgust.

Creating a Treaty he did not believe in after a Great Victory we had not won. Enforcing a peace that was damned from the start. Early retirement as a mere *capitaine* when the army was cut back in '29. Life in Évian as a useless cripple in the care of his mother, like a child again. One blinding flash.

Pierre's face began to tremble.

'And for what?' He wept on to my shoulder, shaking. 'All the sacrifices of Verdun retaken by a few motorcyclists across the Meuse during one single night?'

Then he held himself very still, eyes closed, hard against me now.

'I was not brave during this last war,' he said into my ear. 'I just did not care whether I lived or died.'

We came slowly out into the light again and I packed him into the car. He pointed out the other infamous sites as we pulled away. Le Mort Homme, le Bois des Caures.

And being so close, Pierre said, there was no excuse. Sedan, a place he had never been. The site of national disaster, three times: 1870, 1914, 1940. We entered the town and drove slowly along boulevards of imitation

Haussmann. Then through the old streets of Louis XIV behind. A place in permanent shadow it seemed, under an invisible cloud.

We in England, we did not understand frontiers, protected as we are by the sea. How many mistakes had we made, *les Anglais*? But each time we could retreat across the Channel. While for France a mistake was fatal.

And, Pierre said, France had not made just one mistake, but three.

1870. A war of movement. But Napoleon III had kidney stones, his face rouged to hide the pain. He could not sit on his horse for a moment longer. So the French Empire had surrendered to the Prussians, out in an open field.

In 1914, therefore, the great French commanders set out to win that same war of movement, to redeem French *honneur* with *l'attaque à outrance*. Up through Sedan with maximum force in response to the Germans in Belgium. But the *boche* was coming around by the Channel coast and Sedan must be abandoned, again. This time it was to be a war of defence and the French had made few preparations. For four years France had almost lost and millions had been killed.

So in 1940 the great French commanders would win that same war of defence. The Maginot, the most magnificent defences ever built. But this time it was to be back to a war of movement: the Allied armies trapped in Belgium with Panzers crashing to the sea and the French defences useless.

Three invasions, three mistakes, three occupations. And not one was a war that France had started. Even as a *rosbif* could I not understand the extremes of French emotion? Vengeance, defeatism, indifference, anger.

Shooting Pétain would change nothing.

We looked for our lunch and a place to stay. Pierre recovering, waving his arms now, talking fast about what we would find: the cheeses of the Ardennes, the famous biscuits of Reims.

I saw that Pierre had been freed in the reeking bowels of the fort and on the river where the avalanching nightmare had begun. Now, maybe, a future could start.

We ate fried *fretin de Meuse* and we drank more champagne. Pierre behaved, beginning to enjoy his *libération*. He had faced them down.

Then he turned on me, like a boy who has successfully performed a dare.

'And yours, *mon rosbif*? Where are yours?' He fixed me with a flinty stare, chin forward to keep the question warm, a little smile, but nothing that would let me avoid him. It was my turn. Time, money, transport, food, there were no excuses.

I began to be afraid, tears burning my eyes, liquor loosening my resistance. Now it was me who reached for him.

'Poland,' I said, 'to stand on free Polish soil. Before the war, I … I was part … there was a chance, a letter, a woman, but I …'

Then a long pause while my confessor held me in the grip of his implacable gaze.

'And La Wantzenau,' I added softly.

Pierre looked away, his face shaded, dark.

We drove through forests of pine and beech, rolling out over the hills of the Vosges. We followed the Rhine canal down on to the plains of Haguenau. Timbered houses in greens and yellows began to appear, thatched roofs on tall gables. I wanted to stop, admit defeat, tell my djinns that they could have me, I was a coward, I was theirs. My heart came up my throat with every mile, with every familiar sight.

In my anger I had said things that could not be forgotten. In fury at my failure I had done things that could not be erased. Vengeance, I could not give back what I had taken from the Lord.

Strasbourg is a beautiful city, not an imitation, a character all its own. Built of *grès*, a local stone of purple grain. The impression of looking down boulevards or up at the cathedral through a glass of pinot noir. Canals from the Rhine running through the centre, past working buildings from the sixteenth century, past houses, shops and warehouses packed together along quays.

The city seemed untouched, as if both sides had been careful with the heritage they both claimed. War seemed distant again until we followed the River Ill, north to where the smaller river meets the Rhine. A deep khaki green flowing into clear fast blue.

Here the retreating German Army had blown the Rhine dykes to create flooded obstacles for the advancing Allies. Two years later repairs were still under way and no crops could be planted again that year. Fields were being drained, revealing a tangle of abandoned matériel covered in fine river silt. Tanks, gun carriers, artillery still harnessed to horse carcasses. The bodies of a few soldiers in their full equipment, sprawling outlines in the flotsam as if exhumed for Judgement Day.

There were Baileys at most crossings on the Ill and longer floating bridges wiggled precariously across the Rhine, pontoons held against the flow by a double row of outboard motors. A permanent girder bridge was still under construction.

The rounded blockhouses of the Maginot Line stared impotently over the destruction. Faded slogans had been painted on to every surface. SEE GERMANY AND DIE! LONG LIVE THE FÜHRER!

At La Wantzenau we crossed the Ill and I turned right along the river bank. Automatic, as if there were no other way.

Black ruin stretched along the edge of the village. Piles of scorched beams and baked plaster, cowsheds reduced to char ankle high, fences, trees, everything was gone. A wide black swath up the river. New green was shooting through here and there, adding to the mournful sight, as if the remains were about to be overgrown, disappear for ever. I crept along until I came to the little farmyard. That too was gone, a cinder. Gone.

An old woman in black was pulling a trolley of bricks. She stopped to watch us. I climbed out of the car and walked toward her. She hurried screaming into the nearest ruin. A younger man came out to the street.

'Do not be concerned about *mamie*,' he said twisting his hand by his temple. '*Les canons.*' The man took us for officials in the Quinze and he started to explain: he was counting the bricks, he would pay.

'Are you from here?' I asked, immediately afraid of the answer.

'Yes,' he said, 'in the army, back last June. Prison in the south, after Africa.'

So I asked him my question and stood watching his jaw, his yellow teeth snatching up and down, hat off his balding head. A wipe, then back on again as the story became difficult.

October 1944. By then it was headlong defeat, the Germans wishing only to be on the other side of the Rhine defending the Fatherland.

As they tried to cross the Ill, then prepared to cross the Rhine, they were strafed continuously by American planes. This was not 1918, men against artillery and an orderly retreat. Now the Germans had no air defences and American advanced fighters were attacking at will. A bridge had been laid but very soon it would be gone. The German Army needed cover urgently. A company of specialists with flame throwers was brought up and the burning of the village began. Smoke poured out over the line of retreat, allowing many of them to get away before the French 22nd arrived. The houses and farms along the river had been the first to go.

I asked about Jeanou and Patouche. He knew them and now he understood that I was not from the government.

'*Vous êtes de la famille?*' he asked before he went on. I nodded. Son-in-law.

He looked down and shook his head. He had seen flame throwers in action, in Marseille along the old port. For those in the houses there was no hope: old people taken by surprise, wood and thatch, a dry autumn. He needed to go no further.

'They have searched the ruins,' he said. There were no bodies to be found, but there will be a memorial...'

'... and the daughter?'

The evening sun warm against my face, the world renewing all around me without pause, the planet turning steadily through unmoved heavens, stretching into a heartless blue. Wishing that I could wait to the end of time before I heard my answer.

'But that was later. There was an investigation, after a few months. You must speak to the mayor, he was present.'

I turned away to the car.

'*Mais elle est morte,*' he said to my back. A sniper's bullet, a crack of death through summer air.

The mayor was polite. Asking who we were and why the questions, addressing Pierre and his ribbons. I watched my friend as he talked, a ghost again on an upright wooden chair. With him she would still be alive, his farm and his name would have had an heir. Pierre nodded toward me and I turned back to the mayor.

'I was her husband.'

The mayor was a soldier, *alsacien* himself, he told us, a major in the 22nd wearing American two-tone khakis. Alsace had been incorporated into the Reich in 1940, not treated by the Germans as part of Occupied France. And now Alsace was not treated by the French as part of the defeated Reich. There had been no military government in Alsace. *France, French, always was, always would be*... I heard the words again.

But because Germany was so close, so many refugees, such large movements of people in both directions across the river, officers had been appointed in each border town, as *maires de la Libération*. Elections would be held later when they had decided who was who again.

After the accident the mayor had ordered an inquiry. There was the possibility that the ambulance had been carrying others. He searched in his file cupboard and found a large grey envelope. He read for a moment.

The story was short.

11 May 1944. Infirmière-Major Katrina Combères of the French Army, driving an eight person Delahaye ambulance without passengers or invalids. Proceeding in a westerly direction over Rhine bridge BG6. Wet surface, loss of control. The vehicle had fallen into the river. Action was taken by the sergeant in charge of the bridge but no body was seen. The next day equipment was brought up and the ambulance was recovered, over a kilometre downstream. Certain recommendations from the investigating panel: the condition of the bridge surface, improved safety equipment and so on. Conclusion: death by accidental causes. The body was never found.

The mayor returned the envelope to the cupboard.

'There was some further evidence which is not in the file,' he said as he walked back to his seat, accepting a Celtique from Pierre. 'From the deceased's staff at the hospital and from an American officer who was French liaison in Munich. It was not important to the investigation so I did not feel that the information should be recorded.'

The mayor fiddled with cigarette and matches as if not wanting to continue.

'But from what they said it may not have been an accident. In April 'forty-four, the month before, we had had an emergency call from the Americans. They had liberated a civilian camp near Munich where there was a typhus epidemic. They needed assistance urgently, trained staff to administer a quarantine, medicines, evacuations. We were the closest here in Strasbourg. Infirmière-Major Combères was the senior nurse among the French volunteers to go.'

He looked out of the window from behind his smoke, avoiding my paralysed stare.

'There was something about our people who went to help the Americans. When they returned they would not talk, they had seen something which they could not describe. They had been changed, turned in on themselves. Living each in their own thoughts, with some terrible experience. We heard only the smallest parts: trains, piles of corpses, thousands and thousands of starving skeletons.'

The mayor shuffled at his desk again, coughing and flicking ash into his ashtray.

'We in Alsace ... our, er ... association ... with, with...' He seemed to search for a long time, as if he had lost the thread. 'With ... with over the river. Some of us with ... with ... common ancestry. We take these things ... these things ... very hard. Later, of course, the whole world saw the pictures.'

I could not speak. I knew nothing, I had spent the war *in Africa*, I came *from Canada*, but the mayor's voice turned me to stone.

'Since the liberation of Alsace,' he continued, 'Infirmière-Major Combères had been searching for her son. There had been difficulties. She had refused to have him speak German before the war. But the son had rebelled. Affected by what he had heard at school: France weak and defeated, Germany strong, the future. The boy was in the Hitler Jugend like so many others in Alsace after the Occupation. Then into the SS at 17.

'In Munich, with the Americans, it is possible that Infirmière-Major Combères had found the answer to her questions about her son and possibly about his war service. There had also been the death of her parents the year before, with the burning of the farm. If it had been important to the inquiry the verdict would have been different.'

The mayor seemed to rush to the end of the story, but now he sat back in his chair. He paused, his face had turned white.

'The answer lies within,' he said finally, tapping a finger at his temple. 'Suicide.'

Then I could hear the other two talking and I could see Pierre pulling on his jacket, coming up on to his crutches. Words that were passing by me, military talk, an exchange of names, of regiments from *la Grande Guerre*. All over my frozen head.

We were leaving. An invitation, soldier to soldier, Pierre shouting as if to wake me.

The mayor's mess was a hotel on the river, converted from a maize mill and granary. The tall brick structure had a standard-tragic Alsace history. French, German, French, German, now French.

The roar of a large party in progress came from every window on every floor of the building as if about to raise the roof. With the mayor I lifted Pierre and his chair, up the steps and in through the front door.

Uniforms of all colours and designs filled the main rooms, shoulder to shoulder. Away left and right through door after door, then into a deep haze of smoke at the back. Beyond the foyer a twenty- or thirty-piece American band was playing swing on the upper balcony of an open courtyard. Waiters, young boys and girls in black jackets moved expertly through the throng carrying full trays of bottles: gin, whisky, wine and cognac. Bottle necks were grasped as the trays went past, liquor splashing into glasses. Other trays were moving through loaded with loose cigarettes.

'We have our meetings every month,' the mayor said. 'The Allied Forces of Occupation. Then afterwards, we invite everyone we can. *Pour la morale.*' He laughed.

I edged my way through, looking at faces, at insignia, rank and lapel badges. Britain, France, New Zealand, Australia, Canada, South Africa, India, all the old Empire. The United States in full force. Belgium, the Netherlands, one or two from Scandinavia, Russia, even Korea.

Mess staff were laying out a huge buffet in dining rooms on the first floor. Meats, fish, pâté, whole hams, bread and fresh vegetables. Even butter.

It was early evening but the party had been going on for some time.

I knew little of the war, its character or its campaigns. But through the fog I began to understand: *World. World War.* A letter, a golf game, cracks in a pavement. A war around the entire world.

Here the volume was turned up to the limit, survival and victory were being celebrated. An ambulance into a river, one life, tens, thousands, millions. Once again it was over.

In the dense crowd, through my dreams, a finger tapped me on the shoulder and I turned. Browning: large, mature, filling out his Number Ones above and below his Sam Browne. Smoking a cigar with an air of authority and success, like an estate agent with an expanding office. Captain Browning, from Isiolo, from Moyale. Now Lieutenant Colonel Browning, 1st Battalion, West Yorkshires.

'Well, Exeter,' he said, looking down at my workman's blues, 'you here about the plumbing?'

4

'Browning had a very good war. Dreadful expression but you heard it a lot. Plenty of action, different theatres, fast promotion, no injuries. And by 1946 he was stationed in Berlin, something important.'

Elaine passed the door and caught Morley's eye without Graham seeing. She pointed to the bed and put her hands together to the side of her head. Graham should be resting.

'I'm going to give you one of these elephant pills,' Morley said to the old man. He dissolved a tablet into a glass then held the concoction to Graham's lips. 'You don't have to drink it all but Elaine says you should sleep for a bit.' Half went down in small sips. He started to splutter. Morley wiped his face, then rubbed more conditioner into his lips. He was ready for sleep.

'After meeting up with Browning again,' Graham continued very quietly, 'there was no difficulty at all. Germany was the New Raj. But this Raj was intended to keep the natives at the starvation line, as punishment. They talked of twenty-five years or more before Germany would be allowed to recover. Many people I met cheered the stories from the Russian zone. Avenging Angels let loose without any of our constraints.'

The old man's head slumped back, then he started again.

'But it was the Russians, Morley, who brought prosperity back to West Germany. By standing up to the Americans. Vengeance ended and competition started. We had to make the Germans prosperous, to show that our system was better than theirs. The Germans were even re-armed.'

'Did you ever get to Poland?'

'Browning was a Big Bwana. In the German Raj the White Man's word was law. He gave us letters and passes to say that we were his liaison with UNRRA, the Relief and Rehabilitation Administration. Doors opened, messes took us in everywhere. With our UNRRA papers it was like travelling from farm to farm through Kenya, very effective, wonderful hospitality. Worked right across Germany. Except in the East.'

Morley wanted Graham to stop, to get some rest. Let him leave, feed his alibi. But the old man was still going.

'UNRRA had an impossible job. Sixty million DPs in Europe after the war. Eleven million German POWs held by the Allies. Another ten million Germans living in areas that the Reich had invaded. They all had to come home. Then ten million slave labourers trying to leave Germany and more millions in the liberated concentration camps. Then millions of Russians outside Russia, millions of Poles not in Poland, a million or more Jews trying to get to Palestine.'

The acid of anticipation began to run through Morley's joints. Falkland Road, standing in the shadows as a skunk waddles across damp grass. A West End Indian mining a dumpster under orange lights. But this time it was going to be different.

Graham continued to talk.

About the officers' mess in Strasbourg, how well the Allied occupiers treated themselves, taking over the castles and the big country hotels. About him and Pierre preparing for the journey across Germany with forty bottles of Naafi vodka under the front seats of the Citroën as their currency.

An entirely new reality. Morley would actualize an entirely new reality for both of them. As victims, as real victims.

'Before we left Alsace there was a film show in the mess dining room. Browning ran some newsreels for us from 'forty-four and 'forty-five. Bring us up to date, he said: the Normandy Landings, the advance into Germany. The war that Pierre and I had both missed.

'Pierre took to the movies right away. *Les films, c'est ça le truc, c'est çale truc*, he said. Couldn't see too many of them, he said.

'Then close to the end, a reel about our propaganda. The role of the BBC before D-Day. The soundtrack started with just four notes. Dah-dah-dah-DAH.

'I was out of my seat immediately. That's Beethoven, I shouted, his Fifth Symphony. What was Beethoven doing on D-Day? Browning looking up, surprised. Beethoven? Oh, didn't you know? Bloody colonial. Been in the

NFD too long. Now a Frog plumber. Loud laughter. That was the BBC's call-sign for our broadcasts to Occupied Europe. Dah-dah-dah-DAH. Those four notes, same as V for Victory in the Morse Code. Dot dot dot dash. Was I *completely* ignorant? But quite the coincidence, wasn't it?'

The old man seemed wide awake again. But Morley would wait, his alibi would wait. The elephant pills would work on them both. There was all evening, he would get to where he was going. And there would be no more weekends like this one: sunshine, cool air, tennis balls echoing. Never, never.

~

From our first day across the Rhine Pierre began to laugh. At the endless damage, Germany broken and occupied. At the new German *Untermenschen.*

A nation on the move. Lines of carts, starved horses, human mules pulling the barrows of a defeated people and their woeful possessions. And millions more on the railways packed into cattle cars heading west. Now it was the Germans' turn to be human freight in some vast continent-wide retribution.

The *Herrenvolk*, the Eastern Empire, the *Großdeutsche Reich* had all been damned on Judgement Day. Where were the arrogant profiles now, riding their plunging half-tracks? Or the rows of heartless steel helmets speeding by in columns of grey Henschels.

Pierre laughed some more when we stopped at the first crossroads inside Germany, where a British armoured car was on guard. We watched a large sergeant, a New Conqueror in well ironed serge, white webbing and shiny boots. He was considering a line of shrunken Germans in the shabby remains of their Sunday best. Humbly displaying passes and ragged identity papers for the sergeant to decide. Could they possibly, please, visit a sick relative? Might they, please, go to church?

Then Pierre laughed again at the queues waiting for soup, or outside shops, lined up for goods that never came. Snakes of exhausted faces holding battered chamber-pots or a chipped water jug from a long-demolished wash-stand in imitation baroque.

He laughed at tree-cutters through the forests. Men hauling logs with ropes over their shoulders, others trimming and hacking. Many clearly new to the work: clerks, schoolmasters, *petit bourgeois* with soft hands, labouring in return for a few extra calories a day.

'In 'twenty-three it was they who jeered at us,' Pierre scoffed, 'when we came for the Reparations due to us. You will never cut our wood with your bayonets, they shouted.'

He rolled down his window, awkward across the car with his left hand. He leaned out, Celtique held carefully clear of the wind. Moustache blown back up his face like Zeus himself.

'*Branlaires!*' He roared, hook waving. '*Chourmo de feiniantas!*' The Reaper speeding by on his black catafalque.

'What was that you said?'

Pierre repeated the phrase.

'*Ça, c'est le dialecte provençal,*' he said proudly. 'The language of the south, of Provence. I learned it in hospital near Avignon, in St Rémy-de-Provence.'

Pierre had solved the mystery of the Chicken-Gutter's language: Provençal. In those few words the past had met the present. It was an omen for our journey, a sign.

We worked our way across the country south of Dusseldorf and south of Hanover, avoiding the cities. Then we came to the Russians at the *Land* border of Thüringen.

At first there were no difficulties. But as we moved deeper into the Soviet zone and closer to the Polish border, our story and Browning's papers mattered less and less in a kingdom of all-powerful Russian commanders. Tight oriental faces, omnipotent in their conquered domain like Asiatic warlords. At Gorlitz we were turned back, sent north toward Berlin. We saw the River Nieße but the Russians would not let us cross. I never did stand on Polish soil.

~

The flow stopped and Graham closed his eyes.

Morley rearranged the bed without disturbing him, tucking bedclothes up to his chin. The old man's face twitched slightly, eyes flickering for a moment. Searching Morley's face as he drifted off.

What are you doing?

Where are you going?

Susan peered cautiously around the restaurant. She put on her most winning look. This was the right picture of herself.

'Oh, Morley, why can't it be like this always? Have you any idea how happy I'd be?'

The glossy magazine elements of an Italian trattoria ree'd and dee'd into the sanitized set for a trendy American soap. Stucco in carefully varnished waves, floor tiles artificially countrified so that the tables always wobbled. Canned opera highlights going round for the second time.

Morley could imagine their married life. His weekly treat: Saturday candlelight dinner at La Piazza to catch up on her office gossip. Or to hear about the latest in self-help for a continent of confused females, still dissatisfied post-liberation.

'Mmm,' Susan hummed with her first forkful, 'you could show me how to make this, Morley, I'd have it ready for when you got in.' Pesto by the *maestro capo cuoco* of Vancouver. Years of experience, flats of fresh basil in by air from Florence twice weekly. 'I'm sure it's just a matter of adding enough salt,' she said.

Susan took in the room again.

'So, who *are* all of these people, Morley? Do you actually *know* many of them?'

Morley poured Susan another glass of wine. She was doing well, right up to his expectations.

Outside the front door of the house Susan tripped.

'Jeesh, Morrey, really had a skinful. And long walkies. Why not put the truck into the garage?'

'Didn't want to cross 33rd. I've been at it too. Wouldn't want the cops to stop us.' He pecked her on the cheek. Eau de Lifebuoy Soap.

'Wecked,' Susan admitted as they entered the house. 'Weally wecked.'

'I've just the thing for that,' Morley said, heading into the kitchen. 'A newly discovered vitamin. Enhances the blood's own natural hyper-regenification. I was told it would deal with an elephant. I'm sure it'll take care of you.'

Susan sat prim and isolated in the living room facing the ugly red stain in the carpet. Ready for a drunken sofa courtship scene, Morley wobbling out his proposal down on one knee.

But the setting was not conducive. Garbage bag furniture unchanged round the walls, an entire room of empties and dirties, an entire house. Morley's still life: *Post Split*.

He brought Susan a fizzing glass.

'Drink up. Good for you.' Standing over her.

'Oh Morrey,' Susan intoned between gulps, 'come back to the master bedroom. Girl's not shposed to admit this, but I miss Big Fun.' His script right down to the dialogue.

He lay against her, feeling her slide into deep limp sleep. Not even enough time to remove her Y-fronts.

Morley filled his place in the bed with pillows, well away on the far side. Lumpy enough for a reaching hand attached to a groggy head to be reassured.

He dressed carefully, tracksuit, runners, cap, an entire black outfit from his designer jogging days. PORTLAND 45+ HALF MARATHON. A disturbing stranger in the mirror. But a sense of mission was taking over. His design finished and now into delivery. Printing, binding, practical matters to absorb tension.

No ID, no money again. He fumbled with the contents of the jumbo sandwich box from under his pants and socks, trembling as he loaded the chambers. Counting under his breath, one, two, three ... six. The gun was small and cool in his hand. He slipped the pistol down into a deep pocket, Jane's garage remote control into another.

Morley ambled back three blocks from the house. A late night walk, nothing suspicious. Past the Landcruiser, up the street and back again. Nobody watching.

Down Burrard and across the bridge. Light traffic, jazz: turned off. Less pressure through his chest and down his arms. This was the action that his primeval system craved. Fight or flight. Both.

He parked by the tennis courts, opposite the fire exit to the silent apartment building. Backed in and hidden behind a Parks Board van, pointing out, ready to leave. Keys in the ignition, less bulk to carry, quick departure, no fumbling. He wouldn't be long.

Morley took a wide route out through the park walking slowly, approaching Falkland from the north. The evening stroller again. Everything was quiet. None of his exaggerated nightmares of alarms, tripwires, cameras, policemen hidden among the rhododendrons. The windows of 205 were dark but open. Jane in bed with Donald. Right over him as he walked by and past the garage door.

The lane down the back of the building was empty. Morley took up a position behind a dumpster in shadows cast by amber streetlights. All remained quiet. He pressed the button on the remote and the garage door started to open. White light falling across orange as if a car was about to pull out into the lane.

The rattle of rollers over tracks, the metallic echo of the door hitting its stops, these were the reverberating sounds from his sweated dreams. He dropped the remote into the dumpster and moved across the lane, flitting into the building just before the door ground back to a close.

The lovebirds were both in, Jetta and Bimmer in their stalls on opposite sides of the aisle.

At the same moment the far door swung open, from front lobby to garage. Morley ducked between two cars, heart pounding, his vision suddenly blurred. A man came down the steps and into the aisle, sorting through his keys as he walked towards his car. Morley waited for the engine to start, but the man was fiddling. Morley could see him three cars away, a dark figure through compounding rows of tinted glass. Now he was opening the back doors of the car, followed by the trunk. Then the man seated himself, but there was still no sound of the motor turning. Morley breathed deeply, trying to slow the air-hammer beating through his entire body.

He slumped onto the concrete floor, down between two mags, black with disc-pad dust. He took the snubnose out of his pocket and held the gun out in front of him, the way the clerk in Dallas had shown him. Out from the body at right-angles, palm around the butt, finger on the trigger, left hand clasping his right wrist. Loaded, pointed, ready for action. Hammer still forward.

Rathkin would come to the door. In Jane's towelling gown, NORFOLK HOTEL on the chest and a little crest over crossed spears. Knot in the belt accentuating his stomach.

'I'm Morley. We haven't met.'

Rathkin is half asleep. He looks down at what Morley is holding. His little red face and bald head turn puce. Standing back to let Morley in.

'Where is she?'

Rathkin points with a terrified limp arm. Morley waves the gun, Rathkin walks ahead of him into the bedroom. Piled clothes overflowing a chair, towels thrown over the open door, pantyhose hooked on the handle. Magazines, used coffee cups and breakfast plates, dirty glasses on a table, on the floor. Jane's new paradise. Another still life: *No More Mr Control Freak.*

'Jane, it's Morley.' Rathkin's voice is trembling.

'Turn on the lights,' Morley says.

There's Jane sitting up in bed. Rathkin's bed. Movements he knows like his own, blinking, looking surprised. But she takes in what's happening immediately. She's trying to draw the blankets up over her breasts. Simultaneously Rathkin is threatening to call the cops.

'What do you want, Morley?' Jane takes over. She's smart, Jane knows not to dial or to scream. 'Shut-up Donald.' Talking it out would be her way. No accidents.

Morley looks at her.

I love you as much as anything in the whole world. And I hate you even more.

Then Morley is pulling away the covers, Jane trying to huddle over a pillow. But the picture is always confused. Sheets tugged, ripped, the gun in his other hand. And what's he going to do? Have them perform while he watches? Kneecaps like Ireland? Take her home at gun point?

Imagined shots and he's running for the door. Down the corridor to the fire exit and out into the park. Lights are coming on all over the building. Shrieking from the windows of 205. But in the confusion he's away. He meets a cruiser coming in the opposite direction, lights and siren rousing the neighbourhood. But Vancouver's Finest are intent on reaching the scene of the crime and the criminal gets away.

Through the West End, slowly, slowly, following all the rules, braking for stale greens.

Then onto Lion's Gate Bridge and the gun goes out through the sunroof and into the harbour below. Still hot.

Round the North Shore and back over Second Narrows. The same parking space is still there. Walking back three blocks to the house. In through the back door and under the duvet with his snoring alibi.

How long will it take them to get to the house? As he's calculating he can hear a cruiser pull into the driveway.

'Oh no. That just can't *be* officer, he was here, in bed with *me*. All night.' Little sleepy smile. Then she begins to understand, waking up, awake. Holding her head. 'Oh, no, officer, that's basically impossible.'

The Landcruiser will be cold by the time all the talk is over and they go looking. Can't remember where I parked exactly, officer, let me see....

And Susan is right onto it by now. 'It was the right decision to park there, officer. He really shouldn't have been driving in the first place.'

Picture of herself: *Mrs Morley*.

Morley didn't know, didn't know. But it was going to unfold, go wherever it wanted to go. Isn't that what Jane liked to say?

The man in the car was still searching.

Morley was sweating on the cold hard floor, tracksuit prickled with damp. His palm against the gun wet and slippery.

More confused pictures. Graham's head sunk back into the pillows, eyes sweeping Morley's horizon. You made me a *promise*, Morley, you made me a *promise*. A little jewel that I can carry in my pocket. Jane on the crumpled bed, lights on, legs open. Khaki skin, bad breath. Rathkin starting to take off the dressing gown. For your tricks and your lies. Everything justified from now on. He could go up there and make them do it. Now, right now, while he watched. He had the power, the power.

Vengeance is Mine saith the Lord.

A power stronger than life itself. Mine, mine, mine, now. Now.

Or over to the Jetta, break the window, open the door and into her seat, her scent, Jane, Jane, barrel cold and metallic between his teeth. The end of everything, this, here, now. The means in his hand. The power. The place. Now. Mine, mine.

In the nano-second after the horn went off Morley remembered the keys in the ignition. Site-Alert. The blaring from the Landcruiser seemed to fill the garage, shrill and persistent like a ship not a vehicle. Honking out across the still of the park.

Morley was on his feet and through the fire exit by the second blast, racing through rhododendrons and over wood chips. Tearing at the door handle, throwing himself across the seat and over to the console. Hitting the release button. Gun falling to the floor. Phone into his hand and the braying had stopped.

Behind him lights had come on, a car thief caught in the act. The man in the garage frozen as he ran out. Her remote in the dumpster. Fingerprints.

Starting the motor, tyres squealing. Still no light from 205.

Everything together. Away.

'H'llo, h'llo.'

'Morley? It's Elaine.'

5

As green forests to charcoal as pink flesh to bones, Berlin was a ruin.

Apocalypse had come.

An endless catacomb of crumbling brick and masonry filling our view in every direction. Up and down what used to be streets. Across what were once squares and parks, now shoulder high in rubble and the detritus of a defeated army. Any building left standing had no roof, no windows and no doors. Stone openings hanging high in the air, floors and frames gone, transfigured by beams of dusty light, like cords through a giant's needle.

A vast flat of lifeless stalagmites, a metropolitan desert.

The destruction of Ypres ten or twenty times over. More. A city where one million defeated troops of the German Army and the SS had tried to hold back two and a half million Avenging Angels in Russian uniform. A city pounded to pieces from the air for three years: low level, high level, by night and finally by day. More bomb damage than all the cities of England combined.

Then this city had been contested to complete devastation. Street after street, building by building, room by room, by infantry and tanks, by heavy artillery over open sights.

We drove in from the East back from the River Neiße. Through the forests of the Spreewald, through Lichtenberg and into Wasteland Berlin.

The road was a pumping artery of vehicles and equipment travelling in both directions at high speed. The supply line for one thousand kilometres of Russian advance starting from the turning point of the war within sight of Moscow.

Convoys of T-34s and A-25s bore down on us from front and back. Stone-faced drivers in leather helmets ready to crush the Quinze and sweep her under their tracks without a second thought. Doze her away into the twisted scrap that ran in wind-rows along both sides of the road like an endless derailed train.

Then the procession would stop for no apparent reason, squeezing us between transports, surrounded by soldiers, some friendly, some suspicious. But all smiles and the offer of a pinch of tobacco wrapped in a strip of *Pravda* when we showed our passports. Or cheers for Pierre as I helped him from the car, waving his hook at them, staggering on his crutches, over to piss against an upturned chassis that was once a Stalin Organ.

Every mile or two bulldozers had cleared ground for a staging area. Women in battle order regulated traffic, Pepesha automatics hanging down their backs. Breasts swelling out tunics, a flag waving in each hand.

Soldiers in groups stoked fires in front of their vehicles, turning the transport parks into Soviet settlements. Laughing, dancing to an accordion, in the morning, in the evening, singing in the middle of the night.

And behind the army the population was moving again, termites emerging from dead wood. Teams of German women labouring over broken bricks and knotted steel, wrapped in kitchen aprons and headscarves, the fashion of '46. Pulling rubble away on adapted mine railways like pit ponies. In human chains up and down building frames, passing buckets and boxes hand to hand.

Shops had opened in cellars: used soap stolen from the American Army, water delivered by horse and cart, tobacco collected from fag ends. Tables for re-sharpening razor blades. Stands for anything of value which had been hidden from the Angels now sold to raise a little cash. Living out an existence in the least damaged buildings. Ignored, left to starve by their conquerors unless taken for labour, or worse. Browning's rumour that over two million German women had been raped. An Angel's finger pointing and the piercing words: *Kom-frau.*

We passed back into the British sector, from Weissensee over to Wedding. Here conditions were better but the Russians had the harder job: the most civilians and the densest parts of the city. At a barrier made by two half-tracks a Russian soldier poked the seats of the Quinze with his bayonet ripping the upholstery. He made a joke that we did not understand. He and his comrades laughed. But we were leaving and they were not much interested. Pierre shrugged, the car had been a wreck before.

Then south through the Tiergarten toward Browning's barracks following signboards we could read: C-in-C BF of O.

The Allies had searched for Foch's *wagon lit,* planning a third capitulation. Hitler had brought the railway car back to Berlin after the fall of France. For his public to enjoy his great moment with him. Now the coach could not be found: burned, destroyed in an air raid, nobody knew.

But the Russians had their own idea of symbolic vengeance.

We drove slowly along Charlottenburger Chaussee, lined with parked tanks and Allied flags. Victory parades were being held daily, each regiment by turn following Napoleon through the Brandenburger Tor and up Unter den Linden. Led by the ghost of Haig on his chestnut mare.

The Siegessäule was still where Hitler had moved it for his Fiftieth, scarred but standing, now topped with a French flag. Surrounded by a Tiergarten of toothpicks, denuded by firestorm. Further down I looked for the site where the monument had once stood and the path leading to Beethoven's statue. And here was the most amazing spectacle in Berlin.

A large cenotaph had been built to commemorate the 2,200 Soviet soldiers killed during the final attack on the Reichstag. Lives wasted in an unnecessary assault so that Stalin's red flag could be hoisted by May Day. The last thousand metres of their thousand kilometre advance.

The monument was the only squared structure in the city. Shining white stone in six porticos translucent against the grey despoliation all around and the death skull of the Reichstag dome behind. The names of the dead Russian commanders and their brave words in golden Cyrillic script. Two light tanks and two field guns up on pedestals. A Red Army guard goose-stepping over a pavement made of pink marble torn from the Reichstag walls.

The work had been completed in six months, crews working night and day to be ready for 11 November 1945. And sited precisely over the pit where the Siegessäule had once stood.

Victory was not complete until every orifice of the vanquished had been penetrated and all their sacred holes filled up.

Browning arrived the next day while Pierre was arguing with me about leaving.

My wife was dead. And as to Poland the Red Army had said *Nyet!* No mazurkas on Polish soil. The largest army in the world. *Nyet!* Was there more?

He was tired and malign, bad after drinking, jealous of the marching victors. His war was worse and he had been given no Berlin parade.

But I had yet to stare them down. They were aroused, their faces haunting me round every mess bedroom across Germany and now through the city I used to know so well. Djinns leering back at me night and day, reflected in our silver vodka lake.

And Browning insisted: another night or two. To visit the American Army cinema. More film was to be shown, he told us, some captured at the end and never screened before. *Les films*, I taunted Pierre when still he talked of leaving, *c'est ça le truc, c'est ça le truc.*

The US Army Information Service cinema sat alone against a far perimeter fence, a prefabricated structure of galvanised metal. Part of an overnight American city built around Templehof airfield.

Rows of tip-up seats off a central aisle marched down a concrete ramp. A table had been set up at the back where clerks were cataloguing German films as they were shown, working under low table lamps in the dark theatre. Figures came and went, soldiers off duty taking seats then shuffling out again when they were bored. The air was dense with cigarette smoke, Luckys competing with Pierre's Celtique, the floor sticky with chewing gum.

On the first day Browning drove us over and he stayed for an hour. On the second day we were delivered by his driver in his jeep. Complete with Pierre's supply of *maïs* and a haversack of vodka.

We watched German films until late into the afternoon. From the other side of the war we had missed. *The Maginot: A Common Grave for French Defenders. Rommel Over Africa. Let Them Come, We Are Ready.* A clerk's American monotone announced each film in English.

We drank from the haversack, fumbling between us in the dark, transfixed by the screen. Pierre alternating with his good hand: bottle, Celtique, bottle. And with every picture of France Pierre jeered his insults: at the occupiers, at Frenchmen caught on German film, going about their daily lives.

An officer from the table, then the GI from the foyer came down the aisle. Put a chill on it, guys.

Then through my blur upside-down numbers flashed. 4 3 2 1.

The flat drone from the back.

'Untitled but dated, 8 August 1944. Location of capture, Sachsenhausen.'

From the whirring start of the projector, white light through blue smoke, the film was dark and raw. A flickering intensity that seemed to tell the viewer to prepare.

We are in a room, the camera does not move. Only fluttering frames show that time is passing, that the camera is running. More than a room, a small barn. The walls show signs of damage then rebuilding.

We can see one entire end of the barn. Black curtains are drawn back against the wall on either side of the picture. An impression that we are looking at a stage.

Two narrow windows in the far wall, arched at the top and barred. The pattern of bars follows the curve of the windows. Matching shutters have been opened inwards to give light. The roof is more black, timbers possibly, open trusses and beams to a high ceiling like a stable. The floor is bare. On the right-hand wall a metal door to the outside is fitted with a locking bar like a fortress. The door is wide, as if for manoeuvring bulky objects.

The camera remains steady.

We have time to take in the furnishings of the room. On the left side, opposite the metal door, a hand sink is attached to the wall, set in a square of shiny tile. Next to the sink, a table and chair. A glass stands on the table next to a bottle of clear liquid that could be schnapps. The bottle has no label. Now every detail starts to take on some meaning, some foreboding that we do not understand.

On the right side in the foreground we see a contraption that is half work bench, half a reminder of village stocks. An oval hole between boards set up at one end of the bench could hold an arm or a leg.

As more seconds pass horror floods the picture. The contraption is a guillotine. An angled blade catches the quivering light, partly recessed into a dark frame high above the boards, ready to drop across the oval hole. The bench is a platform for a prostrate body.

Then the beam. Across the room, wall to wall above the rounded tops of the windows, the beam is hard to see at first against the dark roof. Deep and strong like the rail of a gantry, a piece of industrial equipment. Eight sturdy hooks evenly spaced are shackled to the lower flange, capable of taking substantial weight without deflection. Like a butcher's storehouse.

Still the camera does not move.

But now all the elements of the room are clear. Already the most terrifying picture I have ever seen.

Pierre's hand takes my shoulder, squeezing me hard.

'*On s'en va,*' he says struggling for his feet, pushing down on me as he comes out of his seat. I hold him back. He thinks that I want to stay.

'The world is already bad enough, no?' loud, ready to argue again. Like me, very drunk. He too feels evil flowing out of the stationary picture.

I push past him stumbling into the aisle.

'Your chair,' I say.

As I turn away for the door I catch that the film has jumped. Now we are looking at a face. The camera has focused so that the face fills the screen. A man in his sixties I think, thin, a large beaked nose. A man I might recognize, a famous actor perhaps. But distinguished, a defiant look for the camera, a man used to command.

I press through swinging doors and out into the foyer. Intense sunshine through windows and I am blinking. Pierre's chair has gone. Even in my stupor I am sure that the chair is not there because the GI is standing in the very place where I had left it. White spats strapped under his crêpe heels, hand on his holster. One of us is swaying backwards and forwards.

'Kindavahaz'rd,' he explains. 'Cap'n told me ta take it over to da eatery, park it with da ja-*a*nitor.' He points across the assembly area outside.

I weave over fresh macadam following the GI's finger.

But the janitor has locked the chair away. Weren't told nutt'n' ab*a*-*a*t it, he says. Plann'n' on return'n' da ting to da infirmary, he mumbles. Was gonna do dat tom-orra. Then he tells me he was just off duty and has already signed the keys to his closets back into the brig. I have to wait another few minutes until he returns. He wheels Pierre's chair out of a door marked JC-6. But there's this pr*a*-*a*blem see? He had listed the chair under PROPERTY, LOST. So now the chair has to be signed for. Because it ain't no longer lost, right? But his clipboard is in his office. I wait again. He returns, yerautogra-*a*ph mister, he demands.

Back at the cinema the GI in his spats holds the swinging door open for me. The clerks around the table look up with a jerk as I start down the aisle holding the chair back against the incline. I can tell something has happened in the theatre while I was out. Maybe Pierre has been swearing and shouting again. One of the clerks has his head buried in his arms.

I look up at the screen as I roll the chair slowly toward Pierre. Now there is another man in the picture. The first face, the commander has gone. This man is standing by the sink drinking from the glass which was on the table. He has poured himself some of the schnapps. He is wearing an apron like a butcher, in a heavy dark material, black leather. Black shirt and tie, silver piping and silver badges glint on his collar.

On the right side of the room the curtain has been drawn out a few feet from the wall behind the guillotine. Part of the beam is now hidden. Only seven hooks remain visible.

The side door opens and another face appears, pushed along roughly by a second man in a leather apron. This face too is closely scrutinized by the camera, filling the screen so that we can examine him just as we examined the commander. Tall sunken cheeks of a shocking hollow grey, but eyes that are calm, returning the camera's steady stare, defying some viewer beyond. This face knows his audience.

By now I have reached the end of our row. Here two things overwhelm me simultaneously.

Pierre has vomited over the seat in front of him, then on to the floor.

And the face on the screen is Werner.

The camera pulls away and the picture of the barn returns. Yet another man appears, stepping forward into the picture from behind the camera, showing only his back. He stands in front of Werner and reads from a paper. I can see the outline of his jaw move but the film has no sound. Werner stands straight, his hands must be tied behind his back but this makes his frame taller, his shoulders square, defiant to the man who is reading. Werner is wearing a shirt buttoned up to the neck, a rough jacket and trousers like a workman. A prison uniform. The jacket is too small, but this only adds to Werner's dignity because the humiliation has not succeeded.

The silent reading ends with the reader raising his right arm in salute before he moves back out of the picture. So that I know which two words will be the last that Werner will ever hear.

The schnapps drinker, the first apron, is still by the sink. The second apron is a tall man, as tall as Werner. The second apron is holding something in his right hand that is hard to make out.

The schnapps drinker walks behind Werner and unties his hands. Then the two aprons together take off Werner's jacket followed by his shirt. The clothes are dropped into a pile on the floor. Werner's body is as thin as his face. The camera catches his ribs in lines edged with black shadow. Still Werner stands upright, still he is unmoved.

The schnapps drinker moves in front of Werner, his back to the camera. When he steps away we can see that Werner's hands have been retied, this time to the front, wrists together, the end of the rope hanging loose. There is no change in Werner's expression, not a muscle moves in his face. The

511

camera learns nothing, the camera is given not one frame of satisfaction.

Now as I watch, the two aprons are working in concert. I am aware of Pierre's distress. Wanting his chair, clothes covered in vomit, hammering my arm with his hook. Stench cutting through cigarette smoke. And at the same time a clerk from the table is behind me and the GI from the foyer is at my side.

But I have no idea what they are saying, I cannot hear, I can only see. For me they do not exist. I grip the handles to the chair like a lifeline in a tempest. I am a pillar of salt.

Werner is hustled over to the right of the screen under the next hook, against the partly drawn curtain. Then he is backed up on to a little stool brought out from behind the curtain by the second apron. A foot high, less.

Werner turns his head sideways. So that I can see his sallow profile, while Werner can see what is behind the curtain. Then he looks straight at us again, he does not even blink.

Still his face will tell the camera nothing. But I know, I know that Werner is fighting a terrible battle. A battle in a war that he will not lose.

Now the taller apron is standing on the chair behind Werner, preparing to secure to the hook the object he has been carrying in his hand. The object is a wire. But first a noose is formed through an eye woven into the end of the strand. The apron leans forward to place the ring over Werner's head. Then the wire is wrapped over the hook. The line is so thin, that to the camera the wire is not visible as it passes under Werner's jaw and around his neck.

The taller apron at the back completes his connection, wire to hook, vertical and taut, no slack. The apron steps down and replaces the chair at the table.

The GI and the clerk have encountered Pierre's vomit and they are retreating. Pierre has rolled over off his seat, on to the floor and into the slop. I am aware of his sobbing. But I cannot look at his condition.

The first apron has his back to the camera again. He is stooped over, standing in front of Werner. Werner's head and bare shoulders show pale and clear above. The apron is removing Werner's trousers. I see that Werner is wearing wooden clogs which fall to the ground as his trousers come off.

And now, as the short apron moves to one side, Werner is revealed. Standing naked on the stool, the wire a narrow filament straight up behind his head, his hands tied. Long seconds pass as the camera watches. But still Werner is defiant, still he is holding straight, still the lens can take nothing from him. Werner is not me.

Then the two aprons are working in concert again. From behind, the tall one bends over to remove the stool at the same moment as the short apron unties Werner's hands. The knot, prepared for this moment, is released with a quick tug on the loose end of rope.

A different clerk is standing next to me. He too has encountered the vomit and he too can see Pierre on the floor. But this one is prepared. He is telling me to leave, he is asking who we are, he is very angry, he is shouting, he wants me to clean up the mess, he is calling for the GI again. But it is still as if I cannot hear and his ranting has no effect.

In that instant Werner becomes a demonic sprinter. Up from his blocks and violently into action. Suddenly he is thrashing wildly with arms and legs as if at an invisible attacker.

I know that Werner wants to die immediately, I know that he wants to remain still and defiant. But I know that he cannot do either. And without any deflection the camera begins to capture its long moment, record its sustained satisfaction.

Werner's arms shoot upward for the beam, for the hook. But the executioner is an expert. Werner's frame arcs like a satanic dancer. He cannot reach. He must jig the jig that has been prepared for him. Sprint his last race.

His legs kick in spasms sideways, then furiously in the air like a running jump, scrambling wildly at nothing, for relief, for purchase that is not to be found. Now his hands know that the beam is beyond his grasp and he is scratching frantically, trying to snatch the wire that is embedded into his flesh. Long fingers ripping down the side of his neck with a violence that tears his skin, black blood spurting over silvery shoulders.

His body fishes maniacally on the wire, twisting around, away from the camera then back toward us. As he turns we can see that Werner is ejaculating and fouling himself, both at the same time.

Then his actions begin to lose intensity and over a time movement comes to an end. The time is the years of my life which will never be the same. The time is the years of Werner's life which is gone for ever. The time is so fast that it cannot be measured. So long that it is eternity.

Then as the body swings gently to and fro, arms to the side now, shoulders drooped, coming down to stationary, the camera takes its last reading. Focusing up to Werner's face again until he fills the screen once more.

The story has come back to the beginning. But now the face has changed, unrecognizable. Black, mouth wide open, tongue hanging like a shaving strap, eyes bulged and staring. Agony contorted across the features, written more horribly than any words.

The camera has seen all it wants. An apron draws the curtain along further.

Six hooks remain.

Then all my surroundings crash in on me. The stench of Pierre, shouting angry voices front and back, close air, dense smoke. The GI has my arm.

Now I too am going to be sick. My stomach is about to come up through my mouth, inside out like a dirty sock. I push away from my belligerents, running up the aisle for the door marked WC-1. On my knees I retch into the bowl: splattered greens and purples, bile that stinks and tastes of fermented vodka. Lumps that catch in my teeth, dribble that runs down my chin.

I am exhausted, I should die, I will die, now, head resting on the wooden seat. Vomit down my shirt, vomit on the floor.

Scenes flood in from Tricia's bathroom: the *Hauptsturmführer* in his black leather coat behind me, the smell of lavender. Silver badge, his ring catching the light. My screams. Being tied, absolute terror, etched glass against my face, unbearable pain. Shaking and screaming, trying to form the words of betrayal. I would have done anything, anything.

Werner upright, proud, not a muscle moves. In a flash, with a single shutter he is the Devil's athlete at a frantic run, sideways, round, spinning away and back. Winding down slowly like a clockwork toy, twisting on the wire. Penis half erect, shit down his legs. Black gargoyle face. The curtain pulled along the beam.

I am trying to hold my body steady, encompassing the putrid bowl with my arms. As the images burst like shrapnel, exploding inside me. Those hundred Christmas crackers from over my trench, those thousand razor edges about to smear a million shards of my flesh against the toilet walls.

But before I blow I am gripped ferociously by the back of the neck, forced to my feet and propelled through the foyer, doubled down. Bent over by a large hand, a steel vice. The other vice has my wrists behind my back. Halfway to the main doors before I understand what is happening. The US Military Police have arrived.

I try to ask about Pierre but there is no answer. I try to say that the man on the end of the wire is my friend, my *Kamerad*. From the War, the *First* War. The hero of my story. That I caused his death, that I caused them all. I scream out loud, I scream. *My fault, everything is my fault.* Then I cry and I slobber, more retching. That is the reason why I am being held face down.

But there is no answer to any of it.

Into a jeep, thrown hard over the back, red and white markings, sparkling white-painted tyres. Silver helmets up above me.

At the entrance to the camp the gates are opened. I am taken off the jeep and pushed out on to the road. The haversack thrown after me. They are too angry to inspect the contents.

Another American monotone warns me what will happen if I attempt to return.

6

At first I can remember the way. Another refugee with his little bag of belongings, shuffling head down through the scree.

I cross the Landwehr Kanal into Mitte. Horses, carts with rubber tyres made from gun carriages. The trams are running again, roofs showing just above the rubble on each side of the road like boats in the trough of a congealed high sea. Military everywhere, red stars in the broken Berlin streets. Groups of old soldiers from the German Army, bandages over bare feet. Dirty and wretched.

Alles kaputt.

Ah, this is my Berlin and I'm back. Back on Friedrichstraße walking up from Hallesches Tor. I'm late but not far now. I know that he is waiting for me at the Adlon. Impatient. Five o'clock tea. The secret pact, we have the secret pact. Pianist's fingers drumming on the table. Da-da-da DAH. Then he is knocking, demanding a drink. Da-da-da DAH. Da-da-da DAH. Our fate in four notes. Fingers. Neck. Fingers. Neck. Da-da-da DAH.

Trill me a trill for what could never be. Jig me a jig for the end of the world. Fusillades out over the water. We talk: all is ready down to the last gaiter button. I have it. Appendix N, the map, the River Vistula. Their nibses at Hendon airport. They must board the plane, now, now. Peace for Our Time.

The Victory that was never won, the Peace that started War. I can even remember the song, so I sing.

> We are a class of working folks
> With hands all hoof'd and brown'd
> By getting coal with heavy strokes
> Deep down beneath the ground.

Then he is saying goodbye, to me, to his *Kamerad*. I watch his profile. But he can see what is behind the curtain. The taxi turns and he is gone.

Back up to Leipzigerstraße, I must see Tricia. Frau Karen has the day off, I am to go directly to the shop. There she is, holding her scissors, red on silver. Flash, flash. Red on red, on Leonardo's man.

Just a quick visit, a peck on the cheek, there is danger. The war she cannot see. Shiny Beholla in a pool of its own reflection. Quick, it's Anna, slide the gun under the hat.

But Tricia is not there, the shop has been closed. I turn, the answer lies within. The answer lies within.

And there's Katrina pushing her pram. Piled with bundles and boxes, her baby balanced on top. A large nose, chewing on the brim of a sun hat. Wheels skidding on the slippery surface. Topple, topple, splash splash. Into blue water. Down down, away, away with the flow. Her baby a shadow in a desert between lava rocks.

Danger, danger, the S-Bahn is flooded under Anhalter Bahnhof. Do not go down. *Do not go down, I say.* A shell has penetrated the main entrance. Women and children stuck to the walls. I run to her to save her but she is moving fast, ahead of me away, away through the blasted forest. Then I am up to her but I cannot stop. I career into her at full speed.

'Кто Вы черт лобери?' She says.

No, not Katrina, this is a soldier. But a man I cannot understand. Helmet, rifle, sounds from the back of his throat like an Eskimo. But a *Kamerad* I am sure. Someone I know, a man who will stop the war with me. Take my arm, put it there, pal, right there, tell me that I will do. But no, not too fast, we haven't been introduced. You Imperials. And now he has my hands up and he's searching my body. Very sensible precaution in such dangerous times. I compliment him.

'Закрой ебалвник.' He replies.

But I'm confident, even if I don't understand his words. This is just his way of being friendly.

Now he's found the vodka in my haversack and there is no doubt that we are going to get along very well indeed.

He holds up the bottle and smiles. He removes the cork and he puts the bottle to his lips. But *ah ah!* There is *another* bottle in the haversack and now we *each* have a bottle. To England he says. To Never Again, I reply. Mr Lloyd George told me that himself. Never Again. But I do not know if my new *Kamerad* believes me.

A circle is forming around us, more *Kameraden*. They are all welcome, welcome I say. And now it is a contest. Between friends. He has his bottle and I have mine and we are starting. Heads back, eyes up at the evening sky. I watch air gulping into clear liquid as fire pours down my throat. I concentrate, swallowing, gasping, another gullet full, another, liquid bubbling down low in the glass now, more than halfway through. I am winning. Cheering and chanting around me. I am winning. I am winning.

Then suddenly the bottle is empty and I am omniscient.

My new *Kamerad* is a Russian. Moscow, I tell him, now there's another great city. Was he in Moscow when the Condors landed? He is thinking. Did he see the streets decked out in swastikas? The champagne salesman was coming. Champagne, Herr von Ribbentrop, more champagne. But did you notice? All up and down Lyusinovskaya Street, both sides. Did you notice? *THE SWASTIKAS WERE BACKWARDS.* Didn't that tell you something? Didn't they teach you *anything* at OCB? Quick, get those flags up. The champagne salesman cometh. Backwards, backwards, made for a propaganda film. Made for a betrayal. A betrayal within a betrayal. A plan that was a betrayal. A betrayal that was a plan.

Paris a trick. Cambrai a defeat. Everything the opposite of how it seems. Think about that, little man.

My *Kamerad* is impressed that I know all these things, that I was there.

Why? Why to all this?

I also know why.

The answer lies within. The era of Pan-Europa is about to dawn. Quick, before Mr S kills us all. Here I come, wait, wait. I am running toward the building. Only a few metres to go. Uncle Joe has issued his orders. Flag up by the First of May, on the roof. By the First! Лонял? Scrambling up rubble, over bricks. I have taken his rifle. If he's not going to the rescue, then I am. They are all in there, waiting for me to fetch them. There's a tank, those T-34s again. Come on boys, get that old bus moving.

Can't you see we're almost there? Only a few metres more. But this gun is useless, out of SAA. Bricks will do, just as effective. And heavier.

Now there is enemy fire, but no, fire from my *Kamerad,* not from the enemy at all. Idiots. Signals crossed, Reichstag is objective Number One. DEM DEUTSCHEN VOLKE. Mighty columns, Prussia, Rome, copies of copies. Imitations of imitations. Don't these people read their orders?

Now my *Kamerad* is very angry. I can see it in his face. But he won't catch me, won't catch me. Through the gate: Victory. Haven't been through the gate. Must go through the gate. Do it properly, trousers down to the count of four. Victory's not a victory 'til all their holes are filled.

You will do very nicely, she says. A gloved hand through my arm. Then she unbuttoned my shirt, like this, like this. Trousers, shoes.

Now I am him, naked like him, now I can jig like him, here, this is how.

Here is the jig for the end of the world. And look, I am wounded too, look, look. *Ah, mon pauvre rosbif,* I see, but you still have all your limbs.

And now we must run. Yes run, bullets flying, smacking through the leaves. I know how it goes, I know what to do. Pictures of your children, show them your family. Show them your son, show him Emma. Where is she? Where is she? The answer lies within.

Then a voice spoke to me.

'You're in a bad way, mate,' standing over my head. 'And who was shooting then? What unit's yer with anyway? And where's yer trousers? An' yer shirt? Not properly dressed. Can't 'ave that, can we now?'

He helped me to my feet, one arm over his shoulder and we staggered back across the river, north into Wedding.

'Firstied, right over 'ere.' Then as we approached a tent marked with a large red cross he said, 'Better do something about yerself before reporting in, stinks to 'igh 'eavens, yer does. Not to mention the other.'

The nurse began.

'Rank?' Looking down her nose and on to her form.

White sheets, kindly words in English, the smell of laughing gas. Gentian violet on my cut hands.

Then all was black. And later I was vomiting again. Nothing but liquid. Pure vodka. Later again I was shaking, crawling on hands and knees under the bed and over to the door marked WC.

On the way I met a pair of shoes, brown shoes, shoes that I knew. I tapped them to see if they were real.

Da-da-da DAH. Fingers. Neck. Fingers. Neck. Da-da-da DAH.

～

'Elaine, tell Elaine I want to do it now.' Almost no voice left. From down in his throat and his chest, but a determination riveting out through whey-blue eyes.

Morley found Elaine sitting at the office computer, keying-in the night's medication reports. He leaned through the door-frame at her and she looked up. Before Morley could speak she was on her feet and they were both back by the bed.

Elaine felt Graham's face then searched for his pulse. She smiled down at him, it wasn't what she had thought.

'How's the pain?'

'I want you to turn me over, take this cast off,' Graham whispered.

Elaine looked over at Morley.

'We'll need wheels,' she said. They seemed to agree without speaking that there would be no argument in the room. In the corridor they moved to opposite ends of the stretcher.

'What's going on?' Elaine asked, holding back. 'He's almost gone, he'll never survive this. Without the cast he'll be in agony, or drugged to the eyeballs.' She clutched the trolley bar to prevent Morley from moving.

'It's what he wants,' Morley said weakly. 'He's so sure of what he is doing. But the pain ... what will..?'

Elaine paused then she seemed to relent.

'There's little point in refusing anything at this stage, I suppose. Like a few last smokes.' She gave her shrug then guided the stretcher through the door and over tight to the bed.

'Do you want anything before we start?' The old man shook his head. A slight movement that was no more than the flicker of his eyes. Like a mute animal that knows what is to come.

Elaine pulled back the covers and moved Graham's yellow urinary bag onto the far side of the trolley. Morley felt more capable, ready at Graham's shoulders; he had done this before. The old man raised shaking hands behind him, up and over Morley's arms. The hard shape in Morley's pocket wedged itself awkwardly between them as Morley started to lift. Then slowly the body was worked over to the edge of the bed.

Elaine untied the cord of Graham's gown, slipping the flimsy green cover off his arms and onto the floor. The entire body lay exposed, straps for the cast across his chest, stomach and hips. A dressing like the front of a pair of shorts covering his lower abdomen. Morley had almost forgotten about the operation. In from the front, through the stomach wall like a cutting torch applied to the structure of a building. Sort past intestines like a tripe sausage, open the obstruction, decide it was hopeless and sew him up again. Cancer released like angry bees from a raided hive, the old man was convinced of it.

Graham's penis protruded below the dressing and into a catheter, a tiny face in a miniature oxygen mask. The bandages came off and Elaine re-dressed the long purple cut, angry and inflamed. She taped the dressing on firmly. Then she unbuckled the cast straps. She nodded at Morley.

'You ready?' she asked Graham. There was a faint grunt in reply.

'Do it and don't stop for anything.'

Morley started with the shoulders, rolling Graham towards him, up onto his side along the edge of the bed, slowly, imperceptibly, over toward the trolley. Elaine followed with the feet and hips, trying to keep the body in line, not to hurt, not to press. The old man's torso starting to heave, then a subdued scream and a mumbled cursing, telling them no, no.

Elaine giving encouragement. Almost there, hang-on, hang-on, ignoring what Graham was saying through gasping breaths. Talking fast to Morley: keep him straight, now hold him back, gently as he comes down. Watch the pipe and the bandage. Keep the trolley tight to the bed. Gently, gently.

Then the old man was over, winded, face down. The cast an empty shell left behind, a shadow haunting along the bed. And on the stretcher the bare fragile figure was a fish out of water, twitching and flapping, sucking for life itself on the far bank.

Elaine crouched down at the old man's head, face to face. While Morley stood staring, transfixed, mouth open, clenched fists up by his forehead.

The form on the trolley was utterly white, the underside of something that lived on the bottom. And from hairline at the back of the head down to buttocks, the surface was furrowed. Ploughed and uneven, edged and callused from side to side. Splattered with clusters of smooth scar tissue. Like lead on a concrete floor dripped from a plumber's torch. Like wet paper towel, like melted plastic, like rough stucco, like new snow over excavated ground. But not any one of those things. No shallow simile from Morley's shallow life could describe the sight.

It was human, alive, attached to a body, it was the body itself, beyond all comparisons. A record of trauma, of blood, infinite pain. Hatred, regret, a life pivoted around a single act of vengeance.

Elaine stood up next to Morley and she stared too. One hand over her mouth, the other reaching out for Morley's arm.

Then Graham was trying to speak and Elaine bent down face to face with him again. She looked up at Morley. 'He wants you to run your fingers over his back.'

Morley stood still for a moment, petrified between repulsion and obligation. Then slowly he stretched out his hands.

A sleepwalker, Morley was a pilot in the night sky. His fingertips drawing lightly over the destruction below. Starting at the shoulders, the surface was hard then soft, scaly then smooth on the inside of horizontal Vs. Silken but uneven, over scarred bumps and rounds, into grooves. A Braille of anguish so plain that even the untrained could read.

Morley's fingers worked down through the middle of the back, over more furrows. Down again to the last lines and onto the wasted translucent skin of Graham's buttocks.

'Again,' Elaine said, 'palms flat, let yourself feel it. Like a massage. Take it right in.'

Morley held his arms out again, still rigid, still reluctant. Elaine came round the stretcher, hands on Morley's elbows, trying to soften him up. Then she was pressing her hands over his and onto the scars. She was warm, understanding, seeing at a glance what was needed.

'There,' she whispered, 'just this little bit of the journey. Let him feel that you're there with him, that's all it takes.'

Morley passed his hands up and down over the fractured surface. Over valleys, plains, deserts, mountains. Flesh. A life that would soon be gone, a warning, a message that would soon be lost.

He was back on the concrete floor in the garage, prickled with sweat down between two tyres. Road smell, rubber, gasoline, oil. Down between two cars thinking that he could win with a pistol in his hand.

Morley's motions became slower, harder. Taking it in through his hands and down in to his middle. Then he was pressing, kneading like one of his pastries, skin flaking under his fingertips. Stu in his bomber, Werner's neck. Tricia in a cattle car. Water imploding through windows under the Rhine. A tribe in an endless circle of desert. Thompson's hand on the handle of the tank door.

Morley as the inheritor, handed a baton. Like a resistance to cancer. No, like some vast ancestral treasure only discovered as the paterfamilias dies.

He is me, I am him. Your scars, my hands. Your death, mine. My life, yours.

Then the inheritors are left on their own. A black man climbs out of his 500, stepping over bodies to collect his pay-off. A white man hides in a garage with his gun.

They have learned nothing. They are nothing. No gun, no bank account, nothing could ... there has to be ...

Graham was struggling to talk.

Elaine bent down to the trolley again.

'He says the world is bad enough already,' looking up at Morley. 'Do you know what he means?'

~

Browning was decent right to the end. He had me discharged from hospital and drove me back to his office. I told him that I had known Major Schacht before the War. And his commanding officer, the Chief of the General Staff, General Halder. Through the Embassy, I said.

Browning shook his head at me, exaggerating the movements.

'Glad I didn't watch that film. I have to carry on here you know, Exeter. Occurs to me every day: damn lucky thing for Jerry that Hitler is dead. He can take all the blame. Incredible the things we've found in this country.

And all done by Der Ruddy Few-rah. Single-handed, of course. Nobody admits to a thing, not the way to get off to a fresh start.'

British Sector Headquarters, Berlin, was the Haus des Deutschen Sports built for the 1936 Olympic Games, some way north of the centre and almost free of damage. Browning took his seat in a vast chamber of Reich-Roman splendour with desk and furniture to match. A baron of the Raj. Two maids from the subject race brought us tea wearing black servant's dresses and frilly white pinafores.

'But the really odd thing about Germany today,' Browning persisted even though I could hardly hear, 'is that everything is the opposite to how it appears. Ever considered that, have you, Exeter?'

Browning lit himself a cigar, happy to have a captive audience. He was no longer a soldier, not even an estate agent. Browning had become a politician.

Unconditional surrender. All that means is that we have unconditional responsibility.

Poland. Reason for the war. So since we'd won wouldn't I expect Poland to be better off? But not a bit of it. Only country to lose territory from the old Versailles borders, other than Germany, of course. And not saved at all, held right in Stalin's claw. Matching hand motion with his fingers on the top of his desk. Can't imagine why I'd come all this way just to stand on free Polish soil. There isn't any, ha, ha, ha.

But wonderful people the Russkies all the same. Americans have no idea what they're up against. At least twenty-five million Russian dead, maybe double that. Against under five hundred thousand for the US. Could never have landed in Normandy without the Eastern front. Never even climbed out of the boats. Never.

But now the Yanks were playing the big victors. Couldn't even agree with the Russians on an official date for the end of the war. The Russkies won't roll over too easily, though. Just you wait and see.

'And of course, the real joke is,' Browning continued some more, even though my eyes were closed, 'that the Americans will end up rebuilding and re-arming Germany. Just to score a point off the Soviets. All this punishment and starvation will soon be forgotten. Germany as our prosperous ally against the Reds. Just what old Adolf wanted all along.'

Browning's laugh boomed out again in the hard cavernous room. Round and round in my hard cavernous head.

'And what's more,' he added, 'in the process the Yanks'll make damned sure it's good for business. While the British Empire is flat broke. *Alles kaputt,* that's us.' He roared more again, even bigger and even heartier.

I waited for the reprimand that I deserved, but it never came.

'We'll just sweep it under the rug,' Browning told me finally. 'The Russkies have made no complaint, the corporal who found you says that their man's rifle was returned. Got your plumber's uniform back I see. People always shooting around here. Yanks I haven't heard from either. Probably don't even remember how you got into the cinema in the first place. And as to the French, well, I've never seen such a fuss. But not what you think.'

After I had been ejected from Templehof, the Americans had established Pierre's nationality from documents in his jacket. He had been transferred by ambulance to the French Sector at Reinickendorf where his full identity was quickly discovered.

'An authentic twenty-four carat hero apparently,' Browning said, shaking his head again. 'What the dickens were you two doing drunk and disorderly in Berlin?'

But my head was now a black echoing cave and the floor was calling for me to lie down. I tried to explain but I rambled, incoherent.

Browning talked on.

Pierre had already been returned to Évian. And this time there would be no avoiding them, he was their prisoner. Browning laughed again. A staff car, a new uniform, flags flying all the way home. Still some bad feelings in France, people jumping to conclusions. More murders and executions than the French would like to admit. So here was a man they could use to make everyone think again.

Browning had heard the story from his opposite number in the French Army.

During the German occupation, after June 1940, *le Capitaine* had played up the First War, his time at Verdun, respect for Pétain, his amputations. He had even taken a position with the Légion Française des Combatants. First War veterans who supported Vichy and were all for getting along with the Germans.

But still the German governor in Évian had been suspicious: *aide de camp* to Foch in 'nineteen and 'twenty, his decorations, a potential leader. Just to be sure, they took away his foot, his hook and his crutches. Thought they had reduced him to a drunken immobile crank living in squalor. Limbs not even returned for his mother's funeral. He had started filling the house up with rubbish and they were satisfied that he had gone mad.

But the property was the end of a pipeline run by Libération Nord. Fugitives escaping from France and from northern Italy, hiding in the trash. Then from Pierre's boathouse over the lake to Switzerland.

Carlisle

GREAT BRITAIN
Oxford
St Ives
LONDON
Croydon
AMSTERDAM

Hamburg
Bremerhaven
EAST
GERMAN
Leipzig
Weim

Ypres
BRUSSELS
Cologne
Calais
Cambrai
Verdun
Frankfurt
PARIS
WEST GERMANY
Nuremberg

FRANCE

1944
ALSACE-LORRAINE
RETURNED TO
FRANCE

la Wantzenau
Strasbourg
Dachau
Munich
Hohenaschau
SWITZERLAND
GENEVA

1948
IRON CURTAIN
Thoiry
Lyon
Vienne
Evian
Milan
Trieste
Venice
Avignon
St Rémy-de-Provence
Florence
Genoa
Rapallo
Marseilles
Cannes
Monte-Carlo

SPAIN

ITALY
ROME

Key

---- Versailles boundaries
changed 1945

Grossdeutsches
Reich 1942

'We're planning to give him a medal ourselves,' Browning said. 'Quite a number of our aircrew were saved, apparently. And the Germans would have shot him on the spot and burned the house down if he'd been caught.'

Rosé glasses clinking, the little group watching. *Oh! quel feu de joie.* Always on the winning side.

The Quinze looked even sadder than me, grey and out of place. Overwhelmed in the endless Transport compound of Berlin HQ, AMG. Lost behind a long row of khaki wrecks. I cleaned her up inside and out. I started her with the help of a corporal mechanic and I went back for my good-byes.

Browning had renewed my papers. He gave me a requisition for petrol, a map and a pass through the American zone. I planned to enter Switzerland across Bodensee. Then to Luzern, Interlaken, Montreux and around the lake to Évian.

'And here's the address of the chap you were asking about, your pal's general.' Browning passed me a scrap of paper: Halder, F.J. No rank. 'Wasn't hard to find, listed by the International Military Tribunal but never charged. Released a few months ago so he should still be alive. I've written out the name of the village. In Bavaria, in the American Zone, probably on your way.'

Browning came out of his office with me. Into life-saving fresh air. Under a stone swastika in an eagle's claw. Between the columns of megalomania, copies of copies, echoes of echoes, down the steps of the House of German Sport.

'Something I've always wanted to ask you, Exeter,' Browning said as we walked. 'You remember those *banda* that came after you into the desert?' He put his hand to his crotch as if to hitch up his trousers. 'Were they still alive when you fixed them up?'

Browning started to laugh his big quaking laugh again. I went weakly through the motions with him, pretending with a post-diluvial grimace. Then I folded myself into the Quinze.

7

I entered the American zone at the *Land* border of Hessen where I exchanged my British Military Government food book for USFC cards. Then a top-sergeant in another polished helmet glanced over Browning's papers and waved me right through.

Ya take care how ya go now. Still pur-dy Roxy ou' dare.

My reputation had not reached them from Berlin.

I bypassed the cities, Nürnberg, München, working south following Browning's map. This Germany would have disappointed Pierre. Some views, some half hours without any sign of damage.

Then as I approached the mountains, Germany could have been Switzerland. American vehicles filled cracked muddy roads, their signs were nailed to every tree, but insignificant against blue crags leaning high over steep forests of dark green tips.

In the south, German defence of the Fatherland had collapsed with Kesselring's surrender in northern Italy after the stalemated winter of 1944 and into 1945. The countryside of Bavaria had seen little fighting, protected by the peaks and cliffs of the Tirol. Every village house had a roof, windows and a front door.

Even small hotels were operating again. Ten old Reichmark, less than sixpence a night, just a few cents of my American dollars but no meal without a card.

The valley of Aschau im Chiemgau is a form of perfection. Mountains on every side high enough for drama but split and shaped to let in sunshine all day. Woods from a chocolate-box, sloping down to a flat agricultural floor of brilliant greens. The River Alz running next to the road, cascading over white rocks.

Lucerne had recently been harvested leaving the fields like trimmed lawns in a park. And on a low hill in the middle of the valley stood the Good Fairy's castle. Proportions from a story book, creams with red and blue decorations, brown slate spires and a golden clock. Church steeples like twin purple onions. From flowered balconies high in the air she could look out over her Charmed Domain: no fortifications, no cannon, no memories of war.

In the village of Hohenaschau I asked a man wheeling a bicycle for directions to Herr Halder's house. He corrected me immediately.

'*Herr Generaloberst Halder wohnt ein bißchen weiter...*'

Halder's house was similar to the others. Two storeys high, large roof overhanging upper windows. Logs secured across tiles to hold back snow loads. Painted wood exterior, elaborately carved casings and shutters decorated in blue and silver patterns. The sound of rushing water from an ice-clear brook on its way to the river. The scent of pine bark sharp on the breeze.

Halder was more than alive. He was sixty-two that year but he looked younger than at our first meeting, his desiccation in some miraculous mountain-air remission. Hair no more than stubble, pince-nez pressed into his face. The only German I had seen in three weeks who was freshly shaved.

He was another Bavarian picture. Grey jacket adorned with red piping, brass buttons like tiny Morris bells, an embroidered green waistcoat, leather hiking trousers, boots and long stockings.

Halder's eyes darted at me as the door opened, then out over my shoulder before I was recognized. Looking for my escort, his daggers taking in the Quinze. But I was alone, not another Allied official with more questions.

Then everything was remembered, everything understood in a flashed second glance. The Lieutenant from the Great War, the *Herrenhaus*, even why I was there at his door. As if it was 1939 again and the palm extended toward me was waiting for an envelope. The reply to his letters. The answer from Halifax, or from Chamberlain that had never come.

He held my hand between his two as if we were in the long dining room again, a step down from the hearth to greet the lost sinner at the church door.

And here I started to tumble once more. Cascading with the features from a thousand nightmares, there on Halder's doorstep. My fractured face, my drunk's breath, an uncontrollable fatigue melting the gristle of my joints. But he took me in and I sat without being asked, a wooden chair at his kitchen table. My face buried into my hands as I wept.

The film, the gargoyle, the unknown viewer, unexplained events. I was back where it had all started, in Halder's presence. Unable to breathe with self-reproach, feet sliding on slimy black rocks in an underground river of *never* that had risen to flood the world.

A woman came into the room, a resigned face in soft folds. Hair in a faded scarf, more of the fashion of '46. Halder introduced his wife but she quickly turned away and started to move pots around on her stove. Embarrassed by my tears, not a part of the General's affairs. She put some soup on the table in front of me, a crust of black bread.

Everyone was underfed and the old polite questions were meaningless. *Would you care for something to drink?* Or, *Are you hungry?* For all the lush fields, American control of food production and black market forces had left even the country dwellers famished.

Halder listened: Werner, my words failing, actions, hands round my neck like the wire, arms reaching up in a Devil's arc for the beam, out of reach by an inch that was as far as the top of the furthest blue peak. Extruded eyes, fingers ripping into flesh. Fingers. Neck. Fingers. Neck. Satan's runner. The curtain pulled across the lens.

Then I was sobbing into my arms again, Frau Halder's soup pushed away across the table.

Halder was a brilliant and a sympathetic man. Ready for anything, encompassing everything, both his strength and his weakness. Moving millions of men by his direct and unquestioned orders, more than half of them lost as prisoners or casualties. And yet he had survived, able to comfort me, just me the failed and broken-down messenger.

'*Je me souviens de notre première réunion au Herrenhaus,*' Halder started after Frau Halder had left the kitchen, sitting next to me, talking to my slumped back. 'We spoke of the pact on the battleship *Deutschland*, about a General Staff of cowardly Fausts who had sold their ambitious souls.'

His French was hard-edged and guttural, out of practice.

'I have heard about this film, what was on this film. It had to follow. The end of Secret Germany, it had to follow. Nemesis. It had to be. Our reward for service without loyalty, for duty without honour. The traditions of the German Army to nothing brought. Then the entire country. This time there is no Armistice, this time there is not even defeat. For us all, this is *Null*.'

Halder had me eat my soup, a pause in his flow, other conversation. He asked me how I had managed to find him, to travel, where I had come from.

I told him that I had spent the war *in Africa*, that I had come *from Canada* and for the moment that was sufficient. I told him about Wasteland Berlin, about the Russian sector, about Pierre and his djinns, now mine. Then about Browning and his help, about Field Marshal Montgomery as Military Governor in the north.

Later Frau Halder reappeared to light an oil lamp in the growing dark. She spoke to the General who told me that I should spend the night with them, they had a room but no candles.

The next day was not what I had expected. After a breakfast of American biscuits and Frau Halder's coffee made from ground acorns, Halder took me into his study and here our roles reversed.

The room was lined with overlapping maps, right around, on every wall. More lay thick on a small table. A miniature *Lageraum*, the Situation Room from his old domain of the *Generalstab*.

Halder led me to every map in order, pointing with quick jabs like an impatient schoolmaster, his Bavarian suit a caricature of his *Waffenrock*. This is how it must have been at Zossen. Or with Hitler.

Every detail clear in his memory. Poland. The first *Blitzkrieg*: just enough opposition to distinguish the short campaign from a blood sport. Returning victorious with cheeks bloodied, euphoria, everything else, all resistance forgotten. Then time to refit as the Allies responded with *Sitzkrieg*. Norway as a brilliant sideshow.

His campaigns into Holland and Belgium. First the matador's cloak, Rundstedt's Army Group B drawing the BEF and the French up to the north, into Belgium. Then the sword. His Panzers thrusting below them, across to the Channel, clean around the impregnable Maginot Line. The Allied armies trapped.

The greatest challenge of his career, threading the mechanized blocks of the 2nd Army through the Ardennes. Crossing the Meuse with his support lines at breaking point, Rommel as a shooting star, barely under control. Waiting for the French counter-attack that never came.

Hitler's disastrous interference, his halt order when Halder had the British in his grasp. The lost opportunity to capture the whole of the BEF in front of Dunkerque, to put a quarter of a million tommies into German camps.

Then, Halder says, the lecturer at his climax, then your Winston Churchill, your Little England would have been forced into a favourable armistice. But Hitler's fumbling allows the British to get away.

The planning of *Barbarossa* and again Hitler's interference. Delays while Halder is instructed to deal with Italian weakness in the Balkans and in Greece. Finally the invasion of Russia is under way. The largest tank battle of the war, of history, but everything is late and there is a first disaster in front of Moscow. The Russians counter-attack on the outskirts of the city when the Führer has persuaded himself that such a thing is not possible. And after he has told the German people that the Russian army has been destroyed. The delusions have begun.

Halder facing his most formidable adversaries, the unbeatable Russian commanders: General December, Marshal January, Commissar February...

Halder started wringing his hands, his old habit. One into the other, over and over again as if in great pain.

1942. Hitler is the Greatest Warlord in History, but he wastes all the advantages Halder has gained. Stalingrad could have been taken early in the year but at the last minute the objective is changed to the Caucasus. Then suddenly the Caucasus is forfeit and the objective is back to Stalingrad again only to find that it is too late. Again the Russians have shorter lines of supply and yet more divisions that the Germans have not counted. And winter is coming round for the second time.

Halder wants to halt, save his men and equipment for the next year. Save lives, young lives. The Army that the elder Moltke created, the Army that von Seeckt preserved. The Army that is now entrusted to him, to Halder.

Blitzkrieg, he argues, is width, not depth, a fragile weapon of political terror. But his Führer will not have it, not even a pause.

No withdrawal, fight to the last man.

There are tense confrontations every day. Hitler waving his arms in big sweeps over the map, *Push here, push there, move this, move that.* He will not listen to his Staff: supplies, reinforcements, defences, fuel. With another wide sweep of his arm Hitler would like to remove every last one of these doubting Staff Officers in their ridiculous red striped breeches.

Hitler's *Lageraum* is a scene of unending agony. Rambling monologues or infernal rages. It is all the generals' fault, they have twisted Hitler's words. Stenographers are brought in, rows of terrified sheep. Every word, every word of his orders will be recorded and followed to the letter. *Only the cowardice of the army and you white-livered officers has produced def...*

He cannot say the word.

The room is a field of ruined grey statues. No one will speak. The man is Magic, Evil, an Unstoppable Power.

Self-delusion deepens. Von Paulus has been taken prisoner at Stalingrad and VI Army no longer exists. Except on Hitler's map a thousand kilometres away.

Then more waste with what is left of the German Army, to Kiev, to Leningrad, places that are not important. Another disaster before Moscow and the Russian advance begins, the advance that will end at the Reichstag.

'And I was to take the blame,' Halder shouting now, 'because I was the only one who would speak, I was chosen by Hitler as the man who had brought on this catastrophe. When it was his interference. His alone.'

Every day Hitler screams at Halder in front of his personal Staff and the entire High Command, possessed of a demonic rage. He calls Halder an *old woman*, or, *not even a Prussian.* He taunts him, *what does a staff officer like you know of the front?* Not one of the bemedalled mannequins supports their Chief of Staff. At the end of '42 Halder is dismissed, removed to the Reserve.

But by then Hitler has lost the war.

I watched Halder's finger up in the air: the Baptist by the Jordan again pointing the Way.

'I tell you, Lieutenant, without any doubt, if it had not been for Chamberlain there would have been no Hitler and no war. And if it had not been for Hitler the German Army would not have lost. Hitler knew nothing, nothing about staff work, about a strategic plan of war. He had never seen such a plan, he would never have understood. He was a nothing, a criminal with a flair for understanding the weaknesses of his opponents. My plans were perfect creations, works of art, the expressions of their creator....'

I had expected Halder to go on once started, unable to stop. But suddenly it was as if he could hear the bell of some mighty clock of doom. Striking on and on toward twelve, Faust's last hour.

Halder was arrested in full flight, face slack, shoulders down, the invisible hand weighing on his arm. He took off his pince-nez and now it was Halder's face buried into his hands. Then his shoulders were shaking and he turned away from me to the window. Another distorted face brought back to the beginning of the story.

There was a long silence.

Halder started to speak again, quietly, a few words at a time, still drawing heavy breaths and facing away.

'No. With you, Lieutenant, with you coming here for answers, for the sake of Oberst Schacht, for them all. And for the sake of the first face you saw in the film, my *Kamerad*, Generalfeldmarschall von Witzleben, for them, the true heroes, the ones who tried, the only ones who ever tried ... *Ich muß die Wahrheit sagen* ... the truth, the truth....'

Halder gave an involuntary shake, a rattle. As if ridding his mind of the picture. Of Halder himself on the end of a wire.

'The Allies decided at Nürnberg that I would not be charged with planning aggressive war and I did not stand trial. They agreed that I had followed orders. And in front of the de-Nazification tribunal I could say that I was never a Nazi, not even in the Party. I had my record, my papers which I buried there in my neighbour's garden after my dismissal.'

Halder pointed out of the window.

'The Gestapo never found them. Or I would have ...'

The rattle again.

'The senior officers of the High Command have been hanged by the Allies: Keitel, Jodl. All the chief Nazis are gone, suicide or the rope. The Führer abandoned his *Volk* with a pistol, the squalid suicide of a coward.'

In Halder's cramped *Lageraum* we had become a tiny General Staff of the vanquished. The worst events possible bearing down on us but unseen in the silent house, far distant from the front. Tears flowing freely while looking out on the enchanted forest.

'So if now I speak of glory and of works of art, how the war could have been won, I too should be judged with them, as a Nazi. I must say what it was. That it was wrong, evil, even starting with the victory against Poland who had our old lands. I must stand before you, before the world and I must tell what happened. There must be no new *Dolchstoß* that would bring us to war again: that the German Army could have won but for ... that Hitler alone was the cause of...'

Slowly Halder recovered himself, face streaked and cracked, drawing more stuttering breaths.

'The truth,' he added softly. 'I ... I myself, in my history for the Americans, I personally will see to the truth.'

Then he wanted to go walking. There had been rain but the sky was clear again.

'Lieutenant, you must remain with us for a few days,' Halder said as we prepared to leave the house.

Something had grown between us in the little room.

'This is a time when being is better than doing,' he said. 'When finding our *Innigkeit* is more important than any *Tätigkeit*, than any activity. The slate has been cleared by unconditional surrender, by *Null*. What will now be written on this slate must be the truth. That is of the greatest importance. For Germany, for Europe, for you and for me.'

We set off on a path through the forest winding up the Zellerhorn. Past crucifixes and statues of the Virgin Mary newly adorned with tiny mountain flowers and little offerings from the requisitioned harvest. Halder carried a basket, it was mushroom season, he told me, a good wet September. He used the Bavarian word: *Schwammerl*. His favourite type were *Reherl*, small and reddy brown. He showed me where to look among the thickest damp pine needles, at the base of mossy boulders facing north.

Halder had followed this path many times, hiking his beloved mountains, asking himself again and again what he should have done. Always he came back to 1938. The last time when all the conditions for a successful *Putsch* were present. As if from that night, sitting with General von Witzleben and with Chamberlain in the air, he could trace the start of the descent.

He told me of conferences with the Führer. Dates and places known to the Tribunal. But he had not detailed for his interrogators what was really said. 22 August 1939 for example, but there were others.

The Berghof. Halder and members of his Staff. Hitler's talk is of *extermination*. He praises Genghis Khan who had a million men and women killed by his own will, *with a gay heart*. The assembled generals were told *our strength is in our ruthlessness and our brutality*, that Hitler would *eliminate all men, women and children of Polish race and language*.

Halder had said nothing. Now he considered himself to be even more guilty than those who had openly supported their Führer. He knew at the time that it was wrong. Maybe some of the others were blinded by faith. By Great Victories.

But for Halder there could be no excuses. In Czechoslovakia, in March of the same year, 1939, Halder had seen what Hitler meant.

'I knew, Lieutenant,' he said, 'when we last met I knew. I knew and I said nothing.'

But Poland was worse, ten times worse. All possible centres of resistance eradicated again. The same list: mayor, priest, noble, teacher. Town by town, village by village. Then across the prairies of Wielkopolska, peasants routed off their lands, turned into Slavic *Untermenschen*. Slaves for the new order of Aryan colonists. Column upon column of refugees homeless in their own country, starving during harvest. Running in front of the German Army until they were trapped by the Russians coming the other way. Up to the River Vistula just as Ribbentrop's secret protocol had planned. Once again Poland had ceased to exist.

Polish Jews were separated then crowded like rats into mazes. To the troops they were blamed for an uprising in Silesia that had never taken place or for any local sabotage and resistance. Bolshevism and Judaism were made the same thing. Millions into ghettos awaiting a solution.

Halder's flow stopped.

'And soon, Lieutenant,' he whispered, 'all the facts will come from the camps in the Russian zone. Then the world will find out what that solution was.'

But the Ukraine, that was where he had seen things for himself. Where self-delusion had become a disease. On Halder as well.

In his interrogation he had not admitted to any knowledge. And this was believable. There were some senior army officers who had never even heard the words: *Endlösung, Einsatzgruppen.* Housecleaning.

'Like you maybe, Lieutenant, my questioners took me for the Good German. The estranged cousin, maybe, because of where I was found at the end. But starting from Versailles in 'nineteen we all believed in some way, at some time. In me you will find the feelings of the whole country.'

We picked our mushrooms, steadily filling the basket, looking back over the peaceful valley. Now was the time. He must start now, Halder said, with the worst. Now.

It was before the final scene with Hitler in the *Lageraum*. Halder was travelling in his half-track to a meeting with his O.Qu I. somewhere near Dubno. Late in the summer or the early autumn of 1942, already chilly.

Motoring across a captured airfield, Halder had come across a group of civilians under guard. No clothes, standing in a line, bare white frames in front of a mound of fresh earth. A silver-haired old woman was carrying a young child in her arms, no more than a year old. She tickled under the child's arms, singing a little song, the child was cooing with delight. Parents looking on with tears in their eyes. Another boy, a child of about ten, shaking, fighting back his terror and holding his father's hand. Then the father was ruffling through his boy's hair, pointing to the sky as if explaining something. Many others were in the line but this group caught Halder's eye.

A shout from one of the guards and a *TV* counted off about twenty from the line. They were led away around the mound, the family included.

Halder was down from the half-track. A girl near the end of the main group, slim with long black hair, came running toward him. She started to speak, words in German he understood, pointing to herself. Me twenty-two years old. Offering herself in desperation, trying to tell him of her tragedy, Halder was not sure. A guard gripped her arm and she was pushed back into line.

Halder followed around the mound.

Here was a huge pit, maybe six metres by forty metres. But the depth he could not tell because the excavation was packed with bodies. Arms, legs, bleeding heads, shoulders ripped by lines of bullet holes. Some were still moving as if to attract attention. He remembered the grave as about half full. An SS captain sat on the far edge holding a machine pistol with a case of ammunition at his side, boots swinging above the corpses below. When he saw movement he held his cigarette between his lips and fired a burst.

Along the side of the trench more *Totenkopfverbände* were waiting in a row, black field uniforms like overalls, one with an automatic, the rest with rifles. Drinking from green bottles, reloading, telling jokes as the naked group approached.

Commands were shouted and the pale figures were climbing down into the pit by stairs cut into the earth. More orders and they started to lie down on top of the dead. Some were still hesitating when the firing started, unable to let go of each other. Jolts and spasms as the bullets hit at close range. Quiet again. Fresh blood tickling down into the tangle of limbs and torsos.

'I suppose I was taken for an inspecting officer...'

Halder stopped on the path holding the basket full of mushrooms. We had been successful.

He had turned ashen, shaken just at the memory. By the remembering, by the speaking of it. Hearing the words out loud through his own mouth for the first time.

'No notice was taken of me. To them nothing out of the ordinary was taking place. No one needed to explain, no one expected to answer questions.'

Halder had stood staring, unable to move away, obsessed with the captain's boots, soles swinging, grazing the uppermost heads and arms below him in the pit.

'These men were attached directly to the Army. There were four *SS-Einsatzgruppen* between our three armies in Russia, under me and my Staff for logistics. We had deceived ourselves, calling them Anti-Partisan Formations protecting our lines of communication and supply. They dealt with *counter espionage* by *special measures*, they were responsible for *resettlement*.'

But now Halder had seen it with his own eyes.

'Then the call again and another batch came around the mound. The procedure was repeated. And as I returned to the half-track more transport arrived with another fifty or sixty prisoners. Shouted commands and they started to undress.'

This time there were very old and weak among them who were helped by the younger ones. From this fresh load the males were separated. These were the men who would cover the full grave and dig the next. Then they too would be shot.

Halder's face was slate. His white lips hardly moving.

'Here is our Great Victory, this is my work of art.'

We walked on up toward the peak, through the last of the fir trees and out on to bare rock. A wide view to Dagendorf in the west and Chiemsee to the north. Halder said nothing more for the next half hour.

He started to talk again as we made our way off the summit. Ever the analyst Halder had come to the conclusion that there had been three choices.

'My first option, as a Christian, was to strip off my uniform and to follow the line. To suffer the same fate, to bear witness before God. But the numbers, the figures. There were only 3,500 *Einsatzgruppen* in their main force, but in those pits I believe they will find millions. We called them Resisters, Communists, Jews and Gypsies, anyone who was denounced by anyone else. But it was just a way of reducing the population to make way for German Lebensraum. It would have been said that I had broken under strain, become mad. Would one body more in a pit have changed anything?'

The question went out into mountain air. Answered by a stir through trees, by cow bells on the first pasture down off the summit. By the rustle of birds hopping through undergrowth off the pathway ahead of us.

We separated again above and below the trail, each returning with a last handful of prizes. Now the basket was overflowing.

And when all the talk of *Putsch* had failed there was a second possibility.

We were almost down to the road leading into the hamlet of Einfang. Halder stopped and put the basket on the ground. He reached into the pocket of his jacket. The chrome Beholla appeared in his hand, the pistol from the dining room table of the *Herrenhaus*. Sitting in a pool of its own reflection. His personal weapon as a Staff Officer, his last remaining insignia of rank and pride. But never used right up to that day.

Just that little motion, the pistol out of his pocket, held in his hand, safety catch off, finger on the trigger. Halder put the gun away. Then he drew the pistol again aiming at an imaginary head, close, right off the end of the muzzle. No chance of a miss. Just that little motion was all it would have taken.

We started to walk again, down to the Alz, across a carved wooden bridge and into the village. Others were on the street by now.

'*Guten Morgen, mein General. Wie geht es Ihnen heute, Herr General?*' Halder raising his Alpini hat left and right and smiling in response.

'I knew Hitler very well,' Halder began again when we were clear. 'After von Brauchitsch resigned in December 'forty-one broken by the Commissar Order, Hitler was my Commander-in-Chief, in direct control of the Army. We would talk together for hours, reminiscing over many topics. Back over the earlier campaigns, our great successes. France especially and Yugoslavia. It was informal between us, I had arrived at the top of my profession. I even stood in front of him with my hands in my pockets. Can you imagine such a ...?'

But as Halder spoke I could hear Faust's bell tolling again.

He clutched my arm with both hands. He had forgotten already, talking as if he had been in front of Hindenburg himself or Moltke. When this man Hitler was a corporal. Warlord through bluff, through deceit, murder, the mistakes of others. And he, Halder, had been the Station Master carrying out the orders.

How long before he could abandon his vanities? The General Staff was finished, gone, not just hidden from view as in 1920. And the Commissar Order was a directive to the Army for the wholesale execution of civilians. All rules of war suspended. Halder should have gone with von Brauchitsch, just as he should have gone with Beck. He should have used the pistol on himself. But he had stayed for the descent to hell. He had wilfully blinded himself.

Tears filled his eyes again.

Halder alone from the OKH had not been searched as he entered the inner sanctum, enjoying the same status as the two most senior officers of the High Command, Keitel and Jodl. He had the loaded Beholla in his pocket at every *Führerkonferenz*.

So why? Why had he not done it?

We returned to the house and I watched Halder clean our mushrooms at a table outside the back door. We would eat well that night, he said. They had been given four eggs, he would make us the perfect omelette. And I could add the last of the vodka from under the seat of the Quinze.

Why? It was a long explanation.

The French Revolution, the destruction of a thousand years of the old order. Revolutionaries as nothing more than destroyers. Creating only new masses to be manipulated to the will of the new few. We had replaced order with materialism and in one hundred and fifty years look what we had accomplished. What had two world wars cost us including all the civilian victims? Fifty million dead, sixty million? We have no idea of the Russian totals. To come to nothing, to this. *Null.*

He was from an old Bavarian family. Three hundred years of officers serving their rulers. But in the last three generations everything had been laid waste.

Halder's grandfather in his entire career had owned only his uniform. When he went to an inn for a beer after duty, he simply put on his *loden* jacket over his uniform trousers. But by the time Halder was a lieutenant no officer could exist without a day suit, evening clothes, a smoking. Not a big thing perhaps, but a perfect example of the rot of materialism.

His grandfather was a professional soldier, his honour could never have been bought.

And his father in his day would say, *General Staff officers have no name.* But by 1935 it was all show and recognition. Under Hitler the Army was only about uniforms, *aiguillettes,* large service apartments, social life, decorations. And in the last years estates had been awarded, or fat cheques attached to letters of commendation from a corporal. Made out in favour of well paid head-waiters with bartered souls.

Yes, he had deluded himself, confusing Hitler with Napoleon, with the man who made order out of the chaos of the Revolution. Telling himself that Hitler had brought victories, that he had overthrown the lies of Versailles, that he had given back to the German people their self-respect.

Was he, Halder, to become the destroyer himself? With one bullet see this new order collapse? Germany back to the conditions of 1918? The very thing the Army had been struggling for so many years to prevent.

And there was an even stronger reason: a life of following orders, of total and complete belief in the hierarchy. The absolute impossibility of shooting his commanding officer. His oath as a General Staff Officer. Then later another oath, to the Living Hitler. His hand simply would not, could not, reach into his pocket.

He would understand, he said, if I found this to be incomprehensible, especially now, looking back from 1946. He had been called *weakling* and *schoolmaster* before. By Hitler.

But that was the truth. Halder's truth.

He looked at me over his pile of prepared mushrooms. But I had nothing to say. I too had believed and I too had gone to war. I too had been tested and I had betrayed.

So the third option.

Halder had followed his orders. He had implemented the instructions of his Führer right up to the day when his Führer had disposed of him.

'There is an old Prussian expression,' he told me. 'The officer can do no more than his duty: the rest is grace.'

Hitler had been thrown up as an expression of the times, he existed only because he was made possible. By Versailles, by the German myth invented to preserve honour, the stab-in-the-back, that Germany could have won in 1918 but for the civilians. By the Allied lie that a defeated Germany alone bore all the guilt.

'Hitler spoke to the secret emotions and yearnings of our people. He was a brilliant connector, he could feel what was in the air. He simplified and he dazzled.'

The new orderless masses were at Hitler's command.

'All Germans shared some of Hitler's objectives but few could find the point of divergence. And no one could act successfully against him in twelve full years. This was Grace, this was Events, I said to myself and I stuck to my duty.'

We climbed up the back stairs to Frau Halder and her stove. The room was more workshop than kitchen. Frau Halder was infinitely resourceful, far beyond our simple gathering of mushrooms. She prepared dandelions against hunger typhus and dysentery, she made tea from apple skins, she boiled her white wash in potato peelings. She had turned the General's army tunics into walking jackets, dyed brown with walnut shells.

We found her sitting at the table by her steaming concoctions, unravelling knitting wool from a ragged pullover. There were new-borns in the village who would be facing a hard winter.

'Tomorrow we will pay a visit,' Halder told me. 'And there I will tell you about Nemesis. The hand of Fate each time. Until a bigger Fate overtook us all.'

He spoke to Frau Halder who left the room. She returned down the attic stairs a few minutes later, followed by a white haired man wearing another of her coarse dyed creations and a patched leather cap.

Halder turned to me to make the introductions.

'Lieutenant, I believe you two have met. This is Xaver. He will drive us.'

The storm-trooper from Masnières, Werner's taxi driver from Berlin.

8

Dachau is a small community a few kilometres north of Munich where the growth of the arms industry at the turn of the century and through the Great War was the start of the town's infamy. In the 1920s Germany's Versailles army could be supplied with a fraction of the country's capacity for weapons production and many of Dachau's factories were abandoned.

It was in a chain of these empty rusting buildings that the SA started their first KZ, *Konzentrationslager*.

The General and I sat in the back of the Stoewer and the storm-trooper drove. Her plush seats had been re-covered with grey canvas like gas curtain, the floors were now copra matting. But she sped through the Ebersberger Forest like the day she had first been run-in.

Frau Halder had tidied up my blues and Halder wore a dark civilian suit with a high white collar. He looked uncomfortably pre-deluge.

Outside Aschau, then again closer to Munich we had been stopped by US Army roadblocks. Each time Xaver had shown a pass.

'You are wondering, Lieutenant,' Halder said after the first barrier, 'how I am allowed through, where I can find gasoline?' Then before I could answer, 'I am working for them now, for the Americans. I kept a detailed diary through the years to 1943 and I have been appointed to organize their Military History Program.' Halder smiled me his prune smile. 'Historians are important people. I am permitted to go anywhere in the Zone.'

Historians as our guardians, of the truth about Great Victories.

'You cannot imagine the hatred in those days,' Halder began as we skirted north around the ruins of another great city. 'Nazi for Communist, old soldier for striker, starving poor for rich Jew. In the early 'thirties KZ prisoners were unknown to the civil authorities, outside the law. They were housed in workshops unused for fifteen years. And the bestiality, man to man ... the early camps were called *wild* ... using rusty vices for extortion, the old forges ... that is how the Golden Pheasants of the SA became so rich, by torture and blackmail.'

And where was he, Halder, the Christian with his Bible? Each time he came back to the same questions.

But before the pact on the battleship *Deutschland*, the Army had been limited by Versailles to 100,000 men, and they, the SA, were millions. So what could have been done even if the facts had been known? And after the *Deutschland* when so many divisions were added? But by then Faust had bartered his soul.

'After the murder of Röhm and the end of the SA, Himmler's SS took over the camps and all personal violence by guards was stopped. There was a new regime: imprisonment as an industry, inflexible punishments according to a code.'

Prisoners were there for many reasons: anti-socials, common criminals, Jews and Gypsies. Then the ideological enemies and political opponents: Communists, clergymen and Jehovah's Witnesses. Each categorized by an intricate system of triangular badges: red, blue, green, pink for homosexuals, two triangles making a yellow Star of David. And there were no terms, no prisoner was told when or even if, he or she would ever be released.

At first, as we approached over a railway line and a canal, the camp looked like a model housing project edged with Bavarian rococo. A row of comfortable semi-detached villas in red brick like the new areas of Cowley or Croydon built in the 'thirties. Neat fenced gardens. Then a square, well planted and maintained. Blocks of modern flats on the far side.

'Eickeplatz. Residences for the SS,' Halder said as we drove through. 'Named after the mastermind of the KZ system. A man Himmler found in an institution for the criminally insane.'

Behind this suburban innocence a huge plant appeared. Groups of factory buildings and workshops of every description separated by yards and lanes. Denser and denser toward the far back, outlined by a tall chimney and a water tower. Giving the appearance of enormous industrial growth, fast and random.

At the gatehouse a GI let us through with a bored nod of his helmet.

Halder pointed out the principal functions as the storm-trooper cruised slowly through the deserted works: furniture manufacturing, clothing, vehicle maintenance, ordnance assembly, weapons overhaul.

'The SS was a fanatical fighting force,' he told me. 'But also a state within a state, beyond the law. The SS was the biggest and most corrupt industrial organization in the Reich.'

I stared at the ordinary-looking buildings as Halder explained. Corrupt was not the right word, he said. The purifying of the *Volk* was a source of endless wealth.

With many of their materials requisitioned, with no taxes to pay and fuelled by the insatiable demands of war, economic success was already assured for SS enterprises. But without any cost for labour, no wages to pay, the SS industrial octopus spread rapidly into every corner of the country.

Dachau was one of twenty or more such camps, each surrounded by further satellites. Built by slave labour and run with slave labour. Then connected by contracts to the greatest names in German business: BMW, Heinkel, Siemens, Messerschmitt, Dornier, all benefitting from slavery. Providing the SS and its officers with a cascade of cash and benefits.

Back by the canal we left the car and walked through another gatehouse. Here a long low building like a vast stable faced row upon row of barrack huts down a large compound surrounded by barbed wire and watchtowers.

This was where the slaves had lived. Subject to a work routine that began at 3.15 a.m. To punishments that started with beatings and solitary confinement for even a second's delay in removing a cap in the presence of a guard. Then from minor offences the scale worked up to the Post and the execution yard.

The death rate was very high, from disease and exhaustion as well as killings. A crematorium was built, the ovens working day and night. Then capacity was doubled and doubled again.

And a mile or so to the east the *SS Einsatzgruppen* had been busy again. Filling pits with Russian prisoners, thousands upon thousands.

The place clamoured at a sense beyond the others, beyond what could be seen or smelt or touched. A sense of dread taken in through the chest, into veins, down through knees. Hatred, terror, a bottomless chasm of the darkest human suffering and bitterness. Evil released on the world.

Halder led me away from the barracks to another long stable at the end of the compound, divided longways by a central corridor.

'They came for me in the early hours of 22 July 1944 and I was put here. I was a special prisoner.'

He pushed open the barred door to a tiny cell with a single high window.

'The worst was not knowing: why I had been arrested, what event had happened, what would happen now, my wife and my daughter. Then every day the punishments took place right outside my cell. I could hear but not see. Executions would start with music, for the Commandant's amusement. An orchestra of inmates, violins, accordions, a mandolin leading the condemned man to the wall. Then beatings, the standing torture, hangings on the Post by the wrists behind the back. All accompanied by terrible screams, by pleas and oaths in twenty languages.'

The cell contained a narrow bed frame. And there we sat like two Borana, searching for the ear and the tail, for the truth about the end of the German Army.

Even after Munich and the failed coup with General von Witzleben, the last chance, some plots had continued. But just like the war of nerves with England in '37 and '38, once the shooting war started, Hitler had won every campaign. From Poland to France, from Norway to the Ukraine. The vanity of the *Lageraum*.

'Hitler predicted that victories would end discontent among the generals,' Halder said. 'And he was right. With the Reich triumphant we all followed orders. And Hitler had seen the effect of purges on the Red Army. Stalin had no choice but to make peace with us in 1939, he had executed all his generals.'

What plots there were had no chance. Amateur, Halder called them. An attempt to isolate the Führer during an inspection of the western defences or at a display of new uniforms. A bomb in a Cognac bottle delivered to his Trimotor that did not go off.

But through the end of '43 and into '44, when Halder was in disgrace after his dismissal and as the noose was tightening on Germany, conspiracies had started again. And there was another noose: the list of conspiracy suspects known to the SS security service grew longer and longer. By then some members from most of the different resistance circles were already in Gestapo dungeons.

Now that Halder had heard the screams and he had seen the methods for himself, he had no doubt. By July 1944 the plotters had to act immediately or perish.

'We had failed, we the old men who had made the pact with the Antichrist. The men of the *Deutschland*. It fell to the next generation to redeem us.'

Halder leaned back against the wall of the cell. Dried out, shrunken like 1939 again.

'Colonel Claus von Stauffenberg was a born leader, both dreamer and man of action. If he had succeeded, he would have inspired the Secret Germany in us all. This man had lost his right forearm, three fingers on his left hand and one eye in a minefield in Africa. But only he among us all carried out a plan. A mutilated body but an uncrippled spirit.'

On 20 July von Stauffenberg exploded a bomb in the *Wolfschanze*, Hitler's HQ buried in the dark woods of East Prussia.

But on that day the *Führerkonferenz* was held in a wooden hut because of the heat. In the *Lageraum* cellar below the blast would have killed them all.

And von Stauffenberg had been interrupted while setting the fuses in the lavatory. The two bombs were in his briefcase. He uses a special pair of pliers made for his crippled hand. A sergeant was sent to find him, the Führer would soon be ready for his report. Only one charge was activated.

Von Stauffenberg positioned the briefcase next to Hitler. Then he had arranged to be called to the telephone. But after he had left, at the last second, the briefcase was moved to the far side of a heavy table leg away from Hitler. By the same man who had been given the dud Cognac bottle to hold on the Trimotor. The briefcase was in his way.

It was fate, events. Hitler survived.

Halder shook his head. Rushed staff work had been their real downfall.

Even after the unsuccessful explosion the *Putsch* could still have carried. But the arrangements to destroy the *Wolfschanze* communications centre failed. Had Hitler and his staff been out of touch in their distant forest lair, even for a few hours, believed to be dead, the coup would have advanced too far to stop when the truth emerged. But Hitler's voice was heard in Berlin within half an hour. Then key officers started to waver and it was over.

And there were other fatal defects: the troops to be used by the plotters to seal off the centre of Berlin had not been screened. One junior officer was an ardent Nazi. When he received his orders he left on a motorcycle to find Goebbels. Then there were no facilities ready for Field Marshal von Witzleben to make his planned martial law broadcast to the German people as the new head of the *Wehrmacht*. And senior officers in the Bendlerblock who opposed the plot were left alive when the action began. Out of misplaced chivalry they were detained in an office, with their pistols, with wine. With a telephone.

The rout began.

The Bendlerblock was surrounded. All the conspirators were arrested, Colonel Schacht who had been responsible for the outlying areas of the capital was taken with Field Marshal von Witzleben. From Berlin to Paris conspirators committed suicide, others were shot that evening. Then the Gestapo took charge and those who had not used their pistols came to regret that they were still alive.

'I knew Colonel Schacht better than anyone,' Halder said. 'He was participating in the assassination of his Commander-in-Chief. You must understand that his agony would have begun months before, with his oath. *Kadavergehorsam*. Obedience to death.'

The power of the SS was now absolute. Those on the SD list were arrested whether or not they had been part of the plot. Dismissed military men such as Halder and General Thomas as well as civilians who had been too prominent to touch without hard evidence: Werner's uncle, Hjalmar Schacht, Josef Mueller, Fritz Thyssen.

Himmler became Commander-in-Chief of the Home Army. Every officer who refused to join the Party was dismissed. The Nazi arm replaced the military salute. Those who remained grovelled to reaffirm their loyalty to their Führer.

While the noose pulled tighter and tighter around the Reich itself: the Russians at the Vistula, the Allies on the Rhine. There was no escape for Germany, for the Army. The Devil was coming to collect his due. The future was *Null*.

Hitler's vengeance knew no limits. Now he had them: the doubters, the monocled Prussians, the nay-saying Staff men, the monarchists, the vons and the zus. The plotters and their families were to be eradicated root and branch as if they had never been born. And when his Great Victory came, delayed for now maybe, but in which he still believed, madly, fanatically, he would create for his Thousand Year Reich a new military caste and a new aristocracy devoted only to his Person and to the doctrines of National Socialism.

The camps collected Trotts, Becks and von Stauffenbergs, brothers, uncles, cousins. Inge and her children disappeared from Zossen. An obscene show trial was staged and the first eight plotters were executed on the second day.

It was Hitler for whom the film was made. To be screened that same night.

We walked back through the compound. It was a beautiful day. Two rows of poplar trees between the barracks swayed softly in the breeze.

By 1946 all the wartime inmates of Dachau had either died or been repatriated. Conditions had improved but the camp was still a prison, now run by the Allies. For dubious DPs: Russians who had fought for the Germans, Jews caught on the underground route to Palestine. Men and women, thin and ragged, up against the fences. The masked faces of the lost and the damned, a glimpse of how the camp had been.

My eyes darted from face to face. But I knew that it was useless. For all her determination, Tricia and her daughter could never have lasted in the camps for six years.

'I have been lucky, Lieutenant,' Halder said as we came back to the car. 'And every day is precious now. I was not included in the executions during August 'forty-four because the Gestapo could not prove anything right away. But they were going to come for me in my cell before the end. It was not intended that I should live to tell this story. Only chaos as the war ended saved my life. And with the Allies, my arrest and detention in Dachau was in my favour.'

The storm-trooper was waiting. We had hardly spoken to each other then or before. I put my hand into his. I had come to believe that he really was at Masnières. The battle that stood for so many things. The battle that we had both won and both lost so long ago. That had brought us to this, to *Null*. Now we shared our dead hero.

'*Alles kaputt,*' he said. Then I found myself embracing his rough jacket and his thick arms were holding me.

We drove slowly round the outside of the compound, Halder describing the liberation of the camp by the Americans.

By early 1945 executions and punishments had stopped. Sabotage by inmates started, which Halder understood. They were making the ordnance and refurbishing the guns that were being used against the forces trying to liberate them.

Then American fighters buzzed the camp and morale soared. There were no more suicides and the SS guards suddenly tried to be friendly.

Even inmates are humans, they said.

On 28 April the first American arrived.

At the gatehouse, a tableau from the final act of a new Ring Cycle. The prisoners as the chorus, a dense crowd watching from behind the wire. A Mid-westerner from the Thunderbird Division stands by his jeep. Soiled battle fatigues, shirt undone to the navel, sweat pouring, his helmet askew. Facing an *SS Obersturmführer*, blond and tall in his perfectly tailored black uniform, polished, perfumed. And next to him a former Belgian resistance fighter in striped pyjamas, clogs and cap, so weak that he is unable to stand without help. The representative of the inmates' committee which had organized for the take-over during the last week.

'*Heil Hitler,*' the *Obersturmführer* says to the American, clicking his heels together and raising his arm. 'I hereby turn over to you Konzentrationslager Dachau. 30,000 residents, 2,340 sick, 560 garrison troops.'

The American major does not return the salute. He walks up close to this Aryan apparition.

'*Du Schweinehund!*' he hisses.

Then he spits into the German's face.

Liberation begins and horror emerges.

A full-blown typhus epidemic has started. Bodies are lying everywhere, taut skin over skeletons in full relief, flesh and muscle missing in places Halder had never seen before. Corpses heaped outside the unmanned crematoria with more inside, piled against cold ovens. Staring eyes, large shaved heads on child-size bodies, limbs in every contorted direction.

The resources of the American front line are immediately overwhelmed. An SOS is sent to the Allies, the French are the closest.

As we pulled away across the railway line Halder pointed to the marshalling yards.

'That was the worst,' he said. 'Down there among the trees. A train had arrived a few days before the liberation. Fifty or more cattle cars standing on a siding. Most of the human cargo had perished during a journey of one or two months. There was evidence of cannibalism. And the few shadows that finally crawled from the cars were shot by camp guards. The stench of death and rot permeated the entire camp and out to the town beyond. By the day of liberation the train had still not been unloaded and the Americans saw for themselves the fully glory of our Reich.'

And now, as the General talked, I could see Katrina. In her uniform, starting her work. Walking among the corpses. Thousands being stripped and laid out in rows for identification. Up and down the train, through disease-ridden huts.

Niemals! Niemals! Wir werden Ihnen niemals verzeihen!

Across the suicidal bridge, slippery and snaking, on the other side of the Rhine. This is what Katrina had seen.

That night after they were all in bed, I wrote the General a letter, sitting at the kitchen table by the light of the smoking lamp. For his collection as a historian.

Dear Generaloberst,

I am ashamed of myself and I am ashamed of Mankind.

I am a speck of failed insignificance in an intolerable world. I am beginning to understand Null.

I have no idea of what to do. But in the ruins we have all created, I can follow your example. I too must be truthful.

In August '39 Mr Lloyd George arranged for me to deliver your second letter to Chamberlain in person. LG was very old, weakened by an operation for prostate cancer. By then he was living with Frances and he married her during the war when his first wife died. They had a daughter named Jennifer.

LG had been out of office for 17 years, but he understood the situation better than the men running the government. LG told me that he had met Hitler in 1937 and that he too had been bluffed about the new Germany just like everyone else.

In 1939 we fumbled our chance for a treaty with Russia, the dukes still would not have it. After that, LG told me, Britain could never protect Poland. He said that Chamberlain's guarantee of Poland was the act of a weak and beaten man lashing out wildly at his own failure. We had so many opportunities to stop extremism. From Munich right back to Genoa and we had wasted them all. Munich was when to fight. With Poland, our only chance was to negotiate. Could a few changes to the Polish Corridor have been worse than what happened? Chamberlain had it backwards.

'Just look at the face, have you ever seen such defeat?' LG asked. 'We should never ever have let Hitler set eyes on the man.'

If Hitler had believed Chamberlain over Poland, or even if our ambassador had been believed, war would have been avoided. But they truly were the Umbrella Men, the Worms of Munich.

LG distrusted the Chamberlains all his life, starting with Joe, Neville's father. The man who started the Boer War with our own genocide and our own concentration camps.

By the '20s the family manufacturing empire had started to decline. So Joe sent Neville to Jamaica to run a sisal plantation, a big gamble to save their fortunes. It was a complete disaster. LG says that Neville never recovered. The failure of the farm as well as his older brother Sir Austen, being groomed as the favourite left Neville unbalanced, desperate to succeed at any price.

The Czech crisis was Neville's supreme opportunity. He thought that he alone understood Hitler, that he alone would settle the affairs of Europe at Munich. Neville used every form of dishonesty to force his solution on to the Cabinet, on to Parliament, on to the people of Great Britain, on to our Allies and on to the Czechs themselves. He believed that only he knew, madly, fanatically in his way.

Scissors and paste were used on reports that opposed Czech Partition. Our General Staff was coached to say that the German armed forces were a 'terrible instrument' when the Wehrmacht was weaker than even the Czechs. One of Chamberlain's experts who reported to the Cabinet that Czech defences were vulnerable had never even been there. To justify giving in, figures from the Royal Air Force were distorted so that we believed that our cities would be destroyed by a 'knockout blow' within hours of the start of war. Chamberlain repeated Hitler's stories of innocent Germans murdered by Czechs, which they both knew to be lies. The translation of military talks with the French was falsified to make

France look stubborn and weak. The reports of our special envoys to Germany were rewritten to make Hitler appear 'reasonable' or 'quiet and cordial'.

Then Chamberlain's moment came. He flew to Germany to talk terms. But the Cabinet would not agree under Hitler's threats, they resolved to meet force with force. Britain prepared for war. You and General von Witzleben were ready with your coup.

But Chamberlain would not stop, he was determined that he would bring Peace For Our Time. He contacted Hitler secretly behind the backs of his colleagues. He lied to Parliament. He drew a piece of paper out of an envelope in front of a packed House. He read out loud that Hitler was prepared to negotiate. There were frenzied cheers. Chamberlain alone had saved us from war. Lord Mayor of Birmingham, Prime Minister of Great Britain, Sole Saviour of Europe, now even old Joe must concede that his younger son had succeeded.

But the piece of paper in the envelope was blank, Null, a trick, there were no concessions. Chamberlain just flew to Munich and gave in. Hitler won it all. It was we, the British, who completed your pact on the battleship 'Deutschland'. Like you we too wanted to be deceived about the state of the world we had created. And we too sold our souls for an illusion.

They try to talk of Munich as giving Britain a year to prepare. But it was Germany who gained the advantage. In '38 you were unprepared. After '39 only a coalition of the whole world could defeat you.

The day after LG saw me, I went walking with Chamberlain and I handed him your letter. I thought that I had made an impression: Secret Germany, Ludwig van Beethoven. But I too was deluded, my forces existed only on my map a thousand kilometres away.

That was the last time I met Mr Lloyd George. He died last year.

Ever yours,

Graham Exeter

The next morning the General took me walking again, over the river and up to the village.

That was when I handed him my letter. On the carved bridge. And that was when I told him: the railway station, one foot in front of the other along the pavement, following the cracks toward Leipzigerstraße. The *Hauptsturmführer* and the bathroom door.

'I knew they had taken you,' Halder said to me when I had finished and when he had read what I had written. 'Oh yes, Heydrich was very happy to let us know that our plans had been uncovered, although you were carrying nothing that directly incriminated me or Colonel Schacht. But he wanted to show that he had outwitted us and our Abwehr. And for proof he sent me a photograph.'

A long silence as we moved off again. I studied Halder's face beside me, eyes to the front. He had known everything before I had arrived. But I was beyond tears, beyond myself, beyond remorse. I was a blank slate.

He took me into the village *Wirtshaus*. There was nothing to eat, only a watery drink, tepid and tasteless. Boiled up from whatever hops were left after a *Lagerbier* had been brewed. But the good beer had been exchanged with city visitors for soap and cigarettes.

The room was full.

'The dead, they are all around us,' Halder said when we were seated, clenching at his hands again, left then right, right then left.

There was Donat the *Schuster*, four sons, the last one was only fifteen, Josef from the *Molkerei*, his wife and her sister, all his children in an RAF raid on Munich. Then Lorenz...

Sons, fathers, uncles, whole families. Matching La Wantzenau life for life, generation for generation.

'Now we have only ourselves. And we must care for each other.' Halder spoke softly but I could hear every word, all the drinkers in the room were silent, defeated. 'That is our new strength. Villages, towns, neighbourhoods, each other. Without borders, without nations, that is the only chance.' A pavé of microcosms defying any new ideology. 'That way,' he added, 'they will never take us again.'

After our beers we walked on. Halder stopped me at the Aschau memorial to the Great War. German faces chiselled into stone, shadowed, blurred by their helmets. Numbers like France: from these few houses and a scattering of farms there were forty-four names. Johann Decker, Michael Osterhammer, Georg Pfaffinger, Andreas Steindlmiller...

Halder drew a paper from an inside pocket.

'And these are the names from this war,' he said. 'You can see that many are the same. Fathers then sons, uncles and nephews. Steindlmiller, Osterhammer, Wimmreuter ... We are going to erect another memorial. This one will have twenty-eight names. And it must be the same the world over.'

These were the men to blame. Everyone in the world was agreed. Steindlmiller, Osterhammer, Wimmreuter ... Halder. But once again their dead were just as dead as ours. Oh, I should have been angry, I knew. Angry that they even had their names, their beautiful village, that a single one of them was left.

But *Null* is the end of everything. After hatred and vengeance have done their worst.

Halder had been standing silent by my side. He spoke again.

'You must have your names too, Lieutenant. The list of people you loved who have been killed by war.'

The list was my biography. From Fairy's classroom decorated in red, white and blue bunting. From chiselled stones that talk to the secrets of a blue river. From cattle cars rattling over rails. To the Devil's athlete in flickering black and white.

Evil as a poisonous gas, at that moment it was the best that I could do. Enough smaller wrongs one on top of the other. Enough of our lies generating more of theirs, evil begetting a greater evil until the cylinder explodes over us all. War as a Sausage Machine with a life of its own. Events, capital E. The Law of the Unintended Consequence. Oh, there are no words.

Music, beyond the end of words. Beethoven's Fate. The knocking on Faust's door. Dah dah dah DAH. Mr S has come to collect our bartered souls.

And where would Halder's list run? His colleagues, their wives and their children, men he knew better than a family. To faceless millions streaming in front of *Blitzkrieg*, refugees, real victims. To his beloved Army left in his care by Moltke and von Seeckt, disappearing by whole divisions into Russian winters, never to return. *Never.*

'And what did they die of?' Halder asked me quietly. 'Not of any disease to which we do not have a medical answer, not of any famine in a desert, certainly not of old age. I say they died of Isms.'

His accent was softer with each day we talked. Back to how he had learned to speak French from his mother.

Fascism, Militarism, Communism, Imperialism. Americanism in the future maybe. And there were more that I could add. Men who say that they have the answer, who try to make their perfect omelette of the world with other men's lives. But there is no Absolute Truth. There never will be a Perfect Omelette. With each attempt there are only millions of cracked eggs.

'There is not much meaning left in the old Christian words now,' Halder began again. We had not moved: stone faces, blurs, helmets, names. 'But I say to you Lieutenant, *Go in peace*. You have confronted your devils.'

We set off back to the house, down toward the river. I was planning to leave that afternoon, make the crossing into Switzerland before dark.

'You did not cause those deaths.' Halder put his hand on my shoulder as we walked. 'You could not have left Germany with the treaty. They were watching, you would have been stopped. And if you had reached England? The Protocol would only have confirmed in those minds that what they were doing was right. Neither side could have admitted to their deceits. You would have vindicated war for them.'

Halder stopped me in the middle of the carved bridge. Where I had handed him my letter, where I had told him about following cracks in the pavement away from the station.

After a night of rain the river was fast and deep. We watched in silence for a moment. Another delicate shade of living green.

'You must go back to Canada,' Halder continued softly. 'You must make your village, your town. Peaceful, prosperous. Just your one little part of the world. You must. That is your only hope.'

Halder turned to face me.

'I have something for you, Lieutenant.' He drew the shiny Beholla out of his pocket. The General's last remaining insignia of rank and vanity, his personal weapon.

The little motion that his arm would not perform in Hitler's map room. Just that simple movement. Hand into pocket, palm around butt, safety catch off, finger on trigger. Out and up, target just off the end of the muzzle. Aim. Fire.

'Here,' he said. 'I do not deserve …' the pistol loose in his palm, '… *ich war ein Idiot und ein Feigling.*'

Halder stood in front of me, his hand out offering the gun. Daggers glazed with tears, overflowing down to his chin. Pride surrendered: all that he was, all that he had stood for in ruins. He nodded down the river.

Without checking the safety catch I grasped the pistol by the barrel. I took a dancing skip across the bridge and I hurled the gun into the air with all my might.

A sparkling arc against a borderless sky, a covenant for the future. Never again. A rainbow of bright promise.

The splash was lost into white froth a long way down.

9

The dictaphone came to the end of the tape and shut off with a loud click. Reverberating through the bed tray and around the noiseless room.

Morley was asleep on the Lay-Z-Boy. He woke with a start into a moment of complete void. Then his hand felt the snubnose, the outline smooth through his tracksuit and the night came cascading back. The close smell of parked cars in a garage, horn blaring, images, screams rising from windows, swerving wildly over Lion's Gate Bridge. What hadn't happened, what had.

Back to Powell Street. Parked, not followed, suddenly very nervous with the loaded gun. The truck could be broken into or stolen. This is Canada, possession is a serious offence. Back on the night he had driven up from Chilliwack and left the Landcruiser in the street with the gun in the spare wheel cover, that had been risk enough. Into his pocket.

Up to the room where he had found the old man still shaking from a nightmare, Elaine sure it was the end but apologizing for the call. Then Graham's nightmare retold and relived, Morley's hand squeezed until he thought his bones would break.

Tumbling into a prison in Berlin. Naked men dancing on wires, white mushrooms gathered in a basket. Then Morley's hands trembling, his fingers stretched out over another wasteland. Rubble, craters, deserts.

And a voice speaking to him from an infinite distance. A face that Morley could picture exactly: cropped hair, shrivelled face cracked and lined, peering at him through pince-nez. And what would they have died of, Morley? Certainly wouldn't have been old age. Halder's darting eyes waiting for their answer.

Past dawn. The long weekend was over. Tuesday morning, when normal people go back to work feeling refreshed after a three-day break. But M+C+W was on some other shore of the Pacific Ocean in the far far distance.

Morley came to his feet, tingling with perspiration through crawling flesh. What could have happened, what had been prevented by a phone call. He reached for the old man's hand, cold and damp like a fish fillet in the market. He leaned over to put his ear against white cracked lips, a faint gurgling, breathing.

Elaine was at the kitchen table smoking, staring blankly at the first lines of light over the harbour. Container cranes like mechanical trolls frozen in place by dawn.

'I checked him while you were sleeping,' she said. 'I think you've come to the end of the story. Showing you his back was about it.'

Morley assembled water, Ensure and a new jar of lip conditioner from the storage room. Elaine nodded.

'Just a bit of liquid into his mouth even if he doesn't swallow. Easier from a thick cup. That'll make him more comfortable.'

She looked up at Morley. His tray was shaking. I know you can do this. Communication without words.

Morley walked back into the room. He applied conditioner lightly then he felt through pillows for the back of Graham's head. A few drops of water passed into the parched mouth and the eyes opened.

Morley sat on the edge of the chair leaning over toward the bed.

'You're dressed like a commando,' Graham whispered. 'What were you up to?'

Morley tried to smile.

'Just a fantasy,' he replied, 'just a fantasy.'

The old man wanted to speak again. Morley moved closer, his ear almost to Graham's mouth.

'Do you know what a lot of blood looks like, Morley? Have you ever seen someone hurt, close up? Someone who will never be the same again. *Never.*' The whisper was slow but earnest, angry. 'Ever heard the screams, Morley, do you know what those screams really sound like?'

No, Morley didn't know. A lot of blood, a dead body, two, three. Real screams. Only on American television.

A long quiet in the room.

'You have something for me, Morley.' Faint, almost not there.

'I'll do anything you ask, of course.' A message, comfort his wife, talk to his step-sons. Anything.

'When you turned me over. I felt it in your pocket.'

Morley's head fell forward onto the bed. Love, hatred and vengeance all fighting their battle inside him had left him drained. The old man knew it all.

Then the same wizened face again, General Halder speaking to him again across a frozen prairie. His picture of the Ukraine, of Saskatchewan as a boy.

Go in peace.

A hand, cold, tentative like a spider, crept gently over Morley's scalp. The hand came to rest on the back of his neck like a compress, soothing and comforting. A field dressing for his flooding wounds.

Saved, condemned to live.

Without looking up Morley reached into his pocket and passed the hand what it wanted.

The hand knew exactly what to do. There was a click and a metal slap then a click again. When Morley raised his head the empty chamber was out to the side of the gun and six bullets lay in a little pile on the sheet on the far side of the bed. Small, stubby like the gun. No bigger than acorns.

The far hand gathered its prizes, a squirrel in slow motion.

The near hand held up the gun on an open palm, shaking hard.

'Some newspaper, Morley, the dumpster.'

The old man forced out the words and his eyes closed.

Then the hand holding the gun dropped back onto the sheet. There was a faint rattle: from the hinges of the chamber, from the old man's jaw, from bones in the bed, Morley couldn't tell.

Morley picked up the gun and took the weekend *Sun* off the television set.

There was no sparkling arc in the sky, no covenant as this gun disappeared. Just the scrape and squeak of a metal lid against the concrete wall of the dumpster room. Then Morley's head was into the bin like a West End Indian scavenging for empties. Tucking his paper bundle down under black garbage bags, past loose sticky cans and under a layer of heavy cardboard.

He climbed the stairs back to the fifth floor.

Morley knew what he had seen and what he had heard. He took the stairs slowly, one at a time, reluctant, sure of what he would find.

Elaine was in the kitchen, talking. Alyce, the day staff and the cleaners had arrived. They were making coffee before the start of their shift.

'I think...' Morley began. He paused as Elaine came toward him through the people in the room. He backed out into the corridor. I think he's dead and he's clutching six bullets. I bought a ... I didn't know what I was ... but somehow Graham knew...

Morley struggled for a way to start. In the entire world only Elaine would understand. Mouth open but no sounds.

Elaine spoke.

'She's arrived, forgot about the holiday. Very difficult arranging flights at the last minute, through Chicago and Seattle...' Elaine stopped as they entered Graham's room.

A woman was sitting on the Lay-Z-Boy facing the bed, the old man lying as Morley had left him. But both hands were out on the sheets and the bullets were gone. Graham looked quiet, happy from the inside. As if he had just seen something deeply satisfying.

The woman was talking in a soft voice but Morley couldn't hear the words.

Suddenly she sensed them behind her and she turned.

'Oh, doctor…'

'I'm not a doctor, I'm just a volunteer.' Morley was first into the room.

'Have you been here long, do you know him?' the woman asked.

Morley smiled at her.

'You're Mary.'

Tears welled up spontaneously in Morley's eyes, pouring down his cheeks. Mary put her hand over her mouth and looked back at the bed.

Elaine was on the far side of the Lay-Z-Boy feeling Graham's wrists then bending close to his face.

'That's it,' she said quietly. 'He's gone.'

Mary sat again and took up a cold hand.

Elaine looked across at Morley. In the corridor Elaine turned as Morley slumped against her, grasping her shoulders, flooding against her face. But the dark night had passed. *Ich war ein Idiot und ein Feigling.* The night of fools and cowards. Morley had survived. Daylight, incoming staff.

The kitchen had emptied, they sat at the table. Morley still weeping and Elaine waiting for him to speak.

'He used up the last of his strength doing exactly what he wanted to do,' she said finally. 'You were Graham's recording angel.'

And he was my guardian, against my great victory.

Elaine put her hands gently over his then she wiped Morley's face. He could smile at her through his tears but he couldn't stop and he couldn't speak. There would be time in his new future, time to explain, time for everything.

Mary came into the kitchen and sat with them. A tall elegant woman, self-composed. A strong photogenic face, creased but graceful. No tears: that would come later, in private.

They talked slowly in polite turns. There was time, infinite time. About her flight delays, in after midnight and not knowing if she could have come over right then. Her illness in France, his fall. Morley recovering himself, explaining about the *Passion*, asking Mary if he could make copies. The maps that he planned to complete. Elaine made more coffee.

Morley walked back up the corridor again, the *Passion*, his bullets. But Alyce was already arranging the room. The Lay-Z-Boy had gone, the blinds were open, the body had been laid out and covered. She glared at him: not staff, an intrusion on the dead. Morley collected his possessions from the bedside locker, the recorder off the bed tray. He left her to it.

Slowly out through the front door, Powell Street traffic a high volume shock.

Welcome sunshine. Another day being offered bright and new. Cars, semis and buses speeding for a stale green at Main. Street people staggering on the sidewalk after a long night. Morley stood watching. Intent faces off to work, defeated faces asking for spare change. Another day being used up.

He looked up and down the street unable to remember where he had parked. A delivery van was pulled up at the kerb, hazards flashing. Further along a set of orange lights were circling off the roof of a tow truck. There was a break in the traffic and the wrecker made a squealing U out from behind the van. The Landcruiser appeared up on his sling, swinging wide across four lanes. Back end in the air and off crabwise down the street.

Morley looked on impassively. They wouldn't find a gun in the spare wheel cover, not even a few bullets. They could have it. The Matrimonial Vehicle, the Matrimonial Home, the Matrimonial Misery.

Sell it. Keep the money. Give me the life.

Exeter Gypsum Co. Ltd

659 Venables   Phone: (604) 391 2728
Vancouver   Fax   :   398 1228
B.C. V6L 3R9   I/Net : me@van.exgyp.ca

BY HAND

Dear Mr Morley,

I called by the hospice yesterday to collect Graham's last things and Elaine told me that you were leaving on a trip, a long one she says. I hope this reaches you before you go. I'm writing on one of the office machines and Don has promised he will arrange for delivery to your house just as soon as I am done.

I want to thank you for being with Graham through to the end. I heard a lot about it from Elaine. In a way it was almost better that you were there, not me or one of the boys. They didn't explain on the phone how serious he was, on Graham's instructions no doubt. And I didn't realize that the boys hadn't been told. Then over the long weekend they were in New York watching the start of the hockey. So I stayed on in France until I was past the worst of my stomach 'flu. Although he was very old Graham seemed indestructible to me and always happy on his own.

My husband held so much inside, I'm sure it would all have gone with him if you had not been there. Elaine says you recorded some of what Graham told you. I would very much like to know all of what happened in his earlier life and I am sure that my sons feel the same way. Maybe when you are back you would agree to come over to the house. I could cook you one of Graham's favorite meals. And as to the papers, he gave them to you so they are yours. I had never seen that music book before.

When Graham came back from Europe in the fall of 1946 I was twenty-six, the boys were three, four and five. I was just so happy to see him that I was not concerned with where he had been or what had happened before. Then after, we were so busy that it never really came up. I knew that he was in Africa and that he was in a war. And of course, I saw his terrible back every day. All he would tell me was that he was a fool and a coward.

Graham and I did very well right from the beginning. He worked extremely hard almost from the moment his aeroplane landed back in Vancouver. He started with the men nobody else wanted, Quebecers and Indians and he built the business into one of the biggest drywall outfits in the city. Now our company does a lot of the new highrises and most of the hospital work. (Don says he knows your architectural firm well and that you have just been taken over by another group from the East.)

When I complained about the time he spent working, Graham would quote to me about being 'upon a wheel of fire', but I didn't understand. I only found out later the words are from Shakespeare. Now two of the boys run Exeter Gypsum and Don has *his* son starting this year. At the bottom with a broom, of course. I used to be the bookkeeper and I still come in most days to help. (Accounts receivable mostly!)

We bought our house in East Vancouver in 1950 for $7,500 and the boys all went to the local schools. Then when we could afford it Graham didn't want to move, even after the Portuguese and the Italians were replaced by East Indians and Vietnamese. He said it was good to have roots and he enjoyed seeing so many different people living together peacefully in a new world. That is how he came to be in the Powell Street hospice.

I went with Graham to Europe for vacations, starting in 1965. Initially to find the grave of my first husband who was a flyer. He is buried in Berlin, on the road to Spandau, if you are there. Flight Sergeant Stuart McVey, Royal Canadian Air Force. Row S2, Commonwealth Cemetery. They cut the headstones in 1948 and I could choose some words to go on the bottom. I followed Graham's suggestion and Stu's stone just has one word. NEVER. Graham told me that it would help me to understand the joy of being alive, each and every moment and the true meaning of sacrificing your life at the age of 23.

On later trips we went over to the Salzburg Festival, then on other holidays to see some of the great sights of Europe. I was astonished to find that Graham spoke perfect French, enough German, reasonable Italian and that he knew his way around all the big cities.

But the vacations were sometimes very difficult. Graham was like a different person over there, disappearing in the middle of the night to walk the streets, or tears flowing down his cheeks at the smallest things. A German word, the smell of a particular kind of cigarette, music played by a Polish pianist, even German cars on the highways in France. He had some idea about 'peace and prosperity', about everyone being 'middle class' and 'well-to-do' (some of his many quaint expressions). Especially he liked Germans taking their vacations in France. He said it would make the world safe. Even in Canada he would become quite furious with any criticism of the Common Market (which he called 'Pan-Europa'!) defending it passionately, right down to all the bureaucrats and regulations. The political masterpiece of the century, he called it.

Over the years we visited other graveyards and we looked all over for a grave in Bavaria which Graham could not find. We went to the war grave sites in Northern France and to a grave by the lake at Evian, but Graham was unable to explain. For a long time Vancouver was the good new and Europe was the bad old life.

In the early '80s we bought a ruined house and a few fields in France, near St Rémy-de-Provence, outside Avignon. I spent the summers banging drywall! They speak some funny French dialect there which Graham seemed able to understand as well. He used to play cards with the old timers in their cafés. (Although they were probably younger than he was!) We call the house Mas Beauchamp, something else I have never understood.

If we do get to talk, please don't worry about telling me of his other women. I know he was married before, we needed his first wife's death certificate before we could get married ourselves in 1947. And he spent years writing to the International Tracing Center about a woman from Berlin and her daughter who had been in one of those terrible camps. In the end Graham gave up. He was sure that they were both put in under her maiden name which he didn't know, because her married name had some sort of connection. I think Graham had it in his heart from the start that they were both dead.

The mysteries went on right to the end. Did you know that when they came for the body they found six bullets in his bed? I didn't even know he owned any bullets. Now I wonder if there's a gun somewhere in the house and whether it's safe, not to mention legal.

The undertakers wanted to make a fuss, some kind of report, but I told them they were harmless memorabilia from a war. When they had him dressed I slipped the bullets back into his pocket. I only realized later what might happen when he is cremated. He will certainly go with a bang!

If you are still here on Friday there is a memorial. You'll probably appreciate what is planned better than everyone else. We are having a lunch for all his friends and the people he worked with in the business. It's what he asked for and his will says: NO SPEECHES ALLOWED. The boys are setting up tables in our warehouse and an Italian restaurant on Commercial

Drive is catering. I am planning for 100 people but Don says 400 would be closer.

Oh yes! And, of course, a lady pianist from UBC who Graham admired very much, is going to play. Chopin, Bach and Beethoven.

I wish you a wonderful trip and we all look forward to talking to you when you return.

Best regards

Mary Exeter

P.S. The only thing I can find for you among Graham's papers that concerns the past is this certificate that hung on the wall in his study. It came from the Pentagon Library in the middle '70s in response to one of Graham's many inquiries. Graham seemed to think that the German name on an American record of the war was very significant so I thought you might like to have it.

DA2442

THE UNITED STATES OF AMERICA

UNITED STATES ARMY EUROPE

On the orders of the Deputy Chief of Staff for Personnel, ATTN.,
and by authority of the Army General Orders Nos. 32 and 34, 1956,
and following the review and approval of the Secretary of Defence
and the State Department, Washington, D.C.,

THIS WILL CERTIFY THAT :

The Meritorious Civilian Service Award - Army

WAS PRESENTED TO :

Franz Julius Halder
of Hohenaschau, Germany

For significant achievement in the improvement of cooperation
between the Federal Republic of Germany and the member states
of the North Atlantic Treaty Organisation while Chief Consultant
to the Historical Liaison Group, United States Army, Europe
from 1946 to 1961. Through his personal efforts in obtaining the
participation of many prominent German leaders and his
extensive knowledge of military doctrine and strategy, General
Halder has made an invaluable contribution to the creation of an
incontrovertible record of events leading to the defeat of the
German army, for the benefit of all posterity.

DATED :

This 24th day of November 1961

CERTIFIED BY :

Major-General M.G. Doleman
Office of the Assistant Chief of Staff, Operations
G-3 USAREUR

ACKNOWLEDGEMENTS

Wolfgang Ansorge · Kristof Borowski · Bundeswehr Forshampt, Potsdam · Nicole et Alain Caritoux, le Café des Arts · La famille Brini · Ben Brown · Guido Campigotto · Michael Clarke · Jane Coop · Robert Cram · Werner David · Hassan Abdi Dima · Jocelyn Fraser · Susan Hill · Inspector Francis Mugambi Imathiu · The Imperial War Museum: Peter Simkins, James Taylor and Stephen Walton · Tyleen Katz · Kenya National Archives · Christine Kidney · Rudolf Kuhne · Daniel Kulicki · George Laverock · John McCutcheon · Brian Muir · Musée de l'Armée, les Invalides · National Archives at College Park, Md. · John Njenga · Paul O'Brien · Maurice Okombo · Oxford Illustrators, Jonathan Soffe · Georgios Paplexiou · Chef de Cuisine Daniel Portas · Michael Prokopow · Hugh Ruthven · Harvey Sachs · Peter Schimmelpfennig · Capitano Antonio Siviero · Christine Teillard d'Eyry · La famille Vanni · Widener Library, Harvard University · Jane Wilde · Henry Syacuse Zakayo · Wieslaw i Hania Zelazko ·

I also acknowledge my debt to the following works of virtuoso scholarship without which this mere novel could not even have been attempted:

Sir John Wheeler-Bennet: *The Nemesis of Power: The German Army in Politics 1918–1945*

A.J.P. Taylor: *The Origins of the Second World War*

Saint Rémy-de-Provence
Bouches-du-Rhône
France